Pawn's Gambit

The author's career to date has been as an academic scientist, interspersed with periods in Whitehall in various governmental roles. He has published extensively in his research field, and has advised a number of companies and overseas governments. He is married with two children and lives near Oxford. *Pawn's Gambit*, a contemporary political thriller, is his first work of fiction; and the first of a Kate Kimball trilogy.

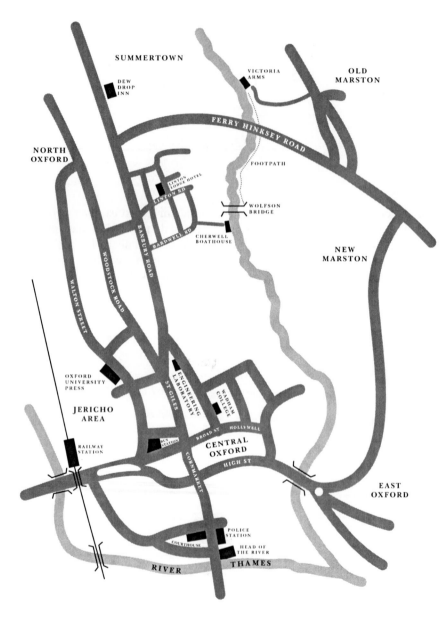

Pawn's Gambit

Harry Armstrong

Arena Books

First published in 2012 by Arena Books *

Arena Books
6 Southgate Green
Bury St. Edmunds
IP33 2BL

www.arenabooks.co.uk

Distributed in America by Ingram International, One Ingram Blvd., PO Box
3006, La Vergne, TN 37086-1985, USA.

Armstrong, Harry
   Pawn's Gambit
   1. Kimball, Kate (Fictitious character) - Fiction
   2. Political fiction.
   I.   Title
   823.9'2-dc23

ISBN 978-1-906791-92-6

BIC categories:- FA, FF, FHP.

Printed & bound by Lightning Source UK

Cover design
by Jason Anscomb

Typeset in
Times New Roman

This book is printed on paper adhering to the Forest Stewardship Council™
(FSC®) mixed Credit FSC® C084699.

PROLOGUE

5.45 pm. 14th November 1983

"There's the turning"

The woman occupying the passenger seat in the front of the van spoke in a flat, expressionless voice, as if rather bored. She pointed to the road junction ahead in an equally off-hand way. The only sign of the rising tension in the van was the fact that she had spoken at all. Unusually for a minor junction, two signs, one on each side of the road, stood out in dazzling white, caught in the main beam headlights of the van. Even without her prompting the driver could not possibly have missed the signs or the turning they indicated. Both recorded that the village of Beckermet was three-quarters of a mile, and the town of St. Bees four miles, off to the right down the B5345. In addition, the sign on the left noted that two railway stations, at Netherton and Braystones could also be found down the same road, as well as a camping site.

The man driving the van absorbed all this sublimally, being acutely familiar with the junction. He said nothing in reply, but slowed and carefully steered the van onto the minor road. Although it was not yet 6 pm., dusk had turned to night. There had been very little traffic on the A595 which they had taken south from their last stopping point at Whitehaven. Nor was there any traffic behind them or approaching them as the van headed onto the St. Bees road. Immediately the headlights picked out a metal fence by the side of the road and, just behind it, a large stone cross in the graveyard of St. John's parish church. This served, and indeed presumably was once at the centre of Beckermet but, over the centuries, or as the result of plague or pestilence, the village must have shifted because, as the sign indicated, Beckermet was now three-quarters of a mile away, with another rather later church now at its centre.

Their destination lay the other side of Beckermet. Next to the later church in the centre of the village was a rather attractive and popular pub; and even on a Thursday in November it could expect to attract a smattering of early evening drinkers, and perhaps a few customers for the pub meals it had recently started serving. But none would recognize the black Ford Transit van, even supposing they saw it; and they headed down the Beckermet road.

The driver remained expressionless, absorbed in his own thoughts. He drove quite slowly, in part because the road, though just about two-way, was quite narrow and twisting; but also because the darkness and the scattered rain which had started as they left Whitehaven made visibility somewhat strained. In addition, however, he was concerned about the equipment in the back of the

7

van, all securely strapped down it was true, but essential for their operation and hence too valuable to take any risk of damaging. He was also mindful of the three men, very much squeezed into gaps between the equipment and the walls of the van and, in their case, only loosely strapped into makeshift seat belts to give them some stability.

The van passed unnoticed through Beckermet and headed on for Braystones. It was along this stretch of road that, nearly two years earlier, they had reached the crest of a ridge and first seen, off to the right, the silver reflecting light of the Irish Sea and, on the left, the target, laid out across much of the horizon, on an almost panoramic scale, looking very much like the set of a futuristic Hollywood film. Now, the absence of moonlight precluded any sight of the sea. But their target was plainly visible, lit by a thousand lights as its workforce went about its twenty-four hour operations. Neither the driver nor the woman in the passenger seat could resist staring at it. Less dramatic, but more important, they saw no other traffic of any kind on the road.

As they approached Braystones the driver could just make out in the dark the outline of a strange ruined tower, a 19th century folly with large barred windows dominating each of several stories. It looked out on the half a dozen or so houses and cottages that formed Braystones, certainly not a village and barely a hamlet, though it had once generated enough business to justify a small halt on the railway line that headed north to Whitehaven alongside, and sometimes virtually on the beach along the coastline of West Cumbria.

Still no one had spoken since they had left the main road but, as they started to climb the no-through-road south-west out of Braystones, the tension, never far from the surface since they had left London that morning, began to be almost tangible. Perhaps to break the tension the driver spoke.
"Five minutes at most"
No one responded, but the woman rubbed her eyes, ran her hands through her short-cut thick dark hair and started to put away various papers and maps that she had been reviewing earlier by torchlight in the glove compartment in front of her. The van headed further up hill, reached a peak and there, despite the hour and the rain, was the very faint sight of the Irish Sea. This, even more than the earlier sight of the target, seemed to engage the attention of the two front seat occupants, and a sense of urgency and energy started to permeate the van. The woman slipped a small pistol out of the bag at her feet and, in a very professional manner that belied her mere twenty-two years of life, checked it, pressed home an ammunition pack and settled it into a leather holster strapped across her chest from shoulder to waist. It was inconceivable that they would come across anyone, but she felt more secure with the pistol, and the others recognised that, as the youngest and a woman, it helped her sense of status

within the team. The driver, at forty-three much the oldest of the team, began idly tapping his fingers on the steering wheel as he went through yet again in his mind the routine to come.

Beyond the hill, the road headed on to a dead-end several hundred metres short of the shingle beach. But just over the top of the hill a large five-bar gate stood open in front of a wide track leading off to the left. This led to a small caravan park, one that in time would become both large and well established. But in the early 1980s there were only ten caravans, all fixed rather than mobile but all used only for brief holiday trips. There was no real prospect that any would be occupied on a bleak Thursday night in November; but Cieran Hughes, the driver and leader of the attack had taken no chances. He knew that the site had been checked discreetly every evening for the last week by Tom Murphy, a local man who had no knowledge of the team's existence and would have no further part to play in the evening's operation. No one had been near the site.

The track led to another gate, this one closed, just in front of the caravan site itself. Hughes slowed the van, then stopped while Mary McGuiness, relieved that they were finally active, jumped from the van, opened the gate and closed it again after the van had gone through. She climbed back in and the van went the last hundred metres or so, stopping just short of a small tunnel which led under the single track railway line to the beach.

The temptation to get on with the operation, now they had arrived, was overpowering. But all five knew the next step, and that it would require great patience. The van's lights were dowsed, the engine switched off and Hughes and McGuiness got out, went to the back and opened the rear doors. The three men inside, Rory O'Halloran, Dougal Hearne and Michael McGuiness, Mary's brother, had already unbuckled their seat belts. All three were evidently rather stiff, but any weariness that they might have felt during their journey from London, with one change of vehicle on the way, was now gone. Over a year of planning, but nearly ten years of forethought were now to be put to the test; and pumping adrenalin was now annihilating any lethargy from the journey.

Nonetheless, when the three of them had climbed out of the van to join Hughes and Mary, all five sat down, leaning their backs against a small stone wall, a long lost remnant of sheep-farming decades or even centuries before, and readied themselves for another half hour of inaction. From now on the operation would go ahead without lights of any kind and so, for absolute accuracy and efficiency, all five would need to have night sight - the power of the human eye, well known to hunters and poachers, to adjust to the dark, like the eyes of a cat, by dilating the pupils to catch and use the limited light available, enabling people to see quite clearly in almost totally black conditions.

It would have been possible to obtain night goggles, and the group had practiced with them; but they were less effective, limited their breadth of vision and generally restricted flexibility. While they had a very precise timetable to meet, to a matter of minutes if not seconds, they had plenty of scope to build in a thirty minute wait to allow their sight to adjust; and knew that, with patience, they would soon be able to see quite clearly despite the darkness of the night. All of them were, in fact, familiar with night sight from earlier times; and Hughes in particular could remember the wonder of it when, as a small boy, he had gone shooting at night with his long since departed father.

No one spoke until, eventually, Hughes said simply
"Everyone OK?"
The other four all nodded, and Hughes, almost in a whisper said
"OK, let's go"
The four men got up, went round to the back of the van and pulled out two large black bags with large strap handles at each end. O'Halloran and McGuinness took one, Hearne and Hughes the other, and they set off, through the short tunnel, onto the beach and headed for the shoreline, just visible in the night about fifty metres away. Mary McGuiness picked up two metal boxes from the back of the van, about the size of small suitcases and headed off after the four men. They, meanwhile, having left the large bags by the water's edge, were headed back to the van, where they unloaded two large compressed gas cylinders, which had been strapped to the inside walls of the van. Between the four of them they carried these down to the sea.

Working in tandem they stripped the bags off their contents. Each contained a small, light but robust inflatable rubber dinghy. Each was connected to a gas cylinder by means of compressor equipment which Mary had brought down in the metal boxes and, in less than two minutes, both craft were fully inflated and ready for service.

Leaving them on the beach, all five returned to the van. Inside, in the centre of the van was an array of aluminium equipment, three rucksacks, a large canister and two large holdalls about one and a half metres long. Mary took the two holdalls; Hughes very carefully secured one rucksack on his back and picked up the two others, one in each hand; while O'Halloran unstrapped and picked up a set of aluminium rods. Hearne and McGuinness gently eased the rest of the equipment out, mainly sections of ladders but also some additional aluminium rods and other pieces, together with the canister, and started to transfer it all down to the waiting dinghies. It took a further trip to get it all to the shore. Then, finally, they all returned to the van and, from two side boxes located against the inner walls of the van, extracted waterproof jackets and trousers. They were not planning to go into the water but, should any of them end up in the Irish Sea, on a cold November night with their clothing dragging them down, none of them was under any illusions as to the difficulty they would face, or how long it would be before hypothermia set in. Within a few minutes, without protection, their bodies would go into thermal shock; and after twenty minutes at most there would be little chance of survival.

The light rain which had been falling when they arrived had virtually ceased. Mary opened the canister, added her pistol to the four others already inside and screwed the watertight lid back on. Then, discreetly, she disappeared around the side of the van to change out of her skirt into the waterproof leggings, not because she felt any embarrassment about changing in front of the men but because she sensed that her brother might feel uncomfortable. Given that, if things went wrong, any of them, perhaps all of them could be dead in a few hours, it was, she knew, a strange thing to worry about; but one's upbringing, one's roots, didn't let you go while you were still alive.

Suitably dressed, they headed back through the tunnel to the beach, roped the two dinghies together; and, while McGuiness and Hearne held the second one steady, Mary climbed into it. Hughes and O'Halloran then carefully loaded all the equipment in with her. All four men then retrieved oars from one of the holdalls, fixed them into rollocks on the front dingy, and climbed into it. It was drifting only slightly in a very mild swell as they took up symmetrical positions both fore and aft and slowly, in the synchronized rhythm they had practiced countless times before, began to row. Imperceptibly at first, but then with gathering momentum, the dinghy moved out to sea, pulling the second dinghy, Mary, their equipment and the rucksacks. It was 6.50 pm. and they were ten minutes ahead of schedule.

Soon they were a hundred metres off shore and, with extensive cloud cover and no moonlight, would already be completely invisible to anyone on shore. Not that there was any appreciable chance that anyone would be looking. Security at the target was probably as tight as anywhere in the United Kingdom – indeed it boasted its own armed constabulary – but they had entered the water almost a mile north of the perimeter fence, and there would be no night time visitors to the caravan site before they returned.

*   *   *

The target, the nuclear installation now known as Sellafield had been through a series of transformations since it started life in the 1950s as the Windscale nuclear plant. Initially it comprised two plutonium production reactors; a chemical plant for separating out the plutonium for bombs; and Calder Hall, an installation designed to produce weapons grade plutonium but also producing electricity as a by-product. In 1963 a new so-called AGR or Advanced Gas-Cooled Reactor was added on the northern edge of Windscale, the new design being preferred because it was less likely to suffer catastrophic failure. Later a much larger re-processing plant, designed to separate out various radioactive elements, was added, enabling Windscale to provide nuclear material for other plants around the country and, later on, around the world. Other new plant was also added, designed to separate out other fissionable by-products, and to store large quantities of material delivered for processing.

In 1973 there was a serious accident in what was known as the Head End Plant; a vast ten storey high plant used for decontamination and treatment of Uranium Oxide prior to it being re-processed. The installation was never used again. In addition, in 1975 Calder Hall was closed. But in 1977, though described at the time as a refurbishment, a large new Magnox power plant was authorized; and in 1978 a new, much larger re-processing plant was approved. However, leakages from some of the ancillary installations continued to occur in the late 1970s; and the new plant was heavily delayed. In view of the increasingly negative impression associated with Windscale, the name of the site was changed to Sellafield in 1981. As Hughes and his team set off from the beach one mile north, the new re-processing plant approved in 1978 had still not reached even the design stage; but the site already covered well over 1000 acres and employed a workforce of over 5000 people.

Given the nature of the operations at the site, security had always been very tight; but it was dramatically overhauled in the late 1970s as Irish terrorist attacks moved to the British mainland. By the early 1980s the three landside perimeters, facing north, south and east, were surrounded by three continuous fences each two and a half metres high, the central fence carrying sufficient electrical current to stun if not completely incapacitate anyone touching it. The inner and outer fences were there primarily to protect the large workforce or any too inquisitive passers by from accidental injury. Covering all of this perimeter fencing were movement detectors which, if activated, set off an alarm in the central security control office and automatically flood lit one hundred metre sections of the fencing around any movement detected. Initially a range of small wild animals kept triggering the system but increased concreting over of the land in front of the fencing, together with improved perimeter roadways both inside and outside the fencing, and the use of much finer mesh in the outer fencing, had largely solved the problem.

This by no means comprised all the site's defences on its landside perimeter. Sellafield's own security police force provided frequent but irregular patrols by car around the perimeter, both day and night; and every inch of the perimeter was covered by CCTV, with a bank of screens being monitored twenty-four hours a day in the central control room, located on the first floor in the security force's own building in the nuclear complex. Even at night the blaze of lights from the thirty or more different buildings on the site provided enough illumination for the CCTV pictures to give good quality, and if the searchlights were triggered, those monitoring the perimeter could have read the labels on an intruder's jacket if it was unbuttoned.

On top of the security building a mini radar station monitored all aircraft within fifty miles of the site; and maintained direct contact with the Kirksdale air force base near Lancaster, including twenty-four hour open channel communication with four aircraft on patrol. Repeated testing had demonstrated that no unauthorised aircraft could reach the site without, if it failed to respond to warnings, being shot down at least ten miles from the site. To complete the security regime, a complex set of codes and recognition mechanisms ensured that no unauthorised personnel could get past either of the two gates into the site. Further security clearance was required by the relatively small number of employees who needed access to the technologically sensitive areas, the nuclear re-processing and reactor areas and the two main control centres which were responsible for different parts of the site.

The western boundary was protected in a slightly different but no less formidable way. The edge of the site ran along the top of a small vertical cliff face twelve metres in height overlooking the Irish Sea. At the foot of the cliff lies a small railway marshalling yard, only infrequently used now for transportation of material to and from the site, but a major portal in the early 1980s. Beyond this the single track railway line runs from Barrow-in-Furness in the south to Whitehaven and Workington in the north. Beyond the track and immediately adjacent to it is the beach.

At the top of the cliff, a couple of metres back from the edge, the electrified fence and the inner protective fence continue on from, and join up with, the northern and southern perimeter fencing, together with the movement detectors, and CCTV. No third, external fence was thought necessary given the proximity of the electric fencing to the cliff top. No external police cars patrolled the area as there is no vehicular access except at the loading and unloading point at the southern end of the goods yard; and no access to the site is possible due to the terrain. However, irregular internal inspections of the perimeter were carried out on foot by members of the security force. In the sea opposite the site, stretching from a point on the beach half a kilometre south to half a kilometre north, and forming an arc nearly half a kilometre out to sea, was a huge boom, a half-metre thick reinforced cable lying on the surface of the water, but anchored to the sea bed and capable of stopping even quite a sizeable ship should anyone think to plan a seaborne attack. Below the surface it supported light but robust reinforced netting down to the sea-bed. A series of sensors would alert security if any part of the cable or netting was broken. This was complemented by permanent radar surveillance covering most of the Irish Sea. The site was regarded as impregnable as it was possible to be. No unauthorised entry had ever occurred in over thirty years and, as far as was known, none had ever been attempted.

*　　*　　*

With the time now just after 7 pm the four men rowed with a slow easy rhythm, the two dinghies moving first due west out to sea and then progressively more southward. They had practiced such rowing in considerably more turbulent seas off the north coast of Northern Ireland, in seas much rougher than they would have contemplated tackling on the operation itself. Hughes had made it very clear from the start, but it was fully accepted by them all, that the operation would not be undertaken, however long they had to wait, until all the conditions – cloud cover, wind, sea swell and tide – were good. But practicing in rougher seas made the operation itself that much easier, one less thing needing any thought as they prepared for the critical phase. They were nothing if not thorough.

Using a watch and compass, Mary McGuiness, perched amongst the equipment a few metres behind the rowers, kept a close track of their movements. Once she had estimated that they were around four hundred metres from the shore-line she raised her arm and called out the one word
"South"
Hughes and O'Halloran, on the shore side of the boat, eased their strokes until Mary dropped her arm, indicating that they were now moving southwards, parallel to the coast. It would now take them about fifty minutes to reach their initial destination.

Over a mile away, a tall, well-built, middle-aged Irishman parked his car in a small lay-by, took out a medium sized case from the boot of the car, and set off on foot into the woods north of the Sellafield site towards its eastern end. He moved slowly, because he had time in hand, and silently, the result of years of experience.

At 7.50 pm Mary saw the defensive boom come into view. She immediately raised her arm to signal that they had reached the cable. They now needed to find a spot on the cable roughly due west of their planned attack point. This would not be difficult because the outline of the various west-facing buildings up on the cliff top, well lit and all by now very familiar to them, were clearly visible four hundred metres away. But, once again, leaving nothing to chance, and needing considerable precision, O'Halloran, the most powerfully built of the four and a good swimmer, had marked the spot two weeks before, swimming out in a wet suit from near the caravan site late one night, taking his bearings with a compass and binoculars, and fixing a small black magnet with a hook on it to the seaward side of the cable at the appropriate spot. He and the others had only to row slowly along the side of the cable until Mary, eyes glued to the bulky black snake-like object, spotted the protrusion.

"We're there" she said, but the others had already seen the small marker as they rowed past it and were starting to bring the two craft to a halt as she spoke. Mary undid the rope connecting the two craft, but kept hold of it as the men steered theirs alongside hers. Then, carefully, one by one, they transferred to her dinghy. This posed no great problem, with the sea quite calm, but even in perfect conditions, with all the equipment crowded into Mary's dinghy, there was always the risk of slipping into the sea as the two craft bobbed up and down. They had thought of using wet suits, but had decided this was too restricting for the operation itself.

With McGuiness and Hearne holding onto the now empty front dinghy, they allowed the second boat in which they all now sat to drift away from the defensive cable; and then edged the other dinghy between it and the cable. McGuiness and Hearne then pressed down on the near side of the empty dinghy, causing the far side to rise up some twenty centimetres or so, while Hughes and O'Halloran, using two of the oars, gently forced the loaded dinghy back towards the cable. This squeezed the empty one against, and then up and onto the cable. A firm push by McGuiness and the empty dinghy flopped into the water on the shore side of the cable, with Mary still holding the loose end of the rope that had initially linked the two craft together.

McGuiness and Hearne now stepped onto and over the cable into the empty dinghy and, while they used their oars to keep it next to the cable Hughes and O'Halloran commenced passing all the equipment from the other boat, over the cable. They worked slowly and carefully, no-one making any sudden movement; but, in practice, the operation proved quite easy. The aluminium equipment was all very light, and the team needed no more than careful timing between whoever was passing it from Mary's boat to whoever was storing it in the other one. It was nonetheless nearly 8.15 pm before all the equipment and all five of them were in the front dinghy and, having tied the other dingy to the hook on the magnet, ready to slide away from the cable towards the shore line.

From this moment on, timing would be critical. They needed to reach the beach by 9 pm. and once there would head straight on; but were confident that they could row to it in 15 minutes at most. This meant waiting for almost half an hour at the cable in a state of extreme tension, but this was the corollary of allowing time for any delays or mishaps on the way, primarily in crossing the cable. And so they waited, rocking gently, occasionally using the paddles to stay next to the cable. Each, even if they didn't know it or express it, was having very similar thoughts about the next hour or so and the vast historical chain of events, of human action and re-action that had led to their present position.

At 8.42 pm. Hughes, without a word, tapped his watch for the others to see and the four men, this time with real power and urgency, began to row. Thirteen minutes later Mary signalled that they were approaching the beach. The men shipped their oars and, a moment later all five quietly stepped into the shallows and pulled the dinghy ashore, some twenty metres of beach separating them from the railway line lying between them and the Sellafield goods yard.

Ironically, they could have arrived at this spot simply by walking the mile or so down the railway line from the caravan site where they had left their van. Passenger trains, though infrequent, passed up and down the line every day and there were no barriers or other type of obstacle to prevent them doing so. But both the north and south perimeter roads of the Sellafield site, on reaching the railway line, ran alongside it for some distance – only half a mile or so to the north but quite far enough to create a real risk of them being seen by a car patrol before they reached the relative security of the darkened goods yard. The approach by sea virtually eliminated the risk of such exposure, allowing the team to reach the perimeter of the site undetected and to a timetable of their own choosing. This was critical, for the key to the whole operation was that for an estimated 28 minutes, from 9.20 pm, the Sellafield western perimeter security system would be blind.

*   *   *

For the man known by everyone on the site as Peter Watson, now sitting with three other members of the Sellafield security team in their control centre, the operation had started over an hour before, when Hughes and the others were rowing steadily south in their dinghies. At 7.43 pm an alarm buzzer had sounded, indicating that something had come into contact with the perimeter fencing in the north-east sector of the site. A movement sensor light had also started flashing for the same sector and, as could be seen very clearly on one of the CCTV screens, the area had been instantly floodlit. The CCTV screens were in two banks, each normally watched by two of the four security team on duty, but briefly all four studied the screens covering, from opposite ends, a 100 metre section of perimeter fencing. There was no sign of any movement.

Instructions for such an event were very clear and well known. First, a standard message went straight through to another building less than 50 metres away, historically always known as the guard house, alerting the twelve or so other members of the security unit on duty - apart from any already out on a patrol - of a 'brown alert', the second of five increasingly serious states of warning. A similar message also went automatically to the security director or one of his two deputies on duty at the time, whose offices and overnight quarters were also in the guard house. Then, for a brown alert, two of the four security officers in the control room would go to the sector from which the warning had come, with open channel communication to the control centre. At no time could there ever be less than two officers remaining in the control centre, to monitor the two banks of CCTVs and the warning systems, and to call for back up from the guard house if either those investigating the alarm needed it, or any other circumstance arose requiring action. For warnings more serious than a brown alert, all four on duty in the control room were required to remain there, with other officers summoned from the guard house to start the process of visual checking.

Perimeter brown alerts were infrequent rather than rare, but there had never been one that did not turn out to be a false alarm, either due to a bird or animal or, on occasion, set off deliberately as part of a programme of testing and evaluating the security team's response times and effectiveness. Each, nonetheless, had to be dealt with as if it were a real alarm. Tony Robinson, a tough, balding and sinewy 42 year old veteran of Sellafield security and in charge of the control room that evening, checked that the alert messages had gone through to the guard room. Watson, choosing his moment carefully – not too quickly but not leaving time for other options to be voiced – said
"I'll go if you want. I could do with some fresh air".

Visual inspections held some attraction for the security officers, as a distraction in the otherwise rather monotonous routine of monitoring the CCTVs and keeping track of the patrol units. But checking for what generally proved to be a dead or dying animal, or very occasionally a system fault, on a bleak November night had its downside as well, and Watson's offer was accepted with a nod from Robinson. No other offer was forthcoming and so Robinson nodded again, this time to Stephen Rigg, a rather gangling, pale faced 28 year who, having become a fully qualified member of the security force eight months before, was only in his second month of duty in the control room.
"You go with him, Steve. See what's up."

Rigg simply said "OK", but was somewhat more pleased than that indicated. It would be only his second activity in any way out of the normal routine, the first being when he had been on gate duty and a truck definitely did not have the correct authorisation papers. He had suffered some abuse from the driver, and the whole matter, inevitably, had been a bureaucratic cock-up; but he had received some much appreciated praise for staying in charge of the situation and playing it strictly by the rules.

Watson and Rigg headed off outside, down the steps and across to one of two Sellafield patrol cars parked in a small yard. For a brown alert, the usual speed limit of 15 mph inside the perimeter fence still applied; and it would therefore take about four minutes to reach the north-east sector, which was at virtually the other end of the site to the control centre.

"What's the betting it's a fox" said Rigg

Watson was not a betting man but, even if he were, he would not have accepted the wager. He knew full well what had triggered the alarm. Someone, though he had no idea who and didn't want to know, had, on cue, fired a bullet from a rifle fitted with a telescopic night sight and silencer, from over 200 metres away in the obscurity of the coniferous trees that form a wood on the north side of the site. This had not hit any of the fences but one of the concrete stanchions that supported the outermost fence, the movement triggering the alarms.

The man was, in fact, Eamon O'Driscoll, a 44 year old senior figure in the IRA who had spent a total of nine years in prison in Northern Ireland but who had disappeared from the British security service's radar some years previously. The rifle and ancillary equipment had been supplied by the IRA's chief armourer three days earlier. Though the armourer had had no knowledge of its purpose he no doubt assumed that it was an assassination. O'Driscoll had crossed the Irish Sea with the weapon, in daylight, in a small fishing vessel and had calibrated the rifle in a heavily wooded area on the lower fells behind Workington. Having fired the single bullet, and seen the lights come on along the section of perimeter fencing he settled down, as comfortably as he could, to wait.

As Rigg and Watson drove, further sections of the perimeter fencing were illuminated by the movement sensors, triggered by their car. After a few minutes they reached the section which had set off the alert, stopped the car and climbed out. Watson knew that they would be monitored by the CCTV system, but nonetheless kept up an irregular flow of comments into the walkie-talkie unit fitted to the collar of his security uniform. Together they walked slowly along the illuminated section of fencing, checking all three fences and keeping an eye on both the external perimeter road surface and the internal one along which they had driven to reach the spot. There was no evidence of anything unusual and they walked back again. Then, following procedure, they contacted the control centre to cut the power to the illuminated section of fencing; got back in the car and headed for the nearest point of access to the area between the inner and outer fences, some 200 metres further on. This comprised a gate in the inner fencing which could be unlocked to allow access to the electric fencing. More sections of lighting came on as they drove.

As they arrived at the access gate, Watson took out a small box from the boot of the patrol car, produced a bunch of keys from his pocket, unlocked the gate and, with Watson carrying the box, they together entered the area between the fences. Again following procedure, Watson obtained confirmation that the power to the section was off and then, with Rigg, walked back to where the alarm had been set off. He then attached electrodes from the box to the now inert electric fence, and then asked control to turn the power back on. Dials on the box then recorded voltage and other details of the current flowing through the wires. This procedure they repeated four times. There was no sign of any system fault that they could see, but recording equipment in the box would be studied later on as a further check. They then requested that the power be cut once again, walked back to the access gate, locked it behind them, contacted control once more to get the power switched back on and got back in the patrol car. They each made short notes in their Incident Books, recording what had happened and how they had responded, before driving back to the control centre, arriving at 8.11 pm. The whole exercise had taken 28 minutes.

As they approached the staircase up to the control room, Watson held back a little, so that Rigg went up the stairs first. As Watson got to the bottom of the stairs his foot slipped and he half fell, grabbing the handrail to support himself.
"Oh shit" he said, pausing on the bottom step.
Rigg looked back.
"Are you OK" he said.
"Yes, I'm fine" replied Watson. "Just slipped on the step. It'll be alright."
He climbed up the steps after Rigg, but with just a hint of a limp, and followed Rigg back into the control room. The night's little excitement appeared to be over.

*   *   *

At 8.57 pm., with three minutes in hand, Hughes, still waiting on the beach with the others, unscrewed the canister lid, took out a pistol which he secured in the belt of his leggings, and handed out a pistol to each of the others. They had no plans to use the weapons, and if they did have to then they all knew that the operation would have failed. The unspoken agreement was that, if things did go wrong, it would be better to try to fight their way out, going down in the process but taking as many with them as possible, rather than face much, if not all of the rest of their lives in prison. Having secured their pistols the team gathered up all their equipment and walked up the beach. They crossed the railway line and then made their way across the seven sets of tracks in the goods yard, reaching the bottom of the cliff just before 9 pm.

The aluminium equipment mainly comprised five lightweight ladders the biggest three of which were each five metres long but hinged in the middle so that no part of the equipment was more than two and a half metres long while being transported, by van or dinghy, to this point. These were unfolded to their full length and the hinges locked. The three were then fitted together like a conventional ladder, with each section sliding through runners fixed to a slightly wider section of ladder. In a procedure which they had rehearsed at least thirty times, they fitted light plastic wire from the bottom of one section, up over small pulleys at the top of the next widest section and back down to the bottom. With two of them holding the wider section and two pulling the wires, the thinner section slowly rose, sliding up inside the runners until, first a nine metre and then a thirteen metre ladder was established. Weight was no problem for the team – each section of ladder weighed less than five kilos – but, even with no wind to speak of, stability was potentially a problem, at least while the ladder was being raised. But raising the second section proved straightforward and, as they had discovered in practice, the secret to raising the third was simply not to rush it. Working together they raised it one rung's length every three seconds, never allowing the ladder to rest against the cliff face. Though it seemed much longer, within four minutes of reaching the cliff the ladder was up, one metre short of its maximum extension, and gently lowered against the cliff face. They could not see the top but, if their calculations were correct – and they had made absolutely sure of them many months before – the ladder now reached to a few centimetres below the top of the cliff face.

Hughes put the lightest of the three rucksacks on his back, attached three small metal devices to his belt and began to climb the ladder, with Hearne and O'Halloran holding the bottom. For the first half of the ascent the ladder was quite stable but, after that, it began to sway slightly, inwards and outwards. Hughes kept going, knowing that if he went very slowly there was little chance of the ladder slipping sideways, which was the only real threat. Rung by rung he edged upwards and finally, after several minutes, his head was just below the cliff top. He consulted his watch. It was 9.08 pm and he had two minutes to wait.

*   *   *

Four minutes earlier, at 9.04 pm exactly, as Hughes was climbing the ladder, Eamon O'Driscoll had fired a second soundless bullet into the same stanchion that he had previously targetted. Like the first bullet, it ricocheted back some thirty to forty metres and was lost in the grass beyond the external perimeter road. The next sixty seconds would determine whether the operation went ahead; but for O'Driscoll, the evening was over. He got up, walked back to his car and drove off. Less than twenty-four hours later he would be back in Northern Ireland and the rifle back in the IRA's arsenal.

A second perimeter alarm in one night, from the same sector, was, as far as anyone there knew, unprecedented; and Watson knew that Tony Robinson, as duty officer in charge for the evening shift, would this time conduct the visual check himself. The question was whom he would take with him.

"Want some more fresh air, Peter?" he said, in an attempt at light-heartedness which did not completely disguise the slight sense of anxiety which was taking hold of him. Clearly something wasn't quite right.

Watson has rehearsed for such a moment more than any actor in a West End production. Striving to ignore the thumping of his heart in his chest he replied, in as casual a tone as he could muster
"Why don't I monitor the screens this time – I've got a bit of a twisted ankle from those bloody steps outside; and it might be an idea if I contact the patrol cars and get one of them to go round on the external perimeter road – see if they can see anything"

They had all known, more than a year previously, when Watson had first got familiar with the job and the plan had been formulated, that it would come down to this moment, to the duty chief's response on a matter that would seem to be of virtually no consequence to him or indeed to anyone. And the half second seemed to hang in the air, take on a discrete identity of its own, separated from time previous or time to come.

"OK" said Robinson "Contact the cars" Turning to the fourth member of the team that night, John Braithwaite, a local man from south of Kendal and another Sellafield veteran, he said
"Why don't you come this time; see if we can find anything these two layabouts missed" He spoke teasingly, promising some caustic ribbing for Rigg and Watson if they returned with some explanation which the first inspection had missed. This time he made a better job of concealing his growing concern.

After all the preparation, with so much at stake, Watson's first reaction was a flood of relief, so intense and overwhelming it was almost physical, surging through his body as he realised that the critical plank in their scheme had held. He instinctively covered this by turning, as casually as he could, towards the internal phone to contact the patrol cars. But barely a second later the relief was replaced by the shock of knowing that they were now, finally, embarked on a mission that would be without parallel in the history of the British Isles, one that would change it for ever.

Robinson and Braithwaite left the room. Watson, again as casually as possible, said to Rigg

"You watch the east bank – see if you can spot anything, while I contact the guard house. I hope we don't have those two crowing all over us when they get back. I'll take the west bank, but let me know if you think you spot anything."

Rigg walked over to the bank of CCTV monitors which covered the eastern half of the site and sat down to watch. Watson alerted first the guard house and then the patrol cars. As he had anticipated, only one was cruising the site at that moment, and he directed it round to the external perimeter road in the north-east sector. He radioed the second car, currently back at the guard house, to be ready to attend if required.

And then, at 9.09 pm precisely, in a movement that would have been virtually imperceptible to Rigg even if he had been watching him rather than the bank of screens, Watson flicked the west central sector perimeter manual override light switch on and off once. It was so fast that the lights did not even come on fully before they went out again, but to five pairs of eyes located by the cliff face below the perimeter fence it was like a flash of sunlight. They too now knew that the operation was on.

Less than a minute later, with occasional comments coming over the loud speaker from Robinson and Braithwaite, and with Rigg following their progress closely on the screens, Watson very slowly moved his hand over the large control board with its array of switches controlling all the various security systems and, coughing slightly to mask the tiniest of clicks, switched off the movement sensors and the electricity supply to the west central sector. Whatever happened he would switch them back on just before Robinson and Braithwaite arrived back in the control room. His part in the night's activities was almost over.

*   *   *

Peter Watson, who sat now staring at the west bank of screens, was, for the first fourteen years of his life, Shaun Riordan, the son of Gerry Riordan, a carpenter in Armagh and his wife Rosin. Those early years were pleasant, uneventful and normal for a healthy young lad growing up in rural Northern Ireland in the 1960s – a village school, the countryside as playground, a poor but not uncomfortable life with devoted parents, and an ever-present sense of excitement, of an unspoken world just out of sight of growing rebellion, of semi-mythical tales of local heroes, danger and death, many episodes of which young Shaun could not tell whether they had happened the week before or nearly two hundred years ago.

Then the night that changed everything, the night which seemingly in an unbroken thread led from then to now, from a country road in Armagh to the control centre at Sellafield 16 years later. Shaun did not know it then but his father was a rather minor though committed member of the IRA, not then a force particularly to be reckoned with. But it was accumulating arms and Gerry Riordan played a not insignificant role in collecting, stockpiling and, occasionally, distributing firearms.

One night in August 1969 he was transporting two armalite rifles and ammunition in his car. With him were his wife, Rosin, Shaun and his seven year old sister Bethany. The impression and indeed the reality of a happy family returning home from a visit somewhere was a convincing cover that Riordan had used more than once in case he was stopped. To date he never had been.

That night, however, a group of four British soldiers mounted an impromptu road check, part of a plan of increasing surveillance of Catholics in the province following the so-called Downing Street Declaration of that same month. It amounted to no more than a small wooden barrier and three lamps, and the soldiers were asking to see some evidence of identity, typically a driving licence. They had no listed of wanted men. It was more just to remind the local community that they might get stopped and possibly searched.

Riordan saw the soldier, rifle in one hand, indicating with the other for the car to stop. Riordan did so and, on being asked for some I.D. handed over his driving licence. It was a scene which was starting to occur frequently throughout the province; but something, some tension in Riordan's stance, perhaps in Rosin's, some atmosphere in the car which even the soldier probably couldn't really describe, led him to become suspicious.

"Will you get out of the car and open the boot please?" he said, in a courteous but firm tone that allowed no misapprehension that this might be a question rather than an order. Riordan knew straight away that if he complied he would, without doubt, face a significant prison term. With his instincts working faster than his brain he released the clutch and hit the accelerator pedal hard. The car, already in gear, shot forward and, in less than two seconds smashed through the temporary wooden barrier. Equally instinctively, two of the soldiers who had remained standing by the barrier raised their rifles and opened fire on the car.

It was later established that probably the only person killed by the shots was Bethany. A bullet hit her in the neck and it was estimated that she would have died a few seconds later. But Riordan was also hit in the shoulder; and the impact was enough to cause him to lose control of the car. It had achieved no great speed, certainly less than twenty miles an hour, but veered off the road and hit a tree with enough impact to crumple the front bodywork of the car and fracture the petrol line. Shaun, badly shaken but virtually uninjured managed to climb out of the offside rear door just before the car burst into flames, incinerating both his parents and the already dead or dying body of his sister.

It is often now forgotten that the Downing Street declaration was primarily designed to help the catholic community by seeking to end discrimination against the catholic population in Northern Ireland; and that the British forces sent to the province at the end of the 1960s were initially welcomed by a substantial cross-section of Catholics. But the searches of catholic homes by British troops, the road blocks and identity searches rapidly undermined this goodwill; and the deaths of three members of the Riordan family were seen as murder pure and simple. It proved to be a trigger for the IRA, whose rather desultory activity up until that point now moved into a much higher gear. Over thirty years of virtual civil war were to follow.

Largely unaware of the shock waves which the incident caused, Shaun, it was decided, would go to live with his aunt Gena in Leeds. She had, several years earlier, married an Englishman, George Watson, whom she had met at the College of Further Education in Leeds when she took a course in business studies. George was taking A levels as a mature student and, the day after being offered a place at Leeds University to study Engineering, he proposed to her.

She had expected strong opposition from her family to the marriage, but George, like Gena, was a rather shy, slightly awkward, but instantly likeable character. He appeared never to have had a political thought or idea go through his head; and they were clearly very happy together. It was, in fact her older sister, Marie who caused the most family heart ache and occasional discord, having emigrated to Canada, albeit with an Irishman from Dublin. Leeds seemed almost next door in comparison.

Gena and George inevitably were seen as the most suitable guardians for Shaun, not only because Gena was his nearest relative but because they had lost their first son, Peter, at the age of two to a crippling bout of meningitis. He would now have been nearly fifteen and, despite a now eleven year old daughter, Marianne, Peter's absence was a daily and permanent fact of their lives. Taking on the care of Shaun could never change this, but it felt the right thing to do in the circumstances. George, in particular, was convinced that both he and Shaun would benefit, and the couple were very happy to take on the responsibility.

Shaun himself responded with a maturity beyond his years. He was far more courteous, pleasant, communicative and generally well-behaved than many an early teenager dealt a far better hand than he had received. He studied, if not hard, then certainly to a level which his teachers found acceptable, even on occasion commendable; and he got on well with his new-found younger sister.

Inside, however, he was close to psychological collapse. In a single moment he had lost his family, and then his friends, his playground, his bearings; and had been moved from a rural existence and a rural pace of life to one of Britain's major conurbations. In some ways it might have been because the shock was so great, the change so total, that he somehow coped and came through - in a sort of numbness of thought, of incomprehension, an absence of feelings – preventing more normal or more predictable reactions to emerge. But somewhere in the centre of this outwardly normal boy, dealing so well as everyone said with the tragedy that had befallen him, entombed in an almost granite-like exterior absence of emotion - fuelled not as many a psychologist might have diagnosed by denial of what had happened but by acceptance - burned an incandescent rage at what the British army had done to his family.

It was Victor O'Connell, a thirty-four year old Republican, until that year deputy commander of the Armagh Brigade of the IRA and a distant relation of both Gerry Riordan and Gena Watson who, on hearing where Shaun had gone, saw with such instant and shocking clarity how this might be used that it seemed almost like a physical blinding flash in his brain. In an instant he knew, beyond any doubt whatsoever, that if Shaun Riordan could, in some way, become Peter Watson, the son of George and Gena Watson, happily settled in Leeds then the boy could be a weapon a thousand times more powerful than all the rifles and explosives that the IRA had accumulated in years. He did not, in that initial dazzling moment of inspiration know how or where, still less when, he could make use of Riordan, but these he knew were mere details. The British had presented him with an opportunity of almost limitless dimensions, and he meant to make sure that it was exploited to the very maximum advantage.

Despite not knowing them at all well, O'Connell sensed, with the type of animal instinct that had saved his life or preserved his freedom on several occasions before, that neither Gena nor George would have anything to do with such a scheme. He also assumed - he did not know because he had never met Shaun - that the boy would be in an unchartered and unpredictable state. And so, to all appearances, he did nothing. He discussed his ideas with no-one; he made no attempt to contact Shaun or the Watsons. To those who knew his past, he seemed to have kept to a decision made earlier, prompted apparently by growing ill health, to withdraw from the high command of the IRA movement. But he made two commitments to himself. The first was to contact Shaun when he was eighteen. The second was, in the intervening six years, to devise the best, the most effective, and the most spectacular way of using this potential new weapon to rid Ireland of the British once and for all.

Unlike the shattering moment when O'Connell saw the scope to use Shaun – a moment he would remember for the rest of his life – O'Connell could not later re-call when he first thought of the nuclear installation located in West Cumbria; but he quickly realised that it was the ultimate, perfect target. An explosion there, releasing radioactivity into the prevailing westerly airflow, would make a substantial area of northern England uninhabitable; and make clear beyond all doubt what catastrophe could and would befall the British if it insisted on its occupation of Ireland. Public opinion would respond to mass, Hiroshima-like death in exactly the way that the Japanese – not known for being supine in the face of attack – had reacted in 1945, by almost instant capitulation.

He needed Shaun to become Peter, and Peter to become a trusted security officer at Windscale, as it was then still called. He provisionally gave himself ten years from when he would first approach Shaun. If the British pulled out of Northern Ireland in that time, he would simply drop whatever specific plan he was pursuing. But if, after that ten year period, the British were still an occupying force in Northern Ireland, then he wanted to have a plan up and ready to go.

The first step, which he took in 1973, with the situation in Northern Ireland deteriorating rapidly, was to contact the now eighteen year old Shaun. O'Connell thought quite hard about trying to find an intermediary of roughly Shaun's age, someone to whom Shaun could immediately relate. He also knew that his own physical presence could be quite intimidating. He was not unusually tall or heavily built, but he was very muscular, in a way that his clothes could not disguise; and there was a hardness in his eyes and in his bearing that deterred strangers and made even old friends cautious. But some instinct told him not to go through a roundabout route, and he had learned to trust his instincts. Shaun would not be 'persuaded'. He either had the inner fire and courage for the project or he didn't; and if he did, then direct contact with a senior IRA officer was what he would need to go forward. And if he didn't – then the project was dead.

O'Connell intercepted Shaun one day on his way home from a summer job in a small local supermarket. Shaun, by now a very presentable six-footer with an intelligent if rather impassive face, thick dark hair, quiet good looks and watchful eyes, had been offered a place at Manchester University to study the newly emerging field of Computing Science and was, like so many imminent students, trying to build up some funds beforehand. O'Connell introduced himself as a distant relation and asked if they could stop off somewhere for a cup of tea and a chat. He had no idea what Shaun's reaction would be to this invitation, but the boy simply said "OK" and they headed for a sandwich bar where Shaun sometimes had his midday lunch.

O'Connell spoke a little of the tragedy of Northern Ireland, of his sorrow at what had befallen Shaun's family, and Shaun himself; but he recognised that this, if not insincere, was rather formulaic, and he sensed that Shaun felt much the same. But such things needed to be said, because the real matter could not be approached without such a pre-amble. After a couple more minutes, in which Shaun said that things had, of course, been difficult, but that he was grateful for O'Connell's words, there was a pause. Then O'Connell said
"You'll know why I am here" There was a slight lilt to his voice, but it was undoubtedly a statement rather than a question. Shaun looked at his cup of tea, said nothing but, almost imperceptibly, nodded his head.

O'Connell had thought hard, over several years, what his next words might be. He had contemplated some history, some modern Irish politics and, most tempting, a call for Shaun to obtain redress for the wanton murder of his family. But in the end he said, simply
"You can do your country a great service". Shaun stared at his cup. Again he said nothing and, for a moment, seemed almost not to have heard. Then, as before, he nodded. It might have indicated no more than agreement that he could, indeed, do his country a great service, but O'Connell new that it was more, much more than that. For O'Connell it was everything.

The two of them sat in silence. There were other things, more practical things, that he needed to say, but the silence was a solidifying of the deal that both knew had just been made. Every second which was not used to qualify in some way their brief exchange was another rod of iron in the scaffolding underpinning the contract.

For Shaun the moment was, in some ways, one of pure release. At some level he knew that the death of his parents and his sister would always be unfinished business. It could not be otherwise. But there was a huge, black hole in his life, a gap in his soul that cried out to be filled with action, not so much revenge – which had little meaning for him – as a need to see their deaths as part of an ongoing history, so that their deaths not only had an explanation but a meaning and a wider purpose of which, in some way as yet unknown to him, he could be an agent.

After some minutes, during which O'Connell made no attempt to imagine Shaun's emotions, but knew this was not the time to discuss matters further, he just said

"I'll get in touch again in a while"

Shaun, for a third time nodded his head and, as if realising that he had said virtually nothing, replied, quietly

"I'll expect you when I see you"

Now it was O'Connell's turn to nod briefly before getting up and heading slowly for the door. The first step taken, he thought, as he disappeared into the crowd of evening shoppers outside.

It was very clear to O'Connell that to get Shaun Riordan inside the Sellafield security force would, as a minimum, require rock-solid documentation that he was Peter Watson, a loyal and trustworthy Brit, and with excellent credentials indicating a good employment record and relevant expertise in security work. A degree in computing would have been a great asset, but the place had been offered to Shaun Riordan, and it could only be Shaun Riordan who would emerge from the course with the knowledge that might make him particularly eligible for security work. Even getting a first job in a security firm would require references from his university, and quite possibly his school; and they would all be in a name that marked him out as of Irish origin.

O'Connell solved all this by thinking on a grander scale. First, he put to the IRA's Army Council that for around £1 million he could deliver a definitive hammer blow against the British Government that would free Ireland. He was not prepared to disclose to anyone what that decisive act might be; and the Army Council was not prepared to allocate such a large sum for an unknown purpose; but three well-connected fund raisers in the United States were alerted to the situation. It took O'Connell three rather circuitous trip to the US, and considerable support for his integrity within the Republican movement before, finally, a self-made Irish immigrant, now in his late 70s - and with a depth of hatred for the British that O'Connell assumed must, in part at least, reflect deep personal loss at some now distant point in the past - agreed to finance his unknown project. The donor assumed that O'Connell would probably use the money to acquire one or more devastating attack weapons, and would have been surprised to know that the money, having been rendered untraceable via a string of overseas banks, was used to set up and then subsidise a perfectly legitimate new security firm in Manchester. The set-up costs appeared in the accounts as a shareholder investment. The ongoing subsidy was provided in the form of a largely ghost client company, set up by O'Connell, which paid for a large scale service from the security firm. This generated sizeable fee income for the security firm, but in practice it provided only limited services, enough to be demonstrable but no more with, consequently, minimal costs involved. The profit generated was then used to pay high wages and salaries, which therefore increasingly attracted experienced and capable staff, while at the same time undercutting, by not too much but nonetheless a significant amount, existing security firms in the Manchester area. Apart from the 'subsidy' the operation was entirely legitimate and was increasingly run by people of some reputation in the business.

Second, he got Shaun to ask Manchester University if they would defer his entry for a year, which they agreed to; and he then enrolled in two courses at Manchester Polytechnic, one in basic computing, the other in business management. He took a series of casual jobs for cash in hand, on a building site, as a waiter and eventually as a stand-in barman. These were mainly so that he had visible means of support, for his living expenses and for a rented room in Manchester; but O'Connell kept him supplied with all the funds he needed. He did all this in the name of Peter Watson, which meant a complete break from his former friends and acquaintances in Leeds. He lived a double life only with his adoptive parents, with whom he spoke on the phone occasionally and visited once or twice. They missed him, but recognised that he was, inevitably growing up and away from them, and were mainly concerned that he was settled and not unhappy. He assured them that all was well, and that he would be going to the University the following year.

Third, and rather to his associates' surprise, he asked the IRA Army Council to use its networks to find a committed supporter in Northern Ireland who was a successful school teacher, one who was prepared to spend some time, several years if need be, in England. The person would continue in his career as a school teacher, and would carry out one, and only one, administrative task for the movement, before returning to Northern Ireland a year or so later. It took nearly a year to identify someone, Patrick Naisbitt, an unmarried man from Belfast who, a year after that obtained a post as deputy headmaster at Hillingdon School, a medium-sized comprehensive school on the outskirts of Leeds.

Meanwhile, the main problem facing O'Connell was documentation. In his new existence as Peter Watson, Shaun would need, most importantly a National Insurance number. Fairly soon afterwards he would need a birth certificate and, ideally, a bank account. Some elements of this were straight-forward. Shaun supplied O'Connell with a key to his home in Leeds and, when George, Gena and Marianne went for a week's holiday walking in the Lake District, he searched the house without disturbing anything. He found little Peter's birth certificate quite quickly, stacked with other poignant mementos of a brief life – some photos, knitted mittens, a cot blanket – in two drawers in one of the bedrooms. O'Connell had been confident of finding it and was also fairly sure that, nearly eighteen years on, its disappearance would not be noticed. Less expected, his searches also found Peter's National Insurance card, a remnant from an earlier age, bearing his National Insurance number. But this, O'Connell knew, was false gold.

In order to tackle the problem of getting the new Peter Watson a National Insurance number, which would be essential if he was to be employed by O'Connell's security firm without any suspicion from the authorities, O'Connell had contacted a number of former Irish associates now living in London. It had taken nearly three months of their rather peculiar brand of networking to identity someone working in Social Security with knowledge of internal procedures relating to a person's first employment. Normal procedure would be for an employer simply to obtain a new employee's National Insurance number, check the employee's name against the file created when the person was borne – computerisation did not begin until seven years later – and the new employee would then be processed both for national insurance payments and for income tax. But where, as in Peter Watson's case, the person had died, the file with its unique number would be removed from the main registry. Any attempt, therefore, by Shaun Riordan to use Peter Watson's original National Insurance number would set alarm bells ringing the moment it was found that no file with that number existed in the main registry. Watson's true fate would almost certainly then come to light.

This was the bad news that O'Connell received from his London contacts. The better news was that, for all sorts of reasons, it was quite common for first-time employees to have no idea of their N.I. number. In most cases the number had either not been noted down by the parents at the time of their child's birth or had been lost some time afterwards. While GPs' files were a usual source of verification, in an increasingly mobile population this was often no longer a traceable source. In such cases, normal procedure was to obtain a birth certificate and use this to locate the appropriate file, and this usually solved the problem. But, in a not insignificant number of cases, no file could be found corresponding to the birth certificate presented. This arose in most cases merely due to administrative error or oversight in communication between the local registration of births and the national social security database. In such cases, the name and details on the person's birth certificate were checked back against the files at Somerset House in London and, if this confirmed the details, a new file was opened and a new N.I. number issued. More detailed checks were reserved for the rather larger number who could produce neither an N.I. number nor a birth certificate. Critically, but not surprisingly, where a birth certificate existed and corresponded with the files in Somerset House, there was not normally a check made against the register of deaths, unless there was some particular reason to be suspicious.

As a result, shortly after being established, Gatehouse Security Ltd., O'Connell's entirely legitimate security company, recruited Shaun as Peter Wilson, the name he had given when enrolling for the courses at Manchester Polytechnic. The company noted in its return to the social security and tax authorities that the new employee had no known N.I. number and supplied the infant Peter's birth certificate. It was found that there was no file corresponding with the certificate and a check was run at Somerset House.

O'Connell knew that there must be some risk, even if small, that, for some reason a check would be run against the register of deaths. At one stage O'Connell had thought to eliminate even this small risk by approaching the official concerned and offering a combination of a large sum of money and what later became known to a wider public as an offer he or she couldn't refuse – probably a photograph of the official's children coming out of school or some such threat – but he knew from his sources that there were several hundred such officials involved in the management of the files, with no way to find out who might process Riordan's registration He therefore had no option but to take the risk. He instructed his people in the company to carry out the administrative legwork, and made sure that Riordan was holidaying in Ireland while the process was in train. In that way, if anything went wrong, Gatehouse Security Ltd. could feign both innocence and considerable annoyance at the attempted fraud; and Riordan would be well away from prosecution. But the project, the grand design, would, he knew, be quite dead. It was, he reflected, the only thing he had left to even a little chance since the day he had first approached Riordan.

O'Connell was not someone to worry greatly about things. He had too much of a sense of the true destiny of his cause, of the inevitable victory whether he was alive to see it or not; but he was both relieved and, he had to admit, hugely excited when, after a seventeen day wait, he heard that Peter Watson was duly registered for employment by Gatehouse Security Ltd., with his N.I. number and tax code. A powerful sense that nothing was now going to stop him gathered force within him, and still no other soul alive, not even Riordan, knew what he was planning.

Riordan phoned Gena and George to tell them that he had decided to take a job with a security firm rather than take up his place at Manchester University. They were supportive in what they said, but he could feel their sense of surprise, perhaps confusion was a better description, at his decision: and he felt some sadness that he was disappointing two people who had helped to save him, turn his life round, provide him with a loving home and a secure upbringing. But, he realised, this was nothing compared to the grief he was likely to cause them at some point in the future when whatever O'Connell was planning came to fruition. He hoped that somehow, at some point, he would be able to explain to them, but doubted whether he had any real prospect of doing so.

Setting up a bank account in the name of Peter Watson was then quite straightforward. Armed with his birth certificate and other documentation, confirmation of his employment and salary from Gatehouse, two letters of reference – one from the company, the other from a solicitor who had acted for an associate of O'Connell – and an initial deposit of £200 from a National Savings deposit which O'Connell had set up in Watson's name some months before, the Ridge Street branch of Barclays, in the Didsbury area of Manchester was very happy to take on its new customer. Riordan's tragic and disrupted childhood, his controlled but unassuagable hatred of the British, and his disciplined and implacable determination to give some meaning to his family's deaths were all now completely hidden behind the rather mild if somewhat sombre air of a 20 year old trainee security officer, with no discernible link to any aspect of Ireland, its politics or its historical enmities.

Over the next three years, O'Connell's men, one by one, backed out of the company except the Managing Director, a man recruited from O'Connell's extensive network of contacts in Dublin, and the Finance Director, a very precise, down to earth Londoner of Irish descent. Meanwhile Peter Watson, as he now thought of himself, learnt the security business – the design of security systems for premises and for the transportation of valuable cargo or people; the manning of security operations; the bureaucracy of running a security firm; insurance; all the ways known to compromise a system and how to minimise the opportunities for this to occur; recruitment, which was particularly ironic in view of his own; preventive strategies; the technology involved; how to deal with attacks; police methods; a whole range of new computer applications then starting to come into the business, and much more. He learnt from the bottom up, spending time on patrol duties but increasingly more supervisory and management aspects, and all in the context of a growing, thriving and effective company, given its secret source of underlying financial strength.

It was then a matter of how well Watson responded, and he did not let O'Connell down. He enjoyed the work, he felt secure in his new identity, and he also felt a sense of purpose in his life that undoubtedly had not existed before. And there was a simmering excitement in knowing that, in a way yet to be explained to him, he would make a major difference to the course of Irish history. O'Connell, for his part, was very pleased at how things were working out. He had spent nearly £1 million to give Riordan an impeccable pedigree, a track record that few if any would seriously think of questioning unless some good reason presented itself, and he regarded the money as well spent. He made one trip to the US to let his benefactor know, face to face, that the project was going well; but refused to make any mention of what the project was, and his US source did not press him.

Riordan had very few meetings with O'Connell. It was in fact at only their fifth or sixth since Watson had started the job that, with three years of excellent training and experience behind him, O'Connell said the time had come to take the next step. He should now, approaching his twenty-fourth birthday, apply to join the police force. This would not only greatly help his record and career prospects when the time came to apply to Sellafield, but would sever his last tenuous links with anything or anyone that could be connected to Ireland.

Watson's experience got him an interview without difficulty, and in fact he was much better qualified than most young recruits interested in joining the police force. The most difficult question he had to face was quite why he wanted to make the move. The pay was no better, indeed initially less good, and he would, no matter what his record showed, have to do two years on the beat before he could hope to start to rise through the ranks. Watson professed a fascination with detective work, a career for which he was quite prepared to make short term sacrifices and, two months later, he became a member of her Majesty's constabulary, based in Manchester.

He endured the work of a bobby on the beat for two years, from 1978 to 1980, before starting in a patrol car, but with the promise of moving to patrol car co-ordination work within a few months. Nine months later he was assigned to work as an assistant to a Detective Inspector. O'Connell envisaged perhaps two more years of this before Watson would have a change of heart and seek to revert to his previous career in security, when suddenly the opportunity that O'Connell had been keeping an eye out for arose – rather too soon from his point of view but it was too good to miss. Sellafield, as it had now become, was still expanding, primarily due to its increasing pre-occupation with nuclear re-processing; and the obvious target which the site presented to Britain' enemies was becoming more and more of a concern to the government. A major overhaul and expansion of its security was put into operation, and recruitment advertised in the trade press.

In the late summer of 1981, O'Connell met Riordan one evening, in a bar in Halifax. Riordan knew the moment they met that something major had happened. O'Connell immediately confirmed this saying that the opportunity he had been waiting for, planning for, had now arrived.

"I want you to apply for a job with the Atomic Energy Authority's security force at Sellafield" he said, in a quiet voice, fixing the young man with his eyes. "This is what it has all been about".

Outwardly, to O'Connell, Riordan seemed not to react. Inwardly, he couldn't count the various reactions he experienced: what a brilliant, what an obvious target; could such a penetration really be possible; what was O'Connell's plan; could he, Riordan, carry out. He said nothing and O'Connell couldn't help but ask

"What do you think?"

Riordan smiled, something that O'Connell had rarely seen him do, and asked "Will I get to walk away"?"

It had several times crossed his mind that whatever O'Connell had in mind for him might involve him losing his life. Whether it was because of all that happened, or whether because he wasn't really facing up to an as yet unknown project he did not know but, either way, the prospect of dying did not panic him. A life sentence in prison held far more fears for him, but there would be time enough to think about these consequences once he knew what O'Connell was planning. Now it seemed as if his life rather than his freedom was more likely to be at stake.

"You will be at least a hundred miles away when things start to happen" said O'Connell. "I give you my word on that".

"Then let's get going" said Riordan. "We've both waited a long time for this".

The pay levels offered at Sellafield were good and, as intended, the number of applications was high; but for a mainstream security officer's job, Watson was well qualified. His time at Gatehouse, backed by a good reference, assured his potential employers that he was well trained in the skills required; and his time in the police force was some assurance that he had a sense of public duty, and an understanding of exacting standards of authority and responsibility. In fact, once again, the toughest question was to explain why he wished to apply, again for no more money, just as his career in the police force was beginning to take off. Watson explained that, after three years in the police force, he had, somewhat to his surprise, found it less challenging and less varied; and he now realised that he had had an excellent start in the security business which would, he thought, stand him in better stead for a good career than in the police force.

He added that he had a fiancée who was a teacher in Kendal and that they wanted to live in the Lake District. A job at Sellafield would be ideal therefore, even if the job turned out to be somewhat more junior in content than he felt qualified to take on. For good measure he added that, if one saw one's future in the security business, there wasn't anything better than to join the private police force guarding Sellafield.

On the day that Watson sent in his application, O'Connell phoned Patrick Naisbitt to initiate his role in the operation. Naisbitt knew absolutely nothing of O'Connell's plans, nor even the existence of Riordan or his new identity. He had simply but firmly been instructed that, on receiving a phone call from O'Connell, he would make it his job to intercept the post to the school where he taught, looking for anything official with a Cumbrian postmark. He managed this by turning up an hour early every day, a change of routine which he explained by saying that he was starting to write an introductory text book on Chemistry, and would make no progress unless he put aside an hour a day when he was not totally exhausted. The letter he had been told to expect would be official and from Cumbria; and he had little difficulty in duly recognising it. He nonetheless steamed it open, in case it was not the letter he had been led to anticipate. It was, however, as predicted, a request from the Atomic Energy Authority for confirmation that one Peter Watson had attended the school from 1966 to 1973, together with a request for any information about his performance or character. Naisbitt duly replied, saying that the headmaster had asked him to do so; that he could confirm Watson's attendance at Hillingdon school, before going on to study in Manchester; and that he had been a bright, normal, reasonably well behaved but otherwise unremarkable boy. He hoped that this would be helpful, and was happy to be contacted if they needed any further information.

The rest of Watson's legend, as the British security services would have called it, was rock-solid. He had had a reasonable education, had a good employment background, appeared reliable and conscientious, was commendably ambitious and financially prudent. O'Connell was finally prepared to admit to the doubts he had resolutely refused to acknowledge over the previous five years, as he saw a vast sum going into a major corporate venture, employing at one stage over eighty people, all of which was merely an enormous sham, designed to give unshakeable credentials to one young orphaned Irish lad who could, nonetheless, change Ireland for ever.

In November 1981, Watson started work at the site, progressively relaying to O'Connell, in now much more frequent meetings, the layout of the site, the nature of the security operations there and the site's defences against penetration and attack. O'Connell began to think out how best to proceed. At this point still no-one other than Riordan and he had any idea of where he was headed. It had become clear to the Army Council back in Ireland that he must be planning a mainland attack. But that was all. O'Connell's American source of funds was anxious – as far as he knew nothing had happened in four years – but his anxiety arose only from the fear that he might die before finding out what he had financed, rather than any concern that his money had been squandered.

*   *   *

Now, two years later, Watson sat staring at the bank of CCTV monitors covering the western half of the site. Those covering various locations within the perimeter fence were brightly lit; those covering beyond it were dark. They would light up if the movement sensors triggered the array of high powered lights along the perimeter fence but, with these disabled, Watson knew that he would see no sign of the incoming attack team until they were inside the fence.

Outside, Hughes took out one of the three metal devices he had taken with him as he climbed the ladder. It was a rod about half a metre long, with a spike at one end curving away 90 degrees and a handle at the other end. Hughes climbed a few rungs up the ladder, so that his chest was level with the top of the cliff face; reached forward, raised the rod and then slammed the spike into the ground in front of him. He then grabbed the handle and pulled himself forward, onto the top of the cliff. If anything had gone wrong, he reflected, if the movement sensors had not been disabled, all hell would be about to break loose.

Silence and darkness continued to rule. He took out the other two devices and, with one of them, knocked very quietly on the top of the ladder. Twelve metres below Mary McGuiness, who had her ear pressed to the bottom of the ladder, heard and to some extent felt the light vibration. She signalled the others and together they eased the ladder away from the cliff face, by only a centimetre or two, and raised the ladder its last metre. Hughes, at the top, steadied the process and, with the ladder now protruding a metre above the cliff top, he secured it with the two metal devices - each with a hook at one end and a spike at the other - firmly to the ground at his feet. At the same time Hearne and McGuiness fixed two devices looking exactly like croquet hoops over the bottom rung of the bottom section of ladder and secured them into the earth at the bottom of the cliff face. These actions had taken less than one of the twenty eight minutes they had available.

O'Halloran then fitted a light metal frame onto his back, the sort that would support a large Bergen-style rucksack but without the rucksack itself, and stepped onto the ladder. He climbed two rungs and then waited while Hearne

36

and McGuiness fitted another folded aluminium ladder, also two and a half metres in length, onto the frame, so that it stretched somewhat above his head and somewhat below his feet on the ladder. McGuiness tapped him on the leg to indicate that the equipment was secure and O'Halloran set of fast up the ladder which, now secured firmly at both ends, was entirely stable.

It took him considerably less than a minute to get to the top whereupon, after another lightly tapped signal, Mary followed him in similar fashion, but with a single two and a half metre section of ladder on her back. As soon as she was at the top, the three of them who had climbed the cliff face moved to the electrified fence a few metres away, leant the first section of the folded ladder against the fence and then, with O'Halloran progressively climbing the rungs of the ladder, swung the other section over the top of the fence until it came to rest, in a horizontal position, supported at the other end by the internal perimeter fence. O'Halloran then cautiously started to move out along this second section of the articulated ladder and, when he reached the far end, signalled for Hearne, who had by now climbed the first section, to pass him the final section of laddering. He then gently lowered this down the inward face of the internal perimeter fence, clipped it into two specially prepared clips on the end of the folding ladder, swung his body round and slowly descended into the Sellafield site. Hughes, standing at the bottom of the fence, was removing the lighter rucksack from his back, but nodded in approval.

Meanwhile, McGuiness and Hearne had each donned one of the two large rucksacks and climbed swiftly up the main ladder. They arrived at the top just as O'Halloran completed the team's entry path, and both moved to join the others at the perimeter fencing. Each rucksack was then passed from McGuiness on the ground to Hughes on the first leg of the ladder, then to Hearne half kneeling half lying on the vertical section and on to O'Halloran on the far side. Mary checked for any instability in the ladder but, as with the countless practices they had carried out, on an exact replica of the situation, the equipment remained robust and secure. When the third rucksack reached O'Halloran, Hearne and then Hughes carefully climbed across and down to join him inside the perimeter fence. Mary descended the main ladder to wait at the foot of the cliff, while her brother climbed onto the main ladder but descended only a few rungs, so that his head was just below the top of the cliff. They had used up less than five minutes of their allotted time.

In the control room, Riordan saw O'Halloran on one of the CCTV screens, and then Hearne and Hughes, as they climbed down inside the perimeter fence. Though the security lighting and alarms had not come on, there was quite enough light from the Sellafield plant itself for them to be visible to anyone who might look at the screens. Rigg, however, on the other side of the room, was watching Robinson's and Braithwaite's progress on the other set of screens If he had detected any uneasiness in Riordan's manner, which was highly unlikely, he would have put it down to the same cause as his own slightly uneasy feeling, that they had somehow missed something out on the north-east perimeter which the other two would find. The reaction, depending on what they had missed, might well be significant in terms of their record of performance at the site, and Rigg therefore watched his screens with more than usual concentration.

Outside, in fact less than three hundred metres away, Hughes, Hearne and O'Halloran each put on a rucksack and set off down a wide path between two windowless blocks, heading for building B701.

*   *   *

Once Riordan had, as Peter Watson, started work at the site, he and O'Connell – and it was now very much the two of them working together - had three problems to solve. The first was how to use Riordan's position to penetrate the site; the second was where to strike; and the third was how to recruit the team that would be needed. It was Riordan who solved the first. After a probationary six month period at the plant, primarily on gate and patrol duties, he was told that his name would be added to the duty roster for shift work in the control centre. As a preliminary, he had to read a 220 page manual covering all aspects of the work of the control centre, the equipment, rules and procedures. He read this, he suspected, with more enthusiasm and concentration than any new security officer had ever read it; and it was while reading it, even before starting work in the control room – though he had been in it a few times, for briefings and the like – that he saw the flaw for which he was looking, the tiny unforeseen chink that he and O'Connell might well exploit. For a low grade perimeter alert there would, for a very limited period of time, be only two, rather than four officers in the control room.

At that moment he had no idea how long or short such a period might be – clearly minutes not hours – but it might be enough to allow a team in. He and O'Connell then had to wait another frustrating four months before there was such an alert. Riordan did not himself go on the visual inspection of the alert, which turned out to be caused by a too adventurous vole, but he timed it at nineteen minutes. This, however, had been relatively near the control building. Riordan was able to estimate that for an alert generated at the far end of the site, they might have a little under half an hour. O'Connell, when Riordan told him about the alert, said with a faint smile that the dead vole would last a very long time in the hearts and memories of the republican movement in Ireland.

The problem was how to ensure that, when the moment came, Riordan would not be sent on the visual inspection. It was O'Connell that came up with the plan for two distractions, the first of which Riordan would contrive to go on; hoping this could be used to steer selection of the officers for the second check away from Riordan, but with the back-up, probably unnecessary as it turned out, of a slightly twisted ankle. With this plan in place, and Riordan checking out the details of how it would work, they now needed to decide where to strike.

O'Connell had always known that entry would have to be secured via the western perimeter above the cliff face. It was partly that this was the only point at which a team could get close to the perimeter fence before their limited window of time would commence; but, more importantly, there was no other section of the perimeter which a team could approach without running a very real risk of being spotted by a random patrol. The distractions would therefore have to be at the far, eastern end, which presented no problems; and the specific target would have to be close to the western perimeter fence.

Initially, when conceiving of Windscale as a target, O'Connell had, in some rather ill-defined way, envisaged an attack with explosives on a nuclear reactor, with a mushroom-like cloud rising into the sky, unstoppable as it started to drift westwards across northern England. His occasional meetings with Riordan, once he was a member of Sellafield's security force, soon disabused him of that aspiration. The two reactors were housed inside enormous concrete blocks, at least two metres thick Riordan estimated, as he went about his duties at the site. It would have taken a large truck load of explosives outside either building to have any chance of making a dent in the reactor itself, and O'Connell had no way of getting such a load into the site. Much less explosive would be necessary if it could be stacked inside one of the concrete blocks, right next to the reactor itself; but this, it soon became clear, was equally impossible. Entry to the reactor buildings was heavily guarded, and armed guards roamed the insides of the buildings in pairs, making any type of successful penetration impossible.

Riordan and O'Connell therefore turned their attention to other possibilities. Their first alternative was one of the re-processing plants which separated out various radioactive elements, but this plan rapidly ran into exactly the same problems – vast concrete buildings, heavily guarded entry and internal security patrols. Riordan looked at some of the storage tanks designed to hold radioactive material, but they were immensely thick, heavily lined structures which they had no confidence they could breach with the amount of explosive they could hope to get into the site. The site also contained large covered 'ponds' for holding and treating lower grade material, but these were set into the ground and there seemed no way of ensuring any significant leakage could be generated.

Eight months after Riordan started work on the site, and two months after he had been introduced to the control room roster, O'Connell, for the first time since he had initially envisaged Sellafield as a target, began to doubt that his grand scheme could be made to work. Despite the enormity of what he was planning, he was not one given to romantic flights of fancy, particularly in relation to operational matters in the war with the British; and he began to think that the nature of the target was such that it was just not possible to bring about the epoch-changing event he had for so long plotted. Riordan carried on looking for potential targets, but he realised, no less than O'Connell, that the whole operation, now nearly ten years in the planning and preparation, might, after all, not be feasible.

It was in July 1982, shortly before Riordan was due to take a summer break, that a change in the patrol roster led him, in company with Harry Motson, a much older man but who had only been with the AEA security force for about four years, past what he later found out was designated as building B701. Motson was not, he said, entirely clear as to its purpose – there were so many buildings on the site and all the security team needed to know was the security classification of each building; but he understood it was, for some reason, called the Export Plant and, as far as he understood, the plant inside had been used in the past to siphon off some by-product which was then shipped to a glass manufacturer somewhere in England. As far as he knew, however, this business was no longer active, and building B701 was not in use. This accounted for its security rating of 'C', a grading system that, confusingly, had nothing to do with the A, B and C designations in front of each building's number, the latter reflecting the operational role of each building on the site.

Buildings with an 'A' security rating, such as the reactors and re-processing plants, had maximum security, with fortified entry, internal patrols and full CCTV monitoring. Those rated 'B' had at least one guard at their entry point and were visited by a roving patrol at least once every half an hour. 'C' rated buildings had no permanent guard, but were visited at least once every hour. In practice quite a number with a 'C' rating were no longer operational and, like B701, received only a cursory drive past to comply with the regulations.

It was another three weeks before Riordan was able to patrol near B701 again, this time with another Peter, Peter Lang, who had joined the service at roughly the same time as Riordan. As they passed the building, Riordan casually said

"Have you ever checked that building?"

Lang replied "No, I don't even know what it's for. I've never seen anyone near it"

"I think its disused" said Riordan "But I suppose we ought to check it occasionally. Let's have a look"

They stopped the car; Riordan got out of the car and went over to the building. It was about twenty metres by forty, single storey, and rather overshadowed by one of the large pylons that carried power lines across the site. To one side there were steps leading down into the ground. Riordan went down the steps to a door some five metres below ground level. It was locked but, through a rather murky window, Riordan could see that the building descended at least another ten metres. Despite its appearance on the surface, it was roughly a three storey building set deep into the ground.

Keys for all security category C buildings were kept in the control room and, the next day, Riordan picked out those for building B701. He told Lang that he thought they should, at least once, check the building out more thoroughly and, although Lang could see little point in the exercise, it was of mild interest and certainly not outside their remit of duties.

On entering the building, they found a metal stairway which allowed them to descend to the bottom of the structure. Most of the building was taken up with various unrecognisable pieces of machinery, storage tanks and pipe work, all of it, they could see, stemming from very large pipes, with a diameter of perhaps a metre or more, running along the floor of the building from one end to the other. The air was cold and the atmosphere quite dank. It was clear that no-one had used the plant for a long time.

"Any idea what any of this is for?" said Lang, wandering idly along one of the catwalks which led off from the stairwell.

"Harry said that they used to tap off some by-product, for making glass I think he said, but not for quite some time. Anyway, it doesn't look like we need bother much with it. I'll just check along the bottom and then we can head on" He spoke casually, but he could feel the tension rising in his body. The moment he had seen the large pipes at the bottom of the building he had begun to visualise the layout of the site; and he could see at once that the pipes ran along a line from building B205, one of the main re-processing plants, to B215, which contained large storage tanks for the material separated out in the re-processing operation. If this was correct, then highly radio-active material flowed through those pipes; and they were vulnerable to attack.

Riordan went down to the bottom of the steps, to find that the pipes, at each end, disappeared into tunnels, no doubt to allow access for inspection purposes, about a metre and a half high. In one direction the tunnel continued for some distance, some thirty metres he estimated, before ending in a concrete wall. The piping headed on, through the concrete, heading directly into building B205. Riordan would have liked to explore further in the other direction, but he knew this was a risk too far with Lang up above him inspecting the inside of the building itself.

That evening, Riordan contacted O'Connell and told him what he had found.

"The piping carrying the stuff from the re-processing plant to the storage tanks is very poorly protected" he said. "It's clear that the building itself is no longer used. I think they must have decided not to have a permanent guard and downgraded its security rating to 'C'. I'll see what I can find out"

"You need to be very careful about that" said O'Connell. "They mustn't get even a hint that you have any particular interest in the building". He mused for a moment. "Are you sure that the pipes do actually go from the re-processing plant to the storage tanks? I know you said that the re-processing plant was quite close, but the storage tanks are some distance away aren't they?"

"I'm not sure, no" said Riordan, "But it's our best chance yet. Don't worry, I won't do anything to raise any suspicion." He paused then added, with a small smile "You know the other great advantage of 701, don't you?"

"No, said O'Connell, "What's its big attraction?"

"It's only about two hundred metres from the western perimeter" said Riordan.

Riordan had no doubt that the pipes he had discovered emanated from building B205, the largest re-processing plant on the site, constructed as Sellafield's role as re-processor for nuclear plants around the world expanded. The concrete wall at the end of the tunnel under B701, where the large underground pipes disappeared, was so near the re-processing plant that it could easily be part of massive foundation works underlying it. He therefore took the opportunity of his next few patrols to examine the area between B701 and the storage tank building some three hundred metres away. It then became immediately obvious that there were two small buildings of a type he had seen all over the site, covering inspection areas, which between them neatly split the distance from the re-processing plant to building B215 - which housed several large storage tanks - into three. He was now more than ever sure that the underground pipes fed the storage tanks, but he knew that he would have to go inside the two small inspection buildings to check.

This took him nearly another month, because both he and O'Connell agreed that each check should be done only when he was with a different patrol member from the security force; someone who knew nothing of his checking of B701 and, equally knew nothing of his checking the other inspection building. Each structure turned out to be identical, basically little more than a large metal staircase descending two storeys into the ground. Though he had had little doubt what he would find, he felt a huge rush of adrenalin as he neared the foot of the staircase and saw the same large pipes that he had seen in B701, running along the bottom of the stairwell. Here also there were tunnels, again running in both directions, and it was clear that it was possible to reach any part of the pipe work as it ran, in a dead straight line, to the storage tanks. They had found no less than three possible attack sites.

O'Connell took an extended trip back to Northern Ireland, to seek advice on how best to breach the pipes. He explained to Sean Cagill, one of the IRA's top explosives experts, the set-up that Riordan had discovered, omitting only the location of the target and the strong likelihood that the pipes would be internally lined with lead or some lead-based material. He reported, however, that the pipe would be double-lined, heavily packed between inner and outer casing, and with both casings being exceptionally thick.

Initially the news was not good. Such a target would need a very large quantity of explosive, not only because of the characteristics of the pipe which O'Connell had described, but because a spherical surface itself needs considerably more force to rupture than a flat surface. When O'Connell said that the explosives would have to be capable of being carried by a small number of men, Cagill began to think that it could not be done. But then he began to focus on the setting. If the explosive was set in the tunnel under 701, not only against and around the pipe but also against the end concrete wall, then the enclosed space would greatly increase the force of impact. This would not, he thought, on its own be enough to ensure success but, utilising the effect of the enclosed space, there might be a way, if O'Connell, or more precisely if O'Connell's team, whoever they might turn out to be, were prepared to use it.

Cagill had assumed initially that O'Connell would need to use Semtex, a powerful but manageable and, above all, very stable explosive, used in a variety of industries and therefore relatively easy to get hold of. But he knew that there was a Czech variant of it, known only as CH10, mainly used in quarrying, which was almost twice as powerful and, moreover, cheaper to produce. Its drawback was that it was somewhat less stable, and two or three industrial accidents as a result of its use had led most countries in Europe and North America to prohibit its use, even for quarrying, on safety grounds. But Cagill knew he could get it if required and, even though it was more unstable, treated carefully there was no reason why it shouldn't do the job O'Connell required. He became still more confident when, in answer to his questioning, O'Connell confirmed that the explosive would throughout the planned operation be in temperatures not much, if at all, above freezing.

Cagill had one further refinement. If, he said, the explosive was laid in two separate blocks, immediately next to each other but each with its own detonator, then it would be possible to wire it up so that one block detonated a fraction of a second before the other. At any safe distance the outcome would sound indistinguishable from a single explosion; but the impact would be quite different. This was because the force of the second explosion would bear down on a structure that would already have started to buckle, and the impact of forty pounds of CH10 on faulty piping, however slight the fault at that moment, would be hugely exacerbated.

Allowing for the greater explosive force of CH10, and the fractional delay in the detonations, together with the enclosed space in which the explosions would occur, Cagill ended up surprising O'Connell with his best estimate of how much explosive would be required. Eighty pounds he said should do it, equivalent to a single block of over three hundred pounds of ordinary Semtex in an unconfined space. O'Connell knew that this could be carried by two men.

O'Connell set in motion the process of authorisation by the Army Council for Cagill to acquire eighty pounds of CH10. He now had almost everything in place, and still no-one other than Riordan and he himself knew the target. The final step in his preparations, however, would, inevitably change that. He had worked out the actual logistics of the attack with Riordan over a period of several months and now needed a team, a minimum of five, and ideally six, in addition to a marksman; and a local man to check the caravan site.

Cieran Hughes was, for O'Connell, the obvious choice to lead the attack Now in his forties, he had been with the IRA for nearly twenty years, had fourteen years' experience of attacks, on British and Ulster Constabulary patrols, vehicles and buildings. He was familiar with the use of explosives; an expert in keeping very tight security and, no less important from O'Connell's point of view, a natural leader. Powerfully built, taciturn, a man who demanded much of those he led, but one who rapidly gained their confidence, through his reputation, his loyalty to them, and his ability to lead in virtually all aspects of clandestine activity through example.

It took a while for O'Connell to contact Hughes, whom he had not seen for nearly two hears and who was no longer living in Northern Ireland. He eventually tracked him down to a pub near the flat he was renting in Kilburn in North London, in the heart of the capital's Irish community. He didn't ask what Hughes was doing in Kilburn, but he was very encouraged by the fact. It suggested that he had some sort of action of his own on the mainland in mind.

After a short conversation about very little, O'Connell explained that he was looking to set up a team to carry out a mainland bombing, and wanted Hughes as its leader. Hughes asked what the target would be. O'Connell paused for a moment. He would clearly have to reveal his plans before Hughes could give any thought to his answer; but, after nearly ten years of nursing his secret, one that still no-one else other than Riordan knew, it was not easy to let someone else in. If only to help himself through the moment, O'Connell said

"Cieran, I've been working on this for the best part of ten years; the operation is worked out at quite a detailed level, and only one other person knows of its existence. It would help me a whole lot if you could give me some sort of.... I don't know what really, some sort of idea if you would be likely to take on something bigger than anything that we have ever tried, as long as you think it looks sound operationally".

Hughes sat, at first just looking at his half-filled beer glass. Then he slowly looked up, straight at O'Connell.

"I'm not going to commit myself without knowing what you've got in mind" he said quietly " but if it is as big as you say, and if it will work, then why would I not take it on?"

"You might not think it *will* work" said O'Connell.

"In that case I won't do it" said Hughes "But knowing you, Victor, if you have been working on it for ten years, it'll work".

O'Connell paused again, then said "It's the nuclear site at Sellafield. I've got a sleeper in there, working for the security force. I've got a route in, and out, and a target that will blast out radio-active material. It should make the whole site unusable, and dependent on the weather conditions, could make a large chunk of Northern England uninhabitable for some while. It will certainly cause mass panic and, quite possibly, a huge exodus of the population in the North-West. But the main thing is that it will show the British Government, once and for all, that the price of staying in Northern Ireland is too high"

O'Connell knew that it sounded rather like a prepared speech which, he reflected, wasn't surprising given that it basically was one. But, if he was going to reveal his years of planning, then he wanted Hughes to feel some element of the awe that he himself felt at the audacity of the plan, and the potential consequences.

Hughes sat, motionless, saying nothing. What O'Connell had said had jolted him mentally, and almost physically; but it was not in his nature to respond quickly. Instead he let the idea wash over him, play over in his mind and, as all sorts of questions came to mind, gently eased them to the back of his brain, while he increasingly concentrated on what actually were the matters which might decide him one way or the other. This seemed to go on for some time, but it was less than a minute before he recognised that, provided the plan looked sound, then there was no question in his mind that he would do it.

"Let's go back to my place" he said eventually "and you can talk me through how you are going to manage it. If I like it, the answer's "yes".

Hughes didn't just like the plan; he loved it. In particular he loved the way it combined a hugely prolonged operation simply to get someone on the inside with just two very slight weaknesses in the site's defences – the rules for dealing with a low level perimeter alert, and the decision not to permanently guard an on-site plant which had ceased operation. All the rest was just consequential logistics. By the end of the evening he was as committed as O'Connell.

It was Hughes who recruited O'Halloran and Hearne. As O'Connell had suspected, Hughes had been starting to work on an operation in London with the other two, but it was very early days, and the chance to move straight in to the active phase of a major operation was irresistible. Both were living in or near Kilburn, heavily ensconced in the Irish community in the area and, like Hughes, thought the plan that O'Connell had devised was perfect.

Rory O'Halloran and Dougal Hearne were both experienced IRA warriors. Both in their early thirties, they had been active for a number of years in Northern Ireland, but had learnt how to survive invisibly in London. Neither was particularly gregarious and neither had as yet put down any family roots, though Hearne had a rather on-off relationship with a woman from County Cork; a friend of a cousin he had met three years before. Both not only trusted Hughes implicitly but to some extent lived in awe of him – his resourcefulness, nerve and his logistical skills. Both were well built, fit and, perhaps a disadvantage in London, had the unmistakable look of men trained in army, or at least military ways.

It was some time before they identified the fourth member of the team; and they discussed at some length whether he was really suitable. Michael McGuiness was certainly very different. Aged twenty-four, he was much younger than the other three. Of average height, thin build but with an athletic agility and with cheery good looks, he could charm people when necessary and was also, by some long way, the best high speed driver Hughes had ever come across. It was this skill that had led Hughes to recruit McGuiness for the operation he had planned in London. He found McGuiness's rather carefree manner grating at times, a youthful exuberance that seemed to suggest a lack of seriousness; and he wondered sometimes if McGuiness wasn't more in it all for the sheer thrill, rather than any great commitment to the cause of Ireland; but his credentials were unchallengeable and he could outdrive anyone if the situation needed it. Hearne, who had known McGuiness since he was very young, liked the lad, ten years his junior and, after a month of thinking about it, Hughes decided to include him in the new team, even though his driving skills were very unlikely to be needed.

The problem was that none of them knew anyone else well enough – and it had to be extraordinarily well – to recruit, even though , having fleshed out the plan in great detail, it was clear to both Hughes and O'Connell that they needed at least five and ideally six altogether. They had to be able to get all the equipment needed at the top – two ladders and three rucksacks of explosives – up the main ladder without anyone having to take the time to descend; but it was thought too dangerous or, perhaps of more concern to the group, running too much risk of failure of the operation, for Hughes to climb the ladder initially, before it had been secured at the top, with a substantial weight on his back. In the end they decided that they would just have to make do with five; and Hughes would practice repeatedly the technique of climbing the ladder with the least onerous burden before he was able to secure the top for the others.

This still left them one short. It was McGuiness who came up with the idea of his younger sister, Mary, still living in Belfast. He knew how committed she was to the cause, and that she regarded herself as no less capable of playing a role in the IRA's operations than her brother, Michael. At first, the others would not countenance the idea; but Michael was able, with relentless logic, to demonstrate that no part of the operation required anything of the fifth member of the team that Mary could not fulfill. Her climb up the cliff face ladder would require care and control, strong nerves and discipline; but no great strength, and Hughes, in the end, was forced to see the sense in this. When he met her in Belfast he immediately recognized, behind the pretty features – long flowing, dark curly hair, large blue eyes and a small, delicate nose - a powerful personality, immense competence and someone who could cope, indeed thrive, on iron discipline in pursuit of the Cause. And he had no other candidate, which eventually clinched the matter.

The four men continued to spend much of their time in London, so as not to raise any question marks amongst their friends and acquaintances in the area; but nonetheless took regular trips back to Northern Ireland to prepare for the operation. O'Connell worked closely with the five of them, in particular preparing the equipment, courtesy of some late night work at a local factory and a sympathetic employee there. Constructing some ladders, slightly specific in design but, after all, only ladders, seemed a relatively easy way to be of service. O'Connell also recruited O'Driscoll, the best man he knew with a rifle; and Tom Murphy, a friend from many years back who now lived near Barrow-in-

Furness, a few miles south of Sellafield. Meanwhile Cagill organised the explosives and Hughes the firearms.

The hardest part of these preparations, unexpectedly, turned out to be the rubber dinghies and gas cylinders; not because these were difficult to find, but because of the need to avoid suspicion in anyone's mind as to their use; and to make no direct contact with Hughes or his team. O'Connell eventually secured them via a series of contacts in Ireland; and the team started practicing in earnest, on a remote beach on the north coast of the Province, always at night and with every aspect increasingly controlled by the clock. Riordan supplied O'Connell with increasingly detailed hand-drawn maps and diagrams of every part of the site that the team would penetrate; answered a multitude of detailed questions which O'Connell relayed from Hughes and his team; and prepared a detailed minute-by-minute timetable of the operation once they stepped onto the top of the western cliff face. He fixed up lodgings in Whitehaven, and rented a large garage lock-up about a mile away. Finally, O'Connell recruited a fishing boat and its owner to transport all their equipment across the Irish Sea. This was stored in the lock-up and, by the late summer of 1983, everything was in place. Meanwhile Mary moved in with her brother in Kilburn.

On the night of the 9th of November, with the light and weather conditions forecast to be favourable, O'Connell drove with Eamon O'Driscoll to Lancaster. O'Connell stopped to let O'Driscoll out, about a hundred metres past a building site near the outskirts of the city. O'Driscoll approached a white Transit van which he had had under observation for the last three nights, always parked in the same spot. In less than forty seconds, O'Driscoll had broken into the van, fired the ignition and sped off. Over the next two days, he and O'Connell re-sprayed it black in O'Connell's Whitehaven lock- up, fitted false number plates and checked every part of it mechanically. On the morning of the 12th of November he called Hughes in London with a brief pre-arranged message. Shortly before noon, Hughes and the other members of his team climbed into his Ford saloon car and headed north.

*   *   *

Hughes, O'Halloran and Hearne walked at a rapid but steady pace, using a rather curious looking gait they had developed some months before, designed to provide a very smooth forward movement of their bodies and, more importantly, their rucksacks. It took them just under two minutes to reach B701. They descended the outside steps and Hughes unlocked the door with a key made from an imprint in a bar of soap obtained by Riordan. Hughes and O'Halloran, carrying the two large rucksacks, then went down the internal steps to the bottom of the building and entered the tunnel which led off towards the re-processing plant in B205. Hearne, with the smaller rucksack, set out across a catwalk and up a separate metal stairway to an inspection area just below the roof of the building.

Cagill's one concern with his solution to the problem of bringing enough explosive power to bear on the pipes in B701 was that the site of the fracture, deep in the bottom of the building and some way into a tunnel, might prevent much of the radio-active material released from fully escaping into the atmosphere. Some would undoubtedly escape, but the location of the explosion might result in only a limited release, damaging no doubt to the operations at Sellafield but with perhaps relatively little impact beyond.

His solution was brutally simple, namely to set a third block of explosive just under the roof of the building, designed to blow most of the roof off and create an outward blast that would suck the radioactivity in the basement of the building up into the atmosphere. This would also greatly inhibit any type of counter-measures which might be deployed to minimise or control the leakage. As therefore, Hughes and O'Halloran started to unload, stack and wire up the two main explosive charges in the tunnel, Hearne set his own explosive charge high up in the building, close to a main supporting girder where it would do the maximum damage. He then headed down to the bottom to help the other two.

All the complex wiring needed to create a double detonation had been built in by Cagill. The stacking of the explosive round the pipe work and the setting up of the detonators was, as a result, fairly straight-forward; and the final step was to set the main timer. At 9.28 pm, exactly eighteen minutes after Riordan had switched off the movement sensors, and one minute ahead of schedule, Hughes set the delay at four and a half hours and pointed to the stairs. The three men ran up the metal steps, through the door which they locked behind them, and started to run the two hundred metres back to the perimeter fence.

Riordan saw them emerge from the building, relieved that no-one had unexpectedly entered the control room. Had they done so he would instantly have re-activated the sensors and the power to the electrical fencing - McGuiness having ensured that he was out of range of the sensors below the cliff top - but knowing that he would have to de-activate them again by 9.28 pm at the latest if Hughes and the others were to avoid setting of the alarms as they made their exit from the site.

One minute later the three men were climbing back over the perimeter fence, McGuiness now back on the cliff top and holding the ladder steady; and Hughes at the rear pulling up the ladder they had used to descend into the site and passing it forwards to the others. Once outside the perimeter fence he rotated the horizontal section of laddering that had taken them across the fences, collapsed it down to its attached section and, with Hearne helping, attached it to the support frame on McGuiness's back. The single section went on Hearne's back and all four started to descend the main ladder. By 9.34 pm they were all at the foot of the cliff and, two minutes later, with still two minutes in hand, they had collapsed the main ladder and were heading for the beach. As they were starting to load up the dinghy, Riordan, now feeling slightly nauseous from the tension, switched on the sensors and the power circuits.

It was, in fact, another seven minutes before a rather disgruntled Tony Robinson and John Braithwaite re-entered the control room to reveal that they, like Rigg and Watson, had been unable to find any cause of the perimeter alert, and would be requesting a full technical examination and testing of that section of fencing in the morning. The rest of the evening was uneventful and, just before midnight, four new members of the security force at Sellafield arrived to relieve the four of them who had been on duty since four pm. Watson and the others wished each other goodnight, set off to their cars and headed for the main gate. Ninety minutes later Riordan and O'Connell were on the small fishing vessel which had brought all the equipment in, heading for Dublin. From there, Riordan would head over to the west coast of Ireland and a completely new identity which O'Connell had set up for him.

*   *   *

Approximately an hour later and over forty miles away, Betty Jones, a retired factory canteen assistant, gently shook her husband, Arthur's shoulder as he lay asleep in his arm chair. The fire was still burning well, but the television programme had failed to keep his attention and he had nodded off, as he frequently did these days.

"Arthur" she said, "Are you going? Its half past ten – you ought not to leave it any later"

Arthur, also now retired for several years, in his case from British Rail, gradually came back to consciousness.

"I've made you a cuppa" Betty said.

"Thanks love" he said as he took the mug of milky tea and stirred it a few times. The truth was that he had definitely meant to visit the badger set that evening. It was only a short walk from their cottage, near enough for him to have become really quite interested in their goings on at night – a change from his main interest of bird-watching, which was rather in abeyance during the winter months – but not so near that the earth works threatened either their small garden or the cottage. He had become rather attracted to their sleek but rather quizzical manner, their awkward movements but impressive efficiency in building defences for their set and, because he didn't sleep too well these days, he visited them several times a week if it was dry.

He did, however, feel rather too warm, cosy and comfortable, in front of the fire with a nice cup of tea. Maybe he would give it a miss tonight. On the other hand, a bit of fresh air before he went to bed nearly always helped him to sleep, and it gave Betty a chance to doze off before he started his sometimes very restless attempts to drop off.

And so he sat there for a moment or two, trying to make up his mind. As he did so, he did not know, indeed there was no possible way in which he could have known that, many years later, long after he himself was in his grave, his decision, there in his comfortable living room, a decision apparently of the utmost inconsequence, would in fact determine the fate, or more precisely the life or death, of several hundred thousand people; and the future of world history.

Twenty- Eight Years Later

CHAPTER 1

" *Paul Emmerson here, or rather not here. Please leave a message after the tone"*
Kate Kimball was gripped by a strong urge to fling her mobile cell phone to the ground and stamp on it. For a second she felt such utter frustration she almost swore out loud, but then, just as quickly, her usual, more controlled, more disciplined persona re-asserted itself and, with the tone only just starting to sound in her ear, she finished the call and returned the mobile to her handbag

For God's sake, where the hell *is* he she thought. At 8.00am. on a Saturday morning you must be at home. This was not just a guess. She had spent enough week-ends with him to know that he regularly caught up on his sleep on Saturday mornings, followed by a long session with the Saturday papers. So where was he? Her mood was not helped by the fact that, with a largely sleepless night behind her, flying back from California, she was now waiting, endlessly it seemed, in the baggage reclaim area of Terminal Three at Heathrow for her luggage to appear or, more accurately, for the luggage carousel to even start moving. And her frustration, she knew, was partly with herself; at the fact that she almost certainly could have avoided the ridiculous situation in which she now found herself.

If only she hadn't been so considerate, so understanding, she thought. To her great surprise she had completed her business trip – and very successfully so – a day early. She had originally expected to be through by Friday afternoon. Given that trips to Los Angeles were *extremely* unusual for a Science Editor at OUP, standing for Oxford University Press, or just 'The Press' as it was generally known in Oxford, she had planned to stay on a day and visit the new Getty Museum, leaving LAX Sunday morning and, with the eight hour time difference, arrive back at Heathrow on Monday morning. But she had done the deal which she had flown to the US to complete – to make, in collaboration with National Geographic and a Californian production company, a film for TV based on a rather dry but learned OUP book about the geology of the San Andreas Fault - by 6.00pm Thursday. She could have rung Paul then and there to say she was just too exhausted to stay on and had decided to come back early, and she was sure she would have found him at home; but to wake him at 2.00am in the morning UK time seemed a little unkind, and she had expected no difficulty in talking to him on Friday, before she took off, with a view to spending the week-end together. However, somewhat to her surprise, she had been unable to get him on Friday, either at home or at work or on his mobile and he had not responded to any of the answer-phone messages she left before she boarded the non-stop flight back to Heathrow.

As soon as she was off the plane, Kate had called Paul's home number on her mobile, confident that she would now find him in if, quite possibly, still asleep. But all she got was the same answer-phone message. His mobile was switched off; and there was no reply when she sent a text message. Ringing again as she waited for her luggage, she realized that there was little chance that he would somehow have materialized in the fifteen minutes since she last rang; but it was just so aggravating that she had given up her planned day out in LA to spend the week-end with Paul and now, here she was, back in England and she couldn't even get hold of him.

The carousel had still not started moving; and Kate went to the bathroom. The face that stared back at her from the mirror as she washed her hands was not, she thought, a pretty sight. Normally, with her aquiline nose, high cheekbones, quite large blue/grey eyes and firm jaw, together with her shoulder length blonde hair, all on the top of a five foot ten inch, well proportioned figure, she knew, and had known since she was a teenager, that she had quite a striking appearance and was naturally attractive to men – which had resulted in her developing a remarkably tough streak to her otherwise rather generous character – but, in the mirror, her hair looked dirty and unkempt, her eyes were quite puffy and her pallor looked anything but healthy.

She went back to the luggage reclaim area to find that the cases from her flight were now appearing. Mercifully, hers was one of the first, perhaps reflecting the 'priority' tag which her club class ticket had warranted; and she headed off for the Central Bus Station. It would have been nice to climb into her own car, a not entirely sensible old convertible Mercedes sports, and escape from everyone around her; but no-one with any sense used a car to go to Heathrow from Oxford. It wasn't just the astronomical cost of parking there for five days but the extreme inconvenience of having to park miles from the terminal, the wait for a bus to ferry you to the terminal and, worse still, have to put up with the whole thing in reverse on arrival back when all she wanted was to get into a hot bath. In contrast, the X70 bus provided a convenient ride directly to (and more importantly from) the central bus station to the centre of Oxford, no more than five minutes from her house.

The journey on the bus gave her the chance to think more clearly about where Paul might be. As a member of the faculty of Engineering at Oxford University, Paul often went on trips, to academic conferences, to visit colleagues at other universities, to meet with people from companies with whom he collaborated or for whom, on occasion, he did consultancy work; but this rarely included being away on a Saturday morning, and he had certainly not mentioned any such commitment before she had left for California five days previously. He might meet up with one or more friends or colleagues, but not at 8 am on a Saturday morning. It was a total mystery to her.

It was with some relief that, just after 10 a.m. she let herself into her house, a small but very adequate terraced cottage in the area of Oxford known as Jericho. Ironically, the criss-cross of rows of such houses had been built in the nineteenth century to house print workers for The Press; and many of the houses had become close to derelict by the 1960s. But they had now become very fashionable – and very expensive for their size – primarily because their owners could walk to work in the centre of Oxford in a few minutes, thereby avoiding the otherwise insoluble problem of where a commuter could park a car for under £30 a day. She dumped her suitcase on her bed, unpacked while she ran a bath and, still feeling much less relaxed than she had hoped, had a long lie in the hot and, to some extent, therapeutic water. She then spent the rest of Saturday in what otherwise would have been quite an enjoyable time pottering around, doing some shopping, tidying up in her small garden, catching up on the newspapers which she had bought at the bus station, and sorting out her own papers from her trip. But she couldn't resist accessing her emails, not least on the off-chance that Paul had sent her one with some explanation for where he was. But there was nothing from him. Instead, she noted, with resignation rather than surprise, that there were over eighty unread, even though she had been keeping up with them in LA. However, she merely scanned them. Monday would be quite early enough to start dealing with them. She twice rung Paul, but was not surprised to get only his answer phones. The first she was likely to hear from him was when he decided to switch on his mobile again and saw that he had both text and answer phone messages.

Around 5 pm she rang two of her friends, Sarah Jennings and Jane Tyson for a chat, catching up on their lives and recounting her trip to LA. Jane asked after Paul, and Kate said that she was slightly miffed. She'd come back early and he was nowhere to be found, probably, she said on some conference trip or the like, though she hadn't known about it before.

As she finished the call, she sat quite still for a moment, not really knowing what to do. Perhaps he *was* on some work-related trip. The only other alternative she could think of was that he had gone off for a week-end walking. They sometimes did this together, usually Dorset or the Devon Coast; and he had once or twice been away with a small group of friends, all of whom he had known since his student days some fifteen years previously. She didn't feel comfortable about ringing round them, asking if any of them knew where Paul was; but reckoned that, if this was the explanation, then his closest friend, Gareth Simpson, would be very likely to be involved.

Kate didn't actually have Gareth's number in her address book, but found it in the telephone book and called him, just after 5.30 pm. Rather to her relief, she got his answer phone and left a message, sounding as casual as possible, and asking if he could give her a quick buzz if he got the message at a reasonable hour. He could, of course, be anywhere, she realized, but it gave a hint of support to the notion that Paul, faced with what he expected to be a week-end without seeing Kate, had gone off with some friends for a night or two.

Kate cooked herself a meal, watched a film on television and, with the lack of sleep the previous night now eating away at her, was in bed before 9.30 pm. and asleep fairly soon afterwards. 30 minutes later she was aroused from an already deep sleep by the phone ringing. Even in such a drowsy state she felt real elation as she reached for the bedside phone.

"Paul?" she said, only to hear Gareth's rather melodious voice reply.

"'Afraid not, Kate" he said "I was just returning your call. I gather you've lost track of him – rather careless if I may say so. You haven't had a row have you?"

"No, no nothing like that. I've been in the States but came back two days earlier than expected. So I was hoping to see Paul for the week-end, but he isn't around and I can't get him on his mobile. I just wondered if he was with you, or if you knew where he might be".

"Did I wake you up" said Gareth "you sound a bit zonked out"

"No I was just about to go off" lied Kate. "I didn't sleep much last night, on the plane, and I'm feeling a bit jet lagged – I'll be fine tomorrow. No idea where Paul might be I suppose?"

"I don't" replied Gareth. "I've not seen him since last week; and he's not with Charlie because we've both been sailing today. Maybe Paul's at a conference, you know what he's like"

"I suppose so" said Kate, clearly not persuaded, "but he didn't mention any business trip".

"Well, there will be a perfectly straightforward explanation" Gareth tried to re-assure her. "Why don't you catch up on your sleep and the chances are he will ring you tomorrow"

"I'm sure you're right" Kate acknowledged. She had begun to feel so exhausted that she let herself, however, subconsciously, be re-assured. She must just get some sleep "I'm sorry to have bothered you".

"No problem" replied Gareth. "I'll give you a call tomorrow, just to check all's well"

"Oh, don't worry" said Kate. "I'm sure you're right", realizing that she was now repeating herself. "Bye". She finished the call and sunk back under the duvet. Now for some sleep she told herself, too tired to worry any more.

The combination of jet lag, however, and her anxiety about Paul combined to give her a very disrupted night's sleep; and she eventually woke just before 10 am. She tried Paul again, with no success, and spent a long time on the Sunday papers. The new Conservative Prime Minister, Alan Gerrard was already beginning to come under attack for his support for the very strong line now being adopted by the not so new Democratic President in the US, Jack Hamilton, over Iran's nuclear ambitions – all so ironic she, like countless others, thought, given how much Tony Blair and President Bush had been criticized for just such a stance over Iraq. Could something similar happen again was the issue that seemed to cover a large proportion of the two very bulky papers she had bought. Despite its significance, Kate repeatedly found her attention wandering off - and then, around midday it suddenly hit her that perhaps Paul had been in an accident of some kind.

She deliberately took a few deep breaths, suppressing any tendency to panic; and then wondered how she could have gone so long without thinking of this possibility. If he had been injured, or even killed, the police would have gone to his home, a spacious flat occupying the whole of one floor of a large Victorian house in the Woodstock Road; but there would be little if anything to signify to them that he had a partner living less than a mile away whom they ought to contact.

Kate immediately left her house. She usually walked round to Paul's house, in well under ten minutes, but with a sense of growing alarm at what she now suspected, Kate headed straight for her car, parked in her resident's parking space and, two minutes later entered the large lobby of the house in the Woodstock Road where Paul lived. She found herself running up the stairs to the door to Paul's flat.

There was no sign of anyone outside his apartment, nor inside. Kate used the key to his flat which Paul had given her several months previously. They had discussed moving in together; and there was certainly enough room for them both in Paul's spacious accommodation; but had decided that, at least for a while, they preferred to keep their own separate spaces. Both lived very busy and somewhat irregular lives; and both felt very comfortable seeing each other whenever they could, but on the basis of their own independence. They had, however, each given the other keys to their homes; and both came and went with a casual ease that reflected their relationship.

Once inside Paul's flat, Kate put on the lights and looked around. Paul was clearly not there; and the place looked just as she had last seen it a week or so ago – understated but elegant modern furniture, everywhere very tidy, and no reason to think anything untoward had happened. Kate looked around for a while, slightly re-assured by the normality of it all, but then began to question why she had come round at all. If Paul had been in an accident, perhaps several days ago now, why would there be any sign of it in his apartment? With a physical pain now developing in the pit of her stomach, she realised that she would have to contact the police if she wanted to check on any road accidents that might have involved Paul. She was just about to summon up the courage to head off to the police station, to see if anything had been reported when it dawned on her that it wasn't Paul's flat she should be looking at but his car, which he regularly parked in a resident parking space in a side road off the main Woodstock Road. If she had had any decent sleep in two nights, she reflected, she might have been thinking rather more intelligently. She headed back down the stairs and forced herself to walk round the corner to where Paul regularly parked his car.

A wave of relief rippled through her as she saw his Series 7 BMW saloon, recognized his number plate, and knew that he hadn't been involved in any accident. Unless, she suddenly thought, he had been a passenger in someone else's car. It was this thought that started to convince her she was perhaps becoming just a little bit paranoid about the whole thing. She really couldn't go on like this. Paul had gone away, and she would just have to contain her impatience until he got back. She knew this didn't feel right, but there seemed nothing else to do. Unless, that was, she decided to call in at the police station in St. Aldate's.

She drove back to her house, went in and called Sarah Jennings again, her closest confidante since they had first met several years earlier at OUP. She said that she was getting very anxious about Paul's whereabouts- she knew it was silly of course – but she just couldn't understand how or why it was that, wherever he was, he was not answering his mobile. Sarah did her best to re-assure Kate, with no great success, but did plant the thought that the best thing was to wait until the following morning before getting too anxious. It was term time in the University and Paul would almost certainly need to be back for Monday. More important, he had expected Kate back early Monday morning and would be awaiting a call around 8 am, when, as he thought, she would have just landed at Heathrow.

"Just wait until tomorrow morning and I'm sure all will be explained" Sarah had said; and invited Kate round for some lunch, which she accepted.

"Do you think it would be silly to check with the police?" Kate asked.

"I really don't think you need to" replied Sarah "It's Sunday; so you've got time if it will make you feel less worried, and I'm happy to come with you, but I really don't think it's necessary, and I'm not sure, just because he's been away this week-end, that they would do very much. If he's not been in contact by tomorrow, then go and see them; and I'll come with you then"

Kate drove round to Sarah's for lunch – a small but very attractive 18th Century house in what many still thought of as the village of Old Marston, even though it was well inside the Oxford ring road, with suburban housing reaching almost to its edge. It was really too big for Sarah, but she had managed to hang on to it when she and her husband had got divorced three year earlier. Kate felt a slight easing of tension as they greeted each other with a hug. Sarah's soft, classically pretty face, reflected well her mild manner and sympathetic personality. With a slim, athletic figure and – much her most distinctive feature – black shoulder-length hair so curly it formed a mass of ringlets, she could not have looked more different from Kate; but they had become very good friends from the moment they met; and both knew that right now Kate really needed Sarah.

As Sarah let her in she could see the strain etched in Kate's face. They went over the mystery of where Paul might be, without any enlightenment; and then managed to spend some of the time talking of other things, in particular Kate's triumph in L.A., which would be the start of a fascinating collaboration with Hollywood. Kate tried Paul's numbers again, hoping, but not expecting that he would now be back, and without success. In the afternoon they played some tennis and, although Sarah said that Kate would be very welcome to stay for supper, Kate said she must get back and sort herself out for Monday morning. After a cold drink she headed back to her house and started to scramble some eggs for her supper. Perhaps it was the fact that Paul had so often done this for the two of them, typically putting all sorts of extra ingredients in, from herbs to champagne; plus her growing sense of despair that she didn't know where he was that, to her surprise, she suddenly burst into a flood of uncontrollable tears, as the accumulating tension of the week-end overwhelmed her. And, as she stood there, trying to wipe her eyes, and get control of herself again, her misery conjured up another thunderbolt – she hadn't, until this moment, considered the possibility that he might be spending the week-end with another woman.

Might he have taken the opportunity of her being away to go off somewhere with an old girl-friend, or perhaps a new one? Was that why he was so completely incommunicado? Her first reaction was to feel almost physically sick. She could feel herself trembling with anxiety. Then she started to tell herself that this was madness. The very fact that it hadn't occurred to her indicated the degree of trust that existed between them. After nearly two years they had, she thought, the strongest relationship of any of her single friends; and rather stronger than a number of her married ones. In all the time they had been together other relationships had never even been a remote possibility. The two of them had been so.... she couldn't think of quite the right word but, well, easy, comfortable, relaxed together. They just got on so well, on so many levels. She couldn't begin to believe that there had been anything false about it, any subterfuge, lying behind their relationship. No, the more she thought about it the more she really couldn't see it as remotely likely; and she began to calm down as she told herself that this was just another silly idea brought on by her anxiety, even more her frustration, at just not knowing where he was. She thought about phoning – wanted to phone - Sarah to talk about this, to get, as she knew she would, a droll laugh and masses of re-assurance; but the very thought of Sarah's reaction was enough to help her out of this latest worry. She could always mention it tomorrow if Paul still hadn't turned up. She ate her supper, drank a substantial proportion of a bottle of white wine with it; and sorted out her papers and thoughts for tomorrow at the office.

Predictably, Kate had another very disturbed night. She had tried to relax before going to bed, taking a long bath, by candlelight, which she often found a rather therapeutic way to end a demanding day; and listened to a CD of choir music which she had recently bought. But her anxiety about Paul and his whereabouts were a physical presence in her gut, and after two hours of restless lying awake she took a couple of diazepam, which she only had on prescription from her doctor to help her sleep on the very occasional overnight flights she made. These brought her some blessed unconsciousness but, by five am. she was awake again and, in a way that the early hours of the morning make worse, spent another two hours becoming more and more convinced that something terrible had happened to Paul. Eventually she dozed, emerging exhausted from the night around 7.30 am. She immediately rang his home and his mobile, with no real expectation that he would have appeared over the intervening eight hours since last she had called; and once again got only answer machines.

As she showered, had some coffee and some supposedly healthy cereal, the awful tension in her stomach gripped her again, but at least now she could start to take some action, which would make things clearer – for better or worse. This thought offered some marginal comfort as she got dressed. She put on a white blouse and dark blue business skirt and jacket, conscious that she would be expected, indeed eagerly awaited at work, to report on her trip to California. And suddenly she felt a surge of anger. The trip had been so successful – an absolute triumph - and she should be getting ready for one of the most rewarding days of her eight years at OUP. But instead, because of Paul, because of what would almost certainly turn out to be some thoughtlessness, even if uncharacteristically so, on his part, she was worried sick and quite unable to focus on the contract she had secured, or what it would mean either for her employer or her own career prospects.

Kate switched on her bedroom radio in the hope that it would be some distraction. She had once been an avid listener to the *Today* programme every morning as she got dressed. Though not someone who was especially interested in politics, she had found it a good way to click her brain into gear; but then, increasingly, found herself agitated by the style of presentation, particularly of its main anchor man, who deployed a bullying, hectoring approach, based on the almost explicit assumption that anyone and everyone in public life were either rogues or fools or, usually, both, so that by the time she left the house she was not at all in the relaxed frame of mind she needed to face the day. Mercifully, this morning it was rather more informative than usual, as a succession of commentators from both the US and the UK tried to make sense of the recent developments in international diplomacy which she had briefly tried to absorb from the Sunday papers the day before. It seemed that Graham Seymour, the new Foreign Secretary, had been pitched straight into the UN's deliberations over Iran's plans to start nuclear weapons testing and, with the new PM's clear backing, was evidently starting to form a strong alliance with the US in favour of a very tough response. But it was the increasing evidence of a strong personal bond between Alan Gerrard and Jack Hamilton, a previously successful Senator from Pennsylvania, that had caught many journalists' attention. As commentators were repeatedly pointing out, their politics were very different, but no more so than those of President Bush and Prime Minister Blair at the time of Iraq; and many thought that their strengthening relationship might be more significant than any amount of UN diplomacy or debate.

The programme provided some diversion for Kate, but not much. She was too much inside her own currently very miserable world. Twenty minutes later, with minimal make-up, her hair pinned up, and stepping into some comfortable low heeled shoes, for the first time since she got up Kate looked outside. It had clearly rained in the night, but was now struggling towards a sunny if breezy April day. Please let it end better than it has started, she thought, as she took a stylish white raincoat from a small cupboard by her front door and, with it over her arm, set off on the short walk which would take her to the new, much less grand, but much nearer entrance to the premises of Oxford University Press, actually located in the Jericho area of Oxford, a mere three streets away from her house. It was 8.25 am.

On arriving at The Press Kate smiled a brief hello to Marian on the reception desk – friendly but not encouraging of any conversation - and went straight to her office. Her secretary, Janice, would not be in until at least nine o'clock, which gave Kate some time to have a quick glance through her gravity-defying in-tray that had built up in less than a week; and switch on her computer. She noted that the list of unanswered emails had grown a little longer since Saturday, though each sender would have received a brief out-of-office reply saying that she would be away until today. She looked through to see if any of the new ones were from, or even to do with Paul, but they weren't; and she hadn't really expected it. If he had wanted to be in touch he could have called, left a message, whatever. Her office email would have been a distinctly odd method of communication, especially as he would have thought she was in the US until two hours ago.

She spent half an hour or so, not so much working as prioritizing what she would need to do during the day; and then, at 9.00 am., still having seen no-one other than Marian, she called the Materials Engineering Department of Oxford University. There was no reply. The Department, not unlike OUP, clearly started at a leisurely pace on a Monday morning. She was just replacing the phone when through her open office door walked her secretary, Janice.

Janice had been Kate's P.A. for nearly four years. She was hugely overqualified, immensely efficient, dramatic in appearance, with positively Slavic cheekbones, long dark silky hair, eye lashes to match – the prettiest woman Kate had ever known – a pneumatic figure; and her name wasn't Janice. This was her chosen anglicisation when she arrived from Warsaw with a degree in English Literature from Krakow University; and Kate had completely forgotten what her Polish first name had been. She had come to Oxford, and had only been able to stay at that time, because she had married a research scientist from the University's Bio-Chemistry Department, Simon MacDonald. He was, by instinct, a rather shy man, but had been so overcome by the sight of Janice in a Warsaw street while there for a conference that, before he had given it any proper thought or known what he was doing, he had approached her, said that he had less than a day free to see the sights of the city and would she mind if he bought her a cup of coffee while she gave him a ten minute run down of the main sights he should see. A fortuitous combination of her surprise, her good English, the man's evident gentility, and the fact that she did, as it happened, have some time free, led her to agree. They married eight months later, she moved to Oxford and got a job with Kate, soon becoming her friend and confidante as well as P.A.

At that time there were very few Poles in Oxford or, indeed, in the UK, as Poland had not then joined the European Union; and that caused her some sadness. But then Poland did join, and everything changed. Soon there was a very lively expatriate Polish community in Oxford, a few of whom she had known before she got married, and she was now, in her own mind, as happy as she could ever have imagined. She got on very well with Kate, whose only fear was that Janice, now in her late twenties, might fairly soon want to have a family and resign from her job, leaving Kate, in vain, she suspected, to seek anyone even half as effective.

Janice's eyes lit up as she saw Kate; and was instantly all questions. How was she, how had the trip gone, was she just in from the airport. But then she rapidly sensed that all was not well, as Kate responded with only the briefest of smiles, and looked increasingly distracted.

"Are you OK?" said Janice. Caught between embarrassment, anger and distress, Kate nodded, but quickly explained about Paul, about her rather awful week-end, and her real fear that something had happened to him. Janice's response was quite different from the one Kate had received from Sarah.

"You must report this to the authorities straight away" she said, not unsympathetically but quite firmly. "They will know what to do. I can put all your meetings on hold"
Kate clearly looked doubtful, but Janice was taking charge.

"You won't be able to work properly until you get this sorted out" she said, with the conviction that comes from unassailable logic. "You must go to the police".

"What have I got on this morning" asked Kate, but knew before she finished asking what sort of answer she would get from Janice.

"Nothing that cannot wait" replied Janice. "Harry wants to hear about California" she continued, referring to Henry Fairbrother, head of the Academic Division at OUP and Kate's boss, "But he can wait until later. The rest is just the usual stuff – I can easily reschedule it". Kate thought for a moment.

"I'll wait until I can get through to his department. That shouldn't be long. If that doesn't produce an explanation, I'll contact the police".
Janice pulled a sceptical look.

"I really will" said Kate, not noticing how completely she had accepted Janice's authoritative stance. But she knew that if Paul did not materialize somehow soon, she would have to do something; and there wasn't really anything else she could think of to do.

The two of them spent nearly half an hour going through arrangements for the week, some relatively insignificant correspondence, and a quick de-briefing from Janice on what had happened while Kate was away. Kate found it difficult to concentrate, but the very normality of it all brought some respite from the anguish she was feeling. At 9.35am she tried Paul's University department again and, such was the context of the call, she practically stopped breathing when a voice she knew very well said

"Materials Engineering. Can I help you?"

"Is that Alice?" said Kate - stupidly, she immediately registered - because she knew immediately that it was Alice Richmond, the long-serving, all-knowing, affectionate dragon-lady of Paul's department – a sweet natured but all-controlling fifty-eight year old, appointed as administrator of the department long before almost anyone there could remember, not particularly imaginative but just the sort of person you would want with you on a desert island, in a plane crash or on a battle field. All-seeing, completely unfazed by anything, and a match for any conceivable crisis that the world or, more likely, the central administration of the university could throw at her, her voice was hugely comforting to Kate.

"Hello Kate" said Alice. "How are you? Are you after Paul?"

"I am" said Kate, trying to sound as normal, as casual as possible. "Is he there?"

"Hang on, I'll see" replied Alice, without any sense that the answer was of stupifying importance to Kate. There was a pause while she clearly tried to connect Kate to Paul's office phone. After what seemed an interminable pause, Alice said

"He's not answering I'm afraid, but he's giving a lecture at ten. Shall I get him to call you, either before if I manage to find him in time, or afterwards if I don't?"

"If you would" said Kate, feeling a wave of relief come over her. Paul would no more miss a lecture than his best friend's funeral. "I'm in my office".

"I'll get him to ring you" said Alice, in a tone indicating that no conceivable hindrance to this would be tolerated. "I'll leave a message on his desk. Have you been in the States?"

"I just got back at the weekend" said Kate. "In fact I got back two days early and have been trying to contact Paul, but he seems to have gone AWOL". If any of the tension behind this carried to Alice, she showed no sign at all of it registering with her.

"Typical" she said. "I'll get him to call you shortly. By the way, are you coming to the first year drinks party next week? Do come. There are never that many women there and it would be good to see a sisterly soul".

Kate said that she hoped she could, without any idea of when the reception was, still less whether she was due to, or free to attend. And that was the end of the call – a minor administrative task for Alice; a ghastly mish-mash of the banal and gut-wrenching emotion for Kate. But she knew she was clutching one priceless piece of information. She knew she would hear from Paul shortly before 10.00 am, or shortly after 11.00 am – all lectures were one hour precisely - or, or what? She would have to take Janice's advice.

The clock in her office ticked more slowly than at any time since the beginning of the world. Once or twice she really wondered if it had stopped, or at least was slowing down. But eventually it reached 10. 00 am with no phone call from Paul. Kate resigned herself to waiting until shortly after 11.00 am. and then, at ten minutes past ten, the phone rang and Janice said there was a call from Alice at Materials Engineering. Kate waited, her head pounding – for a moment she wondered if she was having some sort of attack – and then Alice came through, breezy as ever in manner but clearly quite disconcerted.

"Kate, I can't think what has happened, but Paul hasn't turned up for his second year lecture. It's very odd. There are about 100 of them milling around and I've suggested that they wait for another ten minutes or so and then give up on today. Do you know where else he might be?"

CHAPTER 2

In some curious, inexplicable way, Kate felt a moment, not of relief – that would be impossible – but perhaps of release. A psychoanalyst would probably say that this was the moment when all the pressure, all the tension of the uncertainly Kate had been experiencing since she arrived at Heathrow fell away; the moment when Kate could finally confront, however terrible, the fact that something had, quite definitely, happened to Paul. Somewhere deep inside her brain functions, one whole set of synapses concerned with all the stress of uncertainty were switching off; and another set, concerned with loss, or potential loss were switching on, no better, indeed certainly worse, but different and, just for a fraction of a second, her mental state, in a sort of limbo between two different states, gave her a moment of release.

It did not last long.

"Hasn't he rung or anything?" she asked, knowing the futility of the question as she asked it. "Has he just not turned up?" But again she knew the answer.

"No" said Alice "it's not like him at all. They'll be able to catch up, but it's very strange. You're sure he's not just at home unwell?"

Kate registered, however, briefly, that Alice, for all her administrative efficiency, had not remotely grasped the situation from their earlier conversation, but then that was probably her own fault for making it all so casual. And then she just snapped.

"No, he hasn't been in touch for three days now. I'm sick with worry; and if he hasn't turned up for his lecture then something really serious must have happened. I'm going to contact the police. I'll let you know what happens, but I must go now"

Now aware of the situation, Alice clicked into action

"I'm so sorry" she said "I didn't realize. You go now and I'll contact people here. I'll let you know if I get any information"

"Thanks" said Kate, and put the phone down. For a moment she stood there, breathing heavily. Then she picked up the phone again and called Sarah.

"Sarah, it's Kate. I've been ringing Paul's office and he hasn't turned up for a lecture that he is supposed to be giving. Something is definitely wrong. I've got to go to the police. Will you come with me?"

"Of course" replied Sarah, recognizing the rising panic in Kate's voice. Give me 15 minutes and I will pick you up – are you at work?"

"Yes, I'll see you outside the Jericho entrance. I'm sorry about this but I just don't know what to do"

"It's no problem" said Sarah, "but try to stay calm. There's still likely to be a perfectly straightforward explanation, I'm sure. I'll see you in fifteen minutes".

It took Sarah twenty minutes to get from her house in Old Marston to OUP. Kate spent the time re-organising her day with Janice - who assured her that she had everything under control – all the while feeling a rising tide of grief inside her. It took another twenty-five minutes to thread their way through Oxford's one way system – people said you could die of old age if you tried to navigate it without knowing it – to the police station, a large four-square, stone building several hundred metres south of Oxford's central cross roads. There being nowhere else nearby where they could park legally, they risked parking in the area down the side of the station reserved for the police themselves, and entered the station. They had to wait nearly twenty minutes while a rather formidably large and unsmiling police woman filled in a form with answers to questions which she was putting to a middle-aged couple – neither Kate not Sarah could fathom what the questions were about - and then, as the questions came to an end, the couple got ready to leave.

Kate was not the type to get worried, or feel very intimidated, by officialdom; but she had to admit to a feeling of embarrassment as she stood up. Paul had, unexpectedly, been away for 48 hours, at a time when he thought she was in Los Angeles; and here she was, wanting to check accident reports. She suspected that she was going to get a rather unsympathetic response from the grim representative of the Thames Valley Police force on duty that day. But, just as the couple with whom she had been dealing were leaving, the police woman called out

"Bye now – don't worry, we'll get it all sorted out" and gave them not only a rather cheery wave but a large smile, which completely changed her whole bearing, almost her whole being. She suddenly looked human, friendly, benign; and Kate approached her feeling a whole lot easier in her mind than she had done five seconds previously.

Kate, with Sarah at her side, approached the desk. The police woman looked up at her, not unhelpfully, Kate registered, but said nothing. Kate started off.

"My …….." There are said to be well over 600,000 words in the English Language, three times as many as in French. Some people, by including a huge number of English words spawned by the internet, put the figure much higher still. But there was no reasonable word to describe Paul's relationship to Kate, or that of millions of other couples with a similar relationship. The conventional term would be her boy-friend but, with both of them in their thirties this sounded ridiculously twee, as if she was some disconsolate teenager, here because she had had a row with her adolescent admirer. Paul was neither her husband nor her fiancé; and lover, though accurate, was far too personal, too intimate to announce to the once- again rather stony faced stranger across the desk. 'The man I am living with' would be fine if she was living with him, but she wasn't. 'My man' would sound like something from a bad film, leaving only the increasingly used 'partner' which she would have to use; but that felt odd as well or, at least, ambiguous. One's partner might be a business colleague, or even one's boss. The police woman would not, of course, misunderstand; and none of this thinking ran through Kate's mind in any conscious way. But the lack of an acceptable word nonetheless caused her to dry up after only one word. It was not a good start.

Sarah looked apprehensively at Kate, thinking that sheer emotion had got to Kate; and that she might need to step in herself to explain. But Kate, in what was less in fact than a second, recovered, and started again - with a phrase which, though it got her off on the right tack was, in fact, quite untrue.

"I got back from the United States on Friday and the man I am living with has disappeared. He wasn't expecting me back until today; and so I wasn't worried, but he didn't turn up for work today – he was supposed to be lecturing at the University at 10am this morning but he wasn't there and hasn't been in touch with anyone. She paused for breath, realising that she had in fact lied to a policewoman twice in five seconds – she'd been worried sick all week-end – but at least she had explained.

"He just wouldn't do that if he was alright" she added.

The police woman continued to look impassively at Kate. It was impossible to read what her reaction was. Then she gave a faint nod, a hint of the smile Kate had seen before, not in any way trivializing the moment but in some vague way putting the two of them on the same side. Getting out a large pad she said

"Can I start with your details, please"

Kate gave her name and address and phone number.

"And your friend's name ?"

For a moment, Kate thought she was referring to Sarah, but then saw that the police woman was solving the language problem in her own discreet way.

"Paul Emmerson – Dr. Paul Emmerson – he is a scientist at the University".

"And he lives with you at this address?" asked the police woman. It was almost a statement, merely seeking confirmation of what Kate had said a few moments earlier. And so the first little lie came to light.

"Well, he has his own flat in the Woodstock Road" said Kate, feeling herself flush a little. "But we have been together for nearly two years and we spend quite a lot of time at either his place or mine". She was about to launch into an explanation of their circumstances, living arrangements, career pressures, even financial aspects; but Sarah, subliminally recognizing that Kate was starting to dig a hole for herself, rested her hand on Kate's arm and Kate stopped. But having faced up to the one lie, she then went on to reveal the other.

"I said I wasn't concerned over the week-end, but actually I'm worried sick. I can't get him at any place he might have gone, and he's not answering his mobile. And now he's not at work. Can you help?"

"We'll certainly try" said the police woman, giving the full smile this time. "Can you give me a description of him or, better still, a photograph?" Oh, how stupid of me, thought Kate. What an obvious thing to do, and she began to realise just how much Paul's disappearance had thrown all her natural efficiency.

"I should have thought of that. I'll get you one. But he's about six foot two inches tall, dark hair, very slightly gray at the sides. He's got blue eyes, a straight nose......" She couldn't think what else to say. Sarah came to her rescue.

"He's very good looking, but it will be easier if we get you a photo".
This produced another slightly conspiratorial smile from the police woman, but then she was back to business. As lightly as possible she asked

"Can you let me have his car registration number?"

"Yes I can" said Kate "but I was at his flat on Saturday and his car was there, so he hasn't crashed it or anything like that".

"Well, that's a help" the police woman replied. "Now, if you get me a photo, I will make some inquiries". She had in mind contacting hospitals in a manageable radius, and unidentified passengers in any road accidents in the last seventy-two hours; but she preferred not to spell this out. But the most likely explanation, she thought, was another woman – some affair that had gone stratospheric over the week-end and blown away any normal sense of responsibility towards his girl-friend here in front of her – a strikingly beautiful woman she thought - but there was no fathoming men, especially where sex was concerned; and it probably was sex, the pure, lustful kind, unencumbered by emotional ties that was at the root of all this, if it even involved not turning up to work when he should. Men, as she had discovered more than once in her life, were such idiots. But absolutely none of these thoughts got through her once again impassive face.

"Obviously I'll call you if we find out anything, but could you call back here about the same time tomorrow, with a photo? If we haven't got things sorted out by then, you'll need to talk to one of my colleagues here; and he'll widen things out a little"

The words were all everyday words, and said in a perfectly normal tone; but Kate recognized the enormity of what was being conveyed. If they hadn't found Paul, or at least got some trace of his whereabouts, in the next twenty-four hours, then there would have to be a full scale search. Oh my god, she thought, this can't be happening; and she felt her upper lip begin to tremble. Sarah lightly held her arm again.

"That's fine" said Sarah "I'll bring her back tomorrow if we haven't heard anything; but let's hope you have some news before then. Thanks for your help. Come on Kate, let's go and have a cup of coffee". Kate thanked the police woman as well and, just about in control of herself, she and Sarah walked out of the police station and up the street to a St. Aldate's coffee shop together.

"What can they do?" asked Kate, as they sat opposite each other in the window seats in the coffee shop. Sarah knew as well as the police woman that it wouldn't be pleasant to spell this out, but there was no point in ducking it. Kate knew the answers anyway.

"They'll check out road accidents, the hospitals, things like that" said Sarah. "I suppose he could conceivably already be.... with the police" She was thinking that Paul might have been arrested for some reason; but the only thing she could think of was drunk-driving, but he hadn't taken his car. Could he have been driving someone else's car?

"But that makes no sense" she added quickly; and went rapidly on. "How do you want to deal with today? Go home, or go to work; or why don't you spend the day with me. You need some support until you hear something".

Kate was grateful for the offer, but knew she would rather be at work, with as much normality and as much distraction to take her mind off Paul as possible. She explained this to Sarah and, having finished their coffees, they went back to Sarah's car, miraculously not clamped, towed away or plastered with rude notices or a ticket, and Sarah dropped Kate back at OUP. It wasn't yet 11.30 am; and Kate didn't know how she was going to get through the rest of the day.

As she headed for her office, Kate wondered if there might be a message of some sort from Alice, a message that could end the nightmare she was now in, but there was none. She spent some time talking it all through with Janice, and this gave her some resilience. At some point, as they talked, about Paul, about what might have happened to him, about what Kate could do – she passed a point she didn't realize she'd reached until later – that she would just have to put the whole terrible situation, all her anxiety, all her incipient panic on hold; not gone – not remotely - but just suspended, to be worked around for twenty-four hours, to be tackled anew tomorrow if it needed to be. In this not exactly positive, but slightly less debilitating frame of mind she set off upstairs to see Harry and report on her trip to L.A. – so successful but now of very little consequence to her.

Harry Fairbrother was in his mid 40's; but his fair, slightly curly hair, a boyish unlined face and a youthful manner all conspired to make him seem much younger; and even his most ardent admirer would not claim that he had great presence. But he was a remarkably innovative publisher, with a rarely erring instinct in developing OUP's strategy for academic publishing, seeking to square the circle of publishing important works across the whole range of arts and science without losing more money than the other divisions of OUP could make, from reference books and dictionaries, from English language teaching books that sold in huge numbers around the world and from more popular non-fiction works. He was also a natural manager, of people, finance, logistics; and he had a charm which carried him a long way. He had risen to a very senior position without, as far as anyone knew, ever making an enemy; and he and Kate had become good friends despite their very vertical business relationship.

"I gather there is a problem about Paul" he said as soon as Kate entered. Clearly Janice had conveyed at least an outline of what had been happening. Kate briefly explained, adding that she felt sure that it would all be sorted out soon. Why, on earth, did she say that, she wondered. She didn't remotely believe it any more, and so why was she seeking to re-assure him? Presumably because an element of her professionalism had returned; and she didn't want Harry, however understanding he would be, to think that anything would interfere with her putting one hundred percent into the job.

No doubt it was due to the same motive that she quickly moved the conversation on to her U.S. deal, the contract she had agreed and the way she planned for the whole project to run. Harry listened, delighted with what he heard, and surprised; not because he had any doubts about Kate's expertise or, indeed, her flair for publishing in general and this very path-breaking deal in particular; but just because it was such a new step for OUP. He had been rather doubtful as to whether anyone could pull it off once they were actually faced with what he thought of as the moguls of Hollywood, albeit a documentary on the San Andreas Fault was hardly Terminator 4; but there was no doubt Kate had set it up with National Geographic and a film production company; got agreement to a tight timetable with every one signed up in all the right places, and the whole thing likely to be quite profitable. More than that though, it was a new departure, a whole new line of business that could be repeated for other learned books with the potential for wider interest; and Kate had also established a set of highly valuable business relationships in the process.

Considerate as he was of Kate's concern about Paul, he was soon fully focused on the project; and as Kate explained more of the detail, his enthusiasm led Kate herself more fully into the excitement of the whole project.

They finished shortly before lunch and both headed for the company's restaurant. Here they met numerous other colleagues and the meal passed quite quickly. Returning to her office, Kate checked that there had been no calls from the police, realising to her dismay that she had not noted the name of the police woman to whom she had spoken at the police station, nor even a phone number; but no doubt she could track her down if it became necessary. The afternoon passed in a series of meetings, some correspondence, most of it email and, later on, a pre-arranged call to L.A. to finalise some further details on the film project, catching her contact at a civilized 8.30 am in the morning, California time.

She left shortly after 6.00 pm and went for a drink with two of her staff team, partly social but partly to catch up on several items of work that she had not been able to cover during the day. She got home at 7.45 pm, relieved that she had got through the day but now acutely conscious that she had heard nothing from the nameless police woman. She rang Sarah to tell her that nothing had come through. Sarah tried as best she could to see the brighter side of this – clearly they hadn't found any road accident victims that fitted his description; because they certainly would have contacted her if they had. Kate saw the logic of this, but it hardly helped, much as she appreciated Sarah trying. They agreed that it was unlikely Kate would hear anything that evening; and Sarah arranged to pick Kate up at 9.00 am the next morning to go back to the police station.

Somewhere at the back of Kate's mind, as she made herself a light supper, she began to formulate an explanation for Paul's disappearance. He hadn't run off with another woman, of that she was sure, certainly not without his car; and it didn't seem as if he had been in a road accident or hospitalized. The only other explanation was that he had been mugged somewhere –maybe by kids looking for money to feed a drug habit, maybe by more professional thieves – and was lying in some undiscovered spot, possibly still alive but probably dead; and he might not be found for a long time, perhaps not ever, At first she thought this through calmly but, as its evident logic overwhelmed her – there really didn't seem to be any other possible explanation – she started to sob, at first small tears which she wiped away but then a flood of tears as she wept, silently but uncontrollably, her half eaten supper cast aside.

Eventually she was too exhausted, or too tense, to cry any more, and began to clear up. She ran herself a bath, and lay in it for a long time, reflecting on her theory of what had happened to Paul from every angle, and trying to ponder any alternative plausible explanation, without success. Wrapped up in a thick dressing gown she watched the ten o'clock news. The prospect was that the US and the UK might attack Iran's nuclear installations, with or without UN backing and, unlike the previous such situation in Iraq, this time there was no question over whether Iran had Weapons of Mass Destruction - Iran was broadcasting to the world that it had them. With Iran promising retaliation on a vast scale, in particular against Israel if any of its installations was attacked, the news could not have been globally more serious; but it passed in a haze for Kate, more concerned about the fate of the man she had met by the merest chance at a book launch; whom she loved with unrestrained passion and who had caused her life to disintegrate by simply not being there, or anywhere she knew. She drank a glass of wine, took two sleeping tablets and headed for another disturbed night.

CHAPTER 3

The next morning Sarah arrived a few minutes early, which was just as well as Kate had been awake, at first rather vaguely but then very definitely, since around 5.30 am. She had dressed for work again, but really didn't know whether she would be able to cope, always supposing that she got to work today. She was not, she told herself, being over-dramatic when she reckoned that today, one way or another, was quite likely to be life-transforming. But she did remember to pick out a picture of Paul.

They parked where they had done the day before – it appeared to have caused no difficulty the day before - and entered the police station. Kate was completely thrown to see a middle-aged man at the desk and five or six black teenagers all talking quite volubly as the policeman sought to take down some details. It looked like it would take some time, Kate took hold of Sarah's arm.
"I can't cope with this" she said, in a whisper.
Sarah sat her down, as far as possible away from the desk and said "Give me a moment" She walked up to the policeman at the desk, fixed him with a piercing look and said
"I am sorry to butt in, but could you tell me if the police woman who was on duty here yesterday morning is around? We have an appointment with her" To her relief, he seemed grateful for the chance to get away from whatever it was that he was trying to note down; said "just a moment" partly to Sarah and partly to the group of youths, who seemed little interested in whether he was there or not; and disappeared through a door at the rear of the desk area. Two minutes later he re-appeared; asked Sarah and Kate to come through a side door to the

left of the desk and, with just a hint of resignation, went back to whatever crime, great or small, he was trying to document.

Through the door, a man in his early thirties came forward and shook Kate's and Sarah's hands.

"Hello" he said "I'm Detective Sergeant Hargreaves. Sergeant Sims, who you spoke to yesterday, has filled me in on the situation. Do come through into this office".

He beckoned them into a room immediately on the left of the passageway into which they had come. It was very small, with just enough room for a table up against one wall, two chairs by it and a third set apart. As they entered he suggested coffee. They both nodded and DS Hargreaves signalled, to someone they couldn't see, to get some coffee.

DS Hargreaves was of medium height but quite rugged build, had a strong but friendly face and a quiet confidence of manner. Kate subliminally registered that he was almost certainly younger than her, but he was welcoming, affable and communicative. Even before they had fully settled themselves down, he and Kate at the table, Sarah in the other chair, he revealed that they had had no luck in tracing Paul. He described how they had worked through all the recorded road accidents of the last five days, seeking anyone fitting Paul's description – by which he meant no more than male, thirties, white and, for some reason, unidentified. This had produced no result. They had contacted 34 hospitals covering a substantial part of Southern England with the same remit. This had produced one possible candidate, a man of more or less the right age who had been admitted to Stoke Mandeville hospital after being found in a semi-conscious state on farmland near the town and with no identification on him. But he had a beard and rather obvious signs of alcoholism; and they were therefore rather certain it was not Paul. They had, as a result, registered him as a Missing Person.

Kate responded to this rather better than she would have imagined. It was, perhaps, the sense that people were on the case, that something was happening rather than just her getting more and more stressed and distressed; and at some level she was probably aware that DS Hargreaves's approach – active, intelligent, helpful – was contributing to this.

"What happens now" she asked, trying to stay calm and focused, but devoid of any suggestions of her own.

"Well, quite a lot, in fact" said Hargreaves. "First we will be putting out an alert to all police stations in the country, giving Mr. Emmerson's description, details, and picture if you have brought one. Every police force in the country will know that we are looking for him before lunchtime. Second, we will start to search his home for any information, in particular whether his passport, credit cards and so on have gone. Third we will check whether anyone with his name has left the country in the last week. If so, we will contact the relevant overseas authorities. We will see if his credit cards or mobile phone have been used recently and, if so, where and when. And we will talk to as many of his friends and colleagues as we can to see if that produces any primary intelligence on where he might have gone. It would be helpful if you could write down as many as you can think of, with addresses if you know them to start us off; oh and his mobile phone number. We will also be checking his bank account, phone calls to his home and work, we'll talk to relatives and so on. We will do everything we can to find Mr. Emmerson".

"*Dr.* Emmerson" said Kate. She wasn't sure how much of what Hargreaves had said had really registered; but Paul was Dr. Emmerson, not Mr. Emmerson. His doctorate had been on the crystalline structure of a class of synthetic materials, and their associated properties, and it somehow seemed important to get it right.

"I'm sorry, *Dr.* Emmerson" said Hargreaves

"And here are two photos" she said, pulling out a family shot of him at a barbecue in the South of France the previous summer, which gave a good impression of him overall; and, although two years old, a very clear studio portrait photograph of him taken for the brochure accompanying a distinguished lecture he had given in New York.

"Ah I see what your friend meant about him being good-looking" said Hargreaves "not unlike the young Paul Newman" at which Sarah blushed somewhat and started to apologise.

"Don't worry" interjected Hargreaves. "As we have these photos I won't treat your description as official. Now Miss Kimball, I need to ask you some questions, and some won't be easy. But they are all designed to help find Dr. Emmerson as quickly as possible. Is that going to be OK?"

"That's fine" replied Kate. "What is it you want to ask?"

"Well, it may help if I give you a quick run-down of what I will need to cover, so that there are no surprises later" He paused to let Kate respond, but she just sat, rather stiff in her chair, and waited for Hargreaves to continue.

"So, first, I will need to know everything you can tell me about Dr. Emmerson – his upbringing, his life-style, his interests, how he spends his time, anything else that comes to mind. Then as much as you can about his job, enough to set us up to pursue inquiries with his employer. Then – I'm sorry – but we will need to know all about you and him, how you met, the – um, state of your relationship. I don't want to give any offence but I'm sure you will see that we need to know about your relationship, if only to close off the idea that that could have had anything to do with his disappearance".

Hargreaves said this with such evident and genuine sympathy that Kate couldn't feel offended. Anyway, the sooner she explained about her and Paul, the quicker they would get on to more productive lines of inquiry. He had mentioned a number of these, but none seemed to her to address the most likely explanation. Before she could say anything, however, Hargreaves was speaking again.

"I will also want you to think whether there was anything odd or unusual in his behaviour, in his manner, his routine, anything at all which might signify some concern or distress on his part; or anything he might have said or done that you are aware of that could have caused trouble, friction with anyone he came into contact with, at work, anywhere really."

Kate was both impressed but also taken aback by the breadth of Hargreaves's interest. She could at once see why. Hargreaves had absolutely no idea what he was looking for; and so would have to throw his initial net very wide indeed. Most, if not all, of what he would be asking, she knew, would lead absolutely nowhere. But then, she had no more clue as to what had actually happened to Paul than Hargreaves did. So, she girded herself up to be as thorough as possible, to give Hargreaves a picture of Paul in as much detail as she could, in the hope that something would make sense, if not to her then at least to him. But first there was something she had to say.

"I appreciate your spelling out just what is involved; and I'm ready to tell you everything I can about Paul. But I'm just terrified that he has been the victim of a mugging – you read about it all the time – and if he has, then none of these inquiries are going to find him. He'll just be lying, dumped somewhere until someone accidentally comes across him. What if that is the explanation?"

Hargreaves looked at her impassively for a moment, clearly making some sort of decision.

"I'll be very straight with you Miss Kimball. That is certainly a possibility. I have already got men taking a first look in all the main open spaces in the city – Christ Church Meadow, the University Parks, Port Meadow, along by the river and so on. But I didn't want to add to your distress; and we may well get some indication of whether that explanation is likely from some of the other investigations I mentioned earlier". He paused. "Was there a particular walk that Dr. Emmerson liked to take, perhaps in the evening, after work?"

"He ran several mornings a week, usually round the University Parks, and sometimes round Port Meadow, though not at this time of the year. But he ran in shorts and a T-shirt, or a track suit – it would have been obvious that he didn't have anything valuable on him"

Kate did not fully register that Hargreaves had moved on from setting out his agenda to actual questioning. But for the next two hours, broken only by the arrival of coffee, she tried to answer every question Hargreaves put to her, while he made copious notes. She covered as much as she knew of Paul's upbringing in a North London suburb – no siblings - of his father and mother, now dead, of the two years they had been together, of his time as a student, studying Engineering at Merton College, Oxford; of his graduate work at St. John's College, the switch being occasioned by his winning a graduate scholarship at St. John's Then a research fellowship at Imperial College, London before returning to Oxford six years previously, as a University Lecturer in the Materials Section of the Engineering Department of the University, with a Fellowship at Wadham College attached. Within the academic world of Engineering he had had a fairly meteoric career; and Kate provided all the details she could as to how Hargreaves could follow up on it. In fact, as she pointed out, one call to Alice would set quite enough balls rolling.

She also described how Paul's life very much revolved around his research work, some occasional consultancy projects and, when they could co-ordinate their very hectic lives, even more occasional holiday trips together. These were rarely more than a week at a time, usually in Europe, and often linked to a conference that Paul was due to attend somewhere. And she described how they met, their rapport, the instant recognition of similar spirits – rather workaholic, driven even – but recognizing that work alone would never, in the longest of long runs, be enough by itself.

On Hargreaves's last group of questions – any recent odd behaviour, tension or concerns – she wracked her brains, and consulted Sarah, but she genuinely could not think of anything. Paul's last few months had been the usual round of lecturing, research in the department, writing up a couple of research articles, a few conference or consultancy-related trips, and week-ends with Kate which had been pleasant, relaxed as far as she could remember for both of them, and no holidays except for one long week-end in Venice.

Hargreaves asked her if she could remember where Paul, as he was now calling him, had gone when he was away. Kate re-called a trip to Berlin and one to Houston, Texas, and others in the UK; but said that Alice Richmond would be bound to know the full list, because she fixed all Paul's travel arrangements. By 11.30 am, despite a second round of coffee, Kate felt utterly exhausted; and Hargreaves, sensing this, said that she had been very helpful and had given him more than enough to be getting on with. He asked if Kate could let him have her keys to Paul's flat, which she did, and arranged that he would call Kate either the next day or Thursday morning at the latest to let her know what progress had been made. He gave her a number to call if she thought of anything else, however trivial it might seem, that could be relevant; and Kate got up to go.

"Can I ask you" she said "is this situation one that you have dealt with before? I mean, is it at all common for people just to disappear? Surely it isn't?"

"Well" said Hargreaves, deciding once again that the woman in front of him could probably take, indeed would insist on the truth, "more people than you might expect disappear each year –many thousands - but a large number are youngsters. Many aren't found because they don't want to be found – unhappy homes, abusive parents and the like. Others are very troubled – victims of abuse, drugs, alcoholism and so on; and some go because they can't face something in their lives – their marriages, debts, responsibilities of one sort or another; and believe they can start a new life if only they can get away. A number of women disappear into the blurred line between prostitution and kidnapping; and quite a number commit suicide sooner or later, in ways that don't link them back to when or where they disappeared, at least not for some time. But the number of 34 year old professional men in a stable relationship, with no history of depression or mental illness, drug habits or alcoholism disappearing without trace or for any discernible reason is very small. It's only the second or third such case that I have come across in over ten years with the Thames Valley Police force; and all the others, in the end, involved financial problems or a relationship that had gone sour. It could, as you said earlier, be a mugging, and there are cases from time to time in Oxford; but not around where Paul lives, and not without trace". He paused, conscious that he had gone on rather too much; but Kate made no reply, and he added "That is why we will put a lot of resources into this case. Given what you have told me, this one doesn't make a lot of sense".

The next twenty four hours, in as far as Kate fully registered them, were horribly similar to the previous twenty four. She went to work, attended some meetings, did what she had to do with Janice, talked to Sarah on the phone, and felt such an aching in her stomach whenever she stopped for a moment that she felt almost physically sick. She spoke to Alice at the Engineering department, who said that the police had visited, searched Paul's office, and asked her a lot of questions, in particular about recent trips Paul had made. Arrangements had been made for someone else to take over his two lecture courses. Both she and the police had spoken to the Warden of Wadham College, who had informed the other fellows in the college; and made alternative arrangements to cover the tutorials that Paul would have given. The local press had not yet got hold of the story; but Kate knew that it was only a matter of time before they did.

And, hour by hour, step by step, Kate started to accept that she was – was what – somewhere between deserted and bereaved; that she had lost Paul, her friend, her lover, her companion and, increasingly she now realized, her rock of support; and she was having to learn to cope without all those people that he had been to her. It wasn't even so much their physical separation – they had often gone much longer periods of time apart – but the prospect, growing by the hour, that she would never see him again and, worse, without any idea of why, or what had happened to him. Twice she let herself cry, uncontrollably, partly because she couldn't stop herself but also because she needed some release, however temporary, from the appalling stress that was devouring her, physically and mentally, minute by minute, hour by hour.

Everyone she knew, Sarah, Harry, and most of all Janice, could see the anguish eating away at her, but could do little to help. Soothing, re-assuring words would be quite hollow and each of them, at slightly different times but all of them by Wednesday evening, began to recognise that Paul, quite possibly, was not coming back. No-one even knew how to raise this with Kate, let alone discuss it and Kate wouldn't have known how to respond if any of them had. She just lived from moment to moment, increasingly distressed, increasingly numb and, she realized with some shock, increasingly resigned to her new status – a widow who had never been married, a woman who had lost her lover to.....to nothing and no-one, but who had lost him just the same.

On Wednesday evening, Gareth Simpson rang to say that the police had been in touch with him; that he had not been much help he thought; that he was so sorry; and for Kate to let him know if there was anything he could do. He'd been in touch with Charlie Gregson and one or two others of Paul's friends, mainly from student days, and they all sent their best wishes. It was all very well meant, but it largely passed Kate by. She agreed that she would be in touch if she heard anything, but she didn't have any great expectations.

It was a sign of how much she was beginning to accept the new status quo that she felt rather angry when Hargreaves failed to contact her by Thursday lunchtime. At 2.45 pm she rang the number he had given her. She could tell by a change in the ring tone that after a few rings, the call was diverted, and she found herself through to the police station. She asked for DS Hargreaves but was told he was out. She left a message but by the time she left work he had not got back to her. After another Valium-assisted night she went to work on Friday morning in a bitter mood. By 10.30 am Hargreaves had still not called, and another phone call to the police station revealed only that he was busy. With mounting anger she asked Janice to put her commitments for the morning on hold and strode through the centre of Oxford, arriving at the police station a little before 11.00 am.

She asked to see Hargreaves, but was told by yet another desk Sergeant that he was currently in Swindon. However, the new face at the desk, an Asian man of impeccable courtesy but, it seemed to Kate little understanding of the urgency of the situation, said that a Detective Inspector Johnson was fully up to speed with the case and would see Kate if she could wait around 15 to 20 minutes. Kate said she would wait, but was in a paroxysm of rage and anxiety when, nearly forty minutes later, the desk Sergeant led her through to the same room she had been in before with Hargreaves. Johnson, who she guessed was probably in his late thirties, was of medium height and tending to overweight, but stocky with it, a powerful looking man, with a rather square head, dark brown hair cut very short, rather piercing eyes and a manner that suggested a tough, no nonsense approach to the trials and tribulations of life in the Thames Valley Police Force. With him was a woman who he introduced as Detective Constable Sally James, a well built, blonde-haired woman who clearly must have been rather beautiful in her teens, and might even now be so, in her early forties Kate guessed, but for the extraordinarily grim, tight-lipped, almost disdainful look that permeated her face, not helped by the curtest of nods as Johnson introduced her. Kate, in a ridiculous moment of insight, knew that they couldn't have any terrible news for her, because they could never have thought this severe looking woman would be the one to try to soften the blow.

"I'm sorry DS Hargreaves isn't here" said Johnson, in a tone that didn't seem to contain much sense of regret "but he's been down in Swindon and probably won't be back until late tonight. Kate forbore to ask what he was doing in Swindon; whether it was to do with Paul; if not, who was doing all the extensive leg-work he had described to her, and so on. Instead she waited, seething with anger at the wait she had been forced to endure, and impatient to hear what, if anything, had transpired.

"We have carried out a lot of inquiries" said Johnson, in just a shade too officious a manner "but I'm sorry to say that they haven't revealed much. The last we can trace of him is last Thursday, and everything seemed entirely normal. He had a sandwich lunch with two colleagues in the cafeteria in the Engineering department of the University, and left some time after 4.00 pm. He returned to his laboratory building later that evening. We don't know if he went home after that or not, but no-one has seen or heard from him since that we can discover. We will, of course, be making further checks, but at the moment we don't have any useful leads".

There was a long pause. It was clear that Kate was supposed to reply in some way and, equally clearly hatchet-face was not going to offer anything to the conversation; but Kate knew, if she wasn't careful, that she would respond in a way that would be very unhelpful indeed. Where in the hell was Hargreaves, who had been so approachable, supportive even? What exactly had they been doing, or found out, since Tuesday? Why had they been so long in contacting her, in fact hadn't contacted her at all but waited until she came in? And what were they now proposing – sorry miss, he's gone, that's it: and less tangibly but most important of all, why were they being so bloody unhelpful and unsympathetic in manner?

In the silence she concluded, either that they had drawn a blank and that was it – another missing person to note down and then move on to other cases which they might have some remote chance of solving; or, having found no other conceivable explanation for Paul's disappearance, had decided that it must be a case of lovers falling out, maybe she was to blame, and it was a waste of police time to take it further. Finally, as much to disconcert this officious pair as anything else, she said

"Why was I kept waiting forty minutes if you had nothing to tell me?"

There was another pause, from Kate's point of view a rather satisfying one. DC James looked, if it was possible, even more disagreeable than before, but continued to say nothing. Johnson clearly considered his reply and then said, rather stiffly

"I'm sorry about that Miss Kimball. I was trying to make sure that I had all the latest information in from colleagues who have been working on the case". With just a hint of a triumphal look added "I felt that you would want us to be fully up to date on what, I'm sure, is a very distressing matter for you.

Kate strongly doubted if any of this was true, but there was no point in pursuing it. However, anger, she found, was much less debilitating than the gut-wrenching anxiety of the last six days and she asked, as calmly as possible, but with a resolution that neither police officer missed

"What did the tracking of his credit cards and his mobile phone show: and do you have his passport?"

She was quite possibly mistaken, but for a split second she could have sworn that the two officers made the briefest of eye contact, and a scintilla of relief flicker across at least Johnson's face.

"Neither his credit cards nor his mobile have been used since last Thursday" said Johnson. "We haven't found his credit cards, but his passport was in a drawer in his desk at his office".

"So he is unlikely to have gone off by choice then, is he?" said Kate, noting with about as mixed a set of emotions as she could bear that if he hadn't used his credit cards and hadn't even taken his passport with him, this surely killed dead any notion that he had run off with someone or, at least, away from her.

"Probably not" replied Johnson "but if he was planning to disappear he'd know that we could trace him through his phone or his credit cards; so he might have decided to avoid using them".

"You don't seriously believe that, do you?" replied Kate, her anger heading back towards the uncontrollable level. "How would he live? Has he cleared out his bank account? What the hell is going on here?"

"No" said Johnson, ignoring the last of Kate's questions. "He hasn't, as far as we can see, provided for a disappearance, but he could be ....living off someone else's resources".

Kate started to stand up, and if she had made it she would undoubtedly have slapped Johnson. But the reason for DC James's presence finally became clear. In an instant she was by Kate's side with a light but firm hand on her shoulder.

"Please don't think that is what we believe has happened" she said, in a matter of fact tone. "We just have to consider all the possibilities. The problem is that, if he didn't go by choice, then the only other explanation is that he has been the victim of a mugging, but we can find no support for this, despite talking to a large number of ....contacts".

Kate slumped back in her chair. She felt utterly defeated, and knew that nothing more was going to come out of this meeting. She tried to focus on what scraps of useful information she might glean.

"So, you are saying that at some time between 4 pm last Thursday and Friday morning he either chose to disappear completely, with someone who could provide for him - I suppose in Britain unless you think he arranged for a fake passport; or he went out, for a walk, was attacked and left somewhere that none of your men has been able to find. That's it, is it?"

"I don't know" said Johnson, with too thinly disguised exasperation. "If you want a guess, but it is only a guess, the most likely explanation is that, yes, he went out Thursday evening, for a walk, a drink, I don't know, maybe some cigarettes, was attacked for some reason, probably a mugging by some drug starved drop-outs, or even just mindless violence; and whoever did it, left him somewhere hidden. I'm sorry to be so brutally explicit, and I hope I'm wrong but, if your relationship is as you described it to DS Hargreaves – and I have read his notes very carefully - that is far and away the most likely explanation. I'm sorry".

Kate was too stunned to reply What Johnson had just said was, at once, so awful, so unthinkable, and yet so plausible, so unremarkable, indeed precisely what she had feared all along. But the idea of Paul masterminding his own disappearance was just ridiculous; and she saw that the police had simply done their work. They had checked out all the other plausible explanations and now she was left with this. A mindless mugging, or some such incident, Paul gone, and not even a body to mourn over. She felt tears well up in her eyes, but she fought them back.

"How thoroughly have you investigated that possibility?" she asked, trying to keep the venom she felt out of her voice.

"Very thoroughly indeed" said Johnson, with rather more exasperation this time. We have talked to just about all his immediate neighbours; we have been touch with all the taxi firms in central Oxford; and we have talked to, shall I say, some of the less desirable elements around the town that we know only too well. They couldn't keep something like this secret from us for ten minutes. None of it has produced anything".

Kate knew that was it. "I'll go now. Thank you for your help" she added, in an unintendedly but absurdly formal way. She stood up, slightly unsteadily, and headed out of the door. She wondered if either Johnson or DC Sally James would say anything – some parting phrase about not giving up hope, or that they would be in touch; but neither did, the only part of the whole interview for which she accorded them any respect. She was back in her office before 12.30 pm.

Sometime during that Friday afternoon – she couldn't say when - while she was working away at OUP, or at least going through the motions of it, Kate crossed some sort of threshold. She went from hoping against hope that somehow it would all come right to knowing that it wouldn't. She left the office in the clear and certain knowledge that she would never see Paul again, dead or alive. Despite all the nightmare of the last week, it was still a terrible shock, a hammer blow to her nervous system - even, in a way, to her sanity. She went home and cried and cried, for what seemed like hours, but eventually got some sort of hold on herself and at 8.15 pm she rang Sarah, who agreed to come round straight away

They spent the evening talking, drinking, Sarah sometimes holding Kate, occasionally finding herself in tears along with her. She said that Kate must come and stay with her, at least over the week-end, but Kate declined the offer. The stress with which she had been living for what now seemed an age was unabated, but she felt too exhausted to be with anyone else, even Sarah. As she headed home, it crossed her mind that if Paul should suddenly re-appear, from a crazy spur-of-the-moment whim to visit central Peru or some such place, that their relationship would not - could not - survive her fury. But then she reminded herself that he had left his car, his passport, his credit cards, and so he could not possibly have gone voluntarily. There was nothing to stand against what both her own instincts and DC Johnson's oh so logical 'guess' proffered – a random, pointless attack, with Paul just happening to be in the wrong place at the wrong time.

Yet, as she drove, on auto-pilot, she was increasingly aware of another sentiment just touching her consciousness, drifting away but circling back, and she struggled to focus on it. Something else was bothering her; something beyond the loss of Paul. It seemed ridiculous in such a situation that anything else could be, but it was there, and if only she had not been in such distress, she might have grasped it earlier. Something wasn't....right - if that could remotely be the word – about even the grotesquely awful situation into which she had plummeted. DS Hargreaves had not only been helpful in manner, he had laid out a major programme of investigation that the police could pursue, to see if they could get any leads on Paul's whereabouts; and that was on Tuesday. Yet by Friday, in fact probably by Thursday afternoon, DI Johnson was, as far as she could tell, largely winding things up, if not confident then at least heavily suspecting that Paul had been mugged. She could readily accept that, while Hargreaves had, by temperament, appeared to be helpful and sympathetic, Johnson and James were...... well, not helpful and sympathetic: but this left two questions. In the first place, could Hargreaves, or anyone come to that, have really completed all those inquiries so fast, to the point where no further investigation appeared warranted? And in the second place, why had Hargreaves so completely disappeared from the investigation – in practice he must have been assigned to other cases by his superiors – so rapidly? More generally, she realized that she had no idea as to who had done what – who had discovered or not discovered anything; and the more she thought about it the more it seemed odd. Hargreaves had been keen to set balls in motion, see what they could find out. Johnson and James, in contrast, seemed unenthusiastic about the case, and mainly pre-occupied with just getting Kate out of their hair.

Perhaps, she was just being rather paranoid. Presumably the police would have means for carrying out very wide-spread checks in forty-eight hours. She had been impressed that Johnson, or officers working for him at least, had been round to Paul's neighbours, and carried out a range of other checks, all in a very short space of time. No doubt wider checks would largely be computer-based and could, with a few dedicated officers, be carried out very quickly. And yet, some instinct told her that something......'wasn't right' was all she could repeat to herself – a sense that she wasn't being *allowed* to see Hargreaves again. She could, of course, be thinking this just because she had established a rapport with him - more than that, she had confidence in him - which she certainly didn't have in Johnson, although even this might be just because she really didn't like Johnson's manner.

As she parked her car it struck her that there was a very easy way to resolve these concerns. In the morning she would again call the number Hargreaves had given her and somehow try to speak to him, to get his assessment of what might have happened, and where, if anywhere, the case rested. Comforted by this thought, she let herself into the house, made herself a light supper, and went to bed. Mercifully, she got her first reasonable non-drug induced night's sleep since she had returned from California.

CHAPTER 4

O
n arriving at her office the next morning, Kate was alarmed to see how much work had accumulated during the previous week, despite her spending at least part of each day there. She launched into it, racing through a series of quick meetings, sending Janice off on all sorts of missions and even fitting in a meeting with David Hennessy, known officially as the Secretary to the Delegates but in practice the CEO of Oxford University Press, to fill him in on progress on her LA deal. He already knew what he needed to know – it was more an opportunity for him to recognize her success, and to thank her for what she had achieved – but he also knew about Paul. Having himself lost a daughter in a skiing accident several years previously, he knew much about the grief of loss, and spent some time talking to Kate about Paul. Kate, to her surprise, found this helpful, even therapeutic, and somehow all the more so because they did not know each other well; though it might have just been the shared bond of having lost someone so close.

The result of her day's efforts was that it was almost 3.00 pm before she rang Hargreaves's number. A soft female voice replied and Kate asked if she might speak briefly to DS Hargreaves. She added that she understood he had been in Swindon the previous week, but should now be back in Oxford..

"Can you hold and I will see if I can put you through" replied the soft voice.

As she waited, Kate wondered what she would actually say. What she wanted to say was that she was deeply pissed off with Johnson and James, and would Hargreaves take over the case again; but she recognized that this would not only be pointless, but completely counter-productive. Instead, she would merely recount her meeting with Johnson and James, in as anodyne a way as possible, and ask if there was anything new to report.

"I can't seem to find him at the moment" said the voice on the phone. "If you would like me to take a message, I'll get him to call you back". Kate duly complied, leaving her home and office numbers and her mobile. "Tell him to ring as soon as he is free, would you?"

"Shall I say what it is about?"

"No, he'll know" replied Kate, and rang off, mightily disappointed.

With Kate throwing herself back into her work, the only antidote she knew to the overwhelming sense of sadness she felt whenever she slowed down, it was lunchtime on Tuesday before it fully registered that Hargreaves had not returned her call. With a growing sense of frustration if not, once again, outright anger, she again rang the number he had left her. One small victory was that she did, for once, get the same voice. Kate explained why she was calling.

"Oh, yes" said the woman. "I gave him your message, but it was quite late yesterday. I'm sure he'll be in touch soon. I'll tell him you called again".

Kate thanked her and returned to publishing matters.

That evening she had dinner with Janice and her husband, Simon. She hadn't wanted to go, however kindly the invitation was meant and however much she enjoyed their company. She explained this to herself in terms of not being able to think for long about anything except Paul, but with no-one else being able remotely to appreciate or share the agony she was feeling. And so she felt more comfortable on her own. She recognized that this way lay reclusiveness – normally quite alien to her - but she increasingly felt powerless to resist the change. However, she forced herself to accept Janice's invitation; and did in fact quite enjoy the evening, in as far as she still had the capacity to enjoy anything. Only as she arrived home around 10.00 pm did she once again begin to think about Hargreaves, the elusive Hargreaves, whom she had still only met once and who again had not returned her call.

She turned on her television to watch the News. The main item was coverage of a speech, made earlier that day, by the US President about Iran. In it he reviewed what he described as Iran's support for terrorist movements throughout the Middle East and beyond; and Iran's build up of nuclear weapons capability. He said that these two trends, if left unchecked, would result in a nuclear attack, on Israel certainly but also, in time, on other Western targets, particularly in the US and the UK. He called on the UN to take unprecedented steps to address an unprecedented situation; and then said something that riveted Kate to the spot.

"We cannot be certain what is going on in Iran, still less what is going on in the minds of its leading politicians. But we cannot stand idly by, hoping, but with no real basis for that hope, that somehow everything will turn out for the best. We have to seize the initiative, and do whatever it takes, to safeguard our people and our freedoms from this evident threat"

Most of this was familiar rhetoric; and Kate's interest in the Middle East, never huge, had been non-existent recently. But one phrase struck her so forcibly that she couldn't get it out of her mind. "Seize the initiative and do whatever it takes". It might just have been the way the line was delivered, or perhaps the no doubt intended Churchillian undertones. More likely was that she was just psychologically ready for the idea, might even have already entertained it herself but at too sub-conscious a level to notice. Whatever it was, it brought her a clarity of thought and a degree of resolution that she had altogether lost since Paul's disappearance. There was something not right, she told herself for the umpteenth time, and she was going to seize the initiative – do whatever it took, to find out what precisely wasn't right.

The next morning she dressed in a stylish dark blue suit with pencil skirt to the knee, a pale blue blouse, a small, exquisitely crafted silver chain that Paul had given her round her neck and earrings to match. She put her hair up, and completed her outfit by putting on stylish three inch dark blue high heels. She had dressed like this for work before, but only when giving a major presentation. Now she was going to make an impression for a cause closer to her heart.

It was a bright if blustery day, and she put on a white mackintosh. Leaving the house at 8.30 am. she walked into the centre of Oxford and down St. Aldate's to the police station., arriving shortly before 9 am. She did not go in. Instead, she crossed to the Magistrates' Court building opposite, a large white stone building, and stood just inside its large glass doors. She then got out her mobile and rang Hargreaves's number. A different voice from before, female but definitely different, answered. Kate said that she needed to contact DS Hargreaves, and could she suggest a good time to try to contact him? She was put on hold, and then told that DS Hargreaves had been in earlier, but was now out on an assignment. When would he be back inquired Kate, trying to stay as calm and reasonable sounding as possible. After another long pause she was told
"Later this morning apparently".

This, to say the least, was not quite what Kate had expected or hoped for. She had anticipated either finding him in, in which case she would have gone straight across to the police station; or getting an approximate arrival time for him, whereupon she would go across shortly afterwards. She had not anticipated that he might have arrived earlier and already be out; nor that his return would be so uncertain.

Kate thanked the anonymous voice, and asked if there was any idea at all as to what time Hargreaves might be back. Again a long pause and then, finally, some useful information. Apparently he was up at the Blackbird Leys Estate, which had a wretched reputation for violence, drugs and general mayhem, notwithstanding a large population trying to survive with some degree of decency on low incomes in an otherwise very affluent part of the South-East. It was not thought that he would be more than an hour or so.

And so, with a large number of work projects to be pursued, and any number of meetings which she should attend, Kate phoned Janice to say that she would be late; quickly walked up St. Aldate's, bought a paper and a take-away coffee; and returned to the police station, taking up residence on the front corner next to the small side road that led to the police station car park. Here she awaited Hargreaves's return.

By 11 am she had read every word of the newspaper, had done much of the crossword, a Sudoku and several other puzzles, her high heels were absolutely killing her; and she was reflecting on how unbearably boring the life of a private detective must be. More curiously, she noted that, despite lurking virtually on the doorway of a police station for nearly two hours, she appeared to have caused not the slightest interest on the part of anyone – not uniformed police officers coming and going through the front door; not drivers and occasional passengers of cars driven down the side street; nor any members of the public, whether calling at the police station or simply passing by. Kate presumed this was because she looked so presentable – so middle class she thought – with a cup of coffee and a copy of the Times, and no suspicious bags to raise concerns. Just a well dressed thirty-something woman waiting for someone or something.

And then that something, in the shape of a white Vauxhall car, and that someone in the shape of its driver, Detective Sergeant Hargreaves, appeared. She recognized him straight away as he slowed to turn into the side road. Kate immediately darted forward, for a second wondering if she might have to fling herself in front of his car, but he saw her, stopped, leaned across and wound down his window.

"Hello" he said, in a cheery enough voice, but with an air of apprehension as well. "What are you doing out here?"

"I need to talk to you" she said, in a firm, even forceful manner. She was quite exhilarated that her waiting had actually paid off, and it clicked her in to very direct mode.

"It won't take long, but it is extremely important".

Hargreaves opened his mouth to say something, but then shut it again. For a second he just sat there, thinking she knew not what. Kate consciously prepared herself to reject or disregard any reason he might give for not talking to her, or any reason to defer the conversation she wanted. She had been fobbed off too long already.

"How long have you been here?" asked Hargreaves.

"Nearly two hours" said Kate, looking straight at him.

"What out, here?" said Hargreaves, with evident surprise.

"Yes" replied Kate. "And you must know why. I've rung several times and left messages but you haven't returned any of them". She continued to fix her eyes on his.

"I'm very sorry about that" said Hargreaves, quietly. "I'm not actually on the Emmerson inquiry any more, and I have been incredibly busy".

"And you probably still are" said Kate. "But you could have rung, if only to tell me that you weren't involved anymore. Why couldn't you have done that?"

Hargreaves started to say something, something that Kate didn't catch, and then stopped again. There was an awkward silence.

"Look, all I want is a few words, preferably somewhere other than through your car window; and then I can let you get on".

Hargreaves was silent a moment longer. Then he said

"Wait here. I'll park the car round the back and be back in a second".

It was Kate's turn to pause. It was plain that Hargreaves felt some reluctance about talking to her; and she had registered that they were not, apparently, going to talk inside the police station. She hadn't spent half the morning in the hope of seeing him, only to let him slip away again into the bowels of the police station.

"That's fine" she said with a smile, "but I'll keep you company while you park". She walked round the front of the car, not seriously thinking that Hargreaves would take the opportunity to drive off, but not giving him even the slightest chance to do so, opened the passenger door and, her long shapely legs seeming to lead the way, sunk into the passenger seat. She gave a small sigh and looked straight ahead.

"I get the picture" said Hargreaves, with a slight grin, almost to himself. He slipped the car into gear and they moved slowly down the side of the police station.

"Do I detect some loss of confidence in Her Majesty's Constabulary?" he said, but without humour, as they eased into a parking space.

"You clearly are an outstandingly good detective" replied Kate, the words sounding more biting than perhaps she had intended. "I don't want to let you out of my sight until we have had a conversation".

"I rather gathered that" he said in a resigned voice, but then his tone turned more urgent, and more serious. "But I suggest we go somewhere else to talk. As I said, I'm not on the case any more, and it might not go down too well with my superiors if it gets round that I have been interviewing you again. And I should warn you that I'm not sure I can tell you anything useful".

"I'm happy to go somewhere else" said Kate, "in fact I'd prefer it". They got out of the car, Hargreaves locked it, and they set off back down the side road on foot. Five minutes later, a period during which they said almost nothing, they were in the St. Aldate's coffee shop where Kate and Sarah had gone just a few days, but a seeming lifetime ago, and from which Kate had already had some sustenance that morning.

"Fire away" said Hargreaves, in what he clearly hoped was a friendly manner that would keep the atmosphere, if not light then at least informal. The effect on Kate was quite different, compounding her anger at the whole situation. But she was much more in control of herself now, in control of her reactions, and outwardly she remained calm. Despite the strategy not having worked on DI Johnson she decided to try to wrong foot Hargreaves, or at least be unpredictable.

"Why did you want to talk away from the police station?" she started, more abruptly than she intended, but that was probably no bad thing. "I don't believe for one minute that it would create difficulties for you with your superiors. A distraught member of the public, bereaved, accosts you and you say you have to take her somewhere away from the police station in case your boss spots you talking to her? You'll have to do better than that" She positively glared at him.

She had the small satisfaction of seeing that this, indeed, had not been what Hargreaves was expecting and, for a second or two he looked very uncertain what to say.

"Well, it's rather more …..difficult than you think. As you know, I did the initial work on ….. Paul's disappearance. DI Johnson then reviewed the position. He said that in view of the lack of anything concrete he wanted me to switch to a GBH, possibly attempted murder case, in Swindon. He said he would get DC James – you've met her, I know – to follow up anything else that emerged on Paul. But by then I had got very intrigued by the case – I'm sorry, that must sound very detached and clinical – but it is quite an exceptional set of circumstances, and I don't really buy the idea of a mystery mugging in what is a very safe part of the city. So, I asked to stay on the case, said I thought there was more to it and so on. Johnson got quite hot under the collar, asked me for any evidence to support such ideas and, of course, I didn't have any. So he made it very clear that I was to drop it. That's when he said that I should avoid any further contact with you – he knew you would want more from us – to avoid getting our lines crossed. He or James would have any-up-to-date information, and he didn't want you thinking that we weren't doing all we could to find Paul. So, it would be rather embarrassing to be seen with you back at the station, and quite a snub to Johnson's authority". He paused, then added

"As you may have picked up, he is not the sort to take that lightly".
Hargreaves immediately realised that this was a comment too far.

"He's right, of course. He's my boss, and it would be chaos if we all started getting involved in each others' cases. I shouldn't be discussing this with you at all" he added gloomily.

"But you are" replied Kate immediately "and, much as I would like to think different, it isn't my natural charm. You're clearly not comfortable about the case are you? And it's not just that you were taken off it, is it. What's going on?"

"Nothing's 'going on' as you put it" replied Hargreaves, quite forcibly. "and I'm not 'uncomfortable' about the case. He paused. "I was a little surprised at how quickly Johnson concluded that we probably wouldn't make much more progress; and I did ask him about that later. He said that, as far as he could see, I had pursued the matter in a fast but very thorough way, which had not gone unnoticed. If none of the lines of inquiry I had instigated had produced anything then it almost certainly was a mugging, and we didn't have limitless resources. He seemed to think that – I'm sorry – that if he hadn't done a moonlight flit, Paul's body would probably come to light sometime soon, and further action by us was just not a top priority. As I say, I was a bit surprised, but there was some sense in it, and it wasn't as if I had any great ideas as to what to do next". He sat there, looking rather tense. Then, suddenly, his whole manner somehow slackened off. "I'm sorry" he repeated. "I'm talking about this as if it is just another job, which for me it is, but I know that it must be very distressing for you".

Kate appreciated this, but was now far too firmly locked onto her self-appointed task of finding out more – that there was more to this than had so far emerged, she was now quite convinced – and her nod of acknowledgement at his apology was so slight that it was not certain whether Hargreaves even noticed it. But his change of tone led her to change hers as well.

"Can you imagine how it looks to me?" she said in a rather sad voice. "When I saw you, you were keen to help and full of ideas. I really felt that, somehow or other, one of the lines of investigation you reeled out to me would lead somewhere. Then, all of a sudden, I can't get hold of anyone; and the next thing I know, I am being given the brush off by Johnson and that ghastly James woman; not merely that they have nothing to tell me – I could just about have put up with that – but neither of them the slightest bit bothered about the outcome. They couldn't have been more unhelpful". She knew this was a little over the top but, for a moment she lost her composure. As quickly, she regained it.

"I do see that" said Hargreaves. "Johnson's bedside manner does leave something to be desired; and I can't say I like working with him – and Sally James is scary, I agree - but he is good at his job. He gets results, which is why he is a Detective Inspector, and I think maybe the cause of your concern is just the switch from......" He was going to make a small joke about his wonderful customer-friendly approach, in contrast to Johnson's brick wall style, but recognized in time that any hint of humour was completely off limits in this conversation. ".....my enthusiasm" he inserted "at a time when there were lots of things to follow up, to Johnson's pragmatism when it was clear that none of it led anywhere".

"I see that" said Kate, in a resigned tone. "It all makes perfect sense. It's just that somehow, I don't know how or why, but somehow I got the clear sense that Johnson just didn't want any more action, not by him, or James nor, clearly, from you, and not just because you all have better things to do. And he certainly didn't want me hanging around any more". To her amazement, Hargreaves nodded.

"I know what you mean. I don't think that there is any more to be done, and I have seen Johnson's bristling efficiency mode, always upwards and onwards, before. Even so….." He left the thought unfinished.

"Did Johnson contact you?" he asked.

Kate frowned and shook her head.

"No, I thought not" said Hargreaves.

"Why would he" asked Kate.

"Because when I heard that you were trying to contact me, I spoke to Johnson about it and he said he would handle it. I assumed that he would get back to you, but it's clear from what you have been saying that he didn't"

"Damn right, he didn't" exploded Kate. "Why didn't he? Just too bloody busy I suppose".

Hargreaves didn't reply, but sat staring at his half empty coffee cup. Neither of them said anything for quite a while

"So what is to be done?" asked Kate, in a voice that hovered between the imperative and the resigned.

"I wish there was something I could think of" said Hargreaves "But I can't touch the case now. Even if I went through all the files, I'd probably only see what I put in them, and it's all one big nothing. I suppose there may be some other friends or colleagues of Paul that I could talk to if I was still on the case, but we did quite a large trawl – all the names you gave me and quite a few others that they mentioned. Unless someone – to be honest, unless you Kate, can suggest something that we haven't thought of, or don't know about, then I can't see what else there is to be done".

His use of her first name made more of an impact on Kate than she might have expected. It certainly didn't bother her, but it put the conversation on a slightly different footing; and she was aware that she had very slightly blushed. And she knew that the thought might itself lead to a more evident reddening of her features. She recalled that she had deliberately dressed to kill – what a complete irrelevance that had been.

"What other inquiries did you, or Johnson, or James make" asked Kate, partly to cover her embarrassment.

"We searched his office and his flat" said Hargreaves, "and we followed up on his credit cards, bank account, mobile phone and so on. We put his data on the Missing Persons network, notified Passport Control, checked hospitals and so on but, as I've said, none of it produced anything. We talked to his neighbours, things like that, but….. nothing".

"I understand" she said, "and thanks for having this conversation. If anything else occurs to you, I'd be grateful if you let me know".

"Of course, and if you think of anything else, feel free to contact me. I'll give you my personal number. I can't do much, but if there were something else to go on, I'd find some way to get police wheels in motion".

Kate was about to stand up when Hargreaves raised his hand a fraction, indicating that he wanted her to stay.
"You said that Johnson didn't contact you?"
"No" said Kate, in a slightly quizzical way.
"Not at all?" replied Hargreaves.
"No" said Kate, emphatically this time. "If he had just rung to say that he was returning my call to you, it would......
Hargreaves interrupted her. "No, I don't mean that. Did he not contact you about Paul's flat?"
"No" said Kate for the third time. "Why would he do that?"
Hargreaves sat quite still for a moment. Kate couldn't read the look on his face, but he was clearly reflecting on something.
"I searched Paul's flat, with two other officers, the same day that I met you. Everything seemed normal, quite undisturbed, but I didn't really know what I was looking for. I had been planning to go back there - with you - to see if you could identify anything that might be missing; but Johnson took over and said that, if he needed to do, he, or perhaps DC James would do that. She didn't contact you, did she?"
"Not at all" replied Kate. "I'm not sure I could have helped". She thought for a moment. "Paul had a rather up- market TV, a few pictures, and he did have one rather fine Chinese pot. None were worth a great amount, but it is odd that they didn't ask me about his belongings. Did you notice anything strange when you were there?" It escaped her completely that she had referred to Paul entirely in the past tense.
"Not really. And if the Chinese vase was the one on the sideboard in the living room, then it was still there because I remember admiring it. But I am surprised that they didn't think it necessary to get you round".
"You said 'not really'. *Was* there something that bothered you?"
"Not really" he said, and immediately apologized for merely repeating himself. Both of them smiled briefly. "I'm sorry I can't be more helpful".
On this subdued note, Kate got up, thanked him and together they headed out to St. Aldate's. She paused before turning left, away from the police station, and held out her hand. As he shook it she said, in a very level tone
"I don't know what happened to Paul, and I have accepted that I won't see him ever again; but whatever I first thought, I don't believe that he is just lying in some out-of-the-way spot as a result of some casual violence. I know that's the most probable explanation, but I don't believe it and I'm not going to accept it. I'll be in touch" and she swung away from him towards the centre of town.

The next few days were as miserable as any Kate had ever known. She continued to do her job – in fact it was the only thing that brought her any respite from the constant pain she felt as her emotions sought to come to terms with Paul's disappearance. She saw Sarah or Jane in the evenings, because she knew as well as they did that being on her own at home was not a good idea. Alice had rung from Engineering a couple of times, partly to commiserate but also because she was having to cope with all sorts of personal aspects of Paul's affairs – his mortgage, his bank, his salary. Kate tried to be helpful but said, quite correctly, that these were not her affair. If she didn't have any of the privileges of widowhood then she was not going to get caught up in the bureaucracy of it either. She suggested that the bank got together with the relevant departments of the university, and with his mortgage company, to sort it all out. She realised that she had no idea who the beneficiary of his Will was, possibly her, but they had never discussed such things and, in any event, much as DI Johnson had written Paul off, she was quite certain that he would not be declared dead for a very long time, unless his body was recovered.

It was around 11.30 am the following Monday when Janice called through to Kate in her office to say that a Detective Sergeant Hargreaves was on the phone. Kate took the call, surprised because she had not, after their coffee together the previous week, expected to hear from him again. After minimal pleasantries he said

"I really don't think this is anything but, after our conversation, I did look through all the case notes. There isn't anything significant there I'm afraid, but there were a couple of small points I wanted to check with you".

Kate could feel her heart pounding, Hargreaves' attempts to downplay whatever it was he wanted to discuss proving completely unsuccessful.

"Tell me what they are" she cut in.

"Well" said Hargreaves "did Paul have a lap-top?"

Kate almost laughed. Did he have a lap-top? It was the second great love of his life, no, quite possibly the greatest. How often had they spent what for her were moderately precious times together with him glued to some programme or other to do with his work?

"Yes, he had a lap-top. He used it a great deal. Is that significant?"

Well, it's just that I assumed he would have, given his job and so on; and I rather expected it would be at his home, but when we searched the place, we didn't come across it".

"He quite often took it to work" said Kate.

"I thought that was probably the answer" replied Hargreaves. "I mentioned it to Johnson, and he said he would ask you about it, if it didn't turn up at his office or in the Engineering laboratory. As he didn't get back to you, I assumed that they found it in one or other place; but I've now checked; and there is no mention of it being recovered from either location in the case notes, or from his car.

There was a pause in the conversation. Kate had had such a powerful psychological response to Hargreaves' call; and she had expected more than a question about his laptop. Kate felt decidedly anti-climactic.

"Do you think that is significant?" Kate eventually asked.

"I suppose not" said Hargreaves. "If he had it with him it's just conceivably a motive for a robbery, which could have led to an attack on him. Was Paul the sort of person who might put up some resistance in such a situation?"

Kate had to admit, first to herself and then to Hargreaves that he probably was. He was powerfully built, very fit, and would not respond at all sensibly to a gang of youths trying to steal his lap-top. Kate wondered if that was what had happened; and all of her feeling that there must be another explanation was just so much wishful thinking.

"So you think that might be what happened?" she said, resignation clear in her voice.

"I just don't know" said Hargreaves. "But it's odd that Johnson didn't ask you about it though – if they didn't find it.

"Oh, I don't know – he probably just didn't want to have to put up with me again" Kate replied

" Maybe so" said Hargreaves, sounding far from convinced. "Still, there isn't anything I can do about it. I' shouldn't really have bothered you".

Kate didn't mind the bother. She was, in fact, rather pleased that Hargeaves hadn't completely given up thinking about what had happened to Paul, even if the most likely explanation only reinforced Johnson's conviction that Paul had been mugged. She was at a loss what to say to Hargreaves when he abruptly said

"Well thanks, got to go" and put the phone down. Kate actually smiled, a rare event these days. Obviously DI Johnson must have just hove into view she thought, and she wondered if, even at this moment, Hargreaves was having to explain away his phone call. But even as her small smile faded, two queries lodged in her mind. If Paul hadn't been attacked – and she still didn't believe that explanation – then what *had* become of his laptop? And what was the other 'small point' Hargreaves had been planning to raise with her before he was interrupted?

CHAPTER 5

Three calls to Hargreaves that afternoon were all equally unsuccessful in getting hold of him. Not surprisingly, Kate had another restless night – something she was learning to cope with – but the missing laptop was also partly to blame. It niggled away at her, like an itch which, no matter how much one scratched it, was still there, irritating, probably pointless, but not something she could ignore. If it wasn't at his flat, in his car or in his office, and if it wasn't lying around at the laboratory where he worked, then where was it? She had no ideas. But she decided to double-check at the department. This was no doubt equally pointless, but at least it was something she could do, until she found out Hargreaves' other little mystery; and that at least helped her, eventually, to get off to sleep.

The next morning she walked round to the Engineering Department. This was housed in a rather extraordinary seven story building in the Banbury Road, which, by a trick of the architectural design, appeared broader at the top than at the bottom. For some time it was famous, first for having Paternoster lifts – small continuously moving open lifts that one jumped into and out of as they slowly went past the floors of the building - and then for students daring each other to stay in them as they disappeared into the top of the building before tipping over and heading back down. However, their real fame came when some of the rubberised washers on the lifts disintegrated, but could not be replaced because the company that had designed and built the lifts had gone bankrupt. The lifts became inoperable, but the University did not remotely have the money to pay the huge amount necessary to replace the lifts – the space being far to small to accommodate an ordinary lift shaft – and so for several years the members of the Engineering Department, both faculty and students, were amongst the fittest in the whole of the higher education system. Mercifully, two years earlier, the University had finally installed new lifts, and Kate was saved a climb to the sixth floor where both Alice and Paul had their offices.

Alice was genuinely pleased to see her. Kate had noticed how many of her friends and colleagues at work seemed awkward in her presence since Paul's disappearance; no doubt sympathetic, but aware of the great grief that she must be carrying and unable to judge how best to respond – or how Kate would want them to respond – even whether to mention Paul at all. Alice, however, not only had a bright, outward going personality but also a rather thick skin, some would say a rather insensitive aspect. So when Kate went into her office she just reacted instinctively, giving Kate a big hug, asking how she was coping, and rattling on about how devastated the department was, with them all still in a state of shock.

Kate found this effusive and unrestrained welcome rather comforting; and she spoke more to Alice, whom she did not know at all well, about Paul in five minutes than she had said to almost anyone else in the last two weeks. If it occurred to Alice to ask Kate quite why she had called round early in the morning – and it probably didn't - she was sensible enough not to do so; and after about ten minutes Kate asked if she could have the key to Paul's office. She was about to explain that there were a few things of hers that she wanted to pick up, though she wasn't entirely sure how plausible this was, but Alice immediately said

"Of course. I'll get it for you" and produced a small bunch of keys from a desk drawer.

"It's this one" she said, holding the bunch out to Kate by the appropriate key. "I'll come along with you".

This was well meant, indeed it would have been quite odd for Alice to let Kate make her own way to Paul's room; and Kate took it as such, but she really didn't want Alice joining her in Paul's room itself. Fortunately, Alice didn't feel the need to be *that* hospitable and left Kate at the door, saying that she would see her back in Alice's office.

Kate had not been in Paul's office very often; and it had little to commend it as a place to conduct any sort of business. It was small, very rectangular and unremittingly functional. She remembered being surprised at the contrast between Paul's evident international reputation, an increasingly prominent figure in his field, and this rather cell-like base he inhabited and from which much of his stream of ideas and results and academic papers emerged. The other contrast, more familiar in Oxford, was between this room where he did most of his non-laboratory research work and his room in Wadham College where he did much of his tutorial teaching – by no means one of the better rooms in the college and built in the 17th century, but four times the size of his departmental office, with a high ceiling, large windows on facing walls with impressive views of two of the college quadrangles; and with a large, if slightly bizarre, collection of furniture, of styles covering at least three of the intervening centuries since the room was built. But Paul spent much of his time on the sixth floor of this rather ugly albeit distinctive '60s concrete building. He did at least have an attractive view of the University parks, though Kate wondered if he ever noticed it once he was ensconced in his work.

The room contained an L-shaped desk with room for both Paul's desk-top computer and writing space, a bank of three chest-high filing cabinets, an easy chair and a small two-seater sofa under the window, plus some bookshelves fixed to the walls. This more than filled the room. It took very little time for Kate to check, as Hargreaves had said, that Paul's laptop was not in the room.

Kate sat on the sofa for a moment. There was no huge sense of disappointment because she had had few hopes that she would find the laptop. And what would she do if she had found it? It would have wrapped up one of Hargreaves' loose ends, but then what? She could have tried to see what was on it, to see if it held any clue to Paul's disappearance; but there would no doubt be a password she didn't know and, as far as she knew, Paul used it almost exclusively for his work when he was travelling, and quite often in the evenings, transferring it all to his desktop when he next returned to the office. None of it would have meant anything to Kate anyway.

It was, however, this line of thinking that led her to realise that, if there was to be any clue to Paul's last few days it would be in his emails which he regularly dealt with on his desktop, now sitting in front of her. She went over to it and switched it on. A few moments later it invited her to press Control-Alt-Delete which she did and then it asked for Paul's password. Of this Kate had not the slightest idea, and absolutely no prospect of guessing. She stood there for a moment, thinking. Then she switched the machine off, went out into the corridor, locked Paul's office door and went back to Alice.

"Successful?" asked Alice as Kate entered the room.

"Yes" said Kate, lightly tapping her shoulder bag. "Mainly just some photographs. But I was thinking, one or two Paul's colleagues around the world always stayed in touch through email, and I'm worried that they won't have had any reply to anything they sent recently. I'm sure some will have heard about Paul, but not necessarily all of them; and I feel I ought to send them something. The trouble is I can't get access to his emails. Does the department have some IT whizz-kid who could fix this for me? I realise it will need some sort of authorisation"

"Let me see" said Alice, only too pleased to be able actually to do something for Kate. "I don't think it should be too much of a problem. Hold on a second" She picked up the phone and dialled an internal number.

"Steve, Alice here, are you free...... could you pop up to my office...... thanks".

"Steve will know what to do" she beamed at Kate, who vaguely remembered Steve Bates, one of the department's IT specialists and, contrary to much of the imagery surrounding such people, always dressed in a white shirt, sober tie, and dark grey trousers. Combined with hair cut very short he looked much more an IBM style computer man than a university department one.

"You remember Kate, don't you" said Alice, as Steve entered, to which he nodded and smiled at Kate.

"Oh yes" he said "I was sorry to hear about Paul". He was about to add something about how much Paul had been missed in the department, but Alice intervened.

"Kate needs to deal with some of Paul's emails, but doesn't know his password. Can you help at all?"

Steve thought for a moment. "I think the rules are that someone – I guess you Alice – should put in a formal request to the Computing Centre. They have some procedure for deciding what to do, whether there are exceptional circumstances and so on. I would have thought that this counts as exceptional". He paused "But there might be a simpler way – it all depends".

"On what?" asked Alice, before Kate could formulate the same question.

"People sometimes forget their passwords, so there is a procedure for retrieving it. They lodge a piece of personal information, something only they know. Then, if you forget your password, you can register that you have forgotten it, and the system will ask you for that piece of personal information. If you provide it, then the system logs you on and, shortly afterwards allows you to set up a new password. It's quite simple really, but it will only get you in to Paul's emails if you happen to know the answer to Paul's personal question. You shouldn't really do this of course, but in the circumstances I can't see why not, and it would save time – if you can answer the question".

"Kate was, in fact, entirely familiar with the system. They had something similar at OUP. It just hadn't crossed her mind to try out what Steve had suggested but, as he explained, she was already speculating what piece of information Paul might have used, and whether she would know it.

"Can we give it a try?" she said

"Sure" replied Steve "Let's give it a go".

They left Alice in her office and returned to Paul's room., Steve switched on the computer and when it asked for Paul's password, Steve clicked on the "Forgotten Password?" box. Up came a larger box with, written inside it "What was the name of your first cat?"

"Calico!" Kate almost shouted. "I've seen a photo of her – more than once" she added with a grimace and then a grin.

Steve typed in the name and immediately the screen displayed a large number of icons, one or two of which, including Microsoft Outlook, Kate recognised but most of which just had codes underneath them.

"That's great" said Kate "I'll just have a look at his emails" and, taking over the seat from Steve, clicked on Microsoft Outlook. It was quite a shock, though she should have expected it, to see well over 300 emails listed there.

"I'll look through" Kate said. "Don't let me hold you up, but can I come and get you if I need any help?"

"Sure" replied Steve "but maybe you shouldn't actually reply to any until Alice has got some sort of authorisation. It might be a bit awkward otherwise".

"I see what you mean" Kate agreed. "Let me look through, and if I see anything urgent, I'll go and talk to Alice. I'll call in on you before I leave, just to let you know what's happening. What's your room number?"

Having given it to her, Steve left and Kate started to open Paul's emails. Some were just junk mail that had got past the University's filtering system, mainly travel companies. A few were personal but looked completely anodyne. But the great majority were clearly work-related; and Kate passed rapidly over them. What did that leave? Twenty minutes later the answer was – precisely none. There were several wondering about not getting a reply to an earlier email from Paul, but none in the last four or five days. The news had clearly spread. If Kate had hoped for any enlightenment to Paul's disappearance - and she really couldn't tell if she had or not - she was sorely disappointed.

She clicked out of his emails, glad at least that she wouldn't have to ask Alice to contact the University's Computing Centre. The screen went back to its serried ranks of icons, and for a moment she just sat and gazed at them, her mind wandering over random elements of the catastrophe that had overtaken her. But as she did so, some part of her brain managed to register that there was a sort of pattern to the code names for most of Paul's work files, each of them starting with one of five different three letter acronyms, or possibly abbreviations, followed by two digits, which clearly indicated an ordering of the files. On a whim she opened the first one of these, EDM01, and was almost immediately presented with some vast, virtually incomprehensible text. The most she could glean was that the E probably stood for 'electron' something, with links to a number of spreadsheets. She tried EDM02 and got something similar, though this also had some diagrams. She tried PRI02 – there wasn't a PRI01 - and got more scientific terminology and data. What PRI might stand for she couldn't fathom. She was about to pack up, but idly clicked on NEL01, and was mildly surprised that the screen went blank. Maybe some redundant file, she thought, but tried NEL02, with the same result. In growing puzzlement she tried all five NEL files, with the same result. She went back and tried all the EDM files, and all the PRI files and all produced something. She then tried the fourth code, SDM, and found that all the files were there. Finally she tried the fifth set, coded RCL and, like, NEL got a blank screen. For some reason, around two-fifths of Paul's work files weren't accessible, and there was no clue to indicate why not, no little box popping up to explain the problem or to ask for some new password.

Kate doubted that this had any great significance; but it wasn't the first puzzle surrounding Paul's disappearance, and she wasn't just going to ignore it. She got up, went out into the corridor and down two floors to Steve's room. He was on the phone, but waved her in and to sit down. It turned out to be a rather long call, but eventually he finished, apologised for being so long and asked how he could help. While Kate explained what had happened, Steve pulled some overly surprised and glum looks and immediately headed off for Paul's room, with Kate following behind. She had intended to show Steve what had happened, but he was straight into Paul's chair and looking through his files almost before Kate was through the door. Somewhat to her relief – it would have been mildly embarrassing if Steve had found that she had just been making some elementary mistake – he got exactly the same result as Kate.

Steve then launched on a flurry of presumably investigative instructions, his fingers moving too fast across the keyboard for Kate to have any idea what he was doing; with boxes and lists coming onto and off the screen so fast, Kate couldn't even read them. This went on for only a minute or so; then Steve got up and went round the side of the desk to where the computer tower – a curious name given that it was all of 50 centimetres tall – stood. He opened up some aperture, gazed at it for a moment and said, almost to himself
"I don't like that".

It was, Kate always thought afterwards, her 'Desdemona' moment. As a teenager she had always loved Shakespeare, mainly because of an inspirational school teacher who had taught her called David Kincaid; and she and Paul, despite their rather hectic schedules, had been to a number of performances together, including two in Stratford-on-Avon. She particularly loved *Othello* and knew it better than any other Shakespeare play, because she had played Desdemona in a school production the year before she took A levels. Of all the great dramatic moments in Shakespeare the one she adored most – it could still literally send a tingle down her neck – was the single line, said by Othello's servant Iago "I like not that". Such a plain simple, apparently undramatic line, an aside almost, but it was, in a very literal way, the first line of the rest of the play, as it draws Othello's attention to the easy, though innocent relationship between Desdemona and Cassio; plants, as it was intended to, the seeds of suspicion in Othello's mind and, step by step, leads to the collapse of their former lives, to utter ruination and death. One small sentence that changes one's life for ever.

Steve's phrase was equally prosaic, indeed, allowing for 17th century English, the same phrase. Unlike Iago's it was neither contrived nor untrue, but it changed Kate's life beyond anything she could imagine - truly her 'Desdemona' moment.
"What's the problem?" she said, as unaware as Othello at this point of its significance. Steve answered without any further preamble.
"Paul clearly had three hard disks which he stored all his work on: one block of work on one disk and two blocks on each of two other disks. One's missing".

"Are you sure?" was all Kate could think to say in reply, not as yet starting to register what this might mean.

"Oh yes" said Steve. "That's why we couldn't get access to two of Paul's files. The real question is, why is it missing? Paul could have taken it, conceivably to use in another computer; but that would be a very odd way indeed to transfer files".

"Might he have taken it to put in his laptop" asked Kate. "This all started off because no-one can find his laptop".

"No" replied Steve emphatically "no laptop would have been able to accommodate the hard disk that is missing from here. Did Paul have a desktop at home?"

Kate, having spent too many evenings seeing him batter away at is laptop, assured him that Paul didn't; and Steve re-iterated that, even if he did, it would have been a bizarre way to transfer work, rather than send them via the internet from one computer to the other.

"Frankly, there are only two reasons I can imagine that Paul would remove the disk. One is if there was some fault on it and Paul asked someone in IT to look at it. That could be an explanation but, again, it would be very unusual. I haven't come across a case in the three years I've been here; and anyway, he would almost certainly have asked me about it first. I'll check though. The only other explanation is if the desk contained something very sensitive and he was worried that that the disk would be stolen. That also seems very unlikely, unless he had made some sort of Nobel Prize winning break-through and didn't want to run any risk of his ideas being stolen. Does that sound at all plausible?"

Kate really had no idea, though it all sounded rather preposterous; and she felt that, if Paul had been on the verge of such a momentous piece of research, she would have had some inkling of it from him.

"Do academics often go to such lengths to protect their research" she asked. "It seems a bit far-fetched"

"I've certainly never come across anything like it before" mused Steve. "It may be a bit complacent but generally everyone relies on password security; and I haven't ever heard of computer theft as a basis for stealing someone else's research ideas".

Kate thought about this for a moment.

"But if Paul didn't remove it, then someone *must* have stolen it" she said with what seemed like irrefutable logic.

"Unless, as I say, he asked someone to check it for some fault or other" Steve reminded her

Kate felt a distinct sense of deflation at the possibility of such a mundane explanation. Some alternative explanation, completely undefined, but in some way conspiratorial, was much more what her psychological state demanded –

something that might offer some reason for her loss. A faulty hard disk was not what she wanted to hear.

"Could you check?" she asked Steve. "I'm sorry to mess up your morning, but I can come down with you now".

Polite as the tone of this was, Steve recognised that he was being urged, in a way that contemplated little resistance, to check out his suggestion immediately.

"No problem" he responded with a grin. "Leave the computer on, because I haven't registered a new password yet.

The IT section of the Engineering Department was a large open-plan area on the fourth floor of the building. Steve found a seat for Kate and then disappeared off into the middle distance, though not actually out of Kate's sight; and she could see Steve consulting someone and then sitting in front of a computer screen. Ten minutes later he was back.

"Paul definitely didn't bring the disk in here" he said.

Kate, imperceptibly, nodded to herself. She had spent the ten minutes in what she thought of as 'super-rational' mode. If the disk had been here, then there was nothing to explain, and she should force herself to let go. A missing laptop and an unpleasant pair of police officers was not enough on which to base.... to base what? A one woman search, of what or where she had no idea, and with nothing else to go on. But if the disk wasn't here, then there were, she thought, only three possibilities. Either Paul had taken it, or someone else in the department had taken it, or someone had broken into the department and taken it. There were no other options, and it surely shouldn't be impossible to find out which had occurred. How this might help to reveal what had happened to Paul she hadn't any idea; but whichever explanation was right, it was suspicious, it must, she thought, have something to do with his disappearance and, perhaps only dimly recognised, she was now beginning to deal with the emotional strain of Paul's loss by pursuing these increasingly problematic 'loose ends' that DS Hargreaves had referred to. Though it was far beyond her consciousness at that moment, Kate was not going to be able to move on from her life with Paul until she knew more about what had happened to him; and these loose ends were the only threads she had.

"Well, it must be somewhere" she said firmly. "I'll have a word with Alice; see if she has any ideas". Steve recognised this as something of a polite dismissal, but had nothing useful to suggest as an alternative.

"I'm sorry I can't help more" he said, in a genuinely apologetic tone. The truth was that he found the whole thing very strange indeed, and he did not want to leave matters in this opaque and clearly unsatisfactory state but, for the moment at least, did not have any further ideas. "If there's anything I can do to help, just give me a call. By the way" he added "what do you want to do about a new password".

"I'll put one in" said Kate "but I won't use the machine until Alice okays it. I'll just switch it off". Steve said that would be fine.

Kate thanked him for his help and, with a farewell nod from Steve, started to head back upstairs. At the last moment she turned.

"Steve, could you keep this to yourself for the moment, and try to find some way of dampening down any curiosity from whoever you talked to? I just need some time to think about this, and then I'll get back to you". She hoped this little carrot might help.

"Leave it to me" said Steve, who actually winked. "Anyway I only asked Dave whether I could use a station here to check on a missing piece of equipment. That won't set any alarm bells ringing".

Kate thanked him again and headed up to Paul's office. She looked once more at the icons on the screen, with their code numbers and, on a sudden impulse, picked up a biro lying on the desk, and a scrap of spare paper, and wrote them all down. She put the paper in her coat pocket, switched off Paul's computer, locked his door and walked round to Alice's office. Alice asked her how she had got on, and Kate chatted for a while, saying that there were a few emails which she thought she might reply to, but would wait for Alice to get some authorisation first. Then, as casually as she could, though she realised it would make little difference, she asked

"Alice, I know this sounds silly, but has there been any sort of break-in, or even a suspicion of a break-in, in the department recently?"
Alice looked decidedly shocked. "Good heavens, no" she said. "Why, is something missing from Paul's office?"

"Oh, no, no, no" said Kate, rather unconvincingly. "I was just talking to Steve about security. The police were banging on at me about it for some reason when they came round; and so I wondered if there had been any sort of security problem here". It didn't sound all that plausible to Kate, but it seemed to calm Alice's incipient wrath.

"We've never had anything like that" Alice said, rather trenchantly. "In fact the police asked the same question but I told them". Anyway, I don't know how anyone could break in. There are the people in reception whenever the building is open, and a night security team when it isn't; and no-one could ever get past the CCTV cameras without being seen. They cover every part of the entrance, and all of the ground floor. They even have them in the lecture rooms and labs. I think it is all too elaborate myself, and too expensive, but the management group were worried about students causing damage". She looked at Kate more intently. "Do you think someone might have tried to break in?"

"Absolutely not" replied Kate. "I really didn't mean to alarm you. Steve and I were just talking about it – whether the police thought anyone might have been after Paul's work at all. But it clearly isn't a problem. There isn't anything to worry about". Kate realised that this wasn't a whole lot more credible than what she had said before, but again it seemed to satisfy Alice.

Kate was, by now, very late for work, and took off fast for OUP. Janice had, as always, held things together, revising Kate's schedule twice and, by the end of the day she was just about up to date again. But she was aware of what, if she wanted to be overly dramatic, she might regard as an emerging form of schizophrenia. She lived the day in two minds, one coping, almost as competently as ever, with her job at OUP, the other grinding away at the mystery of what had happened to Paul, to Paul's hard disk and, for that matter, his laptop, the whereabouts of which was still unknown. This second side of her brain kept producing one overriding thought. Paul, she was now certain, had not died at the hands of some random mugger.

"The next morning she rang Alice and fixed up to call in. Her first objective, she had decided, was to find out if the police knew about the missing disk and, though she trusted Hargreaves – it was, after all, he who had set her on this particular path, even if he didn't know it - she preferred to pursue the matter her own way. On arriving at Alice's office she asked her if, when the police had come round to the department building, they had played around with Paul's computer at all. Seeing Alice's immediately quizzical, not to say suspicious reaction, she immediately added, in a distressed tone that she knew would elicit Alice's sympathy, that the police had asked her about some emails she and Paul had sent each other, and she wondered what it was all about. She barely noticed, but did nonetheless register, that she had so easily slipped into the art of lying, even to people she knew quite well. Part of her mind asked why – why not just explain about the disk and whether the police had discovered it had gone. But a deeper, more dominant part of her mind supplied the answer – she just couldn't risk, psychologically risk, the ever practical but somewhat unimaginative Alice proffering common-sense explanations that would undermine the fragile prop to her psyche which the mystery had increasingly become. She just hoped that the lie would never come to light.

"No they didn't" said Alice, rather proprietarily. "The first two were here for quite some time, looking through his desk drawers and book shelves, but I was there all the time and they didn't pay much attention to his computer. I didn't really want to stay, but the older one – I can't remember his name but he was a very polite man – had quite a lot of questions, about Paul's comings and goings, his work and so on; and in the end he and his colleague came back to my office with me. The second pair – I can't say I cared much for their manner – were very brief, only about ten minutes at the most I'd say. I didn't stay there, but I'd be very surprised if they looked at Paul's emails in that time. Anyway, they couldn't have got access to them, could they, not without his password". She paused, but then added "This is all a bit odd, isn't it?"

"I think so too" said Kate, fully aware of the ambiguity, not to say disinformation inherent in this reply. "Anyway, that's been very helpful. It's probably just someone covering their backsides, or having to fill out some form somewhere. It's not going to make any difference. I won't ever see Paul again".

It hadn't been deliberate, or at leas not completely so, but this last sentence diverted Alice from interrogative mode, with a growing number of questions forming in her mind, to sympathetic mode.

"It must be so distressing" she said "and I'm so sorry Kate. Do let me know if there is any way I can help, any way at all". Both knew there wasn't anything at all that Alice could do, but it was meant well; and Kate thanked her. Meanwhile part of her mind – schizophrenia again she noted – was wondering why DI Johnson – she was confident that it was Hargreaves who called the first time and Johnson the second – had gone back to Paul's office. Perhaps just to check whether Paul's laptop was there? That would fit with what Hargreaves had said.

Kate left Alice, promising that they would meet for a drink soon, went to her own office and called the number Hargreaves had given her. She wasn't, she realised, going to get much further without talking to him. Rather to her surprise, she actually got through to him.

"Can I ask you something" she said, sounding, she thought, rather American.

"Sure" he replied "anything I can do to help".

"When you went to Paul's office, did you look at Paul's computer?"

"No" said Hargreaves. "It occurred to me, but it would have needed authorisation to get access; and at that stage I still thought we would find some trace of Paul without the need for that. I would have pursued it later – it's quite common, though generally it's when we are looking for paedophiles and the like – but then Johnson took over and that was it".

"I don't think Johnson checked it out. The administrator at the department said that the police called back – it sounded like Johnson and someone else from the description of his manner - but they weren't there long, so I'm presuming that they were just checking on whether Paul's laptop was there or not".

There was a long pause, and Kate knew she had said something more significant than she realised.

"That's odd" said Hargreaves. "When Johnson said that he had 'pulled all the threads together' – that was his phrase - I asked him if he had investigated Paul's emails. He said that he had been in touch with the University authorities, had got hold of Paul's password and was planning to take a look. Maybe he just printed them out?"

"That's impossible" said Kate emphatically. "There were hundreds of them. It would have taken him much longer than ten minutes just to print them. I suppose he might have printed out only those he had some interest in, but it would still have taken him a lot more time just to go through them to decide what he wanted to take a further look at".

There was another long pause, perhaps even more pregnant than the previous one.

"How do you know this?" said Hargreaves quietly.

Kate realised too late that she had gone rather further than she had intended, but there was no point in any subterfuge now.

"I've been through them" she said, without any further explanation.

"I see" Hargreaves was about to ask her the obvious question, but the answer – somehow she had got past Paul's password – was equally obvious, and instead he asked

"Are you sure Johnson wasn't there long?"

"Well, as I said, the administrator told me about your visit – I presumed it was you because she said the lead officer was very polite" - Kate allowed herself a slight laugh - plus another officer with you; and then later two other officers called. She was not at all impressed with them and I assume it was Johnson. She said they were there only briefly – as I said, less than ten minutes. There just wasn't time" she ended, rather lamely.

This was followed by a third period of silence, and then Hargreaves said

"Let me see if I can check this out. All the bloody paperwork and bureaucracy and monitoring we have to put up with these days might just prove useful for once. I'll call you with whatever I find out. Which is the best number to get you on?"

Kate suggested her office or her mobile and was about to ring off when Hargreaves said

"Haven't you forgotten something?"

"What?" said Kate, for a second unsure what he meant, but only for a second.

"You haven't told me why you are so interested in Paul's computer, especially if you have already read all his emails; or, to put it more accurately, why you're so interested in whether *we* are interested in Paul's computer".

When Kate had rung she had been quite clear in her mind that she would have to explain to Hargreaves what had prompted her call. Now that the moment had come, she was, for some reason, very reluctant to say. At present only she and Steve Bates knew that one hard disk was missing – apart of course from whoever had actually taken it she reminded herself – and she really didn't want the knowledge going any wider than that. Maybe having some private information about Paul was some sort of miniscule substitute for the equally private relationship they had had – if so, how sad, she thought – but it was more than that. She trusted Hargreaves, but almost certainly he would feel that he had to let Johnson know – if he didn't already - and Kate needed time to think through for herself what possible explanations there might be, how she wanted this to progress before she felt ready to discuss it with someone else, especially the otiose DI Johnson.

"Would you mind terribly" she started, with such unintended formality that she almost stopped "if I didn't answer that, at least for the moment? It's just a query in my mind and I'm sure it is inconsequential, but it helps me to keep my sanity just at the moment".

"Given that I am not the investigating officer on the case" Hargreaves replied, with deliberately equal formality " I can't see that I have any grounds for locking you up" -   this time Kate laughed out loud - " but" he added, more serious now "if there is something worrying you, I mean really worrying you, about the investigation, I want you to promise me that you will let me know. I'll listen, and I'm not going to – I don't know – hound you, over whatever it is that's bothering you. Is that a deal?"

"A deal" said Kate, more moved than Hargreaves would ever have realised from her response. "And thanks. It's all so awful, I really appreciate your help" She wanted to add more, to thank him for his understanding, for maybe taking risks with his career for her sake, but it would all have been too personal, too intense.

"That's OK" he replied. "I'll get back to you as soon as I can".

Kate was again just about to put the phone down when she remembered that she had another question. "I'm sorry" she said "but there was something else. When we spoke on the phone, before we were…..cut short, you said there were two things you wanted to mention but we only talked about the laptop. What was the other thing?"

"Well….." Yet again Hargreaves seemed reluctant to speak "I just wanted to check…. have the Press approached you at all?"

"No. I thought that was quite strange at first; but I'm relieved they haven't. I don't think I could cope with them at all. Why do you ask? How do they find out about things like this anyway?"

"Oh they find out all right" said Hargreaves, with some passion "usually within a few hours. I'm curious why they haven't this time. I might just look into that as well, if I can".

CHAPTER 6

It was nearly forty-eight hours before he called her; long enough that she began to wonder if, like before, he would appear so helpful and then just evaporate. There was no small talk, nor even any apology for the time he'd taken getting back to her.

"Neil Hargreaves here" – Kate realised that she hadn't known his first name until this moment, and wondered if his use of it was remotely significant, probably not – "Two things" he said tersely, "first, Johnson *didn't* go to the

Engineering building. I asked around a bit amongst a few PCs here, even spoke to Sally James and a couple of other DCs, managed to piece together roughly what he'd done after I was sent off to Swindon, which seems basically to have wrapped things up as quickly as possible. I was so shocked I spoke to him about it. He was really angry of course – he clearly thought I was criticising him for not going to Paul's office – and explained to me as if I was the biggest idiot since PC plod that he had got a print out of all Paul's emails from the university authorities and that, as he had anticipated, there were no leads in any of it. I asked if he had fixed for anyone else to go to Paul's office and he was emphatic that he hadn't – made some snide comments about how he had *hoped* he could rely on my earlier visit, or was I saying that he had to do *everything* himself and so on. I'm quite sure it is true because he looked really sick to the gills when I told him that two other police officers *had* been there, albeit briefly. He tried to avoid what I was saying – asked how the hell I knew – got even angrier, and I think my prospects for making Chief Constable have taken a bit of a dive, but he was shocked, I could tell. Whoever the other officer was, Johnson didn't know about him, and he's pretty mad".

It took a while for Kate to take this all in. she had been so sure that it must be Johnson that she wasn't immediately ready to let the idea go.
"I just don't understand" she said, "but the administrator at the department met the men who followed up your visit. Is there some way we can check if one of them was Johnson?"
"It wasn't him" said Hargreaves, with an air of finality and just a hint of exasperation "but if you're not convinced, I'll try to get a photograph of Johnson from somewhere and you can show it to her".
Neither spoke for several seconds
"Kate, I'm sure it wasn't him. He has been totally cavalier about this case, clearly decided early on that it was a moonlit flit – probably sex related – and I don't know why he should behave like that; but I don't think he is lying when he says he didn't call at Paul's office, and I can't see any reason why he would".
Kate registered the conviction in Hargreaves – in Neil's - voice, and felt any sense of resistance wane. She'd talk to Alice again, but she had crossed some sort of line, from being rather certain that it had been Johnson to being fairly convinced that it wasn't. But if not him, then who?
She heard herself echoing this thought to Hargreaves.
"If it wasn't Johnson, then who was it?"
"I don't know" said Hargreaves "more important neither does Johnson, I'm sure of it. He'll have to re-open the case. And you have got to tell me why you are so interested in Paul's computer. I really do need to know what's going on".

It was now clear to Kate that she would have to be quite open with Hargreaves.

"I looked at Paul's emails" she said. "Like Johnson said, there's nothing of any note there. But I also looked through his work files, and...... a hard disk is missing from the computer. I just wanted to know whether you – whether the police – knew about it". She felt that she had said this in a rather too dismissive tone, and instantly regretted it, but there wasn't anything to be done about it. "That's how I found out that there had been two visitations from the police, only now it seems that's wrong. Do you have any idea who else it might have been?"

"There are any number of weird and wonderful departments that could have muscled in I suppose – Special Branch, the security services, God knows who – but they wouldn't charge in without contacting us plods and warning us they were getting involved. But Johnson was totally wrong-footed when I told him, I'm sure of it. And why would anyone else be involved anyway? Paul was hardly a likely looking terrorist or some post cold war spy". He stopped, puzzling away at his own question. Kate said nothing, her mind lagging behind both the information and the questions, that Hargreaves had thrown at her.

"And you say a disk is missing?" added Hargreaves, unable to keep some incredulity out of his voice. Kate explained how she had found some blank files, talked to an IT specialist at the laboratory, and what he had found; also that Steve was very doubtful there was an innocent explanation. There was another rather ominous silence between them, and Kate found herself pacing round her office clutching the phone as if it might leap out of her hand. She broke the silence.

"This is serious isn't it?" As if Paul's vanishing wasn't serious enough, but Hargreaves knew what she meant.

"I'm afraid so" he said, aware of the extent of understatement. "And there's more. I made some discreet inquiries about why the Press hasn't got the story – they'd love a missing Oxford don. The answer is that they were leaned on. The Home Office used to be able to issue a D Notice, which meant that nothing appeared without their permission. Not legally enforceable, but no editor would dream of ignoring one. The system rather collapsed in the face of mutual suspicion, but it carries on unofficially. Paul must have been involved in something very important though, for them to act – it's quite rare these days".

Kate stopped pacing, dazed and bewildered. For a fraction of a second, she thought she was going to fall over. Instead she sat down, as carefully as she could, on the chair by her desk that Janice normally used. "I don't know that I can take much more of this" she said and, for the second time in three minutes instantly regretted her words, partly because they sounded so pathetic, but more because she had no sooner said them than she realised they just weren't true. Every additional revelation – and they seemed to be coming thick and fast - indicated that something very – *very* – strange was going on; and that was her only hope of salvation at the moment, her only hope that Paul wasn't just the hapless victim of some mindless mugging.

"What do you mean 'important'?" she asked quickly. "You said Paul must have been involved in something important. What does that mean?"

"I don't know" replied Hargreaves. "Something secret, maybe something to do with national security, or industrial secrets which the government has an interest in. I don't know, but, like I say, it has got to be pretty important for a suppression request to be made to the newspapers. Have you any idea what it might be?"

Kate felt she should take time to think before answering, but couldn't stop herself.

"Absolutely none. I can't believe it really. He was – I don't know – just like any other academic. He wrote learned articles and went to conferences and gave lectures. It's crazy to think of him involved in some other clandestine life. I'm sure I'd have known if he was. It doesn't make any sense". She paused. "Can you find out anything more about it, why this has happened? How did you find out about this anyway?"

"I spoke to the deputy editor of the Oxford Mail" replied Hargreaves. "He's a friend - sort of – anyway he's quite happy to help out with information because he knows I can be very helpful, or not very helpful, on other cases. He said he was amazed – it's only a request, but more 'advice-stroke-very strong request'; local newspapers always accept it he said, and his editor was not about to rock the boat. Then the Nationals simply don't get to hear about it. Plus they know that, usually, in the end, there is a bigger story to cover. But I doubt I can find out much more. I wouldn't know where to start frankly, and I'm not even on the case – I'm not even sure that it *is* still a police case - but I'll see what I can do. In the meantime, I really think you should keep well out of it".

Kate thanked him for helping her, and for being concerned about her, but the shocks were, little by little, beginning to wear off; her brain was re-engaging; more significantly, her natural resilience was starting to re-assert itself, and she responded

"The fact remains that a disk appears to have been stolen from his office computer, his lap-top's gone, and someone else called in at the laboratory who said they were police officers, but this is not, apparently, known to the officer in charge of the case. I can't be shocked out of my mind by all this and then just go back to work. I've got to think what to do". She paused. "Look, would you see what you can find out about the D Notice, but otherwise just sit on this, at least for a day or so? I'll have another word with the administrator at the laboratory and see if I can find out anything more. I don't trust Johnson to take this seriously, in fact I don't trust him at all; so could you just keep this between us, at least for the moment?"

Hargreaves saw immediately that there was a right answer and a wrong answer to this, and he paused while part of his mind processed the fact, leaving

Kate in a state of total tension. But another part of his mind, quite sub-conscious, knew just as quickly that he would give the wrong answer, possibly because he didn't trust Johnson either, maybe even because he had come to admire the woman who had had to deal with so much anguish and sense of loss but, more than either of these reasons, because he, like Kate, needed time to think about the situation, time to decide what to do for the best when anything less than that might prove very costly to his career.

"I'm not sure that's at all sensible" he said, "but I don't suppose there is much else I can do, unless I can get Johnson interested again; and I don't think that's a runner at the moment". He paused. "I suppose you could tell the Administrator at the department – Alice did you say her name was – that you are worried about the identity of the two who called after I did, and would she get in touch with Johnson about it? She could ask, pending a formal complaint, that he looks into it. That should produce some action. But whatever you do, will you give me an assurance that you won't go beyond talking to the administrator again, and that you will then get back to me? If there's anything else to be done, you must let me follow it up. You just don't know what you are getting into here".

"What do you think he will do if Alice does complain?" asked Kate. Hargreaves wasn't much more helpful than before.

"I don't know, but he can't just leave it, especially if she says she is very upset, and wants a good explanation or she'll go higher up, or complain to her local councillor, or something like that".

"Let me sleep on it" Kate eventually said. "I'm so confused by everything at the moment. I don't know what's the best thing to do. I'll think about it and then perhaps we could discuss it – maybe another cup of coffee if you have time?"

"Sounds fine to me" said Hargreaves, more pleased at the prospect than his purely professional interest could justify. "Give me a call in a day or two and let's meet". In a more sombre tone he added "There is one thing I should say……" he trailed off.

"I know, I know" said Kate. "Something's not right, but it won't bring Paul back. I know. I just want to know what happened" and to her surprise realised that she was quietly starting to cry. Hargreaves wanted to say something, anything to comfort her, but could think of nothing. There was no telephone equivalent of a comforting shoulder. "Do call soon" he said, hoping that this at least sounded supportive, "any time".

"Thanks" replied Kate. "I do appreciate your help. I'll call as soon as I can think clearly. Bye". She rang off, trying to re-assert some control of her emotions, her head whirling with what Hargreaves had told her. None of it made much sense – correction – any sense at all, and she wondered, in a vague sort of way, whether the two police officers, or officials from wherever, who called the second time, were perhaps some branch of the police force that checked up on the regular officers. That might explain why Johnson didn't know about them, and why he was apparently so angry when he found out. Well, the only way to make progress was by going back to Alice.

That night, after a light supper, she poured herself a glass of wine, sat on her settee with her feet up and thought long and hard about what to do. She even got out a pen and paper to write down notes, to help construct a plan – a technique she often used at work, so why not on this, the biggest problem she had ever faced in her life. The first thing that was clear to her was that, until she had found out what was going on, she was going to be increasingly incapable of focusing in an intelligent way on what, she feared, was starting to become the remnants of her career. Arrangements on the L.A. deal were all going well, and she was keeping everything going at the office; but she knew that she was beginning to lose her more innovative element, her flair and enthusiasm which normally led her to push herself and others to such good effect. Harry and the others would make allowance for her distressed state, in fact quite clearly were doing so, and would for some time to come. It was more a problem of letting herself down, the awfulness of needing people to 'make allowances'. She appreciated the motives but hated the fact that she was not operating at anything like her usual self. But she couldn't just drop the mystery of Paul's disappearance. Someone had removed one of Paul's hard disks; and even if it had been Paul himself, which she doubted, someone else – possibly some obscure department of the country's police force or security services but possibly not – was clearly interested in the matter. It had not escaped her notice that the unexplained visit might have been as brief as Alice had said it was because they had found the hard disk gone. Then again, they might have taken it themselves. Either way she was determined to find out as much as she could about the disk, and Paul's lap-top she remembered. And what possible reason could there be for suppressing any news coverage of what had happened? She felt she had no choice but to try to get to the bottom of it all, which greatly simplified things. Finding out who else might be involved would have to wait.

Another thing that increasingly became clear to Kate was that she couldn't involve Alice in any active way. She could see the logic in what Hargreaves had suggested; but felt very unhappy about dragging Alice more and more into her personal nightmare. She didn't know Alice that well and, from Kate's point of view, was a rather unknown, or at least unpredictable, quantity. They weren't only very different generations, they inhabited quite different worlds. But that, if she was honest with herself, was not the real reason. The real problem was that she had already been less than frank with Alice. This would almost certainly become evident if Kate now tried to get her to do what Hargreaves had suggested, and Alice would, Kate thought, be very offended. Alice had always been entirely friendly towards Kate; but Kate was twenty years younger a highly successful professional, even something of a globe-trotter now, making her own way rather than, as in Alice's case, administratively underwriting the very largely male members of the engineering department. It wouldn't take much for there to be quite some tension between them, and Kate did not want, if she could possibly avoid it, her deception – however justified – to trigger this. Whether this was pragmatic – Alice could be quite important in what was starting to form in the back of Kate's mind – or more due to some deeper sense, even guilt, on Kate's part that she did not want to be the object of Alice's disapproval – justified disapproval – she could not say.

Moreover, she decided that she would have to act alone; or, more specifically, without help from Hargreaves, at least for the moment. She felt this was quite unfair of her, and probably quite unwise. He had been nothing but helpful and straight with her, both as the initial police officer on the case and, more importantly, after he had been removed from it and clearly warned off interfering any further in it. But he was, she reminded herself, a junior officer with a career to pursue; DI Johnson was his superior; and it would not take much for Hargreaves to feel that he would have to talk to Johnson, tell him what Kate and he had found out, and that was not a risk she was prepared to take.

Having convinced herself of these points, she rang Sarah. She made no mention of any of the developments she had discovered, but said she was holding up quite well. Both were pleased she had rung, but neither knew that it was, in some rather abstruse way, Kate touching base with familiar voices before launching herself into a new project, unlike any she had ever contemplated before. She then began to map out a detailed plan of action, the first step of which was to dig out a large shoulder bag that she occasionally used to carry papers to or from her office.

She rang Alice the next morning and arranged to call in to see her around 5.30 pm. Kate felt buoyed by her new found sense of action, limited as it was, and by the feeling that she wasn't just standing on the sidelines watching events. As a result, she had one of her most productive days at the office since Paul had disappeared, but the late afternoon appointment and how she would use it were never far from her mind. When she arrived at the Engineering department, immaculately dressed as ever and with her large bag slung over her shoulder, Alice seemed genuinely pleased to see her, and Kate suspected that Alice warmed to the prospect of helping Kate at such a difficult time, providing the human touch when so much of her work was with paper and computers. After some idle chatter, while Alice made them each a cup of tea, Kate launched in.

"Sorry to bother you again" she said "but I'm having a really hard time with the police. It's all just their bureaucracy I'm sure – 'procedure' they keep calling it – but it's driving me mad. I sort out something with one of them and then someone quite different comes round and doesn't seem to know what's happened. Anyway, I think I need to have a word with the police officers who called here, not the first pair – they've been quite helpful – the second lot. It looks like they're the main two, but I don't even know their names. You don't happen to remember them do you?"

"I don't" said Alice. "I think they said who they were, and they both showed me some sort of identification – a warrant card or something – but I really can't remember their names".

Kate had not expected that she would, but it provided a plausible lead into her next question. "Don't worry. There's no particular reason why you would remember. But can you tell me what they looked like. I might be able to let the officer on duty at the police station know, and track them down that way. If Alice thought any of this strange, she showed no sign of it.

"I really didn't take to them" she said, repeating what she had told Kate before. "The one in charge was a rather aggressive looking type, tall, quite large, sort of barrel-chested and big shoulders. He had very short grey hair, quite a round face but very hard looking. He spoke very quietly though, in fact he didn't say very much at all, and I remember thinking that he had a slight accent, I'm not sure what though. The other one – I don't think he said one word all the time they were here – he was quite tall as well, but much thinner, wiry type if you know what I mean. He had very short hair as well, but it was black. I don't know why I took against them – they weren't exactly rude or anything – actually I do know why, now I think about it. There was something rather menacing about them. That's it. Nothing they said or did, they just had a rather menacing sort of presence. This isn't a lot of help is it?" she added.

"On the contrary" said Kate. I'm sure I can find them based on what you have said. What age would you say they were?"

"Oh, I don't know, late forties maybe fifty, not much less. The one in charge was probably a bit older than the other one. But look, I've just thought, I can do better than that. I should be able to show you what they look like" There was an almost imperceptible, but triumphal pause. "From the CCTV. They spoke to Jeff at reception – he rang me to say they wanted to come up – and we should be able to track back on the tapes and find them". She beamed.

Kate was momentarily speechless. Why hadn't she thought of that, but thank heavens that Alice had. "Alice, that's brilliant. Could you fix it?"

"No problem at all. I'll speak to reception. It may take a day or so. I'll give you a call".

"Well, many thanks, Alice. They do sound a grim pair. But that should make it easier to find out who they are. Let me know when it would be convenient and I'll come over again" She was, in fact, already certain beyond any possible doubt that Hargreaves was right. Johnson had not been anywhere near Paul's office. But it might be useful to have pictures of the two later visitors. Perhaps Hargreaves could use them.

"Just one other thing" she added, her tone artfully pitched between exasperation that the whole thing was still dragging on, and assurance that some sort of end was in sight, "I think I've filled them in on almost everything they wanted to know, but they said they wanted to know about all Paul's recent research work – God knows why. I couldn't help at all, but they said they had a list of all his computer files – I don't know if they got them from his office or at home – but, anyway, they said they didn't know what the headings meant. I was getting so fed up by this stage I said that if they gave me the list and I filled in the details, would that be an end of all their questions. I'm not sure if I believe them – they seem so disorganised – but they agreed that was all they now needed, so I said I'd get it for them. To be honest I did think of just sending them round to you again, but I know this has been very disruptive for you, and its all been going round and round in circles for so long now I just wanted to be done with them".

Kate wondered if she had been just a little too loquacious, but Alice was too busy sympathising, sister to sister, in the face of predictable male inefficiency or worse; and, as Kate had known well, she really didn't want any more police officers round at the department.

"I don't think that should be much of a problem" she said, with a hint of professional pride "I've had to deal with all his research and teaching files, so if you have a list I should be able to tell you what they all are. If necessary I can look them up in my files here". She waved rather majestically in the direction of a bank of filing cabinets on the far side of her desk. Kate got out the list she had made from Paul's computer, now transferred onto a proper sheet of A4 paper, and started to call out the code names she had noted down. Predictably, thought Kate, Alice never once needed to go to the filing cabinets; indeed Alice repeatedly provided far more detail from memory than Kate wanted or could possibly digest.

As they went through, Kate made brief notes against each codename. EDM was, as she had surmised, something to do with electrons or, to be more precise 'Electron Diffraction Microscopy – Stage 2 Trials'. This, according to Alice, had been Paul's main research project in the laboratory in the weeks before he had disappeared. She didn't know much about the specifics of Paul's work, but most of it was to do with what she happily called 'stresses and strains'. The Holy Grail was a material that couldn't break but weighed next to nothing. Apparently, the US space programme had given a huge boost to the type of work which Paul did, and he had had some role in it in the past, going over to Houston, Texas quite frequently, but not recently.

PRI stood simply for Princeton University, and was a collaborative piece of work with two Engineering professors there, one of whom had been Paul's

114

colleague in Oxford until a year or so earlier. The same sort of area of research, Alice thought. And so it went on. NEL, one of the missing files Kate reminded herself, stood for National Energy Ltd., and was another collaborative piece of work, this time with one of the UK's largest energy utility companies, privatised some time in the 1990s. Alice explained that it was a fairly typical arrangement. The Company provided data and research funding. The academics, putting it bluntly she said, provided the brain power. Paul could pursue his research agenda, delighted to get some articles for publication out of it – all-important these days not only for one's career but for future research funding – and the company might get some useful and, if it was lucky, applicable insights from the research, which it might be able to patent jointly with the university or, even where not, getting one or even two year's lead time as a result of the time it often took for an article finally to appear in a learned journal.

SDM stood for S-Function Decay Mapping, in relation to which Alice merely raised her eyebrows; but RCL was straightforward – Redstone Construction Ltd. – originally a small stoneworks producing the distinctive red sandstone of Cumbria but now, fifty years on, one of the largest civil engineering companies in the UK, and Paul's partner in another collaborative effort. Alice thought the collaboration probably might have to do with the resilience of bridges, but was not certain.

Although Kate had planned to ask, it was clear from Alice's response that there were no other projects unaccounted for on Paul's hard disk. Kate had not expected that there would be – and, more important, none of the files she had noted appeared to be secret in any way. The subject matter of S-Function Decay Mapping was clearly way beyond non-scientific mortals, but the project was there in the files, just like all Paul's other projects. The other critical point – one she could not share with Alice - was that the only thing apparently linking the two files on the missing disk was that they were both, in fact the only two, involving collaboration with private sector companies. What the significance of that might be, if any, Kate had no idea.

"That's great" said Kate. "I'll give them all this, and much good may it do them. Then I've had it with them – if they want more they can whistle for it. If I have to direct them to someone who might understand any of this, can you tell me who is currently Head of the Department?"

Alice thought that a sensible idea, but said if the police wanted to contact Professor Howard Ewing FRS, Head of Department and God's representative in the Engineering Department of Oxford University, they should call her number and she would put them through, always supposing she could find him.

"And do you have any details as to who they should contact if they want to follow up the various collaborative projects he was working on" Kate added casually. "I've got a gut feeling that they will ask".

"Oh, yes, I've got all that" replied Alice. She finally headed for the filing cabinets and, after a few seconds, came up with some files. She scribbled some names, addresses and phone numbers, including two for Princeton. "These are the people Paul mainly liaised with. I don't know if he was actually working with them, but they were involved in setting up the projects – I've spoken to them all at some point, and I should think they could tell the police anything they want to know or, if not, who can".

"What has happened about Paul's collaborative work?" asked Kate

"Nothing yet, really" replied Alice. "I ought to sort something out, but I'm not quite sure what to do. I'll talk to someone over at the University Offices in Wellington Square. They should be able to advise".

Kate picked up the piece of paper, made sure it was all legible, and embarked on a long and generous thanks. Alice, for her part, needed no thanks. She was there to make the world and its wheels go round; that was what she was really good at; and much of her joy in life was obtained from doing it, a process of self-actualisation, if she had but known the jargon, which kept her in close harmony with the world. Kate, in contrast, was moving into hunting mode. Paul's disappearance was somehow linked up with one or other, or possibly both, of the files on the missing disk – the collaborative projects - and she now had points of contact with both. Apart from Hargreaves – and not really him even – she was on her own, which suited her perfectly. She didn't feel she needed anyone else to do anything, or not anything she could think of at present. She didn't know how she would explain any of it to anyone else - didn't want to explain to anyone else - which was just as well because she had no explanation to give, for what had happened or for what she was now planning. All she needed was two things. One, she realised with some apprehension, was time – time to follow up the information she had obtained, time away from her office at OUP. She had no doubt that she could get it – compassionate leave they would call it – but whether it was sensible was quite a different matter. The other, with a little luck, she could get right now.

As she got up to go, she asked Alice if she could briefly borrow the key to Paul's office. She explained that there were a couple of photos she was missing, which she hadn't found when she had been in Paul's office before, and which were possibly lying somewhere in Paul's desk. She would only be a moment. Alice, once again, was only too pleased to help, and got the key for Kate.

"I'll drop it back in a few minutes" she said, and headed for Paul's office. Once there she went straight to the first of the three filing cabinets. As she had no doubt would be the case, the files were in alphabetical order. She went straight to the second cabinet, to the letter N, and there, as she had anticipated, was a file on National Energy Ltd. She quickly thumbed through it and in less than ten seconds found what she was looking for – Paul's contract. In fact there were three copies, which she guessed might be slightly different drafts but didn't have time to check. Each, however, was dated and she put the latest in her shoulder bag. Then she was on to the third filing cabinet and in a few more seconds had extracted the contract with Redstone Construction. This time there was just one copy, which joined the NEL one in her shoulder bag. Less than three minutes after entering the office she was back returning the key to Alice.

"No luck, I'm afraid" she said. "They're probably at his flat, but I just can't find them. Not to worry. I've got others" she added rather forlornly.

"I'm sorry about that" replied Alice. She wanted to say that she would have a good look out for anything personal when she cleared out the office; but any reference to clearing the office seemed so tactless as to be quite impossible, and she merely added, rather feebly, that she would be happy to have a look through later. Kate thanked her for this and, noting that she was now quite ready to steal as well as lie, took her leave. Now she needed to solve the time problem.

CHAPTER 7

The next morning she rang the two contact names which Alice had given her at National Energy and Redstone Construction. She gave her name as Jane Mortimer, next to whom she had sat in her final year at primary school. In both calls she said that no doubt they had heard about Paul's disappearance - Alice had confirmed that she had let both of them know some time before – and could she, as one of the University's administrative staff, fix a brief meeting to discuss any consequences of the situation – how to wrap up the work and the contract involved, all the time making it sound as humdrum as possible. She mentioned Alice several times as a vaguely subliminal way of providing credibility, and fixed to visit both of them. All this was clearly a risk, not so much that any such matters had already been sorted out – it seemed fairly clear from what Alice had said that that was not the case – but that it would be apparent at the meetings that she didn't know all about the arrangements which Paul had had with the companies. However, she had done her homework on this, having spent an hour or so the previous evening going through every aspect of Paul's contracts. These were, in fact, quite straight-forward, and added very little to what Alice had said about the nature of such contracts. But she now had all the details in her head, and felt reasonably confident that she could handle it.

She next fixed half a day's absence, to visit the head office of Redstone Construction, once located in Carlisle but now based near Grosvenor Square, Mayfair. Next she arranged two meetings, one of which was in any case due, with two academics at Leeds University, the more urgent one to discuss publication of a book on a remarkable mechanical device over 2000 years old that had been discovered 100 years ago off the Island of Antikithera in Greece, and the purpose of which a professor of astrophysics was beginning to unravel. The other meeting was more to do with mainstream physics, a text-book designed for students but potentially very lucrative. These she timed in such a way as to dovetail with a visit to the regional head office of National Energy plc, in the centre of Leeds, through which Paul had been carrying out his work with the company. She wouldn't say that life was looking up; but at least she was doing something about Paul, and she got her second solid eight hours sleep since she had returned from California.

*   *   *

"My name's Jane Mortimer. I have an appointment with Clive Morrison" It was not surprising, Kate thought, that a construction company should have an inside track on the finest building materials, but the acres of marble in the reception area of Redstone Construction spoke of either great commercial success or hubris on a gigantic scale. The receptionist was no less marble-like, elegant beyond reach or description, and Kate wondered if, rather than go home to family or friends, she was just put in a wardrobe-like box at the end of the day, recharged overnight, ready to deal with any and every request that the following day's visitors would bring. Kate knew this was driven by monumental envy – how could a receptionist be so beautiful, so cool, so completely in charge. That was London as opposed to Oxford she thought, and no doubt a very attractive salary package as well. "Would you take the lift to the eleventh floor, please. Mr. Morrison's PA will be there to meet you". This all proved to be correct and, less than two minutes later, it having been ascertained that she would have coffee, Kate was ushered in by Morrison's PA, another remarkably chic-looking and smartly dressed twenty something, to his spacious, elegant, though minimalist office.

Kate's job led her to meet large numbers of people, mainly though not exclusively academics, budding or established authors, reviewers, teachers, people with all sorts of ideas as to what needed to be published; and she had learnt to suppress her instincts – natural she assumed to many women – to make snap judgments on people, still less let them effect her professional judgment. She had met charming and engaging people who had no idea at all as to what others might be interested to read or, therefore OUP might be prepared to publish; and some of their most successful, most potent publications had emerged from the hand of authors who, at first sight, she would have thought the product of a care-in-the-community programme. Focus on solid content, not impressions or style she often, rather glibly, said to herself; too glibly because, in falling for Paul almost as soon as she met him, she had had no idea of any 'content'. He was pure style, good looking, charming, amusing, exhilarating to be with. Only later did she come to realise that there was much more to it than this. They had had rather similar upbringings, he in North London, she South of the Thames but both very much Londoners. Much more important, he was a clear workaholic and she immediately felt comfortable with that, not because she was similarly workaholic, though she was to date very dedicated to her career, but because her father, as a result of a roller-coaster career as an entrepreneur – one moment taking the family to Monaco, the next moving them into shabby rented accommodation and leaving no forwarding address – had become an alcoholic. There was quite a strong parallel between, on the one hand, the times without number that she, as a little girl, had been left to amuse herself outside a pub, as her father got steadily more plastered inside, with her mother trying to keep some semblance of control of him; and, on the other, Paul's obsession with his work. Even their first week-end together, he had spent more time with his laptop than with her – and she had felt quite at home with that. They had been just right for each other, a match waiting only for an opportunity to spark, but that opportunity had come only because she had acted on her first instincts, allowing his engaging style to triumph over her natural caution.

With this one important exception, Kate was not normally given to instant judgments on people. At the same time, Mr. Clive Morrison, with whom she now shook hands, was one of only two people in the world at the moment who could help her; and she studied him intently as they introduced themselves. He was, she registered, something of a puzzle, not fitting any convenient stereotype. There was no gainsaying that he was fairly nondescript – average height, average build, mousy brown hair and nothing particularly handsome or distinguished about his rather soft round face. But he had an impish manner and a smile to match, quite at odds with his physical appearance; and he welcomed Kate with a warmth, and something more - an intensity was nearer the mark – that was quite captivating. All of which was a great help as Kate embarked on her latest deception, her largest yet by some long way.

"It's good of you to see me, Mr. Morrison" she began, as pleasant as possible, but striving for a faintly official sound. "I'm from the central administration of the University, and Alice Richmond, the administrator at the Engineering Department suggested I contact you, about Dr. Paul Emmerson. You know, I think, about the tragic circumstances concerning Dr. Emmerson; and I have been asked to review and settle the details of his contract with you. I've gone through it all with Miss Richmond, and I don't believe that there are any particular difficulties, but I understand that you were the main contact point at the company end, and I thought it best we meet to sort out the details"

"I quite understand" replied Morrison, the smile no more than sympathy for the unusual, and perhaps rather difficult position Ms. Mortimer found herself in. "We were very sorry to hear what had happened. I gather there is no real explanation for his disappearance". If it was a question, he did not wait for any answer. "He was doing some excellent work for us, quite outstanding, and I don't know that we will be able to replace him. I think in principle we would be very happy to provide the rest of the research funding we agreed with Oxford, if there is some prospect of keeping the project going – I'm speaking without commitment of course – but, as I say, I'm not sure that there is anyone else ready to pick up from where we currently are". It was Kate's turn to say that she quite understood and that, in the circumstances, that sounded very generous on the part of Redstone. She added

"I'm purely an administrator – finance mainly – I'm afraid that I don't really know what the scientific content of the project was". It was as far as she felt she could go, but she had judged the man well enough.

"It was fascinating stuff" said Morrison in a rather gossipy manner, his face now beaming with enthusiasm. "Absolutely cutting edge. It was designed to establish a whole new way of identifying potential weaknesses in construction materials – mainly concrete but not only that – much greater warning of stress failure; and potentially much cheaper as well. It could be a major factor in virtually all our maintenance work, and it might in the end have had some implications for the materials used in a lot of civil engineering projects". He paused, aware that he might already be starting to bore the attractive young woman who had come to sort out a few contract desiderata. Kate wanted to shout at him to go on, but judged that it was probably enough just not to intervene. Her reticence turned out to be stronger than his.

"It's brilliant in concept, but it's actually quite simple to explain. So much of what we do is concerned with guaranteeing the load-bearing strength of the materials we use, but reducing its weight and cost. So we are for ever measuring stresses – the potential for materials to fracture, that type of thing. For years we have relied heavily on ultra-sound techniques that can give you a picture of the resilience, or lack of it, of what looks to the naked eye to be absolutely solid. But it isn't totally reliable – we can still get caught out – and to make sure there is no risk, absolutely sure, means building in a lot of redundancy – extra strength - and that's very expensive. If we had a more certain method of estimating stresses we could probably cut at least 30% out of most construction projects. Dr. Emmerson's work was at an early stage – nowhere near operational – but it held out the prospect of tests a hundred more times sensitive than ultra-sound techniques, based on examining the atomic structure of the

120

materials involved. I won't baffle you with all the science, but it was quite something - will be quite something, if it works".

"I see" said Kate, this being largely if not completely true. "It's a great pity that Dr. Emmerson couldn't complete the work. I'm sure the head of department – I don't know if you know him, Professor Ewing – will want to discuss possible ways forward. My job is mainly to check out the finances. I presume that, for the moment at least, the funding you are providing will cease?"

"Well, the payments Dr. Emmerson – his consultancy fees – will cease because we paid them against invoices sent him by him, for his time and expenses. We aren't due to make another project payment until next year, so there will be plenty of time to see whether further work is feasible. I think that's all on the financial front. But there is the issue of all of his data and research material".

"Yes, I read the contract on that " interposed Kate "but what is your understanding?"

"Oh that's always a ghastly area – too many lawyers involved. Basically, the research is Dr. Emmerson's, for him to publish, or for another academic approved by the University to pick up. Any commercial exploitation is ours. Any patents that emerge are owned jointly by us and the University, all covered by some hugely detailed legal documents".

"So Dr. Emerson's work was potentially very valuable?" asked Kate, focusing on one of the key questions she had identified.

"In principle, yes. But I don't think we were anywhere near exploiting that potential. For a start, he was still on some very preliminary analysis – I was very optimistic from what I saw that it could develop well, but there was absolutely no guarantee that it would lead anywhere, commercially speaking at least. We hadn't even thought about getting a patent claim in, and we would certainly do that before even an academic conference paper on the topic was presented – that's a standard part of such arrangements – so you can see what early days it was".

"I see" said Kate again "but what then should we do with Dr. Emmerson's research material in Oxford?"

"I think the department should just hang on to it, until we know if there is anyone else available and interested to take over the project. We can't restrict the University having access to it – they just can't proceed in any public forum without our agreement".

"But presumably there is some sort of confidentiality, or a security issue involved, with all his files and so on?" She felt her heart starting to hammer against her chest as she said this, only too aware that no-one other than her and Steve in IT knew that Paul's Redstone computer files were already missing.

Morrison looked doubtful. "It's possible, I suppose. But it's not very likely. As I say, he had only just got started but, in any event, all the trial data, that's the really sensitive   – commercially sensitive that is – material, is held here;

and Dr. Emmerson could only work on it here. I think he did a fair amount of the more purely theoretical work in Oxford, but that would all end up in the public domain anyway. *He* might have wanted to keep it confidential, so that no-one else suddenly popped up at a conference with his ideas, or in a journal; but that could only have been the scientific ideas, with no empirical aspect, and that's a bit far-fetched. It's a very small world – I used to be an academic myself – there are probably only a dozen or so people anywhere in the world working on anything related to what Dr. Emmerson was doing; he'd know them all and they'd all know what everyone else was up to. So, I don't see much of a problem. As long as Oxford just keeps the material secure. It will all be password protected anyway".

"I see" echoed Kate a third time, rather disoriented by the chasm that existed between Morrison's rather relaxed approach on the one hand and, on the other, her knowledge that Paul's Redstone files had gone. If everything was at such an early stage, if all the sensitive material was here, at Redstone Construction, and if whatever was on Paul's disk couldn't possibly be passed off, in the apparently tight-knit world of materials engineering, by someone else as their own work, then why had it been removed? And what would happen when, eventually, as it must do, it came to light, and to Mr. Clive Morrison's attention, that the Oxford material had disappeared? And what would happen to Kate?

"I'll follow it up with Miss Richmond" said Kate, suddenly quite anxious to make an exit. "If there's any problem, one of us will get back to you".

"That's fine" said Morrison. "I hope, in time, that we can move ahead, but I'll need to think how best to proceed". They stood, shook hands, chatted briefly about the company and Oxford, and then Kate departed, down eleven floors, back through the acres of marble and out into the fresh air. She felt totally drained, by the stress of the deception and by the weight of her knowledge; and quite downhearted by the lack of any real progress. She did have a rather clearer idea of the sort of work on which Paul had been engaged, but was not remotely further forward on why his lap-top or hard disk were missing, still less what might have happened to Paul. Maybe she would make more progress with National Energy plc, but she was not feeling optimistic.

Kate got back to Oxford shortly after lunchtime and went straight to her office. There she found Janice, who said that Alice had called in quite a state, and had asked Kate to call her back as soon as she could. Kate felt like she had been punched in the stomach. All she could think was that Morrison, quite innocently no doubt, had phoned Alice with some follow-up from their morning meeting and Kate's deception had become immediately obvious.

"What time did she call?" asked Kate, by no means certain that she could deal with the situation.

"First thing, just after nine" replied Janice, and Kate's gut-wrenching feeling eased slightly. She hadn't even reached Morrison's office by then. But what could be the cause of Alice's agitation? Kate rang Alice.

"Oh thanks for getting back to me" said Alice, with such an evident sense of relief that Kate knew she, at least, was not the cause of Alice's concern. "I got Peter – he runs the reception people – to look At the CCTV tapes, and I have got a print-out of the two police officers that you wanted". Kate was about to thank her, unclear as to why this should be a problem, but Alice went straight on. "The thing is, they weren't quite sure where to start looking and reviewed some earlier tapes – just a mistake really – and found out that there *has* been a break-in, or at least an intruder, just like you mentioned to me before. I can't believe it".

"What, someone broke into the laboratory building"?" asked Kate, her heartbeat once again starting to race.

"Well, not exactly. It was the middle of the morning, lots of students around, but the CCTV on Paul's corridor picked up someone going into his office, and coming out about ten minutes later. Pete checked through and has got pictures of the man coming into the building, but he was amongst a group heading for various lectures and just walked up the stairs – no-one really noticed him – and then there is coverage of him leaving the building in the same way, but again it doesn't look at all suspicious. There are hundreds of students and staff coming and going during the day, especially in the morning when most of the lectures are on, and the reception desk people wouldn't know most of them"

"Did he steal anything?" asked Kate. "I mean, was he carrying anything when he left?"

"It doesn't look like it".

"How did he get in to Paul's office?" asked Kate.

"That's the really worrying thing" said Alice. "The CCTV isn't brilliant, but the man just walks up to the door and almost immediately walks in to Paul's office. He must have had a key, or be very expert at picking a lock".

"And when did this happen?" asked Kate, furiously trying to absorb the implications of this information.

"That's very worrying as well. It was the 23rd, the Friday before you got back from America. Paul was in the office the day before".

So many thoughts started competing for Kate's attention that she temporarily became speechless. Someone had been in Paul's office the day after he disappeared – so much for the mindless mugger theory; she felt the need to calm Alice down, but realised that her previous non-explanations for why she had mentioned the possibility of a break-in weren't necessarily going to stand up any longer; still worse, it was clear that the police – which meant bloody DI Johnson – would have to be brought back in; and, most serious of all, she was fairly certain that she knew why someone had burgled Paul's office and what he had taken, but she had told no-one precisely because she didn't trust Johnson.

Alice sensed that Kate was very shocked by what she had said, as she herself had been when Pete had come to see her earlier that morning; but was temporarily bereft of any further thoughts. Finally, Kate broke the silence. "Have you done anything yet?" she asked.

"Not yet. I wanted to speak to you first. I'll need to get in touch with the police, but I remembered you asking about a break-in and I thought it would be good to get your advice". Kate had had no time to think up a good answer to this without disclosing the missing computer disk, and she was still reluctant to do so; and she couldn't now properly remember what she had said before.

"Oh, it was just the police who kept asking me if any of Paul's things were missing. So I wondered if anything had gone from his office. That was all". It was fairly lame, but she thought it would suffice.

"I see" replied Alice. "Well, I'd better get in touch with them to let them know that they might have been right, though, as I said, it doesn't look as if anything was removed. Who do you think I should contact?"

Kate's first instinct was to talk to Hargreaves, but she quickly recognised that, while this might make her feel a little better, it would not achieve anything, indeed it could be a lot worse than that. Hargreaves would have to pass the information on to Johnson, who would want to know why Kate, or Alice, was still talking to a detective no longer on the case. Johnson couldn't ignore the new evidence of.... something – it was all still a complete mystery to Kate – but he had seemed very determined not to pursue the case before; and Kate anticipated that this would be his overriding objective again. All of which left her only one option. Johnson would have to be told about the break-in, but he could find out about the missing disk himself – always assuming that he didn't already know - and in the meantime, Kate would have to stay at least one step ahead.

"I'm sure you should let them know straight away" said Kate. "The person to speak to, I think, is Detective Inspector Johnson – you probably won't be able to get hold of him yourself, but if you leave a message about what's happened, they'll get it to him I'm sure. Let me know what happens".

"I will" agreed Alice. "Will you call in to get the photo I got for you, or do you not need it now?"

Kate, in the shock of Alice's information, had quite forgotten that this had all been triggered by her attempt to get a photo of the two officers who had called. More than ever she wanted to see what they looked like, not because she anticipated that this would help at all, but because it would, for the first time, give some tangible quality to whatever - or whoever – she was up against.

"Thanks, I'll call over when I finish work. If you've gone by then, can you leave them at reception for me to pick up?" This was fine by Alice and she rang off. Kate immediately called Janice in.

"Could you try to re-arrange my visit to Leeds? I need to see Curtis and Edmunds as soon as possible, this week if possible". The two budding authors would no doubt be pleased at the apparent urgency with which an OUP editor wished to see them, and Kate would not disabuse them of the reason. Two hours later, Janice had re-arranged her meetings, one for Thursday, the day after tomorrow, in the morning, and the other for Friday – that was the best Janice could do - and Kate had similarly re-arranged her visit to National Energy for Thursday afternoon, on the simple but now true pretext that she was going to be in Leeds earlier than she had expected.

For a day and a half, her life followed as normal a path as was possible for a bereaved young woman. She saw little of her friends, took no part in any of the activities that she might have pursued if Paul had still been there – not necessarily with him, but happy in the knowledge that she would see him. No tennis, no theatre, no meals out. She cooked in the evenings, listened to some music, watched no television except the news, which generally chimed with her unhappy mood. This included daily coverage of apparently motiveless crimes of violence which, she reminded herself, was still how most people thought Paul had died; and a growing shadow of international tension over Iran – as far as she could see, and as far as most commentators could see, a chilling repeat of Iraq, with growing evidence that Iran not only had, but was quite prepared to use, nuclear weapons, combined with considerable scepticism as to the reliability of this information. The UN seemed quite undecided about what to do; the US was increasingly sabre-rattling and, once again a critical question was whether the British Prime Minister, Alan Gerrard, would, on the basis of an unlikely but clearly very strong personal relationship with the US President, offer support, both militarily and diplomatic to a so-called coalition of the willing. None of it kept her attention for more than a few seconds.

CHAPTER 8

Kate travelled by train to Leeds the following afternoon, and booked into the Excelsior Hotel, a rather brash but very comfortable four star hotel in the now very fashionable heart of a massively renovated city centre. After a restless night she had a light breakfast and headed for the University. By lunchtime she had discussed a book, essentially a text book for undergraduates on sub-atomic physics, with one of her authors - level, target readership, time scales, contracts and related matters and, after a brief sandwich lunch, set off for NEL's headquarters.

David Nicholls was a very different proposition from Clive Morrison. Though probably just the right side of forty and about average height, he was carrying too much weight and losing his hair – not, Kate thought, an attractive sight. He might once have had a somewhat rugged look but, if so, it had long gone to flab. Rimless glasses gave him slightly more gravitas than he might otherwise have had, but he had a fussy, almost twitchy, manner and, Kate noticed, he was clearly quite taken with her figure. She was used to men looking at her breasts – as if somehow she wouldn't notice – but even though she had a high collar blouse on, under a business-like jacket, and with a pencil skirt to her knees - not a hint of cleavage or thigh to distract him - Mr. David Nicholls was not to be deflected from a visual tour. So be it, she thought. I need you to talk to me, and gave him a broad smile.

Nicholls asked her if she wanted some tea. Kate had only just finished off a coffee after her sandwich but, in her role as Jane Mortimer, accepted the offer as a small way of putting the conversation on an easy-going basis. Nicholls put this in train over an intercom on his desk and then, with a broad smile of his own, threw open his arms as a gesture for Kate to start. "How can I help? I'm all ears". And eyes, thought Kate, also registering that Nicholls had made no reference to Paul – no questions, no commiseration. Kate reprised her role as some sort of financial administrator from the University's central offices, there in part at Miss Alice Richmond's suggestion, to deal with the contractual and related fall-out of Dr. Emmerson's strange and tragic disappearance. Interrupted only by the arrival of tea, Nicholls spent most of the time Kate was talking nodding, rather energetically Kate thought, but at least he seemed fully to understand why she was here – perhaps, Kate began to think with just a hint of alarm, rather more than she did.

When she finished speaking, Nicholls, still smiling and nodding, said "It's all pretty straight-forward, I think. We set up the consultancy arrangement with Dr. Emmerson around six months ago. We agreed to pay him in three equal tranches, one at the beginning, one after a progress report and one at the end – but you'll know all this. We were awaiting the progress report when we heard that he had gone missing. Has there been any progress on what happened to him?" he added.

"I don't really know " said Kate. "I think the police suspect that he was the victim of a mugging – something like that – but I don't think anything much has come to light. Did you work at all closely with Dr. Emmerson?"

"Good heavens, no" said Nicholls. "I'm not on the technical side here. I'm a lawyer by training, but have increasingly moved into the management side. I'm responsible for the overall area which Dr. Emmerson was advising. It was our Chief Engineer, Richard Werner, who proposed contacting Emmerson. I think he knew Emmerson from when he was a student – Emmerson that is".

"I see" said Kate. "Do you know if they had made much progress?"

Nicholls looked rather pensive, and Kate feared that that had been a step too far, or at least too soon. "I don't know the first thing about Dr. Emmerson's work" she added lightly, "I just wondered, as you said you never got the progress report, whether the company got some value from the project, or has it all been wasted?"

Nicholls visibly relaxed, but said "I can't discuss the actual work at all– that's completely confidential – but I know Werner was very disappointed. I don't really know how well they got on – Werner's a rather remote figure, absolute genius but too up-tight for my liking - but he had got quite enthusiastic about Emmerson's ideas and, as I said, he was very disappointed at what happened. So I don't think he got much out of the project".

Kate nodded. Where to go from here? Paul had been doing some sort of consultancy project; it sounded fairly short-term; was, what, half way through, maybe less; and hadn't got round to providing any great insights to National Energy before he disappeared. But it was confidential, and Kate's instinct was that she was now, however, loosely, on a more productive track. But how to find out more? The work was no doubt on 'stresses and strains' but it didn't look like she was going to find out anything more specific about it from Nicholls – so where to go next?

"I'm sorry it didn't work out. It all seems straight-forward on the administrative and financial side. There's just one last point. Dr. Emmerson had a number of computer files, on all his research projects, and I presume that this includes data on the work he was doing for you. What would you like us to do with it – you said the project was confidential?"

"There won't be anything in Oxford on this project" said Nicholls firmly. "I can't go into details. Although Emmerson was contracted by NEL, all the actual work was with another organisation, and there was a very strict agreement that all his work would be carried out at their premises – everything. So it won't be a problem".

Kate hoped she didn't look as stunned as she felt. There certainly *had* been a set of NEL files in Oxford. What on earth was Paul doing? No doubt it would have been more convenient to have whatever data or other material he needed for the project in Oxford; but Paul was not the type to break an agreement. He wasn't that irresponsible, and he wasn't that stupid either. So what had been going on? She had to find out more but, she told herself again, she wasn't likely to find out much more from Nicholls.

"That solves that then" said Kate "I must let you get on" She stood up.

"Are you off back to Oxford now?" asked Nicholls casually. Kate was momentarily caught by surprise. She certainly wasn't going back to Oxford, not only because of her second author's meeting next day – not a meeting she could mention to Nicholls – but also because she knew she had to talk to Richard Werner somehow – and that was another reason which she clearly couldn't give Nicholls. So the answer had better be a 'yes'.

"Err, yes" said Kate, but she had been too unprepared to lie convincingly, and she heard the lack of conviction in her own voice.

"You don't seem too sure" Nicholls said in a slightly teasing voice. "Not going to go on a little shopping spree? Leeds is quite the Paris of the North these days"

Nicholls didn't know how relieved Kate was to be given an excuse for how she had responded to his query.

"It had crossed my mind" she replied with a conspiratorial grin.

"If you would like a drink later on – something a bit stronger than tea - I'd be happy to buy you one. I'll be away from here around six".

So that was the way things were moving, thought Kate. I should have seen that coming. Kate was very used to men trying some form of pick-up, had been since her mid-teens, and for a while it had been rather flattering. She had thought some of her attractive friends rather silly, one moment dressing to kill and the next feigning, or perhaps not feigning, annoyance at some approach, subtle or otherwise. After a while it became a bit of a bore, but she got used to it. Now it was the proverbial water off a duck's back. Kate didn't even have to think consciously about her reply, launching into an automatic rejection – polite, neutral, but 'no'.

"That's very kind of you" she said, disingenuously treating the invitation as entirely innocent. The next word was 'but' – but I'll be headed back by then, but I've got work to do, but I'm going on to see my grandmother in Scotland, but something, anything. But the correct next word did not emerge. In the time that it had taken Kate to thank Nicholls for his oh so kind invitation she had figured out, somewhere subterranean in her mind, that she was unlikely to be able to get hold of Werner, still less get him to talk about a clearly confidential project. Even if she did, it would get back to Nicholls, and that might well trigger a call to the University and to Alice, and a general unravelling of her fictions. This she was prepared for if it was the cost of tracing what had happened to Paul, but not if she had gained no further information. That being so, then this rather horrid man in front of her, inviting her for a drink, was her only identifiable way forward. Not a very promising one, to be sure but, right now, all she had.

Kate had no qualms about handling Nicholls or, rather, not handling him. He might leer, be suggestive, he might well be a groper – well, she had dealt with all those types, and ones with much more forceful personalities than Nicholls, men with too much testosterone and too much sense of their own macho attractiveness to women. And if Nicholls thought there might be something to gain, be it a barely plausible mild flirtation or a delusionary night of rampant sex, then there might be something more to be learnt, even if it wasn't remotely clear how.

"Can I give you a call in a couple of hours?" she continued. "I think my plans will be a little clearer then".

From Kate's point of view, as against the automatic rejection she had started out on, this was a possible 'yes', though even as she said it she registered that it gave her a good opportunity for second thoughts. For Nicholls it was an almost certain 'no'; a polite, convenient way for Miss Jane Mortimer to extricate herself from an unwelcome invitation. Ah well, he hadn't really expected more. What he really needed was some reason to see her again, but everything seemed to have been resolved, at least everything that Oxford's administrative offices were interested in. With no time to think he said

"Do that. We were all very shocked when Miss Richmond contacted us. Did you know Dr. Emmerson?"

"I met him once" lied Kate, not grasping that Nicholls didn't expect her to call back, and was desperately trying to find some common ground that might persuade her to do so.

"Our people thought he was brilliant" Nicholls went on. "A real star. I didn't have much contact with him myself, once we set the project up. I don't even know if he had a wife or family – awful for them if he did".

"No, he wasn't married"

"Oh, well, that's some small consolation I suppose. If you are free for a drink, I'd be interested to know more about him, and why the police suspect a mugging. I'm surprised they haven't followed things up with us". It wasn't much of a bait. Nicholls had no reason to think that Emmerson's disappearance had anything at all to do with National Energy; and he'd be hard pushed to develop any sort of line on this if Miss Mortimer pursued it. She was, in any case, just an administrator trying to tie up loose ends. But the question dangled there, requiring some sort of answer; and Nicholls had been genuinely surprised that, after one cursory phone call from the Thames Valley police, asking if he had any information on the whereabouts of Dr. Paul Emmerson, he had heard nothing more.

Kate was also surprised. "Didn't the police contact you?" she asked, with rather more intensity than was appropriate for an administrator from central finance. Nicholls explained that they had called; it was just rather perfunctory and they hadn't followed it up. Given that Dr. Emmerson was spending at least one day a week, occasionally two, on the project, that seemed just a little casual. Kate only just managed to stop herself from saying that she hadn't been aware

Paul had been spending such a large amount of time in Leeds – how would a financial officer at the University know of such things – and instead just nodded in agreement. Paul was always zipping around the country, and abroad – she'd often seen him trying to fit it all in with his teaching schedule in Oxford - and he'd been both to glorious places, mainly for conferences, and prosaic places to say the least; but she couldn't remember him singling out Leeds.

"Oh, so did he spend a lot of time up here?" she asked. This followed on very naturally and, this time, she didn't think she was pushing too hard.

"No, not at all" said Nicholls, picking up, in some instinctive way that, for some reason, Miss Mortimer was starting to become interested. "We employed him, but to work with another company. Look, I'm going to have to run now – I'm a bit late for a meeting with the energy conservation lot. I can't think why we, of all people, want the public to conserve energy, but we must do our bit for the planet I suppose. Let's talk more if you're free later". He edged towards the door, giving himself a metaphorical congratulatory slap on the back. He'd played his decidedly unpromising hand really very well. It was still probably fifty-fifty that she'd call back, but that was a whole lot better odds than five minutes ago. It wasn't just that they clearly had something, namely Emmerson, that they could talk about, but there was more of a rapport than before, based around a common interest – of sorts – rather than being hungry predator and wary prey. You haven't totally lost your touch, he thought.

"OK" said Kate. "I'll call you around 5, maybe 5.30 pm or so. I'd quite like to know more about what Dr. Emmerson did, in a general sort of way. Everyone says how clever he was, and I don't know anything about him as a person". She hoped that this just sounded rather gushing, but she was, with ice-cold calculation, laying down some chips in whatever poker game was to come. Nicholls immediately thought that he recognised the lure of the confidential. Secrets could be sexy. The secrecy associated with Emmerson's project was, alas, not remotely sexy, and would, even if he told her, have precious little impact on this rather gorgeous, if slightly naïve, creature in front of him; but she was not to know that. There might be some mileage there. He wouldn't mind it being six-mile-high mileage he thought, with an inward smirk, but outwardly he remained all sympathetic smiles.

"Well, as I say, I can't discuss anything to do with the work he was doing for us – very market sensitive – but I know something of his career, why we hired him. Give me a call" he re-iterated, trying to sound faintly mysterious, and Kate headed out of his office, glad to give herself time to think carefully about where she was and where she might be going with this...... with her own project as she now thought of it. One thing was certain. She wasn't going shopping.

She went back to her hotel and just sat there for a while, trying to think through what to do next. One thought very rapidly formed in her mind. If the Thames Valley police had not followed up their initial call to Nicholls – which she was presuming that Nicholls would have known if they had spoken to anyone else in the company – then they had not contacted Richard Werner, which might just give her an entry point. Without hesitating, lest she lose her nerve, she rang a Directory Inquiries number, got from India or somewhere similar the general inquiries number for National Energy's offices in Leeds, then rang and asked to speak to Richard Werner

"Just a moment" said a pleasant female voice. "May I say who is calling?"

Kate was perfectly aware that impersonating a police officer was very serious stuff – an entirely different league from little Miss Finance; but she really didn't care much any more. If the police had been more concerned, less pathetic, she wouldn't be in this position. So, she'd give it a go. She doubted, from what Nicholls had said, that anything less than officialdom – and perhaps not even that – would get Werner to talk.

"Detective- Sergeant Sally Weston" she replied. Another primary school friend dragooned into service.

"One moment please" There was a pause and then another female voice said

"Can I help you?"

"Is it possible to speak to Mr. Werner?" asked Kate, trying to sound like polite but firm officialdom.

"It's Dr. Werner, actually" said the voice, not unkindly, but in the tone of someone who would not make that sort of mistake. "and he's in the States at the moment. Can I help? I'm his P.A.

"No, it will wait" said Kate. "can you let me know when he will be back?"

"Not until Monday week, I'm afraid. But I am in daily contact with him. Can I give him a message?" Kate's spirits fell and, with them went all the nervous tension that had got her to this point. In any case, asking Werner to contact her would be suicidal.

"No, I'll call again when he's back. Thanks for your help" and Kate put the phone down. So, no full-scale police impersonation after all, she thought and, Mr. David Nicholls, this is your lucky day, or at least as near to it as you are likely to come.

She closed her eyes and tried to think through her forthcoming encounter with Nicholls. The promise of sex for information about Paul's work was an absurd scenario. She could just about imagine gurgling that she'd do anything to find out what had happened to Paul but, given her Miss Finance subterfuge, this would be totally implausible; and she certainly wasn't actually going to be dishing out sexual favours to anyone, least of all the clearly over-sexed and rather disagreeable Mr. Nicholls. And, at a more pragmatic level, even if she had been prepared to let him… let him what – she certainly wouldn't dream of letting him fuck her – presumably let him work out his sexual fantasies over her, there was no way that they could ever do a deal. She wouldn't let him touch her without having the information she wanted; and she was quite sure he wouldn't divulge anything until he had got his leg over her. So it was all out of the window, and she was quite shocked to realise that she was actually working through these possibilities, however unrealistic. She might pick up something from loose, particularly alcohol-fuelled chatter, with just a little physical contact helping the process along; but she couldn't see it being more than that. Unless…..

She suddenly had a thought so inspirational, so shocking, so absolutely off-the-wall that she felt physically sick for a moment. What had President Hamilton said ? *"Seize the initiative and do whatever it takes…"* Ten minutes ago she had been preparing to impersonate a police officer, but maybe she didn't need to; and she certainly didn't want to hang around for however long it took to hook up with Werner in the US. But could she really carry off what had just burst out of the depths - indubitably the depths - of her mind. Don't think about it or you won't; just do it, get on with it. This self-addressed call to action, combined with the quite contradictory thought that it might well not work out, was enough.

There wasn't a telephone directory in her room, and for what she planned, India was not going to be much help. She went down to Reception, who duly obliged. She noted down four numbers from the residential section, and three from Yellow Pages. She went back to her room, made five calls and then left the hotel. She took a taxi to an office about three miles away and spent the best part of an hour there. She followed this up with some shopping in the centre of Leeds – with a wry smile she thought how Nicholls would have be impressed at his own foresight – including a trip to a bank, and by 5.15 pm she was back at her hotel. Part of her kept asking if she had any idea what she was doing. But part was sheer exhilaration. Her life had fallen apart; and no-one, not even the rather nice Neil Hargreaves, had really done anything about it. The greatest thing in her life, ever, had gone and the response was – tough. There had been oodles of well-meaning sympathy but nothing actually useful, and bugger all from the police. But there was clearly more to it, much more, than anyone knew – certainly more than she knew – and now she could do something to get rid of the stultifying sense of helplessness that had been driving her mental these last few weeks. Some action, quite like her old self, if just about as far away from publishing academic texts as you could get.

At 5.30 pm she rang Nicholls.

"I'm going to stay in Leeds tonight" she said. "I'm in the Hotel Excelsior. Maybe we could meet for a drink in the bar – if you're still free".

"Definitely" replied Nicholls, hardly able to believe his luck – no, it wasn't luck, at least not entirely. "The Excelsior's very grand – Oxford must be very generous on expenses".

Kate's instant re-action – what a patronising bastard Nicholls was – was quickly replaced by the thought that she had potentially made a big mistake. She surely wouldn't be on expenses to stay overnight if she was who Nicholls thought she was; and if she was staying over at her own expense then Miss Jane Mortimer would never have booked into just about the most expensive hotel in town. But, with what she increasingly realised was absolutely instinctive criminal deception – maybe she had been in the wrong profession all along – she said

"I rang the office and told a little white lie" She was pure saccharine now. "I said it was all a bit more complicated than I'd expected, and that you had a meeting – which you did" she added defensively, as if this remotely justified everything "and that we'd need to get together again tomorrow morning. So I am on expenses, and the Excelsior isn't at all expensive by London standards. Any way, I'll say it was all I could find at short notice in the respectable part of town. A girl's got to be careful". Next time I'm back in L.A. I'm going to go for a screen test, she thought. Pure Hollywood. And Nicholls will love it.

Kate didn't know the half of it. Nicholls became aware that he was softly massaging his crotch. Clearly not a woman with any great scruples. A day away from the office, a load of retail therapy, and getting her employer to pay for overnight luxury. He could fall in love with Miss Mortimer.

"I'll be there just after six. Is that OK?"

Kate confirmed that that would be fine. They rang off and both, for radically different reasons, sat at their respective ends of the line breathing rather more heavily than was usual. It's all in the lap of the gods now thought Kate; while a rather similar sentiment was going through Nicholls' mind. He picked up the phone to tell Pat he'd be late home, knowing that she would probably regard this as good rather than bad news.

CHAPTER 9

Kate was sitting on an enormous leather settee in the bar area of the hotel when Nicholls arrived. She looked the same of course, and she looked totally different. Largely the same clothes, though she now wore an elegant pair of high heels, her hair now up, and Nichols could swear that she was now wearing a tighter, more revealing blouse under her jacket; but, most of all, this was a woman sitting in the bar of a rather good hotel, not in his office, and that changed everything about her. He was surveying her figure again even as he approached her. God, if he could just get his hands on her breasts. He was realistic enough to know that the prospect was vanishingly small – he had learnt the hard way that for such purposes he needed to meet nymphomaniacs and, sadly, there weren't any in his experience. But it was a glorious sight before him, and a dreamy prospect wouldn't do any harm. Something to think about when, or increasingly if, he and Pat both got drunk enough at the same time to have some brief, restorative, almost medicinal sex. It had gone downhill soon after their first child was born. He sometimes wondered how they managed two more. Still, this was not a night to mope. He was having a drink in a fashionable hotel with a strikingly beautiful, sexy lady, and life didn't get a whole lot better for David Nicholls these days.

"What will you have to drink?" he asked as he sat down.

"Gin and tonic please"

Nicholls managed to catch the waiter's eye almost immediately, and ordered two gin and tonics. He must be on a roll. How often had he been able to get served so quickly – he usually felt quite invisible and totally inaudible to waiters, who never seemed to grasp the one single, simple rule of waiting – keep looking around. Most of the ones that he came across seemed to have escaped from a school for the blind and, just in case they could see, would traverse the tables with their eyes firmly glued to the floor. But for once, thank God, and when it really mattered, he had found the one truly professional waiter in Leeds. It didn't occur to him that it was perhaps Miss Mortimer's presence which had led to a monitoring eye being cast in his direction. He was just having a really good day.

"Did you have a successful afternoon?" he asked; and Kate launched into a simple fantasy of clearing some work out of the way, phoning Oxford, and then shopping here, there and everywhere, including her new shoes. She dropped the name of a few fashion store chains, quite certain, though she had never seen them, that the centre of Leeds would have them all; and equally certain that Nicholls wouldn't have a clue which shops were there and which weren't. She said that she had had no idea how very elegant the shops were, playing up the blinkered southern girl who might still think most if not all northern cities were coal black dumps of grim streets and huge unemployment. As she anticipated, this allowed Nicholls to get into his stride, explaining how the North in general, but Leeds in particular, was now a far better place to live than in the South. He asked Kate where she had been brought up, and how she came to be working for Oxford University. Kate gave a fairly accurate, if rather vague, summary of her childhood, and said that she had worked at Oxford University Press for a while – keep it is as truthful as possible – but the prospects weren't great, she had acquired some financial expertise and, not wanting to move away from Oxford, had jumped at the opportunity to join the University's finance section.

"Any family?" asked Nicholls casually, looking for the waiter again.

"No, not married" said Kate. "I was engaged, but I got cold feet, and he then immediately waltzed off with someone else, so I think it was a lucky escape". That would be enough temptation she thought, enough apparent availability.

"But that's enough about me. Tell me what you do at National Energy. You said you were a lawyer, but not now?"

The waiter re-appeared and Nichols ordered two more gin and tonics without consulting Kate. He then launched into a quick life history, the main points of which, Kate noted, were that, like her, he had been brought up in London, had moved straight into law after leaving Nottingham University, and had achieved quite a senor position in 'external relations' whatever that covered, fairly fast. He clearly had ability.

"Do *you* have a family?" she asked. In fact she knew the answer, and anticipated that Nicholls might want to slide around the issue somehow; but it was still a bit of a bombshell when he replied "I was married, but it didn't work out. Maybe it would have done if we had had kids".

So, Kate thought, this is a very high stakes evening; and he didn't blink an eyelid. Mr. Nicholls, you are a much cooler customer than you look. Time to move on and time to start getting serious.

"So, tell me about Dr. Emmerson. What sort of person was he?"

Nicholls re-iterated that he hadn't known Emmerson very well – they'd only met a couple of times when the project was being set up; but he was quite a name, and a nice guy, and Werner had been delighted to recruit him. When he paused to sip his drink, Kate said

"I know it's all confidential but what sort of things did he do? I presume it was all 'stresses and strains' stuff – he had another consultancy project in that area – you probably know about it". She hoped that this degree of familiarity with Paul's work, slight as it was, might encourage Nicholls to talk.

"Yes, with Redstone Construction. Their interests are rather different from ours, but from Emmerson's point of view it was all similar science. He got much more data, and more varied data, to test his theories; and both companies gained because he could do more comprehensive analysis. Win-win all round" he added, beckoning the waiter over again.

Kate admired his timing. He clearly wanted to get her drunk, but never pushed it, in fact never ordered until she had nearly finished the previous drink. And she was deliberately knocking them back quite fast – otherwise she couldn't plausibly start to seem a little drunk. She indicated that she'd like another drink.

"But you said at the office that Dr. Emmerson wasn't actually working for National Energy; and that you were paying him to work for someone else. I don't really understand. Was it Redstone Construction?" she added – a hint at what a confused little Miss she was becoming.

"No, no, no" said Nicholls jovially, nicely relaxed now. "No, we're nothing to do with them. It's just that - how shall I say – we had a little interest in another company and Dr. Emmerson was helping us check out things there, at a greater level of detail than we could have done". He stopped, more than dimly aware that he might have gone a little too far, but quickly re-assuring himself that it couldn't cause any trouble, especially not to someone as remote from the business world as Jane Mortimer. He hadn't mentioned any names and, anyway, the whole thing was dead now, so no harm done. He was more concerned that he still had no clear idea how to pursue matters with her, as he watched her cross and uncross her long, unquestionably sexy legs, in that tight black skirt she was wearing – but he'd just have to be patient. Dinner was his intermediate target.

"It all sounds very mysterious" said Kate, heading into her third gin. "What sort of 'little interest' does National Energy have?" almost simpering. Then, much more forcefully, "God, this makes a change from bloody university finance".

"I really can't say" Nicholls replied. "We just…. had an interest – the possibility of doing some business together – with another company. It was potentially a big deal and we were, sort of, getting to know each other. Emmerson was helping us on the technical side – some really very advanced stuff that we couldn't do ourselves, nor anyone else. He got some funding, research staff and so on, but I can't really say any more".

Kate nodded. "I quite understand. But might his disappearance be somehow tied up with the work he was doing for you? Might he have found out something they didn't want you to know?"

"We did think about that" replied Nicholls, feeling more and more at ease with her. "But it wouldn't have made any sense. We were all very open – co-operative - about what we were doing, very transparent. No-one expected any problems from Emmerson's work but, if there were any, then we all knew that the deal would be off, or at least, back to square one. So, if he found out anything earth-shattering, getting rid of him wouldn't have helped. We wouldn't go ahead in such circumstances – we haven't – the deal's dead, more's the pity, and anyone would have known that. So whatever happened to him couldn't have been anything to do with the deal we were working on. He might have found out something that was a problem for the other company irrespective of the deal; but both we and Emmerson were operating under strict confidentiality, so there'd still be no advantage to anyone in getting rid of him. I presume that's why the police didn't pursue it with us. Didn't you say they thought it was a mugging or a burglary gone wrong, or something like that? Bloody bad luck for us. I suppose we might resurrect things eventually, but not for a while".

Kate nodded, not sure what to say next. He sort of made sense, if not entirely, but it certainly didn't suggest that there was anything in what Nicholls knew that might lead somewhere in terms of Paul's fate.

"Not sure I really understand all that". She needed more, and for that she needed to get closer to him, emotionally but, she recognised with some distaste, physically. "It all sounds a lot more interesting than how I spend my time".

"Which is how?" asked Nicholls. Keen to get on to another topic.

"Oh, you don't know how boring most of it is" said Kate. "All wretched form filling, spreadsheets, ticking boxes. You don't know. And I could go under a bus tomorrow and nothing would be any different. You know, I get a good salary, I never do overtime, it's wonderful; and a complete bloody waste of time. A trip like this is such a relief, but it's once in a blue moon". She stopped, finding it surprisingly easy to make her eyes start to water. She put one hand over them. "I'm sorry, how embarrassing. It's just the gin talking. As you may detect, I am not wild about my job. I really must get into something more ...... I don't know, just more exciting".

Nicholls sensed that he wouldn't get a better opportunity.

"I am sorry. Look, I can't do much to solve your problem, but if you'd like a spot of dinner, I'd be happy to provide a sympathetic ear. I've got a horribly early start tomorrow – I've got to go to Berlin first thing – so maybe not anywhere too fancy – there's an Italian place almost next door, if you don't have any other plans". He didn't know if it would work but it was, he thought, a masterstroke. All that rubbish about an early start – just a quick meal was the antithesis of anyone seeking the wine-dine-recline routine. Totally unthreatening.

"That's very kind of you" said Kate "But I'll be terrible company if I get going about my job, my whole bloody life frankly at the moment. I'll join you if you promise to tell me to shut up if I start moaning away".

"It's a deal. I'll just settle the bill and then let's go" said Nicholls, thinking – we have lift off!

"Well then I'll pay for dinner" said Kate, for the first time beginning to feel just a hint of dizziness.

"OK" replied Nicholls, "but I'll buy the wine".

While Nicholls paid, Kate went to the lavatory. She needed Nicholls drunk, and she couldn't achieve this without risking – no, getting – drunk herself. She just had to stay sober enough to keep a close eye on the clock. So far they were on schedule and proceeding according to plan.

They arrived at the restaurant, got a table and ordered. Nicholls chose an expensive bottle of wine but also, with Kate's blessing, ordered two more gin and tonics. Drunk is one thing, she thought. I just hope I'm not going to be sick. That was not at all on the menu. Then Nicholls went off to the lavatory and, marvelling at what her world had come to, Kate emptied her gin and tonic into the base of a vine and refilled her glass from the bottle of mineral water. A small victory she thought.

"So" said Nicholls, when he returned "is it really so grim at work?"

"No, I shouldn't have gone off like that. It's just what you were saying about your organisation, your work, the world of business deals, doing things that make a difference; it all sounded great, and I was just struck by the contrast with what I do. I ought to move, but I've probably left it too late now".

If Nicholls hadn't been on his fourth G and T, and if he hadn't in any case experienced a complete collapse of his critical faculties as he rode his luck with this clearly rather vulnerable woman then he might, just might, have seen through this less than subtle ploy. But, in the circumstances in which he found himself, he had no chance. He felt in control, and he was going to play it long.

"That's probably a bit too black and white" he said, in rather Olympian fashion. "To be honest, a lot of what I do is very tedious, very routine. There is so much red tape stuck over just about everything we do these days – I swear I'll end up murdering one of those Health and Safety freaks. Actually, it may sound strange, but that's the core of what's bothering you".

Kate, just starting on the melon and ham which had arrived, looked astonished.

"No, it is. What's exciting about my job – some of the time at least – is taking risks, gambles. You don't make money without taking risks. I think that's why you are fed up with your job. You said there's no excitement; well there's no excitement without taking risks, and that's why Health and Safety are the curse that they are. They just want to get rid of any risks at all. My…." He almost said 'wife' - "sister went to some woodwork evening classes and they had all these fabulous machines, automatic lathes, power drills, you name it, and they couldn't use any of them – bloody health and safety. They had to have a skilled techy person around to be able to use the stuff and the cost of that would have finished off the night class. Of course, they could all use chisels and saws and what have you instead– quite enough to kill themselves". He stopped, aware that he was getting a little carried away. "Sorry, my turn to get fed up. But it's the same thing. The business world is exciting because you have to take risks. That's what makes you feel alive". He stopped. Don't dot the i's and cross the t's; let her work it out.

"I hadn't thought of it like that" said Kate "but you're right. And the project Dr. Emmerson was working on was a risk that didn't come off?" She hadn't meant this to sound slightly slurred, but the wine was beginning to mix with the gin, and it couldn't have been better timed.

"Afraid it didn't" said Nicholls. "I can't go into the details, but it was potentially very big, in the billions. I can't see why we don't go ahead anyway, and maybe we will, but the board got in a right old state when they heard Emmerson had vamoozed. They didn't like it one bit and......" He wasn't quite sure what he wanted to say next, but quickly recovered. "They just panicked. I'm determined to get things moving again" he said, in an understated but overtly self-important manner. "But they need time to think it through. It would be a great help if the police could come up with a perfectly normal explanation".

Kate knew that by now she was not functioning too well, but she hadn't totally lost it. As she had suspected from their earlier conversation, it sounded very much as if National Energy had been planning some sort of merger, or maybe a takeover bid, and Paul must have been employed to do some sort of assessment of the other company's facilities. So, it was clearly going to be an agreed bid. Paul wouldn't have been able to get access to the other company otherwise. Now, with Paul's disappearance, it had fallen through, though not, perhaps permanently, and somewhere in all of this, Kate was now certain, was an explanation for what had happened to him. But even as this thought permeated through her rather inebriated brain, she recognised that, no matter how drunk Nicholls got, he was very unlikely to tell her who the other company was, and why Paul had been working with them; and she knew that, without this information, she was not going to get any further. So it was time for stage two.

They ate and drank and talked some more. The food kept them from getting totally drunk, despite Nicholls ordering another bottle, part of which went to water the vine when Nicholls went to relieve himself again. Then he suggested liqueurs. Kate had a Grand Marnier with ice, Nicholls a Cointreau. At just past 9.15 pm they settled the bill, the alcohol element for Nicholls substantially exceeding Kate's food bill, and they got up to leave. Kate was less steady on her feet than Nicholls, her gender-related genetic deficit in coping with alcohol more than offsetting Kate's lower consumption, courtesy of the restaurant's natural flora. As they left, Nichols took her arm, and Kate was aware that this worked on two levels. She needed a steadying hand, and it was one step nearer to a successful outcome to the evening. Whether she would have thought this in a more sober state did not occur to her.

Neither had mentioned that he would see her back to the hotel. It just happened quite naturally. When they got back Kate said
"I've so enjoyed the evening. Do you want to come up and have some coffee; or we could raid the mini-bar" she added with a giggle.
Christ almighty, we are in orbit, Houston, thought Nicholls. Fucking brilliant he said to himself. Maybe brilliant fucking. Brilliant.
"Lead on" he said, with mock formality. He hoped she wouldn't remember his supposedly early start next morning.. In fact he really didn't care if he didn't

make it through to the morning. He just wanted to get her clothes off, get her into bed, and fuck the night away. Tomorrow, the rest of his life, could take care of themselves.

As they entered the lift, a man who had been sitting in the bar joined them. He had a large brief case and looked very bored. Clearly an overnight business trip. I've been there so many times, thought Nicholls, just wishing that there was some attractive single woman to chat up or more, and it's finally happening. Eat your heart out he thought as they all got out on the fifth floor, he and Kate heading for room 507, the man trudging behind. Kate opened her door and stood back. "After you" she said with exaggerated politeness and a hint of a hiccup. Nichols went in and Kate followed. The man who had been with them in the lift headed on down the corridor. It was, Kate noted, 16 minutes to ten. She would dearly have loved to kick off her high heels, but she knew that they were - in every sense - the last things she should take off. Nicholls headed for the large cupboard under the TV and opened the mini-bar.

Kate took off her jacket and sat down on the small two seater sofa, the king size bed a looming presence in the quite spacious room. Nicholls also took off his jacket and loosened his tie, got out some spirits and mixers, saying that they had a bottle of champagne, but it would probably need a second mortgage to pay for it. He got some glasses and sat down beside her.

"I really don't think I should drink any more" Kate said. Nicholls looked at her somewhat drooping eyes and rather deflated stance as she lolled on the sofa, and decided that he didn't need to push it.

"Are you serious about wanting to change your job?" he asked. "I could certainly keep an eye out for anything going in the company. I don't necessarily mean here in Leeds – this is just a regional office – although it is our research centre as well and there's a lot going on. But we have offices all over the place, as well as the Head Office in London". Kate let her head fall back on to the back of the sofa.

"I don't know" she mumbled, her eyes now more than half-closed. Nichols put his arm lightly across the back of the sofa, just touching rather than holding her shoulder. She didn't move, didn't appear to notice even. He took a swig of his drink, another gin and tonic, and they sat there, in an alcoholic haze, in touch – just – and in silence. Kate stirred very slightly, looking down at her watch, though Nicholls didn't register it. Time was marching on. With her eyes now completely shut, she said, quietly,

"If we're going to have sex, the bed would be a lot more comfortable".

So there it was. He'd actually fucking well done it. No persuasion, no angst, just chat, drinks and into bed. Very adult, he thought. Now don't blow it. A bit of TLC was what the situation called for. He gripped her right shoulder a little

140

more firmly with his right hand, gently putting his left hand under her left elbow, and lifted her up on her feet. He wondered if she'd make it to the bed, but she walked with the extraordinary care of someone who knows they have drunk too much. She slumped on the bed, managing to retain her high heels, and was aware of Nicholls getting onto the bed beside her. She lay there, slowly opened her eyes and gave him an embarrassed smile. He gave her an exploratory kiss on her forehead, ran his hand down her arm, and then put a hand on her breast. He felt the substantial, soft, warm presence through her brassiere and blouse, and felt an erection starting to manifest itself. Please God don't let her suddenly back off now – it would be more than he could bear. Perhaps more than he would bear. After all, she had just agreed to sex; hell, she'd actually proposed it.

Kate didn't respond. He gave her another kiss, this time on her cheek, and carefully undid the top button of her blouse. She still didn't move, and he checked that she hadn't passed out; but she lay there, with her eyes, certainly slightly glazed, but open, watching his hands moving in front of her. He took his time, but four buttons later her blouse was undone and her really magnificent breasts, in a quite flimsy, slightly elastic but clearly very supportive bra – Dr. Emmerson would have been impressed with the combination of strength and lightness he thought – came more fully into view. He stroked one of them. Kate didn't stop him, but she slowly sat up more, eased her blouse off, letting it drop to the floor. She then undid the top of her skirt and eased it off, losing her shoes in the process.

"Don't want to get it crumpet" she said, as much to herself as to Nicholls. It was everything he could do not to burst out laughing. He didn't care if it was a Freudian slip, *double entendre* or just Kate's inebriated state; he'd dine out on that for years. And she wasn't wearing a slip, Freudian or any other sort. What she was wearing, for Christ's sake, was stockings and a suspender belt! You have died and gone to heaven, he thought. She couldn't have come to Leeds like that. She must have bought them that afternoon, which meant she was either very mixed up, or one hell of a sexy lady; and he didn't care which. If Nicholls had had an ounce of sobriety left, or even an ounce of self-knowledge, he would, at this point of no return, have registered at least the merest pang of suspicion. He was not paying for a night with a high-class Leeds prostitute; he was seducing a low level administrator from the finance department of Oxford University – someone who hadn't even met him before today. But his mind was quite elsewhere – how to get his clothes off and hoping he wouldn't ejaculate before he'd got inside her.

For the moment he seemed mesmerized by her bust. He leant over and kissed one of her breasts, just above the top of her bra and, in an action which Kate seemed not to notice, but amazed him, he yanked his shirt, only unbuttoned at

141

the top, plus his loose tie, over his head and off. He ran a hand down one of her thighs, then briefly sat up, kicked off his shoes and slipped effortlessly out of his trousers.

Kate lay there, prone and, he noticed that she was even less eyes-open than before. She may not remember too much about this, he thought, but she's there for the taking. He lay back by her side, then leant half on top of her, and moved his hand towards the crotch of her knickers.

Kate intercepted his hand. "Now, now, not so fast" she said, "not so fast. This isn't wham-bam- thank-you-mam. You wouldn't want me to think you were trying to take advantage of me" she giggled. Vaguely, at the back of her mind, she made a note that perhaps she wouldn't after all be going for that screen test in Hollywood. Only a total idiot would believe such a load of bullshit. But she had gone as far as she was going, and it was now time just to hold out.

There followed several minutes in which Nicholls indulged in increasingly persistent groping; and Kate felt herself start to panic. She managed to keep his attention, or at least his hands, above her waist, but she had, she now realised, moved a little too fast, and she was under no misapprehension of the difficulty she could soon be in. Then, at last, she heard a tiny click. Nicholls, now fully on top of her, and finally managing to pull her bra down to expose her nipples, was breathing heavily and didn't notice it. The door opened and Nicholls became aware that they were not alone. He swung back, heaving his body off Kate's, and Kate swung her head sideways, her hair falling across her face. Almost instantly the room seemed to explode. A large burst of light, then another and another, accompanied by a loud clicking, at a rate of three per second but Nicholls was not to know this. Even Kate, who had been expecting it, in fact waiting for it with increasing desperation, was shaken. Nicholls just lay there, completely stunned. It was barely three or four seconds, but it was enough for around a dozen photographs to be taken before Nicholls began to realise what was happening. Even then, like Kate, he was completely blinded by the flash bulbs and couldn't see much of the room, still less the man with the camera.

"What the hell...." He started to say as Kate, shaking and feeling quite drugged, which in a way she was, leapt off the bed and grabbed at her blouse and skirt. "I'm sorry Mr. Nicholls, but that is as far as it goes. We need to talk".

Nicholls' eyesight had recovered enough for him to recognise the photographer as the man who had come up in the lift with them. Kate must have handed him the little plastic key after she had, oh so cleverly, ushered him into her room.

"You fucking bitch" he screamed. "You fucking, fucking bitch. I'll fucking well kill you". He got off the bed and started to move round to where Kate was beginning to put her blouse back on.

"I don't think so" said the man with the camera, and Nicholls sensed that he was rather formidable looking. "You've had more fun than most men get without paying for it; and I suggest we all calm down a bit". Drunk and angry, Nicholls made to go past him, heading for Kate, but the man put out his arm. "Mr. Nicholls, sit down or I will beat you to a bloody pulp". He said it quietly, not particularly menacingly, but he accompanied it with very intense eye-contact that left Nicholls in no doubt that he was very serious.

"You fucking bastard" said Nicholls, but he was sobering up fast, or at least trying to come to grips with the situation. He sat down on the bed. "What the fuck is this all about anyway? I took her out for dinner, and she invited me up to her room. She even suggested having sex with me. So if this is some sort of attempt to blackmail me over a rape charge you can go fuck yourself. I'll bloody well sue the pair of you, and when it comes to suing people, I know what I'm doing".

As he spoke, the photographer produced some sheets of paper which he had retrieved from some equipment he carried with him, while Kate put her skirt back on. "Have a look at these Mr. Nicholls. They show you in your underpants – in this one at least it is very evident that you have an erection – next to Miss Mortimer, who is dressed only in her underwear, with her breasts exposed. There will not be the slightest doubt to anyone who sees these that you were interrupted in a sexual encounter with her. This will not be a source of great embarrassment to her as – look – you can barely make out her face. In any event she is unmarried, does not have a partner. She is just a thoroughly normal, heterosexual 33 year old woman wanting some sex. You, however, Mr. Nicholls are married with three children. Can we move on?"

"You'll show them to Pat?" scoffed Nicholls. A vicious smile crossed his lips. "Bloody well show them to her. I'll probably go up in her estimation. You haven't done your homework very well, have you?" he spat the words out with all the venom he felt at how he had been set up, and robbed of a night of sex. He started to get dressed. "Go on, show them to her" he almost shouted. "See if I care".

"Please don't underestimate me, Mr. Nicholls" said the man calmly. "That would be a serious error. Pat will certainly get a copy. So will your children, the parents of their friends, your friends and your work colleagues. They will show you attempting to have sex with someone very much dressed as a professional sex-worker. If none of that causes you any concern, then I think our business is concluded".

"Business, what business?" exploded Nicholls. "Anyway, it will be bloody obvious that it is some sort of blackmail. I don't know if the police will be able to track you down, but they'll certainly get bloody fucking little Miss Mortimer here. She's in the photographs too, in case you hadn't noticed" he sneered.

"I did tell you not to underestimate me, Nr. Nicholls". There are at least three in which Miss Mortimer's own mother wouldn't recognise her; and if there were any doubt, I can touch them up digitally, just to make sure. So, I think we are done here. Mr. Nicholls clearly likes taking risks". He gathered up his equipment and moved towards the door.

"I'm sorry" said Kate again. "It could have been so much easier, and we could have avoided all this; but you have clearly made your mind up". She turned to join the photographer.

"You bitch" re-iterated Nicholls, now almost dressed. "What is it you want? It's not money is it? It's something to do with Emmerson isn't it? And you are no more a finance officer from Oxford University than you are a good fuck". His rage was now really building, but the prospect of the photos being distributed so widely was beginning to rattle him. It would mean his job, and his marriage and, rather to his surprise, that suddenly felt very bad. Moreover, he dimly began to see that there might be some sort of way out.

Kate spoke as calmly as she could, still trembling with shock from everything that happened. "I want to know four things. If you tell me them and if, when I follow up on them, what you tell me proves to be accurate then the photos will never be seen again, provided no-one ever hears anything about tonight

"And the four things would be what?" snarled Nicholls.

"The company Dr. Emmerson was working with on your behalf; the nature of your 'interest' in the company; the nature of the work Dr. Emmerson was doing for you; and the main point of contact with the other company in relation to Dr. Emmerson's work. No mention will be made of your name; in fact if I contact them I will deny all knowledge of you. My name is not Jane Mortimer; so there is no way anyone could trace our connection. That's it".

"Why do you want to know" said Nicholls, "and who the hell are you. What do you want? There would have been some money to be made before Emmerson disappeared – a bit of profitable insider trading - but that's all gone now. I told you before, there's no deal anymore".

"Well, it can't be much of a problem to tell me what I want to know then, can it?" said Kate, surprised to find that she was beginning to feel just a flicker of sympathy for this rather pathetic man, because he clearly couldn't understand what was going on.

"You set all this up just to get this information?" he asked.

"I'd hoped that you might just tell me" replied Kate. "But I needed a back-up plan. I checked you were married via the telephone directory – if you wife says that the secretary of an old colleague of yours, just in the UK for a day or two, called, I wouldn't bother to follow it up. At least you will know what it is about, which two other D. Nicholls won't. And then I found, lets call him Dave here, who does security work. It only took two calls to find someone who knew him and his….. relevant skills. His is a purely professional interest by the way. But this isn't really moving us forward, is it? I do need that information".

"Would you have let me screw you - if you had to - to get the answers" asked Nicholls. "You've got a fucking sexy body – I'd have told you everything for another half hour".

Kate managed to resist most of the sense of degradation he was deliberately heaping on her, though not all of it. She was beginning to see what a truly awful thing she had done, started to be shocked at her capacity to carry it through. She needed to recall the sense of loss and helplessness that had set her on this path and, just at this moment, with Nicholls steadily deflating in front of her, she was having some difficulty in doing that.

"There was never any chance that I would have had sex with you" she said "and I'm sorry that I suggested it. You were supposed to do that, but I was getting as sloshed as you were, and we were starting to run out of time".

"I hope you feel really good about all this tomorrow" said Nicholls. "What a bitch" he added, half to himself, and then finally succumbed. "The company is British Nuclear Ltd. We were thinking of making an agreed takeover bid. Emmerson was part of a programme of checking their sites, all their main installations. Structural integrity is vital, and he was helping us with that. I don't know the details. Only Werner does. But I told you, the deal's off since Emmerson disappeared. It can't be anything to do with the deal because we are all pissed off – we've all lost an opportunity to make big money. Why do you need to know more? Why all this fucking charade?"

It had, in the end, been no big deal to tell her. He wasn't making anything up. There wasn't anything to go for, whoever she was – journalist maybe, free-lance money-grubber. The increasingly pre-dominant thought in his mind was her wonderful breasts popping out of her bra. It would, he hoped, be a long time before he forgot that.

"And who would Dr. Emmerson have worked with at British Nuclear?" Kate asked, bringing him back to the here and now. "Or who, at least, was the main contact?"

"A guy called Brasher, Colin Brasher. In fact he is Sir Colin Brasher, their Chief Scientist; but he's one of those Whitehall warriors, don't ask me what or why. Now give me the photos and sod off".

The photographer, who by now had packed up all his equipment, handed them over. "You realise that the lady will have copies, just as insurance against you contemplating anything foolish?"

Nicholls didn't bother to reply. "You bloody well make sure you don't mention me…" he said to Kate belligerently, but couldn't complete the sentence with any credible threat. "Now fuck off the pair of you" he said and walked out. He started planning what he was going to say to Pat.

"Thank you for your help" said Kate, to Christopher Barnett, ex-Special Air Services, now security-cum-private detective, not listed in Yellow Pages but a well known specialist amongst that fraternity. She took a thick envelope out of a drawer and handed it to him. He had cost her £500 for three hours work, two and a half of which had comprised sitting in the lobby of the Hotel Excelsior but it had been well worth it.

"A pleasure, Mam. I have as little idea as he has as to why you want to pursue all this, but I hope it works out. Let me know if I can be of further service"

Barnett left, and Kate collapsed onto the bed, utterly exhausted. But she forced herself to get out of her clothes, wondering why men were so obsessed with suspenders and stockings. Sexier than tights, she could see - even so. But they made sure the photos looked very sleazy, and that had been the main thing. Two minutes later, she passed out.

CHAPTER 10

The meeting next day with her putative author at Leeds University was a real trial. She was hung over, a condition that neither black coffee nor croissants had much corrected; but more difficult was her complete lack of concentration. She could bring none of her expertise to bear on the value of the book under discussion. She had risked a lot to get to where she now was in relation to Paul's disappearance, and she could think of little else but following up the information she had obtained as soon as possible. Above all, who would gain from Paul's disappearance? Nicholls had said no-one. She could readily see that if Paul had found some sort of problem at British Nuclear, then the deal was finished anyway. Paul disappearing would make no difference. And if he hadn't found any problems then his vanishing act was a disaster, putting paid to a merger which could otherwise have gone ahead, to both sides' benefit. Equally, if he had discovered something that was bad news specifically for British Nuclear, then that was precisely why there would have been the confidentiality arrangement to which Nicholls had referred. Major companies didn't go around bumping off distinguished scientists just on the off-chance that they might break such an agreement. It was ridiculous. At this rate it wouldn't be difficult to slip back into thinking that DI Johnson was right after all. Paul, and the takeover bid, were just victims of a random act of violence.

It wouldn't be difficult, but it would be wrong, she told herself – of that she was certain – because his office had been broken into, his laptop and hard disk had gone, and two completely unknown people either pretending to be police officers or from some unknown section or department had been at Paul's office. Someone was very interested indeed in what Paul had been doing, and Kate was confident that it related to his work at British Nuclear. In between these lines of thought, Kate agreed to look at some material supplied by the author in front of her, commission some referees reports and get back to him in due course. The author, who had had dealings in the past with both Cambridge University Press and Manchester University Press came away from their meeting pleased, but aware that publishers could sometimes be a rather flaky lot.

Kate spent a day shoring up her job in Oxford – increasingly it seemed that Janice was doing her job for her – but it increasingly held no interest for her. So she went to see Harry. She re-called that he had offered her some leave if she felt that she needed it. She'd been grateful for the offer but had hoped not to take it up; but was not sleeping at all well, was on prescription drugs – basically Valium – and felt she was letting OUP down. So perhaps she should take three or four weeks off, if Harry thought this could be covered. Harry confirmed that he thought this could be, in fact he was certain because he had become increasingly concerned about Kate, and had actively explored some alternative arrangements prior to 'suggesting' that she took some time off. He was rather relieved that she had taken the initiative herself.

Kate spent the rest of the day handing over all her projects to various others in the Press. Maybe they were overstaffed, as was all too frequently alleged, she thought, given the apparent ease with which her senior role was re-assigned and absorbed by others. But it was only for three or four weeks. Her main conundrum was Hargreaves. She clearly ought to tell him what she had found out, but she remained as reluctant as before, and for the same reasons. He was just too close, maybe not by inclination, but unquestionably too close to Johnson. In any event, the information she'd got from Nicholls wasn't by itself very profound. She would need to see where it led before having anything much useful to tell Hargreaves. That settled in her mind, she tracked down the Head Office address and phone number of British Nuclear Ltd. easily enough, in Victoria, opposite the back of the grounds of Buckingham Palace; called the main switchboard and was put through to the office of the Chief Scientist, Sir Colin Brasher. With a sense of relief at not having to lie quite so much as before, she introduced herself as Anne Williamson, and said that she was an associate of Dr. Emmerson, the Oxford University scientist who had been working with Sir Colin and who had tragically disappeared. Might she fix an appointment to see Sir Colin as certain aspects of the matter – she deliberately left it vague whether this related to their collaboration or the fact that Paul was missing – had emerged which it might be important to discuss with him.

Whoever the representative of Sir Colin's office was, he made no reference to whether the Chief Scientist was there or not, saying that he would consult and ring Miss Williamson back in the morning. Kate left her home number and her mobile number. She then went home and started an internet search on everything she could find out about British Nuclear Ltd. or BNL as it was generally called. It has started life as the Atomic Energy Authority, the governmental body covering both nuclear power and atomic weapons development. It had, over fifty years, become a huge, sprawling empire, its reputation sporadically damaged by accidents, pollution problems, growing awareness of the problems of nuclear waste disposal and the public's increased apprehension about safety issues. The nuclear power stations had eventually been split off into a separate organisation and then, some eighteen years earlier, had been privatised. The sale to private investors had become viable only because the government had agreed to underwrite around £45 billion of eventual de-construction, waste disposal and de-contamination costs, spread over nearly 40 years. With soaring energy prices, the consequence of another bout of severe unrest in the Middle East, in particular the US-led threat to Iranian oil supplies, the privatisation had raised almost a third of the government's underwriting costs for the public coffers, and Her Majesty's Treasury was delighted to have got out of a potentially open-ended commitment so lightly.

Meanwhile, the investors were equally happy. With oil prices over $100 a barrel, and with the ever growing tide of environmental concern about fossil fuels, the government had recently decided, in principle at least, to end its moratorium on the building of new nuclear power stations; and while there were a number of contenders around the world to pursue this opportunity, none was remotely as well-placed as BNL. Its share price had accordingly done quite well. Kate did not expect to find, nor did find, any hint anywhere of any possible bid for BNL by National Energy.

There was a lot more, but she next followed up on Sir Colin Brasher, googling him, noting his heavyweight career, first as an academic, then as a senior scientific civil servant, then Chief Scientist at BNL. Kate wondered to what extent his appointment to the post was down to BNL's trying to expand its networking and PR, rather than Brasher having hands-on control of the company's technical and research capability, because he seemed to have a almost limitless number of other posts, primarily non-executive directorships of other companies but also membership, or in some cases the chairmanship, of at least half a dozen scientific committees of one sort or another. She felt considerable apprehension at the prospect of meeting him; but also felt that she had rather more cards to play than before. She had no confidence that DI Johnson would do much if provided with all the information Kate had gathered, with its collective finger starting to point in some way towards BNL; but she had rather more confidence that Brasher would not know this fact. In the absence of any answers to her questions, therefore, she was quite prepared to intimate that she'd have to leave it to the police to follow the matter up.

Over the next two days her apprehension turned to exasperation as Brasher's office failed to get back to her, not even her answer-phone. Eventually she rang back, was told that, as she would no doubt appreciate, Sir Colin was very busy, but they hoped to get back to her as soon as possible. This sounded as if she was going backwards, and Kate became increasingly sceptical that Brasher would make contact. But then, early the next day, already the Thursday of Kate's first week of leave, Brasher's office called back. Kate's momentary relief soon dissipated, however, as the voice asked if she could please explain what it was that she wanted to discuss with Sir Colin. Kate replied that she had already explained – it was in connection with Dr. Paul Emmerson. Yes, the voice conceded, they understood that, but what specifically was it about Dr. Emmerson that she wished to discuss, and could she please identify what organisation she represented.

Kate dealt with the first question simply by saying that it was a matter on which she would prefer to speak to Sir Colin in person; and parried the second by saying – it being the only thing she could think of quickly – that she worked with the Engineering Department in Oxford. Why did it take so many lies to get to people, she wondered. It was, she added, a matter of some importance and some urgency. The net result was where she had been before, that Sir Colin's office would get back to her. Christ, if it was this difficult even to contact him, what chance did she have of actually having a useful conversation with him? Fortunately, and to her great surprise, she got a call back that afternoon, proposing a meeting at noon the next day, in Sir Colin's London office. It was slow progress but it was, she hoped, progress.

BNL's Head Office was, predictably, all glass and marble, very pale, quite tasteful, Kate had to admit, with a few well-chosen pieces of modern art on display, together with several models of nuclear power stations. She was logged in and tagged and ushered up to the eighth floor, offered coffee and finally, on the dot of noon she noted, led through into a huge modern office. Sir Colin rose from behind a large Georgian partners' desk. He was around sixty Kate guessed, tall, in good shape, distinguished by immaculate silver hair, and with a rather granite-like air, which was exacerbated by a hostile, frowning stare. He indicated for Kate to sit across the desk from him and, without preamble said

" I'd be grateful if you would start by telling me who you are and what this is all about. If you are from the Press, I will certainly be speaking to your Editor".

Kate felt herself blanche, and then start to redden, though noting the irony that she *was* from an organisation known as the Press, in Oxford, but it wasn't the Press that Sir Colin meant; and in any event she had said she was from the University.

"No, I'm not from the Press" she said.

"Well you're not from the Engineering department at Oxford either. I got my PA to check".

Kate wondered briefly whether Alice had put two and two together and was even now waiting to have a showdown with Kate.

"That's correct" said Kate. "I'm sorry that I misled you. I am a friend of Dr. Emmerson's".

"Then why didn't you say?" Brasher responded, still sounding quite angry, but a fraction milder in tone than before. And, Kate noted, a look of genuine puzzlement began to replace the hostility that he had initially exuded. To that thin straw Kate decided to clutch, not that she had much alternative.

"I'm really very sorry about the deception" Kate repeated. "I can see that it was quite wrong, not to mention very rude. It's just that I did need to see you, and I thought that if you knew my only connection with Paul was personal, you might well not see me". She forbore to mention the weeks of no-one offering any help, which had driven her down the path, probably now fruitless, that she was on. Brasher seemed to soften a little, and she pressed home what miniscule advantage she might still have.

"Can I ask why you *did* agree to see me, once you found out I wasn't from the University?"

For a moment Brasher sat in silence, just looking at her. "Let's go and sit over there" he said, pointing to a large leather sofa with two arm chairs, overlooking a rather spectacular view of south west London. He went on "I've known Paul since he was a student" he said. "Not well. We didn't often get the chance to meet up; but I liked him, and admired him as a scientist and as a person. I was delighted when we got the chance to do some work together. You obviously know about that, though how I don't know – I'd be surprised if Paul told you, but we can come back to that – and I was very saddened by what has happened. So although, as you will have gathered, I have a very busy schedule, maybe I would have been quite happy to meet up with someone who knew Paul. But, there again, maybe I wouldn't, so perhaps your … approach…. worked out. Not quite as you planned – virtually no-one outside BNL knew Paul was working for us; so I was curious to know who was willing to risk arrest for impersonation to talk to me about Paul. Which brings us back to where I started – what's this all about, and how *did* you know about his work for BNL?" This time, however, it was said as a real question, and with even an element of sympathy.

150

Kate's instinct was to trust Brasher, and she decided that she would try to be truthful in whatever she said to him. But she couldn't rule out the possibility that BNL was behind Paul's disappearance – indeed it was currently her only hypothesis – and she was not, therefore, by any means ready to tell him everything she knew, not until she knew a lot more about Brasher and about BNL.

"The police think that Paul was just in the wrong place at the wrong time, attacked by someone on drugs or after money to buy drugs, something like that anyway. Well, I don't think they're right – in fact I know they're not. I think it had something to do with his work, quite probably what he was doing here, and so I wanted to talk to you about it. Do you think there could be any reason, stemming from his work at BNL, for his disappearance?"

Brasher sat back, silent, looking thoughtful, even slightly bemused.

"I presume you weren't just a 'friend' of Paul's?"

"No" Kate replied. "We'd been together for some time. Maybe he mentioned me when he met up with you again? My real name is Kate Kimball"

Brasher digested this piece of news impassively. "He mentioned that he had rather settled down. I think I asked him if he had got married yet" There was another pause. "How did you know Paul was working here? Did he tell you? It was commercially very sensitive indeed. So much so that we didn't have any formal contract with him, and I'd be surprised if he was so indiscreet as to tell you, not even pillow talk"

Kate shot him a glance, but saw that he was smiling, at least with his eyes if not his mouth, and she became less tense.

"No, he didn't tell me" she said. "I found out myself – I hope you will forgive me but I'd rather not say any more on that score. I'm sorry" she added rather lamely.

Kate thought that he might revert to a more hostile manner, or at any rate make clear that he wasn't going to be much help to her if she wasn't going to be open with him, but neither happened.

"If you're not with the University, and you're not with the Press, what *do* you do when not engaged on your own private detective agency work?" Again the smile in the eyes, even a slight grin this time.

"I work in publishing, the academic division of Oxford University Press. That's how I met Paul". Another pause

"I see. Why do you think his disappearance has something to do with his work?"

Kate wanted to explain, about the missing laptop and Paul's consultancy files, about the break-in, the lack of police interest, the unexplained callers at the laboratory, but it was too much to give away, especially to someone in BNL, even if she was beginning to warm to this scion of the scientific establishment.

151

"He had some files in Oxford, files he shouldn't have kept there. You said that you've known Paul a long time; so you would know that he is honest and responsible. He wouldn't do something like that unless there was a very good reason. And then he disappears, without trace. I just don't believe the police theory".

"Do you mean computer files?" asked Brasher. Kate nodded.

"How did you get access to them?"

"I didn't. I haven't, but I know they exist" She could almost feel him sizing her up, wondering whether to push her further or not. Before he could she attempted, for the first time since she'd entered the room, to gain the initiative.

"I'm not a scientist, I have only the vaguest idea of Paul' work, and I know almost nothing about BNL. But I'd like to know what he was doing, maybe talk to whoever he was working with him at BNL, and see if it throws any light, any at all, on why it might have put Paul in danger. I came here to ask if you can help me – either what you know yourself, or through any contacts you can give me"

"I'd need to think about that" said Brasher

"I understand that, but I don't have much time before I have to go back to work" Kate noticed a rather unattractive pleading tone in her voice. She played her one remaining card.

"It wasn't easy coming to see you. I'm putting a huge amount of trust in you; and if I'm wrong in that judgment, I may even be putting myself in danger". Brasher raised an interrogative eye-brow.

"Paul worked on structures, stresses on them, fractures, structural integrity. He must have been doing similar sort of work on some of your installations. If he came across something irregular, or maybe something dangerous, BNL would have a big incentive to keep it quiet. I don't mean ignoring something that was unsafe, but you wouldn't want the world knowing about the problem, maybe mistakes made by BNL, the costs of putting things right. If Paul knew about such things he might become a real threat, to you, to your company. And then he disappears. So, will you tell me, did Paul discover something harmful to BNL's interests?"

Even as she spoke, she realised the likely futility of her question. If there was something suspicious – if Paul had come across something unpalatable to BNL, it was not very likely that Brasher, the Company's Chief Scientist, was going to tell her. And she hadn't been melodramatic in speculating that she might even be putting herself in danger.

"That was quite a little speech" replied Brasher, in a neutral tone. He stood up and walked to the window, obviously thinking hard before replying. Kate literally held her breath. Then he turned.

"I'd like to help you" he said. "I'm not just saying that. I admired Paul, a lot; and I can see how distressing this is for you. But you must understand that I can't discuss BNL business with you. All I can say, if it is any use, is that nothing Paul was doing here would have led to his disappearance. It's just not realistic. I know you only have my word for that, but please believe me. I'm sorry I can't say more".

So, thought, Kate, this is how it ends. She wouldn't be able to find another way into BNL. Any inquiries she made would undoubtedly end up on Brasher's desk. She sat there, silent, devastated beyond words, looking down at her hands in her lap. Slowly, a tear trickled down her cheek. Brasher, embarrassed, started to say something.

"No, no" said Kate, holding up her hands "I'm sorry, I just can't ......" What she couldn't do was left unsaid. "It's just that..... I can accept Paul's loss if I know what happened; and I can even accept that he was the victim of a mugging if there is no other explanation. But unless I know that it couldn't have been anything else, I'm in a sort of terrible limbo, a......" again words failed her. "Could you not help me just a little, enough to know, for myself, that it was nothing to do with BNL. I'm not going to say a word about this to anyone else – no-one else is involved – and if there really is nothing sinister about it, surely there can't be any problem about telling me?" Please" she added; and it was no contrived effect that her voice cracked with emotion, and her shoulders beginning to shudder as she started to cry. "I'm sorry" she repeated.

"Please don't" said Brasher. "I'm the one who's sorry. Look, if I tell you the background, will you please keep it confidential? It's not the matter itself – just that I shouldn't be talking outside the company. I don't want to add to your..... distress" was all he could think to repeat. Kate looked up.

"I give you my word, I will not repeat anything you tell me. I just need to know".

"Well" said Brasher "you ask whether Paul found anything damaging to BNL's interests. The answer to your question is 'yes' " he said, "and 'no'". Kate said nothing, aware that she was quite disoriented, as much by the admission that she might, just conceivably be on the right track as by the ambiguity of Brasher's answer.

"Yes" continued Brasher "in that Paul's work did reveal a significant problem for BNL that we would not have otherwise been aware of - a serious structural weakness in one of our re-processing plants. We estimate it will cost around £150 million to correct. And, no, this discovery - the fact that Paul knew it - did not remotely put Paul in any sort of danger. The extra cost is a nuisance, but we currently plan to invest nearly £4 billion in our existing or new plant over the next three years; so this extra cost is fairly much at the margins – at worst it might delay a smaller project or two by a year. In fact we already had plans to spend over £300 million on renovation and improvements in the re-processing plant where the problem was identified; so the extra cost is hardly earth-shattering. We've closed it down of course, and that could lose us some revenue but, again, not much. We've just brought forward the work we planned anyway, so the additional lost revenue will be fairly minimal. We haven't made any public announcement, and we don't intend to, but if we did tomorrow, the share price might wobble a few per cent for a few days and then revert to roughly where it was. I can see that you might have thought BNL could have had something to do with Paul's disappearance; but it didn't, it couldn't have had, and I'm afraid that the police explanation, however banal- and all the more tragic for that – is probably the correct one".

Kate felt stunned, almost literally, just as if someone had hit her on the head. There were too many unanswered questions for her to accept the random mugger theory; but if what Brasher had said was true, she was truly at a dead end. Yet, inexplicably, she felt hugely invigorated.

"Quite a little speech of your own" she said eventually. "You're certain it's all true?" What she meant to say - wanted to say - was 'why should I believe all that?' but didn't have the resilience to question his honesty so directly.

Brasher smiled, a rather sad smile, seeing Kate's dilemma and her rather unsuccessful attempt to deal with it.

"Yes, quite certain" he said, very calmly "In the circumstances, I'd be happy to provide you with the evidence – it's not that difficult to understand - but the clearest evidence is the fact that I've told you all this. I've no way of stopping you from talking to the Press – the story would make an inner page of the *Financial times;* and possibly the Business Section of the *Daily Telegraph* – but, as I said, we'd come through it fairly easily. It's simply not something that anyone would commit murder for".

Kate's mind, in turmoil, was still in questioning mode, but her instincts were clear – she had little doubt that Brasher was telling the truth. So, what now?

"Does National Energy know about this?" she asked, clutching at straws. Brasher, barely perceptibly, nodded to himself.

"I thought you must know about the takeover talks. I'm really curious to know how you found out, but I won't push you. And yes, they do know. I told my counterpart there as soon as I heard from Paul, and how we would deal with it. The problem didn't remotely threaten the deal – it was Paul's disappearance that did that. It just raised too many questions in their mind. Werner – he's the man responsible for their research side – visibly got cold feet. I'd hoped that we might pick up the threads again later, but he rang me a couple of days ago in a real panic – said that the police wanted to talk to him. I can't see why that should be a problem for him, and he says that it isn't – just that he doesn't cope with officialdom very well".

With her quest, her project, more or less dead, Kate felt a moment of sheer recklessness.

"You can tell him that they won't be pursuing him" she said, with a deadpan expression. For the first time since they'd met, Brasher's composure slipped. He stared at her, registering the implication of what she had said, mentally rejecting it, realising that he couldn't reject it, slowly absorbing it. Then that smile again. He sat down again.

"My God, you are quite extraordinary. Maybe extraordinarily foolish, but quite extraordinary". He wanted to say how lucky he thought Paul had been, to have a girl-friend like this, but it didn't seem right. "I don't think we should discuss that particular aspect any more".

"I agree" said Kate, but aware that her indiscretion – the vulnerability that she had presented to Brasher - had significantly changed the atmosphere.

"So, if both National Energy and BNL are losers from what happened to Paul, who gains? Your competitors?" Brasher had still not fully got his mind back in gear after what Kate had revealed, but sought to recover his equilibrium.

"In theory, I suppose; but the business we are in is totally global. The merger would have made us the biggest player in the UK, but all our main competitors are overseas – US, Japan, German, and Indian and Chinese pretty soon – and we would have still only been about the fifth or sixth largest. Similar mergers have been going on elsewhere. No-one's going to lose much sleep over this merger; and anyway, we took great care to make sure no-one else knew about the possibility, and none of our competitors could have known that Paul was working on the project. Even if, somehow, they had known, getting rid of Paul would have been a bizarre way to try to kill the deal – at best it will probably only delay matters. It just doesn't add up".

Kate couldn't fault the logic in any way. Maybe it was all bullshit, a convincing performance from a consummate operator but, if so, it *was* convincing, sufficiently so that she didn't have the stomach, the mental reserves, to question it. Time to go, she thought.

"Did *anyone* else know about Paul's work?" she asked, fairly confident that she knew the answer "Apart from National Energy and you?"

"Only a couple of civil servants at the Department of Energy" replied Brasher.

The answer surprised Kate. "How did they know?"

Once again Brasher paused, wondering how much to tell this really rather remarkable young woman. But the chemistry – the alchemy even – had changed, somewhere in the conversation. He had nothing to hide, but he had nonetheless seen her as an intrusion, someone he wouldn't have wasted any time on but for his curiosity. Now he genuinely wanted to help.

"Paul's method of testing materials was revolutionary, and remarkably sensitive. Where it revealed weaknesses - I'm talking about ones too fine to be detected by traditional methods, and far too small to be visible in any way to the naked eye – it could normally distinguish between different causes – corrosion, overload, shock waves, whatever - by the pattern of molecular displacement. He told me that there was clear evidence from his research that the re-processing plant had been subject to some sort of explosive force, and wanted to know if I had any information on that. I was absolutely certain that there hadn't been anything that could have caused such an effect since BNL was privatised; but couldn't be certain before that, when the organisation was in public hands. So, I asked my main contact in the Department of Energy. He had to consult someone else, perhaps a couple of people – I'm not sure - before confirming that there was no record of any explosion in the re-processing plant. Frankly, my contact was rather incredulous at the suggestion, and I mentioned Paul's work as a way of indicating that there was some serious research behind my question. Paul was a big fish in the energy world you know".

"Could the Department of Energy have any reason to want to silence Paul?" asked Kate. "Maybe there was some incident at the plant and they wanted to keep it secret?"

"I really think that is being fanciful" said Brasher. "The Department is as keen for the merger to go through as anyone – creating a so-called 'National Champion' in the industry, even though that's a concept heavily frowned on these days. I explained to them that we would be able to take care of the problem at the plant. Paul was no threat. Frankly, the whole thing is much more likely to become public knowledge as a result of the mystery surrounding Paul's disappearance than if we were just left to deal with the matter as part of the refurbishment plans for the plant. No-one would be any the wiser" He paused, then added darkly "And since we are being very open with each other, let me tell you that there were a number of incidents – potentially very serious nuclear accidents - in the early days, which no-one got to hear about until many years later, including at least one that has caused a significant rise in cancers near one of our installations. Some sort of explosion inside a re-processing plant, presumably a fairly minor one given that the plant has kept going for a good many years – if it happened at all – is not going to be headline news. Anyway, civil servants don't go around knocking people off just because of the potential for some embarrassment long in the past, - at least not in the Department of Energy!" he added with a flourish and a sympathetic grin.

More impeccable logic and, again, Kate did not doubt the truth of what Brasher had said. But it was so frustrating - lots of progress in finding out more about the whole situation, and no progress at all in finding out what had happened to Paul. It was like pulling oneself along a rope, in the hope of finding something at the end of it, only to find each time just another piece of rope.

"Would you let me know the name of your contact in the Department of Energy?" asked Kate, thinking it unlikely that Brasher would divulge the information; and not knowing what she would say to the civil servant even if Brasher did give her his name.

"I can't do that, as I'm sure you realise" replied Brasher. "I've been far too indiscreet as it is – and if you ask why so, it's because I had a very high regard for Paul, I'm really sorry that you have had this loss, and I'd like to help – and so I am trusting you to respect the fact that all this information is in strict confidence. But if the Department was to know that I had talked to you, and told you about my discussion with them, my career would come to a rather abrupt end".

"I could find out, in some other way" said Kate in a slightly mischievous way.

"I have little doubt that you will" said Brasher "I hope you do – but not from me. Now, I think I need to get back to my schedule - it is rather heavy".

"Yes, I'm sorry to have kept you so long. Thank you for your time".

He stood and Kate did the same. Brasher put his hand on her arm and looked intently at her.

"Will you give me your word that you will not tell anyone – and I do mean anyone – about our conversation? I have been very frank with you, because I can see how distressing the situation is for you; but I hope you will respect my frankness, not abuse it".

Kate did not hesitate. "I give you my word" she said, rather solemnly. "And thanks again for your time. I hope we might meet again - if ever the truth comes out".

"I'd enjoy that" said Brasher, and they headed for the door.

"There is just one last thing – where is the re-processing plant that Paul was concerned about?"

"I suppose I can tell you that" said Brasher. "BNL has four main sites, but I'm sure you will find out that all our re-processing work is carried out at Sellafield in Cumbria. I really must go now".

CHAPTER 11

On her train journey back to Oxford, Kate thought long and hard about what to do next. By the time the train pulled in to Oxford station, she had decided on three courses of action. The first was simply to avoid Alice. What she would make of someone contacting Sir Colin and pretending to be from Alice's department, heaven only knew. At some point Kate would have to decide whether to admit to the deception or not but, for the moment, she couldn't really face this; and so she would give the Engineering department a wide berth. Fortunately, she was on leave - it would not be surprising therefore if she was not around for a while. Second, she decided she would call Hargreaves, to see what, if anything more, he had found out; but she placed no great weight on this producing much useful information. More promising in her mind was the other decision she had taken.

She arrived home, rang Hargreaves and, predictably, couldn't get hold of him. She left a message for him to ring her. Next, she went to the Bodleian library – as the Press was wholly owned by the University, senior members of the OUP management were entitled to have a so-called 'Bod-card' which allowed access to the Bodleian Library. There she settled herself at a computer station and in a few minutes had accessed the archive service of *The Times*. She typed in 'Atomic Energy Authority' and was rewarded with the information that there were over 7,000 references to the AEA in the previous fifty years. She wasn't interested in the last eighteen years when BNL had been in private hands, but then she anticipated that relatively few of the references would be in that period. If she could check them at the rate of three a minute – she only needed to scan each one quickly to se if it referred in any way to an accident of some sort at Sellafield, or Windscale as it had previously been known – then it would take her about 40 hours to check the lot. But it might be a lot quicker. It sounded from Brasher as if Paul had been fairly confident concerning the cause of the structural weakness he had found, yet the Department of Energy had come up with nothing. So perhaps the event she was looking for was quite a long time ago. If she started in the fifties – as early as she could go – then she might discover something in rather less than 40 hours. She mentally set aside the next few days and returned home.

To her surprise, she had a message from Hargreaves. She rang him back and was put through. He asked her how she was, and she said she was fine – which was ridiculous but she didn't want to get side-tracked – and asked him what information he had gathered.

"I've nothing new on the media coverage I'm afraid. Just like a standard D notice, no explanation given, and no-one I have spoken to has any explanation either. There's slightly more on Johnson and the inquiry. He's opened a file on the unauthorised entry into the Engineering laboratory, and linked it to the Emmerson file; and he has been to see the Administrator at the laboratory. But there doesn't appear to be anything missing, no damage, so it's not being given much attention. Johnson seems rather bemused, but I can't discuss it with him. Now, why don't you tell me what you have been doing?"

"Not a lot" Kate lied. "But the break-in, Paul's missing lap-top, gagging the Oxford Mail, the two other officers who visited his laboratory, all say that something was going on – is going on – and that's why Paul was not a mugging victim, whatever it may suit Johnson to believe. So, I have been finding out more about what Paul was doing in recent months".

"And what have you found out?" asked Hargreaves.

"About his work, quite a lot. About why he might have disappeared, very little, if anything. But there is a reason tucked away somewhere, and I'm going to plod on until I find it".

For a moment, neither spoke, then Hargreaves said

"Do you want to tell me about it – what you have found out - not officially of course, but maybe over a drink? Two heads and all that. I won't say anything to Johnson – indeed he'd blow my head off if he ever found out I was still…. pursuing the matter. Whatever Rules of Engagement you want".

Kate recognised that this was a critical moment, and her first instinct was to avoid it, to say that she would think about his suggestion. But that didn't solve anything. Either she was going to do this all on her own, or she was going to need help; and if the latter then Hargreaves was the obvious choice – the only choice in fact. There was little to be gained by delaying the issue. Well, she trusted him – that was one thing – and some help would be really good, at the very least someone to bounce ideas off, even just some company in which she could talk about her 'project'.

"That would be nice" she said, feeling that she sounded very prim. How about 6.30 pm tomorrow, the Head of the River pub should be convenient for you".

"Perfect" said Hargreaves, the pub being virtually next door to the police station. And just in case she started to change her mind he said

"Got to go now, see you then" and rang off.

Kate slowly replaced the telephone. I hope that was the right decision, she thought, but her spirits felt somewhat lifted, which was something.

The next day was spent methodically going through the newspaper archive at the Bodleian Library. Kate found she could go much faster than she had anticipated, because the headline alone was usually enough to tell her that the article had no interest for her. By the time she stopped for a late lunch, she had already got through nearly a thousand. The pleasure she felt at moving so fast was dampened only by the fact that, so far, her search had revealed nothing remotely relevant. By the time she left to meet Hargreaves, she was into the 1970s and, while she had found references to two incidents at the Windscale plant, neither concerned the re-processing plant, or any sort of explosion at the site.

When she arrived at the pub, Hargreaves was already there, and offered to buy the drinks. He returned with a relaxed smile.

"We'd better start with names. As this is entirely unofficial – by mutual consent – may I call you Kate? You can certainly call me Neil". He put on a slightly exaggerated quizzical smile.

"That's fine" she replied "But I'm not likely to be much company, and I've no small talk. I'm sorry"

"Understood. Why don't you just tell me what you have been doing? I'm a good listener"

So Kate told him. About the missing computer disks, and how she had visited National Energy and found out about Paul's work at BNL, though omitting to say how she had managed this. She also omitted any reference to her meeting with Sir Colin Brasher, saying only that she hadn't discovered any reason why BNL might want Paul gone. But she told him that she thought the answer might relate to some problem that had occurred at the Sellafield plant some years ago, and that she was looking back through newspaper archives for any clue as to what it might be. That, she told herself was more or less everything – not the fact that some civil servants in the Department of Energy knew about Paul's work, and not her other plans – plans she would pursue irrespective of whether the archives produced anything tangible – but otherwise, Neil knew as much as she did.

Hargreaves mulled over what she had said. He very much wanted to offer some useful observations, better still some suggestions as to how to proceed but, apart from her continuing to hunt through the archive, he had little - in fact nothing – to add. Eventually he said as much.

"Put that all together and, I agree, it seems much more likely that Paul's death relates in some way to his work – Johnson is way off beam". Both of them noted, without commenting, that Paul's disappearance had now become his death. Much as she had accepted this, the word still shook Kate. But she forced herself to stay calm.

"I'll push on with the archive" she said. "What I don't understand at all is who else is interested in all this. I'm guessing that the man who broke into Paul's office stole the computer disk, but who was he, and why was he so keen to get hold of Paul's results; and why was Johnson so determined to wrap the whole matter up; and who were the other two men who called? Is there any way you can find out anything about them?"

"I'll see what I can do" said Hargreaves, relieved to offer some apparent help, but at the same time realising he had not the slightest idea how to pursue this. Sadly, there seemed little more to say – he had vaguely hoped that they might have some supper together – but the conversation had reached a natural end. They rose, she thanked him for his help and they left, agreeing to stay in touch.

Next morning, Kate went back to the library and headed on through the newspaper articles. It was tiring work because of the need to concentrate; and she had mixed emotions as she sailed through 1981, the year Windscale changed its name to Sellafield. It was progress, but she had come up with precisely nothing so far. Shortly before 1 pm – she was thinking that she would take a break shortly for a sandwich – she came across an article about an electrical failure at the Sellafield plant. She moved rapidly on, had actually clicked to go to the next article, which promptly appeared, but a word in the previous article remained imprinted on her retina – 'explosion'. She clicked to go back. The article, from page 2 of *The Times* for 14th November 1983 was, as the headline indicated, about a rather spectacular electrical failure at the plant. A major transmission line carrying 33,000 volts from the plant to the National Grid had burnt through where it connected to a pylon, which in turn had collapsed, causing the mother of all short circuits. The output of the power station had had to be reduced by 15 per cent for several days until the power cables could be repaired. None of it seemed to relate to anything Paul might have worked on, but a local resident had been interviewed and said that there had been a huge flash in the night-time sky 'like a big explosion'.

That was it, and Kate's spirits, temporarily lifted, sank. No doubt the accident was very dramatic – a huge flash, probably not unlike a massive lightening strike – and one that could easily be mistaken, in the shock of the moment, for an explosion - but nothing to do with Paul. She went to click the mouse to move on as she read the last line of the article 'The pylon was close to the main re-processing plant at Sellafield, but a spokesman confirmed that the plant had not been damaged'.

Kate sat and stared at the sentence. She had virtually programmed herself to focus on, to pick up on the words 'explosion' and 're-processing plant' and here was an article with both phrases in it – but there had been no explosion and no damage to the re-processing plant! It seemed almost like a cruel trick, specifically designed to wind her up into a screwball of tension but with absolutely no actual link to what she was looking for. In fact, the more she thought about it, the more it seemed a complete red herring. If there had been an explosion in the re-processing plant then , unless it had destroyed the plant – which manifestly it hadn't – then it would not be apparent to anyone outside, be it in the middle of the night or not. She sat there, her breath very short as she played around in her mind with all the possible permutations she could think of; but nothing emerged. Could the pylon have collapsed onto the re-processing plant and caused the sort of shock wave pattern – or whatever it was - that Paul had discovered. It wasn't just implausible, it was completely insane. She had never seen a re-processing plant, but had little doubt that they were built on a monumental scale. In fact she doubted that the Titanic or a small asteroid hitting it would do much damage, let alone some twisted pieces of metal. Just not a runner she told herself; and her rudimentary school physics was sufficient to tell her that mere electricity – even 33,000 volts of it – could not produce shock waves in concrete. Reluctantly, she put the matter into a mental file called 'sod's law' or 'irritating coincidence', went and had a sandwich, and, in her own words 'plodded on' throughout the afternoon.

By 5 pm the next evening she had gone through every AEA reference and found nothing that could, by any stretch of the imagination, be a lead to Paul's work. The 1983 incident still riled her, but she knew it didn't fit, and so it was time for plan B. She rang Hargreaves's number and left a message saying that she was going to be away for a few days, and then looked up train times.

Shortly before 11 am the next morning she caught a train from Oxford, changed at Birmingham New Street, and by late afternoon was at Carlisle. There she hired a car and set off west, following the road to Cockermouth, on to Cleator Moor and then to Egremont, past the Eastern end of Sellafield, and eventually turning off right at Gosforth, heading for the small town, not a lot more than a village, of Seascale, a couple of miles south down the coast from Sellafield.

Some large houses along the cliff top above a long sandy beach suggested that Seascale had once been an attractive seaside location; but its character, Kate soon realised, had greatly changed in more recent times. Much of the road into the town comprised long stretches of early post war council housing, no doubt related to the growth of the Sellafield plant; and in the fading light of late afternoon on a grey, blustery day in early April, it held little attraction. But what Kate took to be the older part of the town, lying closest to the sea, did produce two surprises. The first was its layout, which was quite unlike anything Kate had ever seen before. Shaped like an hour glass, it had one section on the north cliffs, with a railway line between the large cliff top houses and the beach; and one section on the south cliffs but this time between the railway line and the beach, with only a minor coast road separating the houses from the sea. Between these two areas, at the centre point of the hourglass, the main road in from the north took a dip, narrowed to single track and, via a Z-bend which, in the circumstances must have been one of the most lethal in the country, disappeared under the railway line, emerging next to a small row of shops and a large car park on the south side of town. Kate discovered all this as she drove round looking for a comfortable looking pub with rooms to let, where she might stay for a couple of nights.

This revealed the other surprise, namely that Seascale appeared to have no pubs at all. Kate stopped in the car park and looked at the ordnance survey map of the area which she had picked up at a newsagent's at Carlisle station, and this also failed to identify any pubs. Only as she gazed across the car park to the row of shops did she notice that none had been built as shops. Rather they were all converted from the ground floor of a terraced row of houses; and Kate began to realise the extent to which the place was really just one big housing estate, laid down as Sellafield emerged from nowhere to become the largest single employer in the north of England.

Kate's map told her that she would find an inn back at Gosforth, on the main road; but she decided to take one more drive through Seascale. Having risked life and limb again by driving back through the chicane beneath the railway, she turned left through the northern part of town and was pleased that she had. A large building on her left, overlooking the sea, announced itself to be the Calder House Hotel which, much to her surprise given the rest of the town, advertised the Chapters Bar as one of its attractions. It was a rather gaunt building – what the local Council might have come up with if it had decided to go in for hotels rather than houses; but she parked opposite and headed for the entrance door at the side. As she arrived, the door swung back and an extraordinarily large man - tall, barrel-chested – and almost completely bald, wearing a white tee-shirt, held it open for her. Kate was somewhat taken aback, but the man smiled, and asked her in a friendly voice and comforting tone whether she wanted to check in. Kate, who had planned to have a drink in the bar first before committing herself, no longer felt this was a viable strategy. She said that she needed a room for a couple of nights, maybe longer and less than three minutes later, courtesy of the man who was as efficient as he was large, found herself installed in an unpretentious but perfectly comfortable ground floor room with a double bed, bathroom next door and a view over the Irish Sea, The sun was now just sinking beneath the horizon, bathing the sea and some windswept clouds in a misty red aura, and she felt decidedly better about Seascale.

A little later she headed for Chapters Bar, which also proved to be a surprise. L-shaped, with a lot of attractive wood panelling, and even some shelves of old books, it had a slightly country house feel to it; and by the time a cheery middle-aged woman behind the bar had poured her a glass of wine, she felt quite at ease in this remote part of West Cumbria. Over the next twenty minutes or so, over a dozen people arrived, in ones and twos and, not surprisingly, they all very such seemed to know each other. Kate sat at a table by herself, wondering how best to make her next move but, in the end, it all happened fairly naturally. She went to the bar for a second glass of wine, and the woman serving her asked if she would be wanting to have dinner. Kate had seen the dining room on her way in – another rather charming room, with immaculately laid tables and its own view of the sea – and readily accepted. This led the woman easily on to ask Kate whether it was work or holiday that had brought her to these parts, and Kate launched in to her prepared piece. She was writing an article about the impact of rapid industrialisation on rural communities; and the coming of Sellafield to one of the most inaccessible areas in Britain, a narrow strip of land tucked behind the hills of the Lake District, might provide some particularly interesting insights. She was hoping to talk to some of those still resident in the area who had lived there throughout the rise of such a major employer, to ask how it had affected their lives and livelihood, and the lives of those whom they knew.

Kate had not the slightest idea of what re-action this little speech might trigger, and only hoped that it at least sounded plausible. A rather quizzical or, worse still, frozen smile by way of reply could easily puncture her fragile grasp of where she was headed; but the woman's reply could not have been more supportive.

"Well, how interesting" she said, with a large grin. "John and me" – she nodded her head backwards to some as yet unseen husband somewhere behind the bar area – "have only had the hotel a couple of years – I'm from Carlisle originally – but there's a lot of folk living in Seascale who work at Sellafield, and I'm sure John could suggest a few. There's Bert Braithwaite for a start – he's quite often in around ten for a pint or two - he worked there for years, retired now but he'll have you up all night if you start asking him questions". She laughed brightly while Kate reflected that she had just swung, metaphorically speaking, from one piece of rope to the next. Where it might lead she again had no idea.

Before she had collected her second glass of wine, 'John' appeared. They were duly introduced, and over the next fifteen minutes he reeled off a number of names of people living in Seascale who worked at the plant, focusing at Kate's request on those who had been employed for some long time. Several customers joined in the game, though only one of them was himself an employee, and only for the last five years. By the time Kate went through to dinner she had acquired six names, though only two addresses, as well as a totally fictitious past as a journalist vaguely rooted in environmental publications. After a dinner which was at once largely bar food and quite delicious she returned to the Chapters Bar to await her luck and Mr. Albert Braithwaite.

Shortly before ten pm, with the bar now quite full, and becoming rather hot and noisy, a short man with a rather wizened face, large ears and swept-back grey hair, quite smartly dressed in tweedy jacket and tie came in, and Kate sensed that her wait was over. The woman who had been behind the bar, but who was now sitting on a bar stool on the customer side of the bar and well ensconced with a group of customers, jumped up, grabbed the new entrant by the arm, called to John to pour a pint and led him over to Kate. She introduced them, giving Bert a very good summary of Kate's fictitious past and present intent; which brought a sparkle to Bert's eyes.
"Well, lass" he said "I've lived in these parts all my life, so there isn't much that's happened I can't tell thee about the place" He drank some beer. "Fire away!"

Kate initially focused on the early days of the nuclear plant, what the local population thought, how many of them took jobs at Windscale as it was then called, and how many 'incomers' as Bert called them arrived; and how did he and others like him take to the new influx of people, the building of new housing estates – were they welcomed, resented, did they make efforts to integrate themselves. Bert had much to say on all these topics and, Kate thought, he would make a good amateur historian; thoughtful, quite balanced as far as she could tell, as he revealed a story of inevitable tensions, for the most part overcome by a fair amount of good will on all sides, and the undoubted economic stimulus to everyone in the communities up and down the coast from the plant, at a time when the only other major industry in the area, namely fishing, based largely at Whitehaven, was in terminal decline. Nearly an hour passed before she asked what those living in the area thought of the risks inherent in having a large scale nuclear power plant and nuclear weapons manufacturing site in their midst.

"Aye, thou'll need to write about that" he said with a more sombre air. "For a long time it weren't a problem. No-one knew about the risks, and the company did a lot to re-assure us all. It were only much later, when we heard about some of the accidents that had happened years before, and when we started reading about more cancers in the area, that we all started getting real concerned, especially those of us working there. But there weren't much we could do, and we all needed the jobs, and I think most others sort of saw that. Anyway, they say the place is as safe as houses now, and we all just pray it's true".

"Were you there in 1973 when there was a major incident?" asked Kate. She was about to elaborate, but Bert cut in.

"At the Head End Plant, yes I was there, but no-one had any idea of how serious it was. At the time we was just told that there had been some operational problem. It was years before we knew the true story, and folk were pretty mad I can tell you. But the Head End was long closed by then, and they did a good job of telling us that things were all different now. Some left their jobs and left the area, but not many as far as I know. Mebbe there's been other trouble we still don't know about, but I don't think it's keeping folk awake at night".

Kate wanted to ask more specifically about the re-processing plants, but knew that would seem very odd given her supposed interest; but she had already worked out a way into the topic.

"Wasn't there an accident in the early 80s which lots of people saw – that must have caused a lot of concern – something in one of the re-processing plants?"

"There was, yes. I was at home here at the time, and it sounds like it was a fair amazing sight, but it were an electrical fault in the high voltage cables. It were near the main re-processing plant, but it wouldn't have done it any harm. But you must talk to Gordon Kidd – he lives over in Gosforth – I'll take you there tomorrow if you like. He were working there that night and has all sorts of fancy ideas about what happened. Says he's sure it weren't no electrical fault. He's not the only one either, but I don't think there's much credit given to it".

Kate decided that she would not get a better moment to take the final step. As casually as possible she asked

"So, has there, in fact, never been any problem with the re-processing facilities?" As she asked the question, it seemed to her to follow on quite naturally from what Bert had been saying. If Bert thought any different, he showed no sign of it.

"None any of us'd know about; and I don't really think so. I never worked there m'self, but I knew those who did and, apart from maintenance and when they modernised it, it's never been out of commission. So folk don't have much reason to worry I'd say". This last was added as if that was the concern behind Kate's question.

Kate sought to overcome the profound disappointment his reply provoked in her. It seemed to confirm what Sir Colin Brasher had told her – there had been no explosion at the re-processing plant; whatever Paul had uncovered had some innocent explanation; and there was nothing here to explain why he was no longer alive. They talked some more, with the bar now thinning out; and Kate resolved to talk to at least some of the other names she had been given, but she had to admit to herself that much of her ... enthusiasm was not the right word but....commitment to pursuing the one lead she had was severely dented. She agreed to pick up Bert from the bar the following evening and drive over to Gosforth to meet Gordon Kidd, but her heart was not really in it.

She spent the next morning tracking down three of the people to whom she had been referred, all retired, but learnt nothing new, or at least nothing new pertaining to her particular interest; and in the afternoon went to the Sellafield Visitors' Centre. This, much to her surprise, had been handed over lock, stock and barrel to an environmental organisation which, therefore, gave a rather balanced view of the pros and cons of nuclear power. It also included a range of hands-on exhibits, and even a large scale nuclear power game that groups of visitors could play, all of which was, she thought, genuinely educational. But none of it was taking her anywhere.

As arranged, she met Bert and together they drove over to Gosforth. This was clearly a much older settlement than Seascale, rather smaller but with five pubs, three of which were all at a small roundabout which acted as the centre of the village. They parked and Bert led them to one of these, the Wheatsheaf, the inside of which was very traditional and much more what Kate had originally expected to find – low oak beams and a roaring log fire. They were quite early and, apart from three young men and a woman sitting at the bar, there was just one man, right by the fire, who Bert introduced as Gordon Kidd. Tall, thin, grey haired and rather ascetic in appearance, he shook Kate's hand very formally and insisted on buying the drinks. He spoke quietly, but with some force and, no doubt having been alerted by Bert, was soon talking about the night of 14th November 1983.

"I was on night shift – I operated a fork lift truck and we were shifting some gear for one of the chemical purification plants. It was around one in the morning, something like that, and I'd stopped to have a cup of tea from my thermos. I was about a hundred yards from the re-processing plant and there was this explosion - took the roof right off a building next to the re-processing plant and brought down one of the main pylons".

"But wasn't it an electrical problem that brought the pylon down onto the building?" said Kate "I've read about it – they said it just seemed like an explosion because it was such a high voltage involved"

"That's the official story, but it isn't right, it really isn't. I was there and I know. And I will tell you how I know - because there were two explosions. Oh, they were very close together, but there was one from inside the building, after the roof had gone but before the pylon had collapsed. The second one couldn't be anything to do with the pylon at all". He sat back with a look that invited Kate to ask any questions she wanted, but there was not a scintilla of doubt in his mind as to what had happened.

"But surely, if that's right, then there would be a lot of people who saw what happened. The company couldn't have kept the matter quiet?"

"It was the Atomic Energy Authority at the time" Kidd reminded Kate "and, no, there wouldn't have been hardly anyone to say what actually happened. Lots of people saw the flash, for some miles around, but at a distance who could tell any different? The night staff at work was quite small, and nearly all of them would have been indoors at the time. I only ever found two others who were outside and near enough…….." His voice faltered and he stopped.

Kate wanted to ask him to go on, but sensed that silence was the better tactic. Bert intervened.

"They're both dead now; one of them….."

"I'll tell it" interrupted Gordon. "One of them, Eric Smith, was a good mate of mine, but we fell out over what happened – he said to leave it alone, but I couldn't; and we didn't really speak to each other much after that. And then he died of cancer, and I haven't felt right about it since" He looked down at his hands, and Kate did not know what to say. Gordon again came to the rescue.

"The other one, a feller called Peterson, he agreed with Gordon; and they did ask about what happened – several times. But they was told they were wrong; and while their bosses said it made no difference to them, it were made pretty clear that they were going to be thought a bit daft in the head if they kept on about it. That's why Eric kept hiself to hiself about it".

Kate said she was sorry to have brought about such unhappy memories, but could not stop herself from asking one further, very obvious question.

"Is there no-one else you know who was there, who saw what happened?"

It was again Bert who answered.

"There's a man I know who works with Sellafield Security – he lives over in Beckermet – who I heard say that he had been on duty that night – feller by the name of Price – but he didn't much want to talk about it, far as I remember - Dave Price I think. Still, this won't help your writing much will it – it were all a nine-day wonder, and it made nowt much difference to Sellafield or to any of us living here".

Kate heard herself saying that, of course, he was right, and repeating that she was sorry to have brought up unhappy times, and she would buy another round of drinks, which task Bert insisted on taking over; but all the time her mind was re-adjusting, processing what Gordon Kidd had said. Maybe there was something to the incident in 1983, though whatever it was, it didn't sound, in any sense, earth-shattering. Still, it was all she had. They had another round of drinks, and talked more generally about the impact of Sellafield on the community. Gordon seemed to cheer himself up, though Kate noticed that he was markedly more pessimistic in tone about what he saw as the overall effect of such a large industrial site on a remote, if quite poor area of the country; and she surmised that this might be not unrelated to his experience back in 1983. Eventually, she thanked him for his time, drove Bert back to his home in Seascale, and was back at the Calder House Hotel just in time for a late dinner.

The next day being Saturday, she managed to track down two more names on her list, but with, once again, nothing new emerging. Around 1.30pm she drove to Beckermet, just north of Sellafield, stopped at the Wild Mare – a quite large and attractive pub in the very centre of the village - and ordered a late lunch. She chatted as much as she could with the waitress, a young woman with a large pony tail and a chirpy manner and, when ordering coffee, asked her if she knew Dave Prince. She didn't but, rather as Kate had hoped, said she'd talk to the landlord – her Dad in fact - who ran the pub, because if the man Kate was after lived in Beckermet then, unless he was tee-total, her dad would know him. Less than five minutes later she returned with an address - not two minutes from the Wild Mare. Then the father himself appeared, obviously curious, and Kate explained that she wanted to ask Price for his views on an article she was writing. She said that she would try to call in on Price.

"Not sure that's the best way to go" said the landlord, pulling a slightly glum face. "Dave's had....is having a bit of a rough time with Jenny – that's his wife – I'm not sure an attractive young lady arrive on his doorstep would go down all that well'' if you get my meaning?"

Kate wasn't about to blush or be thrown by this, but she nonetheless did feel somewhat embarrassed, perhaps on the landlord's behalf, and quickly thanked him for the advice.

"Tell you what" said the landlord "I'll give him a call, see if he is free to come round for a chat with me, and I can introduce you. How would that do?"

Kate could see the sense in this, but her instincts told her not to give Mr David Price an opportunity to avoid her. So she thanked the landlord, but said she was sure it would be okay – if Price's wife was there she could ask her about the significance of Sellafield to life in the area as well.

168

A few minutes later she was ringing the bell of Monk's Cottage. A woman around fifty years old, but with what Kate thought of as striking good looks and a real presence opened the door. Kate introduced herself as Mrs. Mortimer - just in case a woman turning up at the house was going to be any sort of problem – and launched into her story, ending up by saying that the landlord of the Wild Mare had said that her husband had worked at Sellafield for a long time and might be someone who could help her; and perhaps Mrs Price might be able to as well. Mrs Price seemed to take all of this in her stride, invited Kate in to their sitting room, and went to the back of the house and called her husband. Dave Price, when he eventually appeared, was a sturdy looking man, in his late fifties Kate guessed and, unlike almost everyone she had so far encountered in West Cumbria, looked distinctly unsympathetic. Neither Price nor his wife offered her a seat, as Kate apologised for bothering them and launched into her reason for calling on them. At first, neither of the Prices answered, but then Dave Price said that he didn't want to seem unhelpful, but that it really wasn't a good time – this said in a way that clearly hinted that no time would be a good time.

"How did you get my name?" he added, not in a hostile manner, but nonetheless rather unhelpfully. Discouraging as this all was, Kate saw a way that perhaps might turn things to her advantage, and save herself quite a lot of time as well.

"I do understand" she said " I've been talking to a lot of people, in fact; and got your name from one of them – not quite sure who now – and I've got most of what I want. But there seemed to be some disagreement about what happened in November 1983, and how much of a threat to the population there was; and someone said that you were working there that night for the Sellafield security service, and would be the best person to tell me. That's all I really needed to ask. Just five minutes of your time would be great". If he could just answer this, she could cut through all the preliminaries about the impact of Sellafield that she had gone through with everyone else.

Price stared at her, saying nothing. The tension in the room was suddenly electric. Jenny Price spoke first

"Dave, why......" but he cut her off with a look and a flick of his hand. Kate, without thinking, but feeling that she must fill the silent void, blundered on

"The reports I've read said that it was an electrical fault, but I've heard locally that it was some sort of explosion in a building near the main re-processing plant. I just thought that, if you were there on duty that night, you could tell me which version is right". Another unpleasant pause followed.

"I really can't talk about it" said Price eventually, now sounding openly hostile. "It was nearly thirty years ago anyway". He looked at her impassively, and Kate knew that she would get no more from him by gentle persuasion. She would have to go for the jugular.

"I'm sorry if your job means that you can't talk about it" she said "I hadn't realised that a breach of security at Sellafield was involved. I suppose the 'electrical failure' was just a cover story for what happened?"

Kate knew immediately that this hadn't worked. Price's eyes blazed and, for a moment she thought he might physically manhandle her out of the house. Instead he said, very quietly

"As I said, I can' talk about it. I'm sorry. Jenny, would you show Mrs. Mortimer out? I must get back to what I was doing"; and he walked out, retracing his steps to the back of the house. And in that instant Kate realised that she had come to the end of the line. This section of rope had no new one attached to it. She had a couple of other names still to contact; and no doubt she could rustle up some more. But none of the conversations she had had had thrown up anything suspicious except the 1983 incident. If those who were there wouldn't talk to her, then she was at a dead end. As Jenny Price escorted her to the front door, she momentarily saw a glimpse of her future – back to Oxford, back to whatever sort of life she could re-construct for herself, back to a future without Paul. A wave of devastating sadness came over her, and her immediate aim became no more than that of getting out of the house without starting to cry.

CHAPTER 12

"I'm sorry about that" said Jenny Price, as Kate stepped outside.

"Me too" replied Kate. "I was obviously delving into something more…awkward… than I realised"

"Why are you investigating what happened that night" asked Jenny. "I mean why really? If you're a journalist, it's rather late in the day for a big exposé".

"I'm not a journalist, but it would take too long to explain" said Kate, and without any artifice or encouragement, a tear rolled down her cheek.

Jenny looked quickly over her shoulder.

"Talk to Edwin Miller. He lives in Gosforth. You'll be able to find his address. He's retired now, but he was the officer on duty that night at the police station in Egremont, and I've heard him talking to Dave about it. There was something not right, I could tell; but Dave has always just clammed up about it, told me to mind my own business. But the local police don't always see eye to eye with the Sellafield lot – in fact there's a lot of friction there – and Edwin seemed convinced that there was something going on. How he'd know I don't know, but he's more likely to talk to you than Dave was".

Kate could only guess at Jenny Price's motivation – it could be genuine concern that Sellafield might be covering up some risk to the community she lived in, but more likely it was something to do with the clearly rather dysfunctional relationship she had with her husband. How deep a simmering resentment might go she could only guess. Whatever the answer, it had thrown her one more lifeline, and she was eternally grateful. She started to thank Jenny, but the other woman cut her off

"Please, you must go now. Don't let anyone know that I told you about Edwin. I hope you find what you are looking for"; and she closed the door quietly behind Kate, who walked slowly back to the Wild Mare and her hire car.

By 6 pm she had booked another night at her hotel and, by working her way through the Wheatsheaf, the Lion and Lamb and the Globe pubs in Gosforth, had established where Edwin Miller lived. Now in his seventies, widowed, and not in the best of health, his reception of Kate was nonetheless as welcoming and courteous as Price's had been churlish; and within two minutes of knocking on his door she was comfortably installed in a large arm chair by a pleasant wood fire with a large glass of sherry in her hand. When he asked her how he could help, she rather wanted to tell this avuncular old man the whole story, starting with Paul's disappearance and everything that had happened since; but she thought this might easily scare him off, and she could not afford to lose this one last thread. So she rehearsed her story of research for an article on Sellafield, but said, in looking at the safety issues, she had come across the disputed events of 1983. Could he help?

"I certainly can" he said with alacrity. "I didn't see or hear anything myself – I was on duty in Egremont. But I got a lot of calls, and everyone of them said that there had been some sort of explosion. I know that a pylon came down, and I heard all the news stories about some electrical problem being the cause, and mebbe that's right. But it didn't seem like that at the time to them what saw it; and the people working at Sellafield wouldn't say a word – not one word – except that it was the electrics. You could just tell that there was more to it than that. And then Jack Arnison – he was the Inspector at Whitehaven – he's dead now, but he was my boss – told me that George Framwell, the Chief Constable of the Cumbria police, had been livid about it all and good as said to Jack that the Sellafield lot where buggering him about – excuse my language – but there weren't anything he could do about it. And there's more. Jack never got to the bottom of it, but he said that afterwards George wouldn't talk about it at all – got right worked up if Jack mentioned it – and he retired early. Jack said he got very down, started getting very irritated with everyone all the time. Mebbe he was just getting old, and Jack couldn't swear it were anything to do with what happened at the plant. Anyway, he's dead now; and I don't know any more than Jack did what happened, but I say there was something happened that they didn't want anyone to know about and they came up with a cock-and-bull story about the electricity cables". He paused and took a large mouthful of sherry.

"Could whatever happened have damaged the re-processing plant near the pylon that came down?" asked Kate, feeling for the first time since she had come to Cumbria that she could speak freely.

"Well, I don't see as how it could" replied Miller. "If there had been an accident – an explosion in the re-processing plant that lit up the countryside around, then it would have to have breached the walls; and that would have been a major incident, probably the worst nuclear accident ever in Britain. They'd have had to close the plant, move the population, maybe close down the whole site; and we'd certainly have known by now because there'd be a whole lot of people dying – and there hasn't been any of that. So I'd say that there was some sort of explosion, which brought down the pylon, but didn't damage the re-processing plant, and for some reason they decided to say it was the pylon what was the problem. Something odd going on, no doubt in my mind, but not as would worry the locals". For a moment he was thirty years away in his mind, his eyes, if focused at all, fixed on the middle distance; but then he nodded to himself, a firm confirmation that this conclusion, however inconclusive, was not to be questioned.

"But" asked Kate, thinking of Paul's work, "could an incident like that have weakened the re-processing plant?"

"Well, I really don't know. It could I suppose. But if it did, then they'd know to close the plant and repair it – so what's the difference? There's no way they'd keep operating a damaged plant. Even in the 1973 accident, which they kept very quiet about, they still stopped operations in the Head End Plant immediately"

"Maybe they didn't know it had been damaged?" said Kate, but realised instantly the fault in this line of reasoning.

"Well, in that case, there'd be nothing they'd know to cover up, would there; and we'd all be dying as well. Anyway, they monitor the radioactivity coming from that place more closely than anywhere else on earth. If it were one smudge above the proper limits, that would be it. No, I think it was just that they didn't want folk thinking that they didn't know how to run a reliable ship; so an electric failure sounded a lot better than some accident, even though it didn't do much damage" This was followed by, if anything, a still firmer nod of confirmation to himself and, this time to Kate as well.

There didn't seem a lot more that Kate could ask or say, but something was nagging at her, a loose end in what Miller had said to her which she just couldn't get hold of. So, anxious not to depart, she thanked him for his help and asked if, in return for his time and help, she might buy him supper in one of the pubs. This invitation he accepted with such alacrity that Kate felt quite embarrassed – recognising that this was not wholly motivated by the quality of the local cooking – but if it gave Miller an enjoyable evening and served her own purposes there seemed no reason not to; and ten minutes later there were ensconced in the small restaurant area of the Lion and Lamb, ordering what turned out to be exceptionally good pub food. Edwin Miller was happy to talk about his, life, his upbringing in Cumbria, his work for the police, the people he'd known and the wife he had loved and lost to lung cancer ten years earlier. It was when he briefly mentioned Jack Arnison again, the Police Inspector who had been on duty at Whitehaven the night of 'the incident' whatever it was, that she remembered the loose end.

"Tell me" she said when Miller paused "you said that the Chief Constable in Carlisle – I can't remember his name – got very irritable about the whole subject of the explosion and just wouldn't talk about it. Did he not give anyone any clue before he died as to why that might have been?"

Miller's face when quite taut. "Oh my dear" he said "I'm sorry, I must have quite confused you. It's George Framwell, but he's not dead It's Jack that died. George is not well at all, hasn't been now for some while, but he's not died yet."

Kate sat quite still, feeling truly stunned. She could have sworn that Miller had said that Framwell had died but, as she thought about it more, she recollected that it was Jack Arnison who had never worked out why Framwell was so spooked by the events of 1983, before he, Arnison, died. Whether it was the way Miller put it, or the assumption that the Chief Constable would be much older and unlikely to still be alive 30 years later she did not know; but she silently thanked whatever guiding force had led her to hang on to Miller and, by chance had led to this vital new information.

"Oh, I'm so sorry" said Kate. "I quite misunderstood. He must be very old now?"

"Around ninety I should say. He's been in a nursing home at Penrith for a good few years now." Miller seemed about to say something more, but Kate couldn't stop herself interjecting.

"Do you think I'd be able to talk to him?" she said, her heart pounding several beats faster than a minute before.

Miller paused, no doubt no more than a second, but it seemed much longer to Kate.

"I don't really know. I didn't know him very well, and I haven't seen him for a good while – he may not be up to much – visitors, you know. But you could call at the nursing home – they say it's a very good one, up on Beacon Edge just behind Penrith. I can't just remember the name, but Mrs. Lewitt – she's his niece, lives in Seascale – will know. I'll get the name for you." He paused, looking pensive. "He may not …….. you know …… remember a lot."

An unwell ninety year old in a nursing home might well not, but Kate knew that Miller was warning her of something altogether more serious than mere forgetfulness.

"Oh, I see" she said. "Does he suffer from dementia?" Why did it sound so critical, so uncaring she wondered. "A lot of older people do these days, such a terrible thing" she added, as some sort of consolation, though Miller had said he wasn't well acquainted with Framwell,

"Well, Mary – that's Mrs. Lewitt – did say he was getting very muddled, last few times she saw him. Said she wasn't sure he really knew who she was any more. And he sometimes talks to the staff about people in his room when there's no-one there – like he's seeing things. But he still talks to the others there, watches a bit of television she said, so he may not be too bad. I don't really know truth be told."

So there it was. All the elation Kate had felt on hearing that Framwell, who clearly knew something none of the local people she'd spoken to knew, was still alive had collapsed again, her quest to find the truth about Paul now hanging, not by a rope, not even by a thread, but by the microscopic strands of uncontrolled protein clutching, tentacle-like at the brain cells of an old retired police officer with either Alzheimers or some other form of dementia. Even if she got access to him and he was ready to talk, would he be able to remember anything, even understand Kate's questions; and what could she make of anything he said if, as Miller put it, he was 'seeing things'?

Kate and Miller walked back to his house, where Kate had left her car; and Miller rang Mrs. Lewitt to get the address of the nursing home. She thanked him for all his help, and he thanked her for such a very enjoyable evening and she set off back to Seascale, clear on her next move, but with a pain in her stomach at the prospect that it might be utterly futile. The next morning she checked out of the Calder House hotel, and just under two hours later pulled up outside the Beacon View Nursing home, set on a ridge to the East of Penrith with spectacular views across the town, the Eden Valley and on to the hills of the northern lakes.

Without much preparation or thought, and with still less anxiety or guilt, she introduced herself to the receptionist as an old friend of Mary Lewitt, George Framwell's niece. Kate had decided against phoning in advance – she didn't want to leave any opportunity for the staff at the nursing home or, indeed, Framwell himself, to explain why she couldn't see him – and apologised for the surprise visit on the grounds that she lived in London and was unexpectedly in Cumbria on business. She was banking on the likelihood that, when Framwell failed to recognise her, she – and the staff - could put it down to a combination of her not having seen him for a long time and his state of mind. In fact, the receptionist was quite helpful. Clearly Framwell, and perhaps many others at the home, had few enough visitors; and there were no standard visiting hours. The receptionist asked Kate if she knew about George's condition; and Kate said that she did, taking the opportunity to note that he might not recognise her.

She was shown into Framwell's room, a spacious, well decorated room with doors onto a pleasant garden and sunlight streaming in. Framwell was sitting in a large armchair, looking out into the garden, a composed look on his face.

"George, I'm sure you won't remember me" said Kate "but I'm an old friend of Mary's, and she said that you might like a visit. It's a very long time since we met, but I thought it would be nice to call in, see how you are".

"That's very kind of you" said Framwell, in a polite, if slightly wooden way. Kate suspected that he had evolved such phrases to cope with an increasingly incomprehensible world, but it was contact of a kind. She said how pleasant his room seemed, and he nodded, clearly understanding something of what she had said. She tried asking how long he had lived there, to which he replied, with a small smile, that it was very nice. And so they chatted, after a fashion, with Kate mentioning the weather, asking about the staff, did he prefer listening to the radio or watching television, to all of which Framwell responded in some way – a smile, a nod, a phrase which sometimes fitted and sometimes didn't. He then surprised her by asking whether she would like some tea, but responded only with a nod when she said that she would. Kate reflected that, given they had never met before, and given his illness, they were establishing some sort of rapport – certainly Framwell seemed to be enjoying their chat. But how to move beyond a social visit?

After some ten to fifteen minutes, Kate said

"Do you remember the old days at all, when you were working at Carlisle?" Framwell looked down at his lap, pondering for a while, and then gave another of his small nods, but made no reply.

"Mary mentioned Jack, Jack Arnison, who used to work at Whitehaven. Do you remember him?"

"Jack" Framwell said, almost to himself "Jack. Always fish and chips, fish and chips with Jack" He paused. "He died, Jack". "Jack" he said again, as if, Kate thought, he could hang onto some recollection by hanging on to the name.

"Yes" said Kate. "He died. You knew him well, didn't you?"

"Knew him well" repeated Framwell, with what degree of understanding Kate did not know; but she began to think that he perhaps followed more than he could readily articulate, if at all. Perhaps she would need to be the one to spell out the thoughts, in the hope that he might indicate in some way their accuracy or otherwise.

"He said you retired early from the police force. Is that right?"

"I was in the police" replied Framwell.

"You were" replied Kate. "But you retired early. Was it to do with the accident at Sellafield? Jack said you were very unhappy about what happened".

For a moment the words just seemed to hang in the air. Framwell sat, composed, silent, still looking down rather than at Kate. They sat in the silence, neither moving. Then Framwell, very slowly lifted his head a fraction, his eyes slightly more, until he was looking at Kate's face, his own still expressionless.

"Jack didn't know" he said, shaking his head slightly. "Jack didn't know"

"Didn't know what" asked Kate as sympathetically as she could. "Jack didn't know what?"

Another long pause.

" The inspector knew" said Framwell, and this time just a hint of firmness came into his voice.

"Knew what" repeated Kate, but Framwell did the same, repeating "the Inspector knew". Kate remembered that Jack Arnison had been an Inspector at Whitehaven, but she was quite certain that, ill as he was, Framwell was not contradicting himself.

"Which Inspector was it?" she asked. "Inspector who?" This time, Framwell sat looking straight at her, and a slight shadow of ernestness had crossed his face. Kate felt that he was struggling to catch on to the threads of his thoughts, and sensed that he very much wanted to reply to her question, if he could only hang on to its meaning. As he sat there, making what sort of mental effort Kate had no idea, it seemed very natural for her to put her hand on his. As she did so, he smiled, and started to nod to himself again; and Kate suddenly knew what Framwell knew – that the answer was coming, from a long way away it was edging, past all sorts of obstacles, towards the point in his brain when he could say the word. They sat there together, oblivious to all else, just waiting. The answer, when it came, surprised Kate, but Framwell's reaction signified that he was quite certain it was the answer he wanted to give.

"Minogue" he said, settling back in his chair as if slightly tired by the effort.

"Minogue?" Kate repeated."As in……" She stopped. "Inspector Minogue?"

"Inspector Minogue – he told me. That was it – he told me"

"Told you what?" asked Kate but, even as she asked, she could see that Framwell was beginning to lose the connection. Some slight intensity in his eyes had gone. She tried asking again, but his only response was to repeat the name again. At least, she thought, he is very certain of the name. She asked some more questions, about Jack, the days when Framwell was in the police force and, once more about Inspector Minogue, but got only acquiescence, some more nods, no new information. Eventually she said that she should go. He nodded again and thanked her for coming – again rather formulaically – and she took her leave, stopping to speak to the staff person at reception.

"Did he know you?" she asked.

"No, I'm afraid not, but we had a nice chat, mainly about when he was in the police force".

"Yes, it's often the case that patients with some form of dementia have clearer recollections of many years ago than of last week. We have one woman – in her late eighties – quite far gone, but she can chat for ages about her early life, some aspects at least".

"George could remember a little – not much, but something. Well, I must be away. I'm back to London now" said Kate, and was soon on her way back to Carlisle railway station.

Once again, Kate's quest hung by a thread or, more accurately, by one word, a name. But there were two things about that name that gave Kate considerable optimism – more no doubt than it should, but optimism nonetheless. The first was that the name, Kate thought, was a very unusual one – very well known because of Kylie Minogue – but not one she had ever come across anywhere else before; and second, it carried the title of Inspector, and clearly a police Inspector. Surely Hargreaves – she still didn't really think of him as Neil – could track him down if, of course, he was still alive? An hour later she was heading south by train, and phoning Hargreaves on her mobile. Predictably she had to leave a message, but she asked Hargreaves to call her back on her mobile as soon as possible – saying it was very urgent. She had to face the fact that, in practice, it wasn't. Hargreaves could just as well try to find Inspector Minogue the next day, even the next week; but Kate was so buoyed up by what she had found out, through a whole series of meetings since she had come to Cumbria, and she just didn't have the patience to wait. Nearly three hours later, while she was waiting at Birmingham New Street station for her connection to Oxford, he got back to her.

She explained that she was on a train on her way back to Oxford, would be there in an hour and a half, and could they meet up? She had found out that there had been an incident at Sellafield in 1983, some sort of accident involving an explosion. It didn't appear to have caused significant damage but, for some reason, had been explained away as an electrical fault. There was clearly something odd about the event, and she was convinced that Paul had found out something about it, despite it having happened nearly thirty years before. But the main news was that an Inspector Minogue had been involved in some way, knew something that was not generally known, and had to be her next port of call. Could he find out about Minogue – anything at all – but more important, was he still alive and if so, where was he living. She was so carried away with her news that it was only having got this far that she realised the mobile phone signal had, at some point cut out, and she was talking to no-one but herself. For a moment she went back in her mind to Heathrow, furious that Paul was not answering her call, and ready to stamp on her mobile – how completely she had failed to appreciate what his answer-phone had signified. Now, she once again contained her frustration, and spent fifteen minutes trying to get back to

Hargreaves. Eventually, spread over three calls, she got her message through; and he arranged to meet her at Oxford Railway station.

By 5.30 pm they were in the bar of the Randolph hotel, where Kate went through her trip to Cumbria in infinite detail. Hargreaves had only one piece of news, more gossip amongst some of the police based at the Oxford station, to the effect that D.I. Johnson had been acting on instructions from way above him when, as everyone agreed, he had sought to wrap up the investigation into Paul's disappearance as quickly as possible. No-one knew why – it was speculated that some other much more obscure department of the national police force might have been given the job – but it fitted with the surrogate D notice, which had also become common knowledge. Kate absorbed this, but then moved rapidly back to Inspector Minogue – could Neil track him down? Hargreaves replied cautiously.

"It's an unusual name – I doubt there were two Inspector Minogues – and his existence can hardly be thought confidential. So, I should be able to find out something, provided, that is, that someone still has records for so long ago I'll look into it tomorrow; but whether I can find out his current whereabouts is another matter, always assuming, as you say, that he is still alive". That was as much as Kate could hope for. They talked some more, had a second glass of wine, agreed to talk again the next day and then Kate headed back on foot to her house – a walk of less than ten minutes. As she arrived, she realised how exhausted she felt, partly all the travelling, but all the emotional energy she had used up as well. She was far too tired, as she walked past the usual long line of parked cars in their resident parking spaces, to notice that one, parked about fifty yards up from her house, had two men sitting in it, who watched her with intense interest.

CHAPTER 13

Kate slept late, and then spent the morning writing up detailed notes of her trip to the North. She listened to the 1 o'clock news while making herself a light lunch, and was surprised, and disturbed, to hear that war now seemed imminent in the Middle East. So absorbed had she been in her own project that she had totally missed out on the wider world. She learnt that US aircraft carriers had moved into battle station positions enabling them to attack Iran in strength; US and British bombers based in the UK were ready to go; and Israel was on stand by to retaliate if, or rather when, Iran responded with attacks on Israel. But the element she had had no inkling of before, which really shocked her, was Iran's widely reported claim to be able to attack targets throughout Western Europe. Commentators speculated – because Iran had not specified – whether this could include London, and whether Iran's capability was already nuclear. The general opinion seemed to be that London was probably within range, but only for conventional long range missiles; but no one was certain, with several saying that the West should have acted long before Iran got so close to having long range nuclear weapons. The UN had called for Iran to accept a UN team of inspectors, a proposal which Iran had not accepted, but had not completely rejected either. President Hamilton was quoted as saying that this was clearly just a continuation of Iran's delaying tactics; and that Iran's support for terrorism, its threats to Israel, and its continued development of nuclear weapons made war inevitable. However diplomatically put, it was clear that the US might not wait upon the UN, any more than he had done in 2003 over Iraq. Prime Minister Alan Gerrard, interviewed on the programme, said that it was not too late to prevent war, but only if Iran immediately opened its borders to UN troops entering in force, provided complete and unfettered access to all sites, and complied with all orders for destruction of nuclear sites – conditions that no-one on the programme appeared to think Iran would meet.. The alternative, according to Gerard, was the destruction of Iran's military forces as quick and as total as had been the case when the US and Britain invaded Iraq.

Kate listened to all this, feeling more alarmed by the minute. Could London really be threatened? If so, could Oxford, where she sat eating an egg salad and planning her next steps? It all sounded preposterous, ridiculous - probably was – but it was disconcerting nonetheless, shades of a return to the threat everyone felt under during the cold war; and she was amazed at herself, that she had become so focused on her search for an explanation for her loss of Paul, that she had simply not registered how seriously matters had developed over Iran.

Her attention to world events was soon interrupted. Her phone rang and, to her surprise, it was Hargreaves. There was good and bad news, he said. The good news was that he had quite quickly tracked down Inspector Minogue. He'd got on to central records, given them a line about following up a connection with a much earlier crime, and found that there was, as expected, just one Inspector – in fact a Chief Inspector –Minogue on the force in 1983; that he was retired, was still being paid a pension; and, as a result, he had Minogue's address.

"That's terrific" said Kate "In fact, brilliant. What is the bad news – what could it be?"

"In 1983, and for some time before and after, Chief Inspector Minogue was based in north London, at Paddington Green police station, mainly working on organised crime, robbery, some drugs and so on. I can't think of any reason why he would have any connection with an incident, or even the cover up of an incident, at a nuclear power plant in Cumbria. It doesn't make any sense".

Kate had two quite contradictory reactions. She was quite convinced, ill as Framwell had been, that he had remembered Minogue correctly, and that Chief Inspector Minogue, whatever his role in the police force, must hold the key to the matter; and Hargreaves' research had led her right to him. But, it was nonetheless, as Hargreaves had said, bad news that he seemed such an unlikely player in whatever drama had been played out at Sellafield in 1983. Could Framwell have been mistaken – he was certainly moderately demented – and the unusual name could have popped up from any number of sources, even seeing Kylie on television she reflected ruefully. Still, there was only one way to find out.

"It does sound odd" said Kate, "but the only way to find out if it is good or bad news is for me to go and talk to him. Let me note down the address, and I'll go tomorrow".

"If I may quote John McEnroe" said Hargreaves "you cannot be serious. Not only is he very unlikely to talk to a member of the public about what is obviously a very sensitive police matter, but he will want to know how you tracked him down. You would not, of course tell him; but he will be onto central records before you are back in your car, and that will be the end of my career. So, please don't even think about contacting him. I will talk to him – I'm sure I can dream up a plausible enough reason for wanting to go over some possible connection with a past case and, before you ask, yes, I will tell you whatever I find out. But you can't see him yourself"

Kate saw the sense of this and, though Hargreaves hadn't mentioned it, she noted that he hadn't actually given her Minogue's address; so she couldn't get to him anyway. More important, without any prompting from her, he had volunteered to pursue the matter, no doubt at some considerable risk to his future career.

"Where does he live" she asked and, as he paused, added in a deliberately formal way "I faithfully promise not to act on it. In fact I'm really grateful to you for being prepared to go yourself."

"As I said, he's retired, and lives in Swanage. I can't go tomorrow, and I have to be in Court on Thursday, but I can probably get down there on Friday". There was a moment's silence while the same thought pulsed through both their minds, and he added "You can come with me if you want".

Kate, who would have been prepared to follow him if he hadn't agreed, said that would be perfect. Hargreaves said he's call the next day to arrange to pick her up, and rang off.

Kate finished her lunch and went out shopping for groceries. She returned shortly before 4 pm and was just making herself a cup of tea when the doorbell rang. Somewhat surprised she went to the door, wondering if it might be

Hargreaves. As she opened the door, it was thrown open with such force that it knocked her flat on her back and, in the same second, a man was on top of her, his knee in her stomach, a large hand over her mouth. Kate just lay there, winded, utterly shocked, incapable of thought or movement.

"Go on" said the man, which made no sense at all to Kate, until she became briefly aware of another man closing the front door, coming past her and heading up her stairs.

"Do you see this bottle?" said the man, this time very much to Kate, his large, heavily shaven head only inches from hers, and in his other hand he held a small transparent bottle, about the size of a small shampoo bottle. "Nod if you do".

Kate nodded, her head hardly moving, so tight was the grip which the man had on her mouth.

"It contains a very nasty acid. If you do not do exactly what I say, without a sound, I will pour it over your face. If the extreme agony doesn't kill you with a heart attack, you will be horribly scarred for the rest of your life. Do you understand me?"

Again Kate nodded.

"Just to make sure that you do not make a sound, I'm going to gag you. Think of it as helping you to get through this" He put down the bottle and took out a small piece of elastic, with what looked like a large handkerchief sown to one part of it. In an instant he used both hands to pull the elastic down over her head, forcing the handkerchief into her mouth. For a moment Kate thought it would cut off her breathing completely, but she managed to breathe through her nose. The man picked up the bottle again.

"Right. Turn over, very slowly" he said. Kate did as she was told, her mind just starting to function again. All she could think was that she was going to be raped, gang raped if two was a gang; but that she would comply - rather than risk the intruder carrying out his threat - she was already quite clear. The man grabbed her right arm and twisted it up behind her back.

"Now, stand up, very slowly" he said. Again Kate complied. "Okay, very good, now up the stairs, just one step at a time". Kate sensed the strength in the man, that he could practically have carried her up the stairs one-handed. She started to climb, now scared totally out of her mind as to what was to happen when she got to the top. As she trod on the fourth step she heard a sound above her. Looking up she saw the second man standing on the landing at the top of the stairs, holding a rope in his hands. Panic started to course through her body at the thought that they would tie her up, and for a moment she could not go on.

"Keep going" snarled the man behind her. Then, as she took another step up, the man on the landing threw one end of the rope over the banister – the rest of it seemed to trail away into her bedroom – so that the end of the rope was about seven feet from the hall floor. And on the end of the rope was a noose.

CHAPTER 14

Kate was struck by absolute terror. They were going to hang her, and she had no way to prevent it. Despite the gag, she let out a half-strangled scream and shook her whole body in a frenzied attempt to get out of the grip of the man behind her. It made no impact at all. She threw her weight backwards, in the hope that they might both topple over backwards, anything to avoid going further up the stairs; but he was quite ready for this, and his weight held them there. Then he dropped the bottle he had been holding in his other hand, which fell behind him and smashed; and, putting his free arm round her lifted her off her feet and took two more steps up the stairs. Kate screamed a muffled scream, kicking and shaking as much as she could, but she made barely any impression on the man forcing her inexorably up her own stairs to her death.

"Get her legs" said the man, and the other intruder, coming down the six or so remaining stairs, grabbing Kate's ankles. "Get her on the landing. I'll hold her, you fix the rope on her". Unable to resist in any way, Kate was carried the last few steps and onto the landing. She tried to collapse, but the man held her on her feet. The other man pulled up the rope from where it was hanging and, despite Kate shaking her head in a frenzy, pulled the noose down over it, onto her neck, and pulled it so tight she could hardly breathe.

"Now, get her over these railings" said the man, "get the gag off her and let's get out of here". The two men each grabbed one of Kate's arms and started to drag her to the balustrade along the landing edge. Kate, practically passing out in terror, continued to struggle, to little effect. Suddenly there was a noise from downstairs, from the front door. All three of them looked down, to see two more men come through the door. The one in front held a pistol with a long barrelled silencer on it. Without a word he instantly aimed, fired and, with a loud plop, a bullet hit the right kneecap of the man who had dragged Kate upstairs. He screamed and fell to the floor, clutching his knee. The other man instantly disappeared into Kate's bedroom and slammed the door, leaving Kate standing on the landing with the noose round her neck. The two new arrivals, raced up the stairs, whereupon the one with the pistol swung it viciously at the head of the man he had shot, who collapsed to the landing floor. The second man tried the door to Kate's bedroom which opened. He went in and Kate heard another shot, another scream. Only just starting to come to her senses, she loosened the noose and slipped it off her neck, over her head. Then she ripped the gag off.

The two men stood either side of her.

"Guess you could do with a stiff drink" said one in a rather guttural voice, and with an American accent. "Let's all go down stairs". Kate stood there, still absolutely petrified, her brain only just beginning to register that, as far a she could tell, *these* two men meant her no harm, in fact had saved her life, and saved her from an appalling death in the process. Why the first two men should want to kill her, why they should want to hang her, why these two men had saved her, were questions that as yet she couldn't even formulate. She stood there, in a state of utter shock, and realised that she was starting to tremble. The two men gently led her down stairs and, as she went, the trembling got worse. By the time she was back in her hallway she was almost convulsing, her body gripped by such extremes of stress, fear, relief that it could no longer function. They steered her into her sitting room and one of them poured her some whisky and water, which she sipped, still unable to speak, and now shivering uncontrollably. The other went out and came back with a duvet from her bedroom, which he proceeded to wrap round her.

Finally, still shivering, occasionally sipping the whisky, Kate managed to mumble

"Who are you?"

"Think of us as the cavalry – and I don't mean the Household Cavalry" replied the man who clearly was in charge, but without any humour in his voice. He turned to his partner.

"Summon some back-up to get rid of those two bags of shit upstairs, oh, and while you're about it, get the camera from the car. They should make great pin-ups". The other man went outside, taking some sort of communication device from under his jacket as he went.

"Who were the men who tried to kill me" asked Kate, still barely able to get the words out in an intelligible order.

"Like I said, a couple of bags of shit. They won't bother you again, that's for sure, nor any more like them when I'm through".

"But why" said Kate, tears now running down her cheeks. "Why did they want to kill me; no, why did they want to..........hang me?"

"To make it look like suicide. Lost lover boy, off work, bound to be depressed, very easy to tie a rope round your neck and jump off the landing. There'd be nothing, not a mark on you, to contradict it."

"They nearly poured acid over me" said Kate, as near to angry as she was capable of being.

"No chance" said the man. They would never have used it – probably wasn't acid anyway. Just designed to .... get your co-operation".

Kate let it go. It was all too difficult to grasp just now.

"What about you? Why are you here?" asked Kate, at last starting to be able to marshal some thoughts.

"Oh, we've been watching you – watching over you I should say – for days. When we saw these two go blasting through your door, we just checked they were alone, set up our weapons and came on over. I'm sorry we weren't sooner – they worked very fast once they were in. We were barely a minute behind and they almost..... well, what the hell - the good guys won".

Before Kate could string another question together – and about a hundred were now beginning to form in her mind, the other man re-appeared.

"They'll be here in under thirty minutes, and here's the camera"

"Okay, let's get to work. Mam, will you please just sit here while we check on the two upstairs, get a few pictures of them in your house, with the rope there, etcetera, etcetera. That will be an important step in avoiding any more adventures like this. We'll have them out in under half an hour, and you can start to get back to normal". Kate wanted to shriek in his ear that she had just been attacked, threatened with acid – what had happened to that for God's sake – and almost executed like a common criminal; she was in a state of extreme shock; and this man, saviour though he may have been, was glibly talking about her getting back to normal, like she'd sprained her ankle or something. If she had had even an ounce of energy she would have slapped him as hard as she could; but every last drop had drained from her, and she just nodded mutely.

The men were gone only a few minutes, during which time Kate made as much effort as she could to pull herself together. She was now safe, she told herself, or at least she supposed herself to be for the moment; and the top priority was to get some answers to some fairly obvious questions. Four in fact – who were the first two men, who were the second pair, why did the first two want her dead, and why did the second pair want her alive? From the responses she had had so far, she had little optimism that she would get answers to any of them. When they returned, the more junior of the two, whom Kate now registered was tall, well over six foot, quite young she thought, tanned, with tight-cropped hair, and a very athletic build, went to her kitchen saying he would make some tea which she must drink with a lot of sugar. The other man was much older, probably late forties she guessed, rather non-descript in every way, but quite muscular and very much in command. Both were clearly American, unless they were Canadian. The boss came back into the sitting room and asked Kate how she felt

'How the hell do you think I feel' were the words that went through her mind, but she wasn't sure whether she actually said them or not. A type of all pervading exhaustion was settling in on her, mental, physical, emotional – total exhaustion; but she hung on to the fact that, very soon, the two of them would leave, and she had to have some answers before then. Start at the beginning, she thought.

"Please tell me who the two men upstairs are, and why they tried to kill me. Please"

"That's classified, Mam; but all the inquiries you've been making have sure pissed someone off along the way – that's for sure".

"You know about …..what I've been doing?" asked Kate.

184

"Not all the details, but, sure, we know you've been digging away up in the North, and clearly someone didn't like what you were doing, someone with powerful contacts".

"And why have you been watching me? Please tell me what's going on"

"Let's just say that we didn't want anything to happen to you. You being thought a suicide would have been almost as bad for us as it would have been for you" Again he spoke a flippant phrase with no humour. So there it was, as she had expected. She would get nothing from these two. As the other man brought her a cup of sweet tea, she asked, without any forethought

"This is all about Paul isn't it? Dr. Emmerson. Those two upstairs must have been involved in his death, and I must have been starting to get close to why they killed him. Why you want me alive I have no idea, unless it's because you want to find out who killed him and why, and I'm your best bet. Is that it?"

There was a pause, and Kate saw that the two men looked at each other. The boss gave a small nod, and the younger one, who had said very little since they had rescued her, spoke.

"Dr. Emmerson isn't dead. We can't tell you any more than that, but he's definitely not dead".

CHAPTER 15

At any time Kate would have been totally stunned. Given that she was close to a complete mental and physical breakdown, the statement – made so definitively - that Paul was still alive started to eat away at her sanity. She could feel her mind start to fragment, one part becoming quite detached from her current predicament, almost calmly observing the turmoil which now afflicted the rest of her being. Part of her was still just trying to recover from, or even just survive, the assault on her not fifteen minutes before; while another part wanted answers, any sort of explanation of what had happened. Now another, welling up from behind all that, was trying to take on board that Paul was alive, Paul was alive, Paul was alive. But even this strand was itself beginning to fray. If he was alive, where was he, *where* was he alive; and then the terrifying thought – what reason on earth had she to believe what she had just been told? Why should she trust the words of these two men, total strangers, fellow members of the human race but otherwise as alien as if they had landed from another planet, just because, clearly for reasons of their own, they had saved her life? Why would they tell her this if they would not tell her anything else about who they were, what they were doing here? It seemed like her brain was exploding, and yet - no doubt some primeval defence mechanism - it was also closing down in the face of just too much shock to her system.

There was little outward sign of all this. Kate slumped forward slightly, her breathing becoming more tortuous, her face white, a mask except for the tears that started once again to run down her cheeks. But as she sat there one thing – one mental image – came to the fore, of Paul, the love of her life, her friend, her partner; and the calmer part of her rapidly splitting persona told her that she just had to regain control of herself – that the next few minutes might make the difference between seeing him again and never seeing him again. She had to make that effort, however non-existent the resources she had left to do so. Slowly she sat up straight again, took a deep gulp of air to try to get control of her breathing, and looked up at the two men.

"Where is he?" she asked, feeling more exhausted by the effort than she could have imagined.

"That's classified too" said the boss man. "But I can tell you he is quite safe and in good shape".

"Will I ever see him again?" Kate asked, but knowing that the question was a huge risk, even if she could believe the answers.

"I sure hope so" came the devastatingly ambiguous reply. "Yep, I think you might – maybe not for a while – but in time. He's a lucky guy having a gutsy lady like you. So, its good news all round". The compliment was of no consequence to Kate, nor the attempted bonhomie. She was trying to get to grips with the idea that she might see Paul again, might be with him as they had been before; but she was in no state of mind to accept the idea.

"Why should I believe that" she said. "Why would you tell me that when you won't tell me anything else about what is going on?"

"Good question. Well, from our point of view, there is no harm in you knowing he's alive. But, like I said, mam, who we are, where Dr. Emmerson is, are both classified pieces of information. There's no reason why you shouldn't know he's okay – there's nothing that you can do about it".

"I can go to the police – get them to re-open their inquiries" replied Kate without thinking, immediately conscious that this was not a very sensible reply.

"You could, but they wouldn't touch the matter – I think you have probably found that out already. Look, I know it must be tough, but just sit tight on that pretty arse of yours and it might all just work out, okay?" Kate was too shattered even to respond to the ghastly sexism of his reply; but before she could think at all, the front door bell rang, and the more junior of the two men went to open it. Yet two more men came in and, on a signal from the man who had opened the door, headed upstairs.

"They'll just get rid of your two intruders" said the boss, "and then we will be on our way. You need someone hear to look after you. You should ring someone, now". Though it was put as a suggestion, there was no doubting that he was issuing an instruction. Kate's first thought was to call Hargreaves, as the only other person who knew anything about what she had been doing; and who could therefore offer any sort of support in dealing with what had happened. But deeper instincts told her not to. It was partly that she was now thinking clearly enough to know that phoning up a police officer who was free-lancing on her case in front of these two quite frightening men was not wise. But from some even deeper level she needed time to think what to tell Hargreaves – whether to tell him anything – because she knew beyond any doubt that he would then try to stop her doing anything more in relation to Paul; and whatever these men had said, she was not ready to drop her investigations – whether what they had said about Paul was true or not. But if she rang Sarah, what would she say to her? Two men had tried to hang her, and two more had shot them – even now their unconscious bodies were being transported out of her house - but she didn't really know why? Sarah might think she was becoming deranged.

The boss man solved her problem.

"If you get a girl friend round, it would be best just to say that you came in and stumbled across someone intent on robbing the place – maybe he grabbed you or something - but then ran off. It would explain why you are in urgent need of some tender loving care but without going into all the...... details. Much wiser all round". As he said the last words, he looked so hard, so forcefully, into Kate's eyes that she felt herself falling backwards in fear. "We don't want *too* many people knowing about all this. That might not be entirely in Dr. Emmerson's interests". The words hung in the air, full of their intended menace.

"Won't she expect me to report it to the police?" said Kate

"I guess so - so report it to the police. They won't do much about it anyway. But, if nothing's gone, you could say that you don't see much point in reporting it. Better to improve your security, though it was useful that you didn't have a lock on your bedroom door. Saved us having to shoot it off".

"How did *you* get in?" she asked.

"With the possible exception of Fort Knox, we can get in to anywhere in a few seconds. In your case a credit card was enough".

Very slowly, and very unsteadily, she stood up and crossed the room to the phone. She rang Sarah and, once more beginning to cry, said she had disturbed a burglar in the house, who had run off without taking anything, but she was shocked out of her mind, and could Sarah come and pick her up, take her to Sarah's cottage for the night? While she fended off Sarah's questions, and her concern, and gave her assurances that she, Kate, would be okay until Sarah got there, the latest arrivals at her house came down the stairs carrying first the man who had grabbed her, still unconscious, and then the other intruder, who clearly had also been shot in the leg and pistol-whipped, but was now semi- conscious. One of the men also carried the rope, coiled up in his hand. When Kate rang off she sat down again and asked

"What will you do with them".

"Return to sender, plus a few photographs. Then the people who sent them will know not to try anything like it again. Very silly of them".

"But who did send them? Christ they tried to kill me – surely I have a right to know?"

"I'm sure you do, but, like I said, it's classified. What's more, it will be a damn sight better for you if you don't know, believe me".

"Was either of you the man who broke into Paul's office?" For the first time since they had burst into her house the man was slightly non-plussed. For a second or two, Kate noticed, she was not just a pathetic victim. He quickly recovered the initiative.

"I'm impressed. It was...... an associate of mine. I'll knock the shit out of him for not being invisible. Now, we'd best be out of here before your lady friend arrives" and he followed the other men out of the house, quietly closing the door behind him.

Kate sat for a few minutes, thoughts swirling into and out of her head. The first thing she managed to grip onto was, she realised, hardly the most important; but it would do for a start. What had happened to the acid – if it was acid? She found the broken glass at the bottom of the stairs. The carpet was wet, but it wasn't burning up. Gingerly she dipped her finger to the wet area, which revealed that it had, indeed, been only water; and she physically shuddered at the thought of how totally she had been controlled by the intruders through the grotesque deception, broken only be the sight – the appalling sight – of the noose hanging by her stairs. She started to clear up the broken glass and as she did so, moved on in her mind to the next question – who, of the people she had spoken to, could have organised such a fate for her? Her first thought was Nicholls, up in Leeds, because of what for him must have been the very humiliating , not to mention frustrating way, she had dealt with him; but her instincts told her this was unlikely. She had not got that much information from him – certainly he hadn't thought there was much for her to go on – and, while he must have been incandescent with rage against her, that would hardly prompt others, who clearly from what she had been told were not just hired thugs, to try to murder her. In any case, she just knew that someone like Nicholls didn't have it in him. No, much more likely, she speculated, was David Price.

Price had not just been unhelpful, he had been concerned when Kate called on him; and it wasn't just 'a bad time' however tricky things were with his wife. He knew something he didn't want to reveal, and he would know people, at Sellafield, who might well share whatever concerns he had. The more she thought about it, the more logical it seemed to her – not for one minute that Price himself would have dreamed up, still less organised, her murder; but he might well have talked to people who would know people........There certainly wasn't anyone else she had spoken to who she thought remotely likely, or capable, of such a thing.

These thoughts were interrupted by Sarah's arrival. Kate added yet another persona to her expanding array, this time playing the quite false role of the victim of an unsuccessful burglary; but she did not have to play-act the role of someone in complete turmoil. That was totally genuine. Sarah did, of course, say that they must call the police; but Kate said she just wasn't up to it at the moment and, in any case, they wouldn't be able to do anything. She was just thankful that she hadn't lost anything, and that the intruder hadn't trashed the place. Probably just a druggie, desperate for some cash. All of which was not just for Sarah's benefit. Do nothing until tomorrow, was all she could think; let your nervous system calm down before you even try to make sense of what has happened, or consider what you should do. As a result, as they drove to Sarah's cottage, Kate lapsed into near silence, a few monosyllabic answers to questions from Sarah, and occasional assurances that she would be alright. Sarah thought she recognised acute shock, did not press Kate and, an hour or so later, Kate passed out in Sarah's spare room, having drunk more tea, eaten half a jacket potato with some cheese and drunk a glass of red wine.

She had a troubled, nightmarish night, once waking with such a vivid impression of a noose hanging in front of her that she cried out, bringing Sarah running into her room. Another diluted whisky calmed her down and, eventually, her whole being suffering nervous exhaustion, she slept.

She woke feeling surprisingly a lot better, and quickly made three resolutions. First, though she had no idea whether what she had been told about Paul was true, she was, she decided, going to believe it; and this gave her an immense boost, an almost tangible warm feeling inside. What, she now recognised, had been the total resignation she had felt underneath all her recent activity dissipated, to be replaced by a state of limbo – anything might be possible - but uplifting rather than depressing. Second, she decided not to go to the police, and told Sarah so, who clearly wasn't happy about this, but saw that Kate was not to be shifted on the point. And, third, she resolved that she was not going to give up one iota of her efforts, not just to find out what had happened to Paul, but to find him if she could. The man the previous evening had calmly said that she didn't have a chance of doing so; but Kate sensed that he had not known very much about what she had found out, nor that she still had a thread to follow, in the shape of ex-Chief Inspector Minogue.

This, however, raised the issue that she had had to face the night before – what, if anything to tell Hargreaves. She felt some guilt at not telling him what had happened; but she couldn't face him trying to stop her investigations and, she told herself, his conversation with Minogue would probably go much better if he didn't know. This clear in her mind, she thanked Sarah for her help, said that she was feeling much better, and would head home. They arranged to meet that evening. As soon as she got home, she rang Hargreaves, remembering as she failed to get through to him that he was in Court that day.

It was a desperately frustrating day. After all that had happened, she just wanted to move forward as rapidly as possible; but her only lead was Minogue and, she reminded herself, that that only came from a single reference from a very old man suffering dementia. She had to know what his role was, but accepted that only Hargreaves could find this out. She spent part of the day talking to a security firm about Chubb locks, door chains, an alarm system and even CCTV, and provisionally arranged a visit the following week. But it was still a huge relief when Hargeaves rang her around 5.00 pm and they arranged to meet after lunch the next day. Twenty-one hours later, punctuated by supper with Sarah and a surprisingly good night, Hargreaves picked her up and they headed off down the A34. Two hours later, having crossed the entry to Poole Harbour by a small car ferry locked onto a chain across the entrance, they arrived in the centre of Swanage. They had some tea at a small café on the waterfront while Kate gave him a raft of quite unnecessary and, in some cases, quite impractical, advice on how to approach Minogue; and then Kate set off for a walk along the cliffs running north towards Studland. Hargreaves meanwhile headed south, also on foot, towards Dalston Point and, just on the outskirts of Swanage stopped outside a reasonable sized house set above the town with views across the bay.

Hargreaves was very much in two minds how to play the forthcoming interview – not in the usual sense of mere uncertainty, but in the more literal sense of having two quite clear strategies, both of which were compelling, but almost certainly contradictory. On the one hand, he very much wanted to do whatever he could to help Kate. She was undoubtedly on to something; the police force, which he normally felt quite proud of, had been less than helpful; he admired the way Kate had pursued the matter and, if he was honest with himself, he felt some considerable attraction to her – not surprising really, given she was tall, attractive, intelligent, personable and resilient under the most trying of circumstances. So, part of him said that he would not take any prevarications from Minogue. At the same time, Minogue was an ex-Chief Inspector, who no doubt maintained some sort of lines of contact back to the Met; and Hargreaves was quite clear that, if he played this wrongly, too aggressively, he could easily end up losing his job. All his instincts told him to go very cautiously into this particular unknown. All this he had pondered as he had sat outside the courtroom for some long time the previous day, waiting to be called to give evidence. He had been the arresting officer in a burglary case

190

involving the theft of commercial data from the head office of a company based in Oxford; and the prosecution had taken most of the day trying to explain to the jury the significance of the data. Fortunately, with so much spare time on his hands, he had come to a conclusion as to how, caught between the two horns of this particular dilemma, he would tackle Minogue.

He rang the bell, and a man, in his sixties Hargreaves estimated, opened the door. He was tanned, looked quite fit, had well groomed grey hair, and a welcoming disposition.

"I'm really sorry to trouble you, sir" said Hargreaves. "Are you Chief Inspector Minogue?"

"That's correct" said the man "How can I help you?"

"My name is Hargreaves. I'm a DS with the Thames Valley police, based in Oxford – here's my Warrant Card. I wonder if you might be able to spare me a few minutes, perhaps give me some advice? It relates to a very old case which I believe you were involved in". Whatever reaction Hargreaves might have anticipated, it wasn't the one he got. Minogue smiled.

"Why do I have a terrible premonition as to which case this refers to? 1983 by any chance?"

"That's right" said Hargreaves. "How did you know?"

"Oh, let's just say that I thought from the beginning that it would never really go away completely. Frankly, I'm surprised it has been this long until someone came knocking. How did you find me? I had very little to do with the case". Hargreaves, somewhat thrown by Minogue's reaction, saw a way to get back on track.

"There's a member of the public in Oxford - she's been involved in a missing person case. We don't think there is much point in pursuing it - in fact we aren't – but she has kept on about it to me – I was the original officer on the case though, as I say, it isn't active – and then, rather to my surprise, she announced that an Inspector Minogue was involved in some way from over thirty years ago. I wouldn't have followed it up, but your name is sufficiently unusual that it wasn't any problem to track down that there had, at least, been an Inspector with that name. So I thought it might just be worth coming to talk to you. That's just about as much as I know". Hargreaves hoped this exuded the right combination of conscientiousness and wide-eyed innocence.

"It's less unusual than you'd think – the name" replied Minogue. "One or two in nearly every phone book in the country. But I guess not many DCIs. How did she get my name?"

"I have no idea, and she wouldn't tell me – another reason I thought of dropping it. To be honest I expected that you wouldn't know what on earth I was talking about, but there clearly was an odd case of some sort in '83?"

"You'd better come in" said Minogue, and led the way into a large, comfortable looking living room. He indicated for Hargreaves to take a seat.

"Tell me about the missing person" said Minogue.

"Oh, well, there isn't much to tell. It's her boy-friend. Almost certainly a mugging for drug money gone wrong, unless he's done a flit with another woman. I can see why she is so determined to pursue it, but we don't have any leads, and what it has to do with anything that happened before either of them was borne I haven't clue".

"Neither have I" said Minogue. "You said you wanted advice, and my advice is to drop the thing. There was a case in 1983, not one of mine I should add – I was just a conduit for certain communications – but there were some irregularities about it, which I was strongly advised to ignore if I wanted to continue in Her Majesty's police force. I've never been asked about what happened, and I don't intend to say anything even now; but I have always thought that one day, someone would, as I said, come knocking about it. But I really do not have any idea why it might re-surface now. Perhaps it isn't that case at all"

"I think it is." said Hargreaves firmly. "The woman mentioned 1983 quite specifically." Kate had clearly hooked onto something real, but Minogue appeared quite adamant, despite his open manner, that he wouldn't say anything more. "You said it wasn't your case. Whose was it?"

"One of my Inspectors – good man, though he left the force soon after. It came to me because he wanted advice on what to do. I made a few calls, told him the result. That was it. I can't tell you any more, except to repeat that I can see no reason why it should have any relevance today, and you'd be much wiser dropping this line of inquiry".

Hargreaves thought as hard as he could, grasping for any way in which he could keep the discussion going, find some way to get Minogue to say more, but he knew it was useless. More than that, as far as he'd gone he had, he thought, been totally convincing as just a hard-working cop following up a rather unusual lead. If he pressed further, that veneer would begin to crack; and if he pushed Minogue too far, he suspected that the ex-Chief Inspector was quite capable of making life very difficult indeed for Hargreaves.

"Well, thanks for that. To tell you the truth, I'm not keen to pursue it. It's just odd that the girlfriend linked it back to an actual case. Maybe I won't disclose that to her, not unless she comes up with a whole lot more to substantiate her claim, I suspected that she was just saying anything to try to keep us interested; and maybe she just read something somewhere – something quite unconnected - but where she thought she saw some link. Who knows? Anyway, thanks very much for your time". They engaged in some small talk, about Minogue's retirement activities, about Hargreaves' career to date; and then he left.

192

Half an hour later, as previously arranged, he met Kate and suggested they had an early supper in Swanage before heading back to Oxford. She agreed, and they took a table in the Cauldron Bistro, on the main street but only a few metres away from the front. Run by two couples and only open a few days a week in the season, it provided one of the finest meals that either of them had ever had in their lives. Sadly, they both had more immediate matters on their minds. Kate looked at Hargreaves expectantly.

"I know I've said this to you before. There's bad news, lots of it I'm afraid, but just one absolute gem of good news". He filled Kate in on Minogue, that he didn't seem to have anything to hide, in what he said or in his manner, apart from what he quite explicitly said he couldn't tell Hargreaves, which was just about everything – and apart from confirming that he had been involved, at least tangentially, in an odd case in 1983. This had the virtue of confirming that Framwell – ill and forgetful as he was – had got that right. It seemed likely that Minogue had spoken to Framwell, but of the likely contents of the call, Hargreaves had no inkling.

"So what is the gem of good news" asked Kate, rather depressed by everything Hargreaves had so far told her.

"He said the case, whatever it was, belonged to one of his Inspectors". He held up his hands to cut Kate off. "I know, I know, he didn't say who it was, and at a Nick like Paddington Green there must be quite a number of them; but he did say that the Inspector, whoever he was, left the force soon after. It was just a throw-away line, and I hope Minogue is not thinking right now what a mistake that was, but that should be enough for me to track him down. Paddington Green is serious stuff – recruits some of the top guys from around the country. There won't be many at Inspector level who then left - in fact I wonder why he left? It might even be significant, except that I really doubt Minogue would have mentioned it if it had anything to do with the case".

"How long will it take you to find him?" asked Kate

"I can probably do it on Monday or Tuesday. Just a question of pulling out the names of all the DIs at Paddington Nick in 1983 and cross checking it with pensions data. I'll just say what I said to find Minogue – that I'm trying to track down a former officer to help on a cold case. If he was young enough at the time he may not be drawing whatever deferred pension he's entitled to; but they'll have the data anyway".

For a while they talked of other things, even began to appreciate the food and wine. Kate, with the adrenalin of the day somewhat spent, began to relax a little. But the ambiance, the nervous exhaustion of the last two days, and a little too much wine, all combined to make her feel rather morbid – not good company at all. She pointed this out to Hargreaves, who gently brushed it aside, saying he couldn't think of a nicer way to spend a Friday evening. Something about the kindness of this thought, amongst all the horror and tension of the last few days, if not weeks, got to Kate, and she could not stop tears welling up in her eyes. Without pausing to think, Hargreaves stretched his hands across the table and gently covered hers. He said nothing, knowing there was absolutely nothing sayable at this precise moment, but knowing this was not 'a member of the public' as he had described her to Minogue. This was a woman with whom he was falling in love.

Kate sat quite still. The tender touch of another human being - something she had not realised she had missed so much – was comforting; and she did not want to end it. At the same time she recognised that, whatever happened, this changed her relationship with Hargreaves for ever. She looked up, looked into his eyes. There was something she had to tell him.

"Paul's alive" she said.

CHAPTER 16

For the second time in two hours, something Hargreaves had said, or in this case done, had resulted in a response that was completely unexpected. Minogue's knowing response to his inquiry had been a shock, but Kate's words were, in fact, so far outside anything he had anticipated that he couldn't really take them in.

"What did you say?" he whispered.

"Neil, in all this terrible time, you are the only person in a position to help me who has been prepared to; and I know that you have taken, still are taking, huge risks with your career to help me. I am so grateful for that; and sitting here with you now is one of the few enjoyable moments I have had in a very long time. But I believe that Paul is alive, that I will see him again soon, and you must see that……. that's everything to me"

Hargreaves didn't know what to say. He wanted to apologise for being so crass as to make any advance to her if Paul was still alive; but why was she saying that? Hargreaves assumed that Emmerson was certainly dead by now and, more important, he had understood some while ago that Kate accepted that. He hadn't planned to reach out to her, hadn't thought about it, but it would never have occurred to him to do so if he had thought Paul might still be alive, or if Kate still thought that. He kept hold of her hands, and she didn't resist.

"I don't know what to say, Kate. For your sake I hope, I really hope, that you are right; and I don't want to …….. I don't know, sound pessimistic; but I thought you had accepted some time ago that it was unlikely. I'm so sorry not to have realised….." Kate interrupted him.

"No, Neil, it's me who must apologise. I had given up but.....something happened......yesterday. I should have told you". She fought to stay calm, but the effort was not successful. Hargreaves waited for her to explain but, in the silence said

"Should I let go of your hand?"

"Only if you decide that you can't forgive me".

"How am I going to drive home then?" he said, and smiled at her. At this, whatever composure Kate retained, which was little enough, collapsed and she sat there, trembling, thankful that they were sitting in a small alcove, away from the eyes of other diners. And so she told him, about arriving home the previous evening, being attacked by two men, almost murdered, how she had been saved, literally at the last moment by two others, how they had shot her attackers and got them taken away; that absolutely none of it made any sense to her, but that her two saviours had been quite clear that Paul was alive and should, all being well, come back to her eventually. She ended by saying that she hadn't told him, partly because it might have made it more difficult for him with Minogue, but also because she was scared that he might have insisted that they call the whole thing off.

For a moment, Hargreaves recalled how, several years before, the Deputy Chief Constable of the Thames Valley police, a sober, well remunerated and much respected family man, had been accused of some petty shop-lifting at the Sainsbury's supermarket in the centre of Oxford. No-one who knew him was prepared to give the story any credence, but the witness – a shelf stacker in the store and herself a woman of apparently impeccable integrity - was very sure of herself; and the Judge was inclined to believe her. During the case, one of Hargreaves colleagues had summed it up. There was only a 5% chance that it was true, and only a 5% chance that the witness was mistaken. Unfortunately, those were the only two possible explanations. In similar vein, Hargreaves now thought that there was only a 5% chance that this extraordinary story could be true, and a 5% chance that Kate was suffering serious mental illness; but there were no other possibilities. For the moment he'd go with the former.

"That's terrible, appalling." he said. "You didn't call the station?" Kate repeated what she had been told – that the police would not do anything – always supposing they believed her; and she added that, if her experiences with DI Johnson were anything to go by, she thought that was right.

"So no-one else knows about this?" asked Hargreaves.

"No-one except you, and you probably think I'm going crazy; but what happened was real, and so I just hope that what they said about Paul is real as well".

There was a long silence after this. Both had things they wanted to say but neither felt it was the right moment to say them. Kate broke the deadlock.

"I'm so sorry." she repeated "I should have told you before. But all I can think of is whether you will still help me track down Minogue's Inspector from 1983. I know that's really selfish, but at least it is the path of honesty".

"I think we should sort us out first" said Hargreaves. "I know that if Paul is alive, if there is even a chance that he is, then you are his, and I would never – not for one moment – do anything but respect that. But until he is back, I hope you will allow me to look after you as best I can, because I think you are a truly wonderful woman. That's why I am still holding your hand". Again that disarming smile.

"That seems so….unfair" said Kate.

"Not at all. You are going through a very bad time, without Paul, without support. You are certainly going to need my help, but you also need some TLC; and I'm nominating myself. No questions, no commitment. The situation is quite extraordinary, and clearly dangerous; you're extraordinary, the way you've kept going through all of this; so, let's have a slightly extraordinary relationship". He did not wait for an answer. He leaned across the table, gave her a very light kiss on the cheek, and then sat back, finally letting go of her hand. "Now, in answer to your question, yes, I will try to track down Minogue's inspector on Monday; but we are going to have to be very careful. To start with, you are going to have to move out of your house. It's just too dangerous".

"Neil, I know you are probably right, but don't ask me to. I just can't face it at the moment. I feel totally violated by those men; but my home is about my only grip on reality – apart from you – at the moment. I'm already in the process of making the place totally secure". Hargreaves wasn't persuaded – not one bit – but saw that now was not the time to push the matter.

"I won't argue with you, but we do need to think very seriously about your safety. I care about you, and until Paul is back, I'm on point duty".

Kate was more moved by Hargreaves' words than she showed. She still thought that maybe she was being unfair to him, using Hargreaves in her hunt for Paul; but she liked him, and trusted him, they had both been honest about their feelings, and what he had said made emotional sense to her. She might regret it, but for now it felt right.

"Thank you so much" was all she could think to say.

"Believe me, it's a real pleasure" he said. "Now, is there anything, anything at all, that you can remember about any of the men you saw yesterday?"

"Not much. But the first two were British I would say, whereas the two who saved me were definitely American. And they as good as admitted that one of their people – whoever they are - had broken into Paul's office, though why I don't know. Presumably they were after his files, but whether they got them, or they were stolen later, I don't know".

"Do you think they are holding Paul, or just knew someone else was?"

"I don't know, but whoever is holding him, they've got to have the backing of some authority somewhere – someone who can call off Johnson's inquiries, clamp down on the Press. That doesn't sound like Americans".

"The UK and the US are pretty close at the moment." said Hargreaves "But that doesn't take us much further. I think we will just have to wait, and hope that we find out more next week".

They drove back to Oxford, both in different ways comfortable with their altered relationship. Hargreaves dropped Kate at her house, and insisted on coming in to check that everything was in order. Having told her, quite unnecessarily, not to open her door to anyone unless she knew who it was, he left, saying he'd call next week as soon as he had something to report. Kate thanked him more than once for his kindness to her, and his understanding. She said it meant a lot to her, and both knew that it was true.

Kate spent a psychologically draining week-end, fluctuating between hope that Paul might really still be alive and complete despair that she would ever find out what had happened to him – and on Sunday night went to Sarah's for supper. On Monday she went in to OUP, and talked to Harry. She said that, if he agreed, she would stay on leave for another two months; but that she would then definitely return, and put in her usual 110%. Harry sensed Kate's commitment to this and was delighted to agree. Kate had lunch with Janice, who was overjoyed to see Kate, especially as she seemed a little better in herself, recovering some of her old confidence. Tuesday saw her signing a contract for the installation of a series of security measures at her home. Hargreaves rang at 5.00pm.

"I've found him" he said. "His name's Ken Richards. He left the Met in 1984. I don't know what he did then, but I've got an address for him in Henley. I'll go as soon as I finished here tonight – it'll only take 45 minutes to get there. I'll call you as soon as I can".

"Neil, if he left the police in 1984, then there surely can't be any problem about me coming with you, can there? I may be able to help." She didn't attempt to spell out that if Hargreaves ran into difficulty, then an alternative - more feminine – approach could be useful. Whether this was seductive, hysterical or just – literally – a sob story, she was ready to use it; but she also had another possible strategy in mind as well. Hargreaves' instant reaction was that this was a very bad idea; but he very much wanted her to come with him.

"Okay, but you shouldn't use your real name; and we need to think up a reason for you being there. I'll pick you up in an hour or so and we can discuss it on the way there".

On the drive to Henley, Kate spelt out her plan.

"You may be able to make some mileage by waving your Warrant Card; but this thing clearly goes much wider than a police investigation. So why don't I be from somewhere in Whitehall – maybe the Home Office – and make out, in as subtle way as I can of course, that I'm there to keep an eye on you? Then, if he starts to clam up, I may be able to coax him forward a little. What do you think?"

"What if he wants to see some ID from you?"

"I'll tell him my department doesn't carry ID. It may not work, but there's nothing to lose"

"I think there is. He may or may not talk to me, but I am absolutely legit. If he gets suspicious of you he may just clam up". Hargreaves began to realise that Kate accompanying him, however much he wanted it, was not such a good idea after all.

"Then I had better be your junior police officer" said Kate. If you show him your Card, and introduce me, he's unlikely to insist on seeing my ID as well". They debated it some more, and Hargreaves suggested that she wait for him in the car; but Kate was adamant that she hadn't pursued the matter for so long; and - she left unspoken - pretended to be all sorts of people in the process; not to see for herself the man who might hold the key to it all. For Hargreaves, faced with Kate's determination, what she proposed seemed, in the end, the least bad solution, risky though it was.

Richards' house, when they arrived, though single storey, was quite palatial. "Even a garden shed in Henley costs a fortune" said Hargreaves. "This place must have set him back a lot. I can't see me retiring to somewhere like this". They rang the bell and a woman, probably in her sixties if one looked at her neck, but from a distance could well pass for no more than forty, answered the door.

"I'm sorry to trouble you" said Hargreaves. "I'm Detective Sergeant Hargreaves from the Thames Valley police" holding up his Warrant Card "and this is Detective Sergeant Jones. Would it be possible to have a word with Mr Kenneth Richards?"

"Yes" replied the woman, looking slightly puzzled. "Please come in and I will get him. Can I tell him what it is about?" Meaning, thought Kate, can you tell *me* what this is about.

"Certainly" said Hargreaves, in his most disarming manner. "We are working on a case which might – just possibly, I'm far from sure – relate back to a case Mr. Richards dealt with when he worked for the Metropolitan police force. It's a long shot, but I thought he might be able to help us". He hoped this might put any concerns she might have had to rest; but the resulting body language was not encouraging.

"I'll get him - one moment" she said, and disappeared off.

"If his reaction is like hers, we may not get much out of this" said Hargreaves.

"Then you will have to arrest him for withholding information" said Kate. Hargreaves stared at her, unsure whether she was joking or not. He had no time to find out, as Richards walked into the room.

Both Kate and Hargreaves were quite shocked at his appearance. He looked very pale and even slightly emaciated, with tufts of grey hair, and walked slowly with the aid of a stick. He saw their reaction – no doubt one he was used to – and indicated for them to sit down. "As you can see, I'm not in the best of health - prostate cancer I'm afraid. I've had it for years without much trouble, but it's got to me now. They were treating me but it's just pain-killers now. A few months at best I think, if I'm lucky; a few weeks if not. Anyway, how can I help you?"

"I'm very sorry" said Hargreaves. "I hope this won't be too stressful for you?"

"Good God, no" replied Richards. "Anything to take my mind off it is welcome". Hargreaves took this at face value, and embarked on an approach he had agreed with Kate on the way down to Henley, a quite different one from the approach he had adopted with Minogue.

"I'm afraid it's the Sellafield case again. Someone's starting to stir things up again – maybe the Press are sniffing around as well but no-one's sure. Anyway, my governor's been asked to follow it up – actually I think he has probably been asked to close it down if possible; but it was a long time ago, and we are quite in the dark. We've spoken to our people at the Cumbrian end, but they said we should talk to you. Can you fill me in on what happened exactly? It's entirely an internal matter".

Richards sat there in silence for what seemed an eternity to Kate. He looked, if it was possible, even older, more drawn than when they had come in.

"You said 'again'" he said finally. "The Sellafield case *again*. What did you mean by that? Have there been previous attempts to look into it?" Hargreaves wasn't sure how best to answer. He had said it merely to try to convey that he has some familiarity with the case.

"I think so, yes" he said . "I haven't been involved myself before, and it may have been some long time ago; but there seems to be a lot of angst around – I don't think this is the first time".

"You know that I was told never to say anything, ever?" said Richards in a slightly distant manner. Hargreaves looked suitably surprised.

"No, actually, I didn't. Look" replied Hargreaves, turning on a hint of frustration "I know very little. I was told to evaluate what risks there might be if anyone started looking too closely at the 'incident' that occurred at Sellafield.

But the DI whom I spoke to in Cumbria said the real issue was at Paddington, not Sellafield, and to talk to you. So I'd appreciate any help you can give me".

"What did you say your name was?" asked Richards.

"DS Hargreaves. Here is my Card. This is DS Jones. I can't evaluate any risks without knowing the full story" he added, in the hope that it would distract Richards from asking to see Kate's ID. There was another interminable pause.

"This is definitely all internal?" he said eventually

"The whole point is to tie it up without a lot of fuss" said Hargreaves.

"As I'm not that long for this world, I may as well tell you what happened. In fact I'd quite like to tell someone. It was the weirdest day, and it certainly changed my life – for the better I should say. How it can make any waves now I don't know, but that's for you to sort out".

"Do you mind if DS Jones takes notes?" asked Hargreaves.

"No. You won't have much difficulty remembering, I can tell you; but the timing is key. If the timing had been different, everything would have been different".

"Okay" said Hargreaves. "As much detail as you can, up until Minogue rang Framwell". Kate, who had said nothing, was mightily impressed. A masterstroke, she thought. It looked like Richards was going to talk; but if he had any reservations, the familiarity with the case implied by this one sentence would quell them, she felt certain. She got out the small notepad Hargreaves had given her on the way there.

"I was on a night shift" said Richards. "Originally, there was going to be an early morning raid, but it had been stood down, and everything was fairly quiet. Then, shortly after midnight I get this call put through to me, from the Lancashire Constabulary. They're following up a 999 call from some chap who's out watching badgers, would you believe? Told them that, through the trees, he'd seen a van pull up on a very minor road near where he was watching. A group of five people get out and go to a large car which he can see has been parked in the entrance to a small field. But then two of them go back with what turns out are cans of petrol, pour them all over the van and then set fire to it. So, he knows they're up to no good, and by now he's terrified in case they see him. He keeps well hidden, while they make sure the van is well and truly alight but, as they drive off, the light from the burning van is quite enough for him to see the registration number of the car. So, as soon as he gets home, he calls 999, tells them what he's seen, and gives them the number. Lancashire CID find that it's registered to one Ceiran Hughes, living in Kilburn, which is why they are calling us. So, over the next couple of hours or so I call in a team and we stake out Hughes' house. He isn't known to us, but he's clearly been misbehaving himself. Around 3.30 am up he turns, in his car, with the four others. So, we nick the lot of them – four blokes and a girl - and get them back to the station, separate them, and ask them what they've been up to. Couldn't get a word out of them. As miserable, tight-lipped bunch as I'd ever come across. Hughes in particular, just sat and stared me out. Didn't complain, didn't bluster, didn't ask me what it was all about – I couldn't have answered him if he had – didn't demand a lawyer. He just sat there. I was actually beginning to think that the most we'd be able to do him for was destruction of what I was sure must be a stolen vehicle. Then, six o'clock in the morning, the Desk Sergeant comes in and says he's just heard on the news that there's been some sort of explosion at Sellafield, and I know at once that it's them. If I'd had any doubts, their reaction when I told them would have blown them right away. Hughes just couldn't resist a smile; and one of the others, the youngest of them, almost punched the air he was so pleased".

Richards paused. He had become quite animated as he re-lived the events of that night; but the effort was clearly weakening him. Kate was scribbling a summary of what he had said, stunned to realise that there *had* been an explosion that night, but even more so that it hadn't been an accident, but a terrorist attack. Why it hadn't devastated the area – hadn't even stopped the plant running – she had no idea. That would have to wait.

"What happened next?" asked Hargreaves.

"Well, then we got down to serious business. I set up calls to the anti-terrorist unit based at Paddington; and while that was being activated, interviewed each of them formally. I said it was clear now what they had been up to, that there was no point in them not co-operating, even suggested that they'd have a much easier time of it with me than the next lot to interview them. Didn't get anywhere. They all just sat there, saying not a word. I still didn't even know who any of them were except Hughes. But – you get an instinct, a sort of feeling – the young one was starting to fret, starting to realise that they were in very deep shit; and I thought I might just be able to cut him loose. I tried telling him that one of the others had decided to tell all, and that this was his chance to co-operate – you know the routine – but he held out against that. Started sweating a lot, it even got him talking, though only to tell me to fuck off; but it was something. So then I really got to work on him. Told him that it was clear they were an IRA terrorist cell; that I didn't know any details yet, but they had obviously pulled off a major strike, perhaps the biggest of the century if they'd actually blown up a nuclear power plant, and he had a choice. If he refused to say anything, then I had no doubt that he, like the others, would go to prison for the rest of his life, and I also had no doubt that the authorities would make sure it was a prison on the mainland, where he'd not only be beaten to a pulp by the other inmates but – good looking chap that he was - fucked, sodomised within an inch of his life, year in, year out. Total living hell – he'd probably try to kill himself but he'd be lucky to succeed. Or, he could tell me about it – co-operate. It wouldn't make any difference to what they had done, but it could make a whole lot of difference to what happened to him. Maybe a 20 year term –

probably only serve about twelve –but it could be arranged for him to serve it in the Maze. He'd be with other IRA prisoners and would be an absolute star – their biggest success in years - looked after, protected, a real modern-day hero. And out before he was forty. Those were the options, I told him; and he had precisely five minutes to decide. It was all a total load of old bollocks; I was just making it up as I went along; but it could just have been true – certainly he looked like he believed it. Anyway, it worked. He went completely to pieces; said his name was Michael McGuiness, that Hughes was the mastermind, and that they had targetted the pipeline taking radioactive waste from the re-processing plant to the storage tanks. And he also said that they had blown the roof off some building above where they aimed to rupture the pipeline so that the radioactivity would escape more easily". He paused again. "I should have asked you, would you like a drink?"

Neither Hargreaves nor Kate replied. Both were mesmerized by what Richards had told them – so far beyond anything they might have anticipated, with new questions pouring in. Kate found she had almost stopped breathing. Slowly she forced herself to relax, conscious that she was supposed to be no more than a junior officer taking notes. Eventually Hargreaves said he was fine. Richards looked across at Kate, who just shook her head.

"Well, that's the boring bit" said Richards. "You might change your mind when you hear the exciting bit". A mirthless smile signified just how much this was meant to tease them both. Kate couldn't stop a jerk-reaction as she looked up sharply at Richards, realising how hot she felt.

"In that case, maybe I could have a glass of water" she said. As Richards went to get it, she looked at Hargreaves and was about to say something, but he just put a finger to his lips.

"Are you getting this all down?" he asked. Kate nodded. Richards re-appeared a moment later, gave both of them glasses of water and took up the story again.

"You can imagine how I felt. It wasn't yet eight o'clock in the morning and, within a few hours of a major terror attack, I had the bastards, under lock and key and confessed. I just needed McGuiness to sign something – I'd taped everything but I wasn't going to be able to use it, not given the threat – the deal I'd made – and had almost finished writing it when the Desk Sergeant came in again. He's just heard the *eight o'clock* news and there's a Sellafield exec being interviewed saying that it was all an electrical failure – huge short circuit, collapsed pylon and so on. Agrees that it must have seemed a lot worse to anyone who saw or heard it; but there's no cause for alarm, just some reduced output for a few days, no blackouts. Then they have a reporter who's actually at the gates of the plant, large as life. There's a big police presence there he says, but apart from that everything seems to be as normal, trucks in and out, workforce all as normal".

"You're saying that they had a bomb attack, radio-active waste pouring out, and they just went on as normal?" said Hargreaves. "I can't believe it".

"If you can't believe it now, think what I was thinking then, with a self-confessed bunch of IRA bombers sitting in my Nick. It just couldn't be happening. No-one would be mad enough to ignore a nuclear disaster, however inconvenient it might be. I just couldn't make any sense of it. Do you know, I actually went and looked in on them to make sure that I hadn't been hallucinating. I realised, of course, that no-one up in Sellafield would have any idea that I was sitting down here with the bastards under lock and key; but I really didn't know what to do next, I can tell you. That's when I went and saw Minogue. He'd just arrived, and he was my boss – Christ did I need a boss to hand things over to. I told him what had happened and, do you know, I think he seriously considered that I had totally flipped, or got smashed or something. He went and had a look at the five of them – looking for confirmation I don't doubt – and then he rang the Cumbrian CID. Said he needed to speak to the Chief Constable, no-one else. That was Framwell. He'd been in for several hours already. I was with Minogue as he politely told Framwell that the incident at Sellafield, previously reported as an explosion, and now revealed as an electrical failure was, in fact, the result of an IRA attack; and that the Paddington Nick was, at that very moment, holding the team which had carried it out. No doubts, one had confessed and – this was the main thing – he claimed that they had ruptured a major pipeline with radio-active material running through it; so what the hell was going on with the electrics story? Shouldn't they be clearing the workforce out, if not the whole local civilian population?"

So far, for a dying man, Richards had been remarkably resilient; but now he faltered, suddenly looking even greyer than before; and it was clear that reliving that morning was beginning to take its toll. He started to cough. "I need a Scotch" he said. "I'm not supposed to – it doesn't mix with the morphine – but it helps. Sure you don't want one?"

"I think I will have one" said Hargreaves "What a story. How about you Jones? In the circumstances I think we could each do with one".

"Just a small one then" replied Kate. Richards opened up a drinks cabinet, poured them all Scotches, got some more water from the kitchen and sagged back into his chair. Hargreaves and Kate waited for him to go on.

"Framwell said that what he was about to tell Minogue should go no further than him and me – absolutely no-one else. He was aware that it had been an IRA attack; but the local police had no jurisdiction. The sequence of events was that, when the incident occurred, the Sellafield Security team had gone straight through to their equivalents at the Home Office, who had sent a team up – jetted them up in less than forty minutes apparently. But a number of local inhabitants had been calling the police, which was why Framwell, as the senior police officer for Cumbria, had been called in. He'd contacted the Sellafield team to ask what was going on, and what should he tell people. They said, for his ears only, that there had been an attack; but that for some reason, as yet unexplained, at least to Framwell, there was no danger to the population, that he should sit tight, and they would get back to him. A couple of hours later they got in touch with the details of how they were going to play it. The explosion had brought down a pylon and a main overhead cable; so they were going to say it was an electrical failure. They were squaring this with the security people on duty at Sellafield. All Framwell had to do was let his people know this, so they could handle the public in the same way. He was busy doing this when Minogue's call had come through; and that seemed to change everything. None of us, me, Minogue, Framwell, had a clue what to do. In the end, Framwell said to leave it with him – he'd go back to the Security people at Sellafield, ask them what to do, and he'd get back to us. In the meantime, we were to do nothing, absolutely nothing".

Richards was, by now, looking distinctly groggy, and the coughing was becoming more pronounced.

"Are you okay to go on" asked Hargreaves.

"Oh ,yes, don't worry. I get very tired, but I'll be fine" said Richards, as he took a small sip of his Scotch. "Anyway, I'm quite near the end. Framwell called back around 10.00 am and said that an anti-terrorist unit from C19 would be round to pick up Hughes and the others shortly. They would be shipped back to Northern Ireland he said, but gave me no hint as to what would happen to them. It would, however, be an end of it as far as we were concerned; and as far as the rest of the world was concerned, it never happened – none of it. Then a lot of thinly disguised stick and carrot. Big trouble if it ever got out, but very good prospects if we did our duty. We both pledged undying loyalty etcetera etcetera and we handed over the Irish lot about half an hour later, to the most vicious looking bunch of military types I have ever seen in my life – the 'thank-God-they're-on-our-side' brigade if ever there was one. So, now you know".

"And you've never spoken about this before, to anyone else?" asked Hargreaves.

"Well, not quite" said Richards. "At first I was quite happy to keep quiet and, as far as I know, Minogue has never said anything to anyone. Whether it helped his career or not I don't know, but he did quite well for himself. But I began to feel uneasy about it all, In particular about what happened to the IRA guys. Everyone accepted the electrical failure story – they even had the television cameras in to Sellafield to film the pylon – and the Irish just disappeared. We never heard another thing about them. Julie, my wife, could tell I was....I don't know..... troubled I suppose; and in the end I told her. She was pretty shocked, said it stank, that it would come back to haunt me sooner or later, and that I should get out. I talked to Minogue, who sent me to see some high-up at the Home Office. I hadn't planned actually to leave; but he was clearly suspicious.

Bluntly, we did a deal. I'd leave, never talk again, and a previously unknown great-uncle would leave me some dosh – getting on for a hundred thousand which, in those days was a lot of money. I set myself up in publishing, doing readership surveys for magazines – there's a surprisingly large amount of money to be made from it – and that's it, until you two walked through the door. Why has it all surfaced again now?"

"Something has come up as a result of technical checks at the plant; and one of the scientists involved is making waves", said Hargreaves non-committally, but sticking quite close to what he assumed was the truth of the matter. "Do you know how it was that the attack, if it was successful, didn't devastate the region with radioactive fall-out?"

"That's the real joke" said Richards, but without the slightest sign that the matter was anything other than deadly serious. "They were very clever, targetted a main drainage channel – I assume that they wouldn't have made much impression on any of the main buildings themselves – and arranged to blow the top off the building underneath which they had planted the explosives, to make sure the stuff escaped. It was this second explosion which brought the pylon down. What they didn't know was that there had been a serious leak from the drainage channel several years before – kept totally secret of course – but apparently, when the Sellafield engineers looked at it, the whole drainage system was shot to pieces. It dated back to the early days there; and several sections could have gone at any time. Fortunately, the technology had moved on; and it was much cheaper to store the waste at the re-processing plant and remove it periodically. So they just shut down the drainage system. There was nothing going through it. Framwell told Minogue that that was the only reason the Irish were able to get into the building above. If the drainage system had still been being used, the security would have been a hundred times tighter".

"But how did they get in to the site in the first place?" asked Hargreaves.

"Minogue asked that, but Framwell didn't know, or wasn't telling. So, it sounded like a brilliant operation that resulted in the IRA blowing up a disused pipe, the roof of a disused building, and an electricity pylon. I can see why, once they found out, the guys at Sellafield said it was just an electricity cock-up".

"And you've no idea what happened to the bombers?"

"Like I said, none at all. I never heard any more. There obviously wasn't anything in the Press about the attack, once the cover story was accepted; and the IRA didn't make any claims. They would have looked stupid if they had – can you see it: 'it wasn't really electrical, it was us but it didn't quite work' – no chance. And I say the IRA – we all assumed that, and they were clearly Irish – but they could have been some breakaway group for all anyone knew". He finished off his drink. "And that's it. The day that changed my world at least. Funny thing is, if some old codger hadn't been out looking for badgers, no-one outside Sellafield would ever have known what happened; and if we hadn't picked the Irish up and had them sitting in the cells when the news – the true story - first came through, I would never have put two and two together. In fact I've often thought that if the Desk Sergeant had only heard the eight o'clock news, not the six o'clock, I wouldn't have had a clue what they'd been up to".

Hargreaves had no more questions, and asked Kate if she had any.

"Just a couple" said Kate. "Is this right, that apart from the nuclear security people, the only people who knew what actually happened were you, Minogue and Framwell?"

"I think that's right" replied Richards. The locals were all told it was electrical. None of my team was present when McGuiness coughed up. We told the Lancashire Nick that it was a drugs bust, and they offered suitable thanks to the badger man. So, no, no-one else knew".

"And did you ever hear who dreamt up the cover story?"

"No, I didn't. But it must have been either the Sellafield security team or the guys from the Home Office. Whoever first thought of it, I guess it would have to have had Home Office approval. A dangerous game. They must have been shitting themselves when they heard we were getting ready to charge someone".

"But who told them?" asked Kate.

"I don't know, but I assume that once Framwell had heard from us he consulted Sellafield – he must have done – and they would have consulted the Home Office boys. They had had a team there for some hours by then. Why do you ask?" He looked at Kate with a quizzical look.

"I was just thinking about who else we might need to talk to; and who it is safe to talk to". Richards nodded his approval.

"Tell me, if you have talked to Framwell and Minogue, why is this all news to you?" Hargreaves perceived that honesty, or as close to it as he could get, would be the best policy.

"Framwell steered us to you, but he wouldn't discuss it at all. Minogue said he only played a communications role – left the field for you" – which was true, even if Richards' presumption that Minogue had given them his name was quite untrue.

"Well, I hope you deal with whatever has come up. I'm sad I won't be around to hear about it" he added, but without any self-pity. Hargreaves and Kate thanked him for his assistance, hoped he didn't feel too tired by it all, added other kind-sounding but fairly meaningless words, and left. As they got to the car, Hargreaves turned to Kate.

"What in Christ's name have we got ourselves into?"

CHAPTER 17

As they drove back to Oxford, neither of them found it easy to formulate any coherent thoughts, on what they had heard, on what it all meant, and how it related to Paul. The events of that night in 1983 were fairly clear – as Richards had said, it didn't need a lot of notes to remember once the timing was understood – and he had answered most if not all of the questions that Kate had grappled with while she was in Cumbria. What she needed to do was collect her thoughts very systematically in order to understand how Paul fitted in; how it related to the attempt to kill her, and her rescue, why Paul might still be alive and who was driving events now, nearly thirty years later. Plus there was one thing she still didn't understand about 1983. She started to explain her thinking to Hargreaves, but he interrupted her.

"I know we have to have a concerted effort to work out what this all means, and where we go from here, maybe tomorrow evening when we have had a chance to let everything sink in. But the first priority- absolutely before anything else – is you".

"What do you mean?" replied Kate, though she already had a very good idea. It just hadn't been quite as high a priority in her thinking.

"The only people who know I'm involved in this are Minogue and Richards" said Hargeaves. "No-one else at all, and my guess is that neither of them are going to talk to anyone else. Minogue thinks he stalled my inquiries; and Richards is past caring – no, actually, that's not right. He was clearly pleased to have the chance to tell us – anyone – what happened. But someone not only knows you are investigating, they don't like it and they are quite prepared to kill you to stop you. And given what we've just heard, they are likely to be well resourced and very determined. In fact, it's rather suspicious that Richards' illness has suddenly become terminal. It wouldn't have been that difficult for someone to interfere with his treatment. Either that or we were very lucky to have got to him just before he dies. In any event, you can't risk your life on some totally unknown American tough guys telling you that you don't have to worry any more; and they probably won't be around to save you if there is another time. The last thing I want to do is alarm you unnecessarily; and I know what you said about needing your home to be an anchor; but the first thing is to make sure that you are safe. Which means you really can't stay at your place. I shouldn't have ducked the issue before. It's just too dangerous. Not until we get to the bottom of all this".

"Where would I go?" asked Kate, knowing the reply. To her surprise, he said

"I'd thought of my place, but it won't work. If you have been followed at all, then I may have come to their notice, whoever they are; but, in any event, this could take some time. You need your own space, not cooped up with me – however much I might enjoy it" he added, with a rueful grin. "Seriously, this is about you – and Paul – and there's no point in trying to find him if you aren't here to meet him when he returns. So, I'll rent a flat in Oxford, in my name, my references and so on, so there is no link to you; but you can stay there until this is over".

"But I'd have to pay you for it".

"Of course, cash only". He was going to add a facetious remark but instead said

"In fact, thinking about it, it might be better if it wasn't in Oxford. We don't know how determined anyone might be to find you, if they see that you've gone missing. Maybe a town near Oxford would be better. That should put enough distance between you, but still be...... practical". He took one hand off the steering wheel and lightly held hers for a few moments; and Kate, that most resilient, efficient, competent business woman of two months ago realised how much she had had to cope with since then, and how much she was coming to depend on this resourceful and amusing police officer. He could never replace Paul and, thank God, Neil knew that, respected that; but she liked him - a lot. She felt very easy in his company, despite the strange aspect to their relationship, partly because he seemed so very understanding of her situation, but also because, in almost no words at all, they had established an absolute honesty about it. She was not so naïve as to suppose that he didn't want to go to bed with her, and at the earliest opportunity; and, if she was honest with herself, she wouldn't necessarily resist. It would be a moment of welcome intimacy, in some way a re-assertion of her femininity in the totally foreign, brutal world she now found herself in and, more than that, a way of expressing how grateful she was to him, not just for his help but for his understanding, and his restraint. Would it be a betrayal of Paul? At one level, of course it would; and that was why it wouldn't happen. The very fact that she would never tell Paul, and the resulting dishonesty, demonstrated that. But at a deeper level, she thought, it would be no such thing – no betrayal at all. Maybe I have just become so schizophrenic, I can compartmentalise my life in ways I never could before, she thought. But even at this level it wasn't going to happen, because it just wouldn't be fair to Neil. Somewhere at the back of her mind was the nagging question of how Neil himself would answer the question – just one night of passionate love-making or none – but she did not let it surface to the forefront of her mind, where it might pose more problems than she could answer.

Hargreaves had no inkling of what was going through Kate's mind; and feared she might be marshalling her arguments to reject his idea. But, when she eventually spoke, she agreed that it might be best; that she would pack some things and take a hotel room until Neil could fix a place for her; but they now needed, urgently, to decide the significance of what they had just learnt.

"Why don't you talk it through out loud" said Hargreaves, "everything you can think of; and I'll critique it, question everything I can, raise any objection or make any observation; and you note down everything we don't know. Then we can review what comes out of that, and decide how to move forward". It sounded a good idea, and Kate embarked on it with some optimism.

"Five IRA break into Sellafield, planning to bomb it and release radio-activity into the atmosphere. How they got in we don't know, but they made it in and out; and would have been fine if it hadn't been for someone out looking at a badger set. Presumably they had some inside information, because they were able to identify a particular target. It must have been very good information because I doubt it is easy to break into Sellafield – it must have been a prime target throughout the war in Northern Ireland; yet not that good because they hit a pipeline that had been derelict for some time. Unless – do you think it was a set-up? The security people at Sellafield knew it was going to happen, and made sure the target constituted no danger?"

"I don't think so" replied Hargreaves. For a start it's very risky; and they would never have let them get away. Remember without the badger man they would never have been picked up"

"Okay. So their intelligence is good but not that good. But someone in Sellafield must have been working for them; which is a major lapse of security, and might be something for us to follow up". She made a note. "So, then, the bombs go off, no doubt all hell breaks out, but Sellafield's security team find out - almost immediately I would guess - that the attack has gone wrong. Just a power line down, and no radioactive leaks. What puzzles me – it did when we were at Richards' house – is why the cover up? They clearly didn't think of it immediately, or there wouldn't have been the initial news of an explosion – the news that set Richards off. So why change the story? The attack failed. I would have thought there was a lot of mileage in showing how appalling the IRA could be – they must have guessed it was them right from the start – and a lot to be gained from showing how incompetent they had been".

"True, but they would have to have admitted that the IRA had breached the security system at Sellafield. I'm sure they would have wanted to keep that quiet" said Hargreaves.

"And they must have realised that there had been some help from inside the plant. They'd certainly want to keep that even quieter".

"And, like Richards said, they could reckon on the IRA not making any claims".

"But once they heard that the bombers had been caught?" said Kate. "Surely they must have reckoned it would all come out?"

"Well, yes and no" said Hargreaves. "By then they'd gone public with the story that it was an electrical fault; so they would want to stick to that at all costs. But that means they'd have to do something about the IRA men – men and woman – and that raises two very interesting questions. The first is – how did Sellafield manage to arrange for the IRA team to be spirited away? It must have come from very high up indeed – not just the Nuclear people at the Home

Office. Somewhere near Cabinet level I would guess. And, second - were the stakes really so high that they were prepared to go that route? I can see there would be scope for some embarrassment; but don't you think that they could have said that the IRA had attacked the electricity cables and been caught within hours? They just hadn't realised that it was an attack rather than an equipment failure when the first news bulletins went out. I know this is all being wise after the event, but they had some time to think out a strategy. Unless something more was at stake. If so, it had to be a lot, because, moving on to the next question, what happened to the Irish? Richards said that they were going to be taken back to Northern Ireland, but to what? I know they had non-jury trials going in the province at the time - they only came to an end a few years ago - but there was still coverage of who was on trial and for what. So taking them to Northern Ireland for trial doesn't sound very plausible. And even if it was all hushed up somehow, if they ended up in the Maze, the whole story would eventually come out. I can only think that they must have been got rid of somehow. But would the Government really do that – we are talking about murdering people in very cold blood – officially sanctioned murder - just to avoid admitting that the IRA cocked up a terrorist attack. That doesn't sound right either".

"Who knows?" said Kate. "Richards said that the men who took the Irish lot away were military looking. They probably saw us as being at war – a lot of British soldiers died in Northern Ireland – and five dead IRA bombers would be just five more casualties of war. Even so, I know what you mean. I'll make a note to go back through the papers around that time – see if I can get a bit more of the flavour of the times. It may produce something".

" While you're at it, why don't you look up who was responsible for energy, and security, and Northern Ireland at the time. Like I said, a cover-up like this will have had to have come from quite high up. There must be some annual reference book that gives that sort of information; and I think there is a Civil Service publication which gives people's positions. If it isn't in the library, I can probably get one through someone at the station".

"Okay" said Kate, making more notes. "But at least we know *what* happened back then, even if why isn't totally clear. I'm not sure it takes us much further on what's happening now, and where Paul is".

"Why don't you carry on speculating, as much as you can, and I'll interrupt again. I seem to have been quite good at that".

"Fine. Well, Sellafield is privatised, and then National Energy thinks about making a bid for it. They call in Paul as part of their review of British Nuclear, and he works secretly so that news about the bid doesn't leak out. He finds some sign of the bomb attack, which has been conveniently forgotten in the intervening years – no, that's not right. It would have to have been more deliberate than that. If the incident was reported to the world as electrical then no-one could say anything about the attack when British Nuclear was privatised. But presumably they weren't concerned, because the IRA had only blown up a disused drainage pipe and a pylon, which would have been repaired years before"

"Which means" interrupted Hargreaves, "that the explosives must have been planted quite near the re-processing plant. Not so near that it did any identifiable damage to it; but near enough that Paul's latest detection techniques could pick up traces of the impact".

"That's right. Brasher at British Nuclear said that Paul's method could distinguish between different causes of potential weakness in materials. So the problem for the two companies wasn't his finding that there *was* a weakness – that could be fixed - but that, contrary to what had been said at the time, it was caused by explosives".

"But that wouldn't be a problem for *the companies*" said Hargreaves. "They weren't around in 1983".

"Which fits with Brasher saying – and I believed him – that he couldn't understand what anyone involved in the merger had to gain from Paul's disappearance". Kate could hear her voice getting more excited as she spoke. "So someone else knew what was going on – and, Neil, I've just remembered who. I asked Brasher who knew about the merger – apart from executives at the two companies; and he said no-one except someone he spoke to at the Department of Energy – to see if they knew of anything that could explain Paul's results before the company was privatised. They said 'no', and maybe that was the truth; but at least one Department of Energy official knew about Paul's work – maybe others - which hooks up with what you were saying a few minutes ago".

"Okay, so someone in Whitehall is getting seriously concerned that the 1983 attack is going to get dredged up. But why go after Paul? He's acting as a consultant to National Energy. He's not going to be making his findings public, whatever they show". Kate thought for a moment.

"I might have an answer to that. Paul's a very straight sort of person" God, I'm talking about him in the present tense again, she thought. How wonderful. "But, quite against the terms of his consultancy contract, he kept some of the data at his office – he was not supposed to remove any of it from the company's offices. I remember asking myself why he would do a thing like that, and had no answer. But suppose he raised his concerns with National Energy, or British Nuclear – no, suppose he asked them to talk to the Department of Energy, or even talked to them himself – and just got some whitewash in return? That might be what prompted him to keep a separate copy of his results. He might not have had any specific plan; but if he was given the brush off, he's not the sort to let it drop. And, of course" she exclaimed "if he gave even the slightest hint that he was suspicious, then that would be the reason for his office being burgled. Then, once they found that he *had* been keeping his own files, they

211

would have seen him as a very serious threat. So they kidnap him and – of course, of course – they take his laptop in case there is anything on it. It all makes sense".

"It certainly does" said Hargreaves. "And there's more that fits. You reported Paul's disappearance, and I started looking into it; but whoever's involved knew that was going to happen. So they go high up in the force, way above my level, and get the matter switched to Johnson, with clear instructions to him to wrap the thing up. Probably quoting national security or some such line. And that does for the Press as well, all stitched up with a surrogate D notice. What it doesn't explain is the Americans. What's their interest? It looks like they were responsible for the burglary, but how did they come to be involved? And why do they then start watching you? And why, in all this, is there a reason…." He stopped.

"A reason to keep Paul alive? Yes, I have been wondering that. Well, we will just have to wait and see. We've got quite a long way; and we have tracks to pursue. To be honest, I still wasn't convinced about moving out – but I am now. I'm quite determined to follow this through, but I feel quite scared".

It was quite late when they got back to Oxford. Hargreaves drove Kate to her house and waited while she packed some belongings – mainly her most shapeless casual clothes. When she was ready, he went out and checked every car parked in her street. Then instead of driving her back out onto Walton Street, the only way into Oxford by car from her house, they walked in the dark along the track by the side of the canal at the end of her street. This eventually emerged into a new housing estate half a mile north of the Jericho area. Hargreaves then used his mobile to order a taxi which, fifteen minutes later picked them up and took them to the Linton Lodge hotel, in a leafy street just off the main Banbury Road. She paid cash and, when he left her, he was quite certain that no-one knew she was there. Except, he ruefully noted, himself.

With the buy-to-rent boom of recent years having well and truly bust in the previous two years, it took Hargreaves only 24 hours to find several likely apartments; and he was able to arrange to take possession of the one he thought the best in only three days time. It was a comfortable, modernised one-bedroom flat in Woodstock, about six miles from Oxford, situated above a small ladies' clothes shop, in a street running from the main road to the entrance to the grounds of Blenheim Palace. He took Kate to see it; and she thought it very suitable. She had left her car back in Jericho, and would use the local bus service to get into Oxford. She also dyed her hair, got some plain glasses and, dressed in her most unflattering clothes, doubted whether Sarah would recognise her if they passed in the street. But this was all, in her own eyes, peripheral. The next morning, not waiting until she had moved to Woodstock, she set herself up in the Upper Reading Room of the Bodleian Library; and started on some determined research, Her two main objectives were first, to map out who, in late 1983, were the main people in government and the upper echelons of the Civil Service in the departments Hargreaves had listed; and second to read up as much as she could about what was going on in the UK at the time, politically, in relation to the IRA, and in the energy sector. To anyone watching it would have looked very tedious, but Kate was gripped by it.

She fairly quickly came across *The Annual Register,* which apparently had been running for hundreds of years, mainly consisted of articles about everything that had happened in the UK and the rest of the world during the year, but which also listed every member of the Government during the year. But it didn't cover the civil service. However, Kate almost as quickly tracked down the Civil Service Year Book that Hargreaves had referred to. The Librarian at the desk said that it was an invaluable publication, much used by academics in the Politics and Modern History faculties. Armed with these, Kate drew up a list. On it went the Cabinet Minister, every Junior Minister, the Permanent Secretary and every Deputy Secretary for four Departments – Energy, Defence, Northern Ireland and the Home Office. She recognised a couple of the Junior Ministers' names as politicians who had gone on to greater things in subsequent years; but only one did she recognise as someone still active in politics; and at the sight of it she practically fell of her chair. There, staring back at her was a name that she knew only too well, a name that everyone knew only too well – Alan Gerrard.

CHAPTER 18

As she sat there, in the centuries-old grandeur of that most famous of libraries, in the ubiquitous silence, utter panic grabbed her. In 1983 Alan Gerrard, now Prime Minister, had been a Junior Minister at the Home Office. He could barely have been thirty years old she thought; and the *Annual Register* gave no information on what his particular responsibilities had been at the Home Office. But if whatever had happened to Paul was being orchestrated by someone who was around – involved – in the events at Sellafield in 1983, then it looked like there was only one candidate. It can't be true, she thought, over and over, it can't be, it can't be. With a sense of foreboding so heavy she could hardly lift her arms, she reached out for the Civil Service Year Book for 1983. Turning to the Home Office she looked up the list of Ministers at the head of the section; and there was Gerrard's name. Next to it was his title - Minister responsible for Domestic Security Issues.

Kate felt as if she might faint. She stood up, but immediately felt dizzy and sat down again. She held her head in her hands for a few moments.

"Are you alright?" said a voice behind her. Kate jumped slightly, and saw that it was the librarian from the main desk, who had been walking past with several books.

"Yes, I'm okay" said Kate. "I just felt rather hot all of a sudden. Could I get a glass of water?"

"Of course, but you'll need to go down to reception at the main entrance. We don't allow any food or liquid in the library itself. Shall I come with you?"

"Oh, no, I'll be fine" said Kate, and headed downstairs. By the time she came back, she was more in control of herself, but still utterly shocked by what she had just read. She desperately wanted to talk to Hargreaves, but doubted she would be able to get hold of him until they met that evening.

Kate arranged to get copies of *The Times* starting in January 1983, as a start on finding out more about what had been happening politically and on the energy front in the year or so before the attack on Sellafield; but she just couldn't concentrate. The name Gerrard kept blocking out any other thoughts. For months she had been aware that she was up against something, someone, some group of people; but until now the only faces she had been able to give to them were the two intimidating men who had burst into her home and attacked her. Now there was another face, one so familiar – the most familiar face in the country – that she couldn't get past it in her mind. Half of her kept saying that it was quite ridiculous - she couldn't seriously be facing a threat from the Prime Minister. But the other half kept going back to the details she had dug out; and they were very compelling. Eventually she gave up on *The Times,* arranging to look at the copies the next day; and headed back to her hotel. She rang Hargreaves and left a message saying that, if he got it, could he get to her as fast as possible – it was very urgent. She very much needed someone to tell her she was getting things seriously wrong.

Hargreaves arrived at 6.30pm – he hadn't got her message – and they walked round to the Cherwell Boat House Restaurant, a few hundred metres from the hotel. At another time it would have been very pleasant, having an early supper by the riverside; but tonight it was a nightmare for Kate. She told Hargreaves what she had found out; and he was as shocked, and as pessimistic, as Kate. The only names from 1983 which Kate hadn't followed up were those of the senior Civil Servants of the time; but they would all have been much older – you might be a junior minister at thirty but you wouldn't make even Deputy Secretary much before forty-five. So they would be quite old, certainly retired and, quite possibly, dead. The only small spark of hope was the Americans. They clearly seemed, for some unfathomable reason, to be working against those who had taken Paul, and attacked Kate; but Gerrard was very close to the Americans – in fact their only main ally in Europe in relation to events in the Middle East. Something didn't add up there; and that was a tiny, tiny straw for Kate to hold on to. More major plusses were, first, that no-one apart from Hargreaves knew where she was; and in two days she would be in Woodstock in a flat rented by Hargreaves. Second, no-one apart from Minogue and Richards knew how much she knew, nor even that Neil and Kate had talked to the two ex-policemen. If it had been David Price who alerted Sellafield about Kate he wouldn't think that she knew enough to follow up any suspicions she might have. Kate would stake her life that Price's wife wouldn't let him know that she had talked to Kate before she left. But, she reflected, maybe it wasn't Price. Maybe, indirectly at least, it was one of the Department of Energy officials to whom Brasher had spoken. Maybe they had been following up her inquiries, but they wouldn't know she had spoken to Brasher; and would have no reason to think she might start nosing around Sellafield and its local population – unless, somehow, they had followed her there? That was a possibility Kate couldn't begin to take on board, but instinctively thought was unlikely. Third, the Americans clearly had some sort of influence, which might offer some protection, if not as much as they confidently assured her they could give her. But none of this made Kate feel secure; and none of it helped at all in deciding what to do. For the moment, reading back copies of the newspapers was all either of them could think of.

Hargreaves walked back with Kate to the hotel. As they arrived, she thanked him again for all his help. He gave her a small kiss on her cheek.

"I could stay with you".

"I know; and I don't want to be alone. But you are my only source of stability, sanity even, at the moment; and that might change if you stayed. I'm sorry".

"You have nothing to be sorry for. I'm there if you need me, not if you don't". He gave her another small kiss, this time on her lips. She did not respond, but she did not move away.

"I'll see you tomorrow night" Hargreaves said "and let's hope we have some more answers by then".

Kate went back to the Bodleian Library the next day, but she was thinking more clearly now. As she had done a couple of weeks before, she went to a computer terminal, accessed the on-line archive service of *The Times* and tapped in the name of Alan Gerrard. The screen indicated that there were many thousands of references, which she specified should be listed chronologically. She then scanned through and started reading everything she could find about him starting in 1980, when he had first joined the Government. A year on through the archive she came to his appointment as Junior Minister for Domestic Security Issues at the Home Office. From there on she read every word she could find about him, both news items and commentaries, making detailed notes as she went; and, almost like reading a History book – though Kate reminded herself a few times that she had been a young girl in England at the time – a picture emerged. It was one which left her in very little doubt that Gerrard was behind Paul's abduction.

In 1981 there had been a major IRA atrocity in Central London. A very large quantity of explosive, packed with nails, had exploded in a popular pub, killing seventeen people and injuring over one hundred more, some terribly and for life. The outcry, indeed outrage, had been enormous and, although there was some sympathy for the problem the security forces had in stopping such attacks, considerable criticism had been directed at the Home Office. This was not particularly directed at Gerrard, despite his position, partly because criticism was more generally aimed at 'the Government'; and partly because Gerrard was still relatively new in the post. But it was he who had to respond to very critical speeches by the opposition in the House of Commons and, if the Press comment could be believed, he did not inspire a great deal of confidence.

So, when in 1982, the IRA derailed a train, killing thirty three more innocent people and again injuring many more, the political attacks on the government formed a tidal wave of criticism with, this time, much of it focused very much on Alan Gerrard. Few were prepared to concede that, in such an open country, it was going to be almost impossible to stop a determined and well-organised terrorist group from succeeding, at least on some occasions; and no amount of oblique references to the many terror attacks that had been prevented through diligent intelligence work by the security forces cut any ice with so-called 'public opinion'. Gerrard again had to defend the government in the House of Commons and, according to some at least, made a rather better speech this time. But events were against both him and the Government. The traditional attack on Government failure was greatly exacerbated by a real sense of fear that public places and public transport were not and could not be made secure against the IRA. There were calls for major new initiatives, and new laws, designed to protect the UK; unrealistic but damaging calls for the Government to go to the country if it was unwilling or unable to implement much more draconian measures; and explicit demands that Gerrard at least, if not the Home Secretary as well, resign.

The Home Secretary, either by mistake or by design - to try to protect himself - was less than fulsome in his defence of Gerrard; and both Her Majesty's Opposition and the Press scented blood – very much Gerrard's blood. Numerous articles openly stated that his position had become untenable; yet he neither resigned nor was sacked. The arrest of two middle ranking IRA members, who had had at least some involvement in the train wreck, slightly abated the pressure over a critical week-end and, in the end, Gerrard survived.

In a short period he had gone from being far and away the most exciting, up-and-coming young politician in the Party – clearly a potential Prime minister and spoken of as such – to a very suspect member of the Government, his reputation severely damaged and his career prospects heavily circumscribed. The final step in the drama was a speech by Gerrard to that year's party conference, committing the Government to wholesale reform of its policy on terrorism, and a commitment to stop attacks on the Mainland. The Papers speculated strongly – no doubt on the basis of some well-leaked information – that this apparently rather foolhardy speech was the result of a deal with the Prime Minister. Gerrard would stay on in post, take the flak and commit to future success. If this worked, his career would be rehabilitated. If there were further attacks then his career was finished anyway for the foreseeable future; but his resignation would take the heat off the Home Secretary and, indeed, the PM himself.

There was a lot more, but Kate knew that she had found out what she needed to know. When Gerrard heard about the attack on Sellafield, he must have thought that he was finished. He had staked his future on there being no more attacks, and the gamble had failed. It was little wonder then, when more detailed reports came through that the attack had essentially failed, injuring no-one and damaging no nuclear installations and, more important, having had little visible impact beyond a collapsed electricity pylon, that he saw, and then grabbed at, a way back. She neither knew nor cared whether the plan to cover up the attack originated from someone at Sellafield, the Home Office or Gerrard himself. He must have authorised it, with or without the approval of anyone higher in the government. Maybe he rationalised it as an act to prevent mass panic, or to stop an IRA publicity victory of sorts; but the main beneficiary was Alan Gerrard and, as far as she could tell, no-one else involved was still around now to respond when Paul came on the scene.

Gerrard must have been in a state of shock when the message got through to him that the IRA team had been arrested; and that one of them had confessed to taking part in the attack. Now even worse threatened Gerrard – not just the security failure but the attempted cover-up as well. Kate could only speculate at what line Gerrard must have developed to get whoever it was who picked up the Irish – maybe the security services, maybe a Ministry of Defence team – to complete the cover-up; but she imagined that 'national security' would have been to the forefront. And so they had been spirited away, to what fate she could only guess; and Gerrard had survived the day. A cursory look through the later archive revealed that he had moved on two years later to another junior government post, then Financial Secretary to the Treasury, firmly back on an upward career path, culminating in the mid-nineties as a still very youthful Home Secretary. The General Election of 1997 had put paid to this seemingly unstoppable career; and he had to endure the frustration of well over ten years in opposition. But he had age on his side. Twenty-four years after the Sellafield crisis, he became leader of the Opposition and fairly soon afterwards led his party to a resounding election victory. His time as PM had so far been rather well received by the Media; and there was a general sense of satisfaction in having such an experienced politician to deal with the grave problem now emerging in the Middle East. His evidently good personal relationship with the US President was as welcome as it was a surprise.

From Kate's point of view, this last point was the only one she still didn't understand. If the two of them were so much on the same wave length, why had two Americans – from the military, CIA or some such organisation she had no doubt – been so at pains to protect her, which couldn't possibly be in Gerrard's interests? She would need to read up more on the current situation, but for the moment, she felt she had all the information she was likely to get. The big question was – what on earth was she going to do about it?

That evening she discussed it all with Hargreaves in the dining room of her hotel. He agreed that there could not really be in any doubt – Paul had obviously discovered the impact of the 1983 explosion, not particularly damaging but clearly not caused by an electrical fault. This had got back to Gerrard, presumably via Sir Colin Brasher having made inquiries at the Department of Energy; and Gerrard, realising that his position was gravely threatened, had decided to have Paul eliminated. With his database material gone as well, there was nothing anyone could do or say that would carry any credibility, indeed it was very unlikely that anyone else would even know of the possibility of what had occurred. Once it became clear that Kate was on the trail of what had happened, she too was marked for elimination. All that remained unexplained – tantalisingly incomprehensible in fact – was where the Americans fitted in, why they had protected her, and why Gerrard might have kept Paul alive. The last question in particular seemed so intractable that her resolve to believe what the two Americans had told her started to crack. She said as much to Hargreaves.

"I think you have just got to keep on hoping" was his response. "There's something very peculiar about what happened to you. We must just push on until we find out the full truth of the matter".

"And that's the real problem isn't it?" said Kate. "What do we do? I doubt there is anyone in the country who would believe what has happened. Without Paul and his data there isn't a shred of evidence to support such a story. The police clearly wouldn't – couldn't more likely – do anything; the Press wouldn't touch it. They'd just think I was a crank. Lover's run off and it's all a conspiracy by the Prime Minister – I can just see it."

"Well" said Hargreaves "you are right that we would have to have some evidence, so let's get some; and there is only one place to get it".

"Richards" exclaimed Kate. "Of course. Do you think we could get him to come forward, or at least write it all down and sign it? I know he has kept quiet all this years, but he knows he hasn't got that long to live; and he was ready to tell us. Maybe he would provide what we need".

"It's worth a try. It may not be enough because, as far as we know, there is no actual evidence. It's just his story, and it could easily be dismissed as some sort of dementia, or a vendetta. But at least we would have something a little more concrete".

"But there's also the fact that he didn't seem to know who was behind it all" said Kate. "He may have had suspicions, but he didn't give any clue when we saw him that he suspected Gerrard. If he gets wind of that, is he really going to help us?"

"Only one way to find out" said Hargreaves. "I'll ring him now". He got the number from a Directory Inquiries service and rang Richards.

"Could I speak to Kenneth please.........oh, I'm sorry to hear that......no, no, it isn't important.... No, I'll call back. Which hospital......thanks". He looked quite shaken. "His condition deteriorated quite rapidly yesterday. He's gone into hospital again, in Reading, and Mrs. Richards doesn't think he is likely to get out again".

"Do you think we could visit him?"

"I don't know. It's rather strange, isn't it, that he should have a relapse so soon after we saw him. Maybe someone knew we visited him and has got to him?"

"Surely not?" said Kate. "We made sure that no-one knew where I was; and no-one knows you are involved at all. I suppose they might have had someone watching Richards' house; but they would have to have been watching for a very long time. And anyway, the doctors would know if he had been attacked in some way, rather than the cancer having got worse. I'll go tomorrow. It sounds like there may not be much of a chance if I leave it any longer"

"Kate, you can't possibly risk going to see him. If he is being watched then they will be straight on to you. I should go, though that won't be possible tomorrow".

"You can't go" replied Kate. "You've got to keep out of the picture. You must see that. Look, I'll ring the hospital tomorrow and ask to speak to one of the doctors. Let's find out what they think, and how long they think he's got. If it doesn't sound suspicious, then I will go. I'll really work on my disguise" she added with a smile.

Hargreaves was only content to agree the first part of this plan, but it resolved the issue for the moment. They finished the meal and he left, wanting very much to kiss her again, but knowing that, having made his feelings quite clear, any future developments would have to be initiated by Kate. She knew this even more clearly than he did; but the suspended animation of their relationship was all she could cope with. She held his hand for a moment and thanked him again for helping her; and then she was gone.

The next day proved to be utterly frustrating. Kate rang Reading General Hospital and was put through to a number of people there, all very helpful in manner but none of them having any useful information about Richards. The nearest she got was one nurse who said that Kate would need to speak to a doctor, was not sure which one, but that whoever it was would probably not be around until the afternoon . She decided to use the time to bring herself up to date on Gerrard, which very rapidly became a survey of the situation in the Middle East. A combination of *The Times, The Financial Times* and *The Economist* for the last three months gave her everything she needed; and it was not pleasant reading. Despite myriad complexities, the central problem was, as it had been for some years, the development of Iran's nuclear capability. Iran had steadfastly maintained that this was for peaceful purposes only, but US and Israeli intelligence were convinced that Iran had also secretly developed both the materials and the processes necessary to manufacture nuclear weapons. This was bad enough, but became infinitely worse when combined with Iran's stated 'foreign policy'. This included the complete destruction of Israel and the insistence that the rest of the Arab world in the region coalesce, however informally, into one pan-Arab grouping under Iran's leadership. This, it was speculated, would be achieved by a mixture of sticks and carrots – the carrot being the prospect of Iran providing nuclear weapons to other Arab states, and the stick being the threat of intervention, backed by the threat of tactical nuclear weapons, if other countries attempted to thwart Iran's aspirations. Jordan, Syria and Iraq in particular were extremely concerned; but appeared to have little impact on the fundamentalist regime in Tehran.

The response from the UN had initially been quite firm, with an insistence on UN inspection of any sites it chose in Iran and, when Iran refused this, economic sanctions. These, however, had not produced any change of heart in Tehran; and discussions were clearly beginning to develop over the possibility of military intervention by the UN in Iran. But then, in the last three months or so, this concerted front had begun to unravel. Iran had allowed some limited inspection, which UN inspectors were following up. The US argued that this was merely to buy time and that, as the main combatant, it could not keep its military forces – primarily large scale bombing capability - on attack standby indefinitely; while others, primarily France and Germany, argued that Iran's action demonstrated the first real signs that it might be persuaded to co-operate, and that this opportunity for a peaceful solution should not be thrown away. Once this split had developed, other countries lined up for all sorts of reasons unconnected with the main issue. Russia supported France and Germany, concerned about the leadership of the US in the matter, and the likelihood of extended US influence in the region once Iran had been dealt with. Numerous countries joined for no more profound reason than that they were generally anti-American. China hovered, unclear where its best interests lay. But a number of countries saw the danger of a belligerent nuclear Iran, and looked for some leadership to take them into the US camp. This was where the UK was vital. After the problems of Iraq, only a few years earlier, the US was not prepared to act independently; but if a sufficient number of others would back it, including providing some military personnel, however notional the number, then it would act; and it was clear that if the UK supported the US, then at least a dozen other countries, most notably Japan and Spain, plus a number of the newer Eastern European members of the EU, would join the coalition. But without a clear UK lead, supporting US intervention, providing military support and, critically, allowing UK airfields to be used as a base for long range US bombers the initiative, it was widely agreed, would falter.

There was not the slightest doubt, therefore, that Gerrard had become the pivotal figure in the emerging international crisis; and no-one had any doubts either that his own policy instincts were to support the US one hundred percent. He had been a hawkish figure over Iraq, but had escaped any great loss of standing given the focus on Tony Blair's support for that war. He had repeatedly made speeches both at home and abroad, calling attention to what he saw, in Iran and its current leadership, as the single biggest threat to world peace, particularly since the North Koreans had started to co-operate more with the outside world; and he had very quickly developed a close personal rapport with the US President, Jack Hamilton. The problem for Gerrard was that his views were clearly not shared by a substantial number in his party, effectively but not openly led by Graham Seymour, the Foreign Secretary who, whether by personal inclination or as the result of the advice he received from the Foreign Office, was much more pro-Arab; and keen to support an EU initiative sponsored by France and Germany which would have given Iran at least another three months and, quite possibly six months, to comply with the latest UN demand for free inspections. Fortunately for Gerrard, this back-bench sentiment had not yet been widespread enough to deter him or thwart him. In a speech just a week before, noting that Israel might not be habitable in six months time, he stated categorically that he was backing the US, invited other countries to do the same, and demanded that any in his Government who could not or would not support this should resign immediately. Seymour, over the week-end, had the choice of an honourable end to his political career; or a rather less honourable acquiescence which would, at least, still give him a chance, albeit slim, of one day leading the country. He chose the latter; and was duly slated by the Press, but remained a powerful figure in the party.

This had not seen Gerrard home though. Whatever the views of its individual members, Her Majesty's Opposition had, for some months, been losing no opportunity to attack Gerrard, demanding debates and, indeed, a vote in Parliament on the Iranian situation and the UK's stance on the issue of military support for the US. All of this Gerrard had so far successfully managed to contain. The real flash point, politically speaking, had been the use of airfields in the UK from which the US wished to launch its attacks. The nearest US bases to Iran from which its heavy bombers could operate were in Turkey. However, Turkey was to date maintaining a neutral stance, no doubt with an eye to its own position in the Middle East once the Iranian crisis was over. Since Georgia had joined NATO the previous year, the US had an air force base there; but it had very limited capacity and technological capability as yet. The US could, if necessary, strike directly from the US; but this was strategically much less attractive if operations were at all extensive. What it needed was the use of the long established and technologically very advanced bases in the UK; but this had been vehemently opposed by both the Opposition and a number of heavy weight press commentators. By some this was seen as merely woolly thinking. The notion that the UK might support the US over Iran, but deny it the use of its bases in the UK, was seen as, at best inconsistent and, at worst a completely cynical, if not totally hypocritical, approach to the international tensions raging over Iran. But, despite this, the use of US bases in the UK had touched some sort of nerve amongst the Media, and – whether cause or effect no-one could say – amongst the public more generally. There had been demonstrations outside several such bases, which attracted much attention; and, perhaps more significantly, Iran had declared to the world that if the UK allowed US bombers to operate from sites in the UK, then the UK would, after Israel, be its main target. Defence experts confirmed that Iran certainly had the long-range capability to hit targets in the UK. What no-one knew was whether it could deliver nuclear warheads over that distance, but it was certainly not being ruled out; and this had had a very deep impact on public sentiment. It had taken consummate skill and determination on Gerrard's part to avoid a debate and a vote on this in Parliament; and it was generally commented that he had, as a result, significantly jeopardised his prospects of remaining the leader of his party, and hence PM, once the crisis was over.

At an intellectual level Kate took this all in. At an emotional level she veered between incipient hysteria and total numbness. Here was a man at the centre of an international vortex of political and military forces, rightly or wrongly – Kate neither knew nor cared – taking decisions that would affect the lives of thousands, maybe millions; yet, by some strange sequence of events, also someone with whom she was playing a very personal cat-and-mouse game, with Paul as the stake for which they were playing. It was absurd, and yet it was as real as anything she had ever encountered. All she could do was make notes;

and hope that some way of moving things forward would, in due course, emerge.

Kate left the library and tried Reading General Hospital again. This proved as unsuccessful as before; and, in desperation, she rang Richards' home again. All she got was an answer phone. Her sense of frustration was so overwhelming she decided that, whatever she had said to Hargreaves, she would go to see Richards herself, straight away. She headed for the railway station, took the next train to Reading and, less than an hour later was in a taxi from Reading station to the hospital.

On arriving there she asked for Richards, and was directed to a ward. A nurse took her to a bed at the far end of the ward; and there she found Richards' wife, sitting by his side holding his hand. Both experienced some surprise at the other's presence. Kate desperately sought for something to say, to give some reason for her being there; but then she saw Richards. He looked to be asleep, but some sixth sense told her he was not merely asleep.

"How is he?" she asked.

"He's lost consciousness" his wife replied. "He went into a coma late last night – more likely the drugs than the cancer – but they don't think he will come out of it. I thought that......." She couldn't continue, and Kate saw that she was crying..

"I'm so sorry" she said. "I'd better go".

"Why did you come?" asked Mrs Richards.

"Oh, just to check up on a few things Mr. Richards told us when we came to see him. It really doesn't matter. I'm sorry to have intruded". Mrs. Richards made no reply, and turned back to look at her husband. Kate, with as much tact as she could muster, and as silently as possible, left the ward. An hour and a half later she was back in Oxford.

That evening, over a meal at a pub near Oxford, she recounted all she had found out to Hargreaves. When she had finished, they sat in silence for a while.

"It isn't good, is it?" said Kate eventually

"No, I'm afraid it isn't. It still looks very likely that Alan Gerrard is responsible for whatever has happened to Paul. The American angle is still unclear. We have no evidence to go on; and we clearly won't be able to get any from Richards now. I wish I could think of something more positive to add, but I can't".

"Unless...." said Kate.

"Unless what?" asked Hargreaves, not sure what to make of this.

"Well, there is the Irish angle. To be quite honest, I can't really see how it would help; but we could try to find out exactly what happened to them. It might throw up something useful. I know it's rather clutching at straws, but I can't think of anything else".

"How would we do it? You could try going through the papers again; but I can't believe that there would be anything about them; and Richards said that he never heard another word of what happened to them".

"I was thinking more of what we might be able to track down in Northern Ireland. We know the names of two of the five. It's a good bet that they came from there. Someone must know something about them".

"I can't say I like the sound of this" said Hargreaves. "What were their names?"

Kate got out the notes she had made when they had been to see Richards.

"Cieran Hughes and Michael McGuiness" she said.

"There must be a lot of people with those names in Northern Ireland".

"True, but we know a little more about them. They were IRA. They disappeared from view in late 1983. Hughes lived in North London; and McGuiness was probably in his twenties at the time. And we have two advantages. We know what happened – at Sellafield, and to the five people involved. The chances are that no-one in Northern Ireland – friends, family, other IRA – ever found out what happened. If so, we have a few cards to play. And second, the whole thing is over now. Peace and light has broken out. Former top members of the IRA are in the Northern Ireland Government. So people will be more ready to talk about what happened, especially something as long ago as 1983".

Hargreaves did not like what he was hearing one bit. He wanted to say that he thought the whole idea total madness – dangerous, unlikely to produce anything new, at best just a way of avoiding the painful truth, that Kate's hunt for Paul was at an end. But he knew enough of Kate's determination to realise that none of this would persuade her.

"Kate, you need to think very carefully about this. In the first place, the troubles in Northern Ireland may be over, but the feelings, the tensions will still run very deep. We are talking of people who lost their husbands and fathers, brothers and sons, innocent people blown up, terrorised – you can't imagine how dangerous it could be. And second, how is it going to help? You might find out all there is to find out about Hughes and the others; but that won't help you find out about Paul, will it? At best it will just confirm that Gerrard is behind his disappearance, but we're fairly sure that's the case anyway".

To his surprise, Kate smiled.

"I know, I know" said Kate. "You're absolutely right; and I know that you are only trying to help me. But, as you said to me a couple of nights ago, we need some evidence – anything that will allow us to get someone to take us seriously – and I can't think of any other way forward. I'll only go for a few days. If that isn't enough, I'll give it up, I promise".

So there it was. Hargreaves' worst fears realised. He'd known instantly that he wouldn't be able to go with her; and the thought of her going off on such a dangerous trip by herself appalled him.

"It's not just that I want to help you. You know that I care about you – care about you a lot - and this sounds really dangerous. You might not survive it; and that would devastate Paul if he makes it back. Me too as it happens". He looked very directly at her. Kate leaned forward and kissed his cheek.

"You mean so much to me" she said. "I can't fully take in what has been…what *is* happening to me; and I know I couldn't have coped without you. But I can't give up now – you must know that – and this is the only way forward I can see. It will probably be a complete waste of time, I know; but it gives me something to hold on to. I'll be very careful, and I'll consult you every step of the way before I do anything. How about that?"

They both knew that he didn't stand a chance.

"I'm not fully persuaded, but another kiss might help" said Hargreaves with a straight, if slightly wicked-looking face. Kate leaned forward, putting one hand behind his head and kissed him again.

"Thank you" she said

"The thanks are all mine" replied Hargreaves .

The next day, Saturday, Hargreaves helped Kate move to the new apartment in Woodstock. On the way, he drove her to the churchyard in Bladon, a mile or two from Woodstock; and they visited the tomb of Winston Churchill. This, he explained, was not mere interest, though it was certainly that. When they got back to the car park, Hargreaves got Kate to drive off, away from Woodstock, while he waited there, noting every car that passed for the next ten minutes. Kate returned ten minutes later, picked up Hargreaves and they headed for Woodstock. Just outside the village she dropped him off again, outside one of the original, though now unused, entrances to the grounds of Blenheim Palace. Kate drove on and parked in the middle of Woodstock, while Hargreaves again noted every car that came past. When he was certain that no car had followed them from Bladon, he walked into the centre of Woodstock, met Kate and they went to the apartment. After unpacking and having a light lunch in the village, Kate got onto the Internet and found out about trains to Liverpool and ferries from Heysham to Belfast. Hargreaves went off with both his own credit card and Kate's; and obtained six hundred pounds in cash. He was as determined as she that she would leave no trace of her travels. She said that she thought it best to have the evening to herself, and would call Hargreaves on Sunday night.

Twenty-four hours later, after a tedious but uneventful journey, including a remarkably smooth crossing of the Irish sea, she checked into a small no-star hotel – more bed-and-breakfast really – about two miles from the centre of Belfast. She spent the rest of the day walking round the city, which was clearly still in the grip of a massive re-building and refurbishment programme, working out her strategy and, after some supper, called Hargreaves to tell him her plans. By nine o'clock Monday morning, after a second good night's sleep in the city, she was ready for action.

Her first port of call was the library of Queen's University. Producing her Oxford University Bod-card, she said that she hoped she might consult the library's newspaper archive. Queen's was not one of the four so-called copyright libraries in the UK – the others besides Oxford being Cambridge, the National Libraries of Scotland and Wales, plus Trinity College, Dublin in the Irish Republic – which together hold copies of everything published in the English Language. But it was, Kate knew, the leading library in Northern Ireland and, as Kate had expected, the librarian was used to such requests. It was, therefore, not long before Kate, once again, though in very different surroundings, was hunting through old newspapers, this time the *Belfast Times,* looking for anything around 1983-4 on non-jury trials of members of the IRA.

There were, it turned out, a very large number of such trials, which had started in 1972 to circumvent intimidation of juries in terrorist cases; and it took Kate rather longer than she had anticipated to verify that no trial had taken place of any IRA bombers for attacking Sellafield. She kept going through to 1988, but it was a dead end and, increasingly, Kate began to think that the whole idea of any such trial being conducted back in Northern Ireland was odd. Trials of other IRA terrorists for attacks on the mainland had been carried out in England, usually at the Old Bailey. So, Richards was unlikely to have missed anything when he said that he had heard nothing more about the IRA team; and Hargreaves was almost certainly right when he speculated that they had come to an altogether much more untimely end.

If only definitively to strike off another possible line of investigation, she consulted the telephone directories in the library. As she had imagined there were getting on for a hundred Hughes in Belfast alone; and substantially more McGuinesses. Probably three or four times as many again in the province as a whole. This would produce no leads. She went out to get a lunch, unclear what to do next. The only thing she could think of was to go back to the newspaper archive, start in November 1983 and just read, for as long as she could take it. Surely five people who certainly came from Northern Ireland, and some of whom probably still lived there in 1983, couldn't just disappear and there be no record anywhere of it? She kicked off at 2.30 pm, giving herself three hours to see how much progress she could make. Having to look at every single headline made for slow going; and she noted that it took her nearly an hour to complete the copies for the month of November 1983, with nothing to show for it. At that rate it would take her around three days to cover up to the end of 1985. This was not an attractive prospect, but she could think of no other way forward.

Kate left the library at 5.30 pm., none the wiser, and went for a walk. She had supper in a bustling restaurant in the centre of the city, aware that being in her thirties, she seemed to be one of the oldest people around; returned to her hotel and phoned Hargreaves. She had nothing to report; he had no new ideas; and they both felt very flat as she rang off. Kate began to see more clearly that if nothing came of her current trip – and she now increasingly felt that that was the most likely outcome – then she would have to give up. She more or less knew what had happened to Paul. There was nothing she could do about it. He might – just might – come back to her; but if he hadn't in a month or two, she would have to regard him as dead, move on, whatever that meant. It was a bleak prospect, but no other presented itself.

This morose feeling, which lasted through the night and a light breakfast, received a very rude shock just after ten o'clock the next morning. She was working through the *Belfast Times* for late December 1983, feeling in a rather robotic frame of mind when a news item leapt out of the page at her. Kate's heart started pounding. Under a heading 'Five Killed in Car Crash' she read 'Four men and a woman from Northern Ireland were killed when their car left the road on Thursday night, close to Portmarnock, a few miles north of Dublin. The car broke through a low barrier and fell almost one hundred feet down the valley-side before catching fire. Police named the dead as Cieran Hughes, 45, and Rory O'Halloran, 33, from Belfast; Dougal Hearne, 32, from Lisburn; and Michael and sister Mary McGuiness, 24 and 22, from Loughgannon, County Armagh. Next of kin have been informed. A police spokesman said that, according to a witness report, the five had been seen earlier in a Public House a few miles away; and it appeared that Hughes, who had been driving the car, may have lost control of it on a tight bend. No other vehicle was involved".

CHAPTER 19

Kate stared at the page, a tide of conflicting emotions surging through her. The predominant one was, even she noticed, the least important. There really had been an IRA cell – or an Irish terrorist group of some sort – and they really had been disposed of, just as Hargreaves had speculated and she had feared. It had been made to sound like drunk driving; and it had conveniently been carried out in the Irish Republic. An explanation, if that was what in all humanity it could be called, for their disappearance had been provided, with no complicated attempt to implicate the protestant militia in Northern Ireland. No doubt there would be compatriots of the dead five who would suspect the worst; and family and friends who would think the same – that either protestant terrorists or the British Army had got to them and wiped them out; but who could ever demonstrate that, let alone prove it? It was just one more murderous incident in the civil war raging in Northern Ireland at the time, one more appalling set of deaths, grief and misery.

Her mind moved on to the next equally shocking thought though, again, it was no more than confirmation of what she and Hargreaves had anticipated. Alan Gerrard, Junior Minister for Domestic Security Issues at the time, had contrived to have the five murdered, on foreign territory and without any connection back to him, to the British Government, Sellafield, indeed to anything at all on the mainland. And this, she was now quite certain, was the man who had arranged for her to be murdered as well, with her only safeguard being that – as far as she could be sure – no-one knew where she was, plus the less than persuasive assurances of an American agent of some type, whom she had never seen before or since. Not good, Kate, she told herself. Not good at all.

And far worse, when she finally got round to facing it was the underlying question. What difference did this make; what could she do, now that she knew the whole story? Was she, in practice, even one step further forward? Could she go to the Irish authorities and reveal that five people from Northern Ireland, killed in a car crash in the Irish Republic nearly thirty years ago were IRA terrorists and had, in fact been murdered? That would probably be no great surprise; and who would want to re-open such a case? And if, by any chance, they deigned to ask her who the perpetrators of this crime were, she could tell them it was Alan Gerrard, Prime Minister of Britain and, incidentally, guilty of trying to have her murdered as well. She could just see the reaction. Tell us where you are and we will come and pick you up – in white coats, no doubt.

She desperately wanted to talk to Neil, if only to share what she had found out; but would not be able to talk to him until the evening. So she just sat there – to anyone looking at her she might have been in a trance – just waiting, waiting for some inspiration. None came. She went back to the newspapers and carried on reading, looking for any further information on the car accident or the five dead people.. By lunchtime it was clear that there was nothing else to find and, once again, she sat there, thinking about what to do next. But, during the course of the morning, an idea – a very obvious idea – had started to emerge. And then, all of a sudden, she knew she was going to do it - and she was going to do it now, right away, before Neil had a chance to dissuade her, as he very sensibly would try to do. She put away the papers and consulted a map of

Northern Ireland. She left the library and took a taxi to the central bus station, where she had a sandwich for lunch. An hour and a half's bus journey later she was in the centre of Banbridge, where she took another taxi, headed for Loughgannon.

The taxi driver was immensely friendly but alarmingly talkative. Kate could think of no good reason to give why she was heading for this small country town which would not involve someone living there whom, she had a strong suspicion, the taxi-driver would expect to know. She had no idea whether the countryside was exceptionally beautiful or not, whether any exotic flora or fauna inhabited the area. She said that she was just visiting someone; he asked for the address. She said she wasn't sure of it; he said he'd be only too happy to help. She said she really couldn't put him to that much trouble; he said it would be a pleasure. So, in the end, worried sick that she was getting deeper and deeper into a situation for which she was totally unprepared, she decided to go at least half way near the truth.

"An old aunt of mine – she was half Irish - used to know a woman who lived in Loughgannon when she was younger. A Mrs. McGuiness. They went very different ways, although they stayed in touch – Christmas cards and the like – and when I had to go to Belfast on business, I thought I'd just see if she was here, say hello. She'd be very old now, in fact I don't know if she is still alive. My aunt's got dementia, but she used to talk about Mrs. McGuiness – she was obviously very fond of her, or at least the memories of her - even though a lot of it didn't make a great deal of sense". If by any chance she found Mary and Michael's mother, and the taxi-driver was still around, she hoped this would leave her a let-out clause somewhere.

"Well, I'm sure we can find her" said the taxi-driver in a cheery way. "What will her first name be?"

Kate realised what a mistake she had made. Not thinking ahead.

"I think it may have been Aileen, or perhaps Emily – I'm not sure. My aunt always called her 'Mrs. McGuiness'".

"Well, I'll take you to Dermot – Dermot McGuiness. He runs a small garage in Loughgannon. I'm sure he'll be able to sort you out". His manner remained extremely amicable. Kate, now tense as a longbow, tried to continue the conversation as normally and casually as possible, not knowing, however hard she tried, whether his demeanour had, in fact changed at all or not. She mentioned that it was her first trip to Belfast which, as she had hoped, got him on to why she had gone there in the first place. This was easier territory as she described a life in publishing, seeing some academics at Queen's University and, to her great relief, they arrived in Loughgannon without further reference to her trip to the town.

Loughgannon would have been, for generations, a small agricultural centre, with a fine church and even its own castle; but at some point relatively late in the twentieth century had expanded and so, from an architectural point, now appeared relatively modern. There were fewer signs here than in Belfast of the resurgent economic growth which had followed the ending of The Troubles, but it was not unprosperous she thought; and it was clear that McGuiness's garage was doing quite good business, both at the forecourt and on the repair side. Kate very much wanted to pay the taxi-driver off, but anticipated – quite correctly – that he was not going to leave her until she had found out where next, if anywhere, she needed to go. She made one, half-hearted attempt to pay him; but recognised that it was not going to work, as he parked the car, got out, and walked her into the tiny reception area at the side of the garage.

"Is Dermot around?" he asked the pretty young woman who sat there wielding a calculator and some bills. She smiled at him, held up a finger to indicate he should wait a moment, and carried on with the calculation, making big eyes when she thought she might have gone wrong but bringing the maths safely to a conclusion. For a few seconds, Kate felt life was normal, but then told herself she must absolutely focus on the potentially very dangerous game she was now playing.

"He's in the repair shop" she said, and the taxi-driver led Kate round to the back of the garage.

"If you just wait here a moment, I'll go and get him" he said.

"Please don't drag him away if he's in the middle of something" said Kate.

"Oh, he'll be delighted to come and have a crack. Works long hours, but enjoys them" he added with a big grin.

He disappeared into the repair area of the garage and, to Kate's growing alarm, did not re-appear for some minutes. What is he telling him she wondered. Trying to look as if she was just idly loitering while she waited, she eased a few yards back, so that she could see the reception area and the young woman in it and – more important for Kate's state of mind – the young woman could see Kate. The taxi-driver re-appeared, accompanied by a very large, almost bear-like man, in his mid forties she thought, with a lot of dark straggly hair, a large saturnine face and remarkably black but sharp eyes. He must be at least six foot five, Kate thought, and he had a strong muscular stance to him as well. Not someone to be trifled with. Only the cheery smile on his face prevented Kate from total panic.

"I won't shake your hand, because mine are as black as coal with the car grease and all that; but it's a pleasure to meet you – we don't have many English ladies calling at the garage". It was said with no hint of anything other than welcome; but it served to remind Kate how far out of her own territory she now was. "Col here says that you are looking for a Mrs. McGuiness. Well, we have a few of those, and I know them all; so Col has brought you to the right place for sure. But which one? Col says you don't know her first name. So what else can you tell me about her?" This last sentence was delivered in a subtly different tone. Still quite friendly, but a real sense of interrogation behind it.

Kate instantly recognised that there was nothing she could say. The only thing she knew, if the Mrs. McGuiness she wanted to see still lived in the town, was that two of her children, perhaps her only two children, had been murdered nearly thirty years ago; and she couldn't blurt that out. The recognition of this was only momentary because, at that point, her nervous system went into defence mode; and she suddenly felt very faint. She started to fall and, instinctively clutched the taxi-driver – Col's – arm.

"I'm very sorry, I don't feel at all well" she said, too dizzy to note how pathetic this sounded.

"You need to sit down" said Col, and he helped her over to the reception office, where the woman behind the little counter vacated her chair for Kate, and got her a glass of water.

"I'm so sorry" was all Kate could say.

"I think you should take it easy for a few moments" said McGuiness "and then tell us what this is all about".

"I'm sorry" repeated Kate. "This is terrible. I should never have come here". She looked up at McGuiness. "I'm sorry to have bothered you" and then, to the taxi-driver "Could you take me back to Banbridge?" Col looked at McGuiness; and it was McGuiness who replied.

"Don't stress yourself" he said. "Col can take you back; but why don't you tell us why you're here?" It was said as a question, but there was a steely edge to it; and Kate, having no bland answer, saw that she was at a point of no return.

"In 1983, Mary and Michael McGuiness, who came from Loughgannon, were killed in a car crash in the Republic. I .....have a connection with them; and I wanted to say how sorry I was – I know it's a long time ago – to their mother, if she is still alive".

She sat looking at the floor, unable to look either of the two men in the eye. The silence that followed seemed an eternity. Eventually she looked up. The taxi-driver was leaning against the counter, looking at McGuiness, who was looking, in a very determined fashion, at Kate.

"What 'connection' would that be?" he eventually said. "You must have been barely born at the time".

"I don't think the car crash was an accident. My ....partner" – she still didn't know how to describe Paul – "discovered something recently that might have brought that to light. As a result, he has disappeared; and an attempt was made to kill me. I don't know what I can do about it; but I wanted to find out what was known about their deaths in the town they came from. I'll quite understand if you think I'm totally mad – I'm not sure I can cope with any of this anyway".

Another silence ensued. McGuiness put his hand on Kate's shoulder.

"The whole town turned out for the funeral. I was there myself – only a lad myself at the time. I didn't know Mary, but I knew Michael a little. I'm no relation, least not recent – I suppose if you go far enough back we are. Not many thought it was an accident; but there was never anything solid to suggest different. What did your partner find out?" Kate only half registered what he had said.

"Do you know where I would find Mrs. McGuiness, or Mr. McGuiness?"

"He died many years ago; and she died two or three years back".

"Did they have any other brothers or sisters?" asked Kate.

"No. Maggie had an elder sister; but she's dead as well".

"Why did some think it wasn't an accident?" asked Kate, starting to think a little more clearly.

"No-one – as far as I knew anyway – thought Mary or Michael was involved in the Troubles; but the other three were all likely Provos; and there was a rifle salute at their funerals. It was almost automatic that folk thought either the security forces or the Prots had got to them. So, what did your partner find out?" There was a quiet insistence this time which was unmistakable.

Kate, disconcerted as she was by the situation into which she had walked so blindly, still recognised that, apart from those actually involved, only she and Neil knew what had happened; and that broadcasting it to a complete stranger deep in Irish Nationalist territory was unwise, to say the least.

"I'm sorry, I really can't talk about it". She left it deliberately vague whether this was because it was confidential, or just too distressing. "I only came here to see if there was anything else to learn about their deaths. I'm sorry to have taken up your time". As she sat there she didn't know whether the next thing would be assistance back to the taxi, or McGuiness's hands round her throat.

"Well, it's no trouble; but I'm thinking that we haven't been very hospitable. Bridget, will you go over to the house and make us all some tea; and we'll come and join you. Have you got time Col? No, I'll not take a 'no'" he added as Kate started to protest. She didn't know whether she was being detained against her will, or receiving generous and well-meant Irish hospitality; but without insisting on leaving there was no way to find out; and her nerve failed her.

"Bridget's my daughter" said McGuiness. "She'll make us a nice spread. So, let's go over to the house". He didn't actually lift her up out of the chair; but the welcoming tone got her to her feet.

"Where are you staying?" This was added in a casual, chatty style, but it did little to dampen the incipient panic Kate felt.

"In Belfast" she replied, as they left the garage, crossed the road and headed for a detached house a few yards down. "I came over by bus. I really don't want to put you to any trouble" she repeated.

"It's a pleasure to meet you" he replied. "And I'm thinking that I may be able to help. I don't know anything myself – as I said, they weren't family, and I didn't really know them; but there was a man who spoke at the funeral – I don't recall his name but he was very moving and we all cried – no-one there would forget it. You just have some tea with Col and Bridget and I'll make a call or two – see if I can get you his name, maybe a telephone number". Taken at face value, this sounded rather helpful; but Kate liked the prospect of McGuiness bringing others into the situation even less than she wanted to stay and have tea; however there was no plausible way she could see for her to refuse his help.

Once inside the house, Bridget quickly produced a pot of tea, cake and biscuits; and fired a lot of standard questions at Kate – what did she do for a living, where did she live, had she been to Northern Ireland before – all so friendly and normal; and Kate tried her best to respond in kind, and truthfully. She said, in answer to the question, that her name was Kay – near enough to run with; though there was plenty of evidence in her purse of her real name. Col was strangely, indeed worryingly quiet, given how much he had been ready to rattle on in the taxi; and she was aware that he was thinking rather hard about what he had heard. Of McGuiness there was no sound. Eventually, in a small pause in Bridget's and Kate's small talk, he spoke.

"I hope your journey here hasn't been wasted; and maybe Dermot will be able to put you in touch with someone helpful. Did you say you were attacked because of all this? I hope you weren't hurt". It was downplayed, even polite, given that Kate had said someone had tried to kill her; but he clearly wanted to find out more.

"Oh, I'm fine" said Kate. "It was more of a shock than anything else".

"And who was it that did this?" Like Question Time in Parliament, she thought, it's always the second question you should be looking out for.

"I don't know. It was all very quick. Some friends of mine happened to turn up and that saved me. But it made me determined to find out more; which is why I'm here. What a tragedy for their mother" she added, hoping to deflect the conversation away from herself.

"And is anyone helping you; or is this a lone crusade – it seems very hard on you".

Kate was certainly not going to reveal that her partner in this venture - if either was the right word – was a serving police officer, busily moonlighting from his duties; but, on the other hand, indicating that she was quite alone in what she was doing did not seem at all sensible.

"I have a friend helping me" she said. In fact I ought to be going soon. I said I'd ring him when I got back to Belfast"

"Well, we'll just see what Dermot comes up with; and then I can take you back to the bus station". Bridget was just starting to take over the conversation again when McGuiness re-appeared.

"I have good news for you" he said to Kate. "I've made a few calls and found out who it was who spoke at the funeral. But he said there's another man who was there, at the funeral, who'd be more help. He's living in Belfast; so I'll just make a few arrangements and take you to meet him. He should be able to tell you a little more about Mary and Michael, maybe the others too. We can leave in about twenty minutes". As he finished speaking another man came in, a thin, wiry but muscular man, around the same age as McGuiness, with a mass of ginger hair.

"Ah, this is Connor O'Brady, a friend of mine – he'll come with us".

Kate's spirits, which had soared at the prospect of getting back to Belfast, now slumped back to despair. Another person was no big deal; but why would McGuiness have invited him unless to keep close watch on Kate while McGuiness drove? She acknowledged the new arrival, though neither of them said anything.

"Who is the man we're going to see?" she asked, trying to keep her voice very calm.

For a moment it looked as if McGuiness was not going to answer. Then he said

"He's the man to sort all this out. His name is Victor O'Connell".

CHAPTER 20

The name meant nothing to Kate, but she sensed that it meant rather a lot to the three men in the room. Even Bridget, just for a second, seemed slightly taken aback. Kate flirted with the idea of saying that she could not put them to all this trouble; that if they gave her the address, she could call in on Mr. O'Connell when she got back to Belfast; that she had to go now; but, as she looked at the three men, even more as she absorbed the body language, she knew this was pointless. It would merely fracture the façade – the farce really – that this was all just local citizens trying to help a distressed stranger in their midst. She had no doubt that she would be seeing Mr. Victor O'Connell, whether by choice or by force; and the fiction that this was merely her responding to well-meant help was infinitely preferable to the alternative.

"It's very kind of you" she said, bolstering the façade and, by the same token, dampening down her panic. "Tell me about Victor O'Connell. Do you know him?"

"Connor here will do that while I just make a few more arrangements – so I can get away. I won't be long". He smiled at both Kate and O'Brady, and left.

"O'Connell was with the Provos back then" said O'Brady. "On the Army Council for some years. That's all in the past now of course; and he's getting on in years; but he'll be able to tell you more about events in the 80's". He spoke with a curiously deep, gravelly voice that was quite out of keeping with his appearance. McGuiness had obviously filled O'Brady in on Kate and the reasons for her being in Loughgannon. Equally obviously, he was going to keep up the pretence that this was all about providing Kate with some more information about Mary and Michael McGuiness; whereas it was now quite clear to Kate that this was in fact about O'Connell finding out what Kate knew. Well, if she had to, she would tell them the whole story. Then it would at least be clear that they were all on the same side of the fence. That was the only thought of any comfort she could latch onto; but it did give her just enough resilience to introduce a more realistic note into the conversation.

"Should I be frightened of this man?" she asked, in what she hoped was only a half serious tone.

"Not if what you've told Dermot is right. It sounds to me as if you have a shared interest. Maybe you can help each other". While on the face of it this was re-assuring, it left unspoken what the implications might be if what she had told Dermot *wasn't* 'right'; or if O'Connell didn't, for some reason, believe her. Not a line of thought to pursue, she decided.

"I'll just make a quick phone-call" she said, getting her mobile out of her handbag, not knowing if O'Brady would, in fact, allow her to make it. If he didn't, it would at least put their relationship on a rather clearer footing.

"Could you not mention Loughgannon" said O'Brady "or me and Dermot; and definitely not O'Connell. Not until you've seen him anyway. I'm sure he would want it that way". As Kate stared at him, he added -

"I know, like I said, that it's all in the past; but for a man like O'Connell, and for a lot more like him, old feelings and passions are still strong – many died and many more were left behind – so it would be best to talk to him before you talk to anyone else". It was said without menace, without a great deal of logic, but its purpose was clear and, while it vaguely held out the possibility that she could make a call, provided she did not reveal where she was or what she was doing, her nerve once again failed her, and she put the mobile away.

"I understand" she said, in a voice sufficiently glum that it did not risk sounding patronising. "I did say I would call a friend of mine, but it can wait until I get back to Belfast. Do you know O'Connell" she added, seeking to move away from any prospect of confrontation.

"I've met him a few times – I doubt he'd remember me – but I know him by reputation. He was a great inspiration to the Nationalists, in the 1970s mainly. He rather dropped out of sight after that, but he was one of the top figures – no doubt about that. He was one of those who nobody gossiped about, if you know what I mean. I didn't know he was still alive until Dermot rang me".

"How did Dermot find him" asked Kate.

"He called a local man who used to be an active member of the IRA. Mentioned the funeral and got the name of the man who spoke at the funeral.

He immediately put Dermot onto O'Connell. Took a few more calls to get his address, but it wasn't difficult. There are a lot of people round here who fought, in one way or another, for the unity of Ireland. Not all are happy with the outcome".

This last thought brought a definite chill to the conversation. Col, the taxi-driver, broke it, saying that, as Dermot and Connor would be driving their visitor back to Belfast, he'd best be on his way back to Banbridge. They all went outside to see him off and, shortly afterwards, McGuiness reappeared, carrying a holdall, got into a medium sized Mercedes car and drove it over to where Kate, O'Brady and Bridget stood. O'Brady shepherded Kate into the front passenger seat and got in the back. McGuiness gave his daughter a wave, instructing her to tell her ma that he'd be back some time, but probably late; and they left.

The journey back to Belfast was physically very comfortable, as McGuiness drove the Mercedes fast but very expertly. Psychologically, it was extremely painful. They talked intermittently, about Kate, about McGuiness, his family and his business, though not about O'Brady at all; and while they talked it was possible – just – to think that this was all no more than another stage of Kate's gathering of information, though what more she could learn was now completely unclear to her. But as the journey went on, and the silences grew longer, a more sombre air descended on them; and Kate was under no illusion that she remained a free agent. This became all the clearer when McGuiness said -

"I don't want to push you on what must be a painful subject; but I've little doubt that O'Connell will want to know more about how you, or how your man, got involved in all this history. I don't think you need have any worries about him respecting any…….. confidences. You'll see that when you meet him".

Kate thought she saw only too clearly already. But, they were on the same side she told herself again; and, anyway, O'Connell, if he was a senior man in the IRA in the 1970's, must be quite old now – at least late sixties and probably in his 70s, if not more. And the Troubles were over, however deep the scars might run. Wasn't she being just a touch hysterical in thinking that she might be harmed in some way?

It was nearing 7pm as they reached the outskirts of Belfast; the light had faded and the lights of the city were spread out in front of them. Kate's trip to the library, only that morning, seemed an age ago. They drove through some suburban roads, eventually turning into a cul-de-sac of pleasant, medium sized, semi-detached houses. The journey had somewhat dulled Kate's senses; but it now hit her very hard that she did not know where she was in Belfast, was with complete strangers; and about to meet a man who clearly had been extremely dangerous for much of his life – and none of this had been either planned or even anticipated. Once again seeking to quell the panic she was feeling, she got out of the car; the three of them walked to a house near the end of the road; and McGuiness pressed the bell.

The door was opened by a man that Kate judged to be in his early 70s, of above average height but clearly still quite fit and full of energy. He looked at them impassively as McGuiness introduced himself, O'Brady and Kate, as Kay, adding -

"I'm sorry I don't know your other name"

"Madden" said Kate "Kay Madden" using the first name that came into her head.

"Good Evening to you, Miss Madden" said the man, shaking her hand. "I'm Victor O'Connell. Do come in" This was said with a perceptible smile of welcome; and Kate began to feel a little easier. As they went through to a living room at the back of the house, this scintilla of relaxation was rudely smashed. Sitting there, behind a small table, were three men, two probably in their forties and one rather older; and they were certainly not smiling.

"Please, have a seat" said O'Connell, still affable; and Kate almost collapsed into a chair opposite the three men. O'Brady remained standing as McGuiness spoke to O'Connell.

"I think that's our job done" he said. "No doubt you've things to discuss – you won't want us around. So Connor and I'll just head back home". It was a sign of how much worse Kate felt her situation had become that she now saw McGuiness as a lifeline; and she didn't want him to leave. But before she could say anything, O'Connell said -

"That's very understanding of you gentlemen; and we'll see that she gets back to where she's staying" and McGuiness and O'Brady had gone.

"Well now" said O'Connell "let me introduce. These are my two sons, Vincent and Declan" – he pointed to the two younger men, neither of whom moved or said anything; "and this" – he indicated the other man – "this is an old colleague, Shaun Riordan". He also remained impassive. "I understand from Mr. McGuiness that you came looking for relatives of Mary and Michael McGuiness, because you have some connection with their tragic deaths back in 1983. Is that right?" He had lost any trace of a smile or a welcoming manner.

"Yes, that's right" Kate mumbled quietly, looking down at her lap. She felt she must say more, but had no idea what to say; and wasn't sure she was capable of saying more.

"But their relatives are all dead, I understand?" said O'Connell. This was a fraction easier, but again all Kate could do was to say 'yes, that's right'.

"Could you tell me the connection please?" It was phrased as a question but delivered in a manner that did not contemplate any negative sort of answer.

Kate looked up at him, panic starting to show in her eyes; and, almost imperceptibly, began to shake her head.

"I can't" she said, so quietly that there was no certainty that any of the five men looking at her heard.

"I'm afraid, Miss Madden, that you must". The formality was combined with a clear touch of sadness; but Kate visibly trembled. Not really knowing what she was doing any more, she stood up, holding the table with both hands.

"I must go" she said. "It's too painful to talk about, I don't want to talk about it. Please excuse me". She tried to steady herself, to get ready to leave, but before she could do so, O'Connell leaned across the table and put his hand on Kate's.

"I know about Sellafield".

Slowly, Kate sank back into the chair.

"How?" was all she could say.

"I can't really say" O'Connell replied. "But Shaun and I knew about the attack" There was a long pause.

"And we knew something happened. The first reports were of an explosion. But then it was all written off as an electrical fault, no breach of the plant itself, no release of radiation. We never heard anything more of the team who carried out the operation until they were murdered in a fake car crash a month or so later. It must have been the British security service who did that – just five more casualties in a war of attrition, except that I knew them; I was involved in recruiting them to work for the IRA; and I feel, however indirectly, responsible for their deaths. There has not been one day since that I haven't blamed myself, gone over and over and over in my mind what happened, in Sellafield and to them". There was real anger building as he spoke. "So, however painful it may be for you Miss Madden, however much you may not want to talk about it, if you have some 'connection ' as you put it, with what happened, then we need to know what it is. If it is any help, Shaun and I, and my two sons, we four, are the only people who know what I have just told you. No-one else".

Kate didn't have a choice – had never had a choice, she now realised – but what O'Connell had said undoubtedly made it easier for her. Trying to pluck one small victory before she succumbed she said

"I will tell you everything I know; but can I please go then? I'm tired and I'm frightened and…….."

"Don't distress yourself" said O'Connell. Where we go from here rather depends on what you have to tell us; but we mean you no harm". This was nothing like as fulsome an endorsement of her safety as Kate would have liked, but it would have to do.

"My partner is a professor of Engineering at Oxford University. He was doing some work for a company that was thinking about buying Sellafield; and found evidence that there had been an explosion near the re-processing plant. But the pipeline it ruptured had been in disuse for some time before it happened; and the British Government was able to pass it off as just a huge electrical fault. The people who did it were seen destroying the van they had used, and getting into the car to take them back to London. The man who saw them – he was just an old-age pensioner out looking at a Badger set - reported them; they were picked up and at least one of them confessed to the attack when it was first announced. But then, when the attack was covered up, no-one knew what to do with them. They were handed over to some government agency – I don't know which – and then ....well you know the rest. Except, that Paul – that's my partner – has disappeared. I thought he must be dead. But I was attacked, in my home, and then saved by two Americans who told me Paul was still alive. I've been trying to find him".

There was a silence so total, a tension in the room so taut that Kate found it physically painful. To break it she added "That's all I know", but the silence then resumed; and she sat there, exhausted, looking down at her lap, though her eyes were almost closed. It was one of O'Connell's sons, she had forgotten which was which, who finally broke the moment.

"How do you know all this?" he said in a flat, expressionless voice.

"I know, I know" was all Kate could reply in a resigned tone. "Could I have a glass of water please?" Again no-one spoke, but the other son got up, went out and came back with a glass of water, which he set down quietly in front of her.

O'Connell eventually broke the silence.

"Well, Miss Madden, I thank you for that. I have spent much of my life wondering what went wrong at Sellafield, and how five Irish patriots ended up being butchered by the British; and you must see that I will need to know how you came to find this out; but it is some consolation finally to know, even if it relieves the pain of losing them not one jot". And with that phrase, Kate recognised that she would not be allowed to leave any time soon. She was, however, jolted out of this line of thought by O'Connell.

"Why did you come to Northern Ireland?"

"I found out that Mary and the others had disappeared back in 1983; and I thought I might discover something more about her and the others by going through newspapers archives in Belfast. I only found out this morning....... what happened to them. I saw that she and her brother came from Loughgannon; and got the bus there. The place sounded small enough that I might be able to find someone who knew them, maybe their family. The rest you know".

"Tell me more about.... Paul" said O'Connell, and Kate did. It was a relief to get the conversation on to something that seemed so much less threatening to her; but terribly painful too, as she realised that she was not the slightest bit further forward in finding out what had happened to Paul, however much more she now knew about the reasons for his disappearance; and the tears ran down her cheeks as she recounted how she had met Paul, and their time together. Her distress seemed to affect O'Connell who, when Kate had finished, said -

"I'm sorry for your loss. We are all victims, in one way or another, of our history in Ireland. But I must ask you how you know what you know. That will, I think, conclude our business".

"Why do you need to know?" asked Kate. She no longer felt any great reason not to tell O'Connell; but the sheer tension of the afternoon had drained her of the energy she needed to re-tell her months-long quest to find Paul.

"Shaun, you explain" said O'Connell, who seemed almost as drained of energy as Kate.

"You have arrived out of nowhere, Miss Madden, with detailed knowledge of one of the most secret operations of the war over Northern Ireland – knowledge that we have assumed for thirty years was known only to the British military or security services. We have no way of knowing if it is true; and know way of knowing if you are who you say you are. If you are working for the British, then providing a lot of valuable, but unverifiable, information would be a classic way of seeking to get information from us. The war may be over, but there is much unfinished business, on both sides. So, please tell us. I need hardly say that you will not leave here until you do". Riordan spoke quietly, but unambiguously and with undisguised menace.

In a curious way, it caused Kate to relax. Much of her anxiety had come from not knowing what to tell these men. The burden of that decision had clearly been removed from her. So, as briefly as she could, she told them of the help the police had initially given, and then their clear aim of ignoring Paul's disappearance; of the lack of press coverage; of finding out that Paul's laptop had gone, and that there had been a break-in at his laboratory. She told them of the missing disks, her tracking through Paul's files to the companies for which he had worked; her visits to them, to Sellafield, and to the retired police officers who had been involved, first Framwell in Cumbria and then Minogue and finally, critically, Richards. She forbore to give the details of her honey-trap approach towards David Nicholls in Leeds. Otherwise, she was methodical, frank and convincing; except that she did not make any reference to Alan Gerrard having been involved; and not once did she mention a certain Detective Inspector Neil Hargreaves who, even now she knew, would be waiting for a call from her.

"Well, may I say you appear to be a very determined and resilient young lady" said O'Connell. "I'm very impressed, truly I am". Kate gave no sign of having even heard him. Then one of his sons interjected.

"Do you have any evidence, of any kind, to back your story?" It was said flatly, but carried unspecified threats with it. For the first time since she had got in the taxi at Banbridge bus station, Kate felt angry and with enough adrenalin to express it.

"Oh, yes, of course, I've got signed witness statements from all of them, downloads of the missing computer files, CCTV, mug-shots of the bombers, anything you want – don't be so bloody daft. It's probably the biggest secret the British security people have been sitting on for thirty years; they tried to kill me just for trying to find out about Paul; it's taken up my life for weeks on end to find out as much as I have – and you start talking about evidence". She spoke with increasing vehemence; and noted with some satisfaction that O'Connell's son, whichever he was, looked – at least a little – taken aback. He'd probably killed people in the past, for the sake of a united Ireland; and would no doubt kill her without a second thought if ordered to; but the sudden show of defiance, after all the fear, tears, submission, had clearly surprised him.

Once again O'Connell intervened and, as before, surprised her by a sudden switch of topic.

"What do you plan to do now?" he said.

"I'm going to go on trying to find Paul" Kate said, re-energised by her previous outburst.

"And how do you plan to do that?"

It was a simple, very natural question; though one to which Kate certainly at that moment had no answer. But, if all those weeks ago, she had had her 'Desdemona' moment in the Engineering Laboratory in Oxford, which had started everything off, this was, perhaps, her 'Eureka' moment. In the fraction of a second that it took one part of her brain to formulate the obvious answer that she didn't, at the moment, know, but would think of a way forward – she always had before – another fizzing, brilliant, innovative, totally glorious part of her mind was operating on a totally different wave-length. She had, she knew, become a mere pawn in a very deadly game; and she might very easily be swept from the board by the very powerful forces at large upon it. She needed a decisive act – a gambit that would, in one move, totally re-shape the game and her position within it – and her mind was racing to formulate a way forward - in quite some detail she realised later – a route at once enormously risky but so stunning she knew instantly that she would follow it wherever it might lead.

"I was hoping you might help me".

CHAPTER 21

Kate might reasonably have expected the reaction to be disbelief, even ridicule; but so gripped was she by the idea that had now lodged in her brain, so immediately immersed in it was she that she expected them to ask her how – how could they help. Neither response occurred.

"Just when did that idea come to you?" asked O'Connell. Before Kate could answer, he pushed on. "You said before that you only found out this morning what happened to Cieran and the others; and that you went to Tandragee on a whim. So you knew nothing of me, of any of us here, until less than an hour ago, you say, but you want our help? Are you trying to drag us into something here, something…...unwise?"

"I really don't like this" said Declan O'Connell before Kate could answer. "I think we should terminate the whole thing, now" It was left unclear whether Kate was part of 'the whole thing'; but Kate was in orbit now.

"The idea came to me about three seconds ago" she said, defiantly. "I have no interest, nor frankly the slightest knowledge about the struggles in Ireland, either now or in the past. I'm just trying to find Paul. I know he is not of the slightest concern to you. You're Irish nationalists and I am no doubt the hated British. But the most important thing in my life, and what sounds as if it has been the most important thing in your life, tie us together, give us a common objective. You must want to know more about the death – the murder - of your friends; I want to find out how to get Paul back – and those two questions have the same answer. After all this time, today - what I was able to find out - must be a shock for you, but no more than the shock it is for me sitting here – I never expected anything like this, and I'm scared to death – but we could all gain something from this if we just have the presence of mind to grab it". She stopped abruptly, her energy almost visibly exhausted once again.

It was clear that no-one other than Victor O'Connell was going to reply to this. He, meanwhile, sat staring at Kate impassively, his fingers pressed together in front of his jaw.

"Declan, Vincent, will you entertain Miss Madden for a brief while? Shaun, a word, outside please" O'Connell and Riordan got up and left the room. Only then did it hit Kate with full force that, if on their return, they had decided not to co-operate with her, then they might regard her with too much suspicion, as too much of a threat, ever to be allowed to leave. The total silence that followed their exit, with neither of O'Connell's sons saying anything, only increased her anxiety. One sat there motionless, the other idly rubbing his thumb and fingers together; and Kate felt sheer panic starting to well up inside her. She put her hands between her knees to stop them shaking, desperately wanting to say something, to engage these two morose and menacing men in some sort of human contact, but unable to think of anything.

"I need to go to the lavatory" she said

"You'll have to wait 'til they come back" said Declan, without even looking at her. It was quite clear that this was not negotiable, whatever the consequences. So Kate tried to focus on her plan, the steps they could take if only these men – or to be more accurate if only O'Connell, for the others clearly deferred in all things to him – could see the advantage; and she had one – just one – Ace to play. Please God, she thought, let it be the Ace of Trumps.

After what seemed an age, but was in fact under five minutes, O'Connell and Riordan returned. To her utter horror she saw that O'Connell was carrying a small gun in his hand, casually, almost concealed, hanging loosely from his fingers, but a gun nonetheless. Kate almost cried out, but no sound would come from her throat.

"What you suggest has some attraction" said O'Connell "but the answer is 'no'. We have discussed it; and we cannot see how it would be advantageous to us, especially now that a 'solution' has emerged to the Troubles, even if it is one many of us abhor. We are not set up for renewed involvement any more – in short it is all too late. I've no doubt from our short acquaintance that you will go on regardless, which presents us with quite a problem. Fortunately, no-one can possibly know where you are at this moment".

It flitted through Kate's half-paralysed mind that this was the second time in less than two weeks that two men had threatened to kill her; only this time the other two men around would join in the killing. Clearly, no amount of pleading or begging would find even an ounce of sympathy. Time for her final card - risky, but her only real chance.

"I know who was responsible for the murder of your friends – I don't mean notionally or indirectly, I mean actually gave the orders personally to have them picked up from the police station in Paddington, taken to Ireland, put in a car unable to move and the car pushed over a cliff. He's the same person who has hold of, or has murdered Paul. I care about what happened to him. You seem not to care. Christ, with friends like you......".

It was, to say the least, undiplomatic; but she needed to shock these men somehow, get them to think about her – about the situation - differently. It certainly surprised the men in the room. O'Connell leaned forward and, with a speed and force that belied his advanced years, slapped Kate round the face, so hard she was knocked off her chair and onto the floor, her mouth and cheeks screaming with pain from the blow.

"Speak to me again like that, young lady, and you will greatly regret it" he said. Kate, slowly starting to pick herself up sensed, through some quite primeval instinct, that the only way she was likely to get out of the situation alive was to stand up to these men. A submissive stance would get her nowhere; and so she had no other route to go. Slowly she sat back on her chair.

"What a great, brave example of the IRA you are – four of you faced with one woman and you are oh so macho. But you won't lift a finger to avenge – even pay some tribute to - people who died for your cause. I'll do better on my own". She looked as scornful as she could. "Useless bunch of pricks" she murmured dismissively, goading them, the obscenity quite outside her usual language. One of O'Connell's sons moved closer to her, grabbed her shoulder and was clearly about to punch her very hard in the face; but the slightest shake of O'Connell's head was enough to stop him. Totally in control of the situation, fully recognizing the game she was playing; and not a little impressed at her nerve, he ignored the studded insult.

"Who *was* responsible?" he asked, icily.

"That's the real killer" she replied, quite unaware of the *double entendre* she had uttered. "Alan Gerrard".

The men in the room had received quite a few shocks during the course of the afternoon; but none quite matched this one. Riordan muttered a "Jesus Christ"; but otherwise all four were stunned into silence. Kate took a sip of water from the glass which still stood on the table in front of her, her mouth feeling as if it was beginning to swell up. Two questions coursed through her veins – would they believe her; and would it be enough to turn things round?
Riordan spoke first.

"How do you know that?" was the predictable question, and Kate was off, talking to save her life.

"The bombing at Sellafield was reported through to the Home Office Mainland Security section; and it was they who, when they heard that the damage was quite slight – no radiation leaks and basically only one pylon down – decided on the cover-up. It was also they who subsequently received the message from Paddington Green police station that a group of Irish terrorists had already been arrested for the attack; and decided to get rid of them. No-one else below the Prime Minister would have had the authority to deal with the news of the attack as well as override the police follow-up to the arrest. No-one below the post of Minister for Mainland Security at the Home Office could have approved such events. I looked up who it was. It was Gerrard.

"But that's not all. He had every reason – every personal reason – to embark on the cover-up. He was taking the flak for previous failures by the security forces to stop IRA attacks on targets in England. The Sellafield attack would have finished him. So, when he saw a way to avoid revealing it, he took it. But then, if the arrest had gone ahead, which would have revealed the cover-up, he would have not only been finished politically, he would probably have gone to jail. That's why the McGuinesses and the others died – had to die – to save Gerrard's career, maybe his freedom; and it worked brilliantly. He recovered his reputation; and now he leads the nation – and it's still your nation. Then Paul's research started to threaten his thirty year secret and - just like that – Paul disappears. God knows what story Gerrard told whoever it was that took him – danger to the State for some cooked-up reason, I've no doubt. Anyway, you may be able to live with all that, just walk away; but I can't and I won't. If Paul's alive, I'm going to get him back; and if he is dead, then I am going to expose the whole awful truth; and finish off Gerrard in the process. I think I know how it can be done; but I can't do it on my own".

O'Connell stared at her with such intensity that Kate could almost feel it, but now was not the time for even an ounce of weakness; and she just stared back at him, daring him to back off from her challenge to him.

"Is that why you came to Northern Ireland – to seek help?"

"No, I told you, I came just in the hope of finding out a bit more about the group that disappeared. I never expected to meet you, or anyone associated with the IRA, let alone anyone who knew the people who had been killed. But now that we've met, it's become very clear to me that, like I said, we have a shared aim. If you can't see that, I don't know what more I can say".

"So how do you think it could be done?" asked O'Connell, so quietly Kate almost didn't hear him.

Kate had reached her Rubicon. She fleetingly recalled reading that the Rubicon had been a very small stream in north-eastern Italy; so small that no-one now knew of its precise whereabouts. But Caesar had faced a life-or-death defining decision as to whether to stay in the Cesalpine region to the north which he legitimately controlled but where, if he remained, he would not get what he regarded as his due reward from the Senate in Rome; and might in time be tried, exiled or even condemned; or to cross the river into the Roman homeland – an explicitly illegal act for a well armed Roman regional governor – leading without doubt to civil war against Pompey, with death or absolute power and glory as the only possible outcomes.

Kate had no stream to cross, just a question to answer. But it was an equally life-or-death defining moment. If she had no answer, her search for Paul was over but, in addition, she had poor prospects of getting out of Northern Ireland alive. If she did answer – and she certainly had one - then it was war; a war against the most powerful man in the country; and no way back. Kate sided with Caesar.

"We contact Gerrard, let him know what we know. Offer to drop it all in return for Paul's release. Whether that happens or not, we then release the whole story to the Press. Eventually, Gerrard will end up spending the rest of his life in jail for multiple murder".

"But without some indication that you have concrete evidence against him" replied O'Connell "he'll just ignore you or, more likely, get you arrested for harassment; and you said before that you had no evidence at all. It's you who will end up in jail, if not a lunatic asylum. Anyway how would you 'contact' him? He's the Prime Minister. Any attempt would be filtered out by his many minions as just the ravings of a crazy person – they probably get hundreds of such things every day already"

For the first time since she'd arrived, Kate began to feel a sense of calm; and a sense of getting in control of both herself and the situation. What O'Connell had said was all entirely negative, but he was, at last, engaging with her, not dismissing her; and she had answers to his doubts.

"I know I have no evidence, but he doesn't know that. I've discovered every last detail of how events developed, so he'll know that I have talked to a lot of people. He won't know, and he won't be able to find out how many of them wrote down, maybe with witnesses, what they knew of the affair; and for all he knows, I may have contacted some of the people actually involved in the cover-up and the murders. He definitely won't be able to take the chance that we somehow know it all but just can't prove it. So he is going to have to respond and, when he does, we will be in a position to get concrete evidence of his guilt".

"And contacting him?" asked O'Connell.

"Oh, that. Look, I know how to do it – this is details. The question is, are you going to help? I can't do it without a team. If you won't, I'll find someone else; but I think you owe it to Mary and Michael and the others". She banished from her mind the distinct possibility that if they wouldn't help, she might well not be around to recruit anyone else. She also ignored the fact that she had no idea who else she could recruit, though Christopher Barnett in Leeds, who had helped with her blackmail stunt on Nicholls, would be where she would make a start.

"Well, that is something we are going to have to think further about" said O'Connell. Declan here will take you upstairs and show you a bedroom where you can have a rest while we discuss it" He nodded briefly, Kate was relieved to see, not to the brother who had earlier been on the point of knocking her teeth out, but the other one. "But before you go up, I must insist that you give me your mobile phone". Kate appreciated that she had no choice, got it out of her bag and handed it over.

"How long do you expect to be?" she asked

"As long as it takes" replied O'Connell, as he walked out of the room.

As Kate got up, she asked Declan O'Connell if she might have a drink of something stronger than water; and he poured her a whisky from a sideboard.

Clutching this they headed upstairs; and he left her in a small but comfortably appointed bedroom with a tiny but serviceable bathroom next door.

"I'll be just outside if you want anything else" he said, but his intention was clearly to let her know that she wasn't going anyway until the O'Connells approved it. As if to make the point even clearer, he added that his brother, Vincent, would be stationed outside in the street, onto which the bedroom looked. Kate took a tentative sip of the whisky, and then a longer one to steady her nerves; lay down on the bed and prepared to wait to see if her gamble had paid off. She had no illusions that waiting was going to be any easier than the experience of the last hour or so but, to her surprise, the whisky and nervous exhaustion combined to make her feel quite drowsy; and she was soon, if not asleep, then in a sort of semi-comatose state. As a result, although it was nearly an hour before Declan O'Connell came back into the room, it seemed a much shorter interlude to Kate.

"Please come back downstairs" said O'Connell rather curtly; and Kate, trying to shake herself back to full awareness got off the bed, tidied her hair in a small dressing table mirror; and headed back down. The other three were all present as Declan followed her back into the sitting room. Victor O'Connell looked as grim-faced as when Kate had last seen him, which did not bode well she thought; but he then said, with some intensity

"You are a very extraordinary woman, you've got some guts I must say, and you've clearly got a smart brain behind that pretty face. I've talked to Shaun here about what you've suggested and, subject to two conditions, we are prepared to go along with it". He paused, but Kate was just too relieved to be able to say anything, not even to ask the obvious question as to what the two conditions were. O'Connell nonetheless told her.

"The first condition is that we are going to check you out so thoroughly there won't be a thing we don't know about you before we proceed. Heaven help you if you aren't who you say you are; and if you turn out to be with the British security forces, we'll ship you out to the Far East for a very large sum of money, where you can keep a lot of sick perverts very happy. You might survive for five years or so, if you are very unlucky; but it's the last anyone here will ever hear of you". The fact that Kate had no such connection did not stop her from feeling like she had been punched in the stomach – and she had given them a false name.

"And the second condition?" she said, with as much control as she could exert.

"That the plan you have concocted really makes sense – every last dot of it. Shaun and me, and my two boys as well, may have some thoughts, in fact we already do, but by the time we have formulated everything, it has got to be absolutely right. We are, after all going out to get the most protected, best resourced person in the whole country. It had better be good".

"Then we ought to start straight away" said Kate.

CHAPTER 22

If O'Connell was surprised by Kate's desire to get going immediately, he showed no sign of it. Instead, he went over to a desk in the living room and got out a large notebook, plus a pen from his pocket. He sat at the table, with Riordan, while O'Connell's two sons stood nearby.

"So, Kay Madden, tell me about you, and then about your boy-friend. Everything"

"My name's not Kay, it's Kate, actually it's Catherine, but I have always been called Kate; and it's not Madden, it's Kimball. I didn't know what I was getting myself into when the taxi-driver from Banbridge took me to meet Mr. McGuiness – so I just said the first name that I could think of. I'm sorry" she added as O'Connell positively glowered at her.

"Jesus, you're starting to really worry me" said O'Connell "and worrying is not something I do well". There was real menace in his voice. Kate was determined to keep some sort of initiative in the conversation.

"I said, I'm sorry. You'll be able to check out every last thing you want about me. I work for Oxford University Press, commissioning books, mainly science. I've worked there for years, I live in Oxford – I can give you my address, the names of the people I work with, everything. As far as they are concerned I'm on compassionate leave because Paul – Dr. Emmerson – my partner, disappeared. They think I'm distraught, and so I was; but I took the leave to try to find out what happened to Paul – and I succeeded. I can tell you everything you want to know about him as well, how we met…" O'Connell put up his hands.

"Whoa, just a moment. This is no good. I need to have all this information down in black and white. Look, here's pad and pen. Write it all down, all the main points in your whole life, right up until now, plus when you met Emmerson and everything about him as well. The boys will check it out and, while they are doing it, you, me and Shaun can start to talk about the way forward".

"How long are they going to need to check it all?" asked Kate. O'Connell looked at his two sons and raised an eyebrow in question.

"Maybe a couple of days, three at the most" said Victor.

"Does it really need that long?" asked Kate, rather belligerently. "You can have the keys to my house, and to Paul's. You can call OUP, ask to speak to me. My P.A. will tell you why you can't get hold of me there. I'll give you a list of contracts I've been working on. You pick one at random and tell Janice that you're calling about that contract. I can give you names of my friends in

Oxford. You can ring them asking if they know how to get hold of me. It won't surprise them because they all know I've gone AWOL. Say you tried OUP. If this was all some elaborate set-up, none of that would make sense. You could even call Thames Valley police at Oxford – ask to speak to a DI Johnson. You could ask him if there has ever been any further news about Paul, did his irritating girl-friend give up on him or not, anything to confirm what I told you. Same with Paul - call the Engineering Lab, ask to speak to Alice Richmond – she's the administrator there; or call Wadham College. They'll tell you he's not there – they may tell you he's dead – but can't you do it quickly? If Paul is alive, it may only be for so long"

Declan and Vincent looked at their father, who paused, then nodded.

"Okay, write down all the names and addresses and phone numbers you can; and who each one of them is. Declan, you get over to Oxford first thing tomorrow morning. Ask around a bit. Vincent, you can get on the phone, to her friends tonight, to her office tomorrow. One other thing...." He wrote something out on a piece of paper from his notebook, tore it out and showed it to them both, in such a way that Kate could not see what he had written. Both nodded. Kate was very keen to know what he had put to them, but decided she would not give O'Connell the satisfaction of rejecting any request to know what it was, and remained silent. For ten minutes she sat and wrote, consulting her address book as she went. Declan said he would head off and try to book a flight; but first he would get a camera and take a picture of Kate. O'Connell told him where to find one; and five minutes later he had Kate on film. He left, saying that he'd return as soon as he had fixed up his travel. When Kate had finished writing down everything she could think of, she made a second copy, gave one set to Vincent, who left saying he'd work out some lines of inquiry and do the phoning from his own house. Shortly after, Declan returned, picked up the other copy and set off for the airport. For the first time since the early afternoon, Kate was faced with only two potentially hostile men; but she wanted their help as much as they clearly still distrusted her. She entertained no thoughts of trying to escape.

"Right" said O'Connell. "It's getting late. Talk us through your plans, in broad terms at least; and Shaun and me will sleep on them. Then we can get down to detail first thing tomorrow. You'll stay here tonight. I'm sorry you won't have your overnight things. Shaun, do you think Meg could rustle up a night dress and a get a toothbrush from that late night store in Western Road?" That Kate had to stay could have been a shock to her; but she had realised from some long time ago now that these men were never going to let her simply head off back to her hotel. Her only real concern was Hargreaves. It was well past nine o'clock now; and he would be very worried indeed that she hadn't rung. She just hoped he wouldn't do anything that could lead O'Connell to know that a police officer was trying to track her whereabouts. She had contemplated telling O'Connell that she had, in a loose sort of way, been working with Neil; but knew that talk of a Detective Sergeant being involved might just be enough for O'Connell to decide that the whole thing was too risky, with what consequence for her she did not want to think about.

Shaun said he'd call Meg – presumably a wife or daughter – and used his mobile. Kate and O'Connell eyed each other like two predatory but alien species, neither quite knowing what he or she was up against. When Shaun had finished his call, O'Connell said

"Now, let's get to the heart of this" and Kate knew she had arrived at the moment of truth.

"There are three key steps to this" she started. "The first is to make contact and convince Gerrard that, unless he plays ball with us, we can and will release damaging and conclusive evidence to the Press on his role in the initial deception and then in multiple murder. How we do that I'll come back to. Second, he is never going to just roll over and do what we say. He will attempt to outwit us and, given the stakes, I think he will try to eliminate us; and it's important that he thinks he can do this. It's vital that we have a plan A that appears sensible, but which he can see a way to circumvent; and then a plan B that will actually hook him. Once we have cast-iron evidence of his readiness to negotiate with us, or rather, get rid of us, he'll realise that his only chance is to release Paul; and once that has happened, or it has become clear that he can't, because Paul is dead, we will then throw him to the wolves".

"And why exactly is it that you think Paul might still be alive?" asked Riordan. "Because an American told you? I don't understand".

"Neither do I" said Kate. "They turned up out of the blue at my house – they'd been watching it - and came in when they saw two other men break in. They just managed to stop me being hanged – to make it look like suicide – so they seemed to have my interests at heart, or shall I say mine coincided with their own. They quite distinctly told me that Paul was alive; and that there was a good chance that he'd be coming back to me. But I don't know how the Americans fit in. Politically speaking the US President is Gerrard's biggest, possibly his only ally at the moment; so why they might be working against him I haven't a clue. But I can't see any reason for the two Americans to tell me he's alive if he isn't".

"Well, we will find out, all in good time I suppose" said O'Connell. "Now, two things, and then we'll get some sleep. How to contact Gerrard; and what are these plan A and plan B ideas?"

Kate spent the next forty minutes running through, at least in outline what she had in mind. It was a great relief to see how increasingly attentive O'Connell and Riordan became; and even more so as they started to throw in comments, ideas, proposals of their own. Kate was keen to get the whole extended strategy planned in their minds, but recognised that the more interruptions she accepted and incorporated, the more the whole thing became a joint enterprise. She needed that to happen if it was to work; and she needed them to accept that it *would* work if she was to have some prospect of getting through it all. So she encouraged a dialogue, but tried to avoid getting into too much detail. That would all come later.

By half past ten, the two men were on board – she could tell as much by the tone as the content of what they said; and Kate was completely drained. She concluded in what was deliberately meant to be a somewhat Olympian style.

"So, that's the whole strategy. Why don't we all sleep on it and, if it still makes sense in the morning, we can get down to detailed planning. I'm totally shattered". O'Connell couldn't disengage quite so quickly.

"Okay, we can't do any more tonight but, as I see it, the two key issues for me and Shaun to work on are numbers and location; and sooner rather than later".

"That's right" acknowledged Kate, pleased to see the clarity and degree of focus that O'Connell could clearly bring to bear on the matter. "Sort those two out and we are in business". With that, she headed upstairs to the bedroom she had visited before, to find a long blue nightdress laid out on the bed; a small overnight wash bag, a tiny travelling alarm clock, plus a bowl of fruit on the bedside table. The sight of these small items of kindness almost overwhelmed her; but the sight of a small vase of flowers that had been placed on the dressing table was too much; and she found herself in tears – wonderful relaxing, cathartic tears. With Kate having, in the last eight hours, been to all intents and purposes kidnapped, then knocked to the ground, threatened with unspeakable degradation and death, Meg, whoever she was, would never know how much this small gesture meant. Twenty minutes later Kate was fast asleep.

Kate woke quite early and made some careful preparations. After eating some breakfast, the day became an increasing blur of discussions, phone calls, planning and frequent cups of coffee. Initially the three of them were focused on progressively more minute detail but, even before lunchtime, this phase started to give way to phone sessions; with both O'Connell and Riordan on their mobiles talking, talking, always in the most circumspect and even elliptical manner, usually fixing meetings for as soon as possible, conveying instructions and, all the time making notes. Kate, judging the time was now right, then asked if she could have her mobile back, saying that she needed to ring a few friends who would be worried about her – which was the last thing they needed – and that she would make the calls right there in front of them – she had nothing to conceal. O'Connell gave this less thought than she had anticipated, which was a good sign; and agreed, provided she kept the calls very short.

Kate first rang Sarah Jennings; and said that she was calling to let Sarah know that she was fine – just taking a few days off in Scotland. Sarah, as Kate had anticipated, had a lot of questions, but she breezily cast them aside, saying that she'd be back in a week to ten days; and would talk through everything then. She really mustn't worry. She added that her Hollywood contract was progressing well. The call lasted barely a minute. She then rang Janice and gave a repeat performance, ending up by asking Janice to give her regards to various people at OUP. Then she rang Hargreaves' home number.

Kate was fairly confident that, at that time of day, she would get his answer phone, but she was leaving nothing to chance; and had resolved, if Neil answered, to say nothing, pretending that she *had* got through to an answer-phone; and then put the phone down. This, however, was not necessary. She heard his slightly metallic voice asking the caller to leave a message. Kate launched into a message which, earlier that morning she had spent some time constructing and rehearsing.

"Irene, its Kate here" she said". Many apologies for not calling earlier. Off work for longer than I expected. Kicking my heels rather" She paused, and held the mobile away from her as she sneezed twice, got a small handkerchief out from her shoulder bag; and then went back to her call. "Wasn't great I'm afraid. I've taken a few days off, in the Scottish Isles. Then to Edinburgh. Hope to see you soon. I'll call when I get back. Really I will. All's well so" – another pause – "This message is to say don't worry about me – please, no need to do anything, absolutely nothing". She paused again. "By the way, just before I left, I got my first letter from the film director guy in Hollywood I told you about – it was very interesting, could be really significant. Bye".

O'Connell and Riordan seemed not to notice anything significantly different between this call and the first two, other than that it was clearly to an answer-phone. In case they did, Kate distracted them by asking if she could now hold on to her mobile

"Not until Declan and Vincent give you a clean bill of health" said O'Connell, and, Kate having switched the phone off, he took the mobile back from her apparently reluctant hand. The question was, what would Neil make of it? He'd realise that she was being overheard, or she wouldn't have addressed a mythical Irene. He'd realise that Kate must be trying to leave some sort of message; and the last sentence about a letter from Hollywood would make no sense at all. Would the emphasis on the importance of her 'first letter' lead him to note down the message from his answer-phone; and then identify the first letter of each sentence? IMOK followed by a long pause; then WITHIRA; plus, don't worry about me – please, no need to do anything. It was a long shot, but she had to let someone know something of her whereabouts. It might even give

252

her just the frailest of cards to play if O'Connell and his murderous associates had second thoughts about the whole scheme and Kate's continued value to them. At least Neil would know that she was alive and well; and he would know that her call had to mean *something*. Well, there was nothing more she could do; so it was back to planning.

In the afternoon, O'Connell and Riordan increasingly took over the operation, dissecting each and every element, playing with alternative ideas, writing ever more copious notes. Kate saw that they were becoming more and more galvanised, absorbed so completely that she suspected that at some moments she could walk out and they wouldn't immediately notice – not that she was going to risk it. And around 5pm she suddenly knew why they had become so committed. What prompted the insight she did not know; but, once seen, she had no doubts that she was right. These two men had not only worked together on many such operations before – that had been obvious from the start – but they must have been involved in planning the attack on Sellafield. The energy they were piling into the operation could have no other source. And as soon as she saw this, she realised that O'Connell must have been the driving force. He was just not the type to be anything other than a leader. Not a realisation that it would be wise to mention at the moment but, once they trusted her – or trusted her as much as they were ever going to – there was a useful new card to be played here if she needed it.

Shortly afterwards, Vincent O'Connell arrived. There was no small talk, not even a greeting.

"Well?" said his father. Vincent turned to Kate.

"I have two questions for you. First, what roughly was the total of the travel expenses which you claimed through your office last financial year?"

"Good grief, what a question" replied Kate, shocked by the unexpectedly banal nature of the question – but one that she immediately saw might make the difference between life and death for her.

"Let me think" She paused, frantically going back in her mind to the moment, some months ago, when she had signed off on her expenses for the year. Slowly it came back to her - not least because her increasingly frequent trips to the US – club class – had pushed the figure up significantly.

"I can't remember accurately, but it was eleven thousand pound something. I do remember that". Clearly he was using this as some kind of check on her. "How on earth did you come to find that out?"

"I rang your P.A.; said I was working for the company's auditors; and just wanted to check the figure. It was £11,760".

"And the second question?" asked Kate.

"What particular award received by Dr. Emmerson for his research did the Head of Wadham College emphasise in his speech at the memorial service which they held for him?" Kate stared at him; and started to panic. Probably it was his Weldon medal – one of the most prestigious awards in his field – but it wasn't the only one he'd received.

"Christ, I don't know. I never went to it – I didn't even know they had a memorial service. I certainly wasn't invited". Vincent looked unimpressed.

"You have got to believe me. You'll have to ask me another question".

"No need" said Vincent. You're right; they didn't have one. I rang them, said I was a colleague from Ireland, and asked if there had been, or was going to be one. I just wanted to know if you knew. If you'd said his medal, you would have been in big trouble". He finished with what could have passed for an apologetic smile.

Kate wanted to scream at him; but was too relieved to bother. She turned to Vincent's father.

"So, can we trust each other now? It is going to make everything very difficult if you don't". O'Connell, for the moment, ignored her.

"Presumably everything else checked out?" he asked Vincent.

"Everything. I've done checks on her career, her colleagues, I've rung any number of them, and her friends, usually asking for her phone number, but really just checking if they know her and what she does. If it is a set-up, it's the best I've ever come across".

"So" repeated Kate, with some emphasis, can we move on?"

"We can carry on with the planning – bring Vincent up to speed and see what he makes of it – but you're not in the clear yet, not until Declan gets back". He held up his hand as Kate went to reply.

"I've survived over forty years in the Movement; and you know the reason? Caution, checking, double checking, checking until you feel you are going to die of the tedium of it all; and I'm not going to change now". It was on the tip of Kate's tongue to say that it hadn't worked at Sellafield; he hadn't hit the target and he hadn't saved five lives; but she was close now – so close. No point in rocking the boat. They went back to their discussions.

It was nearly 10pm before Declan made it back. He also had two questions – O'Connell had clearly asked both of them to identify something that Kate would know if she was who she said she was, but not otherwise – presumably that was the written note he had shown them both before they left the previous night. First he asked her what was odd about putting the overhead light out if she was lying in Paul's bed at his home. She silently congratulated him on a very clever question; and explained that there was a wall switch, but it had ended up just behind the headboard when Paul had had a new bed installed, which made it difficult to operate. He then asked her -

"Why might Paul Emmerson be careful visiting Staircase 9 in his college?" Kate was so relieved she actually laughed.

"Because a student called Emma something lives there; and she sprayed him with champagne when he went to congratulate her on having finished her final exams last year. How did you find that out?"

"I called in and started asking about him. Said I was an Irish cousin over briefly in Oxford; and very sad about his disappearance".

"So, are you convinced?" asked O'Connell.

"There was a picture of her, along with about forty others – top management – on a board behind the reception desk at her offices; and I found out she had worked there for getting on for fifteen years. And everything else I tried checked out including the messages on her answer-phone at her house. She's kosher". O'Connell smiled, for the first time since Kate had met him.

"Welcome to the Irish Republican Army, Kate".

CHAPTER 23

Riordan drove her to the hotel Kate had been booked into. There; she picked up her belongings and paid the bill. Perhaps it was mere politeness, but Riordan came up to her room to help her with her small suitcase, so that she was never actually out of his sight. When they got back to O'Connell's house, she pointed out that she had come prepared for only a couple of days; and would need more things fairly soon if she was to base herself from now on at O'Connell's house. He acknowledged this, but waved the problem away until the next day. It was rather clear that, now she was regarded as a key member of an IRA operation, minor creature comforts like clean clothes were not high on his list of priorities.

That night, as Kate tried to sleep, the events of the day, not unnaturally, crowded in upon her. But more powerful emotions were also at work. She saw that she would, very soon, be taking part in an almost military-style action, but she couldn't free herself from dwelling on the situation she now found herself in and how she had got there – reflecting on all the points at which she might have held back, called the thing off, or simply collapsed under the weight of imminent failure. But somehow she had come through; and two things above all else were responsible for this – the sense of loss she had felt when Paul had disappeared and her determination to do anything and everything she could to find out what had happened to him; and the support, at great risk to his own career, that Neil had provided. And the two emotions tugged at her relentlessly. Where was Paul – if he was alive – and in what sort of state. Had Neil got her message and, whether he had or not, what was Neil thinking, feeling? Had she used him, used his affection for her, to pursue her single-minded pursuit of

Paul? She hadn't consciously, but that was a very different matter. None of this led to any answers, however, and eventually she slept fitfully.

The next day was spent on four critical elements of her plan: setting out a detailed timetable; trying to locate three suitable locations in the UK for the main action – though two would be easy enough to find when they were in England; preparing the details of the approach to be made to Gerrard; and, in the evening, a first meeting of a group of men whom the O'Connells and Riordan had been contacting over the previous forty-eight hours. Only the first location in England gave them any difficulty. It had to be absolutely right and, given time, there would be no problem about finding the right place. But time was what Kate did not have much of; and they were forced to limit their search to places with which the men were familiar from previous operations. Given thirty years of active struggle, there was, fortunately, quite a lot to choose from, but very little recent information on them. Unknown to Kate, an army of former IRA men or, in many cases just loosely associated sympathisers throughout mainland Britain were, by that evening, exploring all manner of derelict buildings, isolated farmhouses, disused warehouses and the like. The timetable clock could only start ticking once the right place had been identified.

The meeting that evening took place in the main dining area – unused on a Wednesday night - of a pub about ten miles into the countryside from O'Connell's house, near the village of Ravernet, south of Lisburn. Kate, Riordan and the three O'Connells were joined, in ones and two over a period of nearly an hour, by sixteen men, of all shapes and sizes. All that seemed to link them were the fact that they all knew the O'Connells – few seemed to know Riordan well, if at all; that they all knew each other, with varying degrees of familiarity; and the heavily suppressed, but nonetheless almost visible excitement that burst forth from each greeting or introduction. Kate could not help but be swept along by the exhilaration that accompanied each new arrival, often with applause and derisory cheers from those already there. O'Connell introduced Kate to every one of them – though she had no hope of remembering any of their names – and Kate noted how virtually every one of them went through the same routine, first of politeness, then wariness, followed by a glance at O'Connell with silent questions – what was a woman doing here, what was a Brit doing here, had O'Connell taken leave of his senses and so on – but then sufficient confidence in O'Connell to let him take his time to explain.

During a temporary pause between arrivals, Kate asked O'Connell who the men were; and was it really the case that there were still significant numbers of IRA members ready to carry on the fight with the British,
"There were three very different types in the Movement" said O'Connell. "By far the biggest numbers were sympathisers – people who were angry at the

treatment of the Irish in Northern Ireland; and wanting unification with the Republic; ready to help in all sorts of ways, eyes and ears, taking messages, arranging meetings, storing arms and even some gun running; but they were never the backbone of it all; and they have all just got on with their lives since the peace process broke out. Then there were the psychopaths – men who at any time in any place would have been involved in illegal action, including the thrill of shooting and bombing. They were vital to the operations we mounted, but no-one had any doubt as to why they were with us; and they were quite a threat – none too bright in a lot of cases. They have carried on, of course, except that now it is back to more conventional illegal activities, some robbery, some prostitution, but it's mainly drugs. There is just so much money in it; and the coast of Ireland is a perfect way into the United Kingdom. Every year there are huge drug seizures off the shores of this island, but it is just a drop in the ocean as far as the main dealers are concerned.

"And then there was us. Not just sympathisers, but totally committed, and controlling the war. To be truthful with you Kate, we are in disarray. Some think enough has been won through the peace process, plus they point to the demographics – that's the much higher birth rate amongst Catholics than the Prots – meaning you can date almost to the day when we will be in the majority of those voting. So they are content. Others are outraged at what they see as a sell-out; and would start the war again if they thought they could encourage enough to back them. And that's mainly who we have here. They're not active at the moment, but they're likely to find the prospect of taking on the Brits - especially when they find out it's the Prime Minister – distinctly appealing".

To Kate it all sounded only too plausible, but served to remind her just how dangerous a situation she was getting into. So why wasn't she terrified? As more people arrived, and O'Connell went to greet them, she asked herself the question very explicitly. Was it just that she had been attacked, threatened, assaulted; and so things were now, however bizarre, rather less frightening than they had been? She didn't find that convincing. Rather, she thought, she was like an increasingly compulsive gambler. She had lost a lot and now, with increasing abandon, was on a last big throw of the dice. If it came off – which it probably wouldn't – then she would be rich for life, back with Paul and such a story to tell. If, or more likely when, it didn't come off then better to have tried and lost – or some such trite excuse. Or perhaps, more accurately, that if she had tried everything and still lost Paul, then she was past caring what happened to her; and with that came a certain element of inner peace. She would play the game and, if she lost, the future was no less bleak than one in which she just accepted Paul's loss. Such thoughts, in a most curious way, steadied and relaxed her, but were interrupted by O'Connell clapping his hands to get some quiet. The men settled on chairs in front of him.

"You are all welcome to have a drink on me from the bar" he said "but I have a few words before you do". He paused and seemed to look round at every individual in the room before he continued. He certainly had their complete attention.

"The war is over; but there is unfinished business. I will tell you everything about it shortly but, first, I need to know who is with me on this. Like it has always been, if you're in, then there is no out; and if you'd rather not be in then, while we are having a drink, let me know and we'll part as good a set of friends and comrades as we have ever been. All I can tell you right now, to help you decide, is that you will putting right a great wrong; you will be away from your friends and family for, I estimate about two weeks – not less; it will be an armed operation; and we are likely to be up against serious opposition, most probably an SAS unit. Shaun, me and my two lads have made meticulous plans; and I am reasonably confident that we will all walk away after the operation in good health; but with opposition like that, none of us can be sure. One last thing – it is about as high profile as you could imagine. That's it, that's as much as I can tell you now. So, let's each get a drink and, if you're in, be back here in twenty minutes. If you're not, let me know. There's not a man here will think any the less of you".

"Can I ask two questions?" said a voice from amongst the men. O'Connell merely nodded.

"First, is it so high profile that it will undo the peace agreement?"

"I don't think so, no" said O'Connell "but it will generate a lot of public sympathy for us, for Sinn Fein; and a lot of antipathy for the British, all of which might just help a little to steer future developments our way. What's the second question?"

"Can you give us a categorical assurance that the woman is not a threat to us?" There was a clearly hostile silence; and Kate silently begged O'Connell to answer quickly and unambiguously.

"Declan and Vincent have checked her out very thoroughly. She will tell you her role in all this after we have a drink but, yes, I will give you that assurance. She has as strong a reason to be part of this operation as Shaun and I do. Any other questions?" There were none, and they headed through to the bar of the pub.

O'Connell made a point of going round, talking to everyone, giving each man the opportunity, discreetly, to let him know that he would not want to stay. Kate did not know, but guessed that they all recognised only too well from past experience that once part of such an operation, there was no going back, no quitting before the end, whatever that might be. She found herself with Riordan, accepted a small whiskey with a lot of ginger ale; and could think of nothing much to say. The reference to the SAS was not new to her. The five of them had discussed in detail how Gerrard would be likely to respond; but it was still very sobering to hear it announced so starkly to sixteen clearly very dangerous men. Twenty minutes later, some with a beer, some with a whiskey, they trooped back into the dining area. Kate found herself starting to count, but O'Connell cut her off.

"We have a full house, gentlemen. I confess, I am not surprised". This produced a few wry smiles but nothing more . "So, now it is time to get down to business. Tonight I am first going to give you the full background. It's in two parts, the first from me and the second, from Kate here. Then Shaun will outline the operation. We hope to be ready to move forward in a couple of days; so you will have that amount of time to make your excuses, put your affairs in order". He took a brief sip of his whiskey. "Now, here's the problem.

"In 1983, five members of the IRA broke into Sellafield, set explosives, exited and detonated the bomb. It was my operation; and they got in and out unnoticed because Shaun and I had spent the best part of ten years creating a new identity for him; and getting him recruited as part of the Sellafield security force. He was there that night; and that's how the team got in and out. The attack was a terrible failure. The pipeline we attacked, which we thought carried high grade nuclear waste, turned out to be disused; the explosion was explained away as an electrical failure; and the team were not heard of again until, a few weeks later, they were all killed in a car crash near Dublin. A number of the men started to mutter names, names of some of the five whom they clearly had known, or known of.

"That's right" said O'Connell, keen to keep control. "Cieran Hughes, Rory O'Halloran, Dougal Hearne, and Michael and Mary McGuiness. Many people thought, and Shaun and I knew, that they were all murdered by the British – put in a car and pushed over a cliff - but it was my operation. I only found out this week precisely what happened; but not a day has gone by since 1983 that I haven't blamed myself for their deaths. My only consolation was that Shaun got away before the bomb went off. That's all bad enough, but there is worse to come". He looked over his shoulder. "Kate, will you take over?" The combination of what O'Connell had told them, plus the notion that the British woman he had brought along was about to tell them something even more dire was spellbinding to the men sitting there. No-one moved – they barely breathed. Kate thought you could hear a feather drop, never mind a pin. She stood up and faced them. As she did so, her nerve almost failed her. Here she was, in front of twenty men – and not just any men but a highly lethal militia – about to address them on the way in which they could bring down the Prime minister of the UK. She wasn't sure that she could speak at all but, from somewhere deep inside her, some element of the training and experience she had had of being a successful executive in a still predominantly man's world, of countless presentations – to more agreeable but undoubtedly less attentive audiences – found its way to the surface and, with a deep intake of oxygen to fire her up, she started to speak. As she did so, she felt herself gaining in confidence.

"Some time earlier this year, my partner, Dr. Paul Emmerson, who is a research materials engineer at Oxford University, was carrying out some consultancy work at Sellafield; and came across evidence that there *had* been an attack there. Somehow this got back to the authorities and, as a result, two months ago, he disappeared, presumed dead, though that is not certain. I have spent the time since then trying to piece together what happened. From this I have learnt two key things. First, what actually happened. The team of five were, by the merest chance, observed transferring to their own car after the attack; and were picked up the same night. At least one of them admitted the attack to the police, before the Government decided on the cover-up. So it then had the embarrassment of what to do with the five people in custody. The answer you know. They were handed over, either to the security forces or the military, shipped to Ireland, put in a car and killed in a fake car crash.

"Second, I found out who was directly responsible for all this – who gave the specific approval. It was the then Junior Minister responsible for Mainland Security, Alan Gerrard, now, nearly thirty years on, Prime Minister". There were one or two audible gasps at this as she added "What is more, he arranged the cover-up because his career was finished if he had had to admit to another major mainland security failure at the time; and he sanctioned the murder of the five IRA members in order to conceal the cover-up". One or two whispered conversation were just starting to break out as she stopped abruptly and sat down again; but O'Connell immediately took the floor again.

"The operation is to retrieve Dr. Emmerson if he is still alive; and whatever the outcome of that, to bring down Alan Gerrard".

The atmosphere was, literally, electric. Kate could feel the tingling effect on the back of her neck. Everyone went quiet again, as a number of the men sitting in front of her looked meaningfully at each other or, in some cases, at Kate. O'Connell remained silent for the moment, letting the impact of what he had said sink in; but then he took up the reins again, now very much in business mode.

"We have one major problem, but a plan for dealing with it. The problem is that we have no solid evidence of the sort that would persuade a newspaper to publish, or the police to investigate. But, as Kate here realised early on in our discussions, Gerrard won't know that; and just can't take any chances. So, she will contact him and threaten that she will provide evidence unless he releases Emmerson. We don't for one moment expect him to accept this, even if he appears willing to do so; but we are confident he will respond, with the intention of eliminating Kate – he has already made one attempt. Whoever he sends will not be expecting a minor army of experienced IRA veterans; and we intend to use that moment to obtain cast-iron evidence of his guilt. That will then be what we use to free Emmerson, if he is still alive, and to condemn Gerrard".

"Why do you think there is any chance that Emmerson is still alive?" asked one of the men. "Surely there is no prospect of that, given Gerrard's murdering record and what's at stake?" O'Connell turned to Kate, who replied.

"You're right. I have presumed him dead for some while. But two Americans – clearly CIA or some such organisation – saved me from Gerrard's thugs – why I don't know – and they said that he was still alive. I can't see what reason they would have to lie about it. But it is very important to us, because it gives a reason for me to try to bargain with Gerrard. If Paul was definitely dead then, if I had solid evidence of Gerrard's involvement I'd just send it to the papers – there'd be nothing to bargain about".

O'Connell took over again. "As I said before, we hope to be up and running in a couple of days, just as soon as we have found some suitable locations. Kate will offer Gerrard the evidence in return for Emmerson; and we expect that Gerrard will send a team, probably SAS, of around 6 to 8 people would be normal. We need a location that looks to make sense to them, that is, one where Kate could see if Emmerson is being delivered or not; and make an easy exit if there is no sign of him; but also one where they think they can take Kate by surprise. But it is we who will do the surprising; and we will then get enough evidence both to retrieve Emmerson – or find out what happened to him – and to sink Gerrard".

"What armaments do you have in mind?" asked a rather formal looking man in the front row of seats.

"Fergal, over there, will act as armourer" - a large, rather florid, red-haired man near the back waved an arm in acknowledgement. "He has kept his hands on quite a collection of weapons, mainly semi-automatics, but also some high precision rifles with telescopic sights, night scopes, the works. We may need a few bigger bangs as well, at least in reserve, so that we are ready for a better protected attack; but my guess is that they will go for stealth rather than a big show of force. You are all familiar with most of what Fergal can get; but if you have any particular requests, ask him before you go. We will also have some very up to date communications gear; and all the transportation we'll need. Murphy and Malone here" – he pointed to two of the men in front of him – "can do the driving though, if they get excited, it's a lot safer walking". In the tension of the meeting, this minor attempt to amuse caused some ripples of laughter; and, more importantly a wave of relaxation to sweep through the room. All at once, almost everyone it seemed was talking to his neighbour.

O'Connell was content to let them chat. He had said almost everything he wanted to say for the moment; and now it was important for them all to start to feel part of a team. He eyed Shaun and his two sons who, as people started to stand up and stretch their legs, drifted into the group of men, starting to talk a little more about the plans to date. Eventually, O'Connell got their attention one more time.

"Have a few more drinks, it's a free bar. I'll contact you all to arrange another meeting, by Friday I hope, Saturday at the latest. Fix what you need to be away, because we will head straight on to the operation after that meeting. No need to say that this is level 5 security – there's no way back if you let anyone else know, however accidentally, about this". Kate didn't know what level 5 meant, but it sounded extreme; and she had little doubt that 'no way back' involved a particularly gruesome end. She had one more drink; and then together with Riordan and the O'Connells, left the pub and headed back for Belfast.

The next morning was spent going over the details of numerous sites in England; and just before lunchtime, they finally found what they were looking for. Wallington House, in Wiltshire, had originally been built in the 16th Century; and for hundreds of years had been the centre of a large agricultural estate, passed down through generations of the Wardell family. Like many such large houses it had been added to and rebuilt but, eventually, had become too large and too uneconomic to continue as a grand home for one family. However, unlike many such albatrosses, it had not been saved by new money, an American heiress, the National Trust or conversion to a hotel, multiple occupation or a Conference Centre. Presumably, at some point, one or more of these had been considered but, if so, too late to save it. From a distance it still looked fine, except for the deadening effect of all the windows being shuttered. Close up it became clear that it was in an advanced state of disrepair, with crumbling stonework and, apparent only from the inside, a roof which, while solid enough in normal circumstances, could be breached by a particular combination of wind and rain. It was of little interest to its owner, a development company that had bought it for next to nothing in the hope that it might be made to work, though with no initiative to date; but it had been of immense interest and, indeed, use to the IRA in the 1980s, as an arms store and operational planning centre less than ten miles from the M4.

One great advantage had been its remoteness, set in the middle of 1500 acres of farmland now owned by three local farmers who had not the slightest interest in the decaying structure at the centre. But equally, if not more important, was that, in addition to a grand entrance on the East side, complete with gatehouse and long drive to the house, it had two other exits, to the South and West, which the local farmers had maintained for their own purposes and which allowed someone in the house to leave the area of the original estate in less than a minute, and then get lost in a maze of little local roads. Such advantages for the

IRA had never been put to the test; but the O'Connells all concurred that it was very much what they had in mind; and both Riordan and Kate found themselves very much in agreement.

"Well, that's it" said O'Connell, in a rather matter-of-fact way over lunch. "We have the plan, the location and the men. We just have to get the timing right now". This was slightly disingenuous, Kate thought, because every spare second of the last forty-eight hours had been spent on getting the timing pinned down. As if reading her thoughts, O'Connell added -

"I know we have it all clear, but every man in the team needs to understand it – when to move and when not to – but we are ready to go. I'll call them all in tonight. I'll give McVeigh a call first though, so he can get his team organising supplies straight away. The first contact with Gerrard must go off tonight, from Oxford". Two weeks before, perhaps even a few days before, such a phrase would have caused utter panic in Kate's breast. It was a sign of how far along the road she had come that now it caused something much closer to exhilaration. She wanted Paul back; and now, finally, it seemed that she might get the chance, facing up, in the process, to the man who had orchestrated his abduction.

What they wanted was a purely private line of communication with Gerrard; but the prospect of that was, they knew, zero. Even in Kate's blinding flash of inspiration she had realised that that was impossible. But they did need to restrict the number of others in the know as much as they could, because Gerrard's freedom of action would become progressively more proscribed the more people involved. So, the first step was a letter – a letter sent to 10 Downing Street which, though addressed to Gerrard; and marked both personal and strictly confidential, would still no doubt be read by someone relatively junior first; and checked by security. So the letter had to say enough to get passed on, if not to the PM then at least to someone quite close to him, in order that the second phase, which would follow the letter, could work. Kate and the others had worked on it the previous day; and she now sat down at O'Connell's computer to type it out. On the first page she wrote:

This letter is addressed to the Prime Minister; and its contents are for his eyes only. Once the purpose of this letter is clear to him, he will himself wish its contents to be restricted to him alone. Please forward the attached sheet to him, sight unseen. Be under no misapprehension - the PM will wish to know of this letter, its postmark and its contents before it is too late for him to act.

Kate did not for one moment expect that this instruction would be followed; but it helped to build a picture of both seriousness and planning. On the next page, she wrote:

PAWN'S GAMBIT

I need to establish a secure and private line of communication with you to discuss important matters of mutual interest. I therefore need you to contact me by email, letting me have an email address through which I can communicate with you privately. This should be sent to me at kate.kimball@yahoo.com. I will be picking up my messages, very briefly, at various locations; and will not therefore be traceable.

The need for us to communicate arises because of certain events with which you were concerned earlier in your political career, with which I am now fully familiar; and because of Dr. Paul Emmerson. If I do not receive the email contact I have requested by 6 pm on Tuesday I shall release the extensive evidence I now have on these related matters to the National Press. The same result will occur if any attempt is made to disrupt the arrangement. If full and private communication can be established then this outcome may be avoided.

Kate Kimball

She made sure there was a copy retained on the computer's hard disk; and printed out a copy of both documents, which O'Connell took. She then picked up the letter itself, folded it twice, to hide the text, and then fixed it with a small piece of selotape. This would be subject to intense security checking; but Kate and the others were reasonably confident that the wording would at least get them to Gerrard's inner circle of advisers; and that they would see the sense, even if they thought the whole thing the work of a crank, briefly to mention a bizarre letter about 'earlier events' in Gerrard's career and a Dr. Paul Emmerson to Gerrard; and that would undoubtedly be enough for Gerrard to ask to see the letter. He would instantly know that the matter was serious; and the clincher was that Kate had used her own name. He would be familiar with it, having tried to have her eliminated; and almost certainly would know that she had now disappeared. The Oxford postmark would indicate that she was now back in action. If Gerrard ignored all the signs that he was facing a crisis of the gravest kind – one that would reveal him as a multiple murderer in order to save his own political life - then, they all recognised, he would get away with it. But, as O'Connell so eloquently put it

"He may have the balls for it, but he's not stupid. He'll get in touch".

Kate folded the sheet of paper with the first message round the second one; and then put the two sheets of paper in an envelope, sealed it, addressed it in her own handwriting – no doubt that would be checked – added 'personal' and 'strictly confidential'; and gave it to Declan O'Connell, who set off for the ferry and thence to Oxford with it. Victor O'Connell, with Kate, Riordan and Vincent O'Connell in attendance, reviewed the timeline again.

"They will get the letter either Friday or Saturday. One way or the other Gerrard is going to see the letter by Monday morning. We will get a contact address by Tuesday 6pm I'm sure of it. Kate will set up the swap – Emmerson for the evidence – at Wallington House for Friday. We will spell out all the precautions you are taking so that they can see that a double-cross on the day will be risky. But Gerrard is never going to play ball; so they're bound to go in early – reconnoitre, check that the place is empty, obtain advance entry, and wait for you to show up – except that we will be two steps ahead of them, in position by Tuesday evening, before they even know of the location. By the time they're done, we really will have the evidence".

O'Connell then told Kate that she should call her friends in Oxford again, keep up the fiction that she was in Scotland, but say that she was feeling a lot better; and would be back in Oxford over the week-end. When Kate asked why, O'Connell pointed out that the moment Gerrard got Kate's letter, he was almost certainly going to try to find her, and that would probably involve getting the local police to contact her friends, and her office, about her whereabouts.

"If they say that you have been away in Scotland, but are due back, that will be exactly what he would expect if the threat to him is real. Of course, they won't find you, because you aren't going anywhere near Oxford; but it will help to convince him and, more important, there won't be anything to link you to us, to Ireland at all – so he won't be expecting that you have got any sort of back-up. If he checks, not one of your friends in Oxford will be missing; so he will think you really are acting alone".

It all made perfect sense to Kate; but there was one great hole in it. If Gerrard, by some means or another, used the Oxford police force – and he had clearly, at whatever remove, done that already once before – then maybe Neil would hear; and he might just be worried enough about her to say that she had been to Northern Ireland. And if he did, then that would put a whole different complexion on things. Kate saw that she could agonise for some time over this, but there was only one way forward; and the sooner she took it the better.

"There's a problem" she said, feeling herself go pale. "Something I didn't tell you".

The atmosphere turned to stone as O'Connell stared at her, his eyes boring into hers.

"There was someone in Oxford who helped me – helped me quite a lot – to find out things. His name is Neil Hargreaves".

"So?" said O'Connell, spitting the word out. "Call him too, tell him the same thing. You're on your way back from Scotland this week-end. What's the problem?"

"Two things" said Kate. "He's a police officer – a Detective Sergeant at the Oxford station - and I think he knows I'm here".

For a moment no-one moved; no-one even breathed – the four of them, frozen in time, brains momentarily dislocated, trying to re-engage, trying to make sense of what Kate has said. Kate was about to start to explain, but before she could continue, Vincent O'Connell interrupted.

"Holy Mary Mother of God. You've fucked us. You stupid bitch, you've fucked us". He started towards Kate, but it was his father who leapt up first, grabbed her by the wrist, dragged her out from behind the table and, for the second time since they had met, slapped her viciously across the face, once, twice, his hold on her wrist all that prevented her collapsing to the ground. Unlike the first time, which had been a calculated action to assert his authority, this time he was seething with rage. Eventually he let go, and she fell back, a huddle on the ground, only half conscious, her mind numbed. Tears started to well up in her eyes, but it was more the physical effect of O'Connell hitting her than anything else. All she could think of was that this was her own fault – why hadn't she explained about Neil much earlier on, but knowing the answer to that too.

"You'd better explain" said O'Connell. "And it had better be good". The absence of any specific threat made his words no less chilling.

"When I originally reported Paul missing, he was the police officer in charge; and he was very helpful. Then Gerrard, or someone, obviously got wind of the investigation; and the case was handed to a more senior officer, who clearly had instructions – I don't know on what grounds, but presumably some sort of national security line – to wrap the thing up quietly. No fuss, no solution, no nothing. So everything I found out, I found out myself; but I had to get to some of the police officers involved back in 1983; and Neil helped me, because he was so appalled at the cover up of Paul's disappearance. And I told him I was coming to Belfast, to see if I could find out more about Hughes and the others. He didn't think I should do it, but I insisted. He's on my side – the only one who was before I got to meet you; but I didn't mention him because I thought you would be suspicious. I've only told you now because of the risk that he might tell someone I went to Belfast".

Kate made no effort to get up. O'Connell stood over her, glaring down at her, the fury in his eyes quite terrifying. Kate's skirt had ridden up her thighs as she fell; and she slowly pulled the hem down – a purely instinctive reaction rather than any over-riding sense of modesty at such a moment; but stopped as she realised what the next question would be – maybe the last that she would ever hear.

"So this Hargreaves doesn't know about us?" asked O'Connell. "He doesn't know you've hooked up with us?" He hadn't blinked since he'd hit Kate; and his breath was noisy, fast, almost panting. Kate, by now, was too faint, too frightened to reply. She just lay there, silent; but O'Connell saw the almost imperceptible nod of her head.

"Oh, Sweet Jesus" he said, under his breath. He lent forward, grabbed Kate by the wrist again, pulled her up and, with both hands, slammed her back in the seat by the table.

"How? How does he know?" he whispered.

"One of my phone calls. I used a sort of code – in a message on his answer-phone. It wasn't anything we planned. He may not have even have worked it out".

"Why? In God's name, why?" said O'Connell, his voice getting louder again. "Why?" he almost shouted.

"I wanted someone to know where I was; and I wanted him to know I was okay. I thought, if I didn't, that he'd worry that I had disappeared; might start to make inquiries - and that could get dangerous. I didn't tell you because, well, I was just too scared. I knew it would sound really bad; and then I'd be dead, wouldn't I? Well, wouldn't I?" she repeated.

"And why would this police officer get so worried? Asked Riordan. "Has he become a one man mission to right the wrongs of the British Police force?"

"He thinks he's in love with me" said Kate, simply. "He's probably just sorry for me, protective, I don't know. He knows how I feel about Paul – Christ, look at me. Look where my feelings for Paul have got me. How many times do I get beaten up before it all ends? But if Paul's dead, I know Neil will want to.... be with me".

"And you? What do you think about all that?" said Vincent. "What a piece of work you are" he sneered. Something was so offensive about this remark, and the way the younger O'Connell had said it, that it snapped Kate back out of the dazed state she had been in.

"That's none of your bloody business" she shouted at him. She turned to O'Connell senior.

"He helped me. None of us would be anywhere close to getting Gerrard without him. I told him I was coming to Belfast because why shouldn't I have? I told him – if he ever got my message – what I was doing here so that he would stay away; and I didn't tell you about him because I knew what your reaction would be; and I was right wasn't I? Look at us. All we have to do is to let him know again not to do, not to say anything to anyone. Then there's no problem. When Gerrard's finished – when the whole story comes out – how he used the security forces, used the police, for his own ends, they'll probably make Neil fucking Chief Constable. Courtesy of the IRA. That'll be a first in British policing history. Now, can we get back to the real business?" Neither her mild swearing, nor the hint of a joke, could conceal that she was pleading for her life. Again.

She had no doubt that Vincent was all for putting her in a car, taking her to some out of the way spot, and putting a bullet through her brains. For no reason she could think of, she was confident that Riordan would accept what she had said. It all came down to O'Connell; and he just sat there, thinking, thinking.

"Chief Constable, aye?" he said with the hint of a smile; but it was just so much surface chatter, unrelated to what was churning below.

"How did you get a message to this police officer? You only made calls while we were there?" Kate explained, just a short message composed from the first letters of each sentence; and then a reference to a first letter being important. Simple really. O'Connell did not reply; and the moment dragged on. Then, finally,

"Vince, get on to Declan. Tell him what's happened. Tell him to stay in Oxford, until Monday at least. Tell him to trace Detective Sergeant Neil Hargreaves, follow him wherever he goes, but to do nothing, repeat nothing, no matter what; and under no circumstances get himself clocked. Lose Hargeaves rather than be seen. Meanwhile, Kate here is going to talk to Hargreaves. Make sure he doesn't make any trouble for us, intentionally or otherwise".

"You're going to trust her?" asked Vincent, genuinely shocked. "She's leading twenty of us into a shoot-out with the SAS or worse, the first operation we have attempted on the mainland in years, up against the fucking Prime minister himself, and you're going ahead with it? You're the best field commander the movement ever had, by a long way; and I'll go anywhere you lead; but, dad, is this really wise?" The almost child-like incongruity of the way he addressed his father, in what was very much the case for the prosecution – execution to be more precise – did nothing to ease Kate's mind. She was about to respond, with the only point she had going for her; but O'Connell got there first.

"I know it looks bad" he said "but, yes, I am going to trust her; and the reason is that, if she is working against us, then she would never have told us about Hargreaves. He's only a problem for us because he is a problem for her. Out of whatever motives, he could screw up the operation, by letting them know about her trip to Belfast, the possibility that she has help; but why would she tell us that, unless she wants the thing to succeed? But..." he turned back to Kate, "is there anything else, anything else at all that you haven't told us? Think hard because, if there is, and you don't tell me now, I will personally see that you die screaming for someone to finish you off. It will be as unpleasant as it gets".

"There's nothing else" said Kate, gently touching her face where O'Connell had hit her.

"Look at me" snapped O'Connell. "Look me straight in the eyes. Is there anything else, anything else at all? This is a defining moment in your life, be very sure of that. Is there anything else we should know?"

Kate looked up and stared straight at O'Connell.

"You know everything I know. There is nothing else. Like you said, why would I have told you about Neil, except that he has now become a threat to our plans? I'll call him. Say whatever you want me to say. It could even help." She continued to stare at O'Connell, who stared right back.

"Please" she said, knowing she had won if only she could lower the tension. "Don't give up on me now. Together we can bring that bastard down and get Paul back. But I can't do it without you; and the fact is that you can't do it without me."

O'Connell made no direct reply to this. Instead he told Kate that, as soon as Declan was in place, she should ring Hargreaves; tell him she had found out all she could find in Northern Ireland; that the IRA people she had met had confirmed what she knew about the deaths of the Sellafield team, but that was all; and that she was coming back to Oxford sometime the following week. She would tell him she had a plan for what to do next, which she would discuss with him when she got back, to see what he thought, but she would need his help; and under no circumstances should he tell anyone anything. End of message. If any of that got back to the people working for Gerrard, it would tend to confirm that she was largely operating alone. Kate nodded her agreement.

Later that afternoon, O'Connell gave Kate her mobile back; and she phoned Sarah and Janice again, keeping up the fiction that she was in Scotland. She assured them that she was beginning to feel a lot better; and would be back in Oxford soon. The rest of the afternoon and the evening was spent in a flurry of logistical planning, for herself and the twenty men with whom she and her future were now inextricably linked. They needed to travel in small groups, completely unnoticed; and all rendezvous at Wallington House by early Tuesday evening. McVeigh and three others from the group would set off the next morning, intending to have the place ready for occupation, fully supplied and with more detailed operational aspects identified before the week-end was over. Fergal Shannon and two others would work in parallel on the armaments they required, retrieving them from two stores in Northern Ireland, shipping them over the week-end to the mainland in three cars specially modified to hold the weapons. They also would be taking some essential electrical equipment.

Victor and Vincent would travel together the next morning, but Kate and Riordan were ready to set off that evening. Kate had to be in England, near Wallington House and completely hidden from view before her letter arrived, quite possibly the next morning because, once Gerrard saw the letter, she would become, in his eyes at least, the most wanted woman in the country. It would not be that difficult for Gerrard and his closest advisors to fabricate some plausible story in which Kate was some type of terrorist threat, so that both the police and the security services would be on the look-out for her. Kate, to her surprise, had coped with this thought quite well until, in a quiet moment, she realised that there were really only two possible outcomes of the deadly game she was now playing – the fall, imprisonment, or perhaps suicide of the Prime Minister; or her own death. Some intermediate outcome, in which the world carried on very much as before, but with Paul restored to her – the outcome which she had for so long now pursued – was no longer an option; not just because O'Connell and his men, who were essential to her plans, cared little for Paul – they wanted Gerrard; but because, as she now saw, Gerrard could never allow her and Paul, knowing what they knew, to survive - a constant threat to his position and his freedom as long as they remained alive. So, without quite ever registering the process as it occurred, the stakes had become as high as they could get, but there was no going back.

Before leaving, Kate called Neil. She hoped that she would get his answer-phone again - that way she could say exactly what she was supposed to say with no awkward questions – and she rather expected to get his answer-phone. So it was a great shock to her when she heard him answer; and for a moment she couldn't speak.

"Hello" repeated Hargreaves.

"Hello" she said. "It's Kate". Before she could continue, Hargreaves interrupted.

"Thank God you've called" he said. I've been so worried about you. Are you alright?"

"I'm fine" she said. "I'm ringing to say that I'll be coming back to Oxford soon, sometime next week I think. I'm going up to see some friends in Scotland first; but I'll be back soon. I'm sorry I didn't call earlier". It was all rather banal in itself but, in the circumstances, was more dramatic for Hargreaves than anything else he had heard in a long time. However, his professional instincts did not desert him. Something, some minor intonation, some minute difference of tension in Kate's vocal chords, certainly something that the O'Connells did not detect, told him that, despite what she said, all was not fine.

"Are you alone?" he asked. She answered smoothly, instantly

"No, I found out all I could; but there is nothing more to do here now. I have had some thoughts about what to do next; but I want to talk them through with you first – as soon as I get back from Scotland. But please – this is really important – don't tell anyone I was over here. I'll explain when I see you; but I'd rather wait until then. I've really missed you". This was true, of that she was quite certain; but she nonetheless registered the guilty feeling she experienced as she said it, because it was, quite shamelessly, added to try to ensure that he still felt close to her; so that he wouldn't want to go against what she had said. Trying to rid her mind of this thought, she added that she had to go, as she had been invited out for a drink.

Hargreaves was almost flattened by the tsunami of different questions, and emotions, smashing into him. He had had no difficulty in decoding her message; and so knew who she was with – and she clearly could not talk freely in front of them – but why then was she calling? How free to talk was she? Was she really alright? Why go to Scotland? Was it really the case that she would be back next week? What plan did she have that she had to discuss with him; and, above all, had she really missed him – like he had missed her – desperately, painfully? The thought came to him that maybe someone else was on the line; but if Kate was using her mobile, that was unlikely. One thing was certain – he was not going to risk making her life more difficult, perhaps more dangerous, by insisting on a lot of questions.

"I've missed you as well – more than you can possibly imagine. But, if you have to dash, let's talk when you get back. Will you give me a call – maybe on your way back from Scotland? If you're coming by train, I'll come and pick you up at the station".

"That would be nice" she replied. "I'll ring you next week; but this is all just between us. Please don't let me down" and she put the phone down before he could reply, feeling even more guilty at the way she was using their relationship – odd as it was – to further her plans.

"You handled that well" said O'Connell "But had he worked out your coded message?"

"He didn't say; and I didn't ask" said Kate. "I shouldn't think so, or he would have asked about it. I thought the fewer questions the better".

"Well, that would be useful - one less thing to worry about. But Declan will tag him in Oxford, which might give some clue". He held out his hand; and Kate handed him back her mobile. Neither wanted to put into words what this act signified about the way they viewed each other. In fact, there seemed nothing more to say on anything; and, having packed for their immediate needs, including several mobile phones, they set off.

Travelling with Kate and Riordan would be Sean Gannon, one of O'Connell's men. Gannon, a dark-haired man with what seemed to be a perpetual smile on his face – which O'Connell said to be wary of as he was also the most accurate shot with a telescopic rifle he had ever known - had been chosen because he was one of the youngest of the team and, therefore, only slightly older than Kate. The six of them would stay in different pubs in the area around Wallington House, but Kate would be much less noticeable as someone's wife or partner than if she stayed on her own; and they did not want to leave anything to chance. Kate wondered – and probably Gannon wondered – whether the room would turn out to have twin beds or a double but, given she might not survive next week, it didn't seem to matter greatly. The six of them would all meet up on the Friday evening, which would give them a full four days to plan the details of the operation on the ground before Gerrard would hear of the location. O'Connell was fairly confident that they would need far less time than this – he already knew a great deal from those who had used the site many years before – but he wanted the details to be right, down to the last second and the last metre. It crossed his mind again and again how precise, how complete his and Riordan's plans had been back in 1983, but with what terrible result. This time there would be no errors.

CHAPTER 24

Kate, Riordan and Gannon caught the last ferry of the day from Belfast and spent the Thursday night in a Liverpool hotel. Kate had now become Mrs. Gannon; complete with an imitation diamond rind hastily purchased in Belfast, and she hung in the background as Sean booked them in. He secured them a twin-bedded room, and Kate's only thought was that she had at least some chance of a good night's rest. To her surprise, nonetheless, that was exactly what she got, aware as she lay there how much she had come, psychologically – even emotionally – to rely on O'Connell and Riordan. It was not that they were brimming with confidence – indeed if they had been she would have been much more alarmed - and it was not just that they seemed so meticulous in everything to do with the operation, though that certainly helped; nor even their commitment, reflecting a lifetime of guilt and remorse over what had happened to Hughes and the others. More than all these factors, she finally saw, was the way that sixteen men who, through temperament, upbringing, environment, and experiences both violent and tragic, were lethally powerful, independent, undoubtedly brave beyond normal imagining - whatever anyone thought of their cause or their methods - the way that these sixteen had respected the two men on whom her life now depended; had to a man, responded to their call with no idea of what it entailed, and who were now quite ready to risk their lives under the leadership of these two men. Kate might be facing a crisis of unimaginable proportions; but she did so in the company of exceptional men – whatever their past crimes – and that re-assurance was as good as any number of sleeping tablets.

Friday, unexpectedly, was a rather leisurely day. Kate, Riordan and Gannon rose late, had a still later breakfast, and then had seven hours to make the rendezvous with the O'Connells in a pub in Marlborough. They travelled by train, because it was completely anonymous, taking a slightly roundabout route from Birmingham to Bristol, to avoid passing through Oxford – the one city where Kate might be recognised, or where people might be specifically looking for her. With time to kill, they lunched in Bristol; hired two cars, in Gannon and Riordan's names; and were in Marlborough with still more time to spare.

Unbeknownst to them, but not far from their minds, Kate's letter had duly arrived, though not at Number 10 Downing Street as, for security reasons, all mail sent to that address is first opened and checked at an unnumbered location further down Whitehall. Also unknown to them, they had been relatively fortunate. Joanna Rosewell, the young woman who actually received the letter, was new to the job, full of her recent training and keen to be a success. The fact that the address was handwritten, and that the letter was marked both personal and confidential, all set alarm bells ringing; and, without making any attempt to open the envelope, she immediately called the Mail Security Unit. The letter was far too thin to contain any sort of explosive device; but they x-rayed it anyway. More important, they checked the surface of the envelope for any sort of toxin and, when this proved to be negative, wearing rubber gloves, slit the envelope and took out the two sheets of paper inside, one selotaped up. These were also checked for any type of poisonous substance, found to be clean and, some half an hour after she had first picked the letter up, Miss Rosewell read the contents of the first sheet.

Outwardly very calm, she could barely contain her excitement. Like all those who worked in her unit, she was used to crazy letters, many religious, some threatening, others just so absurd as to be almost meaningless. This one was decidedly different; and without a moment's pause she headed for her boss's office a few steps down the corridor. Ralph Barnes was on the phone, but she waited, so that he knew it was important. He rang off after a minute or so; and she showed him the letter, together with the still selotaped accompaniment; telling him that it had been thoroughly checked by Security. Barnes, an experienced hand of some eight years in the job, complimented her on having handled the letter exactly as she should have done; and said he would take the matter from there on. This, she had known, would be the case; but it was still something of a disappointment – a disappointment which he sensed – and he assured her that, as far as was permitted, he would let her know the outcome. It was still most likely to be a crank but, if so, a rather unusual one, which made for some interest in what could at times be a very monotonous job.

When she had gone, her boss sat for a moment, thinking carefully. The natural thing was for him to open and read the second letter; but the emphasis in the first one on the PM himself not wanting the contents to be known by anyone else made a powerful impression. Something vaguely similar had happened in the past – two or three times in fact while he had worked there; but not with this precision and clarity. He thought for a moment longer, then rang Mel, his secretary-cum-administrator and asked her to fix him five minutes with Andrew

Palmer, Head of Communications for Downing Street and a member of the PM's Policy Unit - more than that, a member - in fact the key member - of the PM's inner circle of most trusted advisors.

It was almost lunchtime before Barnes got to see Palmer, in his office at 11 Downing Street. He handed Palmer the two letters, one still unread, and confirmed that they had been cleared by security. Palmer, a man not given to many words that weren't absolutely necessary, read the first letter and, without any hesitation, used a letter opener on his desk to cut through the selotape. He read the second letter once, quickly, then again more slowly. The reference to Gerrard's early career meant nothing to him; nor did the name Paul Emmerson; but all his instincts – instincts which had made him one of the most trusted, and most feared, of the PM's advisors – told him this was important. He thanked Barnes – a genuine thanks but in a manner that made it quite clear that that was the end of the matter as far as Barnes and his staff were concerned – and they left his office together.

The letters bothered Palmer enough that he would have to ask Gerrard about them; but not enough to fix a specific meeting. He would see Gerrard around 6pm that evening – most days they and several others would have a drink and review the day, usually in the PM's flat above 11 Downing Street. Some Fridays, Gerrard went off to Chequers, the Prime Minister's country residence, for the week-end, but this was not one of them. He'd bring it up at the end, when there was just the two of them. So, for an hour or more that evening, Gerrard, Palmer, and three other members of the PM's closest advisors drank gin and tonics and discussed Iran, with the curious pair of letters a mere shadow at the back of Palmer's mind; while, around eighty miles away, Kate and five committed Irish Nationalists drank beer or, in Kate's case, a glass of wine, and discussed their plans for the next four days. Neither group was under any illusion that what they were discussing was not of historic importance.

In the sitting room of Gerrard's flat, Robert Hammond, Gerrard's Chief of Staff, Head of the PM's Policy Unit, and one of Gerrard's three closest colleagues, was in full flow,
"Alan, I know – I know better than anyone, believe me – how committed you are to supporting the US; and you're right to do so. The UN is a busted flush. It'll never act in time. But you've got to have a vote. I know it's a risk; and it will be a bit bloody, but the Whips think they can get you through. I talked to them not three hours ago. And you can't allow the US to use bases here to launch attacks – it'll finish you Alan. There just isn't enough support". Gerrard sat motionless, looking down at his glass. Eleanor Lewis, known to the world simply as 'El', head of foreign policy in No. 10, and another member of the inner circle, all the way back to undergraduate days, looked at Gerrard.

"I hate to say it, but he's right Alan." Gerrard still didn't look up, but he spoke with grim force.

"I can't support the US - wholeheartedly by the way - and then tell them they can't use their bases – *their* bases I should remind you – the only bases in Europe from which they can operate effectively. It makes no sense".

"It makes no sense to you" said Hammond, "and it makes no sense to me, to any of us here - there *is* no sense to it for Christ's sake. But enough of the great unwashed on our back benches don't see it that way. They don't want to go down in history as the morons who let Iran destroy a chunk of the world; but they hate the US no matter what it does – or are convinced their constituents do; and so supporting your stance on Iran but refusing the airbases is a neat way for them to avoid facing up to reality. And if it comes to a Vote of Confidence, there are too many potential defectors. I hoped that the threat of a General Election might bring enough of them to their senses; but the bastards seem quite confident they'd get back in – probably will too given the opinion polls – but it will be with fucking Seymour as PM; and then you can kiss goodbye to any support for the US at all; and the whole thing could unravel. So give them the vote they want, agree no bases - the US can do the job from home – the job will get done and you will still be here. With the vote behind you, you'll be untouchable. I know it's not ideal, denying them the bases; but they can still do it – plus, what's the alternative? Risk a first strike by Iran, while we all sit around playing politics".

"Andy?" said Gerrard, looking up briefly at Palmer.

"Call a vote on the war. That keeps you in the driving seat. Announce that you are dumping the bases during the debate. You'll get a result. The concession gives them an easy way out. If you go it alone and Parliament calls your bluff – sets up a Vote of Confidence, then you are on the back foot. If you give up the bases in a Vote of Confidence debate, they will smell blood. You might still win, but you probably won't. No other options I can think of".

For a while, no–one spoke. The fifth person present, David Morgan, was relatively new on Gerrard's staff, not part of the inner circle that had worked with Gerrard while he was in opposition, who had worked to get him elected, first, leader of his party and then into No. 10. He was also, at 32, much younger than the others; but he nonetheless had an encyclopaedic knowledge in his field – defence and security; a shrewdness that Gerrard much admired; and an ability to reason with, and persuade, much more established figures in Gerrard's team, all of which had been invaluable in the recent months of almost permanent crisis over Iran. Gerrard looked across at him, an invitation to say something.

"Put that way" said Morgan "it's a no-brainer. But it's more than that isn't it? It's personal". The four others all looked at him, waiting for more.

"Alan, we've all been working with the US for months on this; but you've been working with Hamilton. You know him, you're close to him, you like him, like what he is trying to do. For most of that time, the bases weren't an issue – we all just assumed the US would use them. We've never withheld their use before, never. So now, when the Press think it's a great story – Iran will nuke us if we let the US use the bases – and a swathe of the party see an easy option for their consciences, you don't want to let him down, do you; or maybe it's the retreat - in his eyes at least - that you want to avoid; but either way, it's personal isn't it?. If it isn't, then back off on the bases, while it is still an option, a policy decision not a cave-in".

Everyone in the room knew this was dangerous territory; and all of them, including Gerrard, also knew that this was why Morgan was in the room, doing the job he was doing – he would call the situation exactly as he saw it – no gloss, no nuances, no tip-toeing round any issue. Understand the situation first; next bring a powerful intellect to analyse it; and then create options. It didn't always work, but it nicely complemented the much more instinctive approach of someone like Palmer; and if the two came to the same conclusion then it was a brave man or woman who challenged it.

"Maybe it is" said Gerrard, rather carefully "maybe it is. But, if we are getting into the psychology of it all, it's about personal integrity. That's a snotty way of saying that I would personally feel more embarrassment – more humiliation if you like – than I think I could take, flying the flag for the US, leading the support, such as it is, in the rest of the world for the US, facing down the loonies at the UN – but then, sorry, you do understand that we can't actually *do* anything. Israel's right to survive is, of course, sacrosanct, as long as it's only the US who's risking anything. We can't actually have those nasty, dangerous planes touch our virgin soil. Yes, I guess it's personal".

"So, do you want to take the decision on personal grounds; or on the basis of political options and their likely consequences?" asked Morgan, rather as if he was offering him a choice of travelling to some destination by car or train.

"I can't answer that" said Gerrard. "But it's a fair question – it's the right question. I'll think on it".

"So long as it's soon" said Lewis, half to herself, but clearly to Gerrard as well. "Our options are narrowing rather rapidly".

"Point taken" said Gerrard. "Let's leave it there".

As the others started to leave, Palmer said he needed a short but urgent word with Gerrard. He could see that this was not at all welcome, but this had never stopped him in the past; and it certainly wouldn't now. When they were alone, Palmer produced the two letters and handed them to Gerrard, who read them with increasing concentration.

"When did this arrive?" he asked.

"This morning" replied Palmer.

"Who else has read them?"

"Two members of the Mail Unit and a couple of the security people have read the first one. No-one except me and you have read the other one. Does it mean anything? Who's Emmerson? And who's this Kate Kimball?"

*   *   *

In the Castle and Ball, in Marlborough High St., the subject of this inquiry was just starting to eat a large plaice, chips and peas. She, Gannon, Riordan and Vincent O'Connell listened while Victor O'Connell outlined yet again, not so much the detail of the operation – that would start tomorrow – but the overall concept, almost, he thought, the philosophy behind the plan.

"It may be that Gerrard will cave in, play ball and produce Dr.Emmerson; but, as you said right at the beginning, Kate, it's not very likely. His only hope of getting through this is to take you out; and if he wants to do that then he will have to bring in an armed unit. They will be as highly trained as any such force anywhere in the world; they will probably have had a lot of experience in Iraq, maybe Afghanistan, quite possibly in terrorist operations in London; and in normal circumstances we would not have a chance against them – not a chance. But we have one great advantage, which is surprise. They will be very careful – at least we have some familiarity with their training and tactics – but they will nonetheless be anticipating that they will be looking for either a lone woman or perhaps her and one or two friends as well. They will not be expecting twenty experienced soldiers. And if, as I suspect, they go in early, they will be anticipating that the site will be empty, which is how it will appear; but we will be there before them as well as just behind them. The keys to our success will be, first, complete invisibility; second, acute observation; third, perfect communications; and, fourth, split-second timing. Those are all things that we are good at; and that is why we can pull this off".

Everyone there would have been delighted if, there and then, they could have got out the detailed maps and plans that they had prepared; but that was deemed much too risky. They were just five people having an early Friday night supper in a pub; and nothing would be allowed to undermine that happy little picture.

"What about the other two locations?" asked Kate. O'Connell looked at Riordan.

"I've got two of the lads to find some sites" he said. "Not too near Wallington House, but not that far either. Then it's a question of studying road maps to pin-point suitable areas; and then finding the specific spots. They should have places worked out by Tuesday; and can let us know when we all meet up then".

They finished their meal; walked slowly back to the Ailesbury Court hotel where they were staying. The question that kept drilling through Kate's mind was what they would do if Gerrard made no reply. O'Connell seemed quite certain that Gerard would; and Kate reflected that this confidence might stem from the recognition by O'Connell that he and Gerrard were, perhaps, rather similar sorts of people – not given to inaction in the face of peril. They would know within ninety-six hours.

*   *   *

Gerrard sat on his sofa, reading the letter again, looking ashen, saying nothing.

"Alan" said Palmer. "What on earth is this about? Alan, for Christ's sake, talk to me".

"This goes no further, not even to Robert. Is that clear?" said Gerrard. Palmer nodded impatiently.

"You'd better mean that nod, Andy. This could be terminal. Get me another drink". While Palmer did so, Gerrard began.

"Back in 1983, an IRA team broke into Sellafield and tried to blow up one of the re-processing plants. There was an explosion of sorts, but they fucked the whole thing up, did very little damage and there was no risk of a nuclear leak. Everyone was very panicky at the time, because there had been a number of terror attacks by the IRA on mainland cities; and letting the public know that the IRA could somehow walk into one of our nuclear installations was not ideal re-assurance. So, we decided to cover the whole thing up – said there had been a huge electrical failure. There wasn't much of a power loss; and no-one outside could see anything; so it was all very easy. Only trouble was – just as we were releasing the story about an electrical fault – we get a call that some copper in Paddington Green has got the five IRA guys banged up and busily confessing. I was the responsible Junior Minister in the Home Office; and I had about an hour at most to sort the bloody mess out. I called in the Chairman of the Joint Chiefs of Staff, explained that it was as critical matter of national security as could be imagined; and asked him to handle it. Directly. To go straight to the Colonel in charge of the SAS, black ops. procedure, get a unit to pick the IRA guys up and lose them somewhere – not on British soil. As they were Irish, we opted for the Republic; which they did – unfortunate car accident near Dublin". He paused.

"Wouldn't look good in *The Guardian*" said Palmer. "But the press is never going to get hold of it – they didn't then. Why would they now? Did something else happen".

"No, that was the end of it or, should I say, that *was* the end of it – no loose ends, no come-back, no nothing........ until a few months ago. Merest chance really, Sutherland - he's only been Business Secretary six months – mentions that some Oxford scientist, using a new technique which he's just developed, has found evidence of an explosion at the re-processing plant. There's no evidence of it using established techniques, but his work shows that the structure is vulnerable. They've shut the operation down while they fix it, but if it got out, the whole story would unravel. All very neat for thirty years, but you can just see what the papers would do if they got hold of it". He paused again. Palmer waited, but not for long.

"Oh, Christ, Alan, what did you do? Not the SAS again?"

"No. I had no compunction about calling them in to deal with the IRA – bloody murdering bastards. And I knew that Jack Weston – he was the Chief of Staff at the time – thought the same. This was different. It was just an Oxford academic. No-one in the army, not even the SAS, nor in the security services, is going to adopt extreme prejudice against someone like that, not just on my say-so. Even if he was a sleeper, there'd have to be some sort of due process. And anyway, how would I, alone, know about him?"

"Well, thank God for that" said Palmer. "So, how did you handle it? Nothing has come out. Did someone have a suitable word with him?"

"No" replied Gerrard. "I really couldn't risk it. So........"

"So, so what?" said Palmer. "Alan, what did you do?"

"I pulled the Americans in".

"You what?" said Palmer, sounding aghast. What do you mean 'you pulled the Americans in'?"

"I had a meeting here with the US Ambassador – just one-to-one, no-one else at all. I told him it was of the utmost importance and the utmost secrecy – both of which were true. I explained, in outline, the problem; and stressed that if the matter came out, I'd be finished, Seymour would take over, and the US could kiss goodbye to any support for the Iran invasion. He cottoned on to the fact that Emmerson – that's the scientist – would have to go, but I explained how risky that would be. However, if the US carried out the action – scientist disappears, no-one knows anything, and no-one can connect it in any way with me – then it might just work. The operation itself would be easy. Pick the man up at a suitable moment – he's not protected in any way – dispose of him, lift his files, computer etc. and no-one will be any the wiser".

"And he agreed?"

"Not immediately; but less than forty-eight hours later he did". He noticed the look in Palmer's eyes. "Andy, it's done. That's not the problem".

"If getting US Special forces to dispose of a British scientist because he might expose you is not the problem, then I'd like to know what is" said Palmer, looking increasingly agitated.

"There are two problems" said Gerrard; and Palmer collapsed back into his armchair shaking his head. "The first is that the Americans took Emmerson without any trouble; and we were able to close down the police investigation quite quickly – I'll tell you about that later – but.......they didn't, as you said, *dispose* of him".

"What?" said Palmer, almost shrieking the word. "I can't believe what I'm hearing".

"They let me know, with no great subtlety, that they had him on ice, got him holed up in some extra-territorial camp – I don't even know where".

"But why, for God's sake?" shouted Palmer

"Calm down, Andy. He's a hostage - their security that I won't, no matter what the political odds here, walk away from supporting them over Iran. They know the UK is the key to getting enough support – not massive, but enough – to make the attack defensible on a world stage. When I asked for their help, I put myself in their pocket; and they're now playing hardball. If I start to even wobble, let alone do a France or Germany, Emmerson will miraculously re-appear; and I will be dead".

"But if Iran all goes according to plan, then they will....get rid of Emmerson?"

"That's what they say; and I have no reason to doubt it; and then I will be in the clear".

"And the bases – is that part of this... deal? Is that why you are being so stubborn about them?"

"Yes and no. I genuinely believe that we can't support the US and then deny them the bases; but if it helped us through the politics I'd ditch the bases. However, the situation is such that I don't have any choice". For a moment, Palmer was, very unusually for him, completely speechless. Gerrard just sat, staring in front of him. It was Palmer who recovered his thoughts first.

"You're saying that the Americans – our American allies – agreed to help you, and themselves, by taking this Emmerson man out of the picture; but have in fact hung on to him as a sword over your head, to ensure that you will support the attack on Iran, and allow British airbases to be used? Is that what you are saying?" Gerrard merely nodded.

"But that's fucking crazy. You've been a supporter for Hamilton's strategy all along; and you just said yourself, you don't believe you should support the policy and then deny them the airbases"

"I know" said Gerrard "but they're worried that, if I think I can't carry the party with me, I'll back off. You heard what the others said this evening – Christ, you agreed with them – that I *should* back off on the bases. This is their insurance". Palmer still couldn't fully take it in.

"And that's it? You don't waver, the attack goes ahead; and Emmerson disappears for evermore. Is that it?"

"Yes, that's it" said Gerrard angrily, but not looking at Palmer as he spoke. "I thought there might be a further problem, in that the police officers I used said there was no sign of a break-in at Emmerson's office at the University; and I thought the Americans might have left behind evidence about the problem at Sellafield. But I got two security services people to check; and they confirmed that Emmerson's hard-disks had gone - so there was nothing other than Emmerson himself who could cause me any trouble. But, thanks to the Americans, he is big trouble".

Palmer put his hand to his face and closed his eyes. There's something I'm not getting here, he thought. Would the Americans really play so rough with their principal ally, with someone who, at a personal as well as political level had been such a stronger supporter of the US on the most difficult international problem since Iraq? Would Hamilton really go this far to ensure Gerrard's continuing support? Was the use of their bases in the UK so crucial? All Palmer's political instincts were screaming at him that things were worse than he knew. Well, what he knew was bad enough.

"And the second problem – you said you had two?"

"That's the one in your hand right now" replied Gerrard. "The letter. Emmerson has a girl-friend – Kate Kimball – who is clearly very resourceful. She indicates in the letter that she has found out about the Sellafield incident in 1983; and seems to know – or thinks she knows – that Emmerson is still alive. She clearly wants him back or, according to the letter, she will release the whole thing to the Press".

"How could she possibly know that Emmerson is still alive" snorted Palmer. Gerrard remained silent. "How could she know?" Palmer repeated, once again raising his voice.

"The Americans told her" replied Gerrard, starting now to look positively ill.

"Whaaat?" was all Palmer, now beginning to feel almost disorientated as revelation followed revelation. "What do you mean, the Americans told her? When? Why?"

"Kimball was getting too close or, at least, she just wouldn't give up. I thought she could just be left to run into the ground; but she kept on and on - talking to people up in Cumbria who had been around at the time of the attack on Sellafield. In the end I had no choice, Andy. I asked the Americans to take her out too, but they wouldn't. They said, quite rightly I suppose, that if one person goes missing it could be anything - random mugging, secret mistress, amnesia, anything; but if his partner goes too – that's a full scale criminal investigation.

"But I still don't understand" said Palmer "Are you saying that they just marched up to this Kimball woman and said 'Hi, we're from the US. Oh by the way, your hubby is okay – we've got him in Guantanamo Bay or somewhere?' That would be crazy, even for them".

"It wasn't quite like that" said Gerrard. "You'd better know the worst. I decided that the woman was too much of a threat. I could see that if she disappeared as well as Emmerson, then the whole thing would burst open again; but I thought that if she ......committed suicide – she was carrying a lot of grief since Emmerson had disappeared......" Palmer interrupted him.

"Are you absolutely out of your fucking mind, Alan?" He was about to go on, but this time Gerrard interrupted him.

"Shut up Andy. And no, I am not out of my fucking mind, as you so politely put it. The fact is that the US should be ready to go very soon, two weeks at the most; and I can hold the coalition together that long, and yes, the bases as well. Three weeks from now, Iran will have no nuclear capability, in fact no military capability at all. I will face whatever political future I have, or don't have, after that; but the US will have no further reason to keep Emmerson alive. He's off everyone's radar already except bloody Kate Kimball's. She is the only real threat; and if she killed herself while the balance of her mind was disturbed by ongoing grief, then I might just spend the rest of my life out of jail. Suicide would raise no new question marks over Emmerson's disappearance – so it was the perfect answer. But the team fucked up the operation or, to put it more precisely, they let the Americans fuck it up. They thought it was too risky to have another death, even an apparent suicide". Palmer reckoned that he was now in some state of shock – a condition to which he had until this moment firmly believed he was completely immune.

"What happened?" he said, very quietly, resigned to still further bad news.

"I arranged for her to be taken out of the picture, but for it to look like she had killed herself – hanged herself. The team that was supposed to manage it didn't know that the Americans were keeping an eye on her; and they intervened – sent our two back rather the worse for wear".

"But I thought you said you couldn't risk using our own forces – that that was why you went to the Americans?"

"I didn't want to; but I didn't any longer have a choice. She had to be got rid of; and the Americans wouldn't do it".

"Who did you get to do it?"

"I cut everybody out of the loop. I'd stayed in touch – just occasionally – with the Colonel who'd overseen the disposal of the Irish. He's in his late seventies now, but I got in touch with him, explained that there was unfinished business from the previous operation. He's a good man – saw the situation immediately. I gave him the name of the target; and he drummed up two of his former paratroopers, retired from the service, totally loyal to him. They knew they were on their own if they got caught, but it seemed such a simple job. No connection with the victim; and no murder inquiry if it looked a convincing suicide. I hadn't for one moment thought the Americans would be shadowing her. And I'm not convinced it was just because they thought another death would be suspicious. I think they want her on the loose. They're confident she can't possibly find him; but it sort of keeps the pressure on me. Their way of saying that it could all come out if I'm not totally in line".

"Is that why they told her Emmerson was still alive?" asked Palmer.

"I don't know. Maybe it's just that she isn't any sort of threat to them, only to me. Maybe they really don't want her to give up. I don't know; but they told her. And now, contrary to what you were saying, the wisdom of my original plan is very apparent. Because it failed, I now have this Kimball woman breathing down my neck. The Colonel sent another pair to see what she was up to; but she has disappeared. Now this letter has arrived".

Neither of them spoke for a while; but both, in different ways, were reflecting that the situation appeared terminal. Palmer couldn't believe that Gerrard had managed to get away literally with murder for so long; and couldn't see how he was going to survive. Gerrard had lived through all that, night after night. His overriding thought was that, whatever he wanted to do, he wasn't going to be able to produce Emmerson, which must be his wretched girl-friend's objective – which meant she would take whatever evidence she had to the Press, who would crucify him. Nor was it just his political future that was dead in the water. Gerrard was quite certain that if the story came out, he'd spend the rest of his life in jail.

"So what are you going to do?" asked Palmer eventually, aware that this was probably the first time in their working relationship that he was asking rather than telling Gerrard what he ought to do.

"I'll send her an email address – totally secure – you can fix that". It was neither a request nor an order – just a statement of fact. "Let's see how she wants to play it. But she must want Emmerson; and I can't produce him. So, I guess we agree to negotiate; and in the process, finally get rid of her".

Palmer's picture of Gerrard, of a man with so much ability, so much to offer both his country and the world, albeit in need of a man like Palmer to act as a foil, a sounding board, an enforcer, had been stretched by the last few minutes' revelations. But only now, as Gerrard calmly envisaged the murder of a desperate, if resourceful, woman, did it stretch beyond breaking point, as he realised exactly how ruthless the man was. And with that came the realisation that he himself, until now quite unaware of any of Gerrard's terrifyingly dangerous secret, could easily, if he was not very careful, become inextricably involved – an accessory before the fact to murder.

"Alan, I can hook you up; I can negotiate on your behalf; I can try to find some solution to all this; but I can't be party to the murder of this woman. I signed up to get you elected, to deal with the world in general on your behalf; and make you the most successful PM Britain has ever had. But I'm not risking a life sentence to save you from this nightmare. If you have 'plans' for the woman, I don't want to hear about them – not a word, do you understand?"

"Don't worry, Andy. You won't have to risk your thick neck. Just get me in contact with her. I'll take it from there".

CHAPTER 25

Kate and O'Connell's men spent Saturday reconnoitering every last inch of the ground around Wallington House, identifying observation points, lines of fire, access points and the like. At one point in the late afternoon, Kate, Gannon and Riordan headed off for an internet café in Swindon, to check Kate's emails. Gannon went in, ordered a coffee, went to a screen and checked to see if there was any message from Gerrard. They did not expect anything until much nearer the Tuesday deadline; but checked nonetheless. They had decided against using a lap-top or smart phones at this stage of the operation, because they had no confidence that it would not be traced. It was easier to use a succession of internet cafes – they estimated they would only need three or four in total – to avoid being tracked down. The mobiles they carried were for emergencies and, perhaps, for the endgame.

Gerrard and Palmer spent part of Saturday with a senior army general by the name of Sykes. They had originally planned to describe intelligence which Gerrard had supposedly received that a militant Islamic group was preparing for an attack in the UK – all too believable - and that Sykes should have a unit ready to pick up a courier who had been identified and might provide vital information on this latest threat to Britain. But they soon ditched this plan. However plausible such an attack might be, Kate Kimball was so far from being a likely courier for such a group that it would be bound to raise suspicions. Instead, therefore, Palmer concocted a variant in which the intelligence identified a dissident arm of the IRA - unable to accept the peace settlement hammered out between Sinn Fein and the protestants in Northern Ireland - which was planning renewed action on the mainland; and it was a UK based sympathizer who was acting as a low-level courier, but who nonetheless might provide some important leads to what was planned, or at least to others who were involved. Sykes should use a team from the SAS, notionally seconded to MI5 but, in practice, under the General's personal and direct control. This was necessary because of some serious concerns that the usual channels of communication for the operation might have been compromised. General Sykes said he would get on to the job immediately. Palmer had no idea how near the truth he had come with this cover story.

On Sunday, in the pitch black before dawn, O'Connell, Riordan and Kate arrived back at the large gates at the entrance to the grounds of Wallington House; and, with an all-clear torch signal from Vincent several hundred metres down the road in one direction and Gannon a similar distance in the other, used a large pair of chain-cutters to slice through the simple chain holding the gates padlocked. A few minutes later they prized opened a ground floor shutter, selotaped up and then gently smashed the window behind it and, a further five minutes after that, were all gathered in the shambling wreck of a house. It took some time to investigate every part of the house, but it was obviously in an advanced state of disrepair. Some of the upper rooms were clearly subject to leaking; much of the plaster was crumbling; and even some parts of the walls looked unsafe. They also explored the outbuildings – two garages, a barn and some non-descript sheds with odd bits of old farm equipment left in them. They mapped it all on to a master plan which they spread out on a table in a large sitting room off the main hallway; and then, piece by piece, they translated the provisional plans which they had drawn up back in Belfast into a specific set of instructions for their team. By late morning they had started working on five additional variants of the master plan, each of which reflected a different possible approach to the house by whoever Gerrard would send. Whether an attack came from front or back, or from all sides, whether in a substantial group or in ones and twos, O'Connell identified a detailed response, aimed at the same outcome. Everything was noted down, in particular the lay-out of the grounds, the trees, hedges and walls surrounding the house; and even Kate found herself totally absorbed in the logistics. Which was just as well, she noted once or twice because, if she stopped to think what was going on, what would soon be happening here, she might have been very tempted to flee in terror. Not that O'Connell would let here, of course. It had been her blindingly brilliant idea; but she was now no more than the tethered goat designed to attract the wild beasts that O'Connell was hunting.

They spent most of the day defining, refining, assessing their plans and by late afternoon, they all clearly felt quite exhausted – a combination of the focus, the intensity of their work; and not a little tension given the stakes. They took a substantial detour on the way back to Marlborough, driving once again into Swindon and coming to a halt outside another internet café which had been identified by one of O'Connell's men. However, once again there was nothing; and they all went to bed quite early. Gerrard, on the other hand, working in the Cabinet Office in Downing Street, was up until late. There had been no time in the day to even think about the Kimball woman; but he had set up his lines of communication with the military; he had a cover story which was good enough for the moment; and he experienced no doubts about what the best strategy was. She had to be taken, spirited away and, in time, dispatched.

Around 10 pm, Palmer came in to see him in the Cabinet Room.

"Let's go up to the flat to talk" said Gerrard. When they arrived, he poured them both drinks. "Are we fixed?" he asked.

"Yes" replied Palmer. "I have an email address we can send her. It's absolutely secure this end; but there's no way I can make it so at her end. She's using a bloody 'yahoo' address. However, we can be very circumspect in what we say; and advise her to do the same if she wants this to work. And I've got a brand new lap-top for this one use, so we can keep this correspondence completely to ourselves. The only thing is, I don't think you should use it here. In fact *you* shouldn't do this at all – I'll send what you want to say – and not from here. It's too risky".

"I thought you didn't want to get your hands dirty, Andy" said Gerrard, genuinely surprised.

"I don't. I'm just acting as go-between in relation to a renewed IRA threat, which you haven't seen fit to describe in any detail to me. But if you go down, my chances aren't brilliant; so I may as well try to ensure that this all works".

"Thanks" said Gerrard, looking straight at Palmer. "I appreciate that. I never wanted any of this; and I thought it was all long gone. But once it started, there was never a point where I could get out. Talk about 'tangled web'. Anyway, if it all goes pear-shaped, I'll make clear you knew nothing of what actually happened".

"Well, my turn to thank you. Now let's get down to specifics. I'll send her the email address, make it clear it is from an aide, not you yourself, tell her that the subject matter should not be disclosed, ask her what she wants. Is that it?"

As far as the reply is concerned, yes, I think it is. But there is something else. Can you get to the Chief Constable of the Thames Valley police? Say I've been advised that some very discreet checks – a follow-up to the Emmerson affair – should be made on Kimball. Imply that there may be something very dodgy about her. She's not to be alerted, but any idea of her movements recently would be helpful, any possible contacts – you know the sort of thing. I don't think it will throw up much – she's not been seen recently at her home, or anywhere in Oxford come to that; but a police watch might just find something. They could ask her friends – say that they need to talk to her in connection with Emmerson. They might know something".

"I'll get onto it in the morning; and I'll delay sending the email until Tuesday, shall I? Just at the moment, every day counts"

"Good idea; and see if we hear anything from Oxford in the meantime".

Kate and the others spent Monday back at Wallington House, refining their plans, carrying out some minor construction work, primarily designed to provide cover at various locations around the grounds, shipping armaments and supplies, both military and more domestic. A trip to another internet café, this time in Bath proved futile. Gerrard had a full day of running the affairs of the Nation, though he had considerable difficulty in focusing on anything at all. Palmer, meanwhile, made a phone call; and before 10 a.m. DI Johnson, having been briefed by his own Chief Constable no less, was sitting in his office, taking a phone call from someone speaking on behalf of the Head of the Metropolitan Police Force. This had been set up through how many layers of higher responsibility he had no idea; but the speaker said that it related to earlier work he had done; was urgent and very confidential. Johnson had had no doubt that it must relate to the work he had done on Dr. Paul Emmerson; but had no idea at all as to what the further work might entail. He was mildly disappointed when it turned out to be no more than seeing if he could track down Emmerson's girl-friend, Catherine Kimball and, if possible, bring her in for questioning. If he did, he was to report only to the man to whom he was talking on the phone; and on no account was anything she said or did to be made known to anyone other than him. The conversation ended with an acknowledgement that Johnson had handled the Emmerson case admirably – a real feather in his promotional cap – with the clear implication that further success would be equally well regarded.

Johnson quickly cleared, or re-assigned, his desk. Within half an hour he had checked that Kimball was not at her home, nor had been seen there for some time. He next called on Sarah Jennings, whose address was still on their files, gaining entry easily enough on the pretext that there might have been a development – nothing very significant – in relation to Dr. Emmerson's disappearance; and that he would like, if possible, to consult Miss Kimball. Sarah was instinctively hostile to Johnson, and was concerned that Kate might find a new approach from the police at this stage to be very distressing. She said that Kate had rung her a few days ago, that she had taken some compassionate leave and been on holiday in Scotland, but that she was planning to come back to Oxford later that week. Johnson asked Sarah to ring Kate's mobile which, with some reluctance, she did; but got only her answering service. Johnson asked her to leave a message for Kate to call Sarah; and said that it would be very much in Miss Kimball's interest if, as soon as possible, she could be in touch with him. He left Sarah a number for Kate to call and left, heading for Kate's office and the redoubtable Janice at OUP. Less than two hours after his initial phone call, he was reporting back to the officer from the Met what he had found out; and said that he would be in touch again as soon as he made contact with Kimball.

As Sarah closed the door behind him she realised she was shaking, more disturbed by Johnson's call than she had at first realised. She made herself a cup of herbal tea; and then rang Kate's mobile again, this time leaving a message as to what had prompted her earlier one. For nearly an hour she sat in her kitchen, very alarmed by Johnson's visit; and quite distressed that she couldn't talk to Kate. At 11.30 a.m. she rang Oxford Police Station and asked to speak to DS Hargreaves. When she was told that he was not available at the moment, she said that it was extremely urgent, concerning a case he was working on; and could they get a message to him to call her back as soon as possible. These communications, rather to Sarah's surprise, worked very efficiently; and, less than half an hour later, Hargreaves called her. Given the subject matter; and realising how distressed Sarah was, he said he would come straight round. It was not yet one o'clock as he rang her doorbell and an anxious looking Sarah let him in. Neither noticed an anonymous looking car, which had followed Hargreaves from where he had been working in Osney Mead, to the West of Oxford City, glide past her house, do a neat three point turn, and park some metres beyond. Declan O'Connell, with a clear line of sight to Sarah's front door; lit himself a cigarette and settled down to wait.

Inside, Sarah quickly related her worries about Kate. She didn't know where Kate was, couldn't reach her by phone, and now DI Johnson had come snooping round. She didn't like any of it; and hoped Hargeaves, whom Kate always said had been very helpful – more than that, very understanding - might be able to help. Hargreaves, for his part, felt he was in very treacherous territory. He certainly wasn't going to mention Northern Ireland to Sarah; but Johnson's renewed interest, coming so soon after Kate's visit there, was setting off very loud alarm bells. Something – he had no idea what, but something – was happening; and this new interest of her Majesty's Police Force in Kate's whereabouts, he was sure, did not bode well for her.

Hargeaves tried to re-assure Sarah; and when she mentioned that Kate had said she was in Scotland, but coming back to Oxford soon, Hargreaves leapt at the opportunity to sound supportive, confirming that Kate was indeed due back soon from Scotland. Too late he realised the error, as Sarah looked slightly taken aback.

"Have you been in touch with her?" she asked, not accusingly, but certainly with more than a hint of concern. Hargreaves tried to seem very calm.

"I rang her a few days ago, just to see how she was; and she said she was just travelling around, having a short holiday; but, yes, she said she'd be coming back from Scotland this week I said I'd pick her up at the station if she was coming by train". He hoped a little domestic detail would allay any wider suspicions Sarah might have.

"So she is answering her phone?" asked Sarah.

"She did, yes, but maybe she's out of range now – maybe visiting the Western Isles. I don't know". He didn't know whether this worked or not; but changed tack. "Look, I'll go and see what I can find out, from DI Johnson or someone at the Station. If I find out anything, I'll let you know". Whether he *would* be able to tell her anything he doubted; but it sounded helpful; and it got him out of the house. As he left, his mind was racing through options as to how he could find out more. Clearly just asking Johnson wouldn't get him anywhere. He set off back to the police station, unaware of Declan O'Connell starting up his car behind him.

By the time he arrived there, both Hargreaves and Declan O'Connell had decided their next moves. Hargreaves tracked down Johnson; and told him that

Sarah Jennings had rung him. He emphasised that it wasn't anything to do with him, but said he thought Johnson ought to know; and, professing as little interest as possible, asked if the whole Emmerson case was starting up again. Johnson merely said that he had been asked to find Kimball if she was around – there might be some new questions. Hargreaves would dearly have liked to know what questions; but he had got confirmation of the main thing. Someone way above Johnson – and Hargreaves had little doubt who that was – was getting anxious; and he also had little doubt that this must be related in some way to Kate's activities in Northern Ireland. The thought of her linked up with the IRA, under what degree of duress he had no way of knowing, truly shocked him. But if Gerrard knew, then Kate was in even worse trouble. The even bigger question was – did Kate know that Gerrard was on the warpath? He had to warn her, but how? If she would answer her phone he could say something guarded; but leaving a message might drop her into any sort of trouble. He tried her mobile again; but rang off when it clicked onto her answering service.

He didn't know that he need not have worried, as long as he kept silent about Kate. If Johnson had not been Johnson, if he had taken Hargreaves into his confidence at an earlier stage, and if Johnson had then asked Hargreaves for some help, then maybe, just maybe, out of concern for Kate, he might have said something, anything to try to avert the catastrophe he felt Kate was heading towards. But as things were, he said nothing, feeling like someone who could see two trains hurtling towards each other on a single track, unable to do anything about it.

Meanwhile, Declan O'Connell had rung Victor, to tell him that the Oxford police certainly were on the look-out for Kate – the first actual evidence that her letter had got through. Hargreaves had visited Kate's closest friend and returned to the police station. There was no way of knowing what, if anything, he was reporting. If he had the hots for Kate, as she had said, then he would do what she had said and keep quiet; but there was no certainty. Victor mulled this over for a minute or two.

"Change of plan. Keep on him. Talk to him as soon as you can without anyone else knowing. Tell him Kate's fine, that she's a free agent, and that she will ring him tonight, say at 11 pm But make it clear – if anyone else finds out that she is with us, he'll never see her again. Got that?"

"Got it" said Declan

"Good. Soon as that's done, join us in Marlborough"

"I'm on my way" said Declan, and rung off.

Hargreaves didn't re-appear from the police station until mid-afternoon. O'Connell followed him, back to Osney Mead. As Hargreaves parked by the side of the canal and got out of his car, Declan parked behind him.

"DS Hargreaves, could I have a word?" Hargreaves picked up the Irish accent immediately – not the light, almost musical accent of the Republic, but the rather more drawn out, almost oppressive burr of the North. His heart started pounding.

"Who are you?" he said.

"I'm a colleague, so to speak, of Kate Kimball; and I have two messages from her for you. First, she will ring you tonight, at 11 pm – it might have been earlier but I wasn't sure that I'd get a chance to talk to you before then. She's in very good shape by the way – an impressive woman. Second, and this is the nub of it, if ….the authorities let's call them, were to find out that she had been in Northern Ireland – I know that you know where she is – then that would go very badly for her; as bad as it could be if you understand me". He looked hard at Hargreaves, letting the significance of his words sink in. Hargreaves, for his part, stood motionless, silent. Clearly he was faced with a member of the IRA; and a very tough looking member at that. But that wasn't the thought that coursed through him. If Johnson had been tasked with tracing Kate, then someone clearly knew something – and that something, he could only imagine, was that she had hooked up with the IRA. But if 'the authorities', as this chilling figure in front of him had so delicately called them already knew that, and if the man found out, then Kate was as good as dead. Hargreaves forced himself to stay calm. One thing was certain - the less said the better.

"I haven't told anyone. Kate asked me not to, and that's enough for me".

"So I gather" replied Declan with a short smile. And then Hargreaves saw his route forward.

"I don't know where Kate is, or what she is doing; but I want her to survive this – I want her to very much. So, if there is anything I can do to help her, then tell me. I don't care what it involves".

"Well said" replied Declan, with another smile. "But there is only one thing you can do to help; and that is keep quiet. Very simple. She'll be back in no time". This led Hargreaves to an obvious question.

"Is Paul Emmerson still alive?"

"No idea" replied Declan. "Kate thinks he is; but that may just be wishful thinking. Tough situation". Hargreaves wasn't quite sure if he was referring to Kate's or his own situation; but wasn't going to find out. Instead he re-focused on the problem at hand – how to warn Kate that Gerrard must be on to her without thereby risking her life at the hands of the bunch of terrorists she had, apparently, teamed up with.

"Can you tell me what Kate is planning? She told me she would be back in Oxford soon".

"And so she will be. But, no, I can't tell you" said Declan.

"Are you sure the authorities, as you call them, aren't onto you?"

"No-one but you knows that we have – an alliance – with Kate. So, yes, I am sure".

The significance of this hit Hargreaves before he had registered *why* it was significant. But then he saw it. He was desperately worried that Gerrard was on to Kate; and had presumed that the same was true for the IRA. But he and the Irishman in front of him were at complete cross purposes. The IRA's only concern was that Gerrard didn't know about *them*. Kate was the trap, he realised. They *wanted* Gerrard to know about her.

"I want to see Kate" he said. "I'll come to Belfast with you, right now if you want; but I want to see her. She's totally out of her depth".

"You know that's not on. Anyway, she isn't in Belfast, she's not even in Ireland. I know you think we're somehow using her, but you're quite wrong. We may want Gerrard, but she wants Emmerson back; and she's sort of co-opted us to help her. Like I said, she's a very remarkable woman".

"Why should I believe that?" snorted Hargreaves.

"She can tell you herself, tonight" said Declan quietly. "But remember that calls can be intercepted. So, keep it short and say nothing traceable – no names. The best way you can help her is to stay here, keep your ears and eyes open, make sure that no-one does know about our involvement"

"They know something is going on" said Hargreaves, before he had thought it through.

"So they should" said Declan. "Kate's been in touch with Gerrard – don't ask me how – so I'm not surprised they're looking for her. But they aren't going to find her. As they say in the films, I could tell you where she is, but then I'd have to kill you" He smiled again, a smile that did little to obscure the fact that that was exactly what he would do if he had to. Hargreaves could see that the conversation was now going nowhere. In fact he had learnt rather more than he might have expected.

"I'll await her call. But just one thing. If anything happens to her, you'll wish you had killed me. I'll find you, wherever you are; and I'll see you spend the rest of your life in prison".

"Well said" Declan said again with a smile "And not the first to say it. But don't worry. We're on her side as much as you are. So carry on as normal, see what you can find out, and call me on this number" – he wrote a phone number on a scrap of paper taken from his pocket – "if there is any hint that Gerrard knows who he is really up against". With that he turned and headed back to his car, en route to join his father.

The rest of the day went very slowly for Hargreaves. He couldn't locate Johnson; and could think of no way to find out more about Johnson's inquiries even if he had. All he could do was wait for Kate's 11 pm call. In Marlborough, the O'Connells, now including Declan, Riordan, Gannon and Kate were in an otherwise empty bar. Victor O'Connell handed Kate a mobile phone, but not her own.

291

"Yours will be hot now" he said. "Call Hargreaves, but keep it brief, and no mention of us on the airwaves. Declan has told Hargreaves the same thing" Kate made the call. Hargreaves had repeatedly rehearsed what he planned to say, in a state of considerable agitation; but when the call came through and he heard her voice, he forgot most of what he had planned.

"Hello" she said; and before he could reply went on. "I just wanted to tell you that I'm fine – quite safe – and you mustn't worry about me. I've got some plans, but they'll soon be done; and then I'll be coming back home".

"As long as you are doing this of your......" He meant to go on, but Kate cut him off.

"Totally. It's fine. Really"

"Is there anything I can do "asked Hargreaves.

"Only what I asked you before. Let's not go over it again. Now, I'd better go".

"You know that I love you" said Hargreaves simply. For a moment Kate couldn't reply

"Yes, I do know" she replied eventually "I must go now". As she closed the mobile and handed back to O'Connell, she wiped her eyes. No one said anything. Then O'Connell nodded briefly; and they all headed for their beds. Fifty miles away, a youthful intelligence officer whom Johnson had requested that afternoon, after his brief conversation with Hargreaves, started to type up a transcript of the call which had been relayed to him, courtesy of a bug on Hargreaves phone.

CHAPTER 26

On the Tuesday morning, Kate and the others all met up for breakfast; and then the O'Connells headed off to Wallington House, to go over all their placements again; and to make final arrangements for meeting up with their mini-army. Riordan, Gannon and Kate headed off for another internet café in Bath, to check her emails so that, provided there was a message from Gerrard, they could alert O'Connell, who in turn would activate the meeting of his men scheduled for 4 pm that afternoon. They had decided that they would not answer any email from Gerrard until that evening, so that O'Connell's men would be fully operational and deployed before Gerrard even knew the location. The journey to Bath hung very heavy. Gannon turned out to be quite entertaining company; and gave Kate a quite gripping history of the Troubles in Northern Ireland, though he freely admitted that he found the successful conclusion of the peace process there quite unfathomable; and not a little shocking for those such as himself - and most of the others now preparing to face whatever Gerrard would throw at them - who had risked much for Irish unity. Riordan was much more taciturn, but even he opened up a little to talk about his past, the death of his family, the years of planning that went into the Sellafield attack; and the gut-wrenching pain he had felt for years after its failure and the death of his comrades, even though he had never met any of them. But none of their conversation could eclipse the cauldron of emotions coursing through Kate's veins. She had a good, well paid and interesting job; a man she loved dearly, who lived for his academic work in the remote regions of the engineering laboratory at Oxford University; yet here she was, linked up with a truly lethal group of men, some of whom had undoubtedly murdered people with little or no compunction, and many of whom had spent years in prison for their cause, preparing to take on the might of the Prime Minister and a group of highly trained killers. She faced a very distinct prospect of dying in the next few days; and she had absolutely no control over the pace or direction of events.

At one point she did ask herself whether, if she had the chance, she would just run off, away, anywhere, give up on the chance that Paul was still alive – just get out. This prompted two thoughts. The first was that, if she did flee, to Timbuktu and beyond, O'Connell and his men could now carry on regardless. They could continue to send emails from Kate's email address, they could carry out the whole project without her; and no-one would ever believe that she was no longer part of it. There was now a virtual Kate, from whom she could not distance herself. The only way truly to 'get out' would be to go to the police and reveal O'Connell's plan; but that she knew she would never contemplate. It was, after all, really her plan; she could not betray the twenty men she had been instrumental in recruiting and, more than all this, it would probably put an end to all hopes of ever seeing Paul again But the second response to her unspoken question was at once much more opaque and much more important. The fact was, she didn't want to get out. She wouldn't run, even if she had the chance, not just because it was a flawed idea, but because she wanted to see the plan, her plan, through, to whatever end, bitter or otherwise, it might be. She was frightened – terrified – but she was committed, totally, to following the thing through; and that gave her some peace of mind as the three of them prepared to do battle with Gerrard.

Just before 11 a.m., Riordan, Gannon and Kate arrived at the internet café in Bath. As the three of them made their way into the café, Kate was acutely aware that if they had heard nothing by that evening, the whole operation was over. So it was to her immense relief that, having bought coffees, commandeered a screen, and accessed Kate's emails, they saw a short message from an unknown source.

"I have been asked to reply to your letter. You may make contact via this email address. Your address is not secure; and I must ask you, therefore, to communicate in such a way that only you and I will understand. Failure to do so will negate what both you and my principal wish to achieve".

The email was unsigned.

"Yes!" said Kate, surprised at how elated she felt. "Victor was right".

"No great insight" Riordan replied, with a smile "Gerrard didn't have a choice. I'll get a print-out; then let's get out of here and let Victor know". They closed down the connection and, while Gannon paid, the others headed out to the car. As soon as Gannon joined them, they sped off and, while Gannon drove, Riordan called O'Connell to let him know the news. Forty minutes later they joined the O'Connells at a pre-arranged meeting point about a mile from Wallington House. Kate went over with O'Connell both the incoming message she had received and the reply she had worked out in the car. Victor nodded his approval.

"So the game is on" remarked O'Connell. "We all meet up at 4 p.m. and start to deploy around the House by 5 pm. I want us all to be ready by 8 pm tonight. That should be time enough. We can reply to Gerrard, or whoever is acting for him around 5 pm or so. With dusk coming on, we will be well hidden before they have any chance to get any sort of observation going".

*   *   *

Things were going less smoothly for Hargreaves. There was a message awaiting him on his arrival at the station to see DI Johnson, without fail – taking priority over anything else – at 11 a.m. Hargeaves was sure it was to do with Kate; and hoped he might be able to glean something from whatever Johnson had to say. Johnson met him in the corridor and said they would talk in an interview room near the back of the station. On arriving there, Hargreaves was shocked to see three clearly muscular men, all with the same implacable look about them, waiting to meet him. Even Johnson, who normally had a rather brutal presence, seemed quite overawed by them.

"These three officers are from the security service; and would like your assistance into whereabouts and activities of Kate Kimball" Hargreaves could feel his mouth go dry.

"What do you want to know" he asked.

"Not here" said one of then curtly. "Please come with us". He stood and led the way out.

"Where are we going" asked Hargreaves, not moving.

We'll explain as we go" said one of the other two, motioning for Hargreaves to follow the first.

"I'd like to consult Chief Inspector Walters first" said Hargreaves, trying to inject a degree of authority, or at least insistence, that he did not remotely feel.

"That won't be necessary" said the first officer. "He has been consulted already and has agreed to release you for the day. Please come with me" He held open the door.

"I'd prefer to speak to him myself" said Hargreaves, now trying to keep any panic out of his voice.

"That's not possible" said the man, with a brief nod to the other two, one of whom took Hargreaves arm and started to usher him out of the room. As Hargreaves started to resist, the third man took his other arm.

"Please don't make this difficult" said the first man, in a slightly resigned fashion. So it was that Hargreaves left the station, via a backdoor and into a waiting Land Rover, with it never quite certain if he was being taken forcibly against his will or merely 'escorted' to the car. The Land Rover already had a driver. The officer in command got in the front passenger seat while Hargeaves was placed between the other two in the back. Hargreaves didn't even notice if Johnson came outside or not.

In the car no-one spoke. Hargreaves tried asking a few questions – who they were with, where they were going – but the only response was that all would be explained shortly. This turned out to be around forty minutes, when they arrived somewhere in North-West London, perhaps Stanmore or thereabouts Hargreaves judged. They drove through some large gates, down a tree lined drive and arrived at a complex of fairly nondescript modern buildings dotted around an old Victorian mansion. He was taken into a large single story, red brick building, to a large room with little furniture and invited to sit at a metal table in the middle of the room. The three men who had picked him up settled down around him. One carried a small recording machine, which he switched on. To his horror, Hargreaves heard first Kate's voice and then his own – a quite clear recording of his phone conversation the night before.

The officer-in-charge looked at him pensively.

"I needn't have played this to you. I could have asked you a lot of questions first, probably caught you out in all sorts of deception; and then made life really hard for you. I have not done so, first, because I am in a hurry; second because, by all accounts you are an intelligent, well respected and resourceful DS with distinctly good prospects; and I propose to treat you as such. I will also be completely truthful with you. Miss Kimball may, I stress 'may' – no-one is at all sure – be some sort of security threat. I do not know any details. I and my team have been told to find her, in order that others may question her and thereby evaluate that threat. That is all. You clearly have a romantic attachment to her – whether she feels the same or not I do not know – but you are a serving officer in her Majesty's Police force; and will therefore recognise your higher duty, which is to assist us in any way you can to find her. Do I make myself clear?" Hargreaves said nothing.

"Do I make myself clear?" the man repeated, not quite shouting, but very forcibly. Hargreaves nodded slightly.

"Good. Then I just need the answer to three questions; and then you can return to Oxford. You will understand that, until you answer these questions, you will remain here, completely incommunicado. I trust that is clear as well". This time he did not look for any acknowledgement from Hargreaves.

"First, where is Miss Kimball?"

"I don't know. She left Oxford over a week ago. She said she had taken some compassionate leave from her work; and was going to have a bit of a break in Scotland. She didn't say where - as far as I know, she hadn't booked anywhere before she left. I got a strong impression that she was just going to tour around, no set journey".

"But she did not go in her car?" It was just about a question; but his interrogator clearly understood that she had not driven.

"No. She was going to take a train, to avoid a lot of driving; and then hire a car when she got there".

"Can you explain, then, why there is no record of a Miss Catherine Kimball hiring a car in Scotland during the last ten days?"

"No, I can't. Maybe she stayed in one place, maybe she took a bus, went to the Western Isles on a boat. I don't know".

"Did she not call you at any point to talk to you, say anything about her holiday?" Hargreaves was on the point of saying that she hadn't but, just in time, remembered that Kate had said something in her last call about his doing what she had asked him to do earlier – to say nothing about her trip to Northern Ireland. He might have been able to finesse that; but it also went through his mind that they might have checked his phone records and, if so, would know that he had taken an earlier call from her mobile.

"She called me a couple of times. Both were very short. I don't think she wanted to talk for long, because things between us were….uncertain. She just wanted to let me know she was all right. I had bigger things on my mind than where she was or how she was getting around. She said she was okay, feeling somewhat better; and she'd be coming back to Oxford sometime this week. That was more or less it".

"In your call last night, you asked her if you could do anything to help; and she said only what she had asked you before. What was that?" Hargreaves, fortunately, had had a good thirty seconds or more to think up an answer.

"Give her some space, some time. She knows how I feel about her, but she is still very distraught about her partner, not knowing what happened to him. Maybe she and I will get together, but I know it won't be until that is all cleared up" To his surprise he saw, for the first time, a moment's uncertainty and, with it, some hesitation on the part of the man sitting opposite him. They don't know about Emmerson, he thought. They don't know the background. They've just been told to find Kate. It wasn't, as far as he could see, hugely significant, but it gave Hargreaves a small psychological boost – one he very much needed just at that moment. Would they be ready to reveal their lack of knowledge, he wondered.

His interrogator sought to regain the initiative.

"So she gave no indication of where she was, or how she was getting around?"

"None at all"

"Or when she was coming back, other than sometime this week?"

"No"

"Okay, second question. In the phone conversation, she talks of her 'plans'. What plans would those be?" Hargreaves decided to push his slight advantage.

"She has been very distressed since her partner disappeared. It has quite wrecked her life. Part of the reason for the break in Scotland was to think through how she was going to come to terms with this, what her plans were for the future; whether she could just go back to the same job in the same city; or whether she might try to make a complete break, go somewhere different. She had been in California recently and obviously liked it there". He knew this sounded quite plausible. At the same time, he was fairly sure that the man opposite him wasn't buying it. But he was going to have difficulty testing this without admitting that he had no idea about Kate's missing partner. That would rather damage his prospects of intimidating Hargreaves sufficiently to be sure he had got all he could from him.

Hargreaves was right that the man wasn't buying it.

"Hmm, very interesting, but in the call – I have a transcript here, have a look – she says that she has got some plans but, I quote 'they'll soon be done'. Doesn't sound like plans for her future, does it?" Hargreaves was stumped for an answer.

"I didn't really pick up on that during the call. I guess I just thought that she was formulating some plans but they weren't yet finalised in her mind". His interrogator stared at him impassively.

"Try again"

"What do you mean 'try again'? I'm not playing some stupid game. I want her to move in with me; and the chances are that she won't; but I don't know what her plans are. What do you think she meant?" He doubted that the morose lover act would succeed, but it was all he could think of. There was a long pause.

"We'll come back to that. Third question". It was the third one that really floored Hargreaves.

"You ask her in the call whether she is 'doing this of her......' and she cuts you off. You were going to say 'of her own free choice' – or something like that weren't you? What did you mean by that?" Hargreaves could think of no good answer.

"Don't fuck with me, Sergeant. What did you mean by the question, 'of her own free choice'?" Hargreaves snatched at straws.

"Kate knew that she hadn't been performing well at her job. Her employer had been quite sympathetic, at least for a while; but I think they were getting tired of covering for her - or Kate thought they might be – and I didn't know how much her thoughts of leaving, not just the job but the UK, were her idea or more being forced on her. I didn't know how much it was her free choice or her responding to pressure, however subtle, from her boss".

"I don't believe a word of it" said the man opposite him, looking increasingly agitated.

"Frankly, I don't give a fuck whether you believe it or not" said Hargreaves. "You bug my phone, drag me off here, start firing questions at me. I've answered them, as accurately as I can. I'm a police officer, not just some member of the public who you think you can intimidate. I don't know who you are; and you clearly don't know what's going on. So I don't care what you believe. Now piss off and let me get back to my job".

Such an attack was probably Hargreaves best form of defence; but it wasn't nearly good enough.

"You're way out of your depth, Sergeant. Speak to me like that again and I'll have you pummelled to a bag of shit. I'll ask you again, why did you start to ask if she was a free agent. Who might have been restricting her freedom? Think very hard about your position before you answer". Hargreaves swallowed hard. This was going to be unpleasant; but he didn't have a choice.

"She was on holiday, for God's sake. I have no idea what you are talking about. I'd like to go now". One of the other two men got up, walked round the table and smashed his fist into Hargreaves' face. His head snapped back; and he felt blood pouring out, down his nose. Momentarily, he thought of collapsing, as if knocked out; but the thought passed. He looked up at his interrogator.

"You can kick me to pieces; but I can't tell you what I don't know. As far as I know she is on her own. That was the whole point of the trip. She certainly never said anything to me about travelling with, or meeting, anyone else. I'd have gone with her myself if I thought for one moment she'd agree". He got a handkerchief out of his pocket and dabbed at his nose. There was blood all over the place.

There was a long silence, during which Hargreaves contemplated how long, and how much, he could suffer without revealing the truth. Perhaps a similar thought was going through the man sitting opposite him, still looking at him without any emotion. Then he seemed to make a decision.

298

"Lock him up. We'll have another talk later"

"Do you have an Arrest Warrant?" asked Hargreaves, his face now becoming very painful indeed. The man smiled a charmless smile.

"Very amusing. Be very clear, whether you ever see the light of day again is entirely up to me. Get him out of here". He got up and walked out. The other two grabbed his arms; and three minutes later Hargreaves found himself in a concrete, windowless cell, with a bunk bed, a wash basin, a lavatory and a chair. It was barely 1 p.m. It had not been a good day so far.

Two hours later, Hargreaves was taken back to the interrogation room, where the same man was waiting for him.

"I trust you are going to be more co-operative this time" said the man, without looking up.

"I'll tell you anything I can. But I don't know where she is in Scotland; I don't know who with; and I don't know what her so-called plans are". His interrogator, whose name was Swinburne, a Captain in the SAS, shook his head slightly; and the other two launched themselves on Hargreaves. One held him while the other repeatedly punched him, pounding his ribs. Hargreaves fell to the floor in agony, whereupon the two started to kick him viciously, in the ribs, the back and his groin. Hargreaves had no means to defend himself. Eventually they stopped; and dragged him, barely conscious back to the chair. Swinburne looked at him.

"Take him back to the cell. Next time, Hargreaves, they are really going to hurt you".

When Hargreaves had gone, Swinburne pulled out his mobile phone and made a call.

"General, we have had a couple of sessions. I'll find out more, but my initial assessment is that he doesn't know where she is, but believes she is due back here sometime this week. She is clearly planning something; but I don't think he knows what it is, though he may know its purpose; and he is concerned as to whether she is acting under duress or not. That means he knows who might be putting pressure on her; but he is not, as yet, saying. But if you think she may be a courier for the IRA, then that would seem the most likely bet".

"Thank you for that" replied the General. "Let me know what more you get". Five minutes later he was on a private, secure line to 10 Downing Street.

*　　*　　*

A little later that day, between 3.45 and 4.00 pm, three cars arrived and parked in the main car park of the Park Hotel a couple of miles outside Marlborough. No-one paid them any particular attention. Shortly after 4 pm, one of O'Connell's men arrived driving a twenty-four seat bus; fifteen men climbed from the cars, got in the bus and it headed off. Gannon, Riordan and Kate stayed behind in Gannon's hired car. Ten minutes later the bus parked in the half empty car-park of a small industrial estate on the outskirts of the town; and O'Connell handed out detailed plans of Wallington House, its surrounding grounds and a specially constructed map of the roads and countryside around. Each marked out where every member of the team would be stationed, and their lines of observation. O'Connell reminded them of the basic structure of the operation; and then proceeded to convert this into a specific role for each man. He talked them through each of the six possible scenarios, what defined or characterised each; and how each member of the team should respond to each scenario. He then gave out more documents which gave details of their communications strategy; and talked them all the way through the document. The key element of this concerned the reporting of sightings to O'Connell over their short-wave radios, so that he could determine which of the six scenarios was to be deployed; and then he could transmit this information back to the team. No-one would make a move until he gave the command, there being in fact a set of these, one for each of the five units within the team. He went though the whole thing twice; and then asked for any questions, which he dealt with. All in all, it took over an hour. Around 5.30 pm they set off for a small lay-by in a road about a mile from Wallington House.

Meanwhile, Gannon had driven with Riordan and Kate to their fifth internet café, this one in Basingstoke. They parked and entered shortly before closing time. They quickly brought up the email that Kate had received that morning. Kate hit 'Reply' and then, at just about the time that O'Connell and the others were parking in the lay-by, she typed in

"Arrange for the P.E. package to which I referred in my letter to be delivered to Wallington House, off the A4361 in Wiltshire, at precisely 11am this Thursday. Maximum of two delivery personnel. I will let them have all the relevant documents you require. Enter by the main gate. There is a speed restriction of 4 miles an hour on the driveway. If any part of these instructions is disregarded, the transaction will not go ahead. There will be no back-up arrangement. The documentation will then be dispatched to an alternative customer".

KK

She looked to Riordan for approval. He nodded. Kate arranged for a print-out and then hit 'Send'.

CHAPTER 27

Palmer had been checking the dedicated lap-top spasmodically; and saw the email less than ten minutes after it was sent. He printed it out, double-deleted the electronic version and arranged to meet Gerrard thirty minutes later. Neither man was remotely concerned at the frantic re-arranging of Gerrard's diary that this entailed. When the two of them were alone, Gerrard told Palmer what he had heard from General Sykes.

"Well, we now know where she is; and we know what the plan is" said Gerrard. "Is she working alone is the question".

"Sykes' men think she's with the IRA?" said Palmer.

"Yes, but that's only because of the cover story I gave Sykes. I think the only support she has been getting is from this copper in Oxford, Hargreaves, and he is well and truly tucked away at present".

"What will happen to him – when this is over?" asked Palmer apprehensively.

"Don't worry, they'll release him, give him a cover story – a mugging or something like that – and then tell him to stick to it if he wants to have Lady Kimball back in one piece. And before you ask, yes, she might get through this alive as well. I thought that might be too risky, but with Hargreaves we have a lever".

"But I thought her great quest was to get Emmerson back?" asked Palmer.

"True, but he isn't coming back, is he? By the end of next week at the latest, maybe earlier, the US will have had what they want from me; and Emmerson will finally disappear for good. Kimball has got Hargreaves waiting for her on the re-bound, so to speak". Palmer tried not to register how shocked he was at Gerrard's callousness. He himself was no slouch when it came to twisting politicians' arms twice round their necks to get what his master wanted, but this complete disregard for life – and no doubt limb in Hargreaves case – made him feel slightly nauseous. But, he reminded himself, for Gerrard, this was a matter of his survival, not just as PM, nor even as a politician, but as a free man. That could quite warp one's perspective.

While Palmer was musing on such things, Gerrard was contacting Sykes.

"She's expecting a contact to join her at 11 a.m. on Thursday at Wallington House in Wiltshire. I don't know who lives there, but that's where she'll be. The contact, we've discovered, is, in fact, a bloody mole in one of our departments; and we will pick him up early Thursday morning, so he won't actually arrive. The courier, plus anyone with her, is to be apprehended and held in isolation until further notice. The operational details are, of course, entirely up to you and your team. Let me know as soon as it has been accomplished.

"Is she likely to have anyone with her?" asked Sykes.

"I don't think so" replied Gerrard. "Maybe an associate. More likely, just the owner of the house. She's only a courier".

"Don't worry, we'll check it all out thoroughly" replied Sykes.

"I'm sure you will" said Gerrard "and thanks".

Five minutes later Sykes had passed all this on to Captain Swinburne, who quickly hauled Hargreaves back.

"Your lucky day" he began. "We now know where your lady love is; and it certainly isn't Scotland. We know what her plan is; and it seems she is working for some IRA splinter group". So why don't you save yourself a lot of grief and tell me everything you know?"

Hargreaves's resolve to defy these bastards, already weakened by the two hours of contemplating Swinburne's previous parting threat, plunged still further on hearing this. He tried to gather his thoughts. He knew he was in a bad way. His chest and ribs were killing him; and he had coughed up some blood. His head was so painful he could barely think at all. But through all this it registered loud and clear that, somehow, these men had found out about Kate's link to the IRA. Not in a million years would Hargreaves even suspect that Swinburne's 'information' – however close to the truth - was entirely the product of Gerrard and Palmer's collective imagination.

"Where is she?" he whispered, the effort of speaking bringing tears to his eyes.

"Back in England. Are you sure you didn't know?" Hargreaves slowly shook his head.

"Well, I think, for once, I believe you. And she's acting as a courier for the IRA. You knew that, didn't you?" Again Hargreaves shook his head.

"But you knew she was linked to the IRA, didn't you? That's why you asked her if she was acting as a free agent, wasn't it?" By now Hargreaves was very confused. There seemed no point in denying Kate's link to the IRA. They clearly knew about that. But why would they think she was acting as a courier? Why would she? Oh, Kate, what have you got yourself into?

"Wasn't it?" repeated Sykes. "If you do not answer me, these two will beat you unconscious; and, be very certain, you will never have children, with Miss Kimball or anyone else". Hargreaves paused a second; and then, almost imperceptibly, nodded. He saw that he had no alternative. But, as he did so, through the pain, panic and terror, he saw how he might still help Kate. She was out to get Gerrard, of that he had no doubt – because that was her only way back to Paul - and she was going to use help from the IRA to do it. How, he didn't know; but it certainly wasn't going to be by running messages for them. Somewhere along the line these bastards had got the wrong information, maybe even deliberate disinformation; and he just might be able to help the process.

He started to speak, slowly, his throat sore, his voice a hoarse whisper.

"For some reason, she thought the IRA might know something about the scientist she was seeing who disappeared. His name's Paul Emmerson. I don't know why she thought that – it was all before I got to know her – but I think they maybe offered her some information about what has happened to him if she acted as a go-between for something they were planning. I don't know any of the details; and I didn't even know whether she had agreed this voluntarily, or whether they had threatened her in some way – that's why I asked if she was a free agent. But you heard her reply. I think she's offered to act as a go-between that no-one would suspect, in return for some information about Emmerson. I think that was her 'plan'. Only, somehow, you know about her. That's it. You can threaten me as much as you like, but I just don't know anything more than that. I wish I did". The effort of speaking, in the state he was in, exhausted him; and he slumped forward, holding his head up with his arms resting on the table.

There was no doubt in Swinburne's mind that he had finally got to the truth. Not least because it tallied with what Sykes had told him. Now all he wanted to do was to get going with his team, down to Wiltshire for some action. He had alerted a team of seven plus himself and, given what Hargreaves had told him, he was confident that that would be more than sufficient to pick up a female courier.

"Take him back" he said curtly to his two men. "Arrange for him to have some food. Then join me in my office". He walked out, feeling considerable satisfaction at the outcome of the interrogation. He would have been very surprised to know that Hargreaves was feeling a very similar emotion.

During the next three hours, Kate, Gannon and Riordan re-joined O'Connell's men; and they deployed themselves, their weapons and their supplies around Wallington House and its grounds. O'Connell placed six men inside the house, all on the first floor overlooking the main entrance and stairwell. He placed four pairs of men outside, two either side of the front and two either side of the back entrances. All were hidden, at the back in outbuildings and at the front behind bushes, supplemented by some rudimentary landscaping which O'Connell's men had prepared in the previous two days. Four more men were placed individually on the outskirts of the grounds of the house, again covering front and back and both sides. All four were in elevated positions, two in thickly leaved trees; and two on the roofs of outbuildings. All were heavily armed; all had powerful radio transmitters, balaclava masks and night vision goggles; plus some food and water to keep them going for 36 hours.

That left Kate, Riordan and O'Connell himself. They took up position in their command post, which was no more than a thicket some one hundred metres away in the corner of a field to which they had added some overhead cover. It was completely invisible from three directions, and barely visible from the fourth, except from a very short distance. Once in place, O'Connell talked via their radios with all members of the team, checked their locations and lines of sight. By 8 p.m., satisfied that all was ready, he, Riordan and Kate had a sandwich supper. All round Wallington House, various members of O'Connell's team took it in turns to sleep, except for the four corner men on the perimeter. They would need to be awake, very much the eyes and ears of the operation, throughout the night.

Meanwhile, Captain Swinburne had rendezvoused with his team; and, by 9 p.m., the eight of them, having arrived in two long-wheelbase jeeps, had arrived in a lay-by around a mile from the house. He called the men to gather round him.

"Wallington House is essentially a ruin". He had found this out quite easily some hours before. "The person we are due to pick up is expecting to meet someone there at 11 am. on Thursday. So my guess is that she will turn up sometime earlier that morning. But it's quite a well chosen location. No possibility of us approaching the house in numbers without being seen; and at least three routes by which she could exit fast if we do – maybe other more hidden ways out as well. But if she's got the place under surveillance, then if we go in early, she'll see us. So, we need to be one step ahead. We'll do a brief recce tonight; and then keep the place under observation. All being well, we'll go in around 4 am. Thursday morning and pick her up as soon as she arrives.

" Sergeant" he nodded to an athletic looking man to his right "you'll take Remmington and Lees in as soon as we are ready. Check the place out and report back. Any problems we'll discuss, sort out, and then lay up until tomorrow night. Any questions?" One of the men replied.

"How many oppo, Sir? Just the one?"

"Possibly two or three. We're not sure. But we'll put six in the house and have two watching from outside. So we'll know in good time. However many, we pick them all up and we're out of here. Okay?" There were no further questions.

Shortly before midnight, Sergeant Ballack, along with Remmington and Lees, all with blackened faces, armed, and with night-sight goggles which also registered body heat, climbed the wall surrounding Wallington House. Using as much tree cover as possible, they approached the back entrance. Both of O'Connell's men stationed on the rear perimeter observed them; and radioed both the four men guarding the rear of the house and the six men inside. The four outside checked that they were well hidden and, a few minutes later saw the SAS team break in. O'Connell, quite certain that this was a preliminary scouting of the site, sent a message to all his men to remain well hidden and take no action. The six men inside the house took up position behind piles of rusting junk, bags of cement and internal walls in one of the three cellars – some of it genuine, some of it a recent addition. The door to the cellar was locked from the outside, but unbeknownst to anyone examining it from the outside, could be opened from within by the simple expedient of removing the hinges.

It took Sergeant Ballack and his two men around 45 minutes to ascertain that the house was not just a ruin but an empty one. They had no keys to any of the cellars; but had no difficulty in breaking the rather puny padlocks, peering inside and satisfying themselves that the cellars were empty. Had it been Afghanistan, they might have searched more thoroughly, for booby traps, munitions or explosives, but this was Wiltshire and they had no reason to anticipate that the house was anything other than it appeared – a once elegant structure that time and economics had passed by. By 1 a.m. they were back with Captain Swinburne, reporting that the house was derelict and empty. The Captain instructed his men to get some sleep; and O'Connell, less than half a mile away, instructed his men to do the same

Wednesday was a day of enforced idleness for almost everyone involved – for Swinburne's team, O'Connell's men and Kate; and for Hargreaves, who was left entirely alone except for the delivery of some lunch. Swinburne arranged for a plane to sweep over Wallington House, but at sufficient height that no-one would notice. It took over two hundred photos at the rate of six a second; and by mid-afternoon they had been analysed and the results forwarded to Swinburne. There was no sign of anyone or any sort of movement anywhere near the house. This did not surprise Swinburne, but it was useful re-assurance. Otherwise, only Gerrard was busy. The latent tension he felt about the whole operation was compounded by two pieces of information. First, at 3 pm. President Hamilton phoned him to say that the US, along with the Israelis, would commence air strikes on Iran's nuclear sites the following Wednesday. The strikes would be mounted partly from the fifth US battle fleet in the Persian Gulf, but the heavy bombers, essential to the destruction of Iran's nuclear arsenal, would fly from two US bases in the UK. He was also arranging for a meeting of the UN Security Council to be called on Tuesday. Hamilton had no illusions that this would provide the support necessary to pass a Resolution backing international intervention by the UN in Iran; but the meeting nonetheless would play a strategic role in his plans. He looked forward to full support from the UK representative on the Security Council. Two hours later, El and two whips came to see Gerrard, to say that the House of Commons had arranged for a debate on Iran, to be held the following Thursday. There had been pressure to hold the debate on the Tuesday, but Gerrard had been clear that it must, at all costs, be delayed until after the attack, to avoid any possibility of the House of Commons seeking to restrict his scope for manoeuvre. Fortunately, the announcement of the meeting of the Security Council, and the argument that MPs would need time to digest its outcome, were sufficient to get the debate scheduled for the Thursday. By then the attack on Iran would be a *fait accompli.* Gerrard's political future might then be over; but he could at least avoid President Hamilton's threat to his freedom.

Shortly before 4 a.m. on Thursday morning, Captain Swinburne and his team of seven, suitably prepared, approached Wallington House, four from the front and four from the back. They anticipated no resistance; and found none. According to plan, the group at the back went in the same way that Sergeant Ballack had, moved silently across the central hall and let the other group in. None of them knew that they had been spotted ten minutes earlier by O'Connell's perimeter team, nor that their approach had been notified in advance to the men hidden outside the main building and inside. As the SAS team joined up in the main hallway, Vincent O'Connell, leading the six man team inside the house, now with their balaclavas on and in position all round the first floor gallery - but standing back from the balcony itself, out of any direct line of sight from below - gave the signal 'go'. Five of his men wrenched off their night-sight goggles and moved forward to the balcony. Less than a second later, Vincent removed his own night goggles, pulled a switch and ten powerful spot-lamps, erected around the gallery during the day, blazed forth, completely blinding the SAS team in their night-sight goggles. Less than a second later, eight more of O'Connell's men appeared, four at the front door and four from the back. The SAS team, in as far as they could comprehend anything, were blinded, surrounded and, most dangerous of all, sitting ducks in the hallway from the six semi-automatic machine pistols pointed at them from twenty feet above. Vincent O'Connell shouted
"If anyone moves, they are dead. Any movement at all".

All O'Connell's men knew that this was the critical moment. Basic SAS training dictates that, in a tight situation, an immediate response, however dangerous, is likely to be the best option. They were not disappointed. Though totally blinded by the light focused onto their eyes by their night-sight goggles, two of Swinburne's team fell to the floor, rolled over underneath one side of the gallery and started firing upwards, across the hallway. One of O'Connell's men was unlucky, taking several bullets in the arm and shoulder. The response was immediate. Both SAS men were hit by a hail of bullets; and rapid fire sprayed across the hallway above the heads of the others was enough to stifle any further movement.
"Try that again and you are all dead" shouted Vincent; and this time no-one moved.
"Drop your weapons, now, lie on the floor on your bellies with your hands stretched out in front of you. Do it. Now! You have twenty semi-automatics

trained on you". One by one the six members of Swinburne's team still untouched complied.

"Handcuffs" shouted Vincent, "You two" – he pointed to two of his team who had come in through the front door – "check the two who are down". He then radioed his father to come on in. A minute or two later, with the rest of the SAS team sitting up against the hall wall, with their hands cuffed behind their backs, two of O'Connell's men reported that the two injured SAS men were alive; one with a shattered arm but not terminal. The other was unconscious, had taken a number of bullets in his stomach and would, they thought, need fairly immediate treatment. At that point, Victor O'Connell, having checked with his perimeter look-outs that no back-up force was on its way, walked in with Riordan and Kate. The two Irishmen wore masks, but there was no reason for Kate to wear one. Her identity was only too well known already. From where she entered, she could not see the two injured SAS men; and the space looked much calmer than she had expected. Vincent explained the condition of the two injured men; and Kate began to realise that all was not as calm as she thought.

"Which of you is in charge here?" he asked. Swinburne muttered

"I am".

"And what might your name be?" asked O'Connell. Swinburne remained silent.

"Its not important" said O'Connell "I only wanted to know what to call you. Now, let's get down to business. My men reckon that one of those two is going to die soon if he isn't got to a hospital. Well, I can arrange that; but no-one is going anywhere until you tell me who sent you. And it had better be accurate, because I'm going to talk to him before anyone leaves". No-one said anything.

"As you wish" said O'Connell. "That's one dead. His colleague looks like he might lose an arm; and he is shortly going to lose a leg as well, unless you tell me what I want to know". Still no-one else spoke.

"Okay". He took hold of the weapon hanging from a strap over his shoulder; and moved towards the injured man lying on the floor. "I don't know if you have ever seen a knee-capping, but it isn't pleasant" This finally produced a re-action; but it was from Kate.

"Oh my God, no!" she said. O'Connell merely nodded his head to a couple of his men; who gently started to help Kate out of the room.

"No, I'm staying" she said. O'Connell merely shrugged.

"She is rather squeamish, which is very much to her credit. I am not. Five seconds". He pointed the pistol at the leg of the other injured man. "Four seconds......."

"General Sykes" said Swinburne.

"Now you are being sensible" said O'Connell in a matter-of-fact way. "And what were his instructions?"

"To pick up whoever was here tomorrow morning"

"And you thought you'd just come along a little early?" This produced no further word from Swinburne.

"And who did General Sykes say you'd be picking up?"

"Just a courier"

"A courier? I see. A courier for who?"

"For you lot".

That shook O'Connell, but he showed no sign of it.
"And who did he say we were?"

"Fucking IRA. Some splinter group that wants to go on bombing and murdering innocent people. Fucking psychopaths". So, there it was. They knew the IRA was involved. Well, too bad, thought O'Connell; and too late. Like Hargreaves, he did not for one moment contemplate that this was disinformation from Palmer, which ironically had fallen not that far off the mark.

"And from whom did General Sykes get his orders?"

"I have no idea. Now can I get my men to a hospital?"

"Shortly, if you continue to play your cards right. What number do I contact him on?" There was no reply from Swinburne. "If he didn't give you a number, then there are going to be a lot people here who will never walk again, plus at least one who is never going to breathe again; but I don't think that's going to happen, is it? Because this was set up very fast – and the good General is going to want to know what has happened just as soon as he can. I think your colleague over there – the one who is dying – probably wants you tell me quite quickly as well". There was still no reply.

"Look, I know you are brave, well trained men, serving your country and all that. But you've lost this round; and there's no point in compounding that with lots of maimed bodies. I'll smash every one of your men's knee caps, and then yours, if I have too; and you'll tell me what I want to know at some point. Better to tell me now before anyone else gets ready for life in a wheel chair. So, for Christ's sake, give me the number". Whether it was fear or the logic of this which got through to Swinburne, O'Connell didn't know, or care, but Swinburne recited a mobile phone number. O'Connell tapped it into his own mobile.

Sykes knew it was bad news the moment he was woken by his phone before dawn.

"Yes?" he barked into the phone.

"General Sykes, I am currently holding your squad of eight men at gun-point. Two are injured, one seriously. Tell me what I want to know and I will release them; and let them get the injured men to hospital. Any prevarication may cost you the life of one of those injured. It will certainly cost you the lives of the others, at the rate of one a minute, until I hear what I want to hear. Is that perfectly clear?" O'Connell had expected some bluster, swearing, maybe some inability, having just been woken up at 4.30 am fully to comprehend the situation; but General Sykes, however near retirement, had had a life of instantly sizing up life-or-death situations and how best to handle them.

"Put Captain Swinburne on the line so that I can confirm what you say".

"Certainly" said O'Connell, and passed the phone to Swinburne.

"Confirmed, Sir" said Swinburne. It was a set-up. There's about twenty of them here".

"Pass me back to whoever is in charge" said Sykes. Swinburne passed the phone back to O'Connell.

"What do you want to know?"

"Who gave you the instruction to pick up an IRA courier?"

"MI5" said Sykes immediately

"General, you're a credit to your profession; but we both know that isn't true. You see, I know who gave you the order. I just want confirmation. Now...." He nodded to two of his men "Stand that one there up against the pillar. No-one should be shot slumped on the floor. You have ten seconds, General".

"It came from the Prime Minister's office" said Sykes.

"Thank you" said O'Connell "From his office or from the PM direct?" Sykes was silent for a moment.

"General...." Sykes cut him off.

"From the PM himself"

"Isn't that a little unusual?"

"Yes. He said that there were fears that the operation, whatever it is, might have been compromised somewhere in Whitehall".

"I see" said O'Connell. "And you believed he was just trying to pick up an IRA courier?"

"Why shouldn't I? Our own intelligence confirmed it". This time, O'Connell couldn't avoid looking surprised.

"Your own intelligence? What was that exactly?"

"The courier's contact in Oxford".

Until now, O'Connell had been completely in control of the situation; indeed it was vital that everyone recognised that that was the case. He was a man with natural authority; he had twenty heavily armed men in support; he had had the element of surprise and he knew exactly what he wanted to achieve. He would prefer it if the injured man didn't die; but he would get want he wanted before lifting a finger to help him. Above all, he was prepared to execute some or all of the SAS team if he had to, just as their predecessors had executed his Sellafield team; though he knew from experience that the clearer he made this, the less likely he was to have to carry it out. But the General's last reply had seriously thrown him. He had been convinced, both by Kate and by Declan, that DS Hargreaves – for that was who Sykes must mean – was no threat. He had dangerous information, but he was clearly lovelorn and certainly not going to do or say anything to jeopardise Kate – of that O'Connell was certain. So how had the General's team got to him; and why would he have revealed Kate's IRA connection? As these thoughts raced through his brain at the speed of light, he realised that, while he didn't know the answer to the first of these questions, he had an awful suspicion that he knew the answer to the second.

"And what did he reveal?"

"I just told you. He confirmed that the woman was a courier for the IRA"

"To whom did he confirm this?" asked O'Connell.

"To Captain Swinburne". O'Connell breathed an inward sigh of relief. He could now see a way forward.

"Thank you General Sykes. You have acted in the best interests of your men" and switched off the phone. He disconnected a small recording device plugged into the phone and put it in his pocket. Suddenly he was all action.

"Right, uncuff one of these men. You three…." He pointed to some of his own team "go with him. Pick up their transport – it must be somewhere near – bring it back here and then Captain Swinburne can get the two injured ones to hospital. I guess it will have to be Reading General at this time in the morning. The others we take to the dump site". He turned to Captain Swinburne. "I'll let you know where they are in due course". He looked back at his own team. "Make sure we have all their arms and any other gear, in particular their communications equipment". He turned to Kate. "Will you and Mickie here go and get the First Aid Equipment? It's stacked in the first barn out the back".

Kate, though she didn't fully appreciate it, was in a state of shock; at the violence and the threat of much worse, cold blooded savagery. She'd known all along what sort of men the O'Connells, and no doubt the rest of his team, were – Victor had viciously hit her twice; and Vincent had clearly wanted her killed at one stage – but none of that had prepared her for what she had just witnessed. Even so, that was not what gripped at her throat so much she could hardly speak.

"What did who reveal?" she asked. O'Connell appeared not to notice her question.

"What did *who* reveal?" she asked again, this time with an insistence that O'Connell could not ignore. He would rather not have this problem, but there it was.

"Hargreaves. They've talked to Hargreaves in Oxford". Kate felt herself start to feel faint.

"Oh my God, is he alright?" she whispered. She addressed this to O'Connell, but it was Captain Swinburne who replied. He had been thinking for some minutes now that the only card he had to play was the policeman from Oxford they had picked up yesterday, now safely under lock and key in Stanmore. He clearly was in love with the somewhat mysterious woman standing next to the

IRA commander. If she felt the same about him, then maybe, just maybe, he could leverage something out of what was otherwise a complete disaster.

"For the moment" he said. Before Kate could fully absorb this, O'Connell intervened.

"What did he tell you?"

"That she is acting as a courier for you". O'Connell remained deeply puzzled as to how or why Hargreaves would have said this. Kate's concern was more immediate.

"Is he all right?" she repeated, this time to Swinburne, her voice both insistent and tremulous. Swinburne very deliberately turned half away from O'Connell to look at Kate and address her very directly.

"Miss Kimball, members of my team have Detective Sergeant Hargreaves in….unofficial… custody. Be very clear. Unless I and my men are released, without any further harm, now, he is a dead man; and his remaining hours will not be good ones". Kate, if it were possible, turned even more ashen at this pronouncement. She began to feel dizzy; and gently clutched O'Connell's arm – the first physical contact she had had with him apart from his two assaults on her. O'Connell's reaction was quite different. Ignoring Kate, he unslung the machine pistol and, in a fraction of a second, took it by the barrel, swung it and slammed the butt against Swinburne's head. There was a sickening noise as Swinburne, already sitting on the floor, collapsed forward, seriously concussed. Kate put her hand over her mouth to stifle a scream. O'Connell paused to make sure that Swinburne was still conscious.

"Try to negotiate with me again and I'll execute every one of your men – do you understand? In any event, you have no cards to play. I really don't give a shit what happens to this Hargeaves. But I don't really know what he's been telling you; and so I'd much prefer to have him here with me, which is why you are going to release him; but that is a sideshow, I can assure you. Now, where is Hargreaves?" Swinburne neither responded nor moved; and appeared to be having difficulty focusing. O'Connell kicked him hard in the thigh and pointed the machine pistol at him. "Where is he?" For a moment it seemed unlikely that Swinburne could, or would respond. But then he moved, very slightly.

"He's at our base" he said; and then appeared to pass out.

"Which is where?" said O'Connell; but Swinburne was no longer conscious. O'Connell turned to one of Swinburne's men.

"If you want your commanding officer to survive, tell me where your base is". He pointed his weapon at Swinburne's head.

"It's in North London, Stanmore" replied the man.

"Now we are getting somewhere" said O'Connell. Nodding to Declan he continued "Take three of the men, plus two of these shit-arses – these two" he pointed "and go and get Hargreaves". He addressed the two SAS men. "I don't care how you do it, but unless I hear within two hours from my men that Hargreaves has been released, then your commanding officer here is a dead duck. And I will make quite sure the world knows why he died. Do you understand me?" Both nodded. "Good. Go".

The next two hours were both action packed and, simultaneously, rather anti-climactic. Declan O'Connell, with three of the IRA team, headed off with two of Swinburne's men to retrieve Hargreaves. Meanwhile, Victor and the rest of his men took Swinburne, still unconscious, and his five remaining men - one also unconscious and clearly losing a lot of blood, one with a shattered shoulder and the other three with their hands cuffed behind them - outside to wait for transport. One of the SAS men was deputed to drive the two injured ones to Reading General Hospital, being assured that if he did anything other than this in the next four hours, no-one would ever see Captain Swinburne again. The rest of the IRA team, all in very high spirits after their adrenalin-fuelled success, retreated from Wallington House, taking Swinburne - now starting to regain consciousness - and the two remaining members of the SAS team with them. They secured the three of them in a derelict greenhouse on the edge of a disused market garden which O'Connell's men had located three days earlier, about fifteen miles east of Wallington House. An hour or so after arriving there, Declan called to say that they had Hargreaves. One of Swinburne's men had gone into their base, while Declan held a pistol to the head of the other; and returned within a few minutes with a limping and very sickly looking Hargreaves. They had left the two SAS men handcuffed back-to-back in a woodland area on the way back to Marlborough. As soon as O'Connell had heard that Hargreaves was free, he gave instructions for everyone to return to their various lodgings in and around Marlborough. When he, Vincent O'Connell, Gannon, Riordan and Kate arrived back where they were staying, Victor O'Connell called General Sykes again and, in two terse sentences, told him where he could find his men. The five of them spent some time checking their recording of the conversation with Sykes; and going over their next move. An hour and a half later, just before 8 a.m., there was a knock on the door and, for Kate at least, the anti-climax was over. Declan stood there, holding up a very ill-looking Detective- Sergeant Hargreaves.

Kate sprung to her feet and went to him.
"Oh Neil, are you going to be all right?" She held out her hands to him. He managed a smile.
"I will be now" he said, as Declan led him to the bed. Kate noticed O'Connell give Declan a querying look, clearly concerned that Hargreaves might need a doctor.
"They gave him a hard time" said Declan. "He is badly bruised; and he may have a cracked rib. Some internal haemorrhaging, but it seems to have stopped. I've given him some pain-killers. He should see a doctor, if only as a precaution; but I think he'll be okay; and we need to be careful about

explanations. It'll have to be a mugging". O'Connell nodded. Hargreaves managed to look gaunt and bemused at the same time. Kate sat next to him and gently held his hand.

"I'm so sorry" she said "to have got you into this. You must forgive me".

"Hey, I signed up" replied Hargreaves. "There's nothing to forgive. But...." He paused as a cough racked his body "I really would like to know what has been going on". Before Kate could speak, O'Connell intervened.

"We'll explain that in a moment. First, tell us your end of the story." He gave no clue as to what he and the others might already know or not know. Hargreaves, talking slowly, evidently in some pain despite the pain-killers, briefly told them what had happened to him. He said that he had tried to give alternative explanations for as long as possible, until it was clear they wouldn't work any more; but that Swinburne had referred to Kate being a courier for the IRA. He knew that wasn't right, but thought the more disinformation they had the better; and so had 'reluctantly' confirmed that.

"Well, here's to you – you're a bit of a hero" said O'Connell. "I'm sorry they made it so difficult for you; but there is no doubt that feeding them that piece of news helped us a lot". Hargreaves looked less than thrilled by this information. He looked straight at Kate.

"Helped what?" he said. "Kate, tell me what you are doing". Kate looked at O'Connell, who just nodded; and Kate explained; her finding out the fate of the Sellafield team; heading, almost on a whim, to Loughgannon, ending up in Belfast with O'Connell; and their plans since then – her plan to find out the truth about Paul; and O'Connell's plan to bring down Gerrard. She forbore to say that, had she not engaged O'Connell's interest and then his commitment, she would probably now be dead or worse; nor did she even hint at the assaults to which she had been subjected. When she had finished, O'Connell took over to describe the night's activities. Hargreaves looked more and more strained; and not a little aghast, as he heard how Kate had been sucked ever more relentlessly into a nightmarishly violent world of which even he, as a police officer, had virtually no experience. He kept this to himself, however. When O'Connell paused, he asked

"So what happens now?"

CHAPTER 28

"Good question" said O'Connell "you're clearly on the mend; and the answer is that we now contact Gerrard again, point out that he has been a very naughty boy, not to mention a lying, duplicitous bastard; and that he is now in very deep shit indeed. But, we give him one more chance, don't we, Kate?"

"We do indeed" she replied. "Neil, we always knew that Gerrard would never just hand Paul over. But now we have real, hard evidence against him – evidence that directly links him to what has been going on. We think that this time, we may get a rather more positive response".

Having insisted that Neil take her bed and try to sleep, Kate left with Riordan and, by 9.30 am were in yet another internet café, this time in Newbury. Kate typed in a message.

Dissatisfied with very poor delivery service. Unless package is received by 6 pm tonight, documents and recordings will be dispatched to alternative user. Have package in helicopter in London region a.s.a.p. and await instructions as to delivery location.

KK

"To the point" said Riordan.

Palmer saw the email immediately. He had been watching his screen like a hawk for the last two hours. Sykes had called No. 10 around 4.30 am., as soon as O'Connell had rung off, but said not to wake the Prime Minister – just get him to call Sykes as soon as he did wake up, which had been at 6.15 am. Gerrard had contacted Palmer straight away, who had arrived in his office by 7.30 am; and, like Gerrard, had been trying to carry on the business of the day while all the time his mind was totally focused on Kate. What had shaken both men to the core was the news that Kate not only really *was* tied in with the IRA, but appeared to have a substantial military-style unit at her disposal. This, they recognized, totally changed the game; and the failure of their attempt to seize Kate raised the very real possibility that she would now go to the Press. They had discussed the possibility of sending an email to her, if only to give some indication that they were still open to negotiation – surely she wouldn't be stupid enough to blow the whole thing wide open straight away – not with Emmerson still safely tucked away? Perhaps not, Palmer had said, but the IRA might be. On the other hand, what could Palmer say in an email? 'Awfully sorry we didn't wipe you out but, hey, let's get back to sorting this thing out'. In the end they decided that they would wait until midday and, if they had heard nothing by then, would send an email, text as yet to be determined. Kate's email spared Palmer the trouble.

Palmer went straight to see Gerrard; and was frustrated beyond measure that he couldn't get to see him for another hour, because of some visiting dignitaries. When they did finally get together, Palmer read out the email to the PM.

"Well, that's it Andy. There's no way out. I can't deliver Emmerson by 6 pm. I don't have him. I don't even know where he is". He sat down, looking pale, almost grey. "I don't think I can face this". This might have been just emotional distress; or it might have been a suicidal intention; but the distinction by-passed Palmer. To his sometimes brutal but always intensely logical mind it conjured up options. He made no reply, but his brain was galloping.

"Alan, there might just be a way forward. Remember, the US want you around just as much now as before – maybe more. Think what's going to happen to their plans if their number one backer at the UN is busily being accused in the Press of multiple murder. I'll talk to them. Maybe we can work something out". Gerrard sat motionless. At first Palmer wondered whether the PM had taken in what he had said. But then, appearing infinitely tired and with his shoulders slumping lower, he nodded.

"Yes, Andy, do what you can. Thanks"

Palmer spent the next two hours talking first to the US Ambassador and then to a senior member of the US's considerable secret military intelligence forces in the UK. At shortly after 11.30 am. he replied to Kate's email.

Cannot deliver by 6 pm. Package is held by American service. Please call me.

He added the number of a mobile phone which he had obtained that morning.

Kate, with Riordan and O'Connell, were sat in one of their cars just off the M4 near Hungerford. This was the third location they had been at since 9.30 am. They had decided that, as they were now very near the end, they could risk using the mobiles they had brought; and would immediately change location when they had done so. They would not use any of them more than three times. Kate saw Palmer's message as soon as it came in. She read it out to the others. All three were equally stunned. It was Riordan who spoke first.

"That's got to be bollocks. Why would the Americans be holding Emmerson? It makes no sense. This is just a ploy, some sort of delaying tactic. It must be".

"I'm inclined to agree" said O'Connell. "What do you think Kate?"

"Like the man says, why don't we call him and find out? I'll talk to him". Kate realised that she had no way of insisting on this; but she was only too well aware that for O'Connell and the others, Paul was just another pawn in a game. For her he was the only reason she was in this potentially fatal situation; and she wanted to be as certain as she could that Paul would come out of all this alive. To her relief, and also to her surprise, O'Connell nodded.

"It's all been between you and him, who ever 'him' is, so far. You may as well continue the conversation. But you need to cut off after a couple of minutes – they'll be able to locate us almost immediately, so we need to be on our way; and you agree nothing with him without consulting Shaun and me first, is that absolutely clear?"

"Agreed "said Kate, who then took one of a number of mobile phones that O'Connell had in a bag in the back of the car; and phoned Palmer's number. He answered almost immediately.

"Yes?"

"This is Kate Kimball. To whom am I speaking?" How her mother would approve of her diction.

"My name doesn't matter. I have authority to speak and act on the matter in question".

"Good" said Kate. "Then please arrange for the package to be ready to be delivered by helicopter from a London airbase by this afternoon. No tales about him being with the Americans. It's not remotely credible".

"Sadly, it is not a 'tale' as you say; and all too credible. An organisation responsible to the US government is holding the package as security for delivery of a UK contract to support a forthcoming US project. I wish it were not so. My principal wishes to conclude a deal with you; but is not currently in a position to do so. If you give us more time we may be able to work something out". Kate relayed this to O'Connell, who mouthed that she should say she would call back later.

"I will call you back" said Kate and rang off.

"Let's get going Shaun" said O'Connell; and they took off, crossing over the M4 and heading south.

"What do you think?" O'Connell asked Kate. "What's your instinct – true or not true?"

"I don't know" replied Kate "but…..does it matter?"

"I don't follow" said Riordan.

"Well, if what we have been told is right, the US will be every bit as keen as Gerrard not to have his past exposed, at least……oh my God…. at least not until the 'forthcoming' US project is complete. It must be Iran – something to do with Iran. Maybe an attack. The news has been full of it recently. As soon as that, whatever it is, is over, Paul will be completely useless to them. They'll kill him".

Riordan took a hand off the steering wheel and put it on Kate's arm. "Those Americans who saved you said he would be coming back; and if he is being held by the Americans, then maybe they knew what they were talking about".

"And maybe they were talking rubbish, just humouring me. But, anyway, the main thing is that maybe it doesn't matter whether the US is holding Paul or not. The threat we present to Gerrard sounds every bit as big a threat to the US. So why don't we use that? Tell whoever it is on the other end of the phone that if the US really has got Paul, then unless they release him by a certain time – we can give them until early tomorrow – that ought to be enough time to get him from wherever they are holding him - if they are, that is - then we go public; and if Gerrard has him all the time, then the threat still works". O'Connell and Riordan looked at each other for a moment in silence.

"It works for me" said Riordan

"Okay, let's do it" O'Connell responded. "We'll call back in another twenty minutes or so, when we have put some distance between us and the last call".

In a lay-by north of Salisbury, Kate phoned Palmer.

"This is Kate Kimball again. I've no idea whether your story about the US is true or not; but if it is, they will, I'm sure, be very sorry at the consequences of continued non-delivery. So, kindly tell them that it is the same deal. I'll give them until 7 am tomorrow morning to deliver the package, by helicopter, to a location I will notify you of around 6 am. That's it. If they don't accept, please make sure that they know the consequences". Without having planned to, but just because it felt right, she switched off the mobile without waiting for any reply. She handed it to O'Connell, who threw it as far as he could into the trees beside the lay-by.

"That was well done" said O'Connell with a hint of a smile.

"We'll see" said Kate, grinning back and, for the first time for a long time, feeling a moment of satisfaction. She would have felt less so had she known that Palmer was also smiling. Kate had responded exactly as he had anticipated; and he could now proceed.

An hour later, back in Marlborough, O'Connell and Riordan were getting ready to bring their team up to date, when an email came through from Palmer, asking Kate to call him straight away. The three of them went out to the car and, some fifteen minutes later, on the outskirts of Chippenham, O'Connell passed her a new mobile. Kate dialled Palmer's number.

"This is Kate Kimball" she announced.

"I've spoken to the Americans" said Palmer. They are prepared in principle to consider releasing the package; but then they would have no way of preventing publicity which would result in…..let us say a severe reputational loss. Their project will be complete a week from now; and they therefore propose releasing the package a week today". Kate didn't feel the need to even discuss this with O'Connell and Riordan.

"That is not remotely acceptable; and I've had enough of all this code-talk. If what you say is true, then Dr. Emmerson will have ceased to have any value to the Americans by then; and there is nothing to stop them just disposing of him. If that is to be his fate, then be in no doubt, I will terminate their plans, not to mention Alan Gerrard's freedom; and I will do it tomorrow morning". The tone in which she delivered this final threat left no doubt in anyone's mind that she meant it. But Palmer had already anticipated this.

"The only condition under which they will act now is if you, Miss Kimball.... accompany the documents you are due to hand over, and remain their guest for a period of one week. They are confident that, in these circumstances, none of your associates will wish to rock the boat during that time. After one week their interest in the matter will cease; and you may return. As you know only too well, they have had your best interests at heart in the past; and would guarantee that you would come to no harm. So that is the deal they are offering".

Kate was, quite literally speechless. The blood drained from her face; and O'Connell and Riordan could see that she was deeply shocked. They both looked intently at her, awaiting an explanation; but she just sat there, her jaw rigid, her eyes staring at nothing.

"What did he say?" demanded O'Connell. Still Kate could not speak.

"What, for Christ's sake?" said O'Connell, looking straight into Kate's eyes.

"He said.... he said that the Americans will release Paul tonight if I take his place – a sort of hostage for a week. Then they say they will let me go". It was O'Connell and Riordan's turn to be shocked. In the silence that followed, each of the three of them was calculating furiously. Riordan was trying to compute whether the US could just afford to let Kate go after a week. O'Connell was trying to think out whether the US holding Kate would make any difference to the exposure of Gerrard which he was planning, whatever the consequences to Emmerson or Kate. She, on the other hand, recovering her senses a little, was focusing on a very obvious fault line in the plan; and it was she who, in the end, got to speak first, to Palmer, waiting at the other end of the phone.

"That may make sense for the Americans, but you will never just let me return, will you? I'll be the only card you've got to play, to stop me – or my associates – from telling the world what I know".

"I anticipated that you would think that" said Palmer, "but that's not what would happen. My principal's only way forward is to secure the documentation which you have. Whether he can trust you or not I do not know; but there is no other option. If all the documents are secured, then there will be no evidence to support anything you may subsequently say; and no reason to... extend your stay. If you retain any evidence and plan to use it, then all is lost anyway. It is only the Americans who want to shore up their position for a week, not us; and they are confident that this arrangement will achieve that".

O'Connell signalled that he wanted to know what was being said, but Kate, increasingly in command of events, indicated for him to wait.

"But you could use my presence as a lever, to avoid any risk that we might hold back some evidence and use it later".

"That might make sense for a short while, but your ......colleagues would never accept that for long. So it's not a practical strategy. May I also point out that my principal, whatever you may think of him, did not at any point in this whole matter want to take action against innocent members of the public; and would certainly not contemplate taking such steps now. The problem that you have faced in recent months was entirely US-driven; and they will be out of the picture in a week. But, in any event, this is all irrelevant. Whatever you and I may think, you either accept the US proposal or, they have made it quite clear, the package will be disposed of – with extreme prejudice. Don't make the mistake of thinking that is a bluff on their part".

O'Connell would wait no longer.

"Ring off. Tell him you will call back. Now". Kate did as he said and, as Riordan once again drove off, she filled them in on what Palmer had said. For some minutes, as they headed back eastwards, no-one spoke, though for a variety of different reasons. O'Connell was very clear in his mind that he would bring down Gerrard, and very soon. He had the recording of Sykes confirming that Gerrard was directly involved; but he needed Emmerson, with his evidence about Sellafield; and he needed Kate, who had filled in all the rest. He did not like the thought of Kate being held for a week one bit. Riordan had come to the conclusion that only Kate could decide whether to take the risk – did Emmerson mean that much to her? He had little doubt in his mind which way she would jump; and Kate did not disappoint him. Sitting in the front passenger seat and looking straight ahead she said

"I can't risk losing Paul, not now, not after all this. If I don't agree, there is no way that I can see Paul surviving. If I go along with them, we might both just somehow come through it".

She hadn't really thought about whether O'Connell would try to stop her; but he was some way ahead of her.

"If they were all like you, I could learn to love the Brits" he said, without any emotion. "You are one hell of a woman. But...." He was as quickly all business and logistics again "we have a problem. You and Emmerson being, however briefly, in the same location, together with the evidence we have, may be too big a temptation for them. They may just try to wipe you both out".

"I'm prepared to take that risk" said Kate. "I'm sure you can work out some way of handling it".

319

"We can try; but it's one hell of a risk" replied O'Connell "and, I'm sorry, but I'm not just thinking of the risk to you. It's your story – and Emmerson's – that will finish Gerrard. I can tell it; and I can back it up now, but from a washed-up IRA man – it'll be quite easy to discredit. It will be so much more powerful in your voice; and I don't want to risk that". Kate appreciated that this compliment was a rather back-handed way of saying that she might be gunned down when they came to swap her for Paul, but she wasn't going to point it out.

"Well, can't you come up with an absolutely fool-proof way of handling the swap?"

"I doubt it"

"So, you'll just take the chance that they are bluffing? Terrific. If we don't agree the swap, Paul's dead. I know it".

"If we risk the swap, you may both be dead. Maybe that's why they have insisted on the deal".

The three of them sat in silence, their different motives for engaging in the whole operation now brutally exposed. Kate, furious as well as distraught, spoke first.

"I won't help you bring down Gerrard if you leave Paul to die. I just won't do it". O'Connell's lack of a reply was, in some ways, more sinister than anything he might have said. "Surely you can work out something?" she pleaded.

"We may not need to" interjected Riordan.

"Why not?" asked O'Connell.

"We are missing a trick here" replied Riordan. "We said we wanted a helicopter because we can direct it to a precise landing spot where we will be waiting, well away from any ground support they may be planning. But, think about it. The helicopter comes in to drop Emmerson and pick up Kate. We will ensure that it has very little fire power available. We discussed that. Why not just take out the rotor blade? We can have some of our semis all round the plane. Take out the rotor and it's dead. They can't make off with Emmerson or Kate; and any attempt to take them both out would then be sheer suicide".

Kate, not for the first time, had very mixed emotions about this latest suggestion. On the one hand, it sounded a good idea – though a big question mark was already forming in Kate's mind - and, crucially, it would allow her to tell Gerrard's man that they would go along with the deal, which would keep Paul alive. But her own prospects were, she thought, not helped if, at the critical moment, O'Connell's men shot the helicopter to pieces.

"It's a thought" said O'Connell finally "A good thought". He then put into words what had bothered Kate. "I wonder why they haven't thought of it".

They turned north before reaching Marlborough and, as they drove, worked out some logistics for the operation to come. They would agree to go along with the swap; and set things up to go through with it; but, if O'Connell saw an opportunity, he would give the order for his men to open fire on the helicopter rotor. Kate, who was likely to be most at risk in this, agreed, but only on the condition that, if such an opportunity did not arise for any reason, then she would go through with the swap and take Paul's place. O'Connell was unhappy about this; but could see that Kate was not to be persuaded differently; and, in any case, was reasonably confident that he should be able to disable the plane. Twenty minutes later they stopped between Newbury and Abingdon. It was the nearest Kate had been to Oxford for some while; and she could not help contrasting what she had had in mind when she last left Oxford – whether, that was, she had anything very clearly in mind - and what had transpired since then. But she decided this was not good for her anxiety level; and focused on the next step in the pursuit of Paul – another call to Gerrard's man. She rang him and, having announced herself once again, went straight to the point.

"Please tell your US contact that I agree to bring the documents myself, in return for... the package which we are expecting. The details of delivery will be exactly as I specify, which I will communicate to you, as I said before, at 6 am tomorrow. Make sure a US helicopter is ready to move, with the package aboard, whenever I say. Is that all clear?"

"Perfectly" replied Palmer.

"The helicopter should be an Agusta 107, or similar size Sikorsky or Bell, with both side doors removed and fully fuelled. If I see anything larger the whole thing will be aborted. I will give instructions from this phone, via you, so make sure you have direct radio contact with the pilot. As the helicopter comes into land, it will be under intense surveillance, inside and out. Apart from the pilot and Dr. Emmerson there must, at most, be two others in the plane, one in the front with the pilot and one in the back with Dr. Emmerson. Is that all clear?"

"Yes" replied Palmer "but the Americans will not release Emmerson from the plane until you are inside it".

"And I will not enter it until Dr. Emmerson is out of the plane; so he will climb out one side while I climb in on the other. Is that agreed?"

"It is as far as I'm concerned" said Palmer. "I'll check with the Americans".

"I presume that Dr. Emmerson does not know what has been arranged?"

"No, I don't think he has".

"In which case, would you please ensure that he is blindfold? He might become somewhat.....unpredictable if he sees me; and I don't think any of us can take that risk".

"I will pass that on" said Palmer. "Needless to say, if the pilot sees anyone other than you at the landing site itself, the deal will be off; and Emmerson will be

dead. I hope that is clearly understood". Kate said that it was, broke the connection; and another mobile went out of the window into long grass
by the side of the road. Even before it hit the ground, Palmer was picking up the phone to Sykes.

They headed back to Marlborough and, by 2 pm. were busy picking up all O'Connell's men and transporting them and their weaponry to the third and final site which they had identified earlier in the week. This was a very large, flat grassy open field, near Devizes, south west of Marlborough, approached only by one very minor road and a muddy track, at least a mile from any habitation or, indeed, buildings of any sort. Hargreaves was still in quite a lot of pain but, having slept for around five hours, was starting to feel slightly better; and insisted on coming too. Having extracted a promise that he would go to hospital the next day, Kate agreed, but kept a close eye on him, though no more so than he did on her. It was very evident to him that the last ten days had changed Kate, dramatically. Her search for Paul had always been thought out and determined, but there had been a strong element of despair before – an underlying sense, no matter how much she sought to ignore it, that she would not, in fact ever see Paul again. Now, now she was quite different; more hopeful of success, certainly but, much more than that, virtually a military commander in manner, seemingly operating as an equal to, and certainly very well respected by, some of the most brutal militiamen the United Kingdom had produced in recent years. His feelings for her hadn't changed at all; but he recognised that she was now operating in a quite different world from him; and by tomorrow she might well have her beloved Paul back.

O'Connell's team spent the afternoon, checking their weapons and going over the plan that O'Connell and Riordan had made. There was consternation when O'Connell revealed that the Americans had insisted on Kate leaving in the helicopter – unsurprising as far as Hargreaves was concerned, but very revealing as far as O'Connell's men were concerned. None cared much if Emmerson survived – he had never been a significant part of the plan to bring down Gerrard; but most had warmed to Kate in the last week; and some were as reluctant to put her in danger as any of the men themselves. O'Connell, however, explained that, while this had been agreed, they were not in fact planning to let the helicopter leave. It would be disabled as soon as it touched down; and any attempt to attack Emmerson or Kate would result in a barrage of fire that would leave none of the Americans alive to tell the tale. Even then, some were clearly anxious; and Hargreaves hated the whole idea, but he was in no position to influence events; and O'Connell was not about to discuss the matter with any of them.

So, as dusk started to settle in, they went in twos and threes to visit the site itself. Six would be over a mile away, where they would carry out an early inspection of the helicopter with binoculars; and only then would they direct the plane to the main landing site. Kate would be positioned there, surrounded – but only at some distance - by the rest of O'Connell's men. Though it would be daylight – a precaution to make sure they could spot any attempt to send in back-up helicopters – they nonetheless would erect four of the large lamps they has used at Wallington House, shining upwards, to form a square to within which the US helicopter would eventually be directed. When they had all identified their locations, the men split up to return to their accommodation, as did Kate and Hargreaves, although much to his regret, the hotel had another room available for him. They ate together, the O'Connells and Riordan tactfully finding a separate table.

"Are you confident this is going to work?" he asked.

"No, I'm not, but I can't think of anything better" she replied, rather despondently.

"Can't one of O'Connell's men be out front when the plane comes in?" asked Hargreaves. "It's just going to be so dangerous".

"No chance" said Kate. "I'm not sure O'Connell would agree; but the main thing is that the pilot is expecting to pick me up. If there's no sign of me, he'll probably just fly off; and that could be it for Paul. I've got to do it". Hargreaves wanted to argue, but he could see how pointless it would be. They sat in silence.

"I'm sorry" Kate said

"Sorry for what? I said I volunteered".

"But I know why you did; and I'm so grateful – you been such a source of support to me – I'm just sorry that... well... I don't know what to say". He briefly held her hand.

"It's okay. I know. You have Paul; and if any woman ever deserved the man she loves, it's you. I'm just sad I didn't meet you first".

After the meal, they joined the others for a few drinks – perhaps more than was wise given what was planned; but Kate reckoned it would help her sleep. It was nevertheless still not 10 o'clock when they drank up and went to their rooms. They were all going to meet up at 4 am, to be in place at the landing site by 5 am at the latest; and so an early night was the order of the day. Kate got undressed, put on a nightdress; and then sat very still on her bed for a while. She hoped that their plan for the morning would work; but she hadn't, she told herself, come this far to see it all go wrong. It gnawed away at her that, if Riordan could think up a simple way to immobilise the Americans, surely they might as well – and have a way of dealing with it. If so, she would have to go through with what she had agreed with Gerrard's man. She pulled together the few clothes and overnight gear that had served her for nearly two weeks now – maybe they would have to see her through another week. She switched off the light and sank back into the bed, but sleep would not come; and the reason was all too clear. This could be the last night of your life, she reflected. At first it was a rather intellectualised idea, clear in her mind but not gripping her emotions. But, as she lay there, the thought began to seep through her whole being; and soon it began almost to paralyse her brain with fear. So much of the last few months had been looking back, to her life with Paul, wanting to re-create it; but now she was facing the real prospect that there would be no future, with Paul, or anyone. For the first time since Palmer had told her of the US terms, she began to wonder whether she could go through with it; and that simply made her even more fearful.

Shortly before 10.30 pm, as Kate lay there, frightened, her heart pounding, trying to calm herself enough to sleep, there was a light tap on her door. She went to the door and asked who it was .

"It's Neil. Can I talk to you?" She opened the door and he came in. He stood in front of her. "I'm sorry to disturb you, but…." He stopped, noticing how fraught and tense she looked. " Kate, you don't have to do this. Let O'Connell and his men handle it. They're used to all this".

"No, Neil, I have to do this. Don't try to persuade me, especially not now. I couldn't take it". She desperately wanted to change the subject. "What were you going to say?" Neil saw that he would not shake her resolve.

"I was lying there, thinking – thinking anything could happen tomorrow. Anything could happen to you. I'm sorry that sounds scary, but we both know it's true; and I thought, I just thought…..well I just thought that this may be the only remaining chance I have to tell you that I love you. You are the most wonderful, beautiful, amazing woman I have ever met, or ever will meet. I know that if all goes well, you will be back with Paul tomorrow; and I want you to be happy – after all you have been through for his sake I really mean that – but I can't let tomorrow happen without telling you what you mean to me; and I want very much to kiss you again". He moved closer to her and slowly started to put an arm around her shoulder. She stood there, unmoving, making no reply. Her head dropped a little; and he put both arms around her, pulling her gently to him. In the far recesses of her mind, Kate recognised that this was madness; but in her fearful state, the warmth of Neil's body, the re-assurance and support it offered and, at a more instinctive level, just the sympathetic touch of another human being, all conspired to render Kate quite motionless and passive in Neil's arms; and so they stood there, with Neil holding her in his arms, kissing her hair, so lightly she hardly noticed. She looked up at him and he gently kissed her on the lips. She kissed him back. He felt her body through the thin nightdress she was wearing.

"Neil, I can't……" she started to whisper.

"Shhh. Neither can I. Not with what feels like two cracked ribs". He smiled. "If I lie down I can barely move. Not quite how I hoped this moment would be, but....it's still the best moment of my life". He kissed her again; and then he let her go. He could see tears welling up in her eyes. "Don't be sad, Kate. Not now, not now everything is in place. You've got twenty very dangerous men on your side; and only three against them. It will be okay".

"You are a very wonderful man, Neil Hargreaves. I want you to know, if things..... well, if they don't work out tomorrow, how much you have meant to me".

"I'm glad" Hargreaves replied "but it will all work out fine, I'm sure"; and then he left.

CHAPTER 29

Shortly after 4 am, all but two of O'Connell's twenty men, Kate and Neil met up and together travelled to the field near Devizes. The other two, Raymond Fenlon and Willie O'Gara made their way north-east to Wantage, armed, besides their semi-automatics, with two mobile phones and a set of maps. By 5.30 am they were all in position, six of the men around a mile and a half away from the others, the rest of them at the main site. At 6 am Fenlon rang Palmer.

"I am calling on behalf of Kate Kimball. What is the position of the helicopter currently?" he asked, without further introduction.

"It's at the US base at Upper Heyford" replied Palmer.

"Do you have the co-ordinates?"

"Just a moment". There was a pause. "1 degree 12 West, 51 degree 52 North". Fenlon passed this on to O'Gara, who quickly consulted his maps.

"228" he said. Fenlon went back to Palmer.

"Tell the pilot to fly bearing 228 and wait for further instructions. I will call back in fifteen minutes. When I do, let me know his speed". Palmer agreed; and Fenlon called O'Connell to confirm what had happened. He and O'Gara then took off, heading towards Didcot. Fifteen minutes later, from the outskirts of the town, Fenlon called Palmer again, ascertained the speed of the helicopter; and said he would call again with further instructions. Shortly after 6.30 am, having calculated that it would now be approaching the first location, Fenlon called Palmer a third time and gave him the co-ordinates to head for, which he estimated the chopper would reach in about a further five minutes

"Tell the pilot to hover, at about forty feet, at that location. He will see four lights shining up at him and should remain stationary in the middle of them. Under no circumstances should he seek to land. We will then carry out a visual inspection of the plane. Is that clear?" Palmer said that it was and passed the message on. Less than five minutes later, as O'Connell's six men waited and listened, the helicopter came into view.

One of his men called O'Connell to say that the helicopter was coming in. O'Connell could, in fact, just hear the sound of the rotors across the early morning air. The helicopter, as instructed, headed slowly forward, until it was hovering approximately forty feet above the ground, in the middle of the torch beams. O'Connell's advance guard, spread around the plane, used their binoculars to look closely at the plane. They saw the pilot, a co-pilot; and, in the back, through the empty side panels of the plane, two seats with two further men seated on them, one with a blindfold, his hands resting on his lap in front of him. Behind, it was difficult to see in to the very back of the plane; but it was not a large area; and appeared to contain only some medium sized boxes. After a couple of minutes, O'Connell's man spoke to him again.

"Looks all okay"

"Is Emmerson there?" asked O'Connell.

"I can't tell if it's him, but there is a guy sitting there with a blindfold".

"And no sign of any back-up, in the air or on the ground?" asked O'Connell

"No, all clear".

"Good" said O'Connell; and rang Palmer's number.

"Tell the pilot to proceed, on bearing 323, for a mile and a half. The pilot will see four more bright lights. Tell him to put the plane down in the middle of them". Palmer made no reply, but a moment or two later, the helicopter started to move off in the direction of the main landing site. O'Connell handed the phone to Kate.

"You're on" he said. Here's the phone to talk to Gerrard's man; and this one is the open line to me". Kate slipped her large shoulder bag over her shoulder. It contained her clothes; plus copies of all the email correspondence with Palmer; and of the precious tape recording of O'Connell's conversation with General Sykes. O'Connell had said that there was little point in her carrying these with her – she wasn't going anywhere – but Kate insisted she did. They had no idea what sort of checks might be demanded before they would release Paul; and she refused to take any risk that Gerrard's people would see they had been double-crossed before Paul was free. And anyway, she had added, they were keeping copies; and it would be just as well that Gerrard knew precisely what evidence they now had of his actions. O'Connell had seen the force of this; and acquiesced. She nodded to him, taking the two mobile phones, one in each hand; and set off towards the middle of the landing site.

As Kate approached the landing site, she heard the helicopter – at first just a faint throbbing, but then a distinct clatter and finally, as it came in over some low trees at the edge of the field, a deafening roar. She stopped to look at it, less than two hundred feet in the air and descending as it approached; and, although she had been preparing for this moment for what seemed a lifetime, it hit her with an intensity she could barely stand that Paul might be – please God he must be – inside the helicopter and, all being well, they would soon be re-united. As she reached the centre of the four lights which O'Connell's men had switched on - barely seconds before the helicopter did the same, now only around forty feet above her - she realised that she was never going to hear anything on either of the mobiles she was clutching. But perhaps it didn't matter. She was only bait – no doubt already being identified from the helicopter through high-powered binoculars. Once the helicopter landed, O'Connell's men would disable it; and that would be an end to it – to the noise, to the fear shaking her body, and to the whole, terrifying nightmare of the last few months. This thought stuck in her mind as, looking up, she saw a man in some kind of military uniform leaning a long way out of the helicopter. He held something in his hand – it could be a small box or piece of equipment of some sort – and was indicating that he was going to drop it down to her. Kate had no time to think, or to do anything with the two mobiles she held. She simply dropped them on the ground and, less than a second later caught the object from the helicopter. It was a medium sized walkie-talkie radio, with a set of headphones clipped to it. Kate vaguely glimpsed the man in the helicopter indicating that she should put the headphones on, but needed no such instruction. The moment she did she could here a voice telling her to look up. As she did so, she saw, from one side of the helicopter, a harness on the end of a rope snaking down towards her; and from the other side, another harness being very slowly lowered. Strapped in it, looking pale – almost grey in the early morning light – and very stressed, was Paul.

Kate, despite her intention not to startle him, could not stop herself screaming his name; but Paul, even though he had somehow managed to wrench his blindfold off, had not as yet seen her; and certainly couldn't hear her above the din of the helicopter. She was about to shout again, when the voice over the head set said, with an admirable economy of words

"The helicopter will not land. Emmerson will be lowered only when you are ready to be winched on board". Kate stood there, dumb-struck. It took only a fraction of a second for her to see that they had been out-manoeuvred; but she was unable to move. Her body completely resisted the idea of allowing herself to be winched aboard the helicopter; but she was so close to freeing Paul – the only real purpose she had had in her life for months. The voice came again over the headset.

"Put on the harness or we will cut the line holding Emmerson". Kate looked up at Paul, still at least thirty feet above the ground. He still hadn't seen her. She looked at the harness, swinging in front of her at the end of the other line to the helicopter.

"I can't......" she started to say.

"That's it" said the voice. "Cut him loose and let's get out of here".

"No" Kate screamed. "No, I'll come up". She grabbed the harness and, as she did so, in that fraction of a moment, she saw O'Connell, some fifty yards away, racing towards her. She pulled the harness down over her head and shoulders, letting it sit over her chest and screamed again into the walkie-talkie.

"Do it now, let him down, now, now" and, as she did so, saw Paul being lowered rapidly from the helicopter.

It took only a couple of seconds before Paul was dangling just a few feet above the ground.

"Harness on" said the abrupt voice through Kate's headphones. She grabbed her bag and, as she did so, saw O'Connell closing in on her. At the same moment, Paul saw her.

"Kate" he screamed, so loud that she actually heard him. Ignoring O'Connell, now only a few yards from her, she looked at Paul and, through the deafening noise, through the sheer terror of the moment, despite all the pain and anger and despair since he had disappeared, for a second she smiled; and knew that Paul could see – the intensity of the moment acting like a drug on the brain, extending the fragment of time to an eternity of sensation, a suffusion of joy that knew nothing of the danger they were both facing, of the murderous game in which they had become mere pawns.

"I love you" she said, sure that although he could not hear her, he would know what she was saying; and then she saw Paul fall to the ground as someone in the helicopter released the rope above him. At the same moment she felt herself lifted off her feet, still clutching her bag. She didn't see O'Connell make a diving lunge to try to catch her; nor did she hear him yelling her name. She looked upwards, to the helicopter, and then back down at Paul as he scrambled to his feet, his face contorted with rage and despair. She wanted to wave – to let him know that things would be alright – but one hand gripped her bag, the other the harness biting into her chest; even more so as she felt the helicopter start to ascend with her hanging, still some ten feet or so below it.

A few seconds later she was level with the door of the helicopter; and felt strong arms pulling her inside. She was thrust into a seat behind the co-pilot next to a man who, from his build and bearing, was clearly used to being obeyed instantly. As she was registering this, her arms were grabbed from behind her by someone who must have been crouching in the back of the helicopter and, before she had time to realise what was happening, he had handcuffed her wrists behind her back. Her bag fell to the floor, from where it was retrieved by the man at her side. No-one spoke, partly no doubt because of the noise; but Kate doubted anyone would have said anything if they had been in a silent hot-air balloon. This was Gerrard's transport department – and clearly very efficient at it – but no more than that. The nose of the helicopter dipped as it rose rapidly. Kate looked down, but from where she sat she could make out nothing familiar on the ground; not O'Connell or any of his men, nor even the lights they had been shining. But handcuffed as she was, amid all the shuddering noise and vibration of the helicopter as it picked up speed; and amongst a group of men who, she was quite sure, would throw her out of the plane if so instructed, she felt surprisingly calm; and she was now sufficiently on top of the situation to understand, in a vague sort of way, why she was so calm. Paul was not only alive, he was free; and that must, she thought, be a substantial protection for her. She would have to go through with the deal – supply the information she had which Gerrard was clearly hoping, and expecting, would save him – but with Paul free they simply couldn't risk not releasing her afterwards. Whether they had anticipated that she – or rather O'Connell – had retained copies of the material she didn't know; but if she disappeared then Paul's evidence alone would finish Gerrard off. In any case, events were now way beyond her control. She had been prepared to swap places with Paul; and she had done so. The rest was up to Gerrard.

They flew on, the helicopter continuing to make a deafening noise; but Kate was aware only of the silence between its occupants. Her thoughts focused on Paul. He would be with O'Connell now; and she started to feel a new sensation – anger. Anger that she wasn't there with them, to introduce them, to see how they faced up to each other, to find out where Paul had been for the last four months, to hear his reaction to what she had been doing to save him, what she had been through in the process. No doubt O'Connell would be furious – with Kate for going through with the switch; and with himself for not foreseeing that the helicopter might forestall becoming vulnerable by the simple expedient of not landing; but that was too bad. With Paul free and copies of all the material retained, they still had much the upper hand. But she still felt a real rage that she was not there with them; and with that rage came a renewed determination to bring Gerrard down, however great his ability to orchestrate all the resources he clearly could command, to expose what he had done in order to hold on to power. To her surprise she also began to feel impatient. She just wanted to get off the wretched contraption she was flying in, hand over the material she had, get back to Paul; and then crucify Gerrard.

It was as well for her equanimity that she did not, in fact, know what was happening back on the ground. As Kate had anticipated, O'Connell, though outwardly in control of himself, was seething at what had happened; but deeper down his most primeval instincts were telling him that things had gone much more seriously wrong than he quite realised. Even before he got across to where Paul was starting to pick himself up, his inner senses had told him that if Gerrard had anticipated the plan to ground the helicopter, then he would also have anticipated that O'Connell had kept copies of the material in return for which he had released Paul; and if that was the case then both Kate and the project to expose Gerrard were in big trouble – and all the bigger in that he didn't yet see how. But he had lost the initiative; and was too experienced a commander not to realise it. As he got to Paul, his worst fears began to be realised.

"Who are you?" said Emmerson, in a menacing voice that totally ignored the circle of armed men converging on where he stood. O'Connell made no immediate reply. He looked hard at Emmerson, not least out of curiosity to see what sort of man had engendered such devotion – and sheer guts – from Kate, but also to appraise the man with whom he was now going to have to co-operate. He saw someone clearly quite imposing, tall, muscular; not, he thought, that good-looking, but someone like Kate would be unimpressed with the superficial. Making snap judgements in a way that had served him well in the past, he assessed Emmerson as rugged, tough-minded, resilient – not at all O'Connell's preconception of an Oxford academic – but clearly very intelligent. Whether he also had a good sense of humour he thought it unlikely he would discover at all quickly. Overall, though, someone he could work with.

"My name is Victor O'Connell; and I have been working with Kate to secure your release". He was about to go on, but Emmerson interrupted him.

"And you let her be taken – what were you thinking of?"

"That was not planned. My team were under instructions to immobilise the helicopter as soon as it landed. When it became clear that it wouldn't land I held off in order to save your life; and I tried to stop Kate from going through with the exchange; but she was determined to do whatever was necessary to free you; and I couldn't get to her in time. I'm sorry" Emmerson realised instinctively that O'Connell was not someone often given to apologising.

"So what will happen now?"

"I don't think Gerrard will allow her to come to any harm, not with you now free to talk"

"Gerrard, do you mean Alan Gerrard?" asked Emmerson, with undisguised incredulity. O'Connell nodded. "What in God's name has he got to do with all this?" He looked completely stunned. O'Connell shared the sentiment. It had not occurred to him that Emmerson might not know of Gerrard's involvement. In fact, he had no idea just what Emmerson did or did not know.

"Gerrard is why you were seized. I will explain everything to you but, first, it would be helpful if you could tell me just what happened to you; and what you know of the reasons". Emmerson, for the first time since he had stood up, looked around him, at the dozen or more men now standing round him.

"Who are you, and who is this…. team of yours?" O'Connell decided to back his assessment of Emmerson.

"We are Irish Nationalists, all except for Hargreaves there…" - he pointed to one of the younger men standing near by – "who is a Detective Sergeant from the Thames Valley police force, based in Oxford". Emmerson gave no sign that this news had fazed him at all. Maybe it was the resilience O'Connell had suspected or, more likely, the inner fury he felt that, whoever they were, they had let Kate go off alone into harm's way.

"What in Christ's name was Kate doing with the IRA; and how does a policeman from Oxford come into the equation? What is going on?" O'Connell grasped his arm.

"I said, I will explain everything; and then we will work on getting Kate back; but I need to know what you know first".

Whether it was tension or exhaustion, or just the physical contact from O'Connell, Emmerson didn't know; but he suddenly felt totally drained. He wanted to sit down, but there was nowhere to sit. He breathed a deep sigh; and then, with a grim look, and in an almost catatonic tone, addressed O'Connell.

"I answered a knock at my door; some men poured in and overpowered me. That's all I knew for a while. I was unconscious – I'm sure they injected me with something – and I came round in a cell where I have been held ever since. I have no idea where it was, but it took several hours flying last night to get me back to that helicopter. I was comfortable, well fed, supplied with books, allowed daily exercise and the guards – all Americans I think – were friendly enough; but there has never been one word of why I was taken nor, for that matter, why they decided to release me. You say this was the Prime Minister's doing?"

"It was, yes, but is there anything else you can tell me? How are they – or you for that matter – supposed to explain your absence?"

"That was very weird. They said I had to stay low – completely out of the picture – for a week. Threatened that it would be very serious if I showed up in Oxford before then; but after that they didn't seem too bothered. No explanation at all. I played along because I just wanted to get out; but I planned to head straight back to Oxford – couldn't see any reason not to. I didn't know then about Kate".

O'Connell could feel a tension growing in the pit of his stomach. He was now convinced that he was in the process of being out-manoeuvred by Gerrard, even though he wasn't yet clear how. He had had all the cards he needed – Kate, her story and all the evidence necessary to bring Gerrard down. But he hadn't been able to act because she wanted Emmerson back; and clearly wouldn't have played along without achieving that aim. Now they had got Emmerson back; but he'd lost Kate, Gerrard would know what evidence he had; and, most worrying of all, they seemed unconcerned about Emmerson. Everything was going downhill very fast.

"And you have no idea why you were taken in the first place?" he asked.

"None at all. Don't think I didn't ask, not to mention scream my head off at the guards; but I got not a hint of an answer; and in fact I don't think they knew either. All I got was just bemused silence. So, tell me what in hell is going on".

"Okay" said O'Connell. "But let's head up to the cars and get out of here. We're based in Marlborough. We can spend tonight there and then think about where we go from here". He started to head towards the cars and Emmerson accompanied him, with Riordan and Hargreaves a step or two behind. The rest of O'Connell's men started to follow.

"You carried out some research on one of the buildings at Sellafield?" said O'Connell.

"That's right" said Emmerson. "One of the re-processing plants. I'd developed a much more sensitive test for structural weakness, which identified a problem". He paused. "But that wouldn't be any sort of reason to lock me up. I reported my findings, and kept a copy, in case there was any resistance to my results. But there wasn't any problem. They scaled down the operation and arranged to bring forward some major reconstruction work. There wasn't any risk".

"Not to the plant, or the local population, no" agreed O'Connell. "But a huge risk to Gerrard. Your results were picking up the impact of an attempt – a failed attempt – to blow up the plant back in 1983. Gerrard was a junior minister then and set about covering up the attack. Unfortunately for him, through a stroke of luck, the police had, meantime, arrested the five people responsible. Gerrard would have been finished politically anyway – the public was in an ugly mood over the government's failure to stop attacks on the mainland – but if the cover-up became known it would have been ten times more serious for him. So......" O'Connell paused, partly because of the gut-wrenching feeling he felt every time he thought of what had happened, partly to impress on Emmerson the enormity of what he was about to say......."he got custody of the five who had carried out the attack, spirited them away; and had them murdered, in the Irish Republic – made to look like an accident but we all knew the truth. He couldn't risk all of that coming out, so when he heard about your work, he had your research records stolen, no doubt clamped down on any of this spilling out into the press, and then had you to deal with".

They had reached the cars, but they made no attempt to get in. Emmerson leant gently against the car, as if he might shatter otherwise, and stared at O'Connell, trying to take in what he had heard.

"The attack on Sellafield – that was you?"

O'Connell nodded. "Four very brave men and one woman, butchered by Gerrard. I know, we were trying to murder Brits; and they have murdered enough of us; but that is, or was, the war we were fighting. My team were killed in cold blood, not as part of that war, but purely to save Gerrard's career". He

332

fixed Emmerson in his eye. "That's why we want him". Emmerson seemed to slump further against the car.

"But why did they keep me alive then? If what you say is right, I'm a huge threat to him. He could have had me quietly disposed of; and no-one would be any the wiser".

"I can only give you a partial answer to that" O'Connell replied. "Let's get going and I'll explain". They got into the back of one of the cars, with two of his men in the front; while Riordan and Hargreaves took another. As they headed off, O'Connell continued.

"For some reason, Gerrard got the US involved. It was the Americans who took you and, as you said, kept you under lock and key. It seems that they have been holding you as a lever, to get Gerrard to go along with them on some major political issue – Kate reckoned it is an imminent attack on Iran. They evidently thought that your research work could, in fact would, finish Gerrard – not just politically, but end up putting him on a multiple murder charge; and Gerrard clearly believes the same. It's as well the US is involved. I've no doubt that Gerrard would have disposed of you. What's more, swapping you and Kate has only bought Gerrard another week, whereas it sounds like it has bought the Americans all the time they need. If they have got Kate, and reach their endgame soon, then they can afford to let her go in a week's time. Bad for Gerrard, but no-one can touch them. You said you thought your captors were Americans; and Gerrard's man on the phone said the Americans were involved. But that's it. Not a shred of real evidence. They're squeaky clean".

"That's good for Kate then?" asked Emmerson, barely keeping up with O'Connell's logic.

"It would seem so" replied O'Connell. "The only thing is, I don't remotely trust Gerrard just to sit idly by and let this happen; and having no explanation for your disappearance – that doesn't sound good. Well, we will have to go along with them, for Kate's sake; and I can't get Gerrard without her".

Emmerson registered with some relief that they were very definitely on the same side, if for quite different reasons.

"How on earth did Kate figure all this out, about the attack on Sellafield – even I didn't know there had been one – and about Gerrard; and how did she hook up with you? It's all quite incredible".

"You have one amazing woman there" said O'Connell "And I don't know all the details. Basically, she found out that your computer files had gone; and then the police, who had initially been very helpful, turned decidedly unhelpful. She got very suspicious, followed up on some of your consultancy projects, and got on the track of rumours about an explosion at Sellafield, which was passed off as an electrical failure. Somehow she tracked down the policeman who arrested my team, saw that something must have happened to them – there was never an announcement of an arrest, or a trial – and then headed for Belfast. She realised that there had to have been a cover-up; and worked out it could only have been Gerrard – which also explained why you were such a potential threat now. She came looking for relatives of two of the team who were killed; and that led to me. We were all very sceptical at the start – I even wondered if she wasn't some sort of British *agent provocateur* – but we checked her out and realised that we had a ….shared interest so to speak. The only problem was, we didn't have any actual evidence against Gerrard. Fortunately, he didn't know that; and we used that to get some – mainly emails and tapes of our communications with Gerrard's organiser. I'll let you see it. The problem is, Kate has a copy of it with her. That was the deal – the evidence for your release. Then immobilise the helicopter and we'd have been sitting pretty. Now I'm not so sure. They'd be mad to touch Kate – they must reckon we've kept copies of the evidence and if Kate were….out of the picture, there'd be nothing to stop us going public. On the other hand they'd be equally mad to let her go – our story would be all the stronger. The only thing that makes any sense is if the Americans really are holding her to ensure Gerrard supports them on Iran - if that is their strategy - and then are content to throw Gerrard to the wolves. But I can't believe Gerrard will just sit and wait. What does *he* gain from you staying out of sight for a week?"

"I don't know" said Emmerson. "Any way, it would be very hard going back to a normal life at Oxford without any idea of what is happening to Kate. Which leads to another question. How do they expect to explain Kate's absence – even if it is only a week?"

"I think I know the answer to that" O'Connell replied. "Kate realised she was up against some very powerful opposition – in fact at one point Gerrard tried to have her killed……" He meant to continue but Emmerson interrupted him.

"What, what are you saying? What happened?"

Two men broke into her house while she was there – they were going to make it look like suicide, grief at losing you I suppose – but, although she didn't know it, she was being minded by the Americans; and they rescued her".

"Christ, poor Kate" said Emmerson "What she must have been through – I'm surprised she's still sane".

"She's the sanest, and the most determined woman I've ever met" said O'Connell "And I have met a few in my time, in the Cause. You're a lucky man. Anyway, before she took off for Belfast, she took time off work and let everyone know that she was going for a holiday – trying to get herself straight after losing you – in Scotland. Off on the Western Isles. That's where her friends think she is. Gerrard will know that from Hargreaves, so there's no problem for them on that score".

"From Hargreaves?" said Emmerson. "Where doe he fit in?"

"He was the detective who originally investigated your disappearance. But he was soon replaced by someone who was, no doubt, acting on instructions ultimately coming from Gerrard. He helped Kate as much as he could, but then got picked up by some very nasty customers - I'd guess security forces being fed a line that Kate was a danger to national security – and as she had by then joined up with us, that wasn't at all implausible. They worked him over, but we managed to get him away. He'll be a valuable part of the story when we go public". O'Connell decided that that was all Emmerson needed to know about Hargreaves. If there was more he should know – and O'Connell thought there probably was – it would be for Kate to say so.

They talked some more about what had happened, options – for Gerrard, for the Americans, for themselves - but made little progress before arriving back at their hotel in Marlborough. O'Connell arranged for some of his men to head back to Belfast immediately, the rest the next day. He himself would stay in Marlborough overnight; and. Emmerson agreed that, if he was to stay out of circulation for a week, then staying with O'Connell was the best place for him. Hargeaves needed to go to hospital, but did not welcome the idea of going back to Oxford, where he would be very easy to find; and O'Connell agreed that two of his men would accompany Hargreaves back to Belfast straight away. O'Connell reckoned that the hospital in Belfast would probably think Hargreaves was a drug dealer when they saw his injuries, but he'd be a lot safer there. Hargeaves said he would call the Thames Valley Police to say that he was unwell; and would be off for a few days.

Just as they were heading into the hotel, O'Connell's mobile rang. When he answered it, a voice said, without introduction and in a very peremptory manner "Put Emmerson on". It was partly the manner – O'Connell was not used to be talked to in that way – but also the need to get back off the defensive position he now felt he was in, that led to O'Connell's reply.

"Anything you have to say you say to me". There was a slight pause.

"This is not my usual area of operations" said Palmer "but let me be very clear. Miss Kimball will lose a finger for every five seconds I am kept waiting to speak to Emmerson". Even Palmer himself didn't know if he was bluffing. He was very used to bullying and threatening - politicians, civil servants, journalists - and he had on numerous occasions followed through, quite literally ruining careers if he thought the situation warranted it. In recent times his reputation was generally sufficient; and to have someone flatly refuse to co-operate was as unusual as it was irritating. He was now in deeper waters, but had some extremely angry special forces at his disposal; and was not afraid to play hardball. He waited for Emmerson to come on the line. Unfortunately for Palmer, powerful as he was, he had never had to deal with a man like O'Connell before. O'Connell turned away from the others in the hotel lobby, so that Emmerson would not hear him, and started to head back outside. He spoke quietly into the phone.

"Cut her tits off for all I care – she's just another fucking Brit as far as I'm concerned. If you have a message for Emmerson I'll take it – it's you who has five seconds".

Palmer was shocked to the core, not particularly because his threat – idle or real he still didn't know – had failed to get him Emmerson on the line, but at the realisation that holding Kate – what he thought of as his trump card – might cut no ice with the Irish bastards she had teamed up with. Emmerson would be compliant – of that he had no doubt – but how much sway would Emmerson have with committed Nationalists out to destroy Gerrard? 'Not much', was the rather obvious reply. Time to make the best of it.

"Don't fuck me around. I know some people who might well do just that. Meanwhile, tell Emmerson that if he stays completely hidden for a week, Kimball will be released. If he doesn't, then it will go a lot worse for her; and he will certainly never see her again. That may not bother you, you arsehole, but it will bother Emmerson; and without him, you're fucked". Palmer immediately switched off his phone, shocked now at how angry he had become – not used to any opposition he realised, still less failing to get his way – and feeling better for the abuse he'd managed to get in without reply. As for the bigger game, he felt he was still on track.

O'Connell heard the line go dead, and smiled to himself. He'd sensed the bluster in Palmer's reply. Whoever he was, he wasn't now going to risk much more serious retribution if things went wrong by pointlessly mutilating an innocent woman. They had been like two stags; and O'Connell had won – that was all. He turned back to the others, who waited for an explanation.

"Gerrard's man, with a message for you" he nodded at Emmerson. "Nothing new, though. He was just making the threat to Kate explicit, if you show your face in under a week. The thing is, we know that's important to the Americans; and, I suppose, for Gerrard, a week is a week, but what then? It doesn't make a lot of sense".

"Well, we'll just have to see, won't we" said Riordan.

CHAPTER 30

Kate was also in wait-and-see mode. She had been blindfolded for the helicopter journey; and had no idea in what direction they had headed. They landed after what she estimated might be an hour or so. The blindfold was removed, but not the handcuffs; and she was assisted from the plane – none too gently – before being marched off across the tarmac to a waiting 4x4. She thought of asking for her bag, but decided to spare herself the breath – and the anguish. She was clearly at an airfield base – not exactly surprising she told herself – with a collection of nondescript buildings of various sizes. The ground looked very flat as far as she could see – maybe she was in Lincolnshire but, having never been in the county before, who knew? She got into the car, with the two men from the back of the helicopter either side of her, plus a driver; and they headed off into some trees lining the side of the airfield. Almost immediately they stopped, outside a large, rather rambling, Victorian looking building. Kate was taken inside, up two flights of stairs; and handed over to two young but no-nonsense looking women, each with pistols in holsters. Kate was shown into a rather large room, in need of some re-decoration but reasonably clean and comfortable looking, with a row of bookshelves and a selection of books. The room had one good-sized window above a bed on the wall opposite the doorway, but with very sturdy looking bars across it; and the view was almost completely restricted by the trees that grew right next to the house at that point. She could see a bathroom off at the side, which proved to have no windows. One of the women finally spoke.

"Whenever one of us opens the spy-hole in the door, you get over by the window or on the bed. Is that clear?" Kate nodded; and the two left, locking the door behind them

For a moment or two, Kate could feel panic begin to well up inside her. She had no idea where she was, or even any very clear idea who was holding her; and nor would Paul or O'Connell. She was clearly a very major threat to Gerrard; and she had no illusions about what he would be prepared to do to protect himself. In fact, if they really believed that she and O'Connell had been straight with them – brought the material evidence of Gerrard's guilt without keeping copies – then she might as well be dead. The only thing that kept her from freaking out completely was that they had brought her here, clearly, it would seem, for some time. Well, she could tell them, as soon as she got the chance, that destroying the evidence she had brought – and her along with it – would not solve Gerrard's problem; and, no doubt stupidly – but the human spirit soars eternal – she clung to the fact that they had said they would only hold her for a week. She could manage that if she had to. She had a wash, looked idly through the books on the book-shelf – mostly cheap thrillers, but there were one or two that she could use to pass the time – and then, quite suddenly, felt exhausted. She lay down on the bed and, in a few minutes, had fallen asleep.

She was woken by the noise of the spy-hole cover in the door being drawn back. An eye checked she was nowhere near the door, whereupon it was unlocked, one of her two female guards came in and, without a word, deposited her bag on the floor. She was followed by the other guard, who came in with a tray of food. She placed it on a chest of drawers; and they both left, locking the door behind them. 'I've stayed at better hotels' Kate muttered to herself; and then, to cheer herself up 'and I've stayed at worse I suppose'. I must have known, she thought, that it all might come to something like this, though quite when she had contemplated it she couldn't now say. But, she had found Paul, when everyone thought he was dead; and she had got him released – using a bunch of very dangerous men it was true, but it was all her idea; and it had been a great success. She just needed to get back to Paul – Gerrard she would leave to O'Connell – and then life would be, once again, as it should be, as it had been before she went to California. While these thoughts went through her mind, she unzipped her bag. As expected, her own things were there, but of the tapes and email print-outs there was no sign. She unpacked, ate the food that had been delivered – not great but quite edible – lay back on the bed and, no doubt to her surprise if she had noticed, fell asleep again.

As she slept, Hargreaves and two of O'Connell's men set off for Liverpool; and the rest of O'Connell's team packed up and made plans to make their several ways back to Belfast. Meanwhile, the material from Kate's bag was being driven down to Palmer in London. Kate's guess that she was in Lincolnshire was wrong, but not that wrong. She was in fact in the original headquarters of a US air force base in the north of Norfolk, not far from the Lincolnshire border. Palmer and his US contact had agreed that Kate would stay there until the first wave of attacks on Iran were over, whereupon she would be handed over to Palmer or, more precisely, security forces answerable only to General Sykes; and then Palmer would start the next phase of his plan. But he needed to see the evidence that could bring Gerrard down immediately; and as long as the Americans had Kate in exchange for Emmerson, that was fine with them. This didn't stop them making copies of it all before releasing it for shipment to Palmer; but they had little doubt that Palmer would have anticipated that.

Although Palmer had the material shortly after lunch, other commitments – and the need for total secrecy – meant that he did not get round to inspecting the material until later that evening. In some respects it was very much as he expected – not terribly intelligible by itself but, linked to a narrative that Emmerson and Kimball could readily supply, it would finish Gerrard. It would also finish Palmer off; and quite probably General Sykes as well. But in another respect he was aghast. It was clear that, up until the point when Kimball had contacted him – and even more, to the point when he replied – neither she nor her Irish friends had had any solid evidence against Gerrard at all. If he had just ignored her letter, they would have had nothing. He could barely contain the fury he felt at having been duped so easily; and almost hurled the glass of wine he was holding against the wall. Only as he started to calm down did he realise that this did at least increase the chances of his current plan working. Then another thought came to him. He picked up the phone and, twenty minutes later was through to the US Ambassador on a secure line.

"Sam, about our project. It all seems to be going according to plan – the swap's made, you have the Kimball woman as the insurance which will see you through. But there is still my master's position to sort out when the immediate crisis is over. It would help a lot if I could have Kimball as soon as possible, rather than after the attack. The Ambassador's speech is already written for the UN meeting; and the attack will have happened by the time of the Parliamentary debate. So you have what you need: his support - and we are very confident he will take enough countries with him to make the attack defensible – and the use of the bases here. But I need time with Kimball if I'm to salvage his position afterwards". There was a pause at the end of the line. All Palmer's political instincts told him it was an ominous one; and he was not wrong.

"Sorry, Andrew, no can do. The President's instructions were very clear; and he has everything – I do mean everything – riding on this. The day after the attack, she's yours".

"But is that really necessary, Sam? President Hamilton must know that Alan fully supports him. The only risk is the Party, but they are not going to be in a position to cause any trouble until the debate; and by then it will be too late". There was another, even longer pause.

"The stakes are very high, Andrew, maybe higher than you realise. I shouldn't say this, but..... well maybe you should talk it through with Gerrard".

"What does that mean?" said Palmer, his hackles beginning to rise. "How could the stake *be* any higher?"

"Look I'm just trying to be helpful. We can't change the arrangements with Kimball; and if that's a problem, I think you should talk to Gerrard about it. That's all". Palmer recognised he would get no further. Feeling distinctly worried, he rang off and made arrangements to go straight round to Gerrard in his flat over No. 11.

When he arrived, he realised for the first time how much Gerrard seemed to have aged in the last few weeks. Not surprising, he thought, but grim all the same. Gerrard poured him a drink and Palmer pitched straight in.

"Alan, I spoke to Sam Hansmeyer, asked him to release Kimball to us now – so I can sort this bloody mess out – but he wasn't having any of it. I explained that you were 100% behind him; and the party can't derail things now; but he just dug in. Hinted that there might be more to it all than I knew. *Is* there anything more I should know?" Gerrard sat, motionless, looking at his glass of whisky.

"Alan, *is* there? I think I can get you out of this; but not if there is something I don't understand." Again Gerrard said nothing; but he looked at Palmer with such a mournful look that Palmer realised he had been working in the dark.

"Well, that's it. I'm out of this. Sort your own fucking mess out". He got up and headed for the door.

"Don't go" said Gerrard. "I'm sorry, I didn't want to involve you. It won't effect how we deal with Kimball and Emmerson; but there's no way the Americans will release Kimball until after they've dealt with Iran".

"And why is that?" snapped Palmer. If it was possible, Gerrard turned even more ashen.

"You know that the US plan is to take out everything – all of Iran's nuclear capability – in one go. The reactors, bomb factory, heavy water plant, their Uranium mines, even their nuclear research centres, ten sites in all. Well, they've concluded that at least four of the sites – the two mines, one of the uranium enrichment plants and the bomb factory itself, and maybe one of the reactors as well - are so deeply buried that conventional weapons won't cause them much damage. Might slow them by a year or so, but that's never going to stop them; and politically they will never get another chance. So........." he paused as his voice slightly faltered "..... they're going to take them out with nuclear strikes – not huge by current standards, but not far short of Hiroshima. They're going to give the Iranians a few hours notice, which they reckon is long enough for everyone to get far enough away; but it will be only the second time that anyone has ever actually used nuclear weapons in anger; and its going to be a political catastrophe". He paused. Palmer stood rooted to the spot, his whole body rigid. For probably the first time in his life, he was rendered literally speechless. What he had heard was so appalling, so completely insane, his mind couldn't fully take it in. He started to say something – he had no idea what – anything to break the screaming silence, but Gerrard went on before Palmer could get even a sound out.

" The moment I heard it was even a possibility, I told Hamilton he was mad, but they foresaw what I would think. That's why they kept Emmerson alive. That's why they are holding Kimball. They want at least some international support for what Hamilton is planning; and they want the use of their bases to support a nuclear attack. If I back off from either, they'll make sure the Sellafield incident becomes public". Gerrard was about to go on, but abruptly stopped, put down his glass and started to rub his eyes.

Palmer sat down again, transfixed by what Gerrard had said. Beyond shock, still almost beyond thought, he tried to digest the awful, unbelievably dreadful news. A first-strike nuclear attack by the US in the Middle-East, supported by the British Prime Minister. And then, suddenly, just when he thought things couldn't be any worse, he realised that they might be.

"Alan, tell me you didn't give permission for the nuclear weapons to be delivered from here. You couldn't do that – it would be suicide".

"No, they didn't ask that. The nuclear warheads will be delivered by computer-controlled missiles, launched from US battleships in the Gulf. But even they wouldn't be enough on their own. The aircraft from here will be carrying blockbuster bombs, which will, I gather, gouge great holes in the sites – though not enough to destroy the underground facilities – and then the nuclear warheads will be directed into the holes created. Hamilton said they can do this with an accuracy measured in inches; and that's what will destroy the sites completely".

"But you are still giving permission for the US to use British sites as part of a nuclear attack?" said Palmer.

"If I hadn't, then suicide would be far and away my best option. If I pull the plug on their plans while they're holding Kimball, then I'll spend the rest of my life in jail. It's as simple as that".

"But.....Alan.....you can't, I mean, you can't involve the UK in a nuclear strike. We will be a pariah state for decades; and the target for every terrorist group the Middle-East has ever produced".

"Don't you think I don't know that" shouted Gerrard. "I know, its lunacy. When they told me it was the only way to get at the sites, I said Hamilton should back off; but he wouldn't. I asked him why he was so determined. He said that the Israelis had made it very clear that if the sites weren't destroyed, then they would take them out with nuclear missiles themselves. Remember that Iran has pledged to wipe Israel off the face of the earth; so Hamilton doesn't think they're bluffing. But American foreign policy has always been incredibly pro-Israeli, for reasons you know well; and Hamilton isn't going to allow Israel to become the centre of a Middle-East bloodbath. So, he'll do the deed - with British support".

"All because they're holding Kate fucking Kimball somewhere? This can't be happening". Palmer's head was now throbbing so much he was starting to feel a little dizzy.

"No, not just because they're holding her, but because of what she knows and the evidence she has. Oh, I know they've sent it to you; but don't think for one moment that they won't have copied it. I ordered the death of five people, four men and one woman, in cold blood. It was a long time ago; and it seemed at the time the best, in fact the only way out of the situation I was in; and they were a bunch of terrorists, potential mass murderers - for Christ sake they tried to blow up a nuclear power station – but Kimball knows it, she can prove it; and the Americans will use that if I stop them flying from our sites. So, this *is* happening; and there is nothing I can do about it".

Palmer was about to respond, still shocked and incredulous but, rather unusually for him, held his tongue and tried to organise his thoughts. That Gerrard was prepared to go through with the attack, no doubt destroying his political career in the process, was now crystal clear. The prospect of spending the rest of his life in prison, he silently conceded, did rather change one's priorities. Even so, a nuclear attack on Iran did not bear thinking about. Except that it looked like it was going to happen and he *had* to think about it. Maybe one step at a time.

"What on earth possessed Hamilton to buy this?" he asked quietly. "He's no war-crazed madman. It can't just be the Jewish lobby".

"You'd be surprised how powerful it is" said Gerrard, despondently. Very difficult to win a U.S. Presidential election without Jewish money; but, no, it isn't just that. Hamilton has, or thinks he has –or someone has fed him a convincing line – that he has a unique sense of history, in particular US military history. He's quite convinced that every major military enterprise by the United States in the 20th Century has been characterised by being far too late and, as a result, very costly to both US interests and the lives of US servicemen. It's not just that they turned up late for World War 2, hell, World War 1 for that matter because of US isolationism – though Hamilton's in no doubt that Hitler would have been smashed three years earlier if the US had entered the war in 1939. No, his main point is that, if they had been 'realistic' – his word – and therefore prepared, then the US would have taken out the Japanese fleet earlier in 1941 – a sort of reverse Pearl Harbour – which would have reduced US casualties in the Far East to near-zero. He thinks that if the US had taken Vietnam seriously from the start – or been allowed to – including a major US presence in Cambodia and Laos, the war would have been won. In fact, he says, if you go to Vietnam now, it's clear the US did win; but he thinks a lot of American lives could have been saved by early, pre-emptive action. He sees the Iraq war as an entirely avoidable disaster if only the US had gone on to Baghdad in 1991. He now thinks there are only three serious world problems – climate change, African poverty which, by the way, he thinks is purely political, not economic, and the nuclear pretensions of North Korea and Iran. If the attack on Iran works, North Korea will be given six months - if they don't dismantle everything and allow unfettered UN inspection, he'll take out their nuclear capability as well. Bingo – no more problems". Gerrard poured them both more drinks.

"But that's lunacy isn't it?" said Palmer, conscious that despite the drinks, his throat felt very dry. "For a start, it'll be as much political suicide for him as we both know it is going to be for you. Christ, look what Iraq did for Bush".

"He doesn't think so" replied Gerrard wearily. "And he has some heavyweight political advisors who agree with him. He says that Bush was hugely popular when he went into Iraq. The US public were right behind him while he was winning a quick, decisive war. What finished Bush was the years of attrition afterwards. But in Iran, there isn't going to be an afterwards – just wipe out the nuclear threat once and for all and then get out. And that's not all - he says Bush Senior was so popular after winning a quick war in Kuwait in '91 that no-one wanted to stand against him – all the leading Democrats thought they would ruin their chances next time round if they stood and lost. That's why a nobody called Clinton, who had nothing to lose and a name to make, stood. But twelve months on, the economy had gone to pot; and no-one wanted Bush or the Republicans. So Clinton got in. But the point, according to Hamilton, is that the US loves a quick winner; and that's what he plans to be". Palmer sat, nursing his drink, almost mesmorised by what he was hearing. Gerrard went on.

"He's also thought through the party politics of it. He says that Bush was inevitably opposed by Democrats; and then lost some moderate Republicans, so he was bound to go down. Hamilton reckons he'll lose some Democrats, but he thinks – says he knows, though on what basis I don't' know – that a lot of Republicans will support decisive action in Iran – National security and all that – and so the maths works in his favour".

"But surely this will generate the biggest threat to America's national security since 9/11. Every terrorist group in the Middle East and beyond will want some of the action after a nuclear strike on Iran; and there will be no shortage of countries willing to help them".

"That's exactly what I put to him. His oh so reasoned answer was to point to what the US has quietly be doing for the last few years in terms of border security and, less well known perhaps, internal security as well. Their formal checks, massive surveillance – they can, in principle, get to every single electronic communication in the world - not to mention a huge infiltration operation – he said that around one in every five in the terrorist training camps, local cells in the West, even the government officials and not so officials who give them assistance, are now on the US payroll in one way or another. All a response to 9/11 but completely non-partisan policy".

"And if all this doesn't deliver?" asked Palmer. "They may have got rid of Bin Laden, but Al Qaeda is still very much in business".

"That doesn't faze Hamilton at all. He just quoted 9/11. Asked me if I could have imagined a more serious terrorist attack, bringing down the two tallest buildings in New York with the deaths of over 3,000 people – absolutely terrible - and what did it do to America? Nothing, except make its population more ready to attack anyone who they regard as a threat. As long as he stays well away from long, drawn out wars – or a long drawn out peace come to that - body bags coming home every week – he thinks he'll be as popular as can be".

"You said this was all the 'reasoned' answer" said Palmer. "Does that suggest there is an unreasoned one?"

"Maybe" said Gerrard. "Hamilton summed it all up by saying that the US was the only superpower left in the world; and it wasn't going to be jerked about by a bunch of medieval religious fanatics. I said to him that that didn't sound either very accurate or the most sophisticated analysis of the situation I'd ever heard. Do you know what he said? 'Whatever'. Like some fucking teenage imbecile 'Whatever'. Said it with a smile too; so maybe he was just pissing me off deliberately. But there is no doubt – no doubt whatsoever – that he has thought this all through, doesn't give a shit for world opinion; and is going to act like who he is – the leader of the world's only superpower".

"Alan, you said he smiled. You were face to face? This was during your visit in January?" Gerrard nodded. "Then why…….." For the second time, Palmer was so angry he couldn't get the words out. "Why didn't you tell me at the time?"

"Because Hamilton doesn't want anyone – and that includes all but about four of his closest advisers in Washington – to know anything about this until after Iran is dealt with. He knows perfectly well that if people, in the US and everywhere else, start debating such a policy, it's dead. He thinks Kuwait worked because it was a fast response to Saddam's invasion; Iraq because it was a response to 9/11. Christ, do you think we would ever have attacked the Falklands if we had sat about for six months discussing it? His strategy is to do it and it's done. He thinks it'll make him stronger at home; in terms of world opinion he'll settle for another coalition of the willing for the operation against Iran, which is where I come into his plans; and then he'll turn his attention to eliminating poverty in Africa and reversing global warming. He thinks he'll end up a fucking saint; and he might just be right".

Both men sat there in silence. Both were exhausted; and there seemed nothing more to say. Palmer veered wildly in his mind between, on the one hand, the horrific logic of it all and, on the other, the fear that Hamilton might be suffering some form of dementia or, at the very least, incipient megalomania. Only three things seemed certain: that Hamilton was deadly serious; that the rest of the world would be apoplectic come Wednesday evening; and that, even if Hamilton's analysis of how Americans would respond was right, the public in Europe would be at the forefront of the condemnation that would be poured on Hamilton - and Gerrard. Palmer stood up.

"I need to think about this overnight" he said. "See what's to be done".

"Do that" said Gerrard. "If there's any way out of this, I don't know what it is; and God, I've tried to find one".

CHAPTER 31

Few of those concerned, one way or another, about Kate slept well that night. O'Connell and Riordan stayed up late, discussing any number of scenarios, but eventually went to bed and had restless nights, worried that they had, in every sense, lost the plot. Emmerson, who had been set up in one of O'Connell's spare bedrooms, was sick with worry about Kate. Hargreaves had a rather better night, in Belfast General Hospital, but only because he was dosed up on painkillers. Gerrard spent yet another night wondering what he could do and knowing there was nothing he *could* do except go along with Hamilton and then withdraw from politics - the alternative was too horrendous to contemplate. Meanwhile Palmer spent the first half of the night still just trying to assimilate what he had heard; and the second half thinking about what could be done. At one point it occurred to him that he could tell a couple of senior cabinet ministers what he knew; and get them to force a Cabinet Meeting at which the policy of support for the US could formally be rejected. But half an hour later he had rejected the thought. Apart from the fact that they would probably think him quite mad – and Palmer was realistic enough to know that there wasn't one of them who would give him, of all people, the benefit of the doubt – Gerrard could just simply deny the whole thing. 'Poor Andrew, been working too hard, drinking too hard, you know the pressures'. Gerrard would have to go as soon as the attack occurred, of course, but he was clearly going to go anyway, so there was no reason for him to risk exposure by admitting what was going on, allowing the Cabinet time to withdraw support for the US. Maybe, Palmer thought, he should talk to the military, but then saw that that was equally pointless. The policy was to allow the US to use their UK airbases, so the only basis on which Palmer could intervene would be that the aircraft were carrying nuclear weapons, except that they weren't – only conventional weapons, however massive, which would then facilitate the nuclear strike coming in from US warships. So, if he tried to blow the whistle, they'd almost certainly lock him up; and even if he did, somehow, convince them, what could they do? They had no authority to enter the airbases, which were treated as US territory; and the notion that they might seek to intercept the US planes was, as Palmer liked to say, an example of the Shrewburyness syndrome – as far beyond barking as it was possible to get. With these less than comforting thoughts going round in his head, and the first signs of light beginning to appear, finally, he dozed off. The only person to get even half a good night's sleep was Kate herself. Days and days of tension, ever since she had headed for Belfast, following weeks of worry and misery about Paul; and the enforced isolation and calm which she was now experiencing, all conspired to wipe her out both physically and mentally. Supper, a cup of tea and a bath all added to the soporific mood into which she felt herself drifting; and before 11pm she was fast asleep.

For all of them, in different ways and for quite different reasons, the week-end was one of the worst they had ever experienced. Hargreaves started to mend, but was frustrated at having to lie still in a hospital bed; and was worried sick about Kate – a sentiment he only just managed to keep in check when Emmerson and O'Connell came to visit him. Emmerson could at least give vent to his fears for her, while O'Connell, despite his huge capacity for patience – a trait that had not only been critical to his career in the IRA but on more than one occasion, life-saving – found the inaction almost unbearable. Gerrard had a full week-end of commitments, largely based round a set of visitors – all political in one way or another – who had been invited down to the PM's country retreat at

Chequers in Buckinghamshire. In some ways it was a relief for Gerrard. The constant discussion, over meals, during walks between meals, late in the evening, slowly shifted him from the dreadful but justifiable state of denial he was in – denial that there was anything he could do to retrieve the situation – to the more relaxing, even numbing, but totally false state of denial that he faced, at best, the end of his political career. Occasionally the horror of what was to come would hit him; and even one or two guests thought that he seemed, on occasion, a little distracted; but such moments passed quickly. It was still a relief when, as had been arranged some time before, the British Ambassador to the UN, Sir Anthony Bignall, arrived around 3 pm on the Sunday, as most of the other visitors were leaving, to finalise with Gerrard the speech he would give on Britain's behalf to the UN Security Council on Tuesday.

Palmer, meanwhile, had discovered no way in which he could save Gerrard's political career. He prepared a draft of the statement Gerrard would have to give to the House of Commons on Thursday, but knew there was no chance that it would prove acceptable. More constructively, however, he worked on his project to keep Gerrard a free man. He met and briefed both the teams he needed - one technical the other decidedly not – and on Sunday evening went bowling with his wife, two sons and daughter. It was something they all enjoyed, though it happened, due to Palmer's job, all too infrequently. He reflected that if things did not go well, they would be able to spend a lot more time bowling. If things went very badly, he'd only see them at visiting hours. There were so many imponderables, but the biggest was Kate Kimball. She was the key to it all. Fortunately for her peace of mind, Kate did not know this. She spent a boring week-end reading. Once, when food was being delivered, she asked if she could go for a walk, suitably supervised, but this was refused. As Palmer sat watching his children knocking down the skittles, the thought uppermost in Kate's mind was that she was two days down; and only five to go. Palmer's thoughts were not dissimilar.

Gerrard spent Monday on an interminable round of meetings, none of which could remotely engage his interest, except for a further discussion with Sir Anthony Bignall before he took off for the meeting in New York. At the meeting, the US would propose a Resolution that, in the face of repeated failure by Iran to disband its nuclear weapons programme, the UN should authorize an immediate inspection of all Iranian sites, the destruction of any facilities being used as part of a nuclear weapons programme, all backed up by whatever international force was necessary. Bignall had a copy of the near-final text of what the US Ambassador would say; and Gerrard and he worked on polishing the UK speech, designed with only one intent, namely to get as much support for the US as possible. Both knew that this was not remotely a matter of including arguments that would persuade the other members of the Security

Council. Their votes would very largely be pre-determined and, to this end, both the US and the UK had sent advance indication of what they would say and, much more important, vast amounts of information resulting from intelligence-gathering – both satellite based and from espionage inside Iran – to demonstrate beyond doubt that Iran now had, or was on the point of having, nuclear weapons capability. In addition, under Gerrard's direction, the Foreign Office and a whole fleet of Ambassadors had spent many hundreds if not thousands of hours in the last week or so urging other members of the Security Council to support the Resolution. Their first main argument was one that anyone – the US included – might use, namely the imminent threat which Iran posed. The second was more subtle; and very much one that the US would have to leave to the UK to deploy - that it was vital for the UN to take the necessary action. If it failed to respond adequately to the threat Iran posed, then it would, as with the Iraq war, be up to a coalition of the willing to act; and that had been as bad as no action at all. Again and again, spurred on by Gerrard, British diplomats around the world urged that this time, the UN must maintain a firm resolve. If it did so, it was highly unlikely that Iran could or would resist. The point of Bignall's speech was merely to provide an acceptable public banner behind which other countries could feel comfortable about supporting a US led initiative.

It was nearly 9 p.m. before Gerrard could get together alone with Palmer to discuss the even bigger drama that was scheduled to go live in little more than 36 hours time. Palmer had been no less distracted than Gerrard through a day of unremitting meetings; and almost everyone he saw that day noted how even more irascible than usual he was, though few were unwise enough to comment on the fact. But through it all his mind had been churning through every conceivable way out of the crippling dilemma Gerrard faced; and quite a few inconceivable ones as well; and, in the end, had come up with just one possibility. It was a long shot, but it was all he had. Once Gerrard had poured them both whiskies, Palmer went straight to it.

"Alan, I struggled all day to find an answer; and there is only one. You won't like it, but there it is". Gerrard, looking drawn and morose, said nothing.

"Hamilton knows he won't get the US resolution past the vetoes of all five permanent members of the Security Council; and without that the attack can't be legit as far as the UN is concerned. He just wants enough support – the nine votes needed to approve a resolution if it *isn't* vetoed – to give his actions a cloak of international support"

"I know that" said Gerrard wearily. "That's why he's bloody well blackmailing me". Palmer ignored Gerard's dismissive tone.

"And this attack is the absolute fulcrum of what he is no doubt pleased to call his political philosophy – the defining act of his Presidency etcetera etcetera". Gerrard merely nodded.

"Then call him up, tell him that a nuclear attack is not on. He can find a way to pound Iran's nuclear capability into dust using conventional weapons – the Americans are inventive enough given time – but not nuclear weapons and, so you are certain, you want his authority for British military inspection of his planes – both here and in the Middle East - before they take off".

"Are you completely mad?" shouted Gerrard, his eyes blazing and his self-control rapidly disintegrating. "What's Hamilton going to say? Oh, sure, would tea-time be convenient for your guys? Give me one good reason why he would even think about such a lunatic proposal?"

"Because, if he doesn't agree, you'll announce to the world tomorrow morning, before the UN vote, that you have just found out that the US are planning a nuclear attack, that that is clearly unacceptable, that you are dropping all support for the US position, and encouraging all other members of the Security Council to do likewise. Let's see if he has the balls to go through with it then".

It was probably a full minute before Gerrard replied; and it seemed to Palmer like an hour.

"You know what that means don't you, for me I mean?"

"Yes" replied Palmer quietly.

"I couldn't face the rest of life in jail, Andy".

"I know that too" said Palmer. Another long pause followed.

"And that's the only solution?"

"Yes". Gerrard sank back into the settee, his face totally drained, of colour or emotion as he stared unseeing at the far corner of the room. He sighed heavily.

"Is a nuclear strike *so* terrible? Iran has to be stopped; and you said yourself that the Americans will do it somehow, except that later may be too late. They're giving the Iranians due warning, so there shouldn't be any more casualties, in fact there will be less. So why not a nuclear strike?"

"I've thought along those lines as well" said Palmer "That maybe the use of nuclear weapons has become a sort of shibboleth, the Doomsday weapon, forever equated with the mass slaughter of civilians in Hiroshima and Nagasaki but, in the Iranian desert, just a bigger bang, that's all. But it doesn't work, Alan, for two reasons." He was about to go on when he realised that he was about to deliver a mini-lecture to a man contemplating his own imminent mortality. "I'm sorry, Alan, there are reasons, that's all".

"If they form the text of my death warrant, I'd like to hear them" said Gerrard, still staring into the distance.

"The first is that, for more than 60 years, through the cold war and a number of hot wars, it has been the overwhelming destructive power of nuclear weapons, not to mention the effects of fall-out, that has prevented their use. Why haven't India and Pakistan gone to war – in any serious way I mean – despite all sorts of provocation? Because both realise that if the other is just mad enough – or frightened enough – to go nuclear, that part of the world will become the worst holocaust in history. Korea, Vietnam, the cold war itself, all went the way they did because no-one was prepared to use nuclear weapons. If they are ever used again in war, however tactical, however limited in scope or impact, the genie which was so terrifying that we *did* manage to stuff it back in the bottle in 1945 will be out, and it will never go back this time. If the US goes nuclear in Iran, then it is only a matter of time before others use them; and then it is only a matter of time for the human race. It's probably how we will end anyway, but do you want to be the man who triggered it. I don't want to sound too apocalyptic, but we could be talking the beginning of the end of the world here".

While Palmer was speaking, Gerrard seemed to come out of the trance-like state he'd been in.

"That's a load of crap, Andy. Are India and Pakistan going to blow themselves up just because the US used three or four nuclear devices to disarm Iran? Of course not. Is the US going to be any more likely to nuke Al Qaeda's caves just because they need a surgical nuclear strike to stop Iran becoming a nuclear threat to the world? Of course not. The world will loathe the Americans for attacking Iran; and I think Hamilton's mad to contemplate it being nuclear; but the idea that this will then free everyone else up to use nuclear strikes whenever they want – you'll have to come up with something better than that, Andrew". He paused. "You said there were two reasons". Palmer could see that he would make no more headway with his first argument.

"When Hamilton spelt all this out to you, you said to him yourself that the US would become the target for just about every terrorist group in the world; and he said that he'd got that covered. Maybe he has, maybe he hasn't; but we certainly don't have it covered in the UK; and if we support the US, are seen to take enough other countries with us, then we will be as big a target as the US – in fact, if their security is as good as Hamilton claims, then we will be even more of a target because we will be an easier one. If you don't stop Hamilton, there are going to be countless deaths here from terror attacks – and some, no doubt, would see it as no more than just desserts if some of those attacks involved very dirty nuclear devices. That is what you are condemning this nation to you if you support the Americans".

Palmer expected Gerrard to kick this into touch as well but, to his surprise, Gerrard remained silent. Palmer left Gerrard to reflect on what he had said.

"You think that is what would happen?" Gerrard eventually asked.

"Don't you?" replied Palmer, anxious to stop the lecture-mode he was stuck in. Gerrard poured more drinks. His next words startled Palmer.

349

"Are our security services really incapable of finding out where this Kimball woman is? Give me her and I'll do it". Palmer realised that Gerrard was now clutching at very thin straws.

"I've kept in touch with Sykes. Air Traffic Control tracked the helicopter to a US air force base in Norfolk; but we had no-one on the spot there to track her. We picked her up on satellite imagery being transferred to a car, but then lost her. The ops people think she was probably taken out of sight, transferred to another car and then she could have been driven anywhere for safe keeping. I've asked them to do anything they can to trace her; but it seems very unlikely. We're certainly never going to find her in 36 hours". Gerrard looked as if he might pursue the matter, but didn't. Instead, he headed off on another tack.

"What will you do, Andrew, if I can't buy your 'solution'?" The words sounded innocent enough, but they were pregnant with meaning. "You know enough to stop me". Palmer gave a wan smile and shook his head.

"It's you call, Alan. The worst one I can imagine anyone ever having to make, but it's your call. I'm merely an instrument". He was going to add the word 'humble' before 'instrument', but decided now was not the time for humour, however gallows-like. He also forbore to mention that he had been through every permutation he could think of over the week-end as to how he might be able to stop Gerrard, but without success. Gerrard stood up.

"I'm going to bed" he said abruptly. "I'll see you in the morning", and left the room.

Palmer remained seated, thinking over what had been said. Did he really believe that Wednesday might be the beginning of the end of the world? Probably not – far too fanciful – and yet? *Could* the US, or - anyone - use nuclear weapons and then successfully pop the genie back in the bottle again? Palmer didn't know, but it was quite plausible to suggest not. In any event, it seemed as if it was the consequences for Britain that weighed more heavily with Gerrard. What would he make of that overnight? If only he had Kimball. He'd take delivery on Wednesday, but by then it would be too late. He needed her Tuesday; and he wasn't going to get her. How many lives – or deaths - to come would depend on that simple fact?

In Belfast, Hargreaves had had as much as he could stand of hospital life. The bed was uncomfortable, but the real problem was noise. Four other patients in the ward had radios or televisions, which they seemed to keep on permanently, whether they were awake or not, or even, in some cases whether they were there or not. There was nearly always someone asleep and snoring loudly; and he soon exhausted the newspapers which O'Connell and Emmerson had brought him to read. The nurses who came to monitor his condition were the high point of the day, but their visits were infrequent; and when O'Connell called in again, this time with Riordan, around 6 pm, Hargreaves announced that he was leaving with them. The nursing staff were unhappy, but conceded that all he needed was to lie still for a long time; and he might just as well do that at home. This they assumed – not unnaturally since Hargreaves had told them such – was O'Connell's house in West Belfast.

By 7.30 pm he was sitting stiffly in O'Connell's kitchen, with all three O'Connells and Riordan, eating a pizza and feeling distinctly better. The only problem was that Emmerson, who had heard every detail of Kate's story that O'Connell was prepared to report – no reference to his twice having struck her, nor the serious prospect that he might have had her killed - now wanted to hear everything that Hargreaves had to say; and Hargreaves knew this was very dangerous territory. He kept as close to the facts as possible, justifying all his assistance to Kate on the grounds that he was appalled at how DI Johnson had treated her; and, as soon as he could, pleaded the pain-killers he was still on as an excuse to go to bed, in O'Connell's last remaining spare bedroom. The most galling thing, as he lay there in the dark trying to get some sleep, was that he could see why Kate had been so determined in her quest for Paul. He had no way of knowing whether Emmerson's looks appealed to women – he presumed they did – but he could see that he was physically impressive, being tall, well built and in surprisingly good shape given his months of confinement; and a strong character in an understated way, courteous, controlled, someone to inspire confidence in a difficult situation Hargreaves thought; and he didn't need to know that Emmerson was a Professor at Oxford University to see that he was also an intelligent man with a clear, logical mind. As he drifted off, it was not so much the thought that he had no future with Kate which troubled him – though that was hard to bear. Rather it was the deep, gut-wrenching regret he felt that he had not made love to her when perhaps, if he had been more.......
more what? More forceful, ardent, persuasive? None of those was right. It would have had to come from Kate. He loved her, of that there was no doubt; but she loved Paul; and if she had let him have sex with her, it would have been for comfort, security, to overcome fear or despair - or some such reason - and, in the end, none of those had been quite enough. Whoever said a policeman's lot is not a happy one was, he thought, a master of understatement as far as DS Hargreaves of the Thames Valley police force was concerned. Meanwhile, the object of all these men's concern, confined to an increasingly claustrophobic room on the borders of Norfolk and Lincolnshire, ticked off another day in her mind.

CHAPTER 32

Early the next morning, Palmer got a message to see Gerrard straight away. As he headed round to No. 10, Palmer reflected that, whatever Gerrard was going to say, he didn't want to hear it. Gerrard started without any pre-amble.

"As you may imagine, I have not had a great night. I've wrestled with the situation, such options as I have, my conscience; and I'm sorry Andy, but I can't ..... I can't.... back out. I'm not going to make any statement, not with them holding Kimball. I'm sorry" he repeated. "I'll live with what Hamilton's going to do; and as a result, I'll live. But you're right that this could be a terrorist nightmare for Britain; and I want to try to stop that. I thought of denying that I knew the US were going to use nuclear weapons, but no-one would believe it; and even if they did, the US would leak that I knew. So, this is what I'm going to do. I'm going to reveal on Thursday specific intelligence from high up inside the Iranian government that a nuclear attack on Israel has been planned for some time and has been judged imminent. I'm going to say that, in the circumstances, and with there being no other way to hit some of the Iranian sites quickly, I personally agreed the US strategy with Hamilton, without consulting anyone else here; and no-one else, therefore, is responsible; and then I'm going to resign, no doubt to mass opprobrium; and everyone in Parliament, the military, all our Ambassadors can spend the coming hours, days and weeks telling the world what a terrible thing I did. They can censor the US, send aid to Iran, anything they want, to dissociate Britain from the use of nuclear weapons. Lastly, I will urge my successor to adopt a security operation in the UK as tight as the US one. The Americans won't give us any help if we are busy attacking them politically; but it can't be too difficult. It just needs the political will, and I think the events we are about to see might just provide that. All I want from you, Andrew, is to stop Kimball and Emmerson. My retirement will not be a joyful one, but at least then I will have one". He stopped, his face a mask of despair and defiance. "I'm sorry" he repeated again, both emotions evident in the words.

Palmer looked at him grimly, but was surprised at how calm he felt. Perhaps it was because what Gerrard had said was, in some ways, better than he had dared to hope. He had not seriously believed that Gerrard would reveal Hamilton's plan and then commit suicide; and so he had come to accept that the die was cast. Whether Gerrard's strategy would save Britain from future attack he doubted; but it was something - not much, but something. He realised that he only had one question.

"*Is* there any specific intelligence from Iran about Israel?" A ghost of a smile drifted fleetingly across Gerrard's face.

"There will be by tomorrow" he said. "It may not hold up any better than Saddam Hussain's weapons of mass destruction in the long run; but it will do for the moment; and it is eminently plausible, given what Iran has been saying for years about Israel. What's more we really do have an agent in the higher reaches of the Iranian Government; and he really has been saying to us privately what his lords and masters have been saying publicly about attacking Israel. It's only the timing that may have to be subject to some..... interpretation". And that was it. Gerrard had no more to say. Palmer had one more question.

"What about the US and UK personnel in Iran? They'll be crucified".

"Everyone bar the Embassy staffs have been quietly moving out for several weeks now; and the Embassy people will be heading for a helicopter rendezvous up towards the Turkish border some time before the advance warning is given"

"It's all been thought through, hasn't it?" said Palmer.

"Oh, yes. It may be mad, but it is very thoroughly mad". Palmer merely nodded and headed for the door. At the last moment he turned.

"I'm sorry that we won't be working together any more" he said.

"Me too, me too" replied Gerrard. "Thanks for all you've done – all you're doing for me". Palmer nodded again, and left.

Around noon Palmer got an urgent message from the Major in charge of the surveillance team General Sykes had assigned to track the US helicopter and, if possible, Kate Kimball's whereabouts. Palmer excused himself from a meeting he was in, went back to his office and picked up the phone.

"Major Daniels here. We've been going over all the satellite material again, using various diagnostics to see if we could get any more out of it. I'm by no means certain, but there is a possibility that the woman wasn't driven off after all. If she was, we've definitely lost her; but detailed analysis of the surveillance data suggests that she may have been taken only a short distance and then transferred into a building on the edge of the airfield. It's amongst trees, and visibility is very poor; but that's my team's best guess. So there's at least a chance of locating her".

Palmer's heart started to pound in his chest. The Security Council meeting would start in three hours – 10 am New York time. If Daniels was right – if – and if Kimball could be taken in time, then Gerrard might still dissociate himself from the Americans. He recognised that the chances were slim, but now was not the time for defeatist thoughts. Palmer phoned Gerrard. An aide told him that the PM was with the Foreign Secretary and couldn't be disturbed.

"I don't care if he's having a one-to-one with God. If you want to keep your job, get him on the line, now" he almost screamed down the phone. When Gerrard picked up the phone, Palmer pitched straight in.

"We may have found Kimball, on a US air force base in Norfolk; and General Sykes has an SAS ready to pick Kimball up tomorrow. If they could snatch her today, there'd still be time for you to pull out. What do you want me to do?" Gerrard paused for only a second.

"Get her. Any way they can. They've got one hour. After that, forget it".

"It's an act of war against our only real ally" said Palmer.

"Don't you think I fucking well know that?" replied Gerrard, also near screaming pitch. "But if it works, that will be the least of their problems; and if it doesn't they'll want to hush it up as much as I will. So do it".

"Will do" said Palmer, and rang off. Within seconds he was through to General Sykes.

"Palmer here. You have a team ready to pick up Kimball sometime tomorrow". As this was no more than both Palmer and Sykes knew, the General, never a man to use even one word if none would do, remained silent. "Could your team be ready to take her by force today?"

"By force, you mean as in a hostage situation?" asked Sykes.

"Yes"

"What's her location and who is holding her?"

"We think American forces are holding her somewhere on a US air force base in Norfolk". There was a pause as Sykes considered this.

"The team could be ready but, no, that's not feasible - probably not at all without a large force, but certainly not at short notice".

"It is of the utmost importance to the PM, General" replied Palmer, with little prospect of this making any difference. "It's critical to national security considerations".

"Then I'm very sorry" replied Sykes. "SAS operations are normally very well planned. On occasion they will go in fast to a hostage situation if lives are at stake; but that is typically in civilian settings and against a small group of amateurs. Mounting an attack, or even infiltration, of a major and no doubt well protected military installation without due reconnaissance would be an unacceptable risk to the men involved; and with little prospect of success if they don't even know the woman's actual location. You'd need a battalion to hold the place long enough for her to be found. I'm sorry".

Palmer could feel the sense of frustration in him coming to the boil. He wanted to scream at the man just to bloody well get on and fix the operation; but knew this was futile. What the General had said exhibited irrefutable logic; and he could think of no repost.

"Would it make any difference if the PM spoke to you and gave you a direct order?" he asked, clutching at straws.

"Only that I would then have to resign" said Sykes.

"I see" was all Palmer could find to reply to this. "Right, well, I'll get back to you tomorrow morning with details of the hand-over". He thought he heard something that might have been a 'good-bye' just before the line went dead. As Palmer replaced the phone, he felt a wave of anger, less with Sykes, who was merely revealing the sort of judgment that had led him to become a senior army officer; and more with himself, for thinking, even for a moment, that the Americans would have exposed anything so important to Hamilton's plans to any sort of weakness. The die really was cast. Yet Palmer was reluctant to concede that all was lost. Why he really didn't know. It was Gerrard's problem, but Palmer somehow had got totally hooked into trying to save Gerrard. It had started with his total loyalty to the man; but that was based on his belief that Gerrard was, or could become, a great political leader of the 21st Century; and both that belief and that prospect were now dead in the water. Maybe he, Palmer, by great misfortune, had become the only man who could stop the first use of nuclear weapons since 1945; and was furious that he could think of no way to achieve it. But that was wrong and he knew it. It was Hamilton's responsibility - and Gerrard's irresponsibility - that had created the situation. He himself was just a cipher, a very powerful one, he knew, but he hadn't been elected to lead the free world, on either side of the Atlantic; and he wasn't about to become either the great moral or political saviour of the day. No, the fact was much simpler than that. He just didn't like to lose. Hamilton had screwed up Gerrard, maybe screwed up Britain; and Kimball threatened disaster. He had a plan for her that would, with a little luck, save Gerrard's neck; but he doubted if Gerrard's plan would save Britain - and he could find no way to stop Hamilton.

200 miles away, Captain Swinburne and his team were relaxing before getting ready for an early departure the next day to the Framlingham air base. The prospect of having Kimball in his hands gave him an almost sexual thrill. He was under strict instructions that she remain totally unharmed – the last thing Palmer wanted was a deranged Emmerson on the warpath – but Swinburne hadn't forgotten for one second what she and her Irish compatriots had done to his men – not to mention his pride and reputation – and he was looking forward to scaring the shit out of her, a plan which, to his surprise, General Sykes had said Palmer wanted. Why, he neither knew nor cared, but she'd pay – psychologically if he couldn't make it physical – to the maximum extent he could devise.

Shortly before 3 pm , Gerrard, El, Palmer, and around half a dozen senior officials from No. 10, the Cabinet Office and the Foreign Office gathered round a screen, watching the start of the Security Council meeting in New York. Although there are only ever fifteen members of the Security Council, each country has large numbers of officials present; and a meeting of this significance saw over 350 people attending. Fortunately, the Security Council has its own large council chamber, which can easily accommodate such a number. The Council itself, which is in permanent session, and can convene anywhere in the world, was set up to deal with the very evident failure of the League of Nations in the interwar period to be able to respond rapidly to situations endangering life; but the aspiration to do better had, in the view of Hamilton, Gerrard and countless others, been thwarted by the existence of a veto power for each of the five Permanent Members of the Council – the US, the UK, France, Russia and China. Together they had vetoed several hundred resolutions since the Second World War, rendering the views of the other ten members - appointed on a regional basis and in a process of rotation from all the other members of the UN - largely irrelevant. A Resolution needed only nine votes to carry, provided there was no veto; but there were few matters of sufficient urgency and importance to go to the Security Council on which the permanent members would ever agree. It was because it was so widely recognised that the veto power of the permanent five had rendered the Council largely ineffective that Hamilton had decided, if necessary, to disregard a veto. All he wanted was the nine votes. If he got them the US would eliminate the Iranian threat once and for all.

The Presidency of the Council changes every month, rotating through the fifteen constituent Ambassadors; and on this particular morning in New York, five hours behind London, the chair was taken by the Ambassador from Botswana, a shrewd and experienced African politician with a powerful pan-African agenda. This he pursued energetically with other like-minded African States, in particular South Africa; and both had become quite pro-American since President Hamilton had started to take Africa's economic condition seriously. Along with the US and the UK, they would provide four very secure votes. The other current non-permanent members were Austria, Croatia and Turkey, Japan and Indonesia, Costa Rica and Mexico and, the sole representative of the Arab world, Libya. Both Hamilton and Gerrard assumed that, although both Russia and China had been more amenable to a strong line with Iran in recent months, there would nonetheless be no support from either for an attack; and France was an unknown quantity; so they needed at least five from the eight other non-permanent members. Despite all the effort which both the US and the UK had made, it was going to be a close run thing.

The session got under way and, after some introductory noises from the Chairman, the US Ambassador to the UN, Daniel Bernstein, was invited to address the Council. In a slow, deep and rather mellifluous voice, he described the background to the meeting – a background with which everyone was familiar, but this allowed him to stress how reasonable and how patient the UN had been in relation to Iran's nuclear ambitions over many years; and how all this had been completely disregarded by Iran in its single-minded determination to construct nuclear weapons. He reviewed the repeated attempts that the UN had made to come to some accord with Iran; and what he described as the cynical way in which these negotiations had been used by Iran to delay progress, while all the time developing the technology and securing the supplies it needed for its nuclear ambitions to become a reality. All of this no doubt lost some of its impact in the vast array of simultaneous translations going on; and the general body language in the Council chamber suggested no great attention was being paid to all this; but a degree of tension started to become apparent, even on the television screen, as the Ambassador started to quote liberally from Iran's numerous foreign policy statements about its attitude to Israel. He continued, with a sombre air that now gripped the audience that, once permitted to manufacture nuclear weapons, there could be little doubt that, on whatever pretext, manufactured or real, it would only be a matter of time before Iran used those weapons to seek to destroy Israel. This, he intoned, the US could, and would not accept. Israel was a legitimate state, its citizenry must be protected by the international community; and the Middle East must be guarded from the threat of a nuclear war which could decimate the region for several generations. The United States was therefore proposing the present Resolution, which required Iran to make itself immediately and fully open to UN inspectors, who were at that very moment at a Turkish border point waiting to be admitted, with a UN force to protect them; and in the absence of this full and immediate co-operation, authorised the UN to take 'all necessary measures' to ensure that the nuclear threat from Iran was eliminated. No-one listening was in any doubt that this entailed the use of force. Only Gerrard and Palmer knew exactly what Hamilton planned to include under that one word 'necessary'.

As the second proposer of the Resolution, the Ambassador for the UK spoke next – a speech honed largely by Gerrard himself. Much of it repeated what had already been said; but then branched out on a new aspect. The Ambassador quoted intelligence sources and satellite surveillance that confirmed, without any doubt, that Iran had missiles capable of delivering war loads over distances in excess of 2000 miles. Apart from Britain and Scandinavia, the whole of Europe was within its range – a point he made several times over in different ways without ever mentioning the countries that this put at risk. Nuclear capability for Iran would be as destabilising in the Middle East and Europe as that of North Korea's in Asia; and if the UN allowed it, then there would be no effective way to stop the proliferation of such weapons in either the Middle East or any where else. He finished by concluding that if the UN was not equal to this threat, then it was unclear that its Security Council continued to provide any useful function.

The remaining thirteen members then each spoke in alphabetical order. Austria regarded itself as neutral, but wanted no new nuclear power within range; and in what in many ways was a continuation of cold war politics, saw itself as firmly in the western camp. It supported the Resolution. Botswana, one of Africa's economic stars of the previous twenty years, and promised both financial support and a substantial role in Hamilton's plans for ridding Africa of poverty, followed suit; and suddenly there were four votes out of four. Palmer looked across at Gerrard, who showed no emotion. Whatever the outcome, he had delivered on what he had promised. The future of the world, if that is what they were contemplating, was now up to Hamilton. Gerrard's future was in Palmer's hands – and the unlikely shape of a publishing agent from Oxford. But before he could dwell on this for long, the television drama unfolding before them moved on to China. The People's Republic of China rarely deigned to support the US on anything really important but, as one of the few nuclear powers in the world, it did not want to see that advantage eroded any further than it had been already; and so there was genuine uncertainty as to how China would vote. If it used its veto against the Resolution then for most observers, the drama would seem to be over. Only Gerrard, Palmer and a few very senior people in the US administration and military forces knew that this was not the case.

The Chinese Ambassador to the UN seemed to take for ever to get to any point of relevance, before reviewing just about every argument for and against the Resolution, including the threat Iran posed to the world and Iran's right to conduct its own affairs free from international intervention. He concluded by stressing the importance of the Security Council, its role in many previous emergencies and then, to everyone's surprise, just stopped, without any indication of how China would vote.

"What did all that add up?" Palmer asked Gerrard.

"I think an abstention" replied Gerrard. "Interesting.". As he spoke, Costa Rica was reflecting its economic dependence on, and close political ties with the US. Five votes for the Resolution and one abstention so far. It was looking good. Shortly afterwards, Croatia made it six.

"Now it should get really interesting" said Gerrard. "The French will be as discombobulated as the Chinese". He based this on the fact that France was known to be very worried about the prospect of Iranian nuclear weapons – and why wouldn't they be, thought Gerrard. But it went against the grain to be seen to be acting on the coattails of the US; and France had played a major role in both the arming of Iran over the years and in supplying nuclear technology for peaceful purposes. So, here again, the outcome was very uncertain – though Hamilton, Gerrard knew, cared little which way France jumped. To his surprise, France was very clear-cut in what their Ambassador had to say. The threat posed by Iran was simply unacceptable, to the Middle East, to Europe, to the UN; and France fully endorsed the Resolution.

"Is that what finding your capital is in range of a new nuclear threat does?" asked Palmer, only half facetiously.

"Pass" said Gerrard. "We emphasised France's vulnerability; but who knows what machinations have been going on. Maybe they suspect unilateral action by the US if the Resolution fails; and are keen to assert the authority and effectiveness of the UN. They have much more muscle inside it than out. Every time it ducks an issue, it weakens their impact. Whatever the reason, Hamilton's going to get his nine votes".

The momentum towards this notably slowed as, first, Indonesia voted against, Japan said it would abstain; and then Libya furiously denounced the Resolution as a gross act of anti-Arab sentiment. Palmer noted that the Resolution still needed two votes from the last four members, one of which was Russia; but Gerrard gave him a wan smile.

"It's in the bag now, watch". Mexico proceeded, to no-one's surprise, to support the Resolution; and then it was Russia's turn. Russia, everyone knew, did not want a new member of the nuclear club; and it definitely didn't want new nuclear capability on its southern borders. But it saw Iran as a critical player in the Middle East; and one which historically had been very much in Russia's sphere of influence. In the contest between the US-backed Israeli world and the Arab world it knew very well which side it was on; and it was determined to retain that influence at all costs. Its Ambassador spoke at length of the history, of its belief in the long-term peaceful intentions of Iran, of its right to the peaceful use of nuclear power, and its confidence in future discussions with the Iranian government over outstanding differences. It noted that Russia had been increasingly prepared to support detailed talks with Iran, and even the possibility of sanctions if these proved fruitless, but Russia would vote against any Resolution that involved a military infringement of Iran's sovereignty

"No way they could know, but that is just about the biggest mistake Russia has made since it decided Communism was a good idea" said Gerrard. "Even Hamilton would have had to pause if his Resolution had been passed. He must be breaking open the Champagne".

"He still needs one more vote" said Palmer.

"Yes, but with South Africa and Turkey to come, he's got two. Hamilton's Africa strategy will ensure the first; and Turkey is the last place on earth – apart from the Israelis – that will want to see a nuclear Iran on her border. He's got want he wants; and the world is going to know very soon". Over the next twenty five minutes, both countries confirmed what Gerrard had said; and the Chairman then announced that the Resolution had ten votes to three, with two abstentions, but failed due to the veto by Russia.

"God help Iran" said Gerrard.

CHAPTER 33

Several hours later, around 4 pm in Washington, 9 p.m. in London and midnight in Teheran, Colin Abineri, a very senior CIA operative, using a scrambled phone-line, called his opposite number in SAVAK, the Iranian Secret Service. Though mortal foes, they knew each other and, over several years, had had contact with each other, whenever it was in their mutual interest. Their contacts were like one everlasting chess game, but such contacts were not unusual, even amongst the most bitterly opposed intelligence services. Abineri, a man of few words at the best of times, came straight to the point.

"Asad, I'm sure you were very pleased with what happened at the Security Council today; but I have bad news, for both of us. The President is not prepared to accept the Russian veto. A few minutes ago, he authorised the immediate destruction of all your main nuclear facilities. This is to give you sufficient warning to remove all the personnel working in them; and you need to get them at least thirty miles away". Asad Farzan, Deputy Director of one of SAVAK's four main divisions, sat very still, shaken beyond words by what he had heard.

"Asad, did you hear me?" said Abineri.

"I heard you, yes" replied Farzan. "Why at least thirty miles?"

"I can't tell you, but you can guess". Farzan's hand holding the phone started to tremble slightly, but he started calculating furiously. Why would the Americans tell him if it wasn't true; why would they tell him if it was. Above all, what cards did he have to play?

"Is there any way this can be stopped?" he asked.

"None" said Abineri. "It's been planned for months; and the UN vote was the last opportunity to stop it. The President now sees no other way".

"Why are you telling me this?"

The President wants to prevent Iran having nuclear weapons, but he doesn't want to harm any Iranians".

"Because that would greatly increase international condemnation".

"Asad, I didn't call to debate politics. Your people are at grave risk. The President authorised me to contact you, but you are going to have to work very fast. You have a few hours at the most".

"You must know that we will immediately alert every major capital in the world?" said Farzan quietly

"Of course you will" replied Abineri. "And they will all contact Washington; and Washington will deny the whole thing as completely mad, some plot dreamed up by Iran. No-one's going to actually *do* anything until it is too late".

"We might" replied Farzan. "We might make a pre-emptive strike on Israel".

"You might indeed" said Abineri.

Farzan sat rigid. He stared, unseeing, in front of him. The shock of Abineri's reply – what it implied about America' strategy – was surpassed by the even greater shock that he – a man with nearly thirty years' experience of operating in the twilight intelligence world lying between policy and military strategy - hadn't seen that coming. A first strike by Iran on Israel would give the US just the rationale it needed for the extreme measures it was planning. Worse still, it was very uncertain how successful such an attack would be. There was no doubt of Israel's military resources and state of readiness; and the Israelis would no doubt know what Hamilton was planning. They would, right now, be on full scale alert. Even the Yom Kippur war, which had come as a complete surprise to the Israeli government, was nonetheless an embarrassing defeat for Egypt; and neither before or since had any war with Israel ended other than in victory for Israel. An attack on Israel might play right into Hamilton's hands.

"Do you have anything else to say?" asked Farzan coldly.

"No. Just get everyone out, from the reactors, the processing plants, the mines, the weapons bases, the research labs – the lot".

"I will get the Director to call the President straight away. This will be a terrible day, for both our countries".

"I know but, for the moment, there is nothing else to do".

The next three hours went very much the way that their conversation had predicted. Farzan spoke to his Director, who immediately arranged a meeting with the Iranian President, Defence Secretary and Foreign Secretary, plus Farzan, a number of other intelligence officers and all Iran's senior military commanders. Their first decision, after Farzan had described his phone call, was taken in a matter of seconds; which was to get all personnel away from the country's nuclear sites. Instructions were sent to every site, directing the seizure of whatever number of cars and buses were required to move the workforce and all the local inhabitants without delay. The meeting then turned quickly to the problem of how to respond. It was quickly agreed that a message promising the severest consequences if the attack went ahead be sent to Washington; and a large number of other governments would be contacted and invited to protest vehemently at what was planned, adding whatever political or economic threats each country could make. But everyone in the room, some openly, recognised the truth of what Abineri had said; and Hamilton had known from the start – none of it would make any difference. The reality of America's unique super-power status was being exercised by Hamilton; and no-one could stop it.

They then turned to the only remaining possibility – an all-out attack on Israel. A much longer debate centred around a proposal for an immediate air strike; but the President and his political colleagues ruled that out, for precisely the reason that Farzan, too late, had seen – that it would give the US every reason it needed to justify its action. A retaliatory strike was quite different.

Iranian bombers and missiles could, if successful, cause immense damage to Israel's army and air force installations; and cause massive destruction in its town and cities. Given what the US was planning, Iran would have considerable support, not just from other countries in the Middle East, but from around the world for such action; and they might be able to set back Israel's nuclear weapons programme by quite some way in the process. It was while this debate was going on that an urgent message was brought into the meeting; and passed to the President. He paused to read it and, as he did so, the blood drained from his face. He sat motionless, looking stupified, as the others waited for him to say what was in the message.

"Defence intelligence says that two large waves of Israeli planes are converging on Iran, one over Syria, the other directly through Iraq. All our available fighters have been alerted and await instructions to intercept them".

All eyes were focused on the President, who sat looking at the piece of paper in his hand.

"Navid" he said, to the Defence Minister "what is our state of readiness?"

"We can, even with the minimum warning time, put more aircraft up than the Israelis; and our fighters and their pilots are, in general, as good as theirs; but, as we have discussed before, their electronics are superior, they can jam us more effectively; and they have better missile control systems. It is not unlike 1981, when the Israelis mounted a surprise attack on Iraq's nuclear weapons programme; and on that occasion they reduced most of Iraq's main sites to rubble". The Director of SAVAK intervened.

"I don't think they will be going for our nuclear installations. I think the US will do that but, if so, they will want the Israelis to take care of our air defences. I suggest we get them airborne immediately". In the silence that followed, the President looked to Navid Hassan, his Defence Minister, who gave a small nod. The President nodded back. Hassan stood.

"I will see to it immediately" he said, and left the meeting. The President, somewhat calmer now, looked round the remaining attendees, in particular the senior military men.

"Let us prepare to defend ourselves" he said "and may Allah be with us".

The Director's assumption that the Israelis were not themselves going for Iran's nuclear sites was correct, but this was not surprising. It was now common knowledge that the Israelis had bought three submarines and fitted them out to fire cruise missiles with nuclear warheads, each at least as powerful as the bomb dropped on Hiroshima. Less widely known, but nonetheless a fairly open secret, was the fact that in 2005, the Israelis had come very close to using them to destroy Iran's nuclear weapons programme. What very few knew, as a result of SAVAK intelligence gathering operations in Israel, was that that remained Israel's chosen means to eliminate Iran's nuclear installations. Missiles were more accurate; they avoided the risk that an aircraft with a nuclear payload might be shot down over Israeli, Syrian or Iraqi airspace; and they reduced the risks to the lives of Israel's armed forces. This knowledge did nothing to cheer him. The night, he was quite sure, would see aerial combat between the Israeli and Iranian air forces; while all the time either heavy US bombers or missiles or both would be zeroing in to cause havoc and destruction on Iran's fledgling nuclear capability. He started to ask himself why he had had no inkling of this from his extensive intelligence network around the globe, including in Washington, but immediately knew the answer. A decision like this, such a bold military stroke and such a risky political one, could never be debated and discussed. To do so would be to strangle the idea at birth. No, this must be Hamilton – Hamilton and hardly anyone else. It would be a total surprise not only to the rest of the world but to nearly every single American as well. Being the sort of man he was, the Director recognised a grudging element of admiration for Hamilton, for so completely throwing off all the restraints, all the checks and balances so carefully built into the US political system, whatever the cost, to pursue the strategy he wanted; and that was why none of his well-placed agents had heard anything. Whether this would be enough to save his position as Director of SAVAK he rather doubted.

Iranian Government officials started to contact their opposite numbers around the world; and the Iranian Ambassador in Washington sought and obtained an urgent meeting with the Secretary of State. As forecast by Colin Abineri in his conversation with Asad Farzan, the Secretary of State denied all knowledge of any forthcoming attack and, when he demanded to know the source of the Ambassador's information, was openly sceptical. Less than two hours later, Iran suffered two devastating blows from which it would take many years to recover, if at all. While twenty-one Israeli jet fighters were shot down – a much higher number than it had anticipated – the Iranian air force was very largely destroyed, some planes in the air, some on the ground, as a result of precisely those Israeli advantages which the Iranian Defence minister had noted. But the second blow was far, far worse. This was the complete annihilation of its nuclear sites. Two waves of C-47 heavy bombers flew from US airbases in the UK, picking up fighter escorts over Turkey. The first delivered a total of forty BLU-109 so-called 'bunker-buster' bombs to five sites These largely or completely destroyed the enrichment plant at Mu-allimn Kalayeh, the reactor at Nekka, the research and Uranium conversion operations at Esfahan, the heavy water plant at Arak and the missile production factory at Dorkhovin. Meanwhile, the second wave delivered sixty more bunker-busters to five other sites – the reactor at Bushehr on the Gulf coast, the main enrichment plant at Natanz, south of Tehran, the two Uranium mines at Saghand and Yadz in the centre of the country, and Iran's principle nuclear weapons production plant at Kerman, creating huge craters. With the sort of precision that the US had developed for the Iraq invasion, three of these sites were then targeted by cruise missiles with nuclear warheads, fired from the *USS Alabama* stationed in the Gulf. The sites at Bushehr and Natatanz were spared this because of their proximity to centres of population. The one remaining target – the research facility in Tehran - was also spared, even though it could have been destroyed with little damage to the surrounding buildings, because this greatly reduced the extent to which the Iranian population had any direct awareness of the attack. The nuclear blasts elsewhere created damage to the underground facilities on a scale that would render them unusable but, in addition, released enough radiation to make the sites uninhabitable, indeed unapproachable for many years to come. President Hamilton had played his super-power card. He awaited the world's reaction.

This was not long in coming. By the next morning, some five or six hours later in the UK, virtually every government in the world had registered the most emphatic protest with Washington and, to a lesser extent, with London. The attack was variously described as an unprovoked act of war, an atrocity, and as endangering the lives of millions. Arrangements were already being put in place to reconvene the UN; and there were calls for President Hamilton to be indicted for crimes against humanity. To all of this, Hamilton's aides merely responded that the President would make a statement at 11 am Washington time. In the UK, Gerrard announced that he would address the House of Commons at 2 pm UK time, some two hours before Hamilton's statement. Gerrard prepared for what he accepted would be his last day in office. One hundred miles north, Kate awoke, completely unaware of the night's events; and far less well prepared for her own judgment day.

CHAPTER 34

Kate was getting dressed, by now in a state of utter depression, brought on by the boredom of her position and the lack of any exercise. The only slight ray of sunshine was that, by her reckoning, either today or tomorrow, this nightmare might come to an end. Shortly after 7.30 am there was a knock on Kate's door. She waited by the window and two of her guards appeared with breakfast.

"Be ready to leave at 8.30 am" said one of them. The flat monotone in which this was delivered could not, even for a second, interfere with the surge of relief Kate immediately felt. Just to be out of the suffocating confines of the room she had spent almost a week in had been the day-and-night focus of her thinking throughout that time; and the prospect of finally leaving was exhilarating. And then, only a moment behind, was the thought that she might, later today, be back with Paul; and with the terrible events of the last few months finally over. Her yearning for that moment was so strong it was painful, bringing tears to her eyes. With this heady cocktail of emotions swirling through her, she could think of nothing to say in reply; and by the time she had regained control of herself, the guards had gone.

The next hour passed agonisingly slowly. She could eat little breakfast – just some coffee and a piece of toast - and was dressed and packed, ready to go long before 8.30 am. On the dot of 8.30 am there was another knock at the door; and she was slightly surprised that the guard still insisted that she retreat to the window before they unlocked the door and entered.

"Please hold out your hands" she said in a no-nonsense way. Kate took a step backwards.

"Why?" she said, more puzzled than anything.

"Just do as I say" replied the guard. "You will need to wear these cuffs for the journey".

"Why?" repeated Kate, panic beginning to grab her.

"You will not leave here unless you do" was the only reply she got. Nervously, Kate held out her hands and the guard, expertly and in less than a second, had locked her wrists in hand-cuffs. She then, to Kate's utter consternation, turned on her heel and, accompanied by the other guard, walked out of the room. Before Kate could even begin to think about what was happening, a man appeared at the doorway. It was Captain Swinburne.

Kate, already on a knife edge of trauma, now completely lost control. "No" she screamed and backed away, falling onto the bed as she did so. Swinburne stood, looking at her imperviously.

"I can't tell you what a pleasure it is to meet you again Miss Kimball". The tone implied anything but a pleasure. "Bring her to the car". Kate saw that this was directed to several other men who had followed Swinburne into the room.

"No" Kate screamed again, even louder. "Leave me alone. I've complied with everything I was told to do. They said I could go after a week". The two of them stared at each other, the mutual hatred very evident.

"Miss Kimball" said Swinburne in an artificially calm voice "let me give you some good news and some bad. The good news is that if you behave yourself then you will be released, as promised, probably tomorrow, by the day after at the latest". He paused, allowing her to savour this appealing piece of information, but also giving her time to imagine the very worst possible bad news to come. "The bad news is that unless you co-operate with me, my men and my masters - instantly, unquestioningly – then your release is off. In such circumstances I and my men have been given clear instructions that you are to disappear without trace. Where, how and when are entirely up to me and, after what your fucking Irish colleagues did to my men, I'm really hoping that you won't cooperate. As for my team, the situation is going to test their readiness to obey orders to the limit".

Kate, now in a huddle on the bed, was terrified beyond anything she could have imagined. But a tiny flicker of self-preservation in her registered that all was not lost.

"What do you want me to do?" she whispered.

"Anything you are told" replied Swinburne "which, for the moment means getting in the car I have waiting outside".

"Where are we going?" asked Kate. To her surprise Swinburne gave her at least a half-answer.

"We are taking you to meet the person directing these operations. Do what he says and you might just be okay. If you don't then I'm happy to say that your last few weeks on earth will be as my guest". Kate, now shaking and starting to sweat, felt that her breakfast, limited as it as, was about to re-appear.

"May I go to the bathroom first? I think I'm going to be sick". Swinburne merely nodded his head; and Kate staggered into the bathroom. There, with the help of a few sips of water, she managed to keep her breakfast down; and then flipped some water onto her face. She glanced in the mirror to say an ashen, distraught woman, the cheerfulness of ten minutes before completely and utterly gone. When she came out, Swinburne said -

"Right, let's go" whereupon two of his men took Kate, one arm each and walked her out to a seven seater immediately outside the door to the building that had been her home for six long days. She was sat in the back row of seats with two of Swinburne's men either side of her. In front were two more of the team, with Swinburne in the front next to a driver. They set off in silence.

Despite everything that Kate had been through in the last few weeks and months, including an attempt to kill her and a period when she didn't know whether O'Connell might not have the same idea, the next two hours were, nonetheless, some of the worst she had experienced. The six men with her were, everyone of them, powerful, tough-looking, unsmiling men; and the thought of being left in their hands was so unthinkably awful that she could barely stop herself screaming again, that they must let her go. Great deal of good that would do. That she would comply with whatever was demanded of her, rather than face such a fate, was very certain, but what could their 'director of operations' or whatever they called him want from her that was so terrible that these men were the alternative? She knew – had known from the moment she agreed to swap places with Paul – that they could hold her and use that fact to stop Paul talking. But that could never last. Either she would be freed, and the threat to Paul would have passed; or they would dispose of her, and she again could no longer be used by Gerrard to threaten Paul or O'Connell. Such thoughts went round and round in her mind, leading absolutely nowhere. So, she forced herself to breathe calmly, tried to rid her mind of any particular thoughts, even tried to remember some odd bits of poetry she had learnt at school. Sometimes it worked. At other times she was so overcome with the fear she felt that she could barely think anything at all.

Rather to her surprise, Swinburne's men had not blind-folded her; but that was then a new source of panic. Why didn't they care if she saw where they were going? Was it because they knew she would never get the chance to reveal the information to anyone else. Waves of desperation engulfed her, but all she could do was sit, looking at her hands, cuffed together in front of her, and wait. The sign posts she saw indicated that they were heading towards London and, after what seemed to her hours and hours, but was in fact only about an hour and a quarter, she noticed that they were no longer in countryside, but clearly heading into London itself. Swinburne turned and said -

"If you make any attempt to attract the attention of another motorist or pedestrian, the driver will head straight for our base; Sergeant Williams, on your left, has instructions to destroy one of your eyes; and the game will be over for you. Do you understand?"

"Yes" mumbled Kate; and continued to stare down in front of her. No-one else said anything. Nearly an hour later they were at King's Cross, from where they headed towards Westminster, coming to a halt outside a large anonymous white stone office block between Whitehall and the river Thames. It was around 10.45 am; there were very few pedestrians about and, apart from an occasional taxi, no cars. Swinburne waited until there was no-one near, then said "Let's go", and the six men climbed out, hustling Kate quickly into a doorway, through an empty lobby and down some stairs into a basement office. There she was given a chair to sit on at a table, while Swinburne's men stood idly around. Again, no-one spoke. Finally, at around 11.15 am, a tall, confident looking man, probably in his late forties, but with wisps of silver hair, walked into the room, accompanied by two others. To her relief, Kate saw that these, at least, were not more of Swinburne's military types. They were altogether much less intimidating physically, wore dark suits and ties, and glasses. At a nod from the man who was clearly in charge, Swinburne and his men left the room. As they did so the man asked them to remain just outside; and to be ready if he should call them in.

Kate wasn't sure, but she thought she recognised the man from his appearance. What she undoubtedly recognised was his voice. She had finally come face to face with Gerrard's fixer. Palmer focused on Kate; and his eyes bored into hers.

"Miss Kimball, for reasons that may become apparent to you later on, I have very little time today. That is why, despite the clear risk it represents, I have had you brought to the centre of London. Please, therefore, concentrate very carefully. I want you to do something for me. I believe that the good Captain has made clear what the consequences of you declining to assist me will be?" Kate, actually finding it very difficult to concentrate, managed to nod. Palmer's next words completely threw Kate.

"Are you a good actress, Kate?"

"Am I what? Replied Kate, not because she hadn't heard or understood, but because she was so astonished by his question.

"You heard me. Are you a good actress – I suppose I should say 'actor' these days".

"I don't know" said Kate, still quite bewildered. "I haven't done any acting since I was at school".

"Were you good at school?" asked Palmer, direct and grim-looking.

"Quite, I suppose. I played several big parts, in school plays. Why are you asking me this?" she added, with a touch of exasperation coming into her voice.

"You, Dr. Emmerson and your Irish associates represent an extreme threat to the Prime Minister. It is now clear to me that you had virtually no evidence to support the threats you made to me; and all that you now have are the emails and tapes of our correspondence since you first wrote that letter. Unfortunately, that evidence, limited as it is, would be powerfully corroborated if anything happened to you, or to Emmerson for that matter. But I will not allow you – any of you - to destroy him. Do you understand that?" Kate again nodded, wondering where this was all going. "My two colleagues here" – he pointed briefly at the two other men sat beside him – "have, therefore, prepared a little… I don't quite know what to call it…. a script - a script of a number of telephone calls, between you and various other people, which between them establish that you, Emmerson and the IRA planned to fabricate this whole exercise. You will read these scripts – 'perform' them might be a better word - a series of performances you will need to give as if your life depended upon them because, be in no doubt, it does".

"What will you do with them?" was all Kate could think to ask, still unable to focus clearly on what was happening.

"Absolutely nothing" was the - again astonishing – reply. Kate was now in such an overwrought state she could barely think

"I don't understand……" she started to say, but Palmer cut her off.

"It's quite simple. You provide the evidence that this was all a plot against the PM; and you go free. Go back to Dr. Emmerson, have a wonderful happy life. But if you, or Emmerson, or the Irish bastards you've been in bed with give even a hint of moving against Alan Gerrard; then the evidence you are going to supply me with will emerge – from GCHQ naturally – that will not only completely discredit you and anything you try to say about the PM, but will leave you wide open to criminal charges that could see you spend much of the rest of your life in prison. What you are going to provide for me – or more accurately for my two colleagues here – will be my insurance that you will never be able to touch the PM. We all get what we want". He paused.

"But if I do what you want, you will be able to have me prosecuted, sent to jail. No-one will believe me – what's really happening".

"I give you my word that will not happen and, before you ask, let me explain why you can trust me on this. All I want, all Alan Gerrard wants, is to be free of the threat you pose. What I am asking you to do will guarantee that. With the problem solved, it would be sheer madness for us to bring the whole issue back under the spotlight. As you say, it is unlikely that anyone, anyone at all, would believe your story, but why would we take that risk? The only point is to neutralise you or, more likely your IRA pals, if you should ever think of going public. If you all keep quiet, the last thing on earth Gerrard is going to do is open it all up again. That is why you can be assured of an end to all this, provided you never ever breathe a word of it ever again". Kate thought she could see the logic in this, but was equally aware that she was not functioning too well. She could think of no reply.

"This is the point where I should ask you if you will be co-operative" said Palmer "but I think you know that you do not have any choice in the matter. The alternative really is too horrible to contemplate". The reminder of Swinburne and his team, just outside the door caused a new bout of panic to hit Kate but, her heart pounding, finally galvanized her.

"How long will this take?" she asked.

"That very much depends on you. My colleagues here..." he nodded perfunctorily towards the other two men "...you may call them David and John, are ready to go. How long would you say?" he asked them. The one whom Palmer had indicated was to be known as David replied.

"If it goes well we will be finished by tomorrow, Friday at the latest. You will probably need most of today to fully understand the scenario we have constructed; and you will need that if you are to be convincing. Then we can start recording tomorrow. There are a totally of eleven calls, so we might well finish before tomorrow evening. But we won't stop until every call is completely convincing".

"I have to go" said Palmer. "Moment of truth, Kate. You are leaving this room either with David and John here, or with the Captain and his crew outside. Which is it to be?" He stood up. Kate remained seated, rigid in her chair.

"As you said, I don't have a choice, do I.?"

"No, not really. That's settled then. Over to you" Palmer replied, with another small nod to the other two men. He went to the door but, before leaving, turned and looked hard at Kate.

"We will not meet again Miss Kimball. But do not, for one moment, forget that I have it within my power to destroy your life, your reputation, your freedom. Please tell your friends that the same holds for them as well". And he was gone, back to No. 10 to handle the media madhouse that had started up the moment news started to filter through from Iran and various government agencies around the world. Whether it was his parting words, or just the fact that such a menacing man was no longer in the room with her, Kate felt a new emotion rising within her – sheer anger, rage at this man who presumed to control her life, threaten her well-being. The anger was, of course, quite impotent, she realised; but it at least gave her some energy and strength – both qualities she had been desperately lacking so far that day. She swung round to David and John.

"Well, what happens now" she said, knowing she sounded both angry and slightly imperious. Well, no bad thing. This time it was John who spoke.

"We have things set up in the room next door - all our equipment, the texts and so on. There's a camp bed for tonight. Captain Lethal and his men will be taking it in turns to guard you; but they are under strict instructions to leave us to get on with things. So, follow me". He led Kate outside, past several of Swinburne's men, who either ignored her or stared at her, grim faced and threatening. The next room looked a little like some sort of laboratory, Kate thought as they entered, with desks covered with assorted telecommunications equipment, recorder, wires, plugs, speakers and the like. Slightly separate were three desks with large coloured folders. Without any preamble, John started in on Kate's task.

"First we are going to talk you through the thing in outline. Then we will give you an hour or two to read through this file. Together they will give you a complete picture of the scenario we will be duplicating. Later this afternoon, we will talk you through the telephone conversations you are going to have and which we are going to record. You'll see how they fit into the scenario – only by hints, innuendo, and all in coded form. Then you can go over each item in your mind tonight and – this is very important – make them very personal to you. Change the language, as long as you don't change the message, so that you feel comfortable with it, that you are speaking the way you would speak, albeit under stress. If you arouse any suspicion in our minds that you are not doing this to the very best extent that you can, the whole thing will be off. His lordship has made it quite clear that he'd rather have you out of the way than captured on tape in a way that won't stand up. You can try to fool us if you want; but it will be a very dangerous game to play. I hope that is clear. As his lordship said, the performance of your life".

Despite the circumstances, Kate found herself being very impressed with the guile that the two of them had shown. Essentially, they described an operation by a dissident group of ex-IRA members, outraged at the peace settlement in Northern Ireland and still determined to achieve a United Ireland. They had decided that the only way to get Britain once again to think seriously about such issues was to be able to blackmail the PM into a new initiative. The death of five IRA members in a car accident in the Irish Republic had triggered a line of approach – that Gerrard had had them murdered to stop them revealing a failed terrorist attack on the British mainland. They had heard about Dr. Paul Emmerson's work via an IRA sympathiser who worked in the Engineering department of University College, Dublin; and out of that constructed the Sellafield story. They had, according to this script, then seized Emmerson and held him captive, with the intention of getting him to reveal what he had discovered at Sellafield, as the background to the death of the five IRA members. But Emmerson, so the story went, could not be persuaded to go public with their fiction; and would clearly not be credible if tortured into doing this. So his girl-friend, Kate, had been snatched and, under the threat of harm to her, had got Emmerson to agree to confirm the whole story. Fortunately, as the result of both local intelligence gathering and electronic surveillance, Britain's security forces had become aware of the plot; and had followed it closely, allowing the threat to Gerrard to be made in the hope that all of those involved could be identified and arrested. Critically, having seized Kate in order to persuade Emmerson to co-operate, the IRA had recognised the protective value of having Kate act as their intermediary in the blackmail operation against Gerrard. The involvement of the Irish could not be hidden, but using Kate would add to the difficulty of their being identified by the security service. All of the communications which O'Connell – though they still didn't know his name – and Kate had recorded, both what they had said and Palmer's replies, as he played along with the charade, were consistent with this interpretation. All that was needed was electronic surveillance records of other calls made by Kate, which made it unambiguously clear that the whole thing was in fact forged from beginning to end; and Gerrard was in the clear. Those calls were what they were going to construct in the next 24 hours or so.

Kate digested all this. More importantly, she had begun to get her wits together. Getting Gerrard had been high on her agenda when she thought that he might have done away with Paul. But since Paul was alive, and relatively safe, and she, extraordinary as it seemed to her, was unharmed, physically at least, she couldn't give a damn about Gerrard. It was O'Connell and Riordan who wanted him. They would be less than pleased that she had co-operated to get Gerrard off the hook, but that was just too bad. She knew, and they would have to recognise, that she hadn't had a choice. Maybe O'Connell would become vengeful; and she and Paul would have to disappear, but at least they would be alive and together. In any event, her own position could only be improved by making this 'scenario' they had described come alive. If it required the performance of her life, then that was what it would be. Her thoughts were interrupted.

"Do you have any immediate questions?" asked David.

"No, I get the picture – very clever. I'll get going on the details in the folder". David passed it to her and she began to read. She was only a little way through when some sandwiches arrived.

CHAPTER 35

In Belfast, O'Connell, Riordan, Emmerson and Hargreaves, out of hospital but – agreed by all – now convalescing at O'Connell's house, were doing what much of the world's population were doing, namely listening intently to the latest news bulletin – in their case the one o'clock news - on the radio. Since quite early that morning, news programmes and bulletins had been filled with virtually nothing other than the US strike on Iran. A succession of politicians and commentators had been interviewed; and the near universal view was that the attack had been the most calamitous decision by the US since the Vietnam War, an act that would stand in infamy for generations to come. Even the Americans interviewed were, for the most part, apocalyptical; and the few who were not totally critical were very circumspect, in general saying that they would wait for the President's scheduled Press Conference at 11 am Washington time. So universal was the condemnation that the interviewers, whose normal stock in trade was to attack from adopted moral high ground, were struggling to find anyone who would disagree with them. Of all the countless millions listening to the reports, only the small group in a West Belfast house had a more immediate and more personal agenda. As soon as they had first heard the announcement, at 8 am that morning, O'Connell had tried to call Palmer, but got only his answer service. He had left a message, saying that he should be called as soon as possible, to arrange the 'repatriation' project they had agreed. He had phoned a further three times since then, with growing frustration at the absence of any pick-up by Palmer. O'Connell was starting to have a very bad feeling about the situation; and Emmerson, though he said little, was starting seriously to consider whether he would ever see Kate again. They agreed that, if they had heard nothing by 2 pm, O'Connell would leave a message giving Palmer until 4 pm to reply, failing which they would make contact with the Press.

Everything changed at 1.23 pm. All of the news up until that point had been about the attack on Iran. Then, as they listened, aware that the deadline for O'Connell's next and last call was fast approaching, they heard the announcer say

"And now for other news. A woman has been arrested in Scotland under the anti-terrorism laws. The 32 year old, who has not been named, was detained at a holiday cottage near Fife and taken to London, where she is helping the security forces with inquiries. A source close to the investigation said that the woman comes from Oxford; and that the arrest is connected with the abduction three months ago of an Oxford scientist by a dissident branch of the IRA opposed to the Peace Process in Northern Ireland". And then she moved on to some financial news.

"Oh Christ" exclaimed O'Connell. "I think we are in the process of being stitched up".

"What is going on?" said Emmerson, though he realised that he had a fairly good idea.

"Simple enough, I suppose" said O'Connell. "Kate is going to be tarred with some terrorist brush; and your disappearance is clearly going to be attributed to us. Very neat".

"But I can vouch for it being totally untrue" said Emmerson.

"And I can confirm that" said Hargreaves.

"Will you - either of you - while they are holding Kate?" asked O'Connell.

"No" said Emmerson "but once they release her – or it becomes clear that they won't – then we will".

"And what credibility will that have?" responded O'Connell. "A bunch of hacked-off IRA hoodlums and the lover of a woman being held on terrorist charges of some sort. No chance. We are well and truly fucked".

"We still have the tape, of Sykes confirming Gerrard's involvement" said Riordan, "plus the email correspondence between them and Kate. There's a lot there for a journalist to go on, surely?"

"You may be right" replied O'Connell mournfully "but it doesn't feel right. They know we will have kept copies, but they've gone ahead with this announcement anyway. Maybe we should give them another hour; and then, if they haven't released Kate, go to the Press". Emmerson quickly intervened, speaking with quiet authority.

"We can't do anything for the moment, not until Kate's position is clear". He thought of adding that he would not take any part – his crucial part – in any exposure of Gerrard while Kate's life still hung in the balance, but he didn't feel the need to. What he had said – and how he had said it - made this quite clear; and O'Connell would not miss the implication.

A long silence ensued. Both O'Connell and Riordan had a sick feeling in the stomach at the growing prospect that Gerrard was going to escape the retribution he unquestionably deserved. Emmerson and Hargreaves' focus was entirely on Kate, but they felt equally desperate. O'Connell's two sons waited, quite prepared to make suggestions but bereft of any ideas. It was Riordan who eventually broke the silence.

"Do we have any cards to play?"

"Barely" said O'Connell. "But maybe just one. The guy we have been dealing with – Gerrard's man. We don't know who he is, but he must be someone very close to Gerrard on his staff. It shouldn't be impossible to find out who he is but, more important, it should be quite easy to persuade him that we can find out his name. He knows we have a force capable of taking on the SAS. So, maybe we should threaten him direct. Unless he releases Kate as he arranged, we will hunt him down – and his wife and kids if he's got any – however long it takes. Make it clear that none of them will ever be free to go where they want. They'll need twenty-four hour protection; and we will still get him in the end, as nasty as possible; and maybe sell his kids to a paedophile ring, anything to get him to keep to what he said". It was, perhaps, a sign of how shocked – outraged – they all felt that no-one seemed put off by this obscenely ruthless approach to the problem. It was Hargreaves, only loosely still remembering that he was a member of Her Majesty's Police force, who asked

"Would you carry that out?"

"That isn't the issue" snapped O'Connell "only whether the bastard believes it or not".

"I think I'd believe it" said Emmerson "enough to be worried, anyway".

"So would I" added Riordan. "So let's try it". The six men looked at each other. No-one made any attempt to question the implicit decision. O'Connell picked up the mobile he'd been using and rang Palmer's number yet again. To his complete surprise, Palmer answered it. Before O'Connell could say anything, Palmer spoke, fast.

"Thought you'd be in touch. I can't speak now – the PM's due at the House shortly. I'll call you around 5 pm. Have Emmerson with you. I'll not speak to anyone else". And with that he switched off the phone.

O'Connell felt a surge of rage that he could barely control. He hadn't been able to threaten the man, hadn't even said a word; and they would have to wait until 5 pm to pursue matters. But beyond all that was the peremptory tone the man had used; and the less than subtle shift of power inherent in the man's insistence that he would only speak to Emmerson – precisely the proposal that O'Connell had so effectively vetoed last time they spoke. He might have a plan, but he was totally on the back foot; and knew he was not at his best in such situations. The others, noting only that O'Connell had said nothing, looked at him, awaiting an explanation.

"He says he's dealing with the Prime Minister and will call around 5 pm. The bastard's so cocky he hung up on me". The six of them sat silently, grim-faced. It was Vincent O'Connell who re-energised them.

"So, we've got thee hours to find out who he is. We should at least be able to sort out a list of possibles. I'll get googling". O'Connell nodded.

In his office Palmer sat for a second with a quiet sense of satisfaction – not just because all was going to plan but, much more than that, because he'd crapped all over the fucking Irish sod who'd humiliated him before. But he had no more time to enjoy the moment. Gerrard was addressing the House of Commons in twenty minutes; and Palmer had to be there to listen – quite possibly, he recognised, his last act as Gerrard's factotum. Gerrard's chances of surviving the day were, by any reckoning, extremely poor and Palmer was very unlikely to survive whatever would follow Gerrard's resignation. It was a commonplace that all political careers ended in failure. Less widely noted were the hordes of underlings whose careers went down the lavatory with them. And he wouldn't even be able to tell all in his memoirs. How had he got to this point, he wondered. Not for the first time, however, he understood that he was Gerrard's political bodyguard, ready to go down to protect him, albeit with less risk of personal damage than a real bodyguard, but a bodyguard nonetheless; and now the day had come, when he had saved Gerrard as a person, from the madness of what he had done almost thirty years ago, from a fate that had been waiting to happen ever since. The only remaining question was whether he could save Gerrard politically. Together, he and Gerrard had spent the early hours of the morning, planning one last card to play in Parliament. It was high-risk; and whether it would work was far from clear, but it was worth the attempt. Well, he thought, there was no point in speculating. He gathered up a few things and headed off to Parliament Square.

The atmosphere in the House of Commons chamber was simply electric. Virtually all 646 Members of Parliament were present, which meant that a substantial number had to stand at the back, facing the Speaker of the House of Commons, there being too few seats to either side to accommodate them all. As Palmer looked down from the gallery he sensed the animal spirits at large, the combination of shock and anger at what had happened, the uncertainty as to Gerrard's role in it all, the anticipation that his head was due to roll, the sense that they were present on an historic day - one that would echo through the ages; and they'd be able to say that they were there – all heightened by the fact that the President would not speak in Washington for another two hours. Gerrard would be the first to try to explain to an unbelieving world – and the first sacrificial lamb.

At one minute before 2 pm, Gerrard entered the chamber from behind the Speaker's chair. For a moment there was a hush, then some booing, and then a crescendo of braying as the one word 'resign' started to emerge from the Labour opposition, echoed by the Liberal Democrats, repeated again and again, ever louder until it reached deafening levels. Gerrard's Conservatives sat in stunned silence, unwilling to condemn him before he had spoken but equally unprepared to offer any support. Gerrard, pale and grim but otherwise appearing to ignore the uproar, took his place on the Government front bench and sat there, silent, unmoving, waiting for the furore to die away. Initially there seemed to be no prospect of this. The opposition had not had an opportunity like this since they had lost power; and were determined to make the most of it. The Speaker's calls for order were completely inaudible and, in the end, Gerrard sat down and simply waited for the storm to blow itself out. Thus it was some six or seven minutes before, finally, the noise had fallen away enough for the Speaker to call the Chamber to order; and then called the Prime Minister.

As Gerrard stood, the calls started again, not as loud as before, but far too loud for him to be heard; and so, in what might have been a calculated move, or just a spur-of-the-moment decision, he sat down again, making it clear that he could sit there all day if he was not to be given the opportunity to speak. It flitted briefly through Palmer's mind that there was probably no other governmental institution anywhere in the world that allowed, indeed by its layout encouraged, such ludicrous behaviour as here, in the so-called mother of Parliaments. Eventually the noise died down; and Gerrard once again rose to his feet. With a shock, Palmer saw that Gerrard had no notes to put on the Dispatch Box in front of him, no copy of the speech that he and Gerrard had worked on so assiduously during the last twenty-four hours. But, he also noted, many of those present had registered the same fact; and, no doubt as Gerrard had intended, it added – if that were possible – to the gravity of the occasion. A man clearly facing his political demise was going to speak from the heart rather than from notes. Gerrard paused a second, surveying the House in front of him. The silence was now total.

"Mr. Speaker, Members of the House, I wish to make a statement concerning the events of the last twenty-four hours; and the role of the British Government in them. I have asked the Speaker to arrange for a debate at 5 pm tomorrow, once Members have had a chance to digest my Statement. At the end of the debate, I will call for a Vote of Confidence in the Government's actions in relation to Iran. Should that vote be lost, I will notify Her Majesty that I no longer can form a Government which retains the confidence of the House, ask for the dissolution of this Parliament and proceed to a General Election". This quite unexpected announcement stunned the assembled Members of Parliament; and no-one broke the shocked silence that followed it. Gerard continued.

"The background to what has happened will be familiar to everyone here. For most of the last two decades, the Iranian Government has been determined to equip itself with nuclear weapons. This has been clear both from satellite observation and intelligence reports from within the country and, in truth, while the Iranian Government has paid lip service to the notion that its nuclear programme is for domestic energy purposes only, it has barely bothered to conceal its true intent. This has been of the utmost concern to the international community, not only the United States and Britain but to virtually all countries in the United Nations; and there has been concerted and sustained effort by the UN to bring this programme to a halt. This has included offers of support for non-nuclear energy development, and economic aid of various sorts, in return for a cessation of the programme and a series of inspections to verify the matter. It has embraced the threat and the fact of economic sanctions; and attempts to block the importation of expertise and resources necessary for its nuclear programme. And it has included extensive diplomatic pressure, both direct and indirect over a long period of time. Iran has accepted the incentives offered and ignored the pressures and, step by step, has constructed all the facilities it needs, recruited all the expertise it needs, and imported all the equipment it needs, to be able to produce nuclear bombs and nuclear warheads. It was in response to this situation that the UN Security Council met yesterday, a meeting to which I will return in a moment.

"At the same time, the Iranian Government has repeatedly said that, in its view, Israel has no right to exist; and that, given the means, it will seek to destroy the country and its people. Whether this is a genuine policy objective, or more a means to bolster internal support and court a *de facto* leadership of the Arab world has not been clear from the policy statements themselves; but intelligence sources from high up in the Iranian Government machine have, for some time, indicated that this is a serious and determined policy objective. It is for this reason that the United States, with the full backing of Britain, sought a Resolution from the UN Security Council to ensure that Iran's nuclear programme – and its evident threat not only to Israel but to peace and stability in the Middle East – be brought to an end by whatever means necessary.

"As Honourable Members know, the Resolution commanded the necessary majority, but was rendered ineffective by the veto of Russia, as one of the five Permanent Members. Intelligence sources revealed some days ago that the failure of the UN Resolution would be viewed by Iran as, essentially, a green light – a clear indication that neither the UN nor any smaller alliance of nations would be prepared to take any effective action to prevent Iran from pursuing either its nuclear ambitions or its declared objective of destroying Israel. Those same sources, however, also revealed that the Iranian authorities were well aware of Israel's acute concern at the developing situation; and the distinct prospect that Israel would take unilateral action to remove the threat from Iran before it could materialise. Within an hour of the failed UN Resolution, both President Hamilton and I were informed that, in order to counter this threat, the Iranian Government was planning a nuclear attack on Israel at the earliest possible moment, this being within a matter of weeks at the most, perhaps days. Whether delivered by Iranian bomber aircraft or missiles from transportable launch vehicles, there is no way to be sure of neutralising this, neither by attacking Iran's airbases nor its missile delivery systems. President Hamilton therefore took the decision to eliminate Iran's nuclear threat while this was still possible – that is, by destroying all the facilities necessary for the construction, arming and launch of its nuclear arsenal. He requested, and I approved as a matter of course, the use of US airfields in the UK which have for many years been a base for the United States Air force.

"I now come to the heart of the matter. A number of Iran's nuclear facilities are buried very deep underground, beyond the reach of the heaviest block-buster bombs which the US has been able to construct; and for some time I have been kept informed of US efforts to construct ever more effective bombs against such sites. I was, however, informed by the US yesterday that, to date, this programme had not been successful and that, with the dire urgency to act that had now arisen, there was no alternative – on certain sites at least – to the use of nuclear warheads. In a personal conversation with the President, I objected in the strongest possible terms to this development, arguing that such a development could never take place without UN authority, which I very much doubted would ever be forthcoming. The President pointed out that no nuclear devices would originate from their bases in the UK, but I indicated that that was not the point at issue. Rather it was the long term devastation that would be caused to Iran and its population.

"President Hamilton then made me aware of two facts which are very germane to the situation. The first was that the US was giving Iran a number of hours notice of its attack, so that it could remove populations from the vicinity of the nuclear sites which the US was targetting; and, in addition, he let me know that in some cases, where there was too large an adjacent population for this to be a practical solution, the US would, reluctantly, forego the use of nuclear weapons, even though this would reduce the impact of its attempt to end, once and for all, Iran's nuclear pretensions. Second, and perhaps of even more significance, he told me that the Israeli Government had been kept fully informed and, indeed, were an integral part of the plans to attack Iran, with the Israeli air force being the mainstay of the attack on the Iranian air force, thereby protecting the US forces deployed in the operation. The Israeli Government had, he said, made it very clear that, in the absence of a fully effective operation by the US, it would itself deploy its nuclear deterrent to protect itself from imminent destruction by Iran. President Hamilton therefore believed, and I accepted that, in the absence of the operation envisaged by the United States, a nuclear holocaust was both inevitable and imminent in the Middle East. Moreover, unlike the US plan of operation, the civilian populations of both Iran and Israel would bear the brunt, in the major cities and beyond. While, therefore, it was open to me to reject any UK involvement in what was planned,

I have to say to the House that, as the person ultimately responsible for the armed forces of the United Kingdom, I acquiesced in the US operation; and stand ready to defend this position in tomorrow's debate. I believe that what has happened is very much the lesser of two evils – evils that were none of our making and which, for so long, we have tried, by all means possible, to avoid. Mr. Speaker, that is the end of my Statement". In the stunned silence that followed, Gerrard calmly walked the few steps towards the Speaker's Chair and disappeared behind it and on out of the Chamber.

A hubbub of noise grew, as MPs of all parties began to take on board what Gerrard had said; and started to voice aloud their reactions. It was all Palmer could do not to leap to his feet and start applauding. Though he was intimately familiar with the speech, it had gained much in the delivery - the lack of any notes had been merely a ploy to heighten the drama, he now realized and, for a brief, nostalgic moment, he recalled how much in awe he had once been of Gerrard and his political talents. The game was far from won, but Gerrard, in his delivery, had at least put himself back in play. How much of the speech was true he was unsure, but of two things he was certain. The first was that Gerrard had checked it all out with Hamilton, so that in less than two hours there would be powerful support from the President. And the second was that, if any of it was untrue, it would be virtually impossible for anyone to identify that fact, still less by tomorrow. All in all, it had been the performance of Gerrard's life. Now it all hinged on tomorrow's debate. He rose and headed out, glancing at his watch. He had twenty minutes to get to a rather critical meeting. Less than half a mile away Kate, still completely unaware of events, was preparing to make some scripted phone calls.

CHAPTER 36

By the time Palmer joined Gerrard in No. 10, the historically but very appropriately named Chief Whip, responsible for party discipline and his two main lieutenants were already there, along with Gerrard's Chief of Staff and two other Special Advisers. Once all eight of them were seated, Gerrard nodded to the Chief Whip.

"Dennis, talk us through it" he said. Dennis Fairbrother looked round the assembled group. A long-standing party stalwart, he was regarded by all as something of an enigma – florid and bull-like in appearance - straight out of central casting was the general view – but surprisingly polite and mild-mannered in style for one of the most bruising roles in politics. He was, nonetheless, extremely intelligent and absolutely ruthless. If anyone could deliver Gerrard the support he needed, it was Dennis Fairbrother.

"Right, broad picture first, then the details. The key thing, of course, is the threat of a general election. Given that we are behind in the polls anyway - and once everything has sunk in we are going to be a lot further behind - there's a big chunk of the party fighting for their lives. We'll lose a few but nearly all those with government positions will come into line – they're not going to give up their positions without a fight – and that's around one hundred and twenty. Then there's another hundred at least – in fact rather more – who will reckon on losing their seats if there is an election. Again, we may lose a few; but as soon as it becomes clear that you could win the vote, there's only a rump that's going to get caught standing out against you. There is some overlap with the government group, but we estimate that together you've got a minimum of two hundred and twenty. So, we need just over one hundred of the rest – say about sixty per cent – to nail it". He paused, but no-one had any comments so far. "James and Ian…" he nodded towards the two other whips "…have been right through the list. There's a good fifty that will either support what you have done, or will be sufficiently neutral not to rock the boat. It's the other fifty that will be the problem. We've targetted three groups. The first – around fifteen or so – you'll have to offer posts to. I assume I've got *carte blanche* on that?" Gerrard nodded. "There's maybe a dozen where we have enough dirt on them I won't really need to spell it out; and there's maybe twenty where a slightly more subtle touch should do the job".

"What does that mean exactly?" asked Gerrard. It was Palmer who answered.

"Cases where there's something not right; and one or two journalists have sniffed around. But they know that if they plunge in, we'll cut them off from everything; so we are in a position to protect the members concerned. But if we are out of office then, with great regret of course, we won't have any levers; and the members must take their chances. It's worked well before, it'll work again".

"So" said Fairbrother, picking up the thread again "we're close. But I'm going to have to work fast to secure all those we have in our sights; and we may still be a few votes short. However, I've drawn up a list of another twenty or so for you to see, Alan. They're unlikely to support what's happened, they can't be bribed and there are no known skeletons. You've just got to persuade them that what you did was right or, as you so powerfully put it, the lesser of two evils. The office is scheduling meetings as we speak".

"Many thanks" said Gerrard. "As effective as ever, Dennis. Are there any questions?"

"What about Seymour?" asked Gerrard's Chief of Staff.

"That's the other beauty of the dissolution threat" replied Fairbrother. "Without that, there's no question Seymour would attack you, Alan; offer himself as your successor; and he'd win, no question. You'd take all the flak, the party would distance itself under Seymour; and he'd be able to offer all manner of goodies under his new administration. But now, he's got nothing to offer. If he attacks you, he'll just hasten the end of this government; and there's a lot of members who would see him as using the situation to get himself elected party leader even though it consigns the party to opposition. No, he is well and truly buggered. In fact his best hope is to show an utter loyalty that, alas, fails to save you. Then he's the new leader with not a stain on his character. He can support you in public and urge his supporters to oppose you in private of course, but there isn't that many who will play ball with him on that". Gerrard looked round the group, waiting to se if there were any other questions, his face an impassive mask of grim determination. No-one else spoke.

"Okay" he said "let's get going". Palmer contemplated staying on, to acquaint Gerrard with the situation on Kimball, but Gerrard was all action now; and Palmer realised that it would have to wait. Anyway, he'd have more to report later.

"Just off Whitehall, Kate was learning her lines or, rather, getting a feel for how she would deliver them. The first set of three fake calls was going to be the hardest. These were the ones where she was going to have to sound shocked, terrified, distraught, as an unknown interlocutor with an Irish accent told her that his group held Emmerson; and that she would need to comply with their wishes if she ever wanted to see him again; that she would have to take time off work, go on holiday, apparently to Scotland but in fact head for Belfast. But her one objective was to master the task as convincingly as possible. Only once did it cross her mind to try to infiltrate some sort of code into her words – something that could subsequently be used to confirm that she had been providing the evidence under duress; but she dismissed the thought almost the moment it occurred to her. The skill she would need was almost certainly beyond her, even though she had used the technique once before; and the stakes were just too high. If she gave them what they wanted, then Gerrard would be in the clear; and there would be no reason for them not to let her go, to rejoin Paul. But if they caught her out – spotted some irregularity and deciphered what it meant – then she knew what the terrifying consequences would be. Such a fear gripped her that she could barely breathe; and that told her just how incapable she was of any type of deviation from what she had been told to do. She moved on to acquaint herself with the thrust of the later calls – all acquiescence now – as the script led her through her role as the front for the Irishman, seeking to blackmail Gerrard on the basis of the tragic but entirely accidental death of five Irish patriots nearly thirty years ago, plus contrived information from Emmerson. As she looked over the material it struck her that, perhaps, it was not Gerrard's fixer or the platoon of soldiers guarding her she should be frightened of, but O'Connell, when he found out that he had been outwitted – lost any chance of bringing down Gerrard – and found out Kate's role in it. Well, she might have a chance to run from O'Connell – and with Paul at her side. She had no chance of running from her present company; and no-one to help her. A no-brainer, really.

In Belfast, Vincent O'Connell had had some success, but not enough. Working on the principles that whoever was directing Gerrard's operation to save him would have to be very high up, almost certainly in No. 10 itself, a party man rather than a Civil Servant, and of long standing, he had identified six possibles, two of whom were women. But as between the other four, he could make no guess; and Victor would have no cards to play if he couldn't accurately identify the man at the other end of the line. Vincent could get pictures of them, but without hearing them speak, he couldn't see how to narrow the field down any further. And he couldn't be certain that his reasoning was sound. Victor O'Connell looked glum as his son relayed this information to him.

"Well, we will have to play it their way for the moment" said O'Connell. "See what he has to say at 5 pm. Not good, though".

It was no less a frantic afternoon for Palmer than for Gerrard and the whips, as they sought to badger, bribe and cajole more or less reluctant members of the party to support Gerrard. President Hamilton's press conference was, on balance, helpful, as it confirmed all that Gerrard had said but, in addition, talked of the opportunity for a new relationship with Iran and a new settlement in the Middle East. With Iran's nuclear option gone for ever, the US and others could, once the present tensions had died down, seek a co-operative relationship with Iran. With Israel's beleaguered security status now much improved, the time had come for a more general settlement, one that Iran and other Arab nations should be able to accept; with the creation of a Palestinian State, the withdrawal by Israel from both Gaza and the West Bank; and an end to the Jewish settlements that had caused such tension in the region. In short, a much tougher line with Israel was spelt out on the back of the salvation that the US had just provided. Much of it, Palmer thought, was naive bollocks, but it all helped – if not to retrieve then at least to gloss over - the otherwise desperate political situation into which Hamilton had plunged the world. But none of this was the real reason that he delayed calling O'Connell until almost 5.30 pm. He wanted the Irishman, whoever he was, to understand that he, Palmer, was now in control, that the call mattered much more to him than it did to Palmer, that he would call the shots from now on.

O'Connell let his mobile ring a couple of times before answering. It was a quite pointless gesture, but he couldn't stomach the prospect of the caller knowing just how desperate he was to take the call.

"Put Emmerson on immediately, or this call is at an end" said Palmer, as peremptorily as he could, enjoying the moment. O'Connell, as Palmer had intended, was incensed – at the tone, at being cut out, at the whole situation –

but he had the sense to recognise that he was in no position to do anything about any of these problems. He passed the mobile to Emmerson, for the second time that day having had a phone conversation with Palmer which involved him saying nothing at all.

"Emmerson here" said Paul.

"Wherever you are, go to a public call box and call me, now. Fuck me around and you will never see Kimball again. Do I make myself clear?"

"Yes" replied Emmerson, and the line went dead. He reported what Palmer had said to the others.

"Making sure we don't record the call" said O'Connell. "Okay, there's a box about four hundred yards from here. I'll take you there". His two sons, Riordan and Hargreaves all came too. A few minutes later, Emmerson called Palmer's number from the pay phone.

"What's the number of the phone you're on" asked Palmer. Emmerson gave it.

"Stay there. I'll call you back in a few minutes, soon as I've checked it is a public pay phone. If it isn't, this is the last you'll ever hear from me". He paused for a second, giving Emmerson one brief chance to admit it if, in Palmer's phrase, he was fucking him around, but Emmerson said nothing. The line again went dead. A few minutes later the phone rang and Emmerson answered it. Palmer spoke with little preamble.

"Four things, Emmerson" said Palmer. "First, all being well, Kate Kimball will be released from custody late tomorrow afternoon. She will be released at Oxford Police Station. Second, for this to happen, you will make your way there by 2 pm tomorrow, and report that you have just been released by a group of men who have been holding you since they abducted you some weeks ago. A Detective Inspector will be on hand to take a statement from you. Third, you will say in that statement that you have no idea where you were held, and not much idea why. It appears that they were a dissident Irish Nationalist faction who wished to use your engineering expertise in some way, but whatever their plan, it did not, as far as you know, ever fully get off the ground. That is all you will say at the police station; and all you will say to anyone else who asks you about your experience. Is that all clear so far?"

"Yes" replied Emmerson. "But why would you expect me to give myself up, after what happened to me before?"

"Because you don't have a choice if you want to see Kimball again. Now stop wasting my time. Be there or don't be there, but be very clear what the consequences are. If it is any comfort, I don't give a shit what happens to you, or to Kimball for that matter. I'm just preserving my freedom of action; and what I have just told you will do that".

"You said there were four things" said Emmerson, recognising that negotiation with the man on the phone would go nowhere.

"The fourth thing is for your benefit - and for the benefit of your Irish colleagues - rather than mine. I strongly advise you, having made the statement at the Police Station, to say nothing to anyone until you have had a chance to speak to Kimball. She will have information that you will find of interest. That's all" Palmer concluded; and switched off his mobile.

The tension amongst the group of men outside the box was palpable. Even O'Connell, who had joined Emmerson in the phone box, had heard only Emmerson's brief side of the conversation. Emmerson told them what Palmer had said.

"So" responded O'Connell, seeking to sum up the position "you go to Oxford and put us in the frame for your disappearance; and they will then release Kate, who has some relevant information for us. That's it?"

"Sounds like it" said Emmerson, feeling, with every second that went by, that the accord he and Hargreaves had developed with the O'Connells and Riordan was starting to unravel. There was every prospect that, within twenty four hours, both he and Kate would have their lives back; and O'Connell would, in some way not yet clear, be out of the game. One thing was certain – he was not going to betray any sign of the surge of optimism that he felt as a result of the phone call. Instead he waited for O'Connell to say something.

"It's one hell of a risk for you to walk straight into their hands" said O'Connell.

"I know but, like he said, I don't have a choice. I may be being very stupid, but I have a feeling that he may mean what he said. Why, I'm not sure. Maybe just wishful thinking". He waited to see if O'Connell would seek to prevent him from complying with the instructions he had received. When O'Connell did reply, it went some long way towards putting Emmerson's mind to rest.

"Well, it all depends on what Kate has to tell us. I guess we'll have to take the risk in order to find that out. Let's head back. You'd better start for Oxford tonight" he said to Emmerson "and I think we should all come with you".

"Even if they aren't after me, might this not be some sort of trap" asked Emmerson "if they expect you to accompany me?"

"For sure" said O'Connell "but I need to talk to Kate. We'll have to work out some way of making sure they don't get to me and Shaun through you".

"I might be able to help there" said Hargreaves. "I'll work out some details for you".

"Sounds good" said O'Connell. "Let's go".

O'Connell, Riordan, Emmerson and Hargeaves gathered what few things they needed together and climbed into Riordan's car. They took the car ferry to Holyhead and, by ten pm, had booked into a hotel in Birmingham. None of them spoke much on the journey, all too well aware that, in different ways and for different reasons, the next day could well be one of the most momentous of

384

their lives. In Downing Street, Alan Gerrard, having had an exhausting eight or nine hours seeing a large number of his party members, was experiencing a very similar emotion. Not far away, Kate, now well within striking distance of completing her project, could barely contain her feelings. The prospect of being free, of seeing Paul, of finally ending the nightmare journey she had been on to trace him; and the possibility that all this might once again be snatched away from her by Gerrard, made her almost physically sick. She could eat little; and prepared to get what sleep she could in the make-shift bed that Palmer had arranged for her.

In the course of the next morning, Gerrard saw more party members; and worked with his inner group, including Palmer, on the likely course of the forthcoming debate; and how best to deal with each of nearly a dozen scenarios that his staff had postulated. Kate made good progress with the phone calls she was working on, now with a real Irish voice at the other end of the line; and her two script writers-cum-producers expressed themselves very pleased with her progress. To her great relief, she saw virtually nothing of Swinburne, or any of his men; only enough to know that they were still very much in evidence outside her room – a formidable barrier between her and anything to do with the outside world. More than once she panicked at the thought that, having provided all the evidence Gerrard would need to damn O'Connell, she would be handed over to Swinburne and his men and never heard of again; but she retained just enough composure to be able to drive the thought away. Gerrard could expect much more trouble from Paul if it became clear she was gone; and with all the recordings made, what possible threat could she be? She would have been much more assured if she had known of the public announcement that she had been taken into custody – a state from which she would have to emerge at some point, free or not – but she was no more aware of this than of the attack on Iran or its political fall-out.

Meanwhile, O'Connell, Riordan, Emmerson and Hargreaves had breakfast and headed on for Oxford, arriving on the outskirts shortly after noon. Hargreaves and Emmerson had used their local knowledge to work out a means for them all to rendezvous with Kate, assuming she was released, but without taking any risk that Emmerson and Kate could be followed to the meeting with O'Connell and Riordan. With this end in mind, they dropped the two Irishmen at the Dew Drop Inn in Summertown, a suburb two miles north of the Oxford city centre, with instructions how to walk to the Victoria Arms – known to everyone in Oxford simply as the Vicky Arms – in Old Marston, only a few hundred metres from where Sarah Jennings lived - located on the banks of the Cherwell river less than a mile from Summertown. While O'Connell and Riordan had some lunch at the Dew Drop, and prepared for a long wait, Emmerson and Hargreaves drove on in Riordan's car to the centre of the city, parked in the Westgate multi-story car park, and walked round to the old prison area, now a completely redeveloped pedestrian area, with the prison converted to a very up-market hotel and with a range of restaurants around. They had lunch in the hotel itself. Emmerson was now less than a mile from his laboratory, and even closer to his college, but on a Thursday lunch-time in term, there was little prospect of his being seen in such a fashionable – not to mention expensive – location by any of his work colleagues. Shortly before 2 pm, Emmerson walked round to the Oxford Police Station, a few hundred yards south of the main cross-roads at the centre of the city. It had been agreed by all that Hargeaves should not head home before they had met up with Kate, just in case the whole thing was indeed a trap; and Hargreaves' home was being watched. Instead, he sat with a glass of wine and a pot of coffee in the hotel restaurant until well past 3 p.m., before heading off to the Cherwell Boathouse Restaurant, a little under two miles north, close to where he could take up what would be a strategically important location later that afternoon.

CHAPTER 37

On the stroke of 2 pm, Emmerson walked into the police station. It was a little under three months since Kate had done the same thing, to report his disappearance. Unlike Kate, he did not have to wait. A rather large, brooding-looking character, probably around fifty, with very short-cropped grey hair looked up from behind the counter.

"Can I help you?" he said in a polite but no-nonsense manner.

"I need to make a statement" said Emmerson. "My name is Dr. Paul Emmerson. I am a research scientist at the University; and I was abducted from my home several months ago. I imagine that the police will know about this?" The officer behind the counter gave Emmerson a long, penetrating look.

"I see. Will you please wait one moment?" he said; and disappeared out of the back of the reception area. A minute or two later, the door to the left side of the counter opened; and another police officer appeared, carrying a beige file.

"Please come this way" he said, and led Emmerson through the door, past the small room where Kate had been interviewed and on to a larger room beyond. Inside, the police officer indicated for Emmerson to take a seat at a medium sized table, on which stood some recording apparatus, and he then took a seat opposite.

"I'm Detective Inspector Johnson of the Thames Valley Police. I understand that you are Dr. Paul Emmerson, on our Missing Persons list; and wish to make a statement?"

"That's correct" said Emmerson.

"Before we start, do you have any means of identification on you?" asked Johnson.

"No, I don't" replied Emerson. "I had none on me when I was attacked. But I can certainly arrange for someone to identify me".

"It may be necessary later, as a formality" said Johnson "but I have two photographs of you here in your file, which are good enough for the moment". He switched on the recorder. "Please go ahead".

"Some three months ago, I answered a ring on my front door bell. As I opened the door, a group of men burst through and dragged me to the ground. I remember one of them shutting the front door, but that is all. They covered my face with a flannel – I presume soaked in chloroform or something similar – and have no further recollection until I found myself in a small room, where I have been kept ever since, until yesterday. Last night, without any warning, I was blindfolded, forced into the boot of a car, and released a short while ago, round the back of the railway station. I recognised where I was and have come straight here".

"Do you know where you were held all this time?" asked Johnson.

"I have no idea" said Emmerson "but I'm fairly certain it was either France, possibly Belgium, or Ireland, because the car definitely went on a ferry fairly soon after we set off".

"Do you have any idea why you were abducted?"

"Not really. They asked me quite a lot about my research work, some of my projects, but that's all".

"And who are 'they'?" asked Johnson.

"I only ever met two men. I can try to give you a picture of them. Both middle aged I would say, and one at least I think was Irish, maybe both of them".

"I see" said Johnson, non-committally. "Anything else?"

"No, that's it. They provided me with food and clothing, some books to read".

"Were you ever allowed out, for exercise or anything?"

"No. The windows were barred, so they let me open them for some fresh air, but I couldn't see anything except some trees. I spent some time every day doing exercises, to try to keep fit, but it was very monotonous".

"So, you have had no news of the outside world for three months?"

"None at all"

"How about the last twenty-four hours?"

"No" replied Emmerson, with a querying tone, trying to put from his mind the all too familiar details of that period.

"I believe you know Kate Kimball?" asked Johnson.

"She is my girl-friend; and as soon as I'm finished here I will go to see her".

"Did you not think to call her first?"

"I have no phone and no money; and she'll be at work. I think it would better to see her – she presumably thinks I'm dead".

"Well, I'm sorry that I have some rather unwelcome news for you, sir. Miss Kimball was arrested yesterday, in Scotland, and taken to London, where she is assisting the Metropolitan Police with some of their inquiries". The fact that DI Johnson had not got things quite correct – this was nothing to do with the Metropolitan Police – in a curious way helped Emmerson's attempt to look suitably shocked.

"I don't understand. What is she supposed to have done?" he said, staring at Johnson.

"I don't know" replied Johnson, but it may well be connected with your disappearance. That, at least, was hinted at on the news yesterday".

"But that's crazy" said Emmerson. "What on earth could Kate have to do with this? She works in publishing for God's sake".

"I have no idea. But it is probably of some significance that you have been released within twenty-four hours of her arrest".

"No, it's ridiculous. Look, I'm going now, to sort myself out, let people know I'm safe. Can you, in the meantime, find out anything you can about Kate, in particular, where she is being held; and I will come back in a couple of hours time".

"I doubt I will be able to offer much information" said Johnson, in a tone that indicated no great regrets about this.

"Well, I will come back anyway" replied Emmerson. "You presumably want me to construct some identi-kit pictures of then men who seized me". Johnson inwardly winced at the realisation that he had not mentioned this himself, but saw it as a useful distraction from the fate of the Kimball woman.

"Yes we will" he said. "I'll fix it up. Shall we say around 5 pm?"

"I'll be here" said Emmerson. "Please do whatever you can to find out where Kate is and how I can see her".

"I'll make inquiries" was as far as Johnson would go; and switched off the recorder. Emmerson was about to leave.

"I'll need you to write down a summary of what you've said, sir, and sign it. I'll get a pad and pen". As he left, Emmerson allowed himself a small smile. If DI Johnson was asked to report on what Emmerson had said – and he had absolutely no doubt that he would be asked – then the record would show that he had fully met the conditions laid down. All being well, he would see Kate later that afternoon.

Emmerson wrote out what he had said, signed it and barely forty minutes after entering the police station, was on his way out. He wondered whether he would be followed; and assumed that he probably would. Well, no matter. He was going to do exactly what he said he would – head home, re-gain his life, and head for the Engineering Department. Only then did it occur to him that his flat would, for certain, be locked; and he had no key to it on him. He went back inside the police station and asked the duty officer if he might speak again, briefly, to DI Johnson. The duty officer disappeared for a few seconds and then returned to say that DI Johnson was on the phone; and could he perhaps help. Of course, he would be, thought Emmerson, reporting on what he had said in his statement but, hopefully, providing the information needed for Kate's release to be authorised. Emmerson explained his problem to the duty officer, who said he could supply someone who could let Emmerson into his flat, but probably not for an hour or so. Emmerson could, meanwhile, arrange for a locksmith either to provide keys or new locks. Emmerson wondered whether Kate would have her keys to his flat on her, but arranged to meet a police officer at his flat at 4 pm, which would give him ample time to get in the place, pick up his keys and be back at the police station by 5 pm. He left again; and headed for the Engineering Laboratory.

When he walked into Alice's office, she took one look at him and promptly burst into tears. It only took her a few seconds to recover her composure, but the shock of seeing him again, after so long an absence; after becoming reconciled to his never returning; and after hearing only the day before that he had been taken by a dissident Irish group, was quite severe; and she found herself coping the only way she knew, which was to make them both a cup of tea. She fussed over this; and Emmerson, realising that she was finding it difficult to deal with his sudden re-emergence, let her do it. She was full of questions about what had happened to him; and Emmerson stuck to the same story that he had told DI Johnson. She absorbed all this, but it was only a few minutes before she began to look rather agitated.

"Have you heard about Kate?" she asked.

"Yes" he replied. "But I think it is all some sort of device tied in with what happened to me; and I think she will soon be released".

"Oh, that's wonderful "said Alice. "But how is it linked to you – I don't understand".

"Neither do I" said Emmerson "but I've seen the police and they are optimistic". He doubted that Alice would ever discover this blurring of the truth. Then, before she could quiz him any further, he said he must go and say 'hello' to any of his colleagues who were in at the moment. Alice was not to be left out of this dramatic moment; and preceded him as he headed for their office area.

The next half hour saw rather extraordinary scenes, as a large swathe of the Engineering Department of Oxford University stopped whatever they were doing and came to welcome Emmerson back. All expressed how distressed they had been at his disappearance – which Emmerson had no reason to doubt – and how delighted they were to see him back unharmed. Everyone wanted to know what had happened to him; and he re-iterated the story he had given Johnson, of a group of Irishmen, not too clear on what they were doing, but somehow of the view that Emmerson's research might help them on some project they had in mind. He emphasised, apart from the first day or two, how boring and even how ridiculous the whole thing had been, rather than in any way frightening and, by this means, distracted attention away from his detention. The conversation again turned to Kate; and he delivered the same up-beat message he had given Alice, saying that he thought he might understand more in a day or two, after she had been released. And then, as academics do, they began to drift back to their offices and lab work; and Emmerson said to Alice that he had, in any event, a lot to do. Eventually she let him go to his office, where he just sat for a moment, recalling the last time he had been there; and going over in his mind what he had said to Johnson, checking for any errors.

He suddenly realised that time was passing; and that he was due at his flat shortly. He said a quick goodbye to Alice and headed over to the Woodstock Road. He arrived just as a police car drew up and an officer with some skeleton keys let him into his flat. Emmerson thanked him for his help; and then asked if the police officer had some jump leads with which he might give Emmerson's car a start, the battery no doubt being absolutely flat after several months lack of use. The officer was happy to oblige, little appreciating the importance Emmerson attached to having his car ready for action. Only when first the battery and then the engine had stuttered to life did the officer leave; and only then, virtually the first time since he had been lowered from the helicopter a week before – since he had become a free man again, of sorts – was Emmerson, at least for a moment, able to think about what had happened to him, focus on what was still going on, - whether he would, in fact see Kate in an hour or two's time - and, to his surprise, a surge of renewed anger came over him. His life had been ruthlessly disrupted, his friends – and most of all Kate – had no doubt been distraught; and all because of Gerrard. While his only real objective was to have Kate back with him, he was, nonetheless, curious to know what 'news' she was supposed to have; and he was very much looking forward to meeting up with O'Connell and Riordan later that day to discuss how they would tackle Gerrard. Still, that would have to wait. He picked up a spare set of keys to his flat, his wallet and mobile phone, went out to his car and drove towards the centre of town. He parked in the broad, leafy thoroughfare of St. Giles, to the north of the central pedestrian precinct of Cornmarket; and then walked through it and on back to the police station. Shortly after 5 pm he was ensconced with an identi-kit expert; and proceeded to give them as accurate a picture as he could of the two Americans who had been his main guards for all those weeks in God-knew-where. But it was all he could do to concentrate as the time when he anticipated that Kate would arrive at the police station approached.

Kate was, in fact, at that moment, gathering her few belongings together. She had completed the recordings to the evident satisfaction of Messrs. David and John, whoever they were. She had done exactly what they asked; and she had done it very well. She recognised that she had made herself dangerously vulnerable to Gerrard, who now had the means to have her arrested and prosecuted at any time; but her main concern was far removed from that prospect. Her mind was totally focused on the next few minutes. Would she, as promised, be released or, her usefulness now at end, would she be carted off by Swinburne and quietly – or not so quietly – disposed of. She kept telling herself that the latter would raise far more problems for Gerrard than it was worth; and why the charade of the last two days if they were then going to arrange her disappearance? The sheer illogicality of such a strategy was all that kept her from breaking down. Well, now was the moment of truth. She finished packing her bag and went to the door. David was there.

"Thank you Miss Kimball. I've reported to his lordship; and you will now be released. The good Captain and his men will escort you back to Oxford; and you will formally be released from the police station there. No charges will be brought, but you will need to be discharged from police custody; and we would rather that had no connection with us in London. So Oxford it will be. Is that clear?"

Kate's reaction – at least at an emotional level – was completely schizophrenic. On the surface this was exactly what she had been waiting to hear for well over a week, ever since she had sought to save Paul's life at the end of a rope hanging from a helicopter; and it was entirely consistent with what she had been told when first brought to London. But the thought of being, once again, in the hands of – and entirely at the mercy of – Swinburne and his Neanderthal crew was simply too terrifying for her to cope with.

"I can't go with them" she said, as if she had any choice. "What guarantee is there that they will deliver me unharmed to Oxford?" Neither David nor John, also standing there seemed to take much notice of her.

"Will one of you come along as well?" she pleaded. "I can't be left alone with them".

"We've got our job" said John "in fact we've done out job – Swinburne's got his. If it's any comfort, I heard his lordship giving clear instructions to him to take you to Oxford once we'd finished our work. So, off you go. There's a car outside. Enjoy the rest of your life. Maybe someone will read all about this in fifty years, but not, I can most definitely assure you, before then".

Feeling the most extreme trepidation, Kate headed for the front door. As she did so, two of Swinburne's men joined her, one either side, each taking an arm. Neither used a very tight grip, but it was quite clear to Kate that the waiting car was her only possible destination. She was put in the back seat, with the two men either side of her. Swinburne and a driver got in the front; and they headed off, down into Whitehall and into Parliament Square, heading for Birdcage Walk, past Buckingham Palace, up to and then along Park Lane, down Bayswater Road, and on to the A40, heading towards Oxford. Swinburne turned to look at her, with extraordinarily bitter hatred in his eyes. He spoke to the two men in the back.

"Well, you've got about an hour. There mustn't be a mark on her when we get there nothing, you understand - but otherwise, the bitch is all yours".

As they drove round Parliament Square, not one hundred metres away the House of Commons debate and associated Vote of Confidence that would determine Gerard's future political career, if any, were just starting. Gerrard kicked off the debate, with a resumé of what he had said the day before but, echoing President Hamilton, with a lot more about how the way was now open – maybe not immediately but in the quite near future – for a much more general peace settlement in the Middle East. He recognised how serious the action against Iran had been; how he understood Members' concern for he too had wrestled with the dilemma of what to do; but urged that now was a time for innovative thinking, a chance to break out from the destructive stalemate which had emerged in the Middle East. He also made several references to Iran's role in support of terrorist activity around the world, and of the scope to offer very substantial olive branches to Iran if it would cease in this activity.

As he spoke, with Palmer once again listening intently from the Stranger's Gallery, there were some – but relatively few – bouts of jeering from the Opposition. More worrying was the lack of any significant support from Gerrard's own back benches. For the most part he was listened to respectfully, but in almost total silence. This did not, Palmer thought, bode well. Gerrard would need to command – and be seen to command – a groundswell of vocal support from his party if he was to survive the day. There was some braying of 'hear-hear' as Gerrard finished, but he was, as the whips had surmised, a long way from home. Then Colin Williams, the leader of the Opposition, stood and came to the Dispatch Box to reply. Palmer was struck as he had been before, by the presence that Williams – not very tall and rather thin – nonetheless commanded. He had a calmness about him, and a certain gravitas in his appearance, which he had regularly deployed to good effect in his perennial bouts with Gerrard in the Chamber.

"Mr. Speaker, Honourable Members , no-one can be in any doubt that today, this afternoon, we are at a critical turning point in the political life of this country. For the first time in over sixty years one nation – the United States – with the clear involvement and explicitly admitted support of the United Kingdom - has deployed nuclear weapons against another sovereign state. The issue before us is whether we, the elected representatives of this country, acquiesce in this act or not. Do we endorse it as the acceptable way to address the problems we face in the Middle East; or do we repudiate it?

"Let us be clear that a number of fundamental principles are at stake. Is it right that we should support an unprovoked attack on another nation; and offer military facilities in support of it? Much bigger still, will we condone a first-strike nuclear attack, with all the destruction and devastation that has caused, and the death – in many cases a lingering one – it will cause for years to come. And yet even that is not the most important question before us today. The most important question – the one that distinguishes our vote this evening from any we have had in the last half century – concerns what sort of world we wish to strive towards, to nurture and sustain. For, with a clarity that rarely emerges in political discourse, we have two – and only two – paths before us. The first – the one the Prime Minister would have you follow – is one in which the superpowers of the world – currently only the United States – will decide the world's priorities, its course of development, in short its future; and will act, if necessary with all the force at its command, to ensure that its interpretation of that future is imposed on the rest of mankind. The views of other countries, the views of various international organisations will, no doubt be listened to but, in the end, the super power will impose its view. And when China, and perhaps India, and maybe once again Russia, have risen to equal super-power status, then they too will have but one model before them of how disputes are resolved – by persuasion if possible but by force if necessary.

"The second path is based on the non-negotiable belief that the future of the world – of a collection of disparate, often conflicting nation states - can only safely be determined through the mediation of rational multi-national discourse – usually prolonged, always messy, sometimes unsuccessful, but, ultimately, the only way we can all learn to live together with other. A world in which discussion, negotiation, bargaining, increasingly based on shared principles concerning human rights and human endeavour, can and will circumscribe the unrestrained use of force by those with sufficient power to exercise it. To describe this latter path sounds hopelessly grandiloquent, which is ironic given how prosaic it is in practice, how relentlessly tedious and repetitive and unsatisfactory it usually is. But, I put it to Honourable Members, it is, with all its manifest faults, the only path we can, in all conscience support.

"If this is accepted, then the present action of the United States, and the succour and support given to it by our Prime Minister, are the most deeply abhorrent acts, the most shameful betrayal of the trust that the people of this country have placed in us, in living memory. And if we – this House – support that action, then we will not only have made the world an infinitely more dangerous place. We will - I do not think it too dramatic to say – we will have killed any prospect in our life time, and quite possibly for the lives of many more generations, of resolving the great differences of our time peacefully." Williams paused; and a low roar, quiet at first, like the rumble of a distant underground train, but steadily growing, emerged from the ranks of MPs behind him. It coalesced in sustained cheering and then, emerging from within the cheering, a refrain, faint to start with but then growing in intensity and clarity, came - what Williams had hoped for and anticipated – the one repeated word, directed at Gerrard "Resign, resign, resign, resign". Gerrard sat, impassive, unmoving but, of much more concern to both him and Palmer, so did all his own party members. A total silence gripped them; and Palmer, after all the hard work of the last twenty-four hours, could see the premiership slipping away from Gerrard. Unbeknown to him, Williams had much more that he was ready to say – a much more detailed, line-by-line attack on Gerrard's perception and interpretation of the situation in the Middle East, of the likely impact of the US attack on Iran's future politics, on Israel's position and much more. But he sensed that now was a good moment to stop. Gerrard was utterly on the defensive. The mood of the House would make it very difficult for anyone to mount much support for him; and, if necessary, Williams could always return to the affray later in the debate. But, as the noise, finally, started to die away, he had one parting thrust.

"Every Member on this side of the House will, of course, vote 'no' later tonight. What possible confidence could anyone of us have in the Prime Minister, given what he has done? But I also appeal to those on the other side of the House, whether in the Government itself or not. This is not a day to be concerned with party loyalties. The issue quite transcends that; and the world will be watching us very carefully. Are we going to play party politics at such a time; or can we rise to the demands of the occasion? Can we see that this is an issue – by far the biggest issue – of political morality that we have had to face since the last World War; and can we send an unmistakable message, to the US, to anyone at all disposed to support the Prime Minister, that that is not the road we will take?" This triggered a renewed round of cheering from his own members which, once again, gradually morphed into the one insistent word 'resign'.

Palmer was impressed, not just by the panoramic scale which Williams had adopted, the global and historic perspective, nor even the moral high ground that he had mapped on to it. The greatest skill had been in vaunting so persuasively the role of international diplomacy and international organisations – in practice the United Nations – without ever once actually referring to that largely moribund and generally ineffective body. Williams had successfully exploited the fact that there was almost universal support for peaceful negotiation in preference to military action, even though there was much less belief that the UN could ever deliver what this policy required. Well, that was maybe something Gerrard could exploit later in the day.

Most debates in the House of Commons are poorly attended. Whatever the number, the moment the two main opening speeches have been made, a substantial number of those present then depart, to be summoned back later only when it is time to vote, virtually always along strict party lines. Generally, only a few MPs remain, those on either side with a particular interest in the topic of the day, who then engage in the archaic procedure of standing up, to indicate that they wish to speak. One is then called by the Speaker, and all the others sit down again. As soon as the person speaking finishes, all the others wishing to contribute jump up again, one is called and so it goes on. Today, as Palmer watched, increasingly convinced that Gerrard was finished, two things were different. First – and no great surprise – no-one, as far as Palmer could see, left the Chamber. This was high drama, history in the making; and no-one, even if they had other meetings to go to, was going to miss being present on such an occasion. But second, to everyone except Palmer's surprise, Gerrard himself stood. Tense as he was, Palmer breathed a sigh of relief.

Debates in the House of Commons, he knew, rarely if ever made any difference to the outcome of the subsequent vote. Most who voted weren't even there for the debate; and even if they were, strict party discipline ensured that virtually all votes were a foregone conclusion. Even where some MPs were prepared to vote against there own party, which did occur from time to time, this was because of pre-determined views on the topic rather than any powerful persuasion during the debate; and even then it was extremely rare for the outcome to be anything other than victory for the governing party. But today was different. Few of Gerrard's members wanted to vote themselves into a general election; and almost certainly out of power. But, as was now clear, few felt any degree of comfort in supporting Gerrard or his actions; and Williams had played upon these fears. Palmer was in no doubt that, if the vote were to be taken now, Gerrard would go down to a crushing defeat. But the debate itself was unlikely to change much – many points repeated, more detailed but by no means determinative arguments presented and then, little by little, even on a topic of this global importance, the irresistible urge on the part of back benchers to make party political points until, finally, at 10 pm, they would vote. Unless Gerrard could give his party members something – something that would allow them to feel that it was right to support him – and give it to them now, so that the next five or six hours would, in the end and as usual, be so much froth, then he was finished. As Palmer knew, Gerrard had one last card to play; and it had to be played now.

The Speaker was slightly surprised to see that the Prime Minister wished to respond immediately, even though he would have ample opportunity at the end of the debate; and called him. Everyone else sat down and, once again, a hush descended on the Chamber.

"Mr. Speaker, Honourable Members, we have heard wise words and fine sentiments from the Honourable Member – sentiments with which no doubt we would all like to agree. The future of the world order no less; and the dark threat to it posed by what has happened. But they are also something else – the prerogative throughout the ages of those in opposition, of those in politics but not in power, of those who do not have to face – as we on the government benches have to face – the day-to-day realities of impossible decisions in the face of intractable dilemmas". He paused. A few derogatory jeers emanated from the opposition benches but, much more important, MPs on Gerrard's side of the House were paying very close attention. They had no idea where this was leading, but it sounded to be of some spirit and aggression; and they were, metaphorically, crying out for something to latch onto. Palmer could feel, as everyone else in the Chamber could, the atmosphere changing. Gerrard next placed two bulky files on the desk-top in front of him. When he continued, it was, at first sight at least, on a completely different tack.

"I have here, and place before the House two sets of information. Copies of both are being made available at this moment in the Commons library; and honourable members will have an opportunity to consult them before we conclude this debate. Let me tell you now, however, what is in them". He paused again, deliberately cranking up the tension – anticipatory on his side, alarming to the opposition – which everyone sensed. "The first is a set of transcripts of messages received by our intelligence services over the last few weeks from sources within the highest levels of the Iranian Government. Though they have been edited in order not to compromise in any way their origin, they are fully authenticated by the Director-General of MI6 as being from well established, reliable sources. They make clear, beyond any shadow of doubt, that a nuclear attack by Iran on Israel was imminent, because of the perceived threat that Israel, in line with its openly declared and well established policy, would very shortly take action to protect itself against Iran. There are, in addition, documents released earlier today by the US Government revealing that Israel's military forces, including its nuclear capability, were placed on full alert yesterday in readiness to attack Iran.

"The second file contains a detailed assessment by intelligence sections within our armed forces of the Iranian and Israeli locations – both military and civilian – targeted by each side; the destructive power of the armoury deployed; and the likely outcome of the conflict between the two countries. Including the devastation of both Teheran and Jerusalem, together with a number of other towns and cities, their most likely estimate is that well over one million people would have died, quite possibly two million eventually; and their minimum estimate – I emphasise their *minimum* estimate - is almost three-quarters of a million people – people alive today but, for those wishing to follow the lofty ideals of the honourable members opposite --- dead". At this, the chamber erupted, with almost every member of the Opposition on his or her feet, shouting at Gerrard, anger etched into every pore of their faces. This was, Palmer could see, partly an instinctive reaction to be characterised as little better than murderers, but it also had a slight element of panic. They could see which way Gerrard was heading; and they knew in their guts that it might lead him out of the utter pit he had been forced into. Equally important, in fact much more so, Gerrard's side could see just the first hint of salvation and, while still restrained, were starting to shout a few words of support.

The Speaker called for order, four or five times before all the MPs on the opposition benches finally sat down and were once again quiet. Gerrard stood silent and immovable throughout. Finally, he continued.

"The honourable member has spoken of the world order he would like to see. I share that view. But, as I have said, those of us in government, those of us who actually bear the responsibility for the lives and well-bring of people face rather more difficult problems than he is evidently aware of". Then, just as everyone thought Gerrard was going to re-iterate his statements about the numbers who would have died without the intervention of the US and the UK, he changed tack again.

"We, on this side of the House, believe in the absolute sanctity of human rights". Another groundswell of opposition began to arise, but he raised his voice and spoke over it.

"No doubt the same is true of Her Majesty's Opposition. The difference is that we do not believe that those human rights stop at Dover. And the most basic human right – without which all others are meaningless – is the right to life". The opposition began baying again, but now the greater sound was beginning to emerge from Gerrard's own side.

"I do not know what the result of the vote later tonight will be. I hope, of course, to win it but, in the greater scheme of things, it is not critical. I shall be content to know that, in conjunction with President Hamilton, I have acted to save more lives than have been lost in all international conflicts since the last World War put together". Now his side was cheering, not wildly yet, but dignified and loud. "We look forward to the day - the day so ably described by the honourable member..." - at this snide and dismissive aside, the cheering really took off – "..when we can resolve all such difficulties through the good offices of the United Nations but, until that day comes – and it is clear to anyone with eyes to see that that is still some way off – I am content to take my stand with those who will defend humanity's most basic right to life; and am content to be judged by that yardstick". Even as Palmer registered that this was the most shameless playing to the crowd, he could see the dramatic effect it was having. Gerrard's side of the House was now in full voice, cheering him on, delighted that they once again had, or very much appeared to have, right on their side. But Gerrard was not quite finished. As quiet again descended, in a move designed to echo – and mock - what Williams had said earlier, Gerrard half turned.

"I do not expect the honourable members opposite to accept what I have said. They do not have the experience of world affairs which would allow them to appreciate the significance of it, or of the decisions that I have taken on behalf of the people of this country. But I do ask honourable members on this side of the House to reflect carefully on what I have said. We are, without doubt, entering a new phase in international politics, fraught with dangers. I know that, with your support tonight, this Government can move forward. We have demonstrated that we have both the ethical principles and the political resolve; and I ask you to allow me to take the lead in this critical enterprise".

As he sat down, the chamber once again erupted, but this time the noise was entirely from behind him. A few opposition members shouted 'shame, shame' but it was half-hearted and they were completely drowned out by Gerrard's supporters. On and on they went, ignoring all appeals by the Speaker for calm, while Gerrard simply sat, his face once again a mask as he stared at Williams, daring him to reply. For just the reason that Gerrard had replied immediately to Williams - nothing much was going to matter afterwards – Williams saw that he now had to respond if he was to keep alive the prospect of winning the vote. He stood up; and the Speaker called him. Everyone knew that this was the last throw of the dice. Palmer, watching intently, found he was barely breathing, so taught had he become. The whips had planned for just such a moment.

"The honourable member talks of human rights….." he began, whereupon, around twenty government MPs stood up and started to walk out. Seeing this, a number of others, started to get up; and several started to talk amongst themselves. It was, by any standard, unbelievably rude; and to any neutral observer watching, easily interpreted as conceding that the Government could not sustain the line of argument that their leader had presented. But within the ampitheatre of the House of Commons chamber it was the *coup de grace* for Williams – visible evidence that the debate had now entered its boring, insignificant stage, an opportunity for all and sundry to state their views, make their points, in some cases unburden themselves of powerfully held views, but none of it likely to influence anyone or anything. Williams tried to continue, indeed he did continue, but no-one was listening any longer. The chamber was emptying; and it would not fill up again until shortly before ten pm. The outcome of the vote was by no means certain, but it would not depend any more on what was said in the debate. It would be down to Gerrard and the whips' cajoling, bribes, threats and other forms of appeal – and that was a battle, Palmer reflected as he stood to leave, they could probably win. It would be an agonising wait – the sort of situation Palmer hated – but the prospects were good.

As Palmer left the chamber, mulling such thoughts over in his mind, it came as quite a shock to him to re-call that the whole thing was a sham – dramatic politics and dazzling theatre but all, ultimately, a sham. In normal circumstances, Gerrard would not have supported Hamilton's insane policy in a million years, not for the reasons he had so eloquently given, nor for any other reasons. It was all down to the fact that President Hamilton had held, first, Emmerson, and now Kimball. Gerrard might or might not be Prime Minister by midnight; the future of the Middle East might be a whole lot better or an imminent blood-bath – and international politics was certainly going to be different for the foreseeable future – but one way or another it was all because Gerrard had sought to protect his career thirty years ago and, in a fit of madness, pulled the US into the cover up once Emmerson had stumbled on the evidence; and because Kimball had so determinedly pursued the whereabouts of her lover. Would the world ever know? He doubted it. Palmer was also very impressed with the way that Gerrard had played his hand. Almost all of what he had so dramatically revealed to the House could have been written – and defended – at any point in the previous five years, if not longer. The trick had been to suggest that an attack by Iran, or to forestall it, by Israel, was now imminent; and that the procrastination of the past therefore had to end. How Gerrard had got the DG of MI6 to sign up he did not know. The estimates of potential damage from an Israeli-Iran war were almost certainly well-established archive documents, the only new thing being that Gerrard had decided to release them now; but the intelligence suggesting Iran was preparing to go to war? Perhaps, finally, an attack *was* imminent, though Palmer very much doubted it. More likely it would turn out to be a matter of 'interpretation', or even just a money-grabbing mole somewhere in the Iranian government machine anxious to provide something to his spy-master that would prove valuable. If so, the Opposition might try to make something of that later on in the debate, when they had looked at the documents; but Palmer doubted the material could be discredited at all quickly. Gerrard had given himself a chance; and Palmer wouldn't bet against him being able to take it. Plus, there was always the chance that the DG had given full authentication, the result of some deal between Gerrard and him. It wouldn't have been the first time that such expediency and mutual back-scratching had altered the course of political discourse. Whether Gerrard would ever reveal the truth to Palmer was doubtful. In the meantime, he had much to do and some long, tense hours to get through before the decisive vote. He was not looking forward to the next four hours.

CHAPTER 38

The ordeal facing Kate was going to be much shorter, but looked as if it would be altogether more gruesome. Following what Swinburne had said, she had almost fainted in terror. She was so panic-stricken she couldn't speak; and Swinburne had made it worse by saying, quite categorically, that he intended the next hour to be the worst of her life. For several reasons, this turned out not to be the case but, as Kate sat in the car, only one such reason penetrated through her panic. Whatever happened, it would not be the worst hour of her life, because that had been in her flat when two men had all but hanged her from her own banister rail. From what Swinburne had said, her life was not in danger; nor could they risk harming her physically; and if these were both true then, come what may, she would get through it and, she kept trying to remind herself, by tonight she would be back with Paul. So, this bastard Swinburne could be as threatening as he liked. She'd overcome him, and the two gorillas sitting either side of her.

As the car pulled onto the A40 flyover at Paddington, one of them put his arm around her back, grabbed her shoulder and, with his other hand started to undo her blouse. The other man started idly to stroke her thigh. Kate screamed at the first to leave her alone, wrapped her arms around herself and doubled up into almost a foetal position. At this point a second aspect of Kate's salvation clicked in. In such a position, it was virtually impossible for the two men either side of her to molest her without getting rough; and she held on to the fact that they had been given clear instructions not to leave a mark on her. They tried to force her to sit back in the car seat, but she wrapped her arms beneath her knees and hung on as tightly as possible. For some moments, like a hedgehog, she seemed quite invulnerable, despite the precarious position she was in. But she knew, and they knew, that she couldn't keep this up for an hour. As the car sped along the dual carriageway, the two men got hold of her arms and, bit by bit, forced her to let go of her knees, slowly forcing her back to a sitting position. However, the moment they sought to utilise this, fumbling at her breasts or trying to run their hands up inside her skirt, they released her arms sufficiently for her to slam herself back into hedge-hog mode. Kate, now no longer in panic but furious beyond anything she could ever remember, began to think that she might yet beat the two animals beside her; and they for their part, were beginning to find the whole thing rather less attractive, with their anticipated sexual gratification distinctly marred by all the wrestling that was going on in such a confined space.

They had therefore progressed quite some way towards the M25 before one of the men hit on the tactic of forcing Kate to sit up, then putting his arm across the front of her throat, so that she could not double up again, but without the risk of marking her neck. He then invited the other man to take advantage of the situation. Even then Kate fought furiously, but felt it was, finally, becoming a losing battle. As she sat there, virtually unable to move, first one of the men then the other started to undress her, unbuttoning her blouse, pulling her skirt up round her waist. Feeling for the clasp on her bra. She started to scream, but one of them put a burly hand over her mouth and then, to her total horror, began to unzip his trousers.

"This should be fun" he said maliciously. Swinburne looked round.

"Get on with it – we'll stop in a minute so I can get a piece of the action as well before we get to Oxford". As he said this, Kate felt her bra come undone and, in a second, one of the men had his hands all over her breasts.

"Permission to fuck the bitch, Captain?" he said to Swinburne with a laugh. Kate, already distraught, now became utterly traumatized, as it became clear that there was no limit to what these men might do to her. But from somewhere deep within the last vestiges of her sanity, one last, desperate attempt to save herself welled up. She stopped struggling, stopped trying to scream, collapsed back into her seat, all resistance gone. The man gagging her mouth sensed this and released the pressure on her.

"Please, just don't hurt me" she said "Don't hurt me" her voice one of total resignation.

"That's very sensible" said the man. "Just do whatever we tell you and you'll be okay" and he let go of her. As he did so, Kate flung herself forward and to the left, almost onto the lap of the man sitting on her left, slammed her face against the window and started to scream at the top of her voice. The sound just came naturally – what she was really trying to do was the best imitation she could of Edvard Munch's famous painting 'The Scream', with her mouth wide open and her hands over her ears.

That someone would see this she had no doubt. Though they were progressing quite fast, there were three quite full lanes of traffic coming out of London and, given that they were in the middle lane, there was bound to be a car just to their left. It was a bonus that just about registered with Kate that the startled driver of the car they were overtaking was a thirty-something woman with a young son and daughter in the back of the car, who also suddenly saw a distraught if not hysterical woman with her blouse undone, no bra on; and apparently screaming at them from the back of a car with a number of men in it. A second later and Swinburne's car had shot further forward into the distance; and the two soldiers had dragged Kate back into her seat; but the damage had been done; and everyone in the car knew it.

"Shit" shouted Swinburne, who had been starting to get both a vicious and sexual pleasure from Kate's plight. "Shit, shit, shit, you fucking bitch". He seemed, for a moment, incapable of anything except shouting obscenities. He eventually calmed down a little. "If anyone saw that, they'll likely have taken our number, and if they've got a mobile, we're in trouble" Kate saw her moment.

"Oh she saw all right. She practically crashed her car she was so shocked. We're bound....." Swinburne swung round with more malevolence than Kate had ever seen in her life.

"Shut up you bitch, just shut up". He was breathing very heavily. "I might just forget about my career and beat you to a fucking pulp, so shut the fuck up". Kate was now, once again, truly scared. Swinburne was talking pure lunacy, but he was in such a rage that he might be capable of anything. At the same time, she knew she had perhaps one chance and one chance only to save herself from the men sat beside her. She let a moment of silence permeate the car; and then said, very quietly and quickly

"If these two don't touch me again, I'll say it was joke".

Kate would not have been surprised if Swinburne had swung round and punched her; and she dropped back into something approaching the foetal position she had used before. In fact there was a long silence. Swinburne had clearly got just enough hold of himself to think about Kate's proposition seriously and, once he had done so, saw that it was the only way to retrieve the situation. But it was several minutes before he said, without turning round

"Leave her alone for the moment". The words should have been a source of monumental relief to Kate, but her situation, the ordeal she had experienced since they set off, and the drama of the last few minutes had left her mind almost paralysed. She was dimly aware that she had gained some respite; and neither man was any longer trying to get hold of her; but she was quite incapable of properly taking on board what Swinburne had said; and she was only too well aware of how many more miles they were to go to Oxford. Only as the seconds ticked by, turned to minutes and more did her almost catatonic mental state begin to absorb the idea that maybe – just maybe – she was past the worst; and possibly even safe.

"Go on to the M25" said Swinburne to the driver. "We've got to get off this road. We'll go back round to the M4 and then up through Newbury. That should at least keep any police interest off our backs for today. Once we've got shot of her we can face out any bloody plod asking questions". Swinburne didn't deign to say whether he had accepted Kate's bargain, but he could see that if Kate made a complaint, backed up by a witness, he was potentially in serious trouble. He said nothing more to his men in the back, but they could sense his fury and frustration; and, to Kate's great relief, kept their hands to themselves. She inferred that the deal had been done. She continued to sit curled up, her hands behind her knees, mainly staring at the floor, counting the minutes away, occasionally looking up to try to divine where they were. Her spirits started to rise a little as, about twenty five minutes later, they left the motorway, and drove onto the dual carriageway of the A34; and they positively soared when she saw a roadside sign indicating that they were headed for Oxford. She began to tidy up her clothing.

It had taken Emmerson over an hour to complete the identi-kit profiles; and he didn't get up to leave until past 6 pm. He had grown more and more tense as time went on, anticipating that Kate would arrive at the police station, but she hadn't; and he was beginning to have serious doubts over whether she would. He only had the word of Gerrard's man to go on; and that, he suspected, was worth very little. For a second he was at a loss as to what to do, but very quickly decided that he would sit it out until she arrived. He thought of going to buy a newspaper to read, but his heart was not remotely in it. Instead, he took a seat in the spacious reception area in the police station, tried to stay very calm; and started to wait. He tried to reflect on all that had happened, but his thoughts and recollections were kaleidoscopic – not confused or unclear, indeed each memory was very intense – but fragmented, a mixture of history, emotions, regrets, anticipation plus, around the edges, still the great fear that he would not after all be re-united with Kate. To the officer on duty, who every now and then emerged from a back office to attend the front desk, he appeared to be as still as a statue, speaking only once to say that he needed no help and was waiting to meet a friend there who was currently with the police; but inside his nerves were jangling and the tension of waiting mounted.

Unknown to him, Kate's car arrived shortly after 7 pm and was driven round to the back of the station. They had not been stopped on their journey; and Kate had remained free of the attentions of Swinburne's men. The growing realisation that she was about to be free of these men, indeed, free full stop, started to induce a feeling of light-headedness rather than any great delight, and she sensed that she might well break down emotionally, even psychologically, if she wasn't very careful. 'Just hold on' was the mantra she kept saying over and over to herself; and having a mantra – any mantra - was quite a useful crutch to lean on. The car stopped and she was allowed out. She was not confident that her knees would hold her; and she fought to stop herself shaking, but made it across the few yards to a back entrance and into the police station. Only Swinburne came with her. He exchanged a few words with a police officer, who disappeared for a few moments; and then returned with Detective Inspector Johnson. The shock was simply too much for Kate. Fortunately there was a chair just by a doorway; and she sunk into it, unable to look at Johnson. Some part of her wanted to go up to him and slam her fingers into his eyes, but she was too drained by everything; and sat slumped in the chair, staring at her hands in her lap. Swinburne and Johnson talked briefly and, although Kate heard them, she did not take in what they said. Then, suddenly, without a word,

Swinburne was gone, back out through the back door, and Johnson said, in a rather formal tone

"You are free to go Miss Kimball". He pointed down a short corridor towards the front of the station. Kate stood, unsteadily, but Johnson made no move to assist. He stood, still, making it clear that she was now on her own; and Kate walked slowly down the corridor, out through a door at the end and into the reception area.

Kate had, to a considerable degree, ceased to be able to think clearly, if at all, about anything; but some part of her brain registered that she was, finally, free – free from the imprisonment that she had suffered since offering herself up in return for Paul; free from Gerrard's games; and free from the threat of assault from Swinburne's foot soldiers. Emotionally, she was completely unprepared for this and, feeling slightly dizzy, she stopped beyond the doorway and leant awkwardly on the ledge that ran along the front of the reception desk to her left. The only thought that she could cope with was that she must, somehow, force herself to stay standing up, unsupported, and walk out of the police station. This would give her some much needed fresh air but, much more importantly, would convince her, in a way that she was not yet convinced, that her life was once again her own. However, before she could make even the first move towards this goal, she heard, coming through the blank space of her most immediate surroundings, a voice, a word

"Kate"

Slowly she raised her head and, trusting neither her senses nor her situation, looked to the source of her name; and saw Paul, walking towards her, his arms outstretched. Whatever inner strength was holding her together, either emotionally or physically, collapsed as she saw him. She burst into a huge, silent weeping and started to fall forward. Paul caught her as she fell, holding her up, holding her to him, putting his arms around her to comfort her. Kate slumped against his chest, trying to say his name but unable to utter a sound as she convulsed with the shock and the relief and the emotional exhaustion. In the somewhat stark surroundings of the reception area of Oxford Police Station, and under the slightly bemused gaze of the duty officer in the office behind, they stood, motionless, locked together, unable to move, with Paul softly stroking Kate's hair, and repeating her name, over and over, no other words being remotely relevant to the moment.

Finally, Kate managed to string a few words together.

"I need some air" she whispered. Emmerson, with his arms still round her, very gently propelled her towards the front door. They emerged into a warm summer evening, he still with his arm round Kate's shoulder, she with her head buried in his chest and lightly clutching him around his waist. Only when they were right outside did she force herself to look up at him and, as she focused on him, burst into uncontrollable sobbing. Paul clutched her tightly, whispering her name again. Neither noticed a man in his early thirties standing across the road in the doorway of the Crown Court building. He had sandy hair, a rather innocent-looking freckly face and a rapid action zoom-lens camera with which he took over a dozen photos of Kate and Paul in each others' arms, making sure that he had clear shots of both their faces. He wasn't certain at the moment why he was taking them; but, as a photographer for the Oxford Mail, he had a good rapport with the Oxford police; and when DI Johnson had called him to say that he could take some pictures of a couple leaving the Police Station that would be worth more to the national press than all the photos he'd taken in the last few years put together, he hadn't hesitated. Oblivious of this, Emmerson sought to re-assure Kate.

"It will be alright now" he said. "It will be alright. Let's find somewhere to sit". He gently steered her the few yards down the road to the 'Head of the River' pub, right by the river below Folly Bridge. "I think a sip of brandy might be sensible". There were plenty of seats alongside the river, but it occurred to neither of them that Kate might take a seat while Paul bought some drinks. It would be a long time before either would let the other out of their sights. So together they went inside, bought two brandies, and only then settled themselves side by side on a bench overlooking the riverside. Still neither found it easy to speak. There was too much each had to tell, and each knew that some of what they had to say was urgent, but nothing seemed remotely as important as the fact of being together again. Recognising that Kate was in a very fragile state indeed, Paul resolved to say nothing except her name until she gave some sign of being ready to talk. So it was Kate who finally broke the near silence.

"I thought you must be dead. I thought....." her voice trailed away.

"I didn't think I'd make it back either" said Paul very quietly. "And I know that I have you – only you, Kate – to thank that I am back. O'Connell told me the whole thing. You have been... you are.... the most incredible woman. How you managed it is unbelievable. I....I... don't really know what to say, except that I love you and will love you until the end of time".

Kate, for whom a sip of brandy had begun to work wonders wiped a small tear away.

"I can't believe I've got you back, I can't believe it. It was so terrible, so absolutely terrible, not knowing if you were still alive or not, but knowing that I couldn't just give up......" She tailed off again; and they sat in silence, holding each other. Emmerson knew that he and Kate needed to talk - about Gerrard, the situation - needed to meet up with O'Connell and the others, but she seemed just too fragile at the moment. He needed to get her functioning again.

"We ought to let O'Connell know you are safe" he said. "But' let's walk, have some air first".

"Is he here, in Oxford?" asked Kate.

"Yes, he wants Gerrard, but he won't move until he knows you are safe". Kate started to shake slightly.

"It's no good" she said. "We can't touch Gerrard".

CHAPTER 39

E mmerson looked at her quizzically.

"Gerrard's man said that we shouldn't act until we'd seen you; said that you had some 'news' for us". Kate explained.

"For the last few days I've been acting out a fantasy – one that Gerrard's people created. Mainly phone calls which they then 'bugged', the jist of which is that I've been helping an IRA conspiracy designed to make out that Gerrard is a murdering bastard – forced to do so in return for your life. It's all very close to the truth – all the material we've gathered, except that my so-called phone calls make it apparent that we know none of it is true. Just one great fabrication by us. If O'Connell – if any of us – goes to the Press, or the Police, with what we've got, they have enough material to demonstrate that we've fabricated it all, that we're basically a bunch of terrorists out to get Gerrard". Emmerson sat back, looking pale.

"So that's why they announced your arrest......."

"What" interrupted Kate "they announced my *arrest*? It was abduction; and they *announced* it? When, where?"

"On the News, yesterday. They didn't give your name – said a woman your age had been arrested in Scotland under the Prevention of Terrorism Act; but they said it was thought to be linked to my disappearance, in fact *my* abduction by the IRA; and I've had to make a statement implying that it *was* the IRA – or some splinter group that has been holding me".

"It all fits very nicely doesn't it?" said Kate. "The Irish take you; blackmail me into smearing Gerrard, for which they now have all the evidence they need. It all goes sour when I'm arrested; and you're released. So then the authorities release me as having been a mere pawn in the whole exercise. And if we try to activate O'Connell's plan – actually go public with what we have on Gerrard – they have a well documented dossier showing that it is all a plot by O'Connell. Gerard's going to get off, pure as the driven snow. O'Connell's not going to like this one bit. Where is he now?"

"He's at the Vicky Arms, In fact we should go and meet him right now. As you say, he isn't going to be happy".

"Is it safe for us to meet him?" asked Kate. "I've seen how ruthless he can be. He wouldn't blink an eye at sacrificing us if he thought it would help him get Gerrard". Emmerson thought for a moment.

"I think we're safe. The story Gerrard has created puts us fairly much in the clear. O'Connell's the guilty party. I can't see that there is any way he can get round it but, if there is a way, we are his only allies – the only ones who know the truth of what actually happened. So, I think we are safe enough. At least Gerrard's political career is over as of tonight".

"Why do you say that?" asked Kate, genuinely puzzled.

"Because of Iran" said Emmerson; and then saw the look of incomprehension on Kate's face. "My God, you don't know, do you?"

"I don't know anything since they winched me on board that helicopter. What's happened in Iran?"

"Gerrard unilaterally supported a US- Israeli attack – a nuclear attack – on most of Iran's nuclear power and weapons installations. The world has gone overboard in condemning Hamilton and Gerrard – the first time nuclear weapons have been used since Hiroshima and Nagasaki – and as first-strike weapons. There's a No Confidence vote tonight and he will be gone by tomorrow".

It took Kate several seconds fully to absorb all this; and then the more immediate significance of it hit her. She started to frame the words but they wouldn't come; and Emmerson spoke for her.

"That's right, it was insane of Gerrard to do it; and there's only one reason he did. Us. The U.S. held me – and then you – as a straight threat to Gerrard. Support Hamilton or the whole bloody story of what Gerrard did to preserve his career back in 1983 would come out. They must have done a deal with Gerrard that he could have you as soon as the attack was under way; and then Gerrard could use you to construct his get-out-of-jail-free scenario. Hamilton has got rid of Iran's nuclear threat; and Gerrard stays out of jail. All very neat". Kate was still struggling to take it all in.

"So Gerrard only gave the Americans support for a nuclear attack because of you and me – because of what you found out about Sellafield; and what I found out about Gerrard while trying to trace you?"

"I think so. I can't see that he would have committed political suicide otherwise – because that's what all the commentators say he has done. They couldn't find a single contributor to back him on the news programmes earlier. Parliament is debating the matter right now, with the vote at 10 pm."

"I can't believe it" said Kate. "And none of this would have happened if some retired railway worker hadn't gone for a late night walk and come across O'Connell's men changing cars. Without that, they would never have been arrested; and Gerrard wouldn't have ended up getting them murdered. And now you and I – and O'Connell's men – are the only ones who know the truth. We can't let Gerrard get away with it. We can't".

"I'd agree" said Emmerson, "except that I can't see any way of stopping him. Anyway, let's go and meet O'Connell and talk it through. We've fixed things just in case you and I are being followed, as a way for Gerrard's men to get to O'Connell".

They finished their drinks and headed north, back past the police station, up to and across the main crossroads at Carfax, through the pedestrian precinct and on up St. Giles to Emmerson's car. If anyone had followed them through Cornmarket it would have to have been on foot; and they would now be unable to follow them any further. They got in the car and headed for the Cherwell Boathouse. As they first walked and then drove, they began, for the first time, to talk about themselves, in particular Kate's shock at discovering Paul had gone, her anguish as it became clear that the police would offer no help, and then the missing lap-top, her search through Paul's files, and then tracking down what had really happened at Sellafield. She glided over just how she had got hold of the information about Paul's consultancy work, less because of any embarrassment about her seduction of Nicholls – it had certainly been worth it – but more because it all now seemed, not irrelevant, but part of a far away world, a living nightmare that she didn't care to re-visit. She also told Paul how helpful Hargreaves had been, without referring to Hargreaves evident feelings for her – that *was* more of an embarrassment because, in her distress and loneliness at the time, she had gained great comfort from him which, in different circumstances might well have developed into a more reciprocal emotion. And then she related her trip to Northern Ireland, the meeting with O'Connell, and all its ramifications. Here too there were omissions in her account, of how he had threatened her, twice savagely struck her – time to relate that when O'Connell was totally out of their life. It was slightly disturbing just how much she was gliding over – she and Paul each gave the other plenty of space in their lives, but had never had any secrecy between them. Perhaps, in a week or two, when life had started to return to normal, she would feel more able to talk – she would make certain that Paul knew everything. But much was still too raw at the moment. Three hours ago she still hadn't been certain whether she would survive the ordeal at all.

Emmerson, for his part, found it quite unsurprising that Kate should have persuaded people to talk to her, engaged Hargreaves' support and found a common purpose with O'Connell. His overwhelming sentiment was that, faced with people – Gerrard's people - who could manipulate the police, control the Press, activate the security services, have a police officer beaten up with impunity and, it seemed, so completely neutralize a very dangerous team like O'Connell's, Kate had nonetheless survived, through determination, a readiness to use whatever help she could find, and a huge amount of courage. They had both been unwilling players in the deadliest game of international politics and military intervention imaginable, but Kate had played her own game successfully; and he owed is life and their future together entirely to that fact.

By the time they arrived at the Boathouse, Hargreaves was no longer there. As arranged, he had left, some two hours earlier, walked through the grounds of Wolfson College, adjacent to the Boathouse, crossed over a small footbridge which spans the Cherwell river at that point, and settled himself inconspicuously by some trees next to the river bank around thirty metres south of the bridge. There he sat and waited for Kate and Emmerson to appear, knowing that it might be some time before they did. It had been a sobering period, as he realized that this evening was very likely to be the last time he would ever see Kate. This had been a source of great sadness to him. Kate was quite the most extraordinary woman he had ever met; and it was easy to persuade himself that they had been close to developing a more permanent relationship – easy, but foolish he realized. They had only met as a result of Emmerson's disappearance; and had only become close because of Kate's dogged pursuit of him. He was only slightly shocked to realise that he would have been quite happy if Emmerson had not come back – just another life taken to ensure Gerrard's survival – and then maybe, just maybe, in time, he and Kate might have worked things out, in fact he was quite sure that they would have done so. But any such prospect was now gone – that was quite clear – and it was going to be a difficult time trying to forget her.

As he sat there he also reflected on his career. He had absolutely no idea how recent events, including his interrogation by Swinburne and his release into O'Connell's hands, would affect his prospects, but his only chance of holding onto his job was if the full truth of Gerrard's past, and the role Emmerson, Kate and he had played, came out in time to protect him. That would, he presumed, be settled later that evening, once they all met up. If O'Connell's plans didn't work out - more precisely, he reminded himself, if Kate's plan didn't work out – then he recognised that he'd almost certainly be looking for a new job. So, beaten up, losing the most wonderful woman he'd ever met, and facing the end of his career – not the greatest time in his life. And yet he knew he didn't regret a moment of it. He'd come through it, he'd spent time with Kate, and he was part of the greatest conspiracy of modern times – a bit part it was true but nothing in his life before it came close in terms of the excitement and – something more – the value, the integrity, the *rightness* of what he'd done. Whatever else he might do in his life this, he was quite sure, had been – would be - the defining moment.

Such thoughts were going through his mind for the umpteenth time when, lulled by over two hours of inaction, he was suddenly shocked to see Emmerson and Kate slowly walking across the footbridge. They moved slowly, stopped to look at the river, not seeing Hargreaves in the trees but knowing he was there, watching them. They then walked off the bridge and turned left, heading north along the river bank away from Hargreaves, heading for the Vicky Arms about half a mile away. Hargreaves remained motionless, watching, as planned, for anyone following Emmerson and Kate. He had reckoned that the ploy of Emmerson and Kate threading their way through the pedestrian precinct to Emmerson's car would defeat any followers but, as a further safety net, had arranged the route to the Vicky Arms and O'Connell via the Wolfson pedestrian bridge. In the next ten minutes, only one couple crossed the bridge in the same direction as Emmerson and Kate and turned north. Hargreaves was fairly certain that they weren't anything to do with Gerrard but, to make sure, they had arranged that Emmerson and Kate would stop and sit by the river bank for fifteen minutes until Hargreaves caught them up. Anyone following them would have overtaken them by then or, if they really were trying to trace O'Connell, then they would have to stop as well and, in that way, become quite overt. If so, the meeting with O'Connell would be off. But the couple strolled on, with Hargreaves following; went past Emmerson and Kate oblivious, as far as Hargreaves could tell, of either of them; and had soon disappeared ahead. Five minutes later, Hargreaves joined the other two and they recommenced their walk northwards. Arriving at the Ferry Hinksey Road, they found themselves quite alone, crossed and, five minutes later arrived at the Vicky Arms, where O'Connell and Riordan sat, nursing their fifth or sixth round of drinks since they had arrived nearly four hours earlier.

O'Connell was genuinely pleased to see Kate; and not only because she and Emmerson were the key to his planned destruction of Gerrard. He had been furious that she had given herself up to Gerrard's men in the helicopter, but his admiration for her knew no bounds. She had been determined to save Emmerson, at whatever cost to herself and, equally to the point, she had succeeded, against very long odds, in saving both him and herself. This pleasure was dimmed only by the nagging feeling that something – some part of his plan – must be faulty, or Gerrard would never have allowed them both their freedom. He suppressed both his curiosity and his anxiety while the five of them engaged in suitably celebratory pleasantries; and Riordan bought them all drinks. But then, with no more ado, O'Connell fixed Kate with an unblinking gaze.

"They said you would have some news for us" he said, flatly. For a moment, Kate was intimidated, as she had been so often before, by O'Connell, but the feeling lasted only a moment. She was free, Paul was back, she was in a rural, riverside pub in her own home City; and O'Connell would have to make the best of what she was about to tell him. She took a sip of her drink, looked him straight back and said, calmly

"Gerrard has outflanked us – or whoever it's been protecting him" she said bleakly, letting that message seep into O'Connell's consciousness for a few seconds before proceeding; and admiring the fact that neither he nor Riordan made any reply, content to play her game, let her explain in her own good time, which she then did. As succinctly as possible she explained what she had been forced to do, in essence provide evidence that she and O'Connell knew that the damming material they had on Gerrard was false, constructed in order to dislodge him from power and, very probably, send him to jail for the rest of his life. She provided a few examples of what she had been forced to say to the stage Irishmen they had provided, to make sure O'Connell was under no illusion as to just how truly fucked up their plan was to get Gerrard. Only once, seeing O'Connell's implacable face, but reading the seething rage beneath it, did she apologise for her role in destroying what they had planned, but taking the opportunity to remind him that she would undoubtedly be dead by now if she hadn't agreed to the plan. When she had finished, there was a very long silence. All eyes were on O'Connell; and he sat as if turned to stone, glowering at his almost empty glass of beer. Of all the things he might have said in response – regret, an explosion of anger, damming Kate, swearing revenge - his next words, said softly, without emotion, almost to himself, were not what Kate had anticipated.

"It'll just have to be another way" he said. It invited an obvious question from the others, but no-one said anything until Hargreaves intervened.

"I'll get another round of drinks" he said – a statement not a question – and headed off across the lawn to the bar inside the pub. Finally, O'Connell spoke.

"It would have been good to have nailed Gerrard for what he actually did; and that looks unlikely now. But at least I know – thanks to you Kate – who was responsible for the deaths of Cieran and the others. It's somehow a lot easier knowing, even if I can't exact the revenge he is due".

"At least what he did has partly caught up with him" said Emmerson. "I doubt he will survive tonight as Prime Minister".

"Which might, in due course, leave him much less well protected" said Riordan.

"We should all go back to my house to watch the end of the debate on TV" suggested Emmerson "unless you think they have it under observation – in case you both turn up there?" They were still contemplating this when Hargreaves returned, set a tray of drinks down on the table, joined them on the beer garden benches they were all sitting on, and said, quietly but very forcefully

"Everyone look at me, now, and keep looking at me, whatever I say". He saw the surprise in their eyes, but otherwise they all looked at him, expressionless, as he started to pass round the drinks.

"The couple who came across the bridge, after Kate and Paul crossed – the ones I followed as far as the Marston Ferry Road before they disappeared – I've just seen them. They arrived down the footpath, the way we came, looking much less romantic – I saw them as I came out of the bar – and the woman was on a mobile. When they saw me crossing the grass, they promptly sat down at a table near where the path reaches the beer garden and cuddled up to each other, but I'm fairly certain that's a sham. I think they're following us, have spotted you both" - he raised barely the tip of a finger towards O'Connell and Riordan – "and she's been calling up reinforcements".

CHAPTER 40

O'Connell and Riordan exchanged a quick glance.
"*Could* they have followed you?" he said softly to Emmerson. It was Hargreaves who answered.
"If they're serious, then they could have had a team following them on foot through Cornmarket, in touch with a set of cars; and once it was clear where Kate and Paul were heading, send the cars round to pick them up in St. Giles; then follow them to the boathouse and dispatch a couple after you on foot".
"If that's correct" said O'Connell, then we probably do not have much time before a large number of others turn up – Swinburne quite possibly and his team – which would not be good for any of us. So, what ways out of here are there?" Only then did it register that the choice of the Vicky Arms – so convenient for ensuring that no-one followed them – was something of a death trap if, nonetheless, they were followed. It was Kate who spelt it out.
"Not good news" she said. "There's the main drive from the road – it's about two hundred metres – but if Neil is right, they're bound to have that covered. There's the footpath we came along, by the side of the river but, again, they'll have that covered. And that's it. The rest of the grounds of the pub are surrounded by either the river – I suppose you might steal one of the canoes or punts moored down there but you'd be a sitting target – or a few open fields, but you'd stand out a mile there too, until it gets dark. You'd be okay in, say, twenty to thirty minutes but, as you said, we probably don't have that much time".
"There are a lot of trees alongside the river" said O'Connell. "Might we not get lost in those?"
"You could" said Hargreaves "but, from where that couple are sitting, they'd see you head off that way; and there's no way out except back to the footpath, the Ferry road, or the river. So I don't think that will work".

"Tell me where the couple are; and what they look like" responded O'Connell.

"The table right by where Kate, Paul and I arrived. It's on the patio rather than the grass. He's in a dark blue open shirt; and she's in a blue skirt". Without moving his head, O'Connell glanced sideways in the direction Hargreaves had described.

"Got them" he said. "Well" – he turned to Riordan – "its headlights time I think".

"Headlights it is" replied Riordan. The other three, sharing the mounting tension but mystified by this reference, looked at O'Connell for an explanation.

"In our more active days, the first thing when you ambushed a patrol, was to knock out the headlights – sort of levelled the playing field. If those two are the eyes of the opposition until the rest arrive, then they need knocking out. Now listen. You three are fine. They've neutralized you as a threat. It's Shaun and me they want. So, thirty seconds after Shaun and me leave, get up calmly, walk into the pub, call a taxi and go – anywhere. Just go. You'll be fine. If they wanted to hold you they would never have released Kate".

"But what will you do?" asked Kate, with more anxiousness than she thought possible, given their history.

"We'll be fine" said O'Connell "Just watch but, remember, thirty seconds, then go". With that, he and Riordan stood up, very casually, said goodbye to the other three; and started to stroll towards where the two watchers sat, near the start of the riverside footpath, chatting to each other. The couple at the table did not look up, but seemed engrossed in each other's company. As Riordan started to pass by the man at the table he suddenly, in a blur of speed, delivered a savage punch to the man's head, knocking him backwards, only his feet under the table preventing him from ending up on the ground. Riordan followed this up with an equally savage kick to the man's head, which might or might not have broken something but certainly rendered him unconscious. The two blows took less than a second and, as the woman started to rise from her seat, O'Connell struck her hard in the stomach. As she doubled up he brought the edge of his other hand hard down on the back of her neck; and she collapsed, certainly unconscious and possibly dead, onto the table in front of her. It fleetingly crossed his mind that the couple might, after all, just be out for an evening walk, now deadly victims of a terrible misunderstanding, but his whole life had hardened him to such musings. If Hargreaves was right, it was he and Shaun – not Gerrard – who faced the prospect of the rest of their lives in prison; and that was not a prospect with which one took any chances. With the two victims of the sudden onslaught prone, one half tangled in his seat but otherwise collapsed on the ground, the other in a heap on the table, O'Connell and Riordan dashed the few metres to the start of the footpath and, in a few seconds more were into the trees. At the same time, Kate, Emmerson and Hargreaves, stunned by the brutality of what they had just witnessed, got up and slowly headed for the bar, Emmerson using his mobile to call a taxi. As they passed another table, a customer looked up at them and said -

"Were they with you? Did you just see what they did?"

"I did" said Emmerson. "I can't believe it. I'm just calling the police". He saw the evident relief in the face of the customer, that something was being done so he wouldn't have to; and then the three of them were inside.

It was less than two minutes later that the first of the rest of Palmer's team arrived, in a car down the main driveway. In normal circumstances, neither Kate nor Emmerson would have noticed any thing special about them – just two men arriving for a drink at a country pub. But, in the highly charged context, it was all too apparent that the two men, well built, grim looking, menacing in manner, were not out for an idle pint; and if there had been any doubt, the manner in which they started to search the beer garden would have settled the matter. They rapidly identified their two front-line colleagues, slumped by the table at which they had been sitting; and one was rapidly on his mobile – whether ringing for an ambulance or for reinforcements was not clear - while the other examined the condition of the unconscious couple. A number of customers were now standing around, none too closely, but watching, uncomprehendingly, at the two apparently lifeless forms. Then, just as two more distinctly threatening men appeared from along the riverside path, one of the first men on the scene approached a couple of those staring at the scene.

"Did you see who did this?" he said, curtly, and with sufficient authority that he got a reply without even hinting who he was.

"I didn't see it happen" said one of them, but there were two men – I think it was two – and they just took off".

"Which direction?"

"I think down the footpath – but they may have gone off to the car park – the path runs along the side of it for a short distance". Their inquisitor offered no thanks, in fact made no reply at all, but merely nodded to the latest arrivals, who took off in the direction of the footpath. At the same time, another two men arrived in a car down the main drive and, after a few seconds of discussion set off, one in the direction of the river, the other climbing a low fence into the fields behind the pub. By this time the manager of the pub had been called out; and exchanged a few words with two of the men now very much in charge of proceedings. One said that this was clearly a police matter which they would be dealing with – neatly implying that they *were* the police without actually stating as much; and suggesting that both the manager and his customers resume their normal behaviour. Only after another ten minutes, which saw the arrival of yet another two man team, did any of Palmer's men actually enter the pub itself, just as Emmerson's taxi was arriving. Neither Emmerson nor Kate recognized him, but he immediately recognized them, whether from briefing photos or because he had been part of Swinburne's earlier team was unclear. As Kate,

Emmerson and Hargreaves started to move towards the main doorway out to the main driveway and car park, the man spoke into a phone.

"Inside, now" was all he said, but it seemed sufficient; and then he stepped into the doorway to block their exit.

"Where's O'Connell?" he said, in a controlled but unmistakably belligerent manner.

"He left" said Emmerson.

"When?"

"About fifteen minutes ago".

"Where was he going?"

"I've no idea".

"Which direction did he go?"

"Out to the car park".

"What car is he driving?"

"He hired one"

"I mean what make, what colour?"

"Grey, Ford I think". Emmerson decided he had had enough of this or, more accurately, that he should quit while he was ahead in delivering misinformation. "Now get out of the way please". Two others had come in from the beer garden during this exchange and stood watching, so Emmerson was in no position to secure this outcome, but it might distract from further questioning about O'Connell.

The man who had interrogated him paused, looked aggressively at Emmerson.

"The three of you sit down, there…" he pointed to a nearby table and chairs "and shut the fuck up, or I'll smash all your teeth down the back of your throat. Do I make myself clear?" Whether, in the absence of the additional two men, Emmerson would have taken him on he was unclear. He was certainly the larger, better built of the two, though the other man looked extremely fit, and well used to taking care of himself. Perhaps it was fortunate that, with three of them to contend with, he and Hargreaves were in no position to object. The three of them sat down. At the same moment the taxi driver appeared at the door and shouted

"Taxi for Emmerson?"

Emmerson waved to him. "How long is this going to be?" he asked the man in the doorway. "I've told you all I can about O'Connell. It's not our fault if you screwed up your reconnaissance". The man gave Emmerson a murderous glance; and Emmerson got ready to field a blow from him, but kept going. "He'll be well away if you waste your time here". Fortunately for Emmerson's teeth the man had, in the meantime, got on the phone again and did not react. He spoke quietly, in staccato words, so that none of them could properly divine what he was saying; and of the voice at the other end of the line they could hear nothing. Yet it was clear to them that the conversation was causing considerable grief, certainly at the near end and, they surmised, at the other end too. The surveillance team had clearly botched the job, provided that was, if O'Connell and Riordan had made it through the trees; and the only question was whether O'Connell's instinct – that there was no reason or advantage in taking Kate or Emmerson back into custody again, still less Hargreaves – had been correct. Seconds ticked by that seemed like minutes; and, however restrained, the man now seemed to be positively remonstrating with his interlocutor. Eventually he snapped the phone shut. He spoke to the two members of his team in the bar.

"Watch these three for me. Any trouble, you know what to do" and walked out.

The next ten minutes were ones of general confusion. Clearly some sort of search operation was being mounted from just outside the bar; the bar manager and a small number of customers were torn between wanting to get on or get away on the one hand and wanting to find out what on earth was going on – clearly a good story to tell later; Kate and the others sat watching their two guards, who stood staring back at them; while Emmerson managed to persuade the taxi driver to wait for as long as it took and he would pay him for the waiting time. Behind all this inactivity, the three of them anxiously waited, hoping to the point of praying that O'Connell and Riordan would not be apprehended; and that they themselves would soon be released. Eventually another of Palmer's men – not that the three of them had any inkling of the identity of the man who was pulling the strings – came into the bar, clearly in charge, and simply nodded for the two men guarding them to leave. Without a word to anyone else, he followed them out.

"I think" said Emmerson "that we are free to go" and they headed outside with the taxi driver. It was half past nine. "Let's all go back to my place and watch the final moments of the confidence debate" he said. "Neil, will you join us? We can give you a lift home afterwards". Hargreaves happily accepted and they drove off, up the driveway, through Old Marston and onto the Marston Ferry Road, heading round to North Oxford and Emmerson's flat. As they passed the point where the footpath – the footpath that they had walked along earlier – crossed the Ferry Road, they saw three Land Rovers parked, standing out in an otherwise deserted road. One had several people in it but, in the dark, it was impossible to see who they were.

"Do you think they could have caught O'Connell and Riordan?" asked Kate. It was Hargreaves who answered.

"They would have had to cross the Marston Ferry Road, to get out of the trees, and that would have been very risky with those back-up teams on the loose, but I still think it's unlikely. They clearly didn't catch them quickly and, if so, then O'Connell and Riordan could have gone a good half mile or more before crossing the road. Plus they clearly believed you, Paul, when you said they had a car; and had headed for the car park; and why wouldn't they? They wouldn't think for one moment that the pair of them had walked here. So I think they will have been combing the roads around here. The problem for them is that it's less than a minute to Old Marston, and then it's straight onto the Eastern by-pass. From there you could be anywhere – half way to London or to Birmingham in no time – so my guess is that they made it".

"The one certain thing" said Kate "is that we won't ever find out. If they got away, they're never going to risk getting in touch with us again; and if Gerrard's got them, they'll disappear without trace, exactly as the others did in 1983".

"Maybe it doesn't matter any more "said Emmerson quietly. "All three of us have been in their grasp; and not at all certain we'd ever survive. But we have and, because we're no longer a threat to Gerrard, we'll continue to survive, get back to the lives we were leading before this all happened, and long before we knew of O'Connell's existence". There was no denying this; and neither of the others did; but the long silence that followed spoke volumes of the dismay and anger they felt that Gerrard could so effectively cover up his past, multiple murder, the corrupt use of his authority, his advisers and the security services. But all three knew that they would have to learn to live with this knowledge.

They arrived at Emmerson's apartment and went inside. Emmerson switched on the television and said he would get a bottle of wine for them. When he had left the sitting room, Hargreaves looked nervously at Kate, who felt his eyes upon her.

"I'm sorry if this is difficult......" he started, but she cut him off.

"Neil, don't say that. It's me that should apologise. You have been such a source of support to me – I wouldn't be here without you – and I don't want to cause you any grief. It's just.... I don't know what to say....."

"When I leave tonight, I know I won't see you again. I'll have to live with that. It's just that it's all so..... unfinished. Things I want to say before 'goodbye'....." He stopped as Emmerson re-entered. Hargreaves and Kate both turned their attention quickly to the television, which was showing the last few minutes of the House of Commons debate on the Parliamentary Channel. Though they did not know it, the last five hours of debate had added little drama and no new information to what Gerrard and Williams had provided at the beginning of the debate. Numbers on both sides had looked at the copies of the intelligence documents to which Gerrard had referred and, as Palmer had suspected, attempts to discredit them in the absence of any proper investigation of their provenance, though tried by two or three of Williams's shadow ministers, had proved unsuccessful. As they watched, an unknown opposition MP was attacking Gerrard's integrity but with very little variation from what fifty others had said at some point earlier. But when he sat down, the tension began once again to rise as the Speaker of the House called the leader of the opposition, indicating that the final two summing up speeches were under way.

"Honourable Members" began Williams in the time honoured if somewhat anachronistic manner "We fast approach the moment of decision. Much in politics is, inevitably a matter of degree, lighter or darker shades of grey; and any Member of this House who serves his country well must learn discretion, that the best is often the enemy of the good, that compromise is an essential part of the running of a modern state. But every now and then a moment occurs when all this must be jettisoned, when an issue is entirely black and white, a matter of principle to be seen with such clarity that it cannot be obfuscated, hedged around, when there is no fence to sit on; and every one of us must be counted. No-one in this House, no-one watching us in this country or from abroad, can be any doubt that this is such a moment.

"We have heard much argument, on both sides, all of it pertinent, much of it persuasive but, now, at the moment of decision, each of us is faced with a choice not just of dire importance but of stark simplicity. The Prime Minister, without consultation has, in our name, in the name of the United Kingdom, participated in the launch of a first-strike nuclear attack, an act without precedent in history. That this act was illegal there can be no doubt, indeed it followed closely on the *failure* of a UN Security Council vote which might, at least, have sanctioned *an* attack on Iran, though no-one in their right minds supposes that it would have involved the use of nuclear weapons. This act has resulted in many deaths and, no doubt, many more to come, lingering deaths; has completely unbalanced the politics of the Middle East, has not just jeopardized but annihilated any hope of a successful peace process. Why, in God's name, he chose to do this we remain completely ignorant, unless to feed some incomprehensible infatuation with a supposed new world order decreed by the US.

"If we offer our collective support to this madness, we will, of course, earn the undying enmity of the rest of the civilized world but, much worse than this, we will forfeit any right to be heard in the councils of the world. Our moral standing will be non-existent – a pariah state. If, on the other hand, we vote this man down, we reject utterly what he has done, repudiate entirely such an approach to the problems of this world then, while we cannot reverse what has been done, we will, as a House, we will as a nation, still have some shred of integrity on which to build, as we seek to play a part in repairing the indescribable damage that has been done. Everyone on this side of the House will vote against. I once again invite members opposite to put aside mere party allegiance and join us in this historic vote" As he sat down, his party erupted into a deafening and sustained applause. That was to no-one's surprise. But all eyes were on the Conservatives – what response would they give? The immediate answer was, in short, no response. The cynical viewer would guess that, whatever they thought, however they would vote, they would not give Williams the satisfaction of showing him any support. The less cynical observer – and for once this would probably be the safer bet – would recognize that Williams had made a very powerful speech, but there was still one speech to come; and they were going to listen to it before they finally made up their minds.

Gerrard let the general hubbub die down; and even let the subsequent silence hang in the air, to give himself the most powerful presence possible and, with it, absolute control of his audience. He knew from the work of the whips, and from Palmer and his team, that few if any of his own party relished the prospect of voting Gerrard down and, with that, the fairly imminent prospect of once again passing into opposition But Williams had spoken eloquently of the sheer immorality of Gerrard's actions; and, above all, they needed some ethically defensible reason, however much of a fig-leaf it might be, to justify, to themselves and to their families and friends, supporting what he had done. Well, Gerrard proposed to provide them with just that, but he would tease a little first.

"Honourable members, there is at least one – sadly only one – point made by the honourable member with which I can agree; and that is that this is the moment when every one of us has to show his true character, has to stand up in front of the world and declare, by their vote tonight, what sort of person they are. To that end I have some new information for the House but, first, one correction to what has been said". It had been Palmer's idea to whet members' appetites in this way, get them to focus on what was coming rather than on what had been said by Williams.

"I have not, on behalf of the British people, waged war on anyone; I have not committed a single member of Her Majesty's armed forces to Iran; I have not breached any protocol, agreement, still les international law. What I have done is to allow the US to use its airbases in the United Kingdom. It is only too plausible that the Honourable Member opposite, had he been Prime Minister, would have allowed the US to have airbases in this country and then prevent her using them when it needed them – that is quite the sort of double dealing we all know he is capable of". This gratuitous insult was also Palmer's idea, playing to the always latent party animosity and, as intended, getting a low but swelling round of guttural support from his own party, re-establishing traditional lines of dispute and, thereby, starting to unwind Williams' appeal – on which his position depended – to dissident Conservatives ready to vote against Gerrard.

"But" he continued "I do not for one moment seek to hide behind this typical mistake by the honourable member. Let me be unequivocal. I believe that the US action was right. I had no qualms about supporting it, nor about this country's limited but not unimportant role in it". As intended, the combination of this clear hostage to fortune with his earlier hint of new intelligence to come had every single person in the packed chamber hanging on his every word. "I said I had some further news". He paused. In that silence Williams sensed - more than sensed, knew – that Gerrard had some sort of ace up his sleeve. Gerrard continued. "At eight o'clock this evening the Israeli Ambassador called to see me at Downing Street, with a message from the Israeli Government. He expressed their thanks to Her Majesty's Government for supporting the US action; and said that, as a result, for the first time in a generation, the Israeli people were no longer living in the shadow of the threat of genocidal destruction. He went on to say that, much as his Government had worked and indeed yearned for peace in the Middle East, there had never been a realistic prospect of this while Iran was building up its nuclear capability with the quite explicit intention of eliminating Israel from the map and destroying the Jewish nation. Now that that threat had passed, there was, for the first time in many years, the real possibility of a general peace settlement, one that secured the right of the Israeli people to existence in harmony with the Arab countries of the region.

"The Ambassador then told me that a specially convened meeting of the Israeli cabinet earlier today, noting this dramatic change in circumstances, recognized that in order to capitalize on the situation, it was incumbent on Israel to take unilateral steps to re-establish the peace process. To that end it had decided, first, on one condition, within one month to withdraw all Israeli restrictions on the Gaza Strip, the condition being that the UN send in a large peace-keeping force to protect Israel from rocket attack while a permanent Palestinian administration can be formed. Second, all the disputed Jewish settlements on the West Bank will, within three months, be vacated and dismantled. Third, the Israeli government will accord full recognition of a democratically elected government of a Palestinian State; and initiate discussions to determine mutually agreed boundaries for the States of both Israel and Palestine. Fourth, the Israeli government will ask the UN to convene all party talks designed to establish an international administration for Jerusalem, providing freedom of access and freedom of religious practice for all. Through these measures, the Ambassador said, the Israeli government hopes to play as productive a role as possible in bringing about a lasting and secure peace in the Middle East. A similar declaration has also been made to the United States Government, to the EU, to all governments in the Middle East and, of course, to the UN Secretary-General"

Gerrard paused, not expecting any immediate reaction. Everyone present was too stunned by the announcement to respond. The silence provided the perfect moment for the final words of his speech.

"And so, as the Honourable Member says, this is the moment for absolute moral clarity. Members of the House must choose, between the grandiose rhetoric which we have heard tonight, and which has so often, both here and on the wider international stage, stymied any real progress towards peace in our world; and which has brought the nations of the Middle East to the brink of mutual destruction – or, for the first time in a generation, support the reality of a new order in which, under the auspices of the United Nations, those nations can live together, free from the threat of genocide and ready to work together to build the peace that we all want".

It was all just words – words and more words, largely meaningless but, in the charged atmosphere of the Chamber, and following the astounding announcement of what the Israeli Government now intended, it was – ironically –precisely the 'grandiose rhetoric' that Gerrard's party members wanted – needed – to hear; and they responded precisely as Gerrard and Palmer had intended they would, with huge and sustained cheering. It didn't involve everyone in his party – but then it didn't need to. It would be sufficient to persuade most doubters that, if they voted against their own party, they might easily find themselves in the minority, expressing no confidence in a Prime Minister who would still be there tomorrow and, therefore, whatever their individual qualities, destined for a life entirely on the back benches, with no hope – for the foreseeable future at least – of any preferment or promotion.

As the voting started, with the 'Ayes' and the 'Noes' proceeding through different exits before re-entering the Chamber to hear the result, Palmer reflected on Gerrard's announcement; and marveled at the consummate way in which he had played his hand. Hamilton had, of course, imposed the package of measures on Israel as the price of his action against Iran, but knowing that it was a price Israel was well prepared to pay to see an end to Iran's nuclear threat without jeopardizing its own security. Already some MPs queuing to vote were speculating as much, but too late to affect the vote. It would take them a little longer though to realize how, if not hollow then certainly much less dramatic the whole package was than it appeared. Israel had twice before pulled out completely from Gaza, only re-entering because the Palestinian population there took the withdrawal as an immediate opportunity to mount new rocket attacks on Southern Israel. The Israeli government would give much to dismantle its current caging in of the land, with the UN preventing renewed rocket attacks. Whether the UN could or would do this was another matter, but its success or failure- not the attack on Iran - would by then be the issue. Demolition of the West Bank settlements was a real plus, but even here, all was not what it seemed. The continued building of the settlements had been so provocative that even the all-powerful Jewish lobby in the US had begun to recognize their destructive impact on any hope of a peace settlement and, as Palmer but not a lot of others knew, the new administration in the US had made it clear that the substantial financial and military support provided by the US to Israel would be brought into question if the policy on the settlements was not reversed. In essence, Israel had made a virtue out of a necessity. As for the promise of discussions on boundaries and the status of Jerusalem, that was all they were – promises of discussions – nothing actually conceded; and with Gaza and the West Bank settlement issues conceded, Israel would command most of the moral high ground in such discussions. So, all in all, Israel had conceded nothing that she would not have been forced to concede anyway, but Hamilton had secured an agreement that would no doubt play as well in Washington as it had done in Westminster.

The voting completed, the four Tellers approached the Speaker and read out the result. Gerrard had won with a majority of 48, implying that only around 30 of his own side had deserted him. Given that there were almost that number who, for one historical reason or another had it in for Gerrard and would have voted against him anyway on a Vote of Confidence, it was, as Palmer noted with quiet satisfaction, an absolute triumph of an outcome. No doubt the knives would soon come out. The Press would commence an orgy of critical analysis. There would be calls, probably in the long run successful ones, for a full inquiry into what had happened, the intelligence documents; and there remained the court of human history – what would the consequences be in practice for the Middle East, for the UN, for the use of nuclear weapons, for international politics more generally. But none of this would greatly trouble Gerrard. He had been staring at utter disgrace and life in jail; he had been forced through the most blatant blackmail to follow a potentially suicidal policy, one for which he had not one shred of enthusiasm, had accepted that, at the very least, he was finished in politics; and here he now was, accepting the congratulations of well-wishers, the triumphant and comfortable survivor of a Vote of Confidence; and in a much stronger position than he could conceivably have imagined even a week ago. Palmer re-called again that all political careers end in failure; and the same would almost certainly be true for Gerrard; but for the moment, having been in a bottomless pit of despair, albeit not one of the public's knowing, he was now ascendant and, at least for the moment, untouchable. This thought prompted him to make a quick phone call, to see how the tracking down of O'Connell had been going. Not, he thought, that it greatly mattered now. He had completely disposed of any threat from that source. Two Northern Ireland dissidents and three rather resilient residents of Oxford knew more than was good for them but, Palmer was now assured, were completely impotent as far as threatening Gerrard – or himself – was concerned. All in all, it had been a spectacularly successful day, even if key parts of it would never make it into his diaries.

CHAPTER 41

In Oxford, the three residents who had impressed Palmer, though they had nonetheless been completely outwitted by him, sat watching the proceedings on television in a subdued state.

"I can't believe it" said Kate. "He's going to get away scot free". She shook her head grimly. "There's still your data, Paul, from Sellafield, showing that there *was* an explosion. Won't that have to be looked at: and if it is, won't it set the whole thing off again?" Emmerson pulled a long face.

"I'm not sure, but I doubt it. My copies have all gone; and given the way Gerrard has stitched things up, I strongly suspect that any other references to it will have been seized or suppressed under the Official Secrets Act, or some such cloak of inaccessibility. I think we just have to count ourselves lucky that we are still alive; and that we can try to return to some sort of normal life. I guess there isn't a moment in the last few months when we wouldn't have settled for that, is there? Maybe we will just have to live with the knowledge we have about Gerrard. It will certainly be very unwise to talk about it – extremely dangerous if anyone believed us and raising real doubts about our sanity if they didn't. What do you think, Neil?"

Hargreaves' mind was on quite different matters, but he said that he thought Emmerson was right. For his part, he'd be going back to work; and it would be interesting to see how his superiors dealt with the situation. His guess was that he'd be packed off to another branch of the police, with a promotion if they wanted no fuss, though he couldn't see how he could make any waves without making himself look brain-damaged from his injuries. No-one had anything to add; and Hargreaves said that he should head off.

"I'll give you a lift home" said Emmerson. Kate caught Hargreaves' eye as he started to say that that would not be necessary, saw the meaning in them, pleading yet somehow iron-like at the same time.

"No, Paul, I'll take Neil. He's done so much for me, it's the least I can do. You settle in" she said to Emmerson "and I'll be back shortly". She spoke pleasantly, easily, but Emmerson picked up the firmness of tone in her voice, and understood that it was important to her.

"Okay" he replied. "Here are my keys. Neil, I still don't know all the details of how Kate tracked down what happened, how she forced Gerrard's hand, nor just how much you helped her; but I know it was a lot and for that I am eternally grateful to you. I hope you are fully recovered soon; and if there is ever anything we can do for you in return, you have only to say. I hope you know that".

"Thanks" said Hargreaves, feeling uneasy at Emmerson's evidently genuine sentiment, but his heart pounding at the prospect of one final moment alone with Kate, They went to the car and, with Kate driving, headed for Hargeaves' house in the Abingdon Road. With very little late night traffic, Hargreaves knew it would be but a short journey.

"Kate, I'm sorry…….." he started, but she cut him off.

"Don't Neil. Please. It's me who should be sorry. You've risked everything for me, which I had no right to expect, helped me through the most difficult, the most terrifying time in my life, had a pack of savage thugs brutally assault you; and all I've done is take your help and bring you nothing in return. I feel so guilty I…….." This time Hargreaves cut her off.

"You mustn't" he said. "You know why I did whatever I could. You know how I feel about you…." Kate started to speak but he held up his hand to stop here. "It's okay, I know that you can't feel the same about me. I understand that; and I'm not going to be a burden – I know this is the last time I will see you – but I just wanted a little time alone with you, to say 'goodbye' properly – I couldn't have just walked out of Paul's place with a cheery wave to you".

"I know" replied Kate softly. "I know. And Paul knew too. He's very shrewd, perceptive".

"But" said Hargreaves "I will say to you what Paul said to me. If ever you are in trouble – of any sort – come to me and I will help. Anything, anything at all. No strings attached. Just the occasional offer to marry you" he added with a rueful grin. Both knew he was in deadly earnest but, delivered in such a self-deprecating way, with the hint of amusement, it eased the tension in the car; and Kate smiled.

"I'll hold you to that" she said. "What your gorgeous wife and three lovely children will say about that will be interesting to hear. Seriously, though, Neil, I'm sorry this is painful for you, but time is a great healer – god what a ghastly cliché but it's true – you'll meet someone, you'll be fine". For a half second Hargreaves was on the point of declaring undying love for ever, a life of celibacy without Kate, but the moment was too important for that kind of thing.

"I expect – I hope – you're right" he said. "But it will be tough for a while; and these last few minutes together are important to me" He broke off from what he had been going to say next, to indicate that they were virtually there and, as Kate slowed down, he pointed out his house. Kate stopped the car. "Please come in – I can't say goodbye to you properly in the front of a car". His meaning was clear.

"Neil, I'm not sure that's wise. It will only make things more difficult for you".

"Kate, like you said, I'll survive, but leaving you is going to cause me a great amount of grief – I'm sorry, but that's the truth. I will come through it so much better if I have a few moments, holding you, the joy of kissing you farewell, to remember you by. I know it sounds mad but, really, it will sustain me through the bad times ahead. I did what I did because I fell in love with you. I can't, I don't expect anything in return, but it would make me really happy if we just had a few moments together". When Kate made no reply he added, once again with a slight smile "We have quite a history. It's at an end, but surely not with me just climbing out of the car".

One part of Kate's mind remained of the view that this would be unwise. But another had been quite moved by what Hargreaves had said. She felt great affection for him, knew how much she owed him and, as she saw increasingly clearly, she did not want to end their unusual relationship resisting him; and in a curious way she could begin to see that a proper physical ending, an embrace, the feel of their bodies touching one another – which had barely ever happened despite all that they had been through – might somehow make their separation easier for Neil to bear. She switched off the engine and put her hand on his arm.

"Just for a few minutes" she said "That would be nice". They got out of the car, walked to the front door and Hargreaves let them in. Without saying anything he fetched a bottle of white wine from the fridge and poured two glasses.

"To us" he said "and to what we achieved. We still have a psychopath for a Prime Minister but we survived against someone who is perfectly capable of eliminating anyone in his way. Maybe we should write it all down, leave the document in a bank vault with instructions that it be opened in the event of anything happening to us; and then letting Gerrard know". Kate smiled.

"No, I think we are safe now; and I just want to forget the whole thing ever happened".

"I can help you there" said Hargreaves, with a slightly mischievous look in his eye. He put down his glass, came close to her and put his arms round her. Kate stiffened slightly at the contact, but it was not unpleasant. She let her head drop slightly against his chest; and it felt natural, comforting. She looked up at him.

"How so?" she asked. He didn't reply straight away, but kissed her lips. She did not respond, but she did not resist; and she realised that she also wanted their parting to mean something, not in the same way that he did, but it was the passing away of an extraordinary time in her life, with a not inconsiderable part of it spent with the man now holding her, kissing her. His reply suggested that he could read her thoughts.

"Kate, until a few months ago you were Kate Kimball, successful business woman living with a fine man, happy I think, content; and from later tonight, that is what you will start to be again. By tomorrow, the day after, what you have been through will start to fade. You will see your old friends, the people you work with, go back to your life before. But for the months in between, you were another person. Initially, I suppose, a victim, but very soon an extraordinary sort of one-woman commando. You took on some of the most dangerous men in the country, O'Connell and Riordan, Alan Gerrard, the security forces, Swinburne and his men, God knows who else; and you beat them. That's a quite different Kate, that's the one I got to know, the one I fell in love with. And that Kate will disappear tonight, here, now. The main reason I can stand our separation is that I know no-one else will ever share that Kate, what we have, what we have been through. When you leave here, a different person will return to Paul, the person he loves and who loves him. But for a few moments more......" he paused to kiss her again "...for just a few moments there is that other Kate, here in my arms; and we need a proper ending. I need that – it's the only thing I will ever ask, can ever ask of you – but you do too, an ending so that there will be no looking back; which is why we should make love to each other before you go, before you, Kate, my Kate, disappears for ever".

If Kate was surprised, it was at how little surprise she felt. At some level she had known, ever since she got out of the car, perhaps even before she left Paul's house with Neil, that he would want to make love to her, with no thought for the morning, or perhaps with every thought for the morning if, as he said, the Kate he knew would no longer be there, anywhere. Instinctively, she started to formulate a rejection, as kind and understanding a rejection as she could, but a rejection nonetheless, but a wave of sadness swept over her as she struggled to say something, anything; and she realized - through an emotional turmoil of affection for Neil, guilt at what pain she had caused him, and bereavement - how perceptive, how right, Neil had been. The person she had become in recent months, honed by fear and anger and despair it was true had, nonetheless been a new Kate, one she felt some pride in, and one who had shared much with the man now gently kissing her again. She was - Neil was right – losing that self, for sure, but it hurt; and something deep inside her felt a need for emotional release, from all the stress and fear certainly but also from what her life had become. Indeed, as she stood there, holding Neil, with him caressing her hair, she recognized that she *had* to escape – from the life, the events, the turmoil and the emotions that had sustained her through the recent months - if she was to find again the Kate who lived with and loved Paul. Kate had, in her life, slept with relatively few men, five to be precise; and in each case it had been a beginning, of a new relationship, a new experience. Some had been quite short-lived, but that did not alter the fact that making love to someone was, for her, always a prelude and, in an important way, a commitment to the future. Now, Neil had either seen in her, or perhaps planted in her, the idea that such an act could be an ending, a completion - in every sense of the word a consummation - of their time together. And it would be the Kate he knew who would make love

426

to him; and a quite different Kate who would then drive off, return to Paul, to her former life. No betrayal, just the death of one person and a renewed life for another. When she got back it would be the meeting she had hoped for when she first returned from Los Angeles. With the nightmare in between banished once and for all.

How much of all this consciously passed through Kate's mind she couldn't say; and even then she did not know what to do, what she would do. All she did know was that the rejection she had sought to put into words, the words the other Kate, tomorrow's Kate, would say, remained unsaid; and as Neil kissed her again, still very gently, she kissed him back. The impact on Neil was like an electric shock through his body, but he remained calm, almost impassive, holding her, knowing how incredibly fragile were both she and their remaining time together. Then, almost imperceptibly, he let one arm slip from around her, took her by the hand, and slowly moved to the bottom of the staircase. Kate, now seeing more clearly what she had been thinking, and relaxing into the knowledge that her instincts were right, followed where he led. Neither said a word as he led her up the stairs, into his bedroom, and kissed her again. They stood together, both now feeling a total acceptance of the moment, its reasons, its significance for the here and now; and its fleeting nature, very soon to be lost for all time, a door closing that neither would ever be able to open or even find again. Neil released Kate and drew the curtains. At the same time, Kate unhurriedly took of her clothes and climbed under the sheets on Neil's large and well upholstered bed. A moment later Neil joined her and, naked, they clung to each other, not as if it were their last moment together but because they both knew that it really was just that. Hargreaves would have wished to make love to her all night long, but the emotions of the moment, the passion he felt were too strong for that. He caressed her body and, in a very few minutes, was on top of her, embracing her, entering her. Kate held him to her, letting her own emotions flow freely though her, the experience being even more cathartic than she could have imagined. As they neared a climax, she could feel the stresses of her recent life seeping away, could see in her mind's eye people she'd met, places she'd been which were now gone; and all the fears she'd felt - that she'd lost Paul for ever, that she would be murdered by nameless intruders in her own home, or maybe by O'Connell, or Swinburne, or Gerrard – all dissolved as her past life dissolved into a moment of shared sexual release with a brave man who had helped her survive.

Afterwards, they both lay there in each others arms, but only for a few moments. Their aroused emotions would cover the sadness of parting for only a short period; and Kate knew more clearly than Neil, that she must now leave. She got out of bed and, again without a word, got dressed. Neil watched her and, to his surprise, it seemed that what he had said to Kate – that he could cope much better with her leaving if he could make love to her before she left – was to some degree true. When she was ready, she came over to him, still lying on the bed, bent over and kissed him. He kissed her back; and she headed for the stairs. At the door she looked back.

"Goodbye, Neil"

"Goodbye Kate" he replied, and then she was gone. In the car, as she drove back, she felt no anxiety, no guilt. It had been the right thing to do, for Neil she could now see, but also for herself. The emotion of the moment had, in some indefinable but very real way, set a seal on everything she had done to find Paul, everything she had done with Neil and without him. She felt ready to return to the normality of her previous life. Ten minutes later she let herself into Paul's house.

"I'm sorry to have been so long" she said, as Paul came to meet her.

"Was there a problem?" He said

"Neil hasn't had a good time, and there were things….. things we needed to say. Paul……." He cut her off

"It's okay, Kate. It's okay. No need to say anything. I'm not totally blind. I have you back; and that's all that matters. It was only the thought of you that kept me going all the time I was held in that cell. You brought me back, incredible, wonderful Kate; and we are together again, now and for the rest of our lives. Nothing else matters". He put his arm round her. She lent against him, just as she had done at the police station earlier that day, but it was a different Kate, the old Kate who stood there this time; and silently wept.

Epilogue

Eight months later

O'Connell lay in long grass, and peered yet again through a pair of high-powered binoculars at the man on the tractor. In camouflage dungarees he was all but invisible; and the binoculars were cased in non-reflective material, with recessed lenses to avoid any danger of light reflection giving his position away. The man on the tractor was towing a hay baler and working at a steady pace. He had been working for several hours, with a break for lunch; and O'Connell had observed his every move. He had also kept two other men under observation from his slightly elevated position above the farmland – an older man whom he knew from observing them over a number of weeks was the owner or tenant of the farm; and another farm hand, unlike the one he was now looking at, only part-time. A fourth man, no more than a lad, had come to help on a number of occasions, always at the week-end, but those were the days that mattered. O'Connell was quite certain that they were the only people running the farm. One woman had appeared fairly regularly from the Georgian style farmhouse, driving off in a Landrover and re-appearing anything from one to five hours later – without doubt the wife of the farmer. Equally invisible, up in the woods on the other side of the farm, Riordan was somewhere around, also watching minutely, noting the farm workers and, to the extent that there was one, their pattern of working.

He, like O'Connell had noted – crucially – that they did no regular work on a Sunday; some odd jobs, occasional repair work, some new fencing put up, but quite often they were not to be seen at all, except for the farmer himself pottering around the farmyard buildings that formed a courtyard around the farmhouse at the centre of Shrove Farm. Twice, however, there had been visitors for Sunday lunch, quite possibly children and grandchildren. This was not surprising, but it complicated O'Connell's plans. It was now late afternoon on a Friday; and O'Connell had heard, only some ten minutes ago, from one of his team. No more waiting, no more planning. They were ready to go.

O'Connell and Riordan had had what could best be described as a difficult time since they had left Kate, Emmerson and Hargreaves just in time, following Hargreaves' warning. After disabling the couple who had followed them, they had made it into the wooded area between the pub where they had been talking and the Ferry Hinksey Road, had moved a long way eastwards before cautiously approaching the road itself and, in the gathering gloom, had managed to cross it unseen. From there they made it onto the cycle track that rang alongside the road, but hidden from it by a screen of grassy earthwork, varying from six to ten foot high. Once there it was a quick and easy sprint further eastward and into the residential streets of Marston, the suburban area that had grown up after the war, filling in between the eastern fringes of Oxford City and the village of Old Marston. An hour later they were on a bus to London and, the next day, back in Northern Ireland. But the satisfaction they both felt at having eluded Gerrard's men was completely overwhelmed by the news that Gerrard had survived the vote in Parliament, was riding high; and by the full realization that their carefully developed plan – Kate's plan – to bring down Gerrard once and for all had failed, had been totally skewered by some very devious bastard working for Gerrard – they still didn't know who, from amongst a small number, it might be. And, as they sat and reviewed the situation back in Belfast, now knowing, thanks to Kate, exactly who was responsible for the deaths of their five comrades, they became steadily clearer in their minds that this could not be the end of the matter. Gerrard had murdered the five of them in cold blood, not as part of a civil war between Britain and Northern Ireland – they might just have been able to live with that – but simply to protect his political career, oh so successfully; and he would have to pay. If it was not to be through a life in prison, then it would have to be with his life.

Neither could remember later which of them it was who actually first proposed assassinating Gerrard – the idea arose so naturally from their reflections on what had happened that they were thinking about it, contemplating plans without either of them ever stating the objective. But that was what started to fill every waking moment of their lives, and quite a few dreams as well. But how to get at the most heavily defended politician in the country? Initially they had hoped that there would, fairly quickly, be such a backlash against what Gerrard had done that he would, despite having won the confidence vote, be forced from office and, shortly after that from leadership of his party. He would still get heavy duty protection, for many years, perhaps for the rest of his life, but both O'Connell and Riordan felt, not unreasonably, that he would be a much easier target as a backbench MP, or even just a private citizen again if he left politics, even though an ex Prime-Minister. No longer living in the public eye would make him much more accessible; and eventually there was bound to be some significant downgrading of the security detail that would be assigned to him. But all this rapidly became a delusion, for it was quite clear that Alan Gerrard was going to remain Prime minister for a good few years yet.

Not that O'Connell and Riordan's initial assumption had been wrong. There certainly was a major backlash against Gerrard, amongst three very different groups in particular. Most damaging was the British Press which, removed from the emotion, histrionics and party machinery which had carried the day in Parliament proceeded, with very few exceptions, to castigate his actions in the most uncompromising terms. Few commentators said anything new, but the views which they incessantly repeated were delivered with the benefit of time, so as to include the most apt and, more importantly, the most damning phrases. Gerrard was seen, in short, to have acted illegally, with some of the more optimistic and opportunistic writers calling for him to be arraigned as a war criminal; as having created, in Iran, the most implacable foe, dedicated to the waging of a renewed terrorist war on the US and the UK for the foreseeable future; and as having, in cahoots with the US, created the most dangerous precedent in the whole history of mankind, the first-strike use of nuclear weapons. Second, partly fed by this media coverage - which was subtly and sometimes not so subtly sustained by the BBC - and partly stoking it up, virtually all of the right-thinking intelligentsia - the mass of well-educated, opinion-forming critics who dominate the professional cadre in the UK – was appalled by Gerrard's actions. While many had voted for him, indeed been regarded as the critical group of swing voters which had brought him victory in the General election so recently, they now deserted him en masse, so that his actions and the unique nature of his error – iniquity really – became an axiom of their discourse. The attendees of many a dinner party vied with each other as to who could condemn Gerrard the most; and many a hostess just prayed that there would not be a lone supporter – not even a pale apologist – for Gerrard because, if there were, then that was the end of a civilised evening indeed, in some cases, any evening at all. And the third pool of opposition was, not surprisingly, at the UN, where the actions of the US and the UK were formally condemned, though with as little impact on global policy or anything else as Hamilton and Gerrard had anticipated. But it helped to fuel the rage of those who discussed such things, and gave the Press yet more stories on which to hang its righteous indignation.

None of this greatly troubled Gerrard in itself. It was no more than he had expected – quite enough to stop him acting the way he had if he had had any choice about it but, as he hadn't, not of great consequence. All that mattered to him was holding on to the party support that he had achieved or, more accurately, preventing a leadership challenge. In this, however, he had many advantages, the main one being the likely wrath of the electorate if either his Cabinet colleagues or his back-benchers decided to determine the identity of the next Prime Minister rather than the electorate itself. In short, many potential recruits to such a move feared, with considerable justification that, if it were successful, then one way or another they would soon be fighting for their seats in a General Election. And if it were unsuccessful then they would merely have wrecked their future careers. This did not, as Gerrard knew well, eliminate the risk of a coup against him, but it would have to have a credible alternative leader, it would need a lot of heavy-weight support, and it would have to be quick. The first two conditions were not difficult. The obvious leader-in-the-wings was Graham Seymour; and the opportunity to remove a fairly obvious political liability, thereby creating new vacancies all the way down the political ladder, was not lost on a number of Gerrard's senior colleagues. The saving grace for Gerrard was the third condition, speed. He had just won a confidence vote in Parliament; and every one of his senior colleagues had voted for him. To then turn round, on the basis of no new events, and demonstrate the ultimate lack of confidence would appear, would indeed be, the height of opportunism at best and utter hypocrisy at the worst. Whoever spearheaded it would be risking the end of his or her political credibility and, with it, his or her political career. As the hours turned into days, and the days into weeks, Gerrard knew, as did O'Connell and Riordan, that he was going to be around as PM for a good while yet.

In this he was helped by two other factors. The first was that, although most of the press and all of the opinion forming class were entirely opposed to him, both his own standing and that of his party in the opinion polls took much less of a hammering than many had expected. A substantial cross section of what were once regularly called blue-collar workers and now referred to as C's, D's and E's in the country quite openly supported Gerrard's actions, helped by a much smaller and much quieter but nonetheless not insignificant number of white-collar workers or A's and B's. They were mainly men, and no doubt testosterone had a part to play in it all, but they quite liked the direct action involved, the settling of an issue by force of arms, the faint strain that Britain still had the word 'Great' in front of it; and at least three papers, *The Sun, The Express* and *the Mail* – though only the first had enough circulation to offer real political clout – both reflected and encouraged this stance. So, although the slim lead in the opinion polls which the opposition had previously been experiencing moved firmly into double figures, it by no means became catastrophic for Gerrard – certainly the figures remaining well within the range from which parties in the past had frequently recovered; and, most ominous of all for the opposition, stabilizing and then beginning, however marginally, to recede within a matter of weeks, demonstrating yet again, if demonstration were needed, how short memories can be in politics.

The other factor helping Gerrard, not massively, but more than might have been expected, was the march of events. Unlike the Iraq war there had been no regime change to achieve, no subsequent occupation, no drawn out period of civil war and countless deaths for which the victorious forces had been unprepared. In fact the US and the UK, reluctantly supported by the European Union, offered to provide funding and resources directly to the Iranian Government to help it set about decontaminating the various sites which had been bombed. The Iranian Government, unwisely most thought but predictably, refused to accept such tainted money, but a secret conduit via the UN was set up which the Iranian's felt able to accept. The conduit was not, in fact, much of a secret, but it enabled the UN to help Iran at no cost other than to the specific contributors; and provided a face-saving basis for Iran

Much more significant was the Israeli initiative. The UN agreed to a substantial peace-keeping force in Gaza, from which, in a month, the Israelis had left. The beginning of the demolition of the West Bank settlements led to major rioting in Israel but, unlike previously, with the real prospect of a peace settlement, the settlers were unable to mount a powerful enough coalition to threaten the Government. Against this background, every single Arab nation in the Middle East except Iran – even Syria – agreed to take part in a region-wide peace negotiation with Israel, under the auspices of the UN, which also began to consider how it might tackle the issue of Jerusalem. No-one was promising anything; and very little that was actually new – apart from the settlements programme – had happened. Of particular concern, neither wing of the Palestinian body politic was saying anything, but a two-nation solution was being discussed – or at least the possibility of such discussions was being discussed; and that was generally seen as positive.

Further helping Gerrard was the fact that, for obvious reasons, neither he nor President Hamilton were playing any part in all this – that would have been too much a red rag in the face of too many bulls; and this had the slightly curious result of drawing attention away from the two men who had triggered the new situation, for better or worse. The media made sure no-one forgot, but the actual politics – policy formation, negotiation, bargaining and so on - increasingly centered around the UN and its various subsidiary bodies, focusing the world on the new situation rather than the circumstances that had brought it about. President Hamilton and Prime Minister Gerrard were both, for somewhat different reasons, entirely happy with this. Hamilton made it very clear that he had saved the Middle East, perhaps the world, from destruction – a proposition which enough Republicans accepted to offset the Democrats he had lost on the way. He was now moving on to the two other big issues he had identified, climate change and Africa. He already had a major bill ready on the first and, while it ran significant risk of defeat in the Senate, opposed by very well financed oil and gas interests, his policy towards Iran had undoubtedly won him new friends and more influence among the Republican ranks of the Senate. Where his steps to abolish poverty in Africa would take him, no-one knew.

For Gerrard, it was just a matter of getting out of the limelight, letting new events takeover and memories fade; and here his final piece of good luck stepped in. For reasons with which he had little personal sympathy and no actual responsibility, the British economy, after suffering its worst recession since the Thirties; and having made the most anaemic recovery of all the major economies of the world was, finally moving into faster and more sustained growth. And perhaps the most iron law of all in politics was that attention and support tends to follow the state of the economy. For every attack on his Iranian folly, Gerrard was able to point to favourable economic factors that meant much more to most people – falling unemployment, rising living standards, even a slightly stronger Pound. Gerard might or might not win the next General Election, but it was probably nearly four years away; and there seemed very little reason for either he or anyone else to expect that he wouldn't be there – as Prime Minister still – to fight it.

Which was precisely what so horrified O'Connell and Riordan; and drove them on in their determination to deal with Gerrard. Exposing his actions back in 1983 had, they saw, become impossible; and if they had any remaining hopes in this regard they were dashed within two days of their escape from Oxford. All the national papers carried the story of Emmerson's seizure by a dissident wing of the IRA; and the attempt by the Irish to mount some sort of campaign against Gerrard using his expertise and the assistance of Emmerson's long-term girl-friend, Kate Kimball. The nature of Emmerson's expertise was left rather vague – merely referred to as 'scientific' – as was the way in which this might have been of use to the IRA. Kate's possible role was even less clear. But the two killer punches, from O'Connell's point of view, was the rather heroic references to how the British security forces had foiled the whole thing, detaining Kate in the process; and the picture carried by all the papers of Emmerson and Kate leaving Oxford Police Station together, the fact of them having been there carrying so much more weight than the fact of their being released. Even without the recording that Kate had been forced to make, O'Connell doubted if he could make the slightest impression with the evidence he had. With a copy of the recording no doubt sitting in a safe somewhere in 10 Downing Street, he knew that that avenue was completely closed to him.

So, for several months, he and Riordan explored possibilities. It was a gruelling and disheartening process. They had already noted that Gerrard was the most securely protected politician in the country. It rapidly became clear that the security surrounding Gerrard matched that of any Middle Eastern potentate or London based Russian billionaire. But much of this security came not from large numbers of secret service personnel or bullet proof cars and the like, though they had no doubts that all of that played an important role. The main plank in protecting Gerrard came simply from the absence of any reliable intelligence as to where he might be at any particular time. This was the only useful – if very negative – information O'Connell and Riordan were able to glean from three months of very discreet surveillance.

Their first step had been to call another meeting of the team they had recruited earlier. This had been a curious occasion, somehow combining the unstated pleasure they felt at having all survived – the camaraderie amongst them that came from having risked their freedom and their lives together – with the bitter taste of failure, made all the worse by the fact that, as a military operation it had gone rather well, at least up until the moment Kate had hooked herself onto the helicopter harness to prevent Emmerson falling to his almost certain death. When O'Connell explained that he wasn't accepting this, was planning – by some means or other – to finish what they had started, the mood turned electric. All sixteen quickly indicated that they were ready, more than ready, to join O'Connell for another operation. O'Connell, however, counselled caution.

"This time" he said "we aim to eliminate Gerrard. If we succeed it will be the biggest blow to the British since the worst days of the war. They will never let up in their efforts to find us, never. So you need to be prepared for that. It will affect you for the rest of your lives; and your families' lives and, needless to say, if you get caught, you will almost certainly spend the rest of your lives in prison. So, think about it. No-one will think any the less of anyone who sees this as a step too far. I'm doubtful about it myself" he added, in an attempt to dispel some of the tension; and was rewarded with a few low laughs. No-one said anything; and he had his team.

The first thing they did was to recruit another twenty-three people, rather specifically chosen, to help with surveillance. These comprised three couples in their seventies, two families with, between them five small children, and four young couples. Most were related to one or other of O'Connell's men, all were sympathizers and all were keen to help out. O'Connell and Riordan wanted some basic information on Gerrard's comings and goings from Downing Street. The street, less than 200 metres long, is a cul-de-sac, with the purely pedestrian access at the end completed closed off. At the other end, any member of the public could look in at the street from behind the twelve foot high protective railings that normally bar entrance from the wide, majestic sweep of Parliament Street, the extension of Whitehall up to Parliament Square; and many hundreds of tourists did every day. But they were all politely forced to stand far back on the few occasions when the railing gates were opened to allow a car in or out. The only times this happened was for the arrival or departure of the Prime minister or the Chancellor of the Exchequer, both of whom lived in the street; and for visiting dignitaries – if they were important enough. There might also be the wife of the Chancellor of the Exchequer plus his two children, but Gerrard had no children; and his wife had died from ovarian cancer nearly seven years previously.

O'Connell wanted to get some feel for when Gerrard came and went, but faced two problems, one foreseen, the other not. The predictable one, though he had no way of checking it, was that the whole of Parliament Street – and no doubt Whitehall and Parliament Square as well - would be covered to the point of saturation with CCTV cameras, permanently monitored, so that anything unusual would be spotted immediately. This would undoubtedly include someone – anyone – loitering for too long near the entrance to Downing Street, which was why O'Connell had brought in nine teams of innocuous looking tourists. Each team sauntered once up and down Whitehall, stopping to gape at Downing Street on the way, preceded or followed by forty minutes with a drink outside the Red Lion pub on the opposite side of Parliament Street to Downing Street, some one hundred metres along towards Parliament Square, with a reasonably clear view of the entrance to the street. Heavily patronized by tourists at all times of the day and night, with many of them spilling out onto the pavement, it offered perfect cover for surveillance by his watchers, provided none of them lingered there too long. Supplemented by ten of his team who had never had a police record in Northern Ireland, and who followed the same routine except that they did not linger to look into Downing Street, they covered two ten hour days – a Monday and Tuesday. Two weeks later, with all of them in some way changing their appearance – hair dyed, glasses on, beards shaved, quite different clothing – they repeated the exercise for a Thursday and Friday. A month later they repeated the whole exercise. O'Connell had planned to collate what emerged; and then carry out a more focused repeat exercise a month after that. He judged that the risk of someone picking out his people on CCTV over such a period, amongst all the others glimpsing Downing Street, traversing Whitehall, having a drink at the pub, was minimal.

He learned a lot, but not at all what he wanted or expected. It became clear quite early on that Gerrard very rarely left Downing Street, at least by its Whitehall entrance; and only one trip could be matched up to anything approaching a predictable journey. Though Parliament was sitting, Gerrard rarely attended. When he did, for Prime Minister's question time, now reduced to once a week, he once apparently made the short journey – barely four hundred metres – in a cavalcade of three cars, 'apparently' because no-one could actually see who was in the back of the middle car with clouded glass, but it looked to a professional eye as if it were bullet and bomb proof, fit for a Prime Minister. However, that was to be expected. The real shock was that Gerrard attended Parliament two weeks later without ever coming through the heavily manned gates at the end of Downing Street. There was clearly an alternative route in and out, which meant that it was not only difficult to know in advance where the PM might be at a particular time, but virtually impossible to know how he would get there from Downing Street. Dismayed, O'Connell and Riordan went back to the drawing board. They had no idea how to attack Gerrard even if they knew where he was going to be. They had no way of knowing where he would be, apart from Prime Minister's Question Time, a weekly visit to the Queen at Buckingham Palace and, if they waited long enough, the Remembrance Day service at the Cenotaph in Whitehall, almost opposite Downing Street - and they had no illusions as to how tight security would be on such occasions. And now they didn't even know how he managed to come and go when he needed to be somewhere else. All in all, things looked very bleak indeed.

It was Riordan who started to loosen the log-jam in their thinking. As the two of them, for the umpteenth time went over the problem, he muttered – a throw-away line –

"No wonder the boys tried to get him with that rocket, though that got nowhere either". He was referring to the attempt in 1982 by the IRA to attack the then Prime Minister, Margaret Thatcher, by launching a missile from just off Whitehall into the garden of 10 Downing Street. The missile caused no injury to anyone, but the fact that the IRA had got so near to the Prime Minister's home with a rocket launcher, and had actually been able to fire it, was a grave embarrassment to the British security forces. O'Connell thought about this for a moment, then responded

"Now that gives me an idea".

"You can't be serious" said Riordan incredulously. "It was a disaster, a complete, fucking disaster. I don't know whose credibility sank furthest – the Brits for letting it happen or the lads for such a pathetic attempt".

"It's okay" said O'Connell. "I wasn't thinking of trying anything like that. But it strikes me that the team that carried it out must have taken a long and hard look at Thatcher's movements; and maybe they could tell us a lot we don't know".

"Did you know any of them?" asked Riordan.

"No, but I know one or two people who certainly did, probably still do. I'll get onto it".

It took less than two days, using his contacts in the IRA to identify Dermot Hogan, one of the four men involved in the rocket attack. Hogan had spent six years in an H block in the Maze prison for his role in the attack, before being released as part of a cease-fire agreement. O'Connell had no difficulty in fixing a meeting – he remained a legendary figure in the movement – and, the next evening, Hogan was delighted to tell O'Connell about the rocket attack. An intelligent man, he rapidly recognized that O'Connell's interest was not in the attack itself and, out of deference to O'Connell, made little further mention of it. What O'Connell wanted was any intelligence they had gathered at the time on how the Prime Minister of the day moved in and out of Downing Street.

Hogan was quite surprised, though he took precautions not to show it, at O'Connell's lack of knowledge on the matter, perhaps forgetting that, all those years ago, they had needed the help of a sympathizer working as a clerk in the

Cabinet Office to get the information themselves. The answer to O'Connell's query was very simple. In the first place, 10, Downing Street, though it looks quite small from the front, is in fact a huge, rambling building, stretching backwards and then sideways, linking up to the Cabinet Office and a series of other government offices in between Whitehall and Horse Guards Parade. These provide at least two alternative main entrances into or out of the complex – one onto Whitehall the other onto Horse Guards Parade; and there is also, for emergencies, a third exit, an unassuming door near to the entrance to the old underground Cabinet War Rooms. Hagan's team had discovered that no-one other than the Head of Security for the day – not even the PM himself – knew until the last minute which exit or entrance might be used. But that was not all. In the second place, it was always open to the PM to walk out of the front door of Number 10, cross Downing Street and enter the back of the Foreign Office Building complex, the other side of which backed onto King Charles Street, providing another exit route. Gerrard could even cross King Charles Street, walk through the Treasury Building which occupied the other side of the street, and emerge directly onto Parliament Square. A car, even a cavalcade leaving there, would appear as if from nowhere and disappear into the London traffic in a few seconds. Hogan's team had concluded that they would never be able to predict with sufficient notice from where the Prime Minister might emerge; and that had eventually led to them mounting the rocket attack on No.10 itself. He confirmed, in answer to a direct question from O'Connell, that he did not think it feasible to get at Gerrard anywhere near Downing Street.

"Did she ever leave by helicopter?" asked O'Connell.

"No" replied Hogan. "We thought of that and checked it out but, apparently they were worried about the prospect of a heat-seeking missile. Quite right too. If they'd used a helicopter I think we would have got her".

O'Connell thanked Hogan for his help; and was preparing to leave, both disappointed and without any inkling of how he might get to Gerrard. Hogan stood up as well, and added as an afterthought

"We thought about getting to Thatcher at Chequers, carried out quite an extensive surveillance, but that was just as tightly sown up – worse in fact". O'Connell hadn't thought of Chequers, traditionally the Prime Minister of the day's country house residence in the rolling hills of Buckinghamshire, some forty miles north of Central London but, no sooner had Hogan mentioned it than, in the same sentence, he had clearly precluded it. Nonetheless, O'Connell was curious; and asked Hogan what they had found out.

"Thatcher used to use it at the week-ends; and we thought about a heavy duty raid on the house while she was there, but it wasn't on then; and it wouldn't be now. It looks so vulnerable – just wire fencing or low stone walls, all round the estate, with rolling parkland; and agricultural land beyond. But we spent some time checking it out and the reality is – as you might expect – quite different.

Nearer the house, partly hidden in the trees is a very high-security electric fence. The parkland is patrolled day and night by armed security teams with dogs and night vision goggles. They have foot and car patrols on the roads around as well. Plus, we never checked but there's no question it would all be covered by CCTV, day and night; and there are even anti-tank traps dug in, in case anyone tried a full military assault. It all looks vintage upper class Englishman's country home, but it must be one of the most well defended buildings in the world". It crossed O'Connell's mind that he had, all those years ago, successfully penetrated one of the most heavily protected nuclear installations in the world, but that was because he had someone on the inside; and it had taken him ten years to achieve that. He reluctantly concluded that, once again, Hogan's assessment had been correct though, even as he did, something – some unconscious whisper - started to niggle away at his fertile brain. Well, he would let it emerge in its own time. For the present, he was no further ahead, indeed he was rather further behind where he had been. That night, he talked it through with Riordan in a small Belfast pub, and Riordan agreed that they didn't really have anything to work on. A deep gloom sunk over them.

"So, where do we go from here?" asked Riordan. "We knew it would be difficult, but there doesn't seem to be a chink anywhere. We can't get him at Downing Street, nor at Chequers; and we don't have the intelligence we'd need to know where else he'd be at any particular time. I suppose......." He stopped. "No, no, that wouldn't work".

"What wouldn't work?" asked O'Connell, rather despondently.

"I was going to say that we might try something when he is on his way to Chequers, but it doesn't work because we wouldn't know when he was travelling there; and in any case, they are bound to use a variety of routes – most basic rule of security 'don't be predictable'; not to mention that he would go in a bomb-proof car in a well defended convoy". His assessment could not have been more negative, but it sent something like an electric current pulsing through O'Connell's veins, for it had triggered what had been floating just beyond his consciousness for some while, made the thought, for the first time, manifest to O'Connell. Years of experience meant that, for a few minutes, he just let the thought lie there – no exploration, no discussion, just let the unconscious do its work before he took it over. But, as he sat there, saying nothing, Riordan could tell that something in the atmosphere had changed. A series of photographs would have detected not a pixel of change in O'Connell's appearance, but there was now a tension in his body which screamed at Riordan, telling him that, out of the black hole into which their plans had spun, something was beginning to emerge. Riordan knew better than to say anything. Eventually, O'Connell spoke.

"There might just be a way" he said. "It all depends".

O'Connell and Riordan spent the next week reconnoitering the Chequers estate from a suitably discreet distance. As Hogan had said, it looked disarmingly unprotected, but O'Connell reckoned that any attempt to find out more about its defences would almost certainly result in his being arrested. Fortunately, he was not very interested in the electric fences, the men and the dogs that kept Gerrard safe and secure when he visited. Instead he worked his way round the perimeter, usually about half a mile beyond the fencing that surrounded the estate; and well amongst the cover of the trees in the area. This revealed what he had felt was very likely to be the case – that there would be very few entrances to such a secure site, perhaps only one. In fact there were two. One was obviously the main entrance, situated close to a bend in the country road in which it stood. It had powerful looking gates and two substantial gate houses, one either side, with a main drive then going on up to the house itself; but either side, the perimeter of the estate was marked by no more than a wire fence. In fact a public footpath passed through the grounds just *behind* the gate houses. Moreover, the gate houses might accommodate security personnel, but clearly was not built to provide more than cursory protection nor, indeed, built any time in the last century. The security came further up the drive.

The other entrance was to the side of the estate, presumably designed originally for tradesmen, supplies, staff entry and the like; and probably still used for the same purposes. Here there was simply a double gate set under a lych-gate structure, watched by an obvious CCTV camera – again the security machine would start further up the staff driveway. It would be natural to think that Gerrard would arrive and depart by the main gate – and no doubt visiting VIPs all would. But O'Connell did not discount the possibility that, on security grounds, Gerrard might well sometimes leave by the servants' quarters. The main point was, as O'Connell's subconscious had begun to see, that if they could identify week-ends when Gerrard used Chequers – and O'Connell had a plan for that – then they would at least have narrowed down to two locations where Gerrard would have to be; and with at least a rough idea of when he would be there. This, at last, was progress.

O'Connell now changed his surveillance programme dramatically. He stood down his motley collection of sympathetic watchers, telling them that they had played a critical part in a great but, as yet, unfulfilled enterprise. He then arranged for the ten members of his team who had been helping with the surveillance to mount a new watch. This time, each of them, dressed smartly in a suit and carrying either brief case or document bag, would walk slowly up Whitehall from Trafalgar Square, on into Parliament Street, past the entrances to Downing Street and King Charles Street but on the other side of Whitehall, go into the Red Lion for a drink; and then head on – each just another tired office worker heading home for the week-end. The first started at around 3 pm on a Friday and, with each having the entrances to both Downing Street and King Charles Street in view for around 40 minutes they were, in aggregate able to keep both those entrances and the Cabinet Office entrance in view continuously until about 9.30 pm. When not employed on this, the men participated in two other rotas. One involved having a lengthy cup of tea or, later, a glass of beer in the open air café at the eastern end of the parkland to the south of the Mall, from which Horse Guards Parade could be sighted; while the other involved sauntering about with the tourists milling about on the north side of Westminster Abbey, from which the entrance into Parliament Square from the Treasury could be observed.

Meanwhile, O'Connell lay among the Buckinghamshire trees with his binoculars observing the main gate into Chequers; and Riordan likewise at the side entrance. This procedure they followed every Friday for ten weeks. O'Connell then called off the surveillance; and arranged for all members of his team to meet him once again in the dining room of the pub near Ravinet, this time on the Monday evening following the tenth Friday of observation. Including O'Connell's two sons there were twenty of them altogether; and the air of expectation was palpable as they each got themselves a drink before settling down to hear what O'Connell had to say.

O'Connell first pointed out that in all of their nineteen weeks of watching no-one – not one of them – had for certain actually seen Gerrard. Most there might feel reasonably confident that they had seen his comings and goings – such as they were – because no-one else would have the level of security they had witnessed – primarily the fact of three car convoys with one-way glass protection; and there was another reason to infer that these arrangements were evidence of Gerrard himself being chauffeured around, which O'Connell would come to in a moment. But it was worth remembering that everything he was about to say was inferred rather than the result of direct observation. Only then did he go on to summarise the information the watchers had gleaned.

Gerrard, presuming it was him, had left Downing Street three times in the course of the ten Fridays, from three different exits. These corresponded with three arrivals around an hour and a quarter later at Chequers. Curiously, the convoy of cars had arrived a fourth time at Chequers, but whether this was because the watchers in London had missed Gerrard once, or because he had gone direct to Chequers from somewhere else they did not know. O'Connell said that he would have felt happier if the watchers had been able to see the registration numbers of the cars, in order to confirm that they were the same cars he and Riordan had seen arriving at Chequers, but none of the watchers had been able to get near enough to identify the plates. However, O'Connell had little reason to doubt that he had identified correctly Gerrard's week-end use of Chequers. The two immediate problems they faced, he said, were first that there was no pattern to the week-ends Gerrard went to Chequers – he had gone there weeks two, five, six and eight – and, second, there was no pattern to *when* he left – his three observed departure times being logged as 6.45 pm, 3.30 pm and 5.20 pm. As for Gerrard's arrival at Chequers, this had three times been through the main entrance and once to the side entrance, but the latter was the journey that probably had not started from Downing Street; and so it was not clear whether this reflected a security decision or just that Gerrard had been coming from a different direction for which the rear entrance was more convenient. Of Gerrard's route or routes from London to Chequers O'Connell had, of course, no idea.

The men assembled there could not but think that this was all rather disappointing news – over four months of work had provided no insight into when Gerrard might go to Chequers, what time he might leave, from which exit he might set off, how he might get there or even which entrance he would arrive at; and all of them knew perfectly well that they were only ever going to get – at most - one chance to kill Gerrard. O'Connell recognized the growing sense of despondency – had anticipated it given what he had had to tell them so far – but, unlike them, knew there was better to come.

"I know that all sounds very depressing" he said "but now I'll come to the good news". All eyes were glued to him as he permitted himself just the hint of a smile. "In fact, three pieces of good news. The first is that on all the four occasions that Gerrard has spent the week-end at Chequers while we have been watching him, he has always left to go back to London around 4 pm or so on the Sunday. The earliest was just after 3 pm and the latest 4.45 pm. The second is that on each of those occasions he has left by the main drive. I couldn't at first understand why his security people didn't use the side entrance sometimes – it makes for a slightly longer journey home but that wouldn't count for much. However, I think the reason might be that the woods beyond the estate come very close to the road near the side entrance; and while they no doubt could rig up all sorts of surveillance equipment, I suspect that they feel uncomfortable with that amount of cover so near to where they would have to take Gerrard. If they leave by the front drive then, once they are beyond the security perimeter, there is no cover for anyone watching, either inside or once they get outside the estate – just parkland inside and agricultural land outside. Once they leave the estate, between the gate houses, they can turn left or right – actually it's more like straight on because of the bend in the road – but turning left takes you all round the side of the estate, away from London, and they haven't used it. In the other direction – basically south - there are open fields on the left of them and just scrubland – a few trees but not many - on the right; and so it looks a lot safer prospect than the side entrance. And the third piece of good news, which I should have thought about earlier – I'm losing my touch – is that, on the week-ends when Gerrard goes there, there is – of course – much more activity; and it starts quite early on the Fridays involved – probably before that in fact, but we haven't been watching earlier in the week. A lot of extra staff must come in, there are additional supplies, the security people will no doubt be doing all sorts of pre-emptive sweeps for bugs, explosives whatever; and, of course, there are the other guests. Gerrard doesn't go and lock himself away for the week-end. Some of it may be social but my guess is that he does a lot of business of one kind or another, with his staff, people he wants support from, visitors from overseas and so on. The result is that, when we see all this activity during a Friday, then see his car leave London, and see it arrive later at Chequers, we can be reasonably certain that two days later, around 4 pm on the Sunday, give or take an hour or two, he will be leaving by the main gate, then heading right along the road. In short, we will know where he is going to be, roughly when, and with nearly two days notice".

Had he expected a roar of approval he was destined to be disappointed, but he was far too experienced for that. Every man in the room felt some elation that they did, at least, now have an identifiable killing ground but, to a man, were themselves experienced enough in such matters to know that that was barely a start. Gerrard would be in a bomb and bullet- proof car; and he would have a substantial number of security personnel travelling with him. A favourite ploy in Northern Ireland of burying a bomb in the road – or some other type of booby-trap device – and then setting it off remotely at the right moment would be out of the question in such a heavily monitored place as the entrance to Chequers. Most, therefore, remained pensive, unsure where this was leading, wondering if that was all O'Connell had so far. Just a few, mainly the older ones who had known O'Connell longest, permitted themselves a lifting of the spirits. O'Connell would not have called them together and explained his thinking if he did not have answers to the questions now crowding in on all their minds. "So" said O'Connell, no doubt being very aware of the sentiments being silently voiced amongst the men in front of him "we take him on Sunday afternoon, on the road as they come out of the Chequers estate. The next question you'll all be asking is 'how do we do it?' Well, if you all come up to the table here, I've got a map that'll help me explain".

The men all crowded round as O'Connell and Riordan unfolded a large hand-drawn map and stretched it out on one of the tables. "Can you all see?" asked O'Connell. There was a general murmur indicating that they could. "Well, here is the Chequers estate". He pointed to an area near the top centre of the map. "The house itself is right up over here". He pointed to the top edge of the map where he was holding it down. "The drive curves down through the middle of the estate, past the gatehouses and onto the road here". He pointed to the line he had drawn down through the middle of the map; and then to the spot where the drive reached the road. "This road is called Meadow Lane. To the east it runs along the southern boundary of the Chequers estate, with farmland on the other side. In the other direction the road fairly quickly swings south, away from Chequers, and runs for over half a mile towards London before there's any turn-off. Towards the end of this section of road, on the left, is Shrove farm. The other side is just some scrubland and a few trees. The farm has about 800 acres altogether, but the key section for us is the field next to the road running south from the gatehouse. That is where we will strike. Any questions so far?"

"Only the obvious one" said one of the men. "How are we going to reach him in broad daylight with no cover; and how are we going to get through the security net that will surround him?"

"Ah" said O'Connell thoughtfully. "I was coming to that. Like all of you, Shaun and I have been spending every Friday watching what goes on. We've spent the other six days each week working out how to carry out the operation; and it all comes down to Shrove Farm. We've been studying it almost every day for the last two months. It has one small but vital characteristic – you could watch the farm for a year and you'd never notice it – but it suits us perfectly; and it will be our way in. Let me explain". For the next hour and a half, O'Connell, assisted by Riordan, talked the group through every aspect of what they had learned about Shrove Farm, how they planned to attack Gerrard – and live to tell the tale – and what arrangements and supplies would be needed in order to carry it out. As he revealed his and Riordan's thinking, stage by stage, the men, now back in their seats, began to see how it might all work. Even those who had been most sceptical began to become enthusiastic and, by the time O'Connell had finished, the atmosphere in the room was supercharged.. O'Connell concluded.

"We won't meet again as a group until the operation itself. But you all know what everyone is doing; and your part in the operation; and Shaun and I will be meeting up with you in twos and threes to go through every step in detail, quite a lot of training, some practice moves and so on. We will also arrange for each of you, once and on your own, to drive down the road to see the layout for yourself. That will only be after you have absorbed every aspect of the plan, so that you can map it onto the terrain. Are there any more questions?"

"If we succeed" asked one of them "is there anything to link the assassination to any of us? Anything at all?"

"No" said O'Connell. "They may reckon that Shaun and me are behind it, but we aim to become very scarce indeed afterwards; and there is nothing to link the operation or either of us back to any of you. The only way you will get caught is if you talk about it to anyone – and I know no-one will do that. So, it will be a great day; and we will all be clear". In fact, if all went according to plan, the world would never know the identity of the eighteen men seated around him.

Whether O'Connell and Riordan would be so fortunate he was much less certain.

Now, another four months later, they were ready to put those plans into practice. They had, in fact, been ready for three weeks, but on neither of the previous two Fridays had Gerrard gone to Chequers for the week-end; and this was now the third Friday that the team had stood ready to move. But this time, finally, the operation would go ahead. All day there had been more activity, in particular around the rear entrance to the house; and now one of his men, walking up Whitehall, had spotted three cars leaving from outside the Whitehall entrance by the Cabinet Office. O'Connell was confident that within ninety minutes at most, he would see the same convoy arrive at the entrance to Chequers, but he would make his way to a point where he could observe the gatehouses, just to make absolutely sure. The four months had been an intensive period, of obtaining supplies, training his men, creating a legitimate company to front one aspect of their operation, should it be necessary; and planning every last detail and for every possible scenario that might develop. The supplies had included acquiring a large number of vehicles and renting some others which O'Connell's men had then had modified; and which were now standing in a large storage unit some miles away; also some specially designed materials, together with armaments for his men – mainly sub-machine guns but also two pistols, a number of grenades - and, in case it might be needed, a small quantity of explosives.

All this had been relatively straight-forward. The only real problem had been so unexpected it had provoked great mirth amongst his team – even he and Riordan had been forced to laugh. They might need – probably would need – three of the men to sound completely English; and none of them could manage it. However much they tried, the rather low, drawn-out Northern Irish accent with its elongated, even slightly turgid vowel sounds would emerge at some point; and that was something O'Connell couldn't risk. In the end he had solved the problem by recruiting three more members of the team, all Northern Irish and strong supporters of the nationalist cause but who had been living in London for most of the previous ten years and could readily pass for Londoners if they wished. There had initially been some concern amongst the group at the introduction of new faces, but O'Connell had carried out very extensive checks before he even approached them; and more thorough ones still afterwards. Helping the process was the fortunate coincidence that one of the three, Joseph Kelly, was slightly related to the McGuiness family, which had lost Mary and Michael so many years ago and whose deaths – not to mention his own conscience - O'Connell was seeking to avenge. None had any experience of even a quasi-military nature but that, O'Connell assured them, would not be necessary; and they could be well on their way long before the real action started. Now, with all these plans in place, they were ready to act.

O'Connell made his way to where he could observe the entrance to Chequers through his binoculars and, some eighty-five minutes later, saw what he had expected to see – three cars coming down Meadow Lane and swinging into the main driveway. It was nearly 7 pm and already dark, but the scene was quite clear to him. Gerrard, he told himself, now had less than forty-eight hours to live. He headed back to his base above Shrove Farm; put through a call to one of his team, all of whom were in two 12-seater vans, one parked in the railway station car park at Watford Junction, the other in a car park in High Wycombe; and told them the operation was on. They would all meet up at 1 am at a pre-arranged point around a mile from Shrove Farmhouse. He got them to check all the arms and equipment yet again – a needless activity but they were all aware that they would get just the one chance; and it filled up what would otherwise been tedious but very tense inactivity for the rest of the evening. Around midnight the vans left their respective parking slots and drove carefully through the deserted roads to the agreed rendezvous. Two of them would drive the vans off again; park them nearby and stay with them until – for a further critical role in the operation – they were next needed. The other eighteen men – the three additional recruits to the team not being required at this juncture – were all dressed in camouflage combat fatigues, carried sub-machine guns, small backpacks with sleeping bags, food and water; and several of them between them humped large and quite heavy canvas bags. Two others carried two short wooden step-ladders. All of them donned black ski-masks, as did O'Connell and Riordan. When they were all ready, they made their way silently forward, O'Connell and Riordan in the lead, through a number of copses but also behind low hedges running along side fields. They were invisible in the dark; and would have been largely so even to someone observing with infra-red night goggles. But they were well to the east side of Shrove Farm; and there was little risk of being spotted from anywhere on the Chequers estate, however good the security.

Shortly before 2 am, O'Connell paused, some two hundred metres from Shrove Farm. He gave a hand-signal – the whole operation would continue with no words spoken – and eight of his men, including both his sons, plus Riordan, set off behind O'Connell. The other eight remained behind with the canvas bags. Slowly and silently they walked down a slight slope across one of the fields belonging to Shrove Farm, down towards the back of the farmhouse. Unusually, the farmhouse stood a little separate from the farmyard, with its barns and other buildings, but this had no particular significance for O'Connell. There was a small farmyard gate set in a perimeter fence, which provided a back entrance to a small yard which surrounded three sides of the farmhouse.

The gate would have afforded easy entry to the yard, but O'Connell had very early on been concerned that opening it might make a noise. The farmer owned two dogs which, for sure, would soon make a lot of noise, but O'Connell wanted, needed, to delay this until the last possible moment. So, as they gathered by the gate, one wooden ladder was lent up against the fence, the first man up carrying the other section of ladder, which he then lent against the inside of the fence; and carefully stepped down into the yard. From this moment, speed was of the essence. As the first man into the courtyard raced across it towards the back door of the farmhouse, the rest of O'Connell's men started to pour over the wall. Only as the first man reached the back door did one of the dogs appear, barking loudly. O'Connell's man had his pistol ready, a large silencer barrel on it; and instantly shot the dog dead. It had managed only two protests of sound. Almost immediately the second dog appeared behind him; and was dispatched after only one bark by the second man in O'Connell's team. The noise they had made had been so brief that it would not have disturbed anyone much beyond the confines of the farmhouse, but O'Connell was in no doubt that it would have woken some, if not all, the occupants of the farmhouse itself. Almost immediately, two more men stepped forward with a large, powerful, hand-held metal cylinder regularly used by police forces the world over to gain entry to premises which they are raiding; and, with two swings in less than three seconds had smashed in the back door. They stood back as O'Connell, Riordan and the rest of the men poured into the farmhouse behind them.

As O'Connell had surmised, the household was now very much awake. The farmer, a sixty-two year old named Anthony Barker, was coming down the stairs, probably heading for the case where he kept his shot-gun, but he was far too late for that. Behind him, at the top of the stairs, was his son and farm assistant, Graham Barker. Of his wife there was, as yet, no sign. As arranged, two of O'Connell's men grabbed the farmer and yanked him down the rest of the stairs. Two more went straight up the stairs and, as the son turned to go back into his bedroom, grabbed him and pulled him down onto the landing floor. All this was so that, critically, two more men could get into the farmer's bedroom quickly in case his wife – a congenial if rather matriarchal woman named Margaret – had access to a bedroom phone. As they entered, guns at the ready, they saw that she was standing by the window in her nightdress, looking very shocked and pale but, to their relief, with no sign of a telephone in her hand or, indeed, in the room.

"Remain silent, do exactly as we say, and none of you will come to any harm at all" said one of the men. "Do you understand – no harm at all? Just don't make any trouble. Is that clear?" he added as she stared back at him, making no sound or movement. Then she gave an almost imperceptible nod.

"Good. That's fine" the intruder replied, as sympathetically as the situation would allow. "Please put on a dressing gown and then come downstairs and join your husband". This she did; and went down the stairs, one man in front of her but essentially going down backwards so that he could keep his eye on her, the other behind her. Downstairs the rest of O'Connell's men had got Barker and his son sitting on a sofa, covered by a dozen guns. As Margaret Barker entered, both her husband and son started to get up, but were forced back into the sofa by the men behind them.

"Can I let my mother sit with my dad?" said the son. "I'll sit in the arm-chair. I won't cause any trouble".

"That's very thoughtful of you" said O'Connell. "Certainly, but do it very slowly". Graham Barker slowly rose, transferred to one of two large old armchairs; and Margaret Barker half sat, half fell onto the sofa next to her husband, who put his arm around her.

"What in hell is this about" he said.

"I need to borrow your farmhouse for a couple of days" said O'Connell. "That's all you need to know. You three will have to stay here, but you'll be free of us by Monday; and you'll not come to any harm provided you behave yourselves. No amateur dramatics. Let me be a little more precise. If you tell me what I want to know; and do not in any way either interfere with my operation, nor seek to alert anyone else to it, then the most you will suffer is a rather boring and claustrophobic week-end. But if you do not comply with this, it will go very badly indeed for you. Specifically, if you......" he pointed at the son "…. deviate in any way from what I have said, then I will put a bullet in your mother's head. Is that clear?" Graham Barker nodded. "If you…." This time he pointed at Margaret Barker "…if you cause me any grief at all, I will have no compunction at all about killing your husband; and likewise, if you….." this time pointing straight at Anthony Barker "….try in any way to act the brave hero, whether successful or not, you will have no son to tell in future years. Do I make myself crystal clear?" All three nodded.

"Did you have to shoot the dogs?" asked Margaret Barker, tears now beginning to well up in her eyes. "Did you have to do that?"

"Unfortunately, yes, I did" replied O'Connell. "I hope very much that that is the limit of the distress that I will need to cause you. But it should be a small indication that I will not recoil from doing whatever is necessary for my plans to succeed. Hurting you three is no part of those plans, but cross me and I will eliminate another in your family as readily as my men shot your dogs, without hesitation and without regret. Now, three questions. First, do you have a deep-freeze?" Barker was initially quite bewildered by the questions, but eventually said that they did, two cabinets in fact; and showed O'Connell where they were. "Second" said O'Connell when they returned "are you expecting anyone – anyone at all – to call here over the week-end? Please be accurate, for your sakes as well as theirs". It was Margaret Barker who replied, probably no less in shock than the two men in her family, but by nature rather more talkative.

"Our daughter and her husband, plus their two small children are coming for lunch on Sunday" she said. Her husband added

"And Josh – that's my farm hand – he's part-time but he'll be planning to come in to do some work tomorrow".

"Does he live alone or with anyone?" asked O'Connell.

"He lives with his cousin" Barker replied "but they don't see much of each other – don't really get on".

"Will his cousin be alarmed if Josh doesn't go home Saturday or Sunday?"

"Lord, no, Col – that's his cousin – probably wouldn't notice and he'd care less". This was very welcome news to O'Connell. He had a perfectly well worked out strategy if he'd got a different answer, but this made things a whole lot simpler,

"Good" said O'Connell. "Anyone else? Think hard. What about your other farm hand? By the way, what are your names?" They told him. "Well, Anthony, you have another farm worker. I've seen him many times. Will he be in during the week-end?"

"No" replied Barker. "He's usually off at the week-ends. It'll just be Josh".

"Okay" said O'Connell. "Now, Graham, any friends of yours likely to show up?" The son shook his head. "In that case, question number three. Is anyone – anyone at all expecting you anywhere else over the week-end? Work or pleasure, friends, family, anyone, anywhere?"

"I'd planned to go shopping tomorrow morning, and I need to get some food for Sunday" she added, a modicum of normal life seeping back into her being for a second.

"That won't be possible" said O'Connell "but will anyone, maybe in one of the local shops you use, miss you at all?"

"They might notice I hadn't been in, but I don't think anyone would exactly be 'expecting' me as you put it".

"Fine. Anything else?"

"I usually go for a drink with some others on Saturday night" said Graham Barker "We haven't exactly fixed anything, but they'll text me sometime tomorrow I should think". O'Connell was pleased at the amount of co-operation he was getting, but then he had, deliberately, been totally intimidating in what he had said, leaving the Barker family in no doubt whatsoever where their best interest lay.

"If they do, can you send a convincing text message back as to why you won't be joining them this Saturday?" O'Connell asked.

"I'll think of something" he said, slightly resentfully.

"Not good enough" said O'Connell, with a deliberate menace in his voice. "Think up something, tell one of my men here what reply you will make if you need to; and he will text the reply from your phone. I want to know what you will say by ten tomorrow morning. Is that clear?" He got a small but clear nod in reply.

"Right. We are making good progress here" said O'Connell in as encouraging tone as he could muster. "The three of you will spend the next forty-eight hours upstairs, closely guarded by my men. You will be fed and have access to the bathroom. Before you go up, my team are going to do a very thorough search up there, for phones, any means of communication with the outside world, any weapons – or anything that could be used as a weapon – and for any lines of sight by which, in an unguarded but, I'm bound to say, extremely stupid moment, you might try to signal your situation to anyone else. We are going to do this anyway, but it will help if you now tell me the whereabouts of anything I have mentioned. If we then find something you have missed, then you know what will happen". He casually pointed his sub-machine gun at the couple sitting in front of him. The woman looked away, but otherwise, neither reacted.

It turned out that the only threat to O'Connell's plans lurking upstairs was Graham's mobile phone and his computer, both of which he readily declared. Everything else, including three shot-guns, were all downstairs; and none of the three were going to see the downstairs of their home until the operation was over. The search completed, O'Connell urged them all back to their beds. He stationed two men to cover the son and two more to cover his parents, with another one on the landing and one at the bottom of the stairs. O'Connell, Riordan and the remaining two members of his team then in the farmhouse settled down to act as look outs, one in each direction, while O'Connell briefly flashed a torch with a pre-arranged signal to bring the remaining eight members of the team in with their equipment.

By 4 am. all was still. O'Connell and his men took it in turns to sleep, as they waited for the morning's activities to begin. The first of these was when Josh the farm hand arrived at the front door; and was duly taken into the custody of O'Connell's men, searched, dispatched to a spare room and put under guard. Next was the feeding of O'Connell's men and the Barkers. O'Connell asked if there was anything essential that Barker needed to do as far as his animals were concerned, but was not surprised to be told that they could all survive unaided until Monday – had it been different, O'Connell was sure that Barker would have pressed the point with him. In fact very little conversation occurred, between O'Connell's men and the Barkers, between the Barkers themselves or, indeed, amongst O'Connell's men. There really was very little for any of them to say.

Outside, rather more was going on. Around 11 am a flat-backed truck drove up from the south along Meadow Lane, heading for the entrance gate to Shrove Farm. On the back was a small crane, and a large number of sections of concrete pipes about two feet in diameter, all held down by chains. It was driven by two of O'Connell's new recruits. As O'Connell saw it stop at the gate, he summoned Anthony Barker.

"Go out to meet them" he said "as if you know all about it – drainage pipes for one of your fields. Your existing system is crumbling; and some of your fields down by Meadow Lane are getting water-logged. So, you're replacing the drains. The work starts Monday – this is just the equipment being delivered. You don't need to say much, but you have to look the part of a farmer receiving some supplies you've ordered, from a company called 'Scammells' if anyone should ask. Tell them to unload the pipes over the far side of your field, next to Meadow Lane. Needless to say, if you don't do this convincingly, then I wouldn't bother coming back to the farmhouse. The rest of your family will not be a pretty sight". O'Connell had no way of knowing whether such activity would be under surveillance from the Chequers estate. There was a direct line of sight but, nearly half a mile south of the gatehouses, it would be difficult to see much. However, there could well be subsidiary surveillance of some sort on what was the main approach road to Chequers from London; and he had to work on the presumption that this was the case. However, he did not think that the delivery of some drainage pipes would cause much concern; and if it did, then the sight of the local farmer – a man who must, knowingly or unknowingly, have been heavily vetted by the British security forces - coming out to greet the arrival would douse any such worries. Barker duly went out, met O'Connell's men as they were closing the gate behind them, said a few words and directed them as he had been instructed. O'Connell's men knew full well where to place the pipes, but O'Connell wanted a very convincing show. The truck drove across the field and O'Connell's men used the crane to unload the pipes, storing them in a neat pile near the field's perimeter hedge, some 200 metres south of the farm entrance. The delivery completed, they got back in the truck and drove off. Barker returned to the farmhouse. No-one else appeared.

An hour later, two large low-loader vehicles approached the farm up Meadow Lane, again driven by O'Connell's new recruits, this time with the third of them a passenger in one of vehicles. On one was a mechanical digger, with caterpillar tracks and a shovel-like contraption at the end of an articulated arm. On the other was a bulldozer. The third man got down and opened the gate to Shrove Farm, whereupon the two trucks slowly edged their way in. The men then lowered ramps at the back of the trucks and proceeded to unload the two machines they had brought. Back in the farmhouse, O'Connell spoke to Barker.

"Show time again. Go down there and say 'hello'. Then tell them to drive the bulldozer along the edge of the field – along the side of Meadow Lane; and leave it about 100 metres along. The digger should go over where the drainage pipes are stacked. Got it?" Barker nodded and set off. O'Connell turned to Graham Barker. "You as well. You don't have to do or say anything, but just look interested. Then come back. Usual rules. If you do anything unusual, give any sign that we are here and your mother will get a bullet in the head before you get back here. I hope I make myself very clear." Graham Barker set off and found it easy to do precisely what he no doubt would have done if the whole exercise had been legitimate, namely wander over to look at the new arrivals. Meanwhile his father had carried out O'Connell's instructions – not that O'Connell's men needed the directions, but it gave the whole thing a more natural look, and within half an hour, the two machines were unloaded and positioned, the digger near the pile of drainage pipes where, presumably, the digging of a new drainage trench would start, the bulldozer around 100 metres further up the road from where O'Connell's men had left the digger.

Both the Barkers had started back towards the farmhouse when two uniformed officers arrived in a car down the Chequers main drive, through the main gate, which was opened by a uniformed officer from within one of the gatehouses, down Meadow Lane and up to the farm entrance gate. They walked over to where O'Connell's three men were having a cigarette before getting back into the two trucks which had brought the machinery.

"What's going on here?" asked one of them in a casual manner, ignoring that it seemed perfectly obvious what was going on.

"We're just delivering for his new drainage system" said one of them, vaguely pointing towards the farmhouse. "His existing one is caput, apparently".

"Working on a Saturday?" replied the policeman, despite this being even more obvious.

"Oh, just delivering. That's usual. We don't start work until Monday, but we try to get the equipment set up for an early start; and it's better driving these things at the week-end, when there's less traffic".

"Which company are you with?" asked the policeman.

"Scammells, in High Wycombe, but the vehicles are all hired, from Johnson Massey".

"Where are you based?"

"In High Wycombe. Here's a card with the details". O'Connell's man took a slightly crinkled card out of his pocket with the company name and contact details on it. The card was completely genuine. O'Connell had picked it up some weeks before when he went to the main office of Scammell's, or SCS as it was often known, standing for Scammell's Construction Services. O'Connell had rung the company seven Saturday mornings in a row; and always got only an answer-phone in reply. So it would need some determination on the part of the Chequers security people to check much further, but if they did, O'Connell had covered the possibility. He had established a legitimate company and presented himself to Scammells as an agricultural contractor, who organized various types of farm construction and repair work. The drainage pipes, the digger and the bulldozer had all been hired legitimately; and their hiring from Johnson Massey was completely standard. O'Connell was confident that the ignorance of Shrove Farm in all this would not be discovered during the next twenty-four hours. The policeman studied the card.

"Is there a problem" O'Connell's man asked with a slightly quizzical look. "If so, you should talk to Mr. Barker over there". He pointed in the direction of the farmhouse, where the Barkers, father and son, were near the front door.

"Maybe just a quick word. Mason, you go back to the car" he said to his colleague. "I'll just be a moment". He then set off down the drive way and approached the Barkers. "I gather you've got a problem with your drainage?" he asked. Anthony Barker was a reticent man at the best of times, never good at disguising his feelings, and enraged at the intrusion into his life which he was experiencing; but he had enough sense and self-control to realise that the bleak Irishman holding a gun to his wife's head was deadly serious; and that her life very directly depended on how he handled this inquiry.

"Yes" he replied slowly. "There's an old system which collects water from the upper side, channels it over here and it gets drained off down by the road. But it's packed up – some pipe fractures. The lower field area's been flooding and we're losing good land, so I'm replacing the system. Why do you want to know?" he added slightly belligerently, though whether this was the stress of the situation, or just the natural reticence of many a farmer to being interrogated about his actions was not clear.

"It's not a problem" replied the police officer. "I'm from the Chequers estate; and we just like to keep a close eye on any strangers in the area. I understand the work starts on Monday?"

"That's right" said Barker, now almost glaring at the officer.

"Thanks, I won't trouble you further" the officer replied; and slowly walked back to the waiting police car, still clutching the card he'd been given By now O'Connell's men were back in the two trucks; and, as they started up the engines, one of them gave a small wave to the police officer. All three vehicles then left, O'Connell's men driving back south along Meadow Lane, the police car in the opposite direction back to Chequers. The Barkers returned to the farmhouse, where O'Connell just quietly nodded at them, the only acknowledgment that they had done what he had said they must do. The tension that had gripped the men in the farmhouse while the events outside were unfolding began to ease, but not greatly, as O'Connell's men watched carefully to see whether Chequers would continue its investigation of what was happening at Shrove Farm. However, no further visits ensued; and it appeared that the police officers were, for the moment at least, satisfied with what they had heard. The only other excitement of the day was when, as predicted, Graham Barker got a text inviting him out that evening. Riordan told him to dictate a reply to the effect that he had to stay in that night because some family were visiting, reminding Barker that if it wasn't convincing, and anyone showed up at the farmhouse, the result would be fatal; and then Riordan sent the reply.

Around 2 am Sunday morning, O'Connell woke Graham Barker and the farm hand, Josh; and moved them all in with Anthony and Margaret Barker. He left four men to guard them. Then O'Connell, Riordan and the remaining twelve members of his team prepared themselves for the operation itself. They first retrieved the contents of the canvas bags they had brought from the deep-freeze cabinets, where they had been placed on arriving at the farmhouse. These comprised fourteen pieces of thick hessian, each about seven feet by three feet, but with irregularly cut edges. One side was fitted with a thin double layer plastic lining containing a viscous liquid which was close to, but not quite freezing at deep-freeze temperature. The other side was covered with a lot of grass, earth, twigs and some leaves, such that it looked very like the surface of an uncultivated field. Some of the attached camouflage extended beyond the edge of the hessian, further blurring the already indistinct shape of the material. Each man, already dressed in camouflage combat dress, took one of these, plus a semi-automatic, and got ready to leave. In single file, with some ten metres between each of them, they set off behind O'Connell, out of the back of the farmhouse; and set off on a large curving trajectory that would eventually bring them to the edge of the field abutting Meadow Lane, well over half a mile south of the entrance to Chequers and around two hundred metres south of the digger and the drainage pipes. As they left the confines of the farmhouse, each of them, moving only one very slow step at a time, held up the hessian sheet so that it fell full length down the right side of each man, thereby screening him from the direction of Chequers.

In the pitch dark, there was no possibility that anyone could see them - with or without the hessian sheets - with the naked eye. But O'Connell's fears had been, first, of infra-red night-sight surveillance that could pick up his men in the dark. However extensive tests had shown him that the large screens he had had made, moving very slowly were, at the sort of range they would be from any possible observation post within the Chequers estate, virtually impossible to pick up by such means. This was particularly the case in that, as his men started to get nearer to the boundary of the field, and then heading along it, they would be moving almost directly towards Chequers. His men would adjust their hold on the screens accordingly, while still just being able to see where they were headed; but, as again O'Connell had repeatedly tested, there would at that stage be relatively little sideways motion when viewed from the direction of the estate. O'Connell's second fear was heat-detection surveillance which would pick up his men's body heat. But here again, his thorough testing had shown that the viscous liquid in the screen linings, at well below freezing point for at least an hour, would completely negate any such attempt to observe people moving in the dark. They would take a full hour to traverse less than 500 metres, but O'Connell was confident that no-one would spot them as they moved into position.

Where they were aiming for was O'Connell's ace-in-the hole, the one small detail of the terrain of Shrove Farm which would make all the difference to his operation. Meadow Lane, like many – perhaps the majority - of country roads in England, lies somewhat below the level of the surrounding fields. In the case of Meadow Lane it was not particularly sunken, perhaps two feet or so in places. As a result, the top of the low, rather sparse and scrub-like hedging along the side of the adjacent field – generally itself about three feet in height – was around the five foot level when viewed from the road. This, of course, in no way prevented a very clear view of the field and beyond to the farmhouse, but that was of no concern to O'Connell. The key for him was that, again very typically, the ground on which the hedging grew was slightly raised above the level of the field itself, only a small amount - around eighteen inches or so – but it was all that O'Connell needed. For the result was that, from the road, the first couple of feet of the field next to the hedge was close to being a blind-spot. It certainly couldn't be seen over the top of the hedge. It was not entirely invisible through the hedge, particularly given the relative lack of foliage but, to anyone looking down from the road, that narrow strip, where the ground sloped down from the tiny ridge on which the hedge stood, was at a very tight angle to the viewer. However, while it would be quite enough to hide a man lying there from the sight of a casual passer-by, O'Connell saw that it would by no means guarantee safety from detection by a patrol specifically charged with keeping an eye on the surrounding countryside. But – and once again he had checked it thoroughly back in the fields of County Armagh – with the screening provided by the camouflaged hessian lying over him, a man could lie low, tucked into the corner of the slight slope up to the hedge mound, and be completely invisible, even in broad daylight, from either the road or from elsewhere in the field. A searcher would virtually have to tread on someone thus hidden to discover them – an outcome that had occurred more than once in O'Connell's testing of his plan; and O'Connell was reasonably confident that an inspection with that degree of detail would be unlikely. If it did occur, then his men were under clear instruction to shoot their way out, escape with their lives if they could, and lose any prospect of getting to Gerrard. But he had high hopes, based on all the experimentation he had carried out in Northern Ireland, that it would not come to that.

The file of fourteen men, with O'Connell and Riordan in the middle, having slowly and silently made their way in the pitch dark in a curving arc round from the farmhouse, reached Meadow Lane. They then started along the side of it, now heading towards Chequers, passed where the digger had been left earlier.

They now held the hessian sheets in front of them, and so were still screened from observation from Chequers. At roughly ten metre intervals, starting with the back marker, O'Connell's men stopped and slowly lay down in the lee of the small slope at the foot of the hedge, placing the hessian sheet nearby. Each would now have to remain motionless for over 12 hours, but this too they had practiced for, trained until they could do it, literally in their sleep for an initial period. They would wait until 4 am before draping the camouflage sheeting over them, by which time the freezing-cold liquid would have returned to normal temperature – still bitterly cold at that time in the morning, but bearable until the sun came up. Twenty minutes after arriving at the roadside, the fourteen men were spaced out over 100 metres, with the front man very close to the bulldozer, the last by the digger. The trap had been set. There was nothing more to do until they received the appropriate signal.

Sunday dawned and, in the farmhouse, saw much the same routine. O'Connell's team of four kept a very close eye on the Barkers and Josh. One of them brought a light breakfast of toast and tea for them all. Around 11.30 am. the Barker's daughter Josephine, her husband and two small children turned up and, like Josh had been, were taken in by O'Connell's men. Josephine became rather hysterical for a few minutes; and one of them was forced to slap her hard to silence her, so that he could explain that neither she nor her husband nor, most importantly, her children would be hurt, and would be away later that night, provided she kept quiet, kept her family quiet, and allowed all of them to be searched for mobile phones. The last item almost set her off again, but it was pointed out that her children needed her; and they most assuredly would be orphans if she did not co-operate so that, finally, in somewhat of a daze, and having gulped a couple of tranquillisers, she let one of the men search her, before joining the Barkers, Josh and the rest of her family in the bedroom upstairs. It was now very cramped there, with eight hostages plus two guards but they were settled in various corners on the floor as well as four on the double bed; and were assured that they would all be free by the evening. The other two Irishmen remained in the farmhouse but outside the bedroom, as a second line of control in the unlikely event that it was needed.

Shortly after 2 pm, the two men who had driven the vans to bring O'Connell's men to Shrove Farm left the vans in which they had spent the night and walked to a pre-arranged spot amongst some trees, about half a mile from the Chequers estate perimeter. From there they could see along the main Chequers drive, up to a point about 200 metres from the main gate, after which the drive disappeared from view behind some trees. From this vantage point they viewed the driveway through binoculars, each taking ten minute spells of watching closely. Unbeknown to O'Connell, the two police officers who had called in on Shrove Farm had reported back on their visit; and a security officer at Chequers had duly tried to call Scammells. Getting no reply, he had called Johnson Massey's office in Watford and had got a reply. They had confirmed that Scammells were a reputable firm with whom they regularly dealt; and that there had indeed been an order for two vehicles to help on a drainage contract in the district. The security officer had not felt totally comfortable but, as the contract work was not due to start until Monday, he merely made a note to investigate further then. The arrangements for the Prime Minister to return to Downing Street the following day were not, therefore, changed.

However, it was decided that a preliminary check of the road from Chequers should be carried out. As a result of this, at 4.20 pm, a Land Rover with four men in it set off from Chequers, drove down the main drive, through the main gate and then slowly south along Meadow Lane. The three passengers surveyed the fields either side with both the naked eye and through binoculars. The vehicle slowed as it approached the entrance to Shrove Farm, stopped by the gate; and two of the occupants got out, opened the gate and strolled into the field. There was no sign of anyone, apart from a car parked at the Farmhouse. They got back in their car and drove on down Meadow Lane for a few hundred metres beyond the entrance gate, paying particular attention to the two unmanned construction vehicles in the Shrove Farm field. Neither of them came even close to realizing that fourteen men lay motionless in the lee of the perimeter hedge, covered with natural foliage. At one point they were no more than ten metres from the man O'Connell had deputed to stay by the bulldozer but, fortunately for him, he was almost completely shielded from their view by the bulldozer itself. The scene remained one of an idle, empty Sunday afternoon. The men returned to the Land Rover, which started back to the Chequers estate.

At 4.48 pm one of the two men watching the estate saw three cars emerging from the direction of Chequers, and immediately used a bleeper device, similar to those used by doctors on call, to send a bleep to fourteen receivers possessed by O'Connell's men lying stiffly alongside Meadow Lane. The two of them then set off immediately, heading back to where they had parked the two vans. On hearing the small blast, the two men at either end of O'Connell's line slowly crawled forward, still largely invisible but, in any case, completely screened from the approaching cars by the bulldozer and the digger close by them. The three cars carrying Gerrard and his team of bodyguards passed through the main gate, and turned right into Meadow Lane. As they started to accelerate southwards, the two Irishmen discarded their hessian screens, swung themselves up into the driving seats of the two machines and fired the engines. O'Connell had removed the risk that the vehicles might not start by getting two very inventive engineers to modify the ignition systems, using a fuel injection system employed on several very up-market cars. Both machines roared into life and, in a few seconds, the bulldozer had crashed straight through the farm hedge, onto the road and up behind the convoy of cars heading along Meadow Lane. At the same time the caterpillar tracks of the digger drove up over the ridge on which the wire fence and hedging along the side of the road stood, straight through the fencing and hedge themselves; and then swiveled round to face the oncoming three cars. Within a few seconds of having left the main Chequers gate, the convoy was trapped on Meadow Lane by O'Connell's two construction vehicles.

The three cars immediately came to a halt, as the digger and the bulldozer closed in on them. Eight members of Gerrard's security detail leapt out of the first and last cars, each with guns at the ready. Two started to make for the bulldozer, two for the digger, while the other four rushed to group themselves round Gerrard's car, now immovable in the middle of the stationary convoy. At the same time, the driver of the bulldozer sent a bleep to the twelve other men lying prone by the side of the road. Instantly all twelve leapt to their feet and, almost in the same motion, started firing continuous rounds from their semi-automatics. Six of Gerrard's guards fell immediately, their bullet-proof vests providing no protection as O'Connell's men sprayed them from head to toe. The two nearest the bulldozer survived because they had distanced themselves a little from the others before the shooting started. They fell to the ground and started to fire back. One of O'Connell's men was hit, but then the two bodyguards saw the bulldozer bearing down on them. As they rose to scramble out of the way, they too were mown down by the blanket of fire from the roadside. Four more security personnel appeared from one of the gate houses behind the bulldozer, but the vehicle had by then virtually completed a rapid three-point turn; and the security force were immediately pinned down by fire from several of O'Connell's team, firing from the shelter of the bulldozer itself.

Gerrard's car now sat there, unprotected save for one body guard in the front passenger seat and his driver, himself an ex-paratrooper. The latter, realising the near-hopeless position they were now in, suddenly gunned the accelerator and shot the car forward, at the same time slewing the steering wheel right in an attempt to crash the car through the fence and hedge on the other side of the road to where the attack had come from. It was a sensible response. The car was both bullet and bomb-proof; and if he could only drive clear of the armed men now approaching the car, he could still get his vehicle away. And he almost made it. The heavy car with a special six litre engine flattened the light wire fencing; and the front of the car made it through much of the hedge. But the impact slowed the car almost to a halt and, with the centre of the car now sitting on the raised ground at the foot of the hedge, neither the front nor back wheels could get enough traction to complete the transition into the scrubland beyond. The wheels spun, but the car barely moved. While four of O'Connell's men, well protected by the bulldozer, prevented any of the gatehouse security force approaching, another attended to the injured man lying near the bulldozer; and the remaining six gathered round Gerrard's car.

O'Connell shouted as loud as he could to the driver to unlock the doors if he wanted to survive, but the driver sat immobile. He had hit the automatic alarm button in the car, and believed that it could only be a minute or so before help would start to arrive from Chequers. Unfortunately for him, O'Connell knew this too. Without a word he stood back to allow two of his men to start sticking a wad of plastic explosive against the window. This took less than five seconds, with a further two to set the detonator into it. The car might be bomb-proof and the windows bullet-proof, but two pounds of Semtex up against the glass would smash it to pieces and take the head of the driver with it. O'Connell and the others backed away from the car, one of them trailing a wire from the detonator. The driver knew he had seconds before suffering the most appalling death, but it was the bodyguard in the front passenger seat who reacted first. Opening his door a fraction he got off two shots, which felled one of O'Connell's men moving back from the far side of the car. He then swung the door wider open to give him a shot at a second attacker on that side, but in this he was just a fraction of a second too late. The Irishman fired a burst from his semi-automatic and the bodyguard was blown backwards, almost on top of the driver. His car door swung open where he had let go of it. The driver had a pistol, but reckoned his only chance was to sit very still. As he sat there he saw, out of the corner of his eye, what O'Connell and his men had also seen – three cars careering down the main driveway of the Chequers estate. Maybe he might just survive even yet. This thinking, though, was fatally flawed. In the first place, it was the very shortage of time that meant O'Connell could not risk having to deal with any heroics from the driver, or anyone else. His men had had clear instructions on the point and, as O'Connell raced to the front of the car, a single further burst of machine gun fire from one of his men killed the driver instantly. He stood back and O'Connell roughly pulled the dead bodyguard out of the front passenger seat onto the ground. He looked through the open doorway to the seats behind. He could only see one passenger from that angle. He vaguely recognized him, but it wasn't Gerrard.

The three vehicles – two land rovers and a small truck – racing down the drive reached the main gate and headed down Meadow Lane, but the bulldozer was an impenetrable block between the wrecked convoy and the new arrivals. The three vehicles from the estate slewed to a halt and around a dozen men got out, some using open doors for protection, others going behind the vehicles; and three or four making an immediate run for cover behind the hedges either side of Meadow Lane. Joining up with the four security men already there, both groups of men started firing, but there was no unprotected target for them to aim at. Then, without warning, six grenades came sailing out from behind the front of the bulldozer, landing around or, in one case under, the Land Rover at the front. Several of the Chequers security personnel, hurled themselves away, diving over the low hedges. The grenades exploded, almost simultaneously, and the front Land Rover virtually disintegrated. Three of the security team died instantly, and several more were injured. With both the wreck of the Land Rover and the bulldozer – the latter with, by now, five heavily armed men defending it - between them and Gerrard's car, there was no prospect of their getting to him. To make matters worse, it was at this point that they saw more men in combat fatigues leaving the farmhouse and starting to approach the stricken convoy. Their commander gave the order to start to fan out on the opposite side, in order to try to get round the bulldozer, but with continual fire from O'Connell's men, they were forced to go very wide; and it would clearly take some time. Time was what O'Connell wanted, but he did not need much of it.

O'Connell resisted getting into the car's front passenger seat to see who, if anyone else, was in the back of the car – the darkened windows allowed no view at all – in case he was met with a bullet in his face. Instead he held back, outside any possible line of fire.

"Is there anyone else in the car?" he said "Get it wrong and you're dead".

The man nodded. "Who?" barked O'Connell.

"The Prime Minister". It could have been a ruse but, for once in his life, O'Connell acted instinctively and sat down in the passenger seat, going in with his back to the windscreen. He looked into the back of the car and there, sure enough, sat Gerrard, immobile, white faced. O'Connell covered the two men with his weapon.

"Who are you?" he said to the man next to Gerrard.

"Andrew Palmer. I'm the PM's Press Adviser" O'Connell had rehearsed for months the moment when he would be face to face with Gerrard, had dreamt regularly of it, and had planned it down to the last minute detail. But now he was completely thrown as he realised that he recognized the voice – recognised it as that of the man who had thwarted his and Kate Kimball's attempts to have Gerrard brought to justice, who had, therefore, in a very direct way, led to where they all now were.

"We've spoken before" was all he said. Palmer nodded, but said nothing. Well, thought O'Connell, that alters one resolve. He had anticipated that there might be other politicians or civil servants in the car, but had decided that his target was just Gerrard – and any security personnel protecting him. However, as this was the man who had so completely protected Gerrard by thwarting his own plans, he decided that Palmer would die as well. But even as he registered this intention, another plan, so audacious it practically took his breath away, was forming in his mind. He looked back at Riordan, standing by the car.

"How long have we got?" he asked. Riordan surveyed the defensive wall provided by O'Connell's men behind the bulldozer, the four members of the team now coming in from the farmhouse; and the men from the Chequers estate now running fast, fanning out to the other side. He also saw the two vans which had brought them all there just turning into Meadow Lane, about 500 metres up from where the digger still straddling the road. He also saw, to his dismay, a helicopter emerging from behind the trees on the Chequers estate; and that three saloon cars had come along the road, two coming to a halt behind the carnage behind the bulldozer, the other, coming in the opposite direction, behind the digger. They appeared to be unconnected with the attack. The one behind the digger couldn't yet see what was going on. The front car of the two by the bulldozer could see only too clearly that a bloody battle was in progress, but couldn't as yet reverse because the car behind it, which was without a clear view, was sat there, blocking his scope for retreat.

"One minute maximum I'd say, if we're to get the lads out in one piece" said Riordan. "A helicopter's coming" he added. O'Connell decided sixty seconds was enough. He turned back to Palmer and, when he spoke, Palmer was utterly taken aback.

"Do you have a private number for the Editor of *The Times?* If you're Gerrard's Press Secretary you must do" Palmer looked dumbfounded but just shook his head.

"Pity" said O'Connell. "That lack of knowledge has just cost you your life" and he held up the pistol.

"Wait" shouted Palmer. "I've got it listed on my mobile" and he frantically started to fish in his pocket for his mobile phone.

"Get him on the line" said O'Connell. Palmer brought up his electronic address book and hit the number. O'Connell turned to Gerrard. "You've got forty seconds to tell the Editor why I'm here". Gerrard stared back at him.

"You're mad" said Gerrard. "He'll think it's a hoax".

"I think he'll know your voice well enough" O'Connell replied. Gerrard sat motionless for a moment. He stared straight at O'Connell

"Go to hell" he said savagely.

"Then you're a dead man" replied O'Connell calmly.

"I'm dead anyway. I know that. You're murdering scum. Your friends got off lightly – a quick death in a car, but you, you'll rot in prison for the rest of your fucking life......." O'Connell fired the pistol once; and Gerrard slumped back, the bullet lodged firmly in the front of his brain. O'Connell fired another bullet to the head; and one to Gerrard's heart. He turned back to Palmer and pointed the pistol at him.

"You tell the Editor what this all about. Exactly what it is about. Do you understand? You've got..... twenty five seconds. Unlike Gerrard, if you comply

I might let you live to explain it in more detail. Twenty seconds…. ". Palmer spoke into his mobile.

"Alex, Andrew Palmer here…. yes I know… Alex shut up and listen. I'm with Alan. He's just been shot dead by Irish terrorists…. yes, he's dead for Christ's sake; and they want me to tell you that it's because, in 1983, Alan had five IRA members assassinated, nothing to do with the war. They'd been arrested for an attack on Sellafield which Alan had covered up, so he had to get rid of them to protect his own position….." From outside the car, Riordan tapped O'Connell on the shoulder.

"Got to go….now" he added urgently. O'Connell looked one more time at Palmer

"That should be enough to set the Press hounds baying. I should kill you, but it'll need someone to explain more fully what you've just told the Press". Then he got out of the car, leaving a stunned Andrew Palmer and an equally stunned Alex Tyson, Editor of *The Times* sitting on the end of the line in his ample study in his still more ample home in Surrey.

Riordan shouted "Out" very loudly; and O'Connell's men, still firing spasmodically, retreated from the bulldozer, back past Gerrard's three cars, the digger and the passenger car, inside which an elderly couple were now in a state of complete panic. Two of the Irishmen took up a defensive position and started firing at the helicopter which was coming in fast. They missed, but the helicopter veered away. Meanwhile, the farmhouse team had joined them, as did O'Connell and Riordan. Simultaneously, the two vans, which had arrived a few seconds before, did wild three point turns, one behind the other, taking out sections of both fences as they did it. Carrying the two members of O'Connell's team who had been hit in the firefight, the men piled into the vans, which took off fast, tyres screaming. The helicopter followed.

"What in Jesus's name was all that about?" Riordan asked O'Connell.

"Just making sure the world knows what this has been about".

"But that'll help them find us" replied Riordan.

"No it won't. They know we're Irish; but they don't have any names. Letting the world know about Gerrard won't make any difference to us. But it will make a very big difference to Gerrard's legacy. He would have been a fucking martyr. Now there's a good chance the world will know what he was really like. Palmer can't deny any knowledge of it now".

"Palmer?" said Riordan. "Do you mean Andrew Palmer, the Press guy? What's he got to do with it?"

"He was the man we and Kate dealt with, Gerrard's front man, protector – the man who fucked up all our plans".

"How did you find that out?"

"He was in the car with Gerrard". Riordan absorbed this, but said nothing.

"I thought about killing him" O'Connell continued "because of what he did to us, but it's better that he's around to fill in all the answers"

"But won't that help them to find us" Riordan repeated.

"I'm not so sure. That would pull Emmerson and Kimball right back into the picture. Palmer went to great lengths to neutralize the pair of them, discredit them. The last thing he'll want is to bring them back into a blaze of publicity. Given what they know about his illegal use of the security forces and the military, he'll risk a long time at her Majesty's pleasure if he talks about us. So, no, I don't think we have had much to fear from him".

"I'd have shot him" said Riordan. O'Connell looked at him with a raised, questioning, eye-brow. "Because he saved Gerrard from the fate he should have suffered" explained Riordan "exposure, trial, life in prison. A quick bullet was too good for him". O'Connell was silent for a moment, but then with a grim look, nodded in assent. "Now" he said, let's concentrate on losing this helicopter".

O'Connell had foreseen that the Prime minister's security team would not be able to follow his men by road, but had reckoned that there might well be air pursuit; and he now activated the final part of his planning. After barely two miles the vans screeched to a halt by a disused barn where ten cars were parked. The men quickly transferred into them, two to a car; and set off. All this was observed by the helicopter, but each time it came close, it was subjected to a hail of machine gun fire that threatened the rotor blades; and it veered away again. Following a detailed plan worked out by O'Connell and Riordan, the ten cars set off, five in each direction, and at each intersection they came to, they took different directions. They were dispersing far faster than could be prevented through road blocks, even though the pilot of the helicopter had radioed through what was happening. In less than ten minutes, the helicopter had only one car in sight. O'Connell had given instructions that, if they were pursued from the air, whichever car remained in sight of the aircraft would go to the nearest of four sites they had identified, in each of which the road when through thick woods. On the way the car being pursued would phone through to one of the other cars – each site had a designated back-up car – which then headed for a road that ran within a mile or so of the wood. The two in the car being pursued then stopped in the wood, out of sight of the helicopter, and headed off on foot though the trees. Within fifteen minutes they had been picked up; and all twenty had disappeared from the world's view.

*   *   *

Every national newspaper had an appalling Sunday as, with skeleton staff, they desperately tried to recompose their front pages in time to print their Monday editions, with huge headlines announcing that the Prime Minister had been assassinated. Only *The Times,* seeking to maximize its advantage, carried the headline 'Revenge killing of PM' and a lead article describing what Palmer had told its Editor. There were, however, few substantiating details, because Palmer provided very few – just the events of 1983 and that the assassination was in retaliation. However, by 8 am. the next morning, both veteran and aspiring journalists on every paper were quick to start investigating what promised to be the scoop of a century.

In his flat in north Oxford, Emmerson sat with his arm round Kate, watching the television newscaster. The latter was struggling because, having said what little was known of the assassination, which took about two minutes, there was little more to say, but hours of airtime to fill. A steady succession of politicians filled the airwaves, all saying essentially the same thing, how shocked they were, what a fine man Gerrard was and so on, but when faced with the one key question concerning Gerrard's alleged complicity in the murder of five IRA people while they were in custody back in 1983, none had any clue as to what to say. It would have to await further investigation. Kate got up, very agitated.

"We are in trouble aren't we?" she said. "They're bound to find out – about us, O'Connell, the whole thing. We might even be seen as accessories". Emmerson considered his reply. Unbeknown to him, he came to the same conclusion that O'Connell had reached.

"I don't think so. Whoever it was in Gerrard's office that we dealt with isn't going to reveal our role in all this. If he does, he'll not only have to admit Gerrard's guilt, but his own in seeking to prevent it coming out; and he'll know that our credibility – which he spent a lot of time ruining – will be restored. In fact the Press would die for the opportunity to print our story, whether it was true or not. So, no, I think we will be left alone. I suppose......we might ask Neil for advice – should we volunteer evidence, should we disappear perhaps ......" Kate paused only a moment.

"No, let's leave the past behind. Let's just disappear anyway, at least for a few weeks. I need to go to back to California again soon. Let's go early, together, tomorrow. That way I can make sure you won't vanish while I'm away". Emmerson kissed her gently.

"That's a remarkably good idea" he said "but then, you're a very remarkable lady".

Lightning Source UK Ltd.
Milton Keynes UK
UKOW03f0201190713

214015UK00003B/58/P